THE KING'S
General

DAPHNE
DU MAURIER

SOURCEBOOKS LANDMARK™
AN IMPRINT OF SOURCEBOOKS, INC.®
NAPERVILLE, ILLINOIS

Published by Sourcebooks Landmark, an imprint of Sourcebooks, Inc.
P.O. Box 4410, Naperville, Illinois 60567-4410
(630) 961-3900
Fax: (630) 961-2168
www.sourcebooks.com

Originally published in Great Britain in 1946 by Victor Gollancz Ltd.

Library of Congress Cataloguing-in-Publicartion Data

Du Maurier, Daphne
  The king's general / Daphne du Maurier.
     p. cm.
  1. Young women—England—Fiction. 2. Country homes—England—Fiction. 3. Great Britain—History—Civil War, 1642-1649—Fiction. 4. Cornwall (England : County)—Fiction. I. Title.
  PR6007.U47K5 2009
  823'.912—dc22
                                    2009020400

Printed and bound in the United States of America.
VP 10 9 8 7 6 5 4 3 2 1

To My Husband
Also a General, but, I trust, a more
discreet one

Acknowledgements

I wish to tender my grateful thanks to John Cosmo Stuart Rashleigh of Throwleigh, and to William Stuart Rashleigh of Stoketon, for giving me permission to print this blend of fact and fiction.

I trust that they, and especially Aenonie Johnson, whose labour in copying family papers proved so helpful, will enjoy this glimpse of their forebears at Menabilly in days long vanished and forgotten.

I am grateful also to Miss Mary Coats, Mr. A. L. Rouse, and Mr. Tregonning Hooper for their great kindness in lending books and manuscripts.

—D. du M.

One

SEPTEMBER, 1653. THE LAST OF SUMMER. THE FIRST CHILL winds of autumn. The sun no longer strikes my eastern window as I wake, but, turning laggard, does not top the hill before eight o'clock. A white mist hides the bay sometimes until noon, and hangs about the marshes too, leaving, when it lifts, a breath of cold air behind it. Because of this, the tall grass in the meadow never dries, but long past midday shimmers and glistens in the sun, the great drops of moisture hanging motionless upon the stems. I notice the tides more than I did once. They seem to make a pattern to the day. When the water drains from the marshes, and little by little the yellow sands appear, rippling and hard and firm, it seems to my foolish fancy, as I lie here, that I too go seaward with the tide, and all my old hidden dreams that I thought buried for all time are bare and naked to the day, just as the shells and the stones are on the sands.

It is a strange, joyous feeling, this streak back to the past. Nothing is regretted, and I am happy and proud. The mist and cloud have gone, and the sun, high now and full of warmth, holds revel with my ebb tide. How blue and hard is the sea as it curls westward from the bay, and the Blackhead, darkly purple, leans to the deep water like a sloping shoulder. Once again—and this I know is fancy—it seems to me that the tide ebbs always in the middle of the day, when hope is highest and my mood is still. Then, half consciously, I become aware of a shadow, of a sudden droop of the spirit. The first clouds of evening are gathering beyond the Dodman. They cast long fingers on the sea. And the surge of the sea, once far off and faint, comes louder now, creeping towards the sands. The tide has turned. Gone are the white stones and the cowrie shells. The sands are covered. My dreams are buried. And as darkness falls the flood-tide sweeps over the marshes and the land is covered. Then Matty will come in to light the candles and to stir the fire, making a bustle with her presence, and if I am short with her, or do not answer, she looks at me with a shake of her head, and reminds me that the fall of the year was always my bad time. My autumn melancholy. Even in the distant days, when I was young, the menace of it became an institution, and Matty, like a fierce clucking hen, would chase away the casual visitor. "Miss Honor can see nobody today." My family soon learnt to understand, and left me in peace. Though peace is an ill word to describe the moods of black despair that used to grip me. Ah, well… they're over now. Those moods at least Rebellion of the spirit against the chafing flesh, and the moments of real pain when I could not rest. Those were the battles of youth. And I am a rebel no longer. The middle years have me in thrall, and there is much to be said for them. Resignation brings its own reward. The trouble is that I cannot read now as I used to do. At twenty-five, at thirty, books were my great consolation. Like a true scholar, I worked away at my Latin and Greek, so that learning was part of my existence. Now it seems profitless. A cynic when I was young, I am in danger of becoming a worse one now I am old. So Robin says. Poor Robin. God knows I must often make a poor companion. The years have not spared him either. He has aged much this year. Possibly his anxiety over me. I know they discuss the future, he and Matty, when they think I sleep. I can hear their voices droning in the parlour. But when he is with me he feigns his little air of cheerfulness, and my heart bleeds for him. My brother. Looking at him as he sits beside me, coldly critical as I always am towards the people I love, I note the pouches beneath his eyes, and the way his hands tremble when he lights his pipe. Can it be that he was ever light of heart and passionate of mind? Did he really ride into battle with a hawk on his wrist, and was it only ten years ago that he led his men to Braddock Down, side by side with Bevil Grenvile, flaunting that scarlet standard with the three gold rests in the eyes of the enemy? Was this the man I saw once, in the moonlight, fighting his rival for a faithless woman?

Looking at him now, it seems a mockery. My poor Robin, with his graying locks shaggy on his shoulders. Yes, the agony of the war has left its mark on both of us. The war—and the Grenviles. Maybe Robin is bound to Gartred still, even as I am to Richard. We never speak of these things. Ours is the dull, drab life of day by day. Looking back, there can be very few amongst our friends who have not suffered. So many gone, so many penniless. I do not forget that Robin and I both live on charity. If Jonathan Rashleigh had not given us this house we should have had no home, with Lanrest gone, and Radford occupied. Jonathan looks very old and tired. It was that last grim year of imprisonment in St. Mawes that broke him, that and John's death. Mary looks much the same. It would take more than a civil war to break her quiet composure and her faith in God. Alice is still with them, and her children, but the feckless Peter never visits her. I think of the time when we were all assembled in the long gallery, and Alice and Peter sang, and John and Joan held hands before the fire—they were all so young, such children. Even Gartred with her calculated malevolence could not have charged the atmosphere that evening. Then Richard, my Richard, broke the spell deliberately with one of his devastating cruel remarks, smiling as he did so, and the gaiety went, and the careless joy vanished from the evening. I hated him for doing it, yet understood the mood that prompted him.

Oh, God confound and damn these Grenviles, I thought afterwards, for harming everything they touch, for twisting happiness into pain with a mere inflection of the voice. Why were they made thus, he and Gartred, so that cruelty for its own sake was almost a vice to be indulged in, affording a sensuous delight? What evil genius presided at their cradle? Bevil had been so different. The flower of the flock, with his grave courtesy, his thoughtfulness, his rigid code of morality, his tenderness to his own and to other people's children. And his boys take after him. There is no vice in Jack or Bunny that I have ever seen. But Gartred. Those serpent's eyes beneath the red-gold hair, that hard, voluptuous mouth—how incredible it seemed to me, even in the early days when she was married to my brother Kit, that anyone could be deceived by her. Her power to charm was overwhelming. My father and my mother were jelly in her hands, and as for poor Kit, he was lost from the beginning, like Robin later. But I was never won, not for a moment. Well, her beauty is marred now, and I suppose forever. She will carry that scar to the grave. A thin scarlet line from eye to mouth where the blade slashed her.

Rumour has it that she can still find lovers, and her latest conquest is one of the Careys, who has come to live near her at Bideford. I can well believe it. No neighbour would be safe from her if he had a charm of manner, and the Careys were always presentable. I can even find it in my heart to forgive her, now that everything is over. The idea of her dallying with George Carey—she must be at least twenty years the elder—brings a flash of colour into a gray world. And what a world!

Long faces and worsted garments, bad harvests and sinking trade, everywhere men poorer than they were before, and the people miserable. The happy aftermath of war. Spies of the Lord Protector (God, what an ironic designation!) in every town and village, and if a breath of protest against the State is heard the murmurer is borne straightway to jail. The Presbyterians hold the reins in their grasping hands, and the only men to benefit are upstarts like Frank Buller and Robert Bennett and our old enemy, John Robartes, all of them out for what they can get and damn the common man. Manners are rough, courtesy a forgotten quality; we are each one of us suspicious of our neighbour. Oh, brave new world! The docile English may endure it for a while, but not we Cornish. They cannot take our independence from us, and in a year or so, when we have licked our wounds, we'll have another rising, and there'll be more blood spilt and more hearts broken. But we shall still lack our leader... Ah, Richard—my Richard—what evil spirit in you urged you to quarrel with all men, so that even the King is your enemy now. My heart aches for you in this last disgrace. I picture you sitting lonely and bitter at your window, gazing out across the dull, flat lands of Holland, and putting the final words to the Defence that you are writing and of which Bunny brought me a rough draft when he came to see me last.

"Oh, put not your trust in princes, nor in any child of man, for there is no help in them." Bitter, hopeless words, that will do no good, and only breed further mischief. "Sir Richard Grenvile for his presuming loyalty, must be by a public declaration defamed as a Banditto and his very loyalty understood a crime. However, seeing it must be so, let God be prayed to bless the King with faithful councillors, and that none may be prevalent to be any way hurtful to him or to any of his relations. As for Sir Richard Grenvile, let him go with the reward of an old soldier of the King's. There is no present use for him.

When there shall be the Council will think on it, if not too late. *Vale.*"

Resentful, proud, and bitter to the end. For this is the end. I know it, and you know it too. There will be no recovery for you now; you have destroyed yourself forever. Feared and hated by friend and foe. The King's General in the West. The man I love. It was after the Scillies fell to the Parliament, and both Jack and Bunny were home for a while, having visited Holland and France, that they rode over from Stowe to see the Rashleighs at Menabilly, and came down to Tywardreath to pay their respects to me. We talked of Richard, and almost immediately Jack said, "My uncle is greatly altered; you would hardly know him. He sits for hours in silence, looking out of the window of his dismal lodging watching the eternal rain—God, how it rains in Holland—and he has no wish for company. You remember how he used to quip and jest with us, and with all youngsters? Now if he does speak it is to find fault, like a testy old man, and crab his visitor."

"The King will never make use of him again, and he knows it," said Bunny. "The quarrel with the Court has turned him sour. It was madness to fan the flame of his old enmity with Hyde."

Then Jack, with more perception, seeing my eyes, said quickly: "Uncle was always his own worst enemy; Honor knows that. He is damnably lonely, that's the truth of it. And the years ahead are blank."

We were all silent for a moment. My heart was aching for Richard, and the boys perceived it. Presently Bunny said in a low tone, "My uncle never speaks of Dick. I suppose we shall never know now what wretched misfortune overtook him."

I felt myself grow cold, and the old sick horror grip me. I turned my head so that the boys should not see my eyes.

"No," I said slowly. "No, we shall never know."

Bunny drummed with his fingers on the table, and Jack

played idly with the pages of a book. I was watching the calm waters of the bay and the little fishing boats creeping round the Blackhead from Gorran Haven. Their sails were amber in the setting sun.

"If," pursued Bunny, as though arguing with himself, "he had fallen into the hands of the enemy, why was the fact concealed? That is what always puzzles me. The son of Richard Grenvile was a prize indeed." I did not answer. I felt Jack move restlessly beside me. Perhaps marriage had given him perception—he was a bridegroom of a few months' standing at that time—or maybe he was always more intuitive than Bunny, but I knew he was aware of my distress. "There is little use," he said, "in going over the past. We are making Honor tired." Soon after they kissed my hands and left, promising to come and see me again before they returned to France. I watched them gallop away, young and free, and untouched by the years that had gone. The future was theirs to seize. One day the King would come back to his waiting country, and Jack and Bunny, who had fought so valiantly for him, would be rewarded. I could picture them at Stowe, and up in London at Whitehall, growing sleek and prosperous, with a whole new age of splendour opening before them.

The civil war would be forgotten, and forgotten, too, the generation that had preceded them, which had fallen in the cause, or had failed. My generation, which would enter into no inheritance.

I lay there in my chair, watching the deepening shadows, and presently Robin came in and sat beside me, inquiring in his gruff, tender way if I was tired, regretting that he had missed the Grenvile brothers, and going on to tell me of some small pother in the courthouse at Tywardreath. I made a pretence of listening, aware with a queer sense of pity how the trifling everyday events were now his one concern. I thought how once he and his companions had won immortality for their gallant and so useless defence of Pendennis Castle in those tragic summer months in '46—how proud we were of them, how full our hearts—and here he was rambling on about five fowls that had been stolen from a widow in St. Blazey. Perhaps I was no cynic after all, but rotten with sentiment. It was then that the idea came first to me, that by writing down the events of those few years, I would rid myself of a burden. The war, and how it changed our lives, how we were all caught up in it, and broken by it, and our lives hopelessly intermingled one with another. Gartred and Robin, Richard and I, the whole Rashleigh family, pent up together in that house of secrets—small wonder that we came to be defeated. Even today Robin goes every Sunday to dine at Menabilly, but not I. My health pleads its own excuse. Knowing what I know, I could not return. Menabilly, where the drama of our lives was played, is vivid enough to me three miles distant here in Tywardreath. The house stands as bare and desolate as it did when I saw it last in '48. Jonathan has neither the heart nor the money to restore it to its former condition. He and Mary and the grandchildren live in one wing only. I pray God they will always remain in ignorance of that final tragedy. Two people will carry the secret to the grave. Richard and I. He sits in Holland, many hundred miles away, and I lie upon my couch in Tywardreath, and the shadow of the buttress is upon us both. When Robin rides each Sunday to Menabilly I go with him, in imagination, across the park and come to the high walls surrounding the house. The courtyard lies open; the west front stares down at me. The last rays of the sun shine into my old room above the gatehouse, for the lattice is open, but the windows of the room beside it are closed. Ivy tendrils creep across it. The smooth stone of the buttress outside the window is encrusted with lichen. The sun vanishes, and the west front takes once more to the shadows. The Rashleighs eat and sleep within, and go by candlelight to bed, and to dream; but I, down here three miles away in Tywardreath, wake in the night to the sound of a boy's voice calling my name in terror, to a boy's hand beating against the walls, and there in the pitch-black night before me, vivid, terrible, and accusing, is the ghost of Richard's son. I sit up in bed, sweating with horror, and faithful Matty, hearing me stir, comes to me and lights the candle.

She brews me a warm drink, rubs my aching back, and puts a shawl about my shoulders. Robin, in the room adjoining, sleeps on undisturbed. I try to read a while, but my thoughts are too violent to allow repose. Matty brings me paper and pen, and I begin to write. There is so much to say, and so little time in which to say it. For I do not fool myself about the future. My own instinct, quite apart from Robin's face, warns me that this autumn will be the last. So while my Richard's Defence is discussed by the world and placed on record for all time amongst the archives of this seventeenth century, my apologia will go with me to the grave, and by rotting there with me, unread, will serve its purpose.

I will say for Richard what he never said for himself, and I will show how, despite his bitter faults and failings, it was possible for a woman to love him with all her heart, and mind, and body, and I that woman. I write at midnight, then, by candlelight, while the church clock at Tywardreath chimes the small hours, and the only sound I hear is the sigh of the wind beneath my window and the murmur of the sea as the tide comes sweeping across the sands to the marshes below St. Blazey bridge.

Two

THE FIRST TIME I SAW GARTRED WAS WHEN MY ELDEST brother Kit brought her home to Lanrest as his bride. She was twenty-two, and I, the baby of the family except for Percy, a child of ten. We were a happy, sprawling family, very intimate and free, and my father, John Harris, cared nothing for the affairs of the world, but lived for his horses, his dogs, and the peaceful concerns of his small estate. Lanrest was not a large property, but it lay high amidst a sheltering ring of trees, looking down upon the Looe Valley, and was one of those placid, kindly houses that seem to slumber through the years, and we loved it well. Even now, thirty years after, I have only to close my eyes and think of home, and there comes to my nostrils the well-remembered scent of hay, hot with the sun, blown by a lazy wind; and I see the great wheel thrashing the water down at the mills at Lametton, and I smell the fusty, dusty golden grain. The sky was always white with pigeons. They circled and flew above our heads and were so tame that they would take grain from our hands. Strutting and cooing, puffed and proud, they created an atmosphere of comfort. Their gentle chattering amongst themselves through a long summer's afternoon brought much peace to me in the later years, when the others would go hawking and ride away laughing and talking and I could no longer follow them. But that is another chapter. I was talking of Gartred as I saw her first. The wedding had taken place at Stowe, her home, and Percy and I, because of some childish ailment or other, had not been present at it. This, very foolishly, created a resentment in me from the first. I was undoubtedly spoilt, being so much younger than my brothers and sisters, who made a great pet of me, as did my parents, too, but I had it firmly in my mind that my brother's bride did not wish to be bothered with children at her wedding and that she feared we might have some infection.

I can remember sitting upright in bed, my eyes bright with fever, remonstrating with my mother. "When Cecilia was married, Percy and I carried the train," I said. (Cecilia was my eldest sister.) "And we all of us went to Mothercombe, and the Pollexefens welcomed us, although Percy and I both made ourselves sick with over-eating." All my mother could say in reply was that this time it was different, and Stowe was quite another place to Mothercombe, and the Grenviles were not the Pollexefens—which seemed to me the most feeble of arguments—and she would never forgive herself if we took the fever to Gartred. Everything was Gartred. Nobody else mattered. There was a great fuss and commotion, too, about preparing the spare chamber for when the bride and bridegroom should come to stay. New hangings were brought, and rugs and tapestries, and it was all because Gartred must not be made to feel Lanrest was shabby or in poor repair. The servants were made to sweep and dust, the place was put into a bustle, and everyone made uncomfortable in the process.

If it had been because of Kit, my dear easygoing brother, I should never have grudged it for a moment. But Kit himself might not have existed. It was for Gartred. And, like all children, I listened to the gossip of the servants. "It's on account of his being heir to Sir Christopher at Radford that she's marrying our young master," was the sentence I heard, amidst the clatter in the kitchens. I seized upon this piece of information and brooded on it, together with the reply from my father's steward. "It's not like a Grenvile to match with a plain Harris of Lanrest."

The words angered me and confused me too. The word "plain" seemed a reflection on my brother's looks, whom I considered handsome, and why should a Harris of Lanrest be a poor bargain for a Grenvile? It was true that Kit was heir to our Uncle Christopher at Radford—a great barracks of a place the other side of Plymouth—but I had never thought much of the fact until now. For the first time I realized, with something of a shock, that marriage was not the romantic fairy legend I had imagined it to be, but a great institution, a bargain between important families, with the tying-up of property. When Cecilia married John Pollexefen, whom she had known since childhood, it had not struck me in this way, but now, with my father riding over to Stowe continually, and holding long conferences with lawyers, and wearing a worried frown between his brows, Kit's marriage was becoming like some frightening affair of State, which, if worded wrong, would throw the country into chaos.

Eavesdropping again, I heard the lawyer say, "It is not Sir Bernard Grenvile who is holding out about the settlement, but the daughter herself. She has her father wound round her finger."

I pondered over this awhile, and then repeated it to my sister Mary. "Is it usual," I asked, with no doubt irritating precocity, "for a bride to argue thus about her portion?"

Mary did not answer for a moment. Although she was twenty, life had barely brushed her as yet, and I doubt if she knew more than I did. But I could see that she was shocked. "Gartred is the only daughter," she said, after a moment. "It is perhaps necessary for her to discuss the settlements."

"I wonder if Kit knows of it," I said. "I somehow do not think he would like it."

Mary then bade me hold my tongue and warned me that I was fast becoming a shrew and no one would admire me for it. I was not to be discouraged, though, and while I refrained from mentioning the marriage settlement to my brothers, I went to plague Robin—my favourite even in those days—to tell me something of the Grenviles. He had just ridden in from hawking and stood in the stable yard, his dear, handsome face flushed and happy, the falcon on his wrist, and I remember drawing back, scared always by the bird's deep, venomous eyes and the blood on her beak. She would permit no one to touch her but Robin, and he was stroking her feathers. There was a clatter in the stable yard, with the men rubbing down the horses, and in one corner by the well the dogs were feeding.

"I am pleased it is Kit and not you that has gone away to find a bride for himself," I said, while the bird watched me from beneath great hooded lids, and Robin smiled and reached out his other hand to touch my curls, while the falcon ruffled in anger.

"If I had been the eldest son," said Robin gently, "I would have been the bridegroom at this wedding." I stole a glance at him, and saw that his smile had gone, and in its place a look of sadness. "Why, did she like you best?" I asked. He turned away then, and placing the hood over his bird, gave her to the keeper. When he picked me up in his arms he was smiling again. "Come and pick cherries," he said, "and never mind my brother's bride."

"But the Grenviles?" I persisted as he bore me on his shoulders to the orchard. "Why must we be so mighty proud about them?"

"Bevil Grenvile is the best fellow in the world," said Robin. "Kit, Jo, and I were at Oxford with him. And his sister is very beautiful." More than that I could not drag from him. But my brother Jo, to whose rather sarcastic, penetrating mind I put the same question later in the day, expressed surprise at my ignorance. "Have you reached the ripe age of ten, Honor," he inquired, "without knowing that in Cornwall there are only two families who count for anything—the Grenviles and the Arundells? Naturally, we humble Harris brood are overwhelmed that our dear brother Kit has been honoured by the august hand of the so ravishing Gartred." Then he buried his nose in a book and there was an end of the matter. The next week they were all gone to Stowe for the wedding. I had to hug my soul in patience until their return, and then, as I feared, my mother pleaded fatigue, as did the rest of them, and everyone seemed a little jaded and out of sorts with so much feasting and rejoicing, and only my third sister Bridget unbent to me at all. She was in raptures over the magnificence of Stowe and the hospitality of the Grenviles. "This place is like a steward's lodge compared to Stowe," she told me. "You could put Lanrest in one pocket of the grounds there, and it would not be noticed. Two servants waited behind my chair at supper, and all the while musicians played to us from the gallery."

"But Gartred, what of Gartred?" I said with impatience.

"Wait while I tell you," she said. "There were more than two hundred people staying there, and Mary and I slept together in a chamber bigger by far than any we possess here. There was a woman to tend us and dress our hair. And the bedding was changed every day, and perfumed."

"What else, then?" I asked, consumed with jealousy.

"I think Father was a little lost," she whispered. "I saw him from time to time with the other people, endeavouring to talk, but he looked stifled, as though he could not breathe. And all the men were so richly attired, somehow he seemed drab beside them. Sir Bernard is a very fine-looking man. He wore a blue velvet doublet slashed with silver, the day of the wedding, and Father was in his green that fits him a little too well. He overtops him, too—Sir Bernard, I mean—and they looked odd standing together."

"Never mind my father," I said. "I want to hear of Gartred."

My sister Bridget smiled, superior with her knowledge.

"I liked Bevil the best," she said, "and so does everyone. He was in the midst of it all, seeing that no one lacked for anything. I thought Lady Grenvile a little stiff, but Bevil was the soul of courtesy, gracious in all he did." She paused a moment. "They are all auburn-haired, you know," she said with some inconsequence; "if we saw anyone with auburn hair it was sure to be a Grenvile. I did not care for the one they called Richard," she added with a frown.

"Why not? Was he so ugly?" I asked.

"No," she answered, puzzled. "He was more handsome than Bevil. But he looked at us all in a mocking, contemptuous way, and when he trod on my gown in the crush he made no apology. 'You are to blame,' he had the impudence to tell me, 'for letting it trail thus in the dust.' They told me at Stowe he was a soldier."

"But there is still Gartred," I said, "you have not described her." And then, to my mortification, Bridget yawned, and rose to her feet. "Oh, I am too weary to tell you any more," she said. "Wait until the morning. But Mary, Cecilia, and I are all agreed upon one thing, that we would sooner resemble Gartred than any other woman." So in the end I had to form my own judgement with my own eyes. We were all gathered in the hall to receive them—they had gone first from Stowe to my uncle's estate at Radford—and the dogs ran out into the courtyard as they heard the horses.

We were a large party, because the Poilexefens were with us too, Cecilia had her baby Joan in her arms—my first godchild, and I was proud of the honour—and we were all happy and laughing and talking because we were one family and knew one another so well. Kit swung himself down from the saddle— he looked very debonair and gay—and I saw Gartred. She murmured something to Kit, who laughed and coloured and held his arms to help her dismount, and in a flash of intuition I knew she had said something to him which was part of their life together and had nought to do with us, his family. Kit was not ours any more, but belonged to her.

I hung back, reluctant to be introduced, and suddenly she was beside me, her cool hand under my chin. "So you are Honor?" she said. The inflexion in her voice suggested that I was small for my age, or ill-looking, or disappointing in some special way, and she passed on through to the big parlour, taking precedence of my mother with a confident smile, while the remainder of the family followed like fascinated moths. Percy, being a boy and goggle-eyed at beauty, went to her at once, and she put a sweetmeat in his mouth. She has them ready, I thought, to bribe us children, as one bribes strange dogs. "Would Honor like one too?" she said, and there was a note of mockery in her voice, as though she knew instinctively that this treating of me as a baby was what I hated most. I could not take my eyes from her face. She reminded me of something, and suddenly I knew. I was a tiny child again at Radford, my uncle's home, and he was walking me through the glasshouses in the gardens. There was one flower, an orchid, that grew alone; it was the colour of pale ivory, with one little vein of crimson running through the petals. The scent filled the house, honeyed, and sickly sweet. It was the loveliest flower I had ever seen. I stretched out my hand to stroke the soft velvet sheen, and swiftly my uncle pulled me by the shoulder. "Don't touch it, child. The stem is poisonous."

I drew back, frightened. Sure enough, I could see the myriad hairs bristling, sharp and sticky, like a thousand swords.

Gartred was like that orchid. When she offered me the sweetmeat I turned away, shaking my head, and my father, who had never spoken to me harshly in his life, said sharply, "Honor, where are your manners?" Gartred laughed and shrugged her shoulders. Everyone present turned reproving eyes upon me, and even Robin frowned. My mother bade me go upstairs to my room. That was how Gartred came to Lanrest.

The marriage lasted for three years, and it is not my purpose now to write about it. So much has happened since to make the later life of Gartred the more vivid, and in the battles we have waged the early years loom dim now and unimportant. There was always war between us, that much is certain. She, young, confident, and proud, and I a sullen child, peering at her from behind doors and screens, and both of us aware of a mutual hostility. They were more often at Radford and Stowe than at Lanrest, but when she came home I swear she cast a blight upon the place. I was still a child and I could not reason, but a child, like an animal, has an instinct that does not lie. There were no children of the marriage. That was the first blow, and I know this was a disappointment to my parents, because I heard them talk of it. My sister Cecilia came to us regularly for her lying-in, but there was never a rumour of Gartred. She rode and went hawking as we did; she did not keep her room or complain of fatigue, which we had come to expect from Cecilia. Once my mother had the hardihood to say, "When I first wed, Gartred, I neither rode nor hunted, for fear I should miscarry," and Gartred, trimming her nails with a tiny pair of scissors made of mother-of-pearl, looked up at her, and said, "I have nothing within me to lose, madam, and for that you had better blame your son." Her voice was low and full of venom, and my mother stared at her for a moment, bewildered, then rose and left the room in distress. It was the first time the poison had touched her. I did not understand the talk between them, but I sensed that Gartred was bitter against my brother, for soon afterwards Kit came in and, going to Gartred, said to her in a tone loaded with reproach, "Have you accused me to my mother?" They both looked at me, and I knew I had to leave the room. I went out into the garden and fed the pigeons, but the peace was gone from the place. From that moment everything went ill with them and with us all. Kit's nature seemed to change. He wore a harassed air, wretchedly unlike himself, and a coolness grew up between him and my father, who had hitherto agreed so well.

Kit showed himself suddenly aggressive to my father, and to us all, finding fault with the working of Lanrest and comparing it to Radford, and in contrast to this was his abject humility before Gartred, a humility that had nothing fine about it but made him despicable to my intolerant eyes. The next year he stood for West Looe in Parliament and they went often to London, so we did not see them much, but when they came to Lanrest there seemed to be this continual strain about their presence, and once there was a heated quarrel between Kit and Robin, one night when my parents were from home. It was midsummer, stifling and warm, and I, playing truant from my nursery, crept down to the garden in my nightgown. The household were abed. I remember flitting like a little ghost before the windows. The casement of the guest chamber was open wide, and I heard Kit's voice, louder than usual, lifted in argument. Some devil interest in me made me listen. "It is always the same," he said, "wherever we go. You make a fool of me before all men, and now tonight before my very brother. I tell you I cannot endure it any longer."

I heard Gartred laugh, and I saw Kit's shadow reflected on the ceiling by the quivering candlelight. Their voices were low for a moment, and then Kit spoke again for me to hear.

"You think I remark nothing," he said. "You think I have sunk so low that to keep you near me, and to be allowed to touch you sometimes, I will shut my eyes to everyone. Do you think it was pleasant for me at Stowe to see how you looked upon Antony Denys that night when I returned so suddenly from London? A man with grown children, and his wife scarce cold in her grave? Are you entirely without mercy for me?"

That terrible pleading note I so detested had crept back into his voice again, and I heard Gartred laugh once more.

"And this evening," he said, "I saw you smiling across the table at him, my own brother." I felt sick, and rather frightened, but curiously excited, and my heart thumped within me as I heard a step beside me on the paving, and looking over my shoulder, I saw Robin stand beside me in the darkness. "Go away," he whispered to me. "Go away at once." I pointed to the open window. "It is Kit and Gartred," I said. "He is angry with her for smiling at you."

I heard Robin catch at his breath, and he turned as if to go, when suddenly Kit's voice cried out loud and horrible, as though he, a grown man, was sobbing like a child. "If that happens I shall kill you. I swear to God I shall kill you." Then Robin, swift as an arrow, stooped to a stone and, taking it in his hand, he flung it against the casement, shivering the glass to fragments.

"God damn you for a coward then," he shouted. "Come and kill me instead." I looked up and saw Kit's face, white and tortured, and behind him Gartred with her hair loose on her shoulders. It was a picture to be imprinted always on my mind, those two at the window, and Robin suddenly different from the brother I had always known and loved, breathing defiance and contempt. I felt ashamed for him, for Kit, for myself, but mostly I was filled with hatred for Gartred, who had brought the storm to pass and remained untouched by it.

I turned and ran, with my fingers in my ears, and crept up to bed with never a word to anyone and drew the covers well over my head, fearing that by morning they would all three of them be discovered slain there in the grass. But what passed between them further, I never knew. Day broke and all was as before except that Robin rode away soon after breakfast and did not return until after Kit and Gartred took their departure to Radford, some five days later. Whether anyone else in the family knew of the incident I never discovered. I was too scared to ask, and since Gartred had come amongst us we had all lost our old manner of sharing troubles and had each one of us grown more polite and secretive.

Next year, in '23, the smallpox swept through Cornwall like a scourge, and few families were spared. In Liskeard the people closed their doors, and the shopkeepers put up their shutters and would do no trade, for fear of the infection.

In June my father was stricken, dying within a few days, and we had scarcely recovered from the blow before messages came to us from my uncle at Radford to say that Kit had been seized with the same dread disease, and there was no hope of his recovery.

Father and son thus died within a few weeks of one another, and Jo, the scholar, became the head of the family. We were all too unhappy with our double loss to think of Gartred, who had fled to Stowe at the first sign of infection and so escaped a similar fate, but when the two wills came to be read, both Kit's and my father's, we learnt that although Lanrest, with Radford later, passed to Jo, the rich pasture lands of Lametton and the Mill were to remain in Gartred's keeping for her lifetime.

She came down with her brother Bevil for the reading, and even Cecilia, the gentlest of my sisters, remarked afterwards with shocked surprise upon her composure, her icy confidence, and the niggardly manner with which she saw to the measuring of every acre down at Lametton. Bevil, married himself now and a near neighbour to us at Killigarth, did his utmost to smooth away the ill-feeling that he sensed amongst us, and although I was still little more than a child, I remember feeling unhappy and embarrassed that he was put to so much awkwardness on our account. It was small wonder that he was loved by everyone, and I wondered to myself what opinion he held in his secret heart about his sister, or whether her beauty amazed him as it did every man.

When affairs were settled, and they went away, I think all of us breathed relief that no actual breach had come to pass, causing a feud between the families, and the fact that Lanrest belonged to Jo was a weight off my mother's mind, though she said nothing.

Robin remained from home during the whole period of the visit, and maybe no one but myself could guess the reason.

The morning before she left, some impulse prompted me to hesitate before her chamber, the door of which was open, and look at her within. She had claimed that the contents of the room belonged to Kit, and so to her, and the servants had been employed the day before in taking down the hangings and removing the pieces of furniture she most desired. At this last moment she was alone, turning out a little *secretaire* that stood in one corner. She did not observe that I was watching her, and I saw the mask off her lovely face at last. The eyes were narrow, the lip protruding, and she wrenched at a little drawer with such force that the part came to pieces in her hands. There were some trinkets at the back of the drawer—none, I think, of great value—but she had remembered them. Suddenly she saw my face reflected in the mirror.

"If you leave to us the bare walls, we shall be well content," I said as her eyes met mine. My father would have whipped me for it had he been alive, and my brothers, too, but we were alone.

"You always played the spy, from the first," she said softly, but because I was not a man she did not smile.

"I was born with eyes in my head," I said to her.

Slowly she put the jewels in a little pouch she wore hanging from her waist. "Take comfort and be thankful you are quit of me now," she said. "We are not likely to see one another again."

"I hope not," I told her. Suddenly she laughed. "It were a pity," she said, "that your brother did not have a little of your spirit."

"Which brother?" I asked.

She paused a moment, uncertain what I knew, and then, smiling, she tapped my cheek with her long slim finger. "All of them," she said, and then she turned her back on me and called to her servant from the adjoining room. Slowly I went downstairs, my mind on fire with questions, and, coming into the hallway, I saw Jo fingering the great map hanging on the wall. I did not talk to him but walked out past him into the garden.

She left Lanrest at noon in a litter, with a great train of horses and servants from Stowe to carry her belongings. I watched them, from a hiding place in the trees, pass away up the road to Liskeard in a cloud of dust

"That's over," I said to myself. "That's the last of them. We have done with the Grenviles."

But Fate willed otherwise.

Three

$\mathcal{M}$Y EIGHTEENTH BIRTHDAY. A BRIGHT DECEMBER DAY. My spirits soaring like a bird as, looking out across the dazzling sea from Radford, I watched His Majesty's Fleet sail into Plymouth Sound.

It concerned me not that the expedition now returning had been a failure and that far away in France La Rochelle remained unconquered; these were matters for older people to discuss.

Here in Devon there was laughing and rejoicing and the young folk held high holiday. What a sight they were, some eighty ships or more, crowding together between Drake's Island and the Mount, the white sails bellying in the west wind, the coloured pennants streaming from the golden spars. As each vessel drew opposite the fort at Mount Batten, she would be greeted with a salvo from the great guns and, dipping her colours in a return salute, let fly her anchor and bring up opposite the entrance to the Cattwater. The people gathered on the cliffs waved and shouted, and from the vessels themselves came a mighty cheer, while the drums beat and the bugles sounded, and the sides of the ships were seen to be thronged with soldiers pressing against the high bulwarks, clinging to the stout rigging. The sun shone upon their breast-plates and their swords, which they waved to the crowds in greeting, and gathered on the poop would be the officers, flashes of crimson, blue, and Lincoln green, as they moved amongst the men.

Each ship carried on her mainmast the standard of the officer in command, and as the crowd recognized the colours and the arms of a Devon leader, or a Cornishman, another great shout would fill the air and be echoed back to us from the cheering fellows in the vessel. There was the two-headed eagle of the Godolphins, the running stag of the Trevannions from Caerhayes, the six swallows of the numerous Arundell clan, and, perhaps loveliest of all, the crest of the Devon Champernownes, a sitting swan holding in her beak a horseshoe of gold.

The little ships, too, threaded their way amongst their larger sisters, a vivid flash of colour with their narrow decks black with troopers, and I recognized vessels I had last seen lying in Looe Harbour or in Fowey, now weather-stained and battered, but bearing triumphantly aloft the standards of the men who had built them, and manned them, and commissioned them for war—among them the wolfs head of our neighbour Trelawney, and the Cornish chough of the Menabilly Rashleighs.

The leading ship, a great three-masted vessel, carried the commander of the expedition, the Duke of Buckingham, and when she was saluted from Mount Batten she replied with an answering salvo from her own six guns, and we could see the Duke's pennant fluttering from the masthead. She dropped anchor, swinging to the wind, and the fleet followed her, and the rattle of nearly a hundred cables through a hundred hawsers must have filled the air from where we stood on the cliffs below Radford, away beyond the Sound to Saltash, at the entrance of the Tamar River. Slowly their bows swung round, pointing to Cawsand and the Cornish Coast, and their sterns came into line, the sun flashing in their windows and gleaming upon the ornamental carving, the writhing serpents, and the lions' paws.

And still the bugles echoed across the water and the drums thundered. Suddenly there was silence, the clamour and the cheering died away, and on the flagship commanded by the Duke of Buckingham someone snapped forth an order in a high, clear voice. The soldiers who had crowded the bulwarks were there no longer—they moved as one man, forming into line amidships—there was no jostling, no thrusting into position. There came another order, and the single tattoo of a drum, and in one movement, it seemed, the boats were manned and lowered into the water, the coloured blades poised as though to strike, and the men who waited on the thwarts sat rigid as automatons. The manoeuvre had taken perhaps three minutes from the first order; and the timing of it, the precision, the perfect discipline of the whole proceeding drew from the crowd about us the biggest cheer yet from the day, while for no reason I felt the idiotic tears course down my cheeks.

"I thought as much," said a fellow below me. "There's only one man in the West who could turn an unruly rabble into soldiers fit for His Majesty's Bodyguard. There go the Grenvile coat-of-arms—do you see them, hoisted beneath the Duke of Buckingham's standard?" Even as he spoke I saw the scarlet pennant run up to the masthead, and as it streamed into the wind and flattened, the sun shone upon the three gold rests.

The boats drew away from the ship's side, the officers seated in the stern sheets, and suddenly it was high holiday again, with crowded Plymouth boats putting out from the Cattwater to greet the Fleet—the whole Sound dotted at once with little craft—and the people watching upon the cliffs began to run towards Mount Batten, calling and shouting, pushing against one another to be the first to greet the landing boats. The spell was broken, and we returned to Radford.

"A fine finish to your birthday," said my brother with a smile. "We are all bidden to a banquet at the Castle, at the command of the Duke of Buckingham." He stood on the steps of the house to greet us, having ridden back from the fortress at Mount Batten. Jo had succeeded to the estates at Radford, my Uncle Christopher having died a few years back, and much of our time now was spent between Plymouth and Lanrest. Jo had become indeed a person of some importance, in Devon especially, and besides being undersheriff for the county, he had married an heiress into the bargain, Elizabeth Champernowne, whose pleasant manner and equable disposition made up for her lack of looks. My sister Bridget, too, had followed Cecilia's example and married into a Devon family, and Mary and I were the only daughters left unwed.

"There will be ten thousand fellows roaming the streets of Plymouth tonight," jested Robin. "I warrant if we turned the girls loose amongst them they'd soon find husbands."

"Best clip Honor's tongue then," replied Jo, "for they'll soon forget her blue eyes and her curls once she begins to flay them."

"Let me alone—I can look after myself," I told them.

For I was still the spoilt darling, the *enfant terrible*, possessing boundless health and vigour, and a tongue that ran away with me. I was, moreover (and how long ago it seems), the beauty of the family, though my features, such as they were, were more impudent than classical, and I still had to stand on tiptoe to reach Robin's shoulder. I remember, that night, how we embarked below the fortress and took boat across the Cattwater to the Castle. All Plymouth seemed to be upon the water, or on the battlements, while away to westward gleamed the soft lights of the Fleet at anchor, the stern windows shining, and the glow from the poop lanterns casting a dull beam upon the water. When we landed, we found the townsfolk pressing about the castle entrance, and everywhere were the soldiers, laughing and talking, encircled with girls, who had decked them with flowers and ribbons for festivity. There were casks of ale standing on the cobbles beside the braziers, and barrow-loads of pies, and cakes, and cheeses, and I remember thinking that the maids who roystered there with their soldier lovers would maybe have more value from their evening than we who must behave with dignity within the precincts of the castle.

In a moment we were out of hearing of the joyful noises of the town, and the air was close and heavy with rich scent, and velvet, and silk, and spicy food, and we were in the great banqueting-hall with voices sounding hollow and strange beneath the vaulted roof. Now and again would ring out the clear voice of a gentleman-at-arms, "Way for the Duke of Buckingham," and a passage would be cleared for the commander as he passed to and fro amongst the guests, holding court even as His Majesty himself might do.

The scene was colourful and exciting, and I—more accustomed to the lazy quietude of Lanrest—felt my heart beat and my cheeks flush, and to my youthful fancy it seemed to me that all this glittering display was somehow a tribute to my eighteenth birthday. "How lovely it is! Are you not glad we came?" I said to Mary, and she, always reserved among strangers, touched my arm and murmured, "Speak more softly, Honor. You draw attention to us," and was for pressing back against the wall. I pressed forward, greedy for colour, devouring everything with my eyes, and smiling even at strangers and caring not at all that I seemed bold, when suddenly the crowd parted, a way was cleared, and here was the Duke's retinue upon us, with the Duke himself not half a yard away. Mary was gone, and I was left alone to bar his path. I remember standing an instant in dismay, and then, losing my composure, I curtseyed low, as though to King Charles himself, while a little

ripple of laughter floated above my head. Raising my eyes, I
saw my brother Jo, his face a strange mixture of amusement and
dismay, come forward from amongst those who thronged the
duke, and, bending over me, he helped me to my feet, for I
had curtseyed so low that I was hard upon my heels and could
not rise. "May I present my sister Honor, your Grace?" I heard
him say. "This is, in point of fact, her eighteenth birthday, and
her first venture into society."

The Duke of Buckingham bowed gravely and, lifting my
hand to his lips, wished me good fortune. "It may be your
sister's first venture, my dear Harris," he said graciously, "but
with beauty such as she possesses you must see to it that it is not
the last." He passed on in a wave of perfume and velvet, with
my brother hemmed in beside him, frowning at me over his
shoulder, and as I swore under my breath (or possibly not under
my breath, but indiscreetly, and a stable oath learnt from Robin
at that) I heard someone say behind me, "If you care to come
out on to the battlements, I will show you how to do that as it
should be done." I whipped round, scarlet and indignant, and
looking down upon me from six feet or more, with a sardonic
smile upon his face, was an officer still clad in his breastplate of
silver, worn over a blue tunic, with a blue-and-silver sash about
his waist. His eyes were golden brown, his hair dark auburn,
and I saw that his ears were pierced with small gold rings, for
all the world like a Turkish bandit.

"Do you mean you would show me how to curtsy or how
to swear?" I said to him in fury.

"Why, both, if you wish it," he answered. "Your performance
at the first was lamentable, and at the second merely amateur."

His rudeness rendered me speechless, and I could hardly
believe my ears. I glanced about me for Mary or for Elizabeth,
Jo's serene and comfortable wife, but they had withdrawn in
the crush, and I was hemmed about with strangers. The most

THE KING'S GENERAL

fitting thing then was to withdraw with dignity. I turned on my heel and pushed my way through the crowd, making for the entrance, and then I heard the mocking voice behind me once again. "Way for Mistress Honor Harris of Lanrest," proclaimed in high clear tones, while people looked at me astonished, falling back in spite of themselves, and so a passageway was cleared. I walked on with flaming cheeks, scarce knowing what I was doing, and found myself, not in the great entrance as I had hoped, but in the cold air upon the battlements, looking out on to Plymouth Sound, while away below me, in the cobbled square, the townsfolk danced and sang. My odious companion was with me still, and he stood now, with his hand upon his sword, looking down upon me with that same mocking smile on his face.

"So you are the little maid my sister so much detested," he said.

"What the devil do you mean?" I asked.

"I would have spanked you for it had I been her," he said.

Something in the clip of his voice and the droop of his eye struck a chord in my memory. "Who are you?" I said to him.

"Sir Richard Grenvile," he replied, "a colonel in His Majesty's Army, and knighted some little while ago for extreme gallantry in the field." He hummed a little, playing with his sash.

"It is a pity," I said, "that your manners do not match your courage."

"And that your deportment," he said, "does not equal your looks."

This reference to my height—always a sore point, for I had not grown an inch since I was thirteen—stung me to fresh fury. I let fly a string of oaths that Jo and Robin, under the greatest provocation, might have loosed upon the stablemen, though certainly not in my presence, and which I had only learnt

31

through my inveterate habit of eavesdropping; but if I hoped to make Richard Grenvile blanch I was wasting my breath. He waited until I had finished, his head cocked as though he were a tutor hearing me repeat a lesson, and then he shook his head.

"There is a certain coarseness about the English tongue that does not do for the occasion," he said. "Spanish is more graceful and far more satisfying to the temper. Listen to this." And he began to swear in Spanish, loosing upon me a stream of lovely-sounding oaths that would certainly have won my admiration had they come from Jo or Robin. As I listened I looked again for that resemblance to Gartred, but it was gone. He was like his brother Bevil, but with more dash, and certainly more swagger, and I felt he cared not a tinker's curse for anyone's opinion but his own.

"You must admit," he said, breaking off suddenly, "that I have you beaten." His smile, no longer sardonic but disarming, had me beaten, too, and I felt my anger die within me. "Come and look at the fleet," he said. "A ship at anchor is a lovely thing."

We went to the battlements and stared out across the Sound. It was still and cloudless and the moon had risen. The ships were motionless upon the water, and they stood out in the moonlight carved and clear. The men were singing, and the sound of their voices was borne to us across the water, distinct from the rough jollity of the crowds in the streets below.

"Were your losses very great at La Rochelle?" I asked him.

"No more than I expected in an expedition that was bound to be abortive," he answered, shrugging his shoulders. "Those ships yonder are filled with wounded men who won't recover. It would be more humane to throw them overboard." I looked at him in doubt, wondering if this was a further instalment of his peculiar sense of humour. "The only fellows who distinguished themselves were those in the regiment I have the honour to command," he continued, "but as no other officer but myself insists on discipline, it was small wonder that the attack proved a failure."

His self-assurance was as astounding to me as his former rudeness.

"Do you talk thus to your superiors?" I asked him.

"If you mean superior to me in matters military, such a man does not exist," he answered, "but superiors in rank, why, yes, invariably. That is why, although I am not yet twenty-nine, I am already the most detested officer in His Majesty's Army." He looked down at me, smiling, and once again I was at a loss for words.

I thought of my sister Bridget, and how he had trodden upon her dress at Kit's wedding, and I wondered if there was anyone in the world who liked him. "And the Duke of Buckingham?" I said, "Do you speak to him in this way too?"

"Oh, George and I are old friends," he answered. "He does what he is told. He gives me no trouble. Look at those drunken fellows in the courtyard there. My heaven, if they were under my command I'd hang the bastards." He pointed down to the square below, where a group of brawling soldiers were squabbling around a cask of ale, accompanied by a pack of squealing women.

"You might excuse them," I said, "pent up at sea so long."

"They may drain the cask dry and rape every woman in Plymouth, for all I care," he answered, "but let them do it like men and not like beasts, and clean their filthy jerkins first."

He turned away from the battlement in disgust. "Come now," he said. "Let us see if you can curtsy better to me than you did to the duke. Take your gown in your hands, thus. Bend your right knee, thus. And allow your somewhat insignificant posterior to sink upon your left leg, thus."

I obeyed him, shaking with laughter, for it seemed to me

supremely ridiculous that a colonel in His Majesty's Army should be teaching me deportment upon the battlements of Plymouth Castle.

"I assure you it is no laughing matter," he said gravely. "A clumsy woman looks so damnably ill bred. There now, that is excellent. Once again, perfection. You can do it if you try. The truth is you are an idle little baggage and have never been beaten by your brothers." With appalling coolness, he straightened my gown and rearranged the lace around my shoulders. "I object to dining with untidy women," he murmured.

"I have no intention of sitting down with you to dine," I replied with spirit.

"No one else will ask you, I can vouch for that," he answered. "Come, take my arm; I am hungry if you are not."

He marched me back into the castle, and to my consternation I found that the guests were already seated at the long tables in the banqueting hall, and the servants were bearing in the dishes. We were conspicuous as we entered, and my usual composure fled from me. It was, it may be remembered, my first venture in the social world. "Let us go back," I pleaded, tugging at his arm. "See, there is no place for us; the seats are all filled."

"Go back? Not on your life. I want my dinner," he replied.

He pushed his way past the servants, nearly lifting me from my feet. I could see hundreds of faces staring up at us, and heard a hum of conversation, and for one brief moment I caught a glimpse of my sister Mary, seated next to Robin, away down in the centre of the hall. I saw the look of horror and astonishment in her eyes and her mouth frame the word "Honor" as she whispered to my brother. I could do nothing but hurry forward, tripping over my gown, borne on the relentless arm of Richard Grenvile to the high table at the far end of the hall where the Duke of Buckingham sat beside the Countess of Mount Edgcumbe, and the nobility of Cornwall and Devon, such as they were, feasted with decorum above the common herd. "You are taking me to the high table, I protested, dragging at his arm with all my force."

"What of it?" he asked, looking down at me in astonishment. "I'm damned if I'm going to dine anywhere else. Way there, please, for Sir Richard Grenvile." At his voice the servants flattened themselves against the wall, and heads were turned, and I saw the Duke of Buckingham break off from his conversation with the countess. Chairs were pulled forward, people were squeezed aside, and somehow we were seated at the table a hand's stretch from the duke himself, while the Lady Mount Edgcumbe peered round at me with stony eyes. Richard Grenvile leant forward with a smile. "You are perhaps acquainted with Honor Harris, Countess," he said, "my sister-in-law. This is her eighteenth birthday." The countess bowed, and appeared unmoved. "You can disregard her," said Richard Grenvile to me. "She's as deaf as a post. But for God's sake smile, and take that glassy stare from your eyes." I prayed for death, but it did not come to me. Instead I took the roast swan that was heaped upon my platter.

The Duke of Buckingham turned to me, his glass in his hand. "I wish you very many happy returns of the day," he said.

I murmured my thanks, and shook my curls to hide my flaming cheeks.

"Merely a formality," said Richard Grenvile in my ear. "Don't let it go to your head. George has a dozen mistresses already, and is in love with the Queen of France."

He ate with evident enjoyment, vilifying his neighbours with every mouthful, and because he did not trouble to lower his voice, I could swear that his words were heard. I tasted nothing of what I ate or drank, but sat like a bewildered fish throughout the long repast. At length the ordeal was over, and I felt myself pulled to my feet by my companion. The wine, which I had swallowed as though it were water, had made jelly of my legs, and I was obliged to lean upon him for support. I have scant memory indeed of what followed next. There was music and singing, and some Sicilian dancers, strung about with ribbons, performed a tarantella, but their final dizzy whirling was my undoing, and I have shaming recollection of being assisted to some inner apartment of the castle, suitably darkened and discreet, where nature took her toll of me and the roast swan knew me no more. I opened my eyes and found myself upon a couch, with Richard Grenvile holding my hand and dabbing my forehead with his kerchief.

"You must learn to carry your wine," he said severely.

I felt very ill, and very ashamed, and tears were near the surface.

"Ah, no," he said, and his voice, hitherto so clipped and harsh, was oddly tender. "You must not cry. Not on your birthday."

He continued dabbing at my forehead with the kerchief.

"I have n–never eaten roast swan b–before," I stammered, closing my eyes in agony at the memory.

"It was not so much the swan as the burgundy," he murmured. "Lie still now, you will be easier by and by."

In truth, my head was still reeling, and I was as grateful for his strong hand as I would have been for my mother's. It seemed to me in no wise strange that I should be lying sick in a darkened unknown room with Richard Grenvile tending me, proving himself so comforting a nurse.

"I hated you at first. I like you better now," I told him.

"It's hard that I had to make you vomit before I won your approval," he answered. I laughed, and then fell to groaning again, for the swan was not entirely dissipated. "Lean against my shoulder, so," he said to me. "Poor little one, what an ending to an eighteenth birthday." I could feel him shake with silent laughter, and yet his voice and hands were strangely tender, and I was happy with him.

"You are like your brother Bevil after all," I said.

"Not I," he answered. "Bevil is a gentleman, and I a scoundrel. I have always been the black sheep of the family."

"What of Gartred?" I asked.

"Gartred is a law unto herself," he replied. "You must have learnt that when you were a little child, and she was wedded to your brother."

"I hated her with all my heart," I told him.

"Small blame to you for that," he answered me.

"And is she content, now that she is wed again?" I asked him.

"Gartred will never be content," he said. "She was born greedy, not only for money, but for men too. She had an eye to Antony Denys, her husband now, long before your brother died."

"And not only Antony Denys," I said.

"You had long ears for a little maid," he answered.

I sat up, rearranging my curls, while he helped me with my gown.

"You have been kind to me," I said, grown suddenly prim, and conscious of my eighteen years. "I shall not forget this evening."

"Nor I either," he replied.

"Perhaps," I said, "you had better take me to my brothers."

"Perhaps I had," he said.

I stumbled out of the little dark chamber to the lighted corridor. "Where were we all this while?" I asked in doubt, glancing over my shoulder. He laughed, and shook his head.

"The good God only knows," he answered, "but I wager it is the closet where Mount Edgcumbe combs his hair." He looked down at me, smiling, and for one instant touched my curls with his hands. "I will tell you one thing," he said, "I have never sat with a woman before while she vomited."

"Nor I so disgraced myself before a man," I said with dignity.

Then he bent suddenly, and lifted me in his arms like a child. "Nor have I ever lay hidden in a darkened room with anyone so fair as you, Honor, and not made love to her," he told me, and, holding me for a moment against his heart, he set me on my feet again.

"And now if you permit it, I will take you home," he said.

That is, I think, a very clear and truthful account of my first meeting with Richard Grenvile.

Four

WITHIN A WEEK OF THE ENCOUNTER JUST RECORDED I WAS sent back to my mother at Lanrest, supposedly in disgrace for my ill behaviour, and once home I had to be admonished all over again and hear for the twentieth time how a maid of my age and breeding should conduct herself. It seemed that I had done mischief to everyone. I had shamed my brother Jo by that foolish curtsy to the Duke of Buckingham, and further had offended his wife Elizabeth by taking precedence of her and dining at the high table, to which she had not been invited. I had neglected to remain with my sister Mary during the evening, had been observed by sundry persons cavorting oddly on the battlements with an officer, and had finally appeared sometime after midnight from the private rooms within the castle in a sad state of disarray.

Such conduct would, my mother said severely, condemn me possibly for all time in the eyes of the world, and had my father been alive he would more than likely have packed me off to the nuns for two or three years, in the hopes that my absence for a space of time would cause the incident to be forgotten. As it was, and here invention failed her, and she was left lamenting that, as both my married sisters Cecilia and Bridget were expecting to lie-in again and could not receive me, I would be obliged to stay at home.

It seemed to me very dull after Radford, for Robin had remained there, and my young brother Percy was still at Oxford. I was therefore alone in my disgrace. I remember it was some weeks after I returned, a day in early spring, and I had gone out to sulk by the apple tree, that favourite hiding place of childhood, when I observed a horseman riding up the valley. The trees hid him for a space, and then the sound of horse's hoofs drew nearer, and I realized that he was coming to Lanrest. Thinking it was Robin, I scrambled down from my apple tree and went to the stables, but when I arrived there I found the servant leading a strange horse to the stall—a fine gray—and I caught a glimpse of a tall figure passing into the house. I was for following my old trick of eavesdropping at the parlour door, but just as I was about to do so I observed my mother on the stairs.

"You will please go to your chamber, Honor, and remain there until my visitor has gone," she said gravely.

My first impulse was to demand the visitor's name, but I remembered my manners in time and, afire with curiosity, went silently upstairs. Once there I rang for Matty, the maid who had served me and my sisters for some years now and had become my special ally. Her ears were nearly as long as mine, and her nose as keen, and her round, plain face was now alight with mischief. She guessed what I wanted her for before I asked her. "I'll bide in the hallway when he comes out, and get his name for you," she said. "A tall, big gentleman he was, a fine man."

"No one from Bodmin," I said, with sudden misgiving, for fear my mother should, after all, intend to send me to the nuns.

"Why, bless you, no," she answered. "This is a young master, wearing a blue cloak slashed with silver."

Blue and silver. The Grenvile colours.

"Was his hair red, Matty?" I asked in some excitement.

"You could warm your hands at it," she answered.

This was an adventure then, and no more dullness to the day. I sent Matty below, and paced up and down my chamber in great impatience. The interview must have been a short one, for very soon I heard the door of the parlour open and the clear, clipped voice that I remembered well taking leave of my mother, and I heard his footsteps pass away through the hallway to the courtyard. My chamber window looked out on to the garden, and I thus had no glimpse of him, and it seemed eternity before Matty reappeared, her eyes bright with information. She brought forth a screwed-up piece of paper from beneath her apron, and with it a silver piece. "He told me to give you the note, and keep the crown," she said.

I unfolded the note, furtive as a criminal. I read:

> Dear Sister, although Gartred has exchanged a Harris for a Denys, I count myself still your brother, and reserve for myself the right of calling upon you. Your good mother, it seems, thinks otherwise, tells me you are indisposed, and has bidden me good day in no uncertain terms. It is not my custom to ride some ten miles or so to no purpose; therefore, you will direct your maid forthwith to conduct me to some part of your domain where we can converse together unobserved, for I dare swear you are no more indisposed than is your brother and servant, Richard Grenvile.

My first thought was to send no answer, for he took my compliance so much for granted, but curiosity and a beating heart got the better of my pride, and I bade Matty show the visitor the orchard, but that he should not go too directly for fear of being seen from the house. When she had gone,

I listened for my mother's footsteps, and sure enough they sounded up the stairs, and she came into the room. She found me sitting by the window, with a book of prayers open on my knee. "I am happy to see you so devout, Honor," she said.

I did not answer, but kept my eyes meekly upon the page.

"Sir Richard Grenvile, with whom you conducted yourself in so unseemly a fashion a week ago in Plymouth, has just departed," she continued. "It seems he has left the Army for a while and intends to reside near to us at Killigarth, standing as member of Parliament for Fowey. A somewhat sudden decision."

Still I did not answer. "I have never heard any good of him," said my mother. "He has always caused his family concern and been a sore trial to his brother Bevil, being constantly in debt. He will hardly make us a pleasant neighbour."

"He is, at least, a very gallant soldier," I said warmly.

"I know nothing about that," she answered, "but I have no wish for him to ride over here, demanding to see you, when your brothers are from home. It shows great want of delicacy on his part."

With that she left me, and I heard her pass into her chamber and close the door. In a few moments I had my shoes in my hands and was tiptoeing down the stairs into the garden. Then I flew like the wind to the orchard and was safe in the apple tree before many minutes had passed. Presently I heard someone moving about under the trees, and parting the blossom in my hiding place, I saw Richard Grenvile stooping under the low branches. I broke off a piece of twig and threw it at him. He shook his head and looked about him. I threw another, and this one hit him a sharp crack upon the nose. "God damn it," he began, and, looking up, he saw me laughing at him from the apple tree. In a moment he had swung himself up beside me and with one arm around my waist had me pinned against the trunk. The branch cracked most ominously.

"Get down at once; the branch will not hold us both,"
I said.

"It will, if you keep still," he told me.

One false move would have seen us both upon the ground,
some ten feet below, but to remain still meant that I must
continue to lie crushed against his chest, with his arm around
me, and his face not six inches away from mine.

"We cannot possibly converse in such a fashion," I protested.

"Why not? I find it very pleasant," he answered.

Cautiously he stretched his leg along the full length of the
branch to give himself more ease, and pulled me closer.

"Now, what have you to tell me?" he said, for all the world as
though it were I who had demanded the interview and not he.

I then recounted my disgrace, and how my brother and sister-
in-law had sent me packing home from Plymouth, and it seemed
if I must now be treated as a prisoner in my own home.

"And it is no use your coming here again," I added, "for my
mother will never let me see you. It seems you are a person of
ill repute."

"How so?" he demanded.

"You are constantly in debt; those were her words."

"The Grenviles are never not in debt. It is the great failing of
the family. Even Bevil has to borrow from the Jews."

"You are a sore trial to him and to all your relatives."

"On the contrary, it is they who are a sore trial to me.
I can seldom get a penny out of them. What else did your
mother say?"

"That it showed want of delicacy to come here asking to see
me when my brothers are from home."

"She is wrong. It showed great cunning, born of long
experience."

"And as for your gallantry in the field, she knows nothing
about that."

"I hardly suppose she does. Like all mothers, it is my gallantry in other spheres that concerns her at the present."

"I don't know what you mean," I said.

"Then you have less perception than I thought," he answered, and, loosening his hold upon the branch, he flicked at the collar of my gown. "You have an earwig running down your bosom," he said.

I drew back, disconcerted, the abrupt change from the romantic to the prosaic putting me out of countenance.

"I believe my mother to be right," I said stiffly. "I think there is very little to be gained from our further acquaintance, and it would be best to put an end to it now." It was difficult to show dignity in my cramped position, but I made some show of sitting upright and braced my shoulders.

"You cannot descend unless I let you," he said, and in truth I was locked there, with his legs across the branch. "The moment is opportune to teach you Spanish," he murmured.

"I have no wish to learn it," I answered.

Then he laughed and, taking my face in his hands, he kissed me very suddenly, which, being a novelty to me and strangely pleasant, rendered me for a few moments incapable of speech or action. I turned away my head, and began to play with the blossoms. "You can go now, if you desire it," he said. I did not desire it but had too much pride to tell him so. He swung himself to the ground, and lifted me down beside him.

"It is not easy," he said, "to be gallant in an apple tree. Perhaps you will tell your mother." He wore upon his face that same sardonic smile that I had first seen in Plymouth.

"I shall tell my mother nothing," I said, hurt by this abrupt dismissal. He looked down on me for a moment in silence, and then he said, "If you bid your gardener trim that upper branch we would do better another time."

"I am not certain," I answered, "that I wish for another time."

"Ah, but you do," he said, "and so do I. Besides, my horse needs exercise." He turned through the trees, making for the gate where he had left his horse, and I followed him silently through the long grass. He reached for the bridle, and climbed into the saddle. "Ten miles between Lanrest and Killigarth," he said. "If I did this twice a week, Daniel would be in a fine condition by the summer. I will come again on Tuesday. Remember those instructions to the gardener." He waved his gauntlet at me and was gone.

I stood staring after him, telling myself that he was quite as detestable as Gartred and that I would never see him more; but for all my resolutions I was at the apple tree again on Tuesday.

There followed then as strange and, to my mind, as sweet a wooing as ever maiden of my generation had. Looking back on it now, after a quarter of a century, when the sequel to it fills my mind with greater clarity, it has the hazy unreality of an elusive dream. Once a week, and sometimes twice, he would ride over to Lanrest from Killigarth, and there, cradled in the apple tree—with the offending branch lopped as he demanded—he tutored me in love, and I responded. He was but twenty-eight, and I eighteen. Those March and April afternoons, with the bees humming above our heads and the blackcap singing, and the grass in the orchard growing longer day by day, there seemed no end to them and no beginning. Of what we discoursed, when we did not kiss, I have forgotten. He must have told me much about himself, for Richard's thoughts were ever centred about his person, more then than latterly, and I had a picture of a red-haired lad rebellious of authority, flaunting his elders, staring out across the storm-tossed Atlantic from the towering, craggy cliffs of his north Cornish coast, so different from our southern shore, with its coves and valleys.

We have, I think, a more happy disposition here in southeast Cornwall, for the very softness of the air, come rain or sun, and the gentle contour of the land make for a lazy feeling of content. Whereas in the Grenvile country, bare of hedgerow, bereft of tree, exposed to all four winds of heaven—winds laden, as it were, with surf and spray—the mind develops with a quick perception, with more fire to it, more anger, and life itself is hazardous and cruel. Here we have few tragedies at sea, but there the coast is strewn with the bleached bones of vessels wrecked without hope of haven, and about the torn, unburied bodies of the drowned the seals play and the falcons hover. It holds us more than we ever reckon, the few square miles of territory where we are born and bred, and I can understand what devils of unrest surged in the blood of Richard Grenvile.

These thoughts of mine came at a later date, but then, when we were young, they concerned me not, nor he either, and whether he talked to me of soldiering or Stowe, of fighting the French or battling with his own family, it sounded happy in my ears, and all his bitter jests were forgotten when he kissed me and held me close. It seems odd that our hiding place was not discovered. Maybe in his careless, lavish fashion he showered gold pieces on the servants. Certainly my mother passed her days in placid ignorance.

And then, one day in early April, my brothers rode from Radford, bringing with them young Edward Champernowne, a younger brother of Elizabeth's. I was happy to see Jo and Robin, but in no mood to exchange courtesies with a stranger—besides, his teeth protruded, which seemed to me unpardonable—and also I was filled with furtive fear that my secret meetings would be discovered. After we had dined, Jo and Robin and my mother, with Edward Champernowne, withdrew to the bookroom that had been my father's, and I was left alone to entertain Elizabeth. She made no mention of my discourtesy at Plymouth, for which I was grateful, but proceeded to lavish great praise upon her brother Edward, who, she told me, was but a year older than myself and had recently left Oxford. I listened with but half an ear, my thoughts full of Richard, who, in debt as usual, had talked at our last meeting of selling lands in Killigarth and Tywardreath that he had inherited from his mother, and bearing me off with him to Spain or Naples, where we would live like princes and turn bandit.

Later in the evening I was summoned to my mother's room. Jo was with her, and Robin, too, but Edward Champernowne had gone to join his sister. All three of them wore an air of well-being.

My mother drew me to her and kissed me fondly and said at once that great happiness was in store for me, that Edward Champernowne had asked for my hand in marriage, that she and my brothers had accepted, the formalities had been settled, my portion agreed to with Jo adding to it most handsomely, and nothing remained now but to determine upon the date. I believe I stared at them all a moment, stupefied, and then broke out wildly in a torrent of protestation, declaring that I would not wed him, that I would wed no man who was not of my own choice, and that sooner than do it I would throw myself from the roof. In vain my mother argued with me; in vain Jo enthused upon the virtues of young Champernowne, of his steadiness, of his noble bearing, and of how my conduct had been such, a few months back, that it was amazing he should have asked for my hand at all. "You have come to the age, Honor," he said, "when we believe marriage to be the only means to settle you, and in this matter Mother and myself are the best judges." I shook my head; I dug my nails into my hands.

"I tell you I will not marry him," I said.

Robin had not taken part in the conversation. He sat a little apart, but now he rose and stood beside me.

"I told you, Jo, it would be little use to drive Honor if she had not the inclination," he said. "Give her time to accustom herself to the project, and she will think better of it."

"Edward Champernowne might think better of it too," replied Jo.

"It were best to settle it now while he is here," said my mother.

I looked at their worried, indecisive faces—for they all loved me well and were distressed at my obduracy. "No," I told them, "I would sooner die," and I flounced from the room in feverish anger and, going to my chamber, thrust the bolt through the door. To my imagination, strained and overwrought, it seemed to me that my brother and my mother had become the wicked parents in a fairy tale and I the luckless princess whom they were bent on wedding to an ogre, though I believe the inoffensive Edward Champernowne would not have dared lay a finger upon me. I waited till the whole brood of them were abed, and then, changing my gown and wrapping a cloak about me, I stole from the house. For I was bent upon a harebrained scheme, which was no less than walking through the night to Killigarth, and so to Richard. The thunder had passed, and the night was clear enough, and I set off with beating heart down the roadway to the river, which I forded a mile or so below Lanrest. Then I struck westward on the road to Pelynt, but the way was rough and crossed with intersecting lanes, and my mind misgave me for the fool I was, for without start lore I had no knowledge of direction. I was ill used to walking any distance, and my shoes were thin. The night seemed endless and the road interminable, and the sounds and murmurs of the countryside filled me with apprehension, though I pretended to myself I did not care. Dawn found me stranded by another stream and encompassed about by woods; and, weary and bedraggled, I climbed a farther hill and saw at last my first glimpse of the sea and the hump of Looe Island away to the eastward.

I knew then that some inner sense had led me to the coast, and I was not walking north as I had feared, but the curl of smoke through the trees and the sound of barking dogs warned me that I was trespassing, and I had no wish to be caught by keepers.

About six o'clock I met a ploughman tramping along the highway, who stared at me amazed and took me for a witch, for I saw him cross his fingers and spit when I had passed, but he pointed out the lane that led to Killigarth. The sun was high now above the sea, and the fishing vessels strung out in a line in Talland Bay. I saw the tall chimneys of the house of Killigarth, and once again my heart misgave me for the sorry figure I should make before Richard. If he was there alone, it would not matter, but what if Bevil was at home, and Grace, his wife, and a whole tribe of Grenviles whom I did not know? I came to the house then like a thief and stood before the windows, uncertain what to do. It wore the brisk air of early morning. Servants were astir. I heard a clatter in the kitchens and the murmur of voices, and I could smell the fatty smell of bacon and smoky ham. Windows were open to the sun, and the sound of laughter came, and men talking.

I wished with all my heart that I was back in my bedchamber in Lanrest, but there was no returning. I pulled the bell and heard the clanging echo through the house. Then I drew back, as a servant came into the hall. He wore the Grenvile livery and had a stern, forbidding air. "What do you want?" he asked of me.

"I wish to see Sir Richard," I said.

"Sir Richard and the rest of the gentlemen are at breakfast," he answered. "Away with you now—he won't be troubled with you." The door of the dining room was open, and I heard more sound of talk and laughter, and Richard's voice topping the rest.

"I must see Sir Richard," I insisted, desperate now and near to tears, and then, as the fellow was about to lay his hands upon me and thrust me from the door, Richard himself came out into the hall. He was laughing, calling something over his shoulder to the gentlemen within. He was eating still, and had a napkin in his hand.

"Richard," I called. "Richard, it is I, Honor," and he came forward, amazement on his face. "What the devil—" he began. Then, cursing his servant to be gone, he drew me into a little anteroom beside the hall.

"What is it? What is the matter?" he said swiftly, and I, weak and utterly worn out, fell into his arms and wept upon his shoulder.

"Softly, my little love. Be easy then," he murmured, and held me close and stroked my hair, until I was calm enough to tell my story. "They want to marry me to Edward Champernowne," I stammered—how foolish it sounded to be blurted thus—"and I have told them I will not do so, and I have wandered all night on the roads to tell you of it."

I felt him shake with laughter as he had done that first evening weeks ago when I had sickened of the swan.

"Is that all?" he asked. "And did you tramp twelve miles or more to tell me that? Oh, Honor, my little love, my dear."

I looked up at him, bewildered that he found so serious a matter food for laughter. "What am I to do then?" I said.

"Why, tell them to go to the devil, of course," he answered, "and if you dare not say it, then I will say it for you. Come in to breakfast." I tugged at his hand in consternation, for if the ploughman had taken me for a witch, and the servant for a beggar, God only knew what his friends would say to me. He would not listen to my protests, but dragged me in to the dining room where the gentlemen were breakfasting, and there was I, with my bedraggled gown and cloak and my torn slippers, faced with Ranald Mohun and young Trelawney, Tom Treffry and Jonathan Rashleigh, and some half dozen others whom I did not know. "This is Honor Harris of Lanrest," said Richard. "I think you gentlemen are possibly acquainted with her." They one and all stood up and bowed to me, astonishment and embarrassment written plain upon their faces. "She has run away from home," said Richard, in no way put out by the situation. "Would you credit it, Tom? They want to marry her to Edward Champernowne."

"Indeed," replied Tom Treffry, quite at a loss, and he bent to stroke his dog's ear to hide his confusion.

"Will you have some bacon, Honor?" said Richard, proffering me a platter heaped with fatty pork, but I was too tired and faint to desire anything more than to be taken upstairs and put to rest.

Then Jonathan Rashleigh, a man of family and older than Richard and the others, said quietly: "Mistress Honor would prefer to withdraw, I fancy. I would summon one of your serving women, Richard."

"Damn it, this is a bachelor household," answered Richard, his mouth crammed with bacon. "There isn't a woman in the place."

I heard a snort from Ranald Mohun, who put a handkerchief to his face, and I saw also the baleful eye that Richard cast upon him, and then somehow they one and all made their excuses and got themselves from the room, and we were alone at last.

"I was a fool to come," I said. "Now I have disgraced you before all your friends."

"I was disgraced long since," he said, pulling himself another tankard of ale; "but it was well you came after breakfast rather than before."

"Why so?" I asked.

He smiled and drew a document from his breast.

"I have sold Killigarth, and also the lands I hold in Tywardreath," he answered. "Rashleigh gave me a fair price for them. Had you blundered in sooner he might have stayed his hand."

"Will the money pay your debts?" I said.

He laughed derisively. "A drop in the ocean," he said; "but it will suffice for a week or so, until we can borrow elsewhere."

"Why 'we'?" I inquired.

"Well, we shall be together," he answered. "You do not think I am going to permit this ridiculous match with Edward Champernowne?" He wiped his mouth, and pushed aside his plate, as though he had not a care in the world. He held out his arms to me and I went to him. "Dear love," I said, feeling in sudden very old and very wise, "you have told me often that you must marry an heiress, or you could not live."

"I should have no wish to live if you were wedded to another man," he answered. Some little time was wasted while he assured me of this.

"But, Richard," I said presently, "if I wed you instead of Edward Champernowne, my brother may refuse his sanction."

"I'll fight him if he does."

"We shall be penniless," I protested.

"Not if I know it," he said. "I have several relatives as yet unfleeced. Mrs. Abbot, my old Aunt Katherine up at Hartland, she has a thousand pounds or so she does not want."

"But we cannot live thus all our lives," I said.

"I have never lived any way else," he answered.

I thought of the formalities and deeds that went with marriage, the lawyers and the documents.

"I am the youngest daughter, Richard," I said, hesitating. "You must bear in mind that my portion will be very small."

At this he shouted with laughter and, lifting me in his arms, carried me from the room. "It's your person I have designs upon," he said. "God damn your portion."

*O*H, WILD BETROTHAL, STARTLING AND SWIFT, DECIDED ON in an instant without rhyme or reason, and all objections swept aside like a forest in a fire! My mother was helpless before the onslaught, my brothers powerless to obstruct. The Champernownes, offended, withdrew to Radford, and Jo, washing his hands of me, went with them. His wife would not receive me now, having refused her brother, and I was led to understand that the scandal of my conduct had spread through the whole of Devon. Bridget's husband came posting down from Holberton, and John Pollexefen from Mothercombe, and all the West, it seemed, said I had eloped with Richard Grenvile and was to wed him now through dire necessity. He had shamed me in a room at Plymouth—he had carried me by force to Killigarth—I had lived there as his mistress for three months—all these and other tales were spread abroad, and Richard and I, in the gladness of our hearts, did nought but laugh at them. He was for taking horse to London and giving me refuge with the Duke of Buckingham, who would, he declared, eat out of his hand and give me a dowry into the bargain, but at this moment of folly his brother Bevil came riding to Lanrest, and with his usual grace and courtesy, insisted that I should go to Stowe and be married from the

Grenvile home. Bevil brought law and order into chaos; his approval lent some shadow of decency to the whole proceeding, a quality which had been lacking hitherto, and within a few days of his taking charge my mother and I were safely housed at Stowe, where Kit had gone as a bridegroom nearly eight years before. I was too much in love by then to care a whit for anyone, and like someone who has feasted too wisely and too well, I swam through the great rooms at Stowe aglow with confidence, smiling at old Sir Bernard, bowing to all his kinsmen, in no more awe of the grandeur about me than I had been of the familiar, dusty corners in Lanrest. I have small recollection now of what I did or whom I saw—save that there were Grenviles everywhere and all of them auburn-haired, as Bridget had once told me—but I remember pacing up and down the great gardens while Sir Bernard discoursed solemnly upon the troubles brewing between His Majesty and Parliament, and I remember, too, standing for hours in a chamber, that of the Lady Grace, Bevil's wife, while her woman pinned my wedding gown upon me, and gathered it, and tuckered it, and pinned it yet again, while she and my mother gave advice, and a heap of children, as it seemed to me, played about the floor.

Richard was not much with me. I belonged to the women, he said, during these last days. We would have enough of one another by and by. These last days—what a world of prophecy.

Nothing then remains out of the fog of recollection but that final afternoon in May, and the sun that came and went behind the clouds, and a high wind blowing. I can see now the guests assembled on the lawns, and how we all proceeded to the falconry, for an afternoon of sport was to precede a banquet in the evening.

There were the goshawks on their perches, preening their feathers and stretching their wings, the tamer of them permitting our approach, and further removed, solitary upon their blocks in the sand, their larger brethren, the wild-eyed peregrines.

The falconers came to leash and jess the hawks, and hood them ready for the chase, and as they did this the stablemen brought the horses for us, and the dogs who were to flush the game yelped and pranced about their heels. Richard mounted me upon the little chestnut mare that was to be mine hereafter, and as he turned to speak a moment to his falconer about the hooding of his bird, I looked over my shoulder and saw a conclave of horsemen gathered about the gate to welcome a new arrival. "What now?" said Richard, and the falconer, shading his eyes from the sun, turned to his master with a smile.

"It is Mrs. Denys," he said, "from Orley Court. Now you can match your red hawk with her tiercel."

Richard looked up at me and smiled.

"So it has happened after all," he said, "and Gartred has chose to visit us." They were riding down the path towards us, and I wondered how she would seem to me, my childhood enemy, to whom, in so strange a fashion, I was to be related once again. No word had come from her, no message of congratulation, but her natural curiosity had won her in the end. "Greetings, sister," called Richard, the old sardonic mockery in his voice. "So you have come to dance at my wedding after all."

"Perhaps," she answered. "I have not yet decided. Two of the children are not well at home." She rode abreast of me, that slow smile that I remembered on her face. "How are you, Honor?"

"Well enough," I answered.

"I never thought to see you become a Grenvile."

"Nor I either."

"The ways of Providence are strange indeed. You have not met my husband." I bowed to the stranger at her side, a big, bluff, hearty man, a good deal older than herself. So this was the Antony Denys who had caused poor Kit so much anguish before he died. Maybe it was his weight that had won her. "Where do we ride?" she asked, turning from me to Richard.

"In the open country, towards the shore," he answered.

She glanced at the falcon on his wrist "A red hawk," she said, one eyebrow lifted, "not in her full plumage. Do you think to make anything of her?"

"She has taken kite and bustard, and I propose to put her to a heron today if we can flush one."

Gartred smiled. "A red hawk at a heron," she mocked. "You will see her check at a magpie and nothing larger."

"Will you match her with your tiercel?"

"My tiercel will destroy her, and the heron afterwards."

"That is a matter of opinion."

They watched each other like duellists about to strike, and I remembered how Richard had told me they had fought with one another from the cradle. I had my first shadow of misgiving that the day would turn in some way to disaster. For a moment I wondered whether I would plead fatigue and stay behind. I rode for pleasure, not for slaughter, and hawking was never my favourite pastime.

Gartred must have observed my hesitation, for she laughed and said, "Your bride loses her courage. The pace will be too strong for her."

"What?" said Richard, his face falling. "You are coming, aren't you?"

"Why, yes," I said swiftly. "I will see you kill your heron."

We rode out to the open country, with the wind blowing in our faces and the sound of the Atlantic coming to us as the long surf rollers spilt themselves with a roar on to the shore far below. At first the sport was poor, for no quarry larger than a woodcock was flushed, and to this the goshawks were flown, who clutch their prey between their claws and do not kill outright, like the large-winged peregrines. Richard's falcon and Gartred's tiercel were still hooded, and not slipped, for we were not yet come upon the heron's feeding ground. My little mare pawed restlessly at the ground, for up to the present we had had no run, and the pace was slow. Near a little copse the falconers flushed three magpies, and a cast of goshawks were flown at them, but the cunning magpies, making up for lack of wing power by cunning, scuttled from hedge to hedge, and after some twenty minutes or so of hovering by the hawks, and shouting and driving by the falconers, only one magpie was taken.

"Come, this is poor indeed," said Gartred scornfully. "Can we find no better quarry, and so let fly the falcons?"

Richard shaded his eyes from the sun and looked towards the west. A long strip of moorland lay before us, rough and uneven, and at the far end of it a narrow, soggy marsh, where the duck would fly to feed in stormy weather and at all seasons of the year, so Richard told me, the sea birds came, curlews, and gulls, and herons.

There was no bird as yet on passage through the sky, save a small lark high above our heads, and the marsh, where the herons might be found, was still two miles away.

"I'll match my horse to yours, and my red hawk to your tiercel," said Richard suddenly, and even as he spoke he let fly the hood of his falcon and slipped her, putting spurs to his horse upon the gesture. Within ten seconds Gartred had followed suit, her gray-winged peregrine soaring into the sun, and she and Richard were galloping across the moors towards the marsh, with the two hawks like black specks in the sky above them. My mare, excited by the clattering hoofs of her companions, took charge of me, nearly pulling my arms out of their sockets, and she raced like a mad thing in pursuit of the horses ahead of us, the yelping of the dogs and the cries of the falconers whipping her speed. My last ride. The sun in my eyes, the wind in my face, the movement of the mare beneath me, the thunder of her hooves, the scent of the golden gorse, the sound of the sea. Unforgettable, unforgotten, deep in my soul for all time. I could see Richard and Gartred racing neck to neck, flinging insults at each other as they rode, and in the sky the male and female falcons pitched and hovered, when suddenly away from the marsh ahead of us rose a heron, his great gray wings unfolding, his legs trailing. I heard a shout from Richard, and an answering cry from Gartred, and in an instant it seemed the hawks had seen their quarry, for they both began to circle above the heron, climbing higher and still higher, swinging out in rings until they were like black dots against the sun. The watchful heron, rising too, but in a narrower circle, turned downwind, his queer ungainly body strangely light and supple, and like a flash the first hawk dived to him—whether it was Richard's young falcon or Gartred's tiercel I could not tell—and missed the heron by a hair's breadth. At once, recovering himself, he began to soar again, in ever higher circles, to recover his lost pitch, and the second hawk swooped, missing in like manner.

I tried to rein in my mare, but could not stop her, and now Gartred and Richard had turned eastward, too, following the course of the heron, and we were galloping three abreast, the ground rising steadily towards a circle of stones in the midst of the moor.

"Beware the chasm," shouted Richard in my ear, pointing with his whip, but he was past me like the wind and I could not call to him.

The heron was now direct above my head, and the falcons lost to view, and I heard Gartred shout in triumph: "They bind—they bind—my tiercel has her," and, silhouetted against the sun, I saw one of the falcons locked against the heron and the two come swinging down to earth not twenty yards ahead.

I tried to swerve, but the mare had the mastery, and I shouted to Gartred as she passed me, "Which way is the chasm?" but she did not answer me. On we flew towards the circle of stones, the sun building my eyes, and out of the darkening sky fell the dying heron and the blood-bespattered falcon, straight into the yawning crevice that opened out before me. I heard Richard shout, and a thousand voices singing in my ears as I fell.

It was thus, then, that I, Honor Harris of Lanrest, became a cripple, losing all power in my legs from that day forward until this day on which I write, so that for some twenty-five years now I have been upon my back, or upright in a chair, never walking any more or feeling the ground beneath my feet. If anyone, therefore, thinks that a cripple makes an indifferent heroine to a tale, now is the time to close these pages and desist from reading. For you will never see me wed to the man I love, nor become the mother of his children. But you will learn how that love never faltered, for all its strange vicissitudes, becoming to both of us, in later years, more deep and tender than if we had been wed, and you will learn also how, for all my helplessness, I took the leading part in the drama that unfolded, my very immobility sharpening my senses and quickening my perception, while chance itself forced me to my role of judge and witness. The play goes on, then—what you have just read is but the prologue.

Six

*J*T IS NOT MY PURPOSE TO SURVEY, IN THESE AFTER YEARS, the suffering, bodily and mental, that I underwent during those early months when my life seemed finished. They would make poor reading. And I myself have no inclination to drag from the depths of my being a bitterness that is best forgotten. It is enough to say that they feared at first for my brain, and I lived for many weeks in a state of darkness. As little by little clarity returned and I was able to understand the full significance of my physical state, I asked for Richard; and I learnt that after having waited in vain for some sign from me, some thread of hope from the doctors that I might recover, he had been persuaded by his brother Bevil to rejoin his regiment. This was for the best. It was impossible for him to remain inactive. The assassination at Portsmouth of his friend the Duke of Buckingham was an added horror, and he set sail for France with the rest of the expedition in that final half-hearted attack on La Rochelle. By the time he returned I was home again at Lanrest and had sufficient strength of will to make my decision for the future. This was never to see Richard again. I wrote him a letter, which he disregarded, riding down from London express to see me. I would not see him. He endeavoured to force his way into my room, but my brothers barred the way. It was only when the doctors told him that his presence could but injure me further that he realized the finality of all bonds between us. He rode away without a word. I received from him one last letter, wild, bitter, reproachful—then silence.

In November of that year he married Lady Howard of Fitzford, a rich widow, three times wed already, and four years older than himself. The news came to me indirectly, an incautious word let slip from Matty and at once confusedly covered, and I asked my mother the truth. She had wished to hide it from me, fearing a relapse, and I think my calm acceptance of the fact baffled her understanding.

It was hard for her, and for the rest of them, to realize that I looked upon myself now as a different being. The Honor that was had died as surely as the heron that afternoon in May, when the falcon slew him.

That she would live forever in her lover's heart was possible, no doubt, and a lovely fantasy, but the Richard that I knew and loved was made of flesh and blood; he had to endure, even as I had.

I remember smiling as I lay upon my bed, to think that after all he had found his heiress, and such a notorious one at that. I only hoped that her experience would make him happy, and her wealth ensure him some security.

Meanwhile, I had to school myself to a new way of living and day after day immobility. The mind must atone for the body's helplessness. Percy returned from Oxford about this time, bringing his books of learning, and with his aid I set myself the task of learning Greek and Latin. He made an indifferent though a kindly tutor, and I had not the heart to keep him long from his dogs and his horses, but at least he set me on the road to reading, and I made good progress. The family were all most good and tender. My sisters and their children, tearful and strung with pity as they were at first, soon became easy in my presence, when I laughed and chatted with them, and little by little I—the hitherto spoilt darling—became the guide and mediator in their affairs, and their problems would be brought to me to solve. I am speaking now of years and not of months, for all this did not happen in a day. Matty, my little maid, became from the first moment my untiring slave and bondswoman. It was she who learnt to read the signs of fatigue about my eyes and hustled my visitors from the room. It was she who attended to my wants, to my feeding and my washing, though after some little while I learnt to do this for myself; and after three years, I think it was, my back had so far strengthened that I was able to sit upright and move my body. I was helpless, though, in my legs, and during the autumn and the winter months, when the damp settled in the walls of the house, I would feel it also in my bones. It caused me great pain at times, and then I would be hard put to it to keep to the standard of behaviour I had set myself. Self-pity, that most insiduous of poisons, would filter into my veins and the black devils fill my mind, and then it was that Matty would stand like a sentinel at the door and bar the way to all intruders. Poor Matty, I cursed her often enough when the dark moods had me in thrall, but she bore with me unflinchingly. It was Robin, my dear, good Robin and most constant companion, who first had the thought of making me my chair, and this chair that was to propel me from room to room became his pet invention. He took some months in the designing of it, and when it was built and I was carried to it and could sit up straight and move the rolling wheels without assistance, his joy, I think, was even greater than my own.

It made all the difference to my daily life, and in the summer I could even venture to the garden and propel myself a little distance, up and down before the house, winning some measure of independence. In '32, we had another wedding in the family.

My sister Mary, whom we had long teased for her devoutness and gentle, sober way, accepted the offer of Jonathan Rashleigh of Menabilly, who had lost his first wife in childbed the year before and was left with a growing family upon his hands. It was a most suitable match in all respects, Jonathan being then some forty years of age and Mary thirty-two. She was married from Lanrest, and to the wedding with their father, came his three children, Alice, Elizabeth, and John. Later I was to come to know them well, but even now—as shy and diffident children—they won my affection. To the wedding also came Bevil Grenvile, a close friend to Jonathan as he was to all of us, and it was when the celebrating was over, and Mary departed to her new home the other side of Fowey, that I had a chance to speak with him alone. We spoke for a few moments about his own children and his life at Stowe, and then I asked him, not without some tremulation, for all my calm assurance, how Richard did.

For a moment he did not answer, and, glancing at him, I saw his brow was troubled. "I had not wished to speak of it," he said at length, "but since you ask me—all has gone very ill with him, Honor, ever since his marriage." Some devil of satisfaction rose in my breast, which I could not crush, and: "How so?" I asked. "Has he not a son?" For I had heard that a boy was born to them a year or so before, on May 16 to be exact, the same date, ironically enough, as that on which I had been crippled. A new life for the one that is wasted, I had thought at the time, when I was told of it, and like a spoilt child that had learnt no wisdom after all, I remember crying all night upon my pillow, thinking of the boy, who, but for mischance and the workings of destiny, might have been mine. That was a day, if I recollect aright, when Matty kept guard at my door, and I made picture after picture in my mind of Richard's wife propped upon pillows with a baby in her arms, and Richard smiling beside her. The fantasy was one which, for all my disciplined indifference, I found most damnable. But to return to Bevil. "Yes," he answered. "It is true he has a son, and a daughter, too, but whether Richard sees them or not I cannot say. The truth is he has quarrelled with his wife and treated her in barbarous fashion, even laid violent hands upon her, so she says, and she is now petitioning for a divorce against him. Furthermore, he slandered the Earl of Suffolk, his wife's kinsman, who brought an action against him in the Star Chamber and won the case, and Richard, refusing to pay the fine—and in truth he could not, possessing not a penny—is likely to be cast into the Fleet Prison for debt at any moment." Oh, God, I thought, what a contrast to the life we would have made together. Or was I wrong, and was this symbolic of what might have been? "He was always violent, even as a lad," continued Bevil. "You knew so little of him, Honor; alas, three months of happy wooing is no time in which to judge a man."

I could not answer this, for reason was on his side. But I thought of the spring days, lost to me forever, and the apple blossom in the orchard. No maid could have had more tender or more intuitive a lover. "How was Richard violent?" I asked. "Irresponsible and wild, perhaps, but nothing worse. His wife must have provoked him."

"As to that, I know nothing," answered Bevil, "but I can well believe it. She is a woman of some malice and of doubtful morals. She was a close friend to Gartred—perhaps you did not know that—and it was when she was visiting at Orley Court that the match was made between them. Richard—as no one knows better than yourself—could not have been his best self at that time." I said nothing, feeling, behind Bevil's gentle manner some faint reproach, unconscious though it was. "The truth is," said Bevil, "that Richard married Mary Howard for her money, but once wed, found he had no control over her purse or her property, the whole being in the power of trustees who act solely in her interest."

"Then he is no whit better off than he was before?" I asked.

"Rather worse, if anything," replied Bevil, "for the Star Chamber will not release him from his debt for slander, and I have too many claims upon me at this time to help him either."

It was a sorry picture that he painted, and though to my jealous fancy it was preferable to the idyllic scene of family bliss that I had in imagination conjured, it was no consolation to learn of his distress. That Richard should ill use his wife because he could not trifle with her property was an ugly fact to face, but, having some inkling of his worse self, I guessed this to be true. He had married her without love and in much bitterness of heart, and she, suspecting his motive, had taken care to disappoint him. What a rock of mutual trust on which to build a lasting union! I held to my resolve, though, and sent him no word of sympathy or understanding. Nor was it my own pride and self-pity that kept me from it, but a firm belief that such a course was wisest. He must lead his own life, in which I had no further part.

He remained, we heard later, for many months in prison, and then in the autumn of the following year he left England for the continent, where he saw service with the King of Sweden.

How much I thought of him, and yearned for him, during those intervening years, does not matter to this story. I was weakest during the long watches of the night, when my body pained me. During the day I drilled my feelings to obedience, and what with my progress in my studies—I was by way of becoming a fair Greek scholar—and my interest in the lives of my brothers and sisters, the days and the seasons passed with some fair measure of content.

Time heals all wounds, say the complacent, but I think it is not so much time that does it as determination of the spirit. And the spirit can often turn to devil in the darkness.

Five, ten, fifteen years; a large slice out of a woman's life, and a man's too, for that matter. We change from the awakening, questing creatures we were once, afire with wonder, and expectancy, and doubt, to persons of opinion and authority, our habits formed, our characters moulded in a pattern.

I was a maid, and a rebellious, disorderly one at that, when I was first crippled; but in the year of '42, when the war that was to alter all our lives broke forth, I was a woman of some two and thirty years, the "good Aunt Honor" to my numerous nephews and nieces, and a figure of some importance to the family at large.

A person who is forever chair-bound or bedridden can become a tyrant if she so desires, and, though I never sought to play the despot, I came to be, after my mother died, the one who made decisions, whose authority was asked for on all occasions, and in some strange fashion it seemed that a legendary quality was wove about my personality, as though my physical helplessness must give me greater wisdom.

I accepted the homage with my tongue in my cheek but was careful not to destroy the fond illusion. The young people liked me, I think, because they knew me to be a rebel still, and when there was strife within the family I was sure to take their part. Cynical on the surface, I was an incurable romantic underneath, and if there were messages to be given, or meetings to arrange, or secrets to be whispered, my chamber at Lanrest would become trysting place, rendezvous, and confessional in turn. Mary's stepchildren, the Rashleighs, were my constant visitors, and I found myself involved in many a youthful squabble, defending their escapades with a ready tongue, and soon acting as go-between to their love affairs. Jonathan, my brother-in-law, was a good, just man, but stern; a firm believer in the settled marriage as against the impulsive prompting of the heart. No doubt he was right, but there was something distasteful to my mind in the bargaining between parents and the counting of every farthing, so that when Alice, his eldest daughter, turned thin and pale for languishing after that young rake Peter Courtney—the parents disputing for months whether they should wed or no—I had them both to Lanrest and bade them be happy while the chance was theirs, and no one was a whit the wiser.

They married in due course, and although it ended in a separation (for this I blame the war), at least they had some early happiness together, for which I hold myself responsible.

My godchild Joan was another of my victims. She was, it may be remembered, the child of my sister Cecilia, and some ten years my junior. When John Rashleigh, Mary's stepson, came down from Oxford to visit us, he found Joan at my bedside, and I soon guessed which way the wind was blowing. I had half a thought of sending them to the apple tree, but some inner sentimentality forbade me, and I suggested the bluebell wood instead. They were betrothed within a week, and married before the bluebells had faded, and not even Jonathan Rashleigh could find fault with the marriage settlement.

But the war years were upon us before we were aware, and Jonathan, like all the county gentlemen, my brothers included, had more anxious problems before them. Trouble had been brewing for a long while now, and we in Cornwall were much divided in opinion, some holding that His Majesty was justified in passing what laws he pleased (though one and all grumbled at the taxes), and others holding to it that Parliament was right in opposing any measure that smacked of despotism. How often I heard my brothers argue the point with Jack Trelawney, Ranald Mohun, Dick Buller, and other of our neighbours—my brothers holding firmly for the King, and Jo already in a position of authority, for his business was to superintend the defences of the coast—and as the months passed tempers became shorter and friendships grew colder, an unpleasing spirit of distrust walking abroad. Civil war was talked of openly, and each gentleman in the county began to look to his weapons, his servants, and his horses, so that he could make some contribution to the cause he favoured when the moment came. The women, too, were not idle, many—like Cecilia at Mothercombe—tearing strips of bed linen into bandages, and packing their storerooms with preserves for fear of siege. Arguments were fiercer then, I do believe, than later when the fighting was amongst us. Friends who had supped with me the week before became of a sudden suspect, and long-forgotten scandals were brought forth to blacken their names, merely because of the present opposition of their views.

The whole business made me sick at heart, and this whipping up of tempers between neighbours who for generations had lived at peace seemed a policy of the devil. I hated to hear Robin, my dearly loved brother with his tenderness for dogs and horses, slander Dick Buller for upholding Parliament, vowing he took bribes and made spies of his own servants, when Dick and he had gone hawking together not six months before. While Rob Bennett, another of our neighbours and a friend of Buller's, began to spread damning rumours in return about my brother-in-law Jonathan Rashleigh, saying that Jonathan's father and elder brother, who had died very suddenly within a week of one another many years before, during the smallpox scourge, had not succumbed to the disease at all, but had been poisoned. These tales showed how in a few months we had changed from neighbours into wolves at one another's throats.

At the first open rupture between His Majesty and Parliament in '42, my brothers Jo and Robin and most of our closest friends, including Jonathan Rashleigh, his son-in-law, Peter Courtney, the Trelawneys, the Arundells, and of course Bevil Grenvile, declared for the King. There was an end at once to family life and any settled way of living. Robin went off to York to join His Majesty's army, taking Peter Courtney with him, and almost immediately they were both given command of a company. Peter, showing much dash and courage in his first action, was knighted on the field.

My brother Jo and my brother-in-law Jonathan went about the county raising money, troops, and ammunition for the royal cause. The first was no easy matter, for Cornwall was a poor county at the best of times and lately the taxes had well-nigh broken us; but many families, with little ready money to spare, gave their plate to be melted down to silver, a loyal if wasteful gesture. I had qualms about this before following their example, but in the end was obliged to do so, as Jonathan Rashleigh was collector for the district. My attitude to the war was somewhat cynical, for holding no belief in great causes, and living alone now at Lanrest with only Matty and the servants to tend me, I felt myself curiously detached. The successes of the first year did not go to my head, as they did to the rest of my family, for I could not believe, as they were inclined to, that Parliament would give way so easily. For the Parliamentarians had many powerful men at their command, and much money—all the rich merchants of London were strongly in their favour—besides which I had an uneasy suspicion, which I kept to myself, that their army was incomparably the better of the two. God knows our leaders wanted nothing in courage, but they lacked experience. Equipment, too, was poor, and discipline nonexistent in the ranks. By the autumn the war was getting rather too close for comfort, and the two armies were ranged east and west along the Tamar. I had an uneasy Christmas, and in the third week of January I learnt that the worst had happened and the enemy had crossed the Tamar into Cornwall. I was at breakfast when the news was brought to us, and by none other than Peter Courtney, who had ridden hotfoot from Bodmin to warn me that the opposing army was even now on the road to Liskeard. He, with his regiment, which was under the command of Sir Ralph Hopton, was drawn up to oppose them, and Hopton was at the moment holding a council of war at Boconnoc, only a few miles distant. "With any luck," he told us, "the fighting will not touch you here at Lanrest, but will be between Liskeard and Lostwithiel. If we can break them now and drive them out of Cornwall the war will be as good as won."

He looked handsome, flushed, and excited, his dark curls falling about his face. "I have no time to go to Menabilly," he told me. "Should I fall in battle, will you tell Alice that I love her well?"

He was gone like a flash, and I and Matty, with the two elderly menservants and three lads—all that were left to us—were alone, unarmed and unprepared. There was nothing to do but to get the cattle and the sheep in from pasture and secure them in the farmstead, and bolt and bar ourselves within the house. Then we waited, all gathered round the fireside in my chamber upstairs. Once or twice, opening the casement, we thought we heard the sound of cannon shot, dull and intermittent, strangely distant in the cold clear air of January. Somewhere about three in the afternoon one of the farm lads came running to the house and hammered loud upon the entrance door. "The enemy are routed," he called excitedly, "the whole pack of them scattering like whipped dogs along the road to Liskeard. There's been a great battle fought today on Braddock Down." More stragglers appeared who had taken refuge in the hedges, and one and all told the same story, that the King's men had won a victory, fighting like furies and taking nearly a thousand prisoners.

Knowing that rumour was a lying jade, I bade the household bide awhile and keep the doors fast until the story should be proved, but before nightfall we knew the victory was certain, for Robin himself came riding home to cheer us, covered in dust, with a bloodstained bandage on his arm, and with him the Trelawney brothers and Ranald Mohun. They were all of them laughing and triumphant, for the two Parliament divisions had fled in dire disorder straight for Saltash and would never, said Jack Trelawney, show their faces more this side the Tamar. "And this fellow," he said, clapping Robin on the shoulder, "rode into battle with a hawk on his wrist, which he let fly at Ruthin's musketeers, and by God, the bird so startled them that the lot of them shot wide and started taking to their legs before they'd spent their powder."

"It was a wager I had with Peter," smiled Robin, "and if I lost, the forfeit was my spurs, and that I should be godfather to his next baby."

They rocked with laughter, caring not a whit for the spilt blood and the torn bodies they had trampled, and they sat down, all of them, and drank great jugs of ale, wiping the sweat from their foreheads and discussing every move of the battle they had won like gamesters after a cockfight.

Bevil Grenvile had been the hero of the day in this, his first engagement, and they described to us how he had led the Cornish foot down one hill and up another in so fierce a charge that the enemy could not withstand them.

"You should have seen him, Honor," said Robin, "with his servants and his tenants drawn up in solemn prayer before him, his sword in his hand, his dear, honest face lifted to the sky. They were all clad in the blue and silver livery, as if it were high holiday. And down the hill they followed him, shouting 'A Grenvile! A Grenvile!' with his servant Tony Paine waving his crimson standard with the three gold rests upon it. My God, I tell you, it made me proud to be a Cornishman."

"It's in his blood," said Jack Trelawney. "Here's Bevil been a country squire for all his life, and you put a weapon in his hand and he turns tiger. The Grenviles are all alike at heart."

"I wish to heaven," said Ranald Mohun, "that Richard Grenvile would return from slaughtering the savages in Ireland and come and join his brother." There was a moment's awkward silence, while some of them remembered the past and recollected my presence in the room, and then Robin rose to his feet and said they must be riding back to Liskeard. Thus, in southeast Cornwall, war touched us for a brief space in '43 and so departed, and many of us who had not even smelt the battle talked very big of what we had heard and seen, while those who had taken part in it, like Robin, boasted that the summer would see the rebels in Parliament laying down their arms for ever.

Alas, his optimism was foolish and ill judged. Victories we had indeed that year, throughout the West, as far as Bristol, with our own Cornishmen covering themselves with glory, but we lost, in that first summer, the flower of our Cornish manhood.

Sydney Godolphin, Jack Trevannion, Nick Slanning, Nick Kendal, one by one their faces come back to me as I review the past, and I remember the sinking feeling in the heart with which I would take up the list of the fallen that would be brought to me from Liskeard. All of them were men of noble conduct and high principle, whom we could ill spare in the county and whose loss would make its mark upon the army. The worst tragedy of the year, or so it seemed to us, was when Bevil Grenvile was slain at Lansdowne. Matty came running to my chamber with the tears falling down her cheeks. "They've killed Sir Bevil," she said. Bevil, with his grace and courtesy, his sympathy and charm, was worth all the other Cornish leaders put together. I felt it as if he had been my own brother, but I was too stunned to weep for him. "They say," said Matty, "that he was struck down by a poleax, just as he and his men had won the day and the enemy were scattering. And big Tony Paine, his servant, mounted young Master Jack upon his father's horse, and the men followed the lad, all of them fighting mad with rage and grief to see their master slain."

Yes, I could picture it. Bevil killed in an instant, his head split in two by some damned useless rebel, while his boy Jack, barely fourteen, climbed on to Bevil's white charger that I knew so well, and with the tears smarting his eyes brandished a sword that was too big for him. And the men, with the blue-and-silver colours, following him down the hill, their hearts black with hatred for the enemy. Oh, God, the Grenviles, there was some quality in the race, some white, undaunted spirit bred in their bones and surging through their blood that put them, as Cornishmen and leaders, way ahead above the rest of us. So, outwardly triumphant and inwardly bleeding, we Royalists watched the year draw to its close, and 1644—that fateful year for Cornwall—opened with His Majesty master of the West, but the large and powerful forces of the Parliament in great strength elsewhere, and still unbeaten.

In the spring of the year, a soldier of fortune returning from Ireland rode to London to receive payment for his services. He gave the gentlemen in Parliament to understand that in return for this he would join forces with them, and they, pleased to receive so doughty a warrior amongst their ranks, gave him £600 and told him their plans for the spring campaign. He bowed and smiled—a dangerous sign had they but known it—and straightway set forth in a coach and six, with a host of troopers following him and a banner carried in front of him. The banner was a great map of England and Wales on a crimson ground, with the words "England Bleeding" written across it in letters of gold. When this equipage arrived at Bagshot Heath, the leader of it descended from his coach and, calling his troopers about him, calmly suggested that they should all now proceed to Oxford and fight for His Majesty, and not against him. The troopers, nothing loath, accepted, and the train proceeded on its way to Oxford, bearing with it a quantity of money, arms, and silver plate, bequeathed by Parliament, and all the minutes of the secret council that had just been held in London.

The name of this soldier of fortune, who had hoodwinked the Parliament in so scurrilous a fashion, was Richard Grenvile.

Seven

ONE DAY TOWARDS THE END OF APRIL '44, ROBIN CAME over from Radford to see me, urging me to leave Lanrest and to take up residence, for a time at any rate, with our sister Mary Rashleigh at Menabilly. Robin was at that time commanding a regiment of foot, for he had been promoted colonel under Sir John Digby, and was taking part in the long-drawn-out siege of Plymouth, which alone among the cities in the West still held out for Parliament

"Jo and I are both agreed," said Robin, "that while the war continues you should not live here alone. It is not fit for any woman, let alone one as helpless as yourself. Deserters and stragglers are constantly abroad, robbing on the highway, and the thought of you here, with a few old men and Matty, is a constant disturbance to our peace of mind."

"There is nothing here to rob," I protested, "with the plate gone to the Mint at Truro, and as to harm to my person—a cripple woman can give little satisfaction."

"That is not the point," said Robin. "It is impossible for Jo and Percy and I to do our duty, remembering all the while that you are here alone."

He argued for half a day before I reluctantly gave way, and then with an ill grace and much disturbance in my mind.

For fifteen years—ever since I had been crippled—I had not left Lanrest, and to set forth now to another person's house, even though that person was my own sister, filled me with misgiving.

Menabilly was already packed with Rashleigh relatives, who had taken refuge with Jonathan, seizing the war as an excuse, and I had no wish to add to their number. I had a great dislike for strangers, or for conversing with anyone for the sake of courtesy; besides, I was set now in my ways, my days were my own, I followed a personal routine.

"You can live at Menabilly exactly as you do here at Lanrest," protested Robin, "save that you will be more comfortable. Matty will attend you; you will have your own apartment and your meals brought to you, if you do not wish to mix with the company. Set on the hill there, with the sea air blowing and the fine gardens for you to be wheeled about in, nothing could be more pleasant, to my opinion."

I disagreed, but, seeing his anxiety, I said no more; and within a week my few belongings were packed, the house was closed, and I was being carried in a litter to Menabilly.

How disturbing it was, and strange, to be on the road again. To pass through Lostwithiel, to see the people walking in the market-place—the normal daily life of a community from which I had been so long absent, living in my own world at Lanrest. I felt oddly nervous and ill at ease as I peered through the curtains of my litter, as if I had been suddenly transplanted to a foreign land, where the language and the customs were unknown to me. My spirits rose as we climbed the long hill out of the town, and when we came abreast of the old redoubt at Castledore and I saw the great blue bay of Tywardreath spread out before me, I thought that maybe after all the change of place and scene might yet be bearable. John Rashleigh came riding along the highway to meet me, waving his hat, a broad smile on his thin, colourless face. He was just twenty-three, and the tragedy of his life was that he had not the health or strength to join the army, but must bide at home and take orders from his father, for he had been cursed from babyhood with a malignant form of ague that kept him shivering and helpless sometimes for days on end. He was a dear, lovable fellow, with a strong sense of duty, yet in great awe of his father; and his wife—my goddaughter Joan—with her merry eyes and mischievous prattle, made him a good foil. Riding with him now was his companion and second cousin, Frank Penrose, a young man of the same age as himself, who was employed by my brother-in-law as secretary and junior agent about the estate.

"All is prepared for you, Honor," smiled John as he rode beside my litter. "There are over twenty of us in the house at present, and the lot of them have gathered in the courtyard to greet you. Tonight a dinner is to be given for your reception."

"Very well, then," I answered. "You may tell these fellows to turn back again towards Lostwithiel."

At this he confessed that Joan had bade him tease me, and all the company were in the east wing of the house, and no one would worry me. "My stepmother has put you," he said, "in the gatehouse, for she says you like much light and air, and the chamber there has a window looking both ways, over the outer courtyard to the west, and on to the inner court that surrounds the house. Thus you will see all that goes on about the place, and have your own private peep show."

"It sounds," I answered, "like a garrison, with twenty people crammed within the walls."

"Nearly fifty altogether, counting the servants," laughed John, "but they sleep head to toe in the attics."

My spirits sank again, and as we turned down from the highway into the park and I saw the great stone mansion at the end of it, flanked by high walls and outbuildings, I cursed myself for a fool for coming. We turned left into the outer court, surrounded by bakehouses and larders and dairies, and passing under the low archway of the gatehouse—my future dwelling—drew up within the inner court. The house was foursquare, built around the court, with a big clock tower or belfry at the northern end, and the entrance to the south. On the steps stood Mary now to greet me, and Alice Courtney, her eldest stepdaughter, and Joan, my godchild, both of them with their babies tugging at their skirts.

"Welcome, dearest Honor, to Menabilly," said Mary, her dear face puckered already in nervousness that I should hate it. "The place is full of children, Honor; you must not mind," smiled Alice, who since her marriage to Peter had produced a baby every year. "We are thinking out a plan to attach a rope of your own to the bell in the belfry," said Joan, "so that if the noise becomes too deafening you can pull it in warning, and the household will be silenced."

"I am already established, then, as a dragon," I replied, "which is all to the good, for I mean to do as I please, as Robin may have warned you." They carried me into the dark paneled hall and, ignoring the long gallery, which ran the whole length of the house and from which I could hear the ominous sound of voices, bore me up the broad staircase and along a passage to the western wing. I was, I must confess, immediately delighted with my apartment, which, though low-ceilinged, was wide and full of light. There were windows at each end, as John had said, the western one looking down over the archway to the outer court and the park beyond, and the eastern one facing the inner court. There was a small room to the right for Matty, and nothing had been forgotten for my comfort.

"You will be bothered by no one," said Mary. "The apartments beyond the dressing room belong to the Sawles—cousins of Jonathan's—who are very sober and retiring and will not worry you. The chamber to your left is never occupied."

They left me then, and with Matty's aid I undressed and got myself to bed, a good deal exhausted from my journey, and glad to be alone. The first few days passed in becoming accustomed to my new surroundings and settling down, like a hound to a change of kennel.

My chamber was very pleasant, and I had no wish to leave it; also, I liked the chiming of the clock in the belfry, and once I had told myself firmly that the quietude of Lanrest must be forgotten, I came to listen to the comings and goings that were part of this big house, the bustle in the outer court, the footsteps passing under the arch below me, and also—although I would have denied the accusation—taking a peep from my curtains at the windows opposite that, like mine, looked down upon the inner court, and from which, now and again, people would lean, talking to others within. At intervals during the day the young people would come and converse with me, and I would get a picture of the other inmates of the house, the two families of Sawle and Sparke, cousins to the Rashleighs, between whom there was, it seemed, a perpetual bickering. When my brother-in-law Jonathan was from home, it fell upon his son John to keep the peace, a heavy burden for his none too brawny shoulders, for there is nothing so irritating to a young man as scolding spinsters and short-tempered elderly folk, while Mary, in a fever of unending housekeeping, was from dawn to dusk superintending dairy, store, and stillroom to keep her household fed. There were the grandchildren, too, to keep in order—Alice had three small daughters, and Joan a boy and girl, with another baby expected in the autumn—so in one way and another Menabilly was a colony to itself, with a different family in every wing. By the fifth day I was sufficiently at home, and mistress of my nerves, to leave my chamber and take to my chair. With John propelling it, and Joan and Alice on either side, and the children running before, we made a tour of the domain. The gardens were extensive, surrounded by high walls, and laid out to the eastward on rising ground, which, when the summit was reached, looked down over dense woodland across to further hills and the highway that ran down to Fowey, three miles distant. To the south lay pasture land and farm buildings and another pleasure garden, also walled, which had above it a high causeway leading to a summerhouse, fashioned like a tower with long leaded windows, commanding a fine view of the sea and the Gribben Head.

"This," said Alice, "is my father's sanctum. Here he does his writing and accounts, and from the windows can observe every ship that passes, bound for Fowey." She tried the door to the summerhouse, but it was locked. "We must ask him for the key when he returns," she said. "It would be just the place for Honor and her chair, when the wind is too fresh up on the causeway." John did not answer, and it occurred to him perhaps, as it had to me, that his father might not want me for companion. We made a circle of the grounds, returning by the steward's house and the bowling green, and so through the warren at the back to the outer court. I looked up at the gatehouse, already familiar with the vase of flowers set in my window, and noticed for the first time the barred window of the apartment next to mine, and the great buttress that jutted out beside it.

"Why is that apartment never used?" I asked idly. John waited a moment or two before replying. "My father goes to it at times," he said. "He has furniture and valuables shut away."

"It was my uncle's room," said Alice, hesitating, with a glance at John. "He died very suddenly, you know, when we were children."

Their manner was diffident, and I did not press the question, remembering all at once Jonathan's elder brother, who had died within eight days of his old father, supposedly of smallpox, and about whom the Parliamentarian Rob Bennett had spread his poison rumour.

We then went below the archway, and I schooled myself to an introduction to the Rashleigh cousins. They were all assembled in the long gallery, a great dark panelled chamber with windows looking out on to the court and eastward to the gardens. There were fireplaces at either end, with the Sawles seated before the first and the Sparkes circled round the other, glaring at one another like animals in a cage, while in the centre of the gallery my sister Mary held the balance with her other stepdaughter Elizabeth, who was twice a Rashleigh, having married her first cousin a mile away at Combe. John propelled me up the gallery and with fitting solemnity presented me to the rival factions.

There were but two Sawles to three Sparks, and my godchild Joan had made a pun upon their names, saying that what the Sparkes possessed in flame, the Sawles made up in soul. The latter were indeed a dour, forbidding couple, old Nick Sawle doubled up with rheumatics and almost as great a cripple as I was myself, while Temperance, his wife, came of Puritan stock, as her name suggested, and was never without a prayer book in her hand. She fell to prayer as soon as she observed me—God knows I had never had that effect before on man or woman—and when she had finished asked me if I knew that we were all of us, saving herself, damned to eternity. It was a startling greeting, but I replied cheerfully enough that this was something I had long suspected, whereupon she proceeded to tell me in a rapid whisper, with many spiteful glances at the farther fireplace, that anti-Christ was come into the world. I looked over my shoulder and saw the rounded shoulders of Will Sparke, who was engaged in a harmless game of chequers with his sisters. "Providence has sent you among us to keep

watch," hissed Temperance Sawle, and while she tore to shreds
the characters of her cousins, piece by piece, her husband Nick
Sawle droned in my left ear a full account of his rheumatic
history, from the first twinge in his left toe some forty years
ago to his present dire incapacity to lift either elbow above the
perpendicular. Half-stupefied, I made a signal to John, who
propelled me to the Sparkes—two sisters and a brother. Will
was one of those unfortunate high-voiced old fellows with
a woman's mincing ways, whom I felt instinctively must be
malformed beneath his clothes. His tongue seemed as two-
edged as that of his cousin Temperance, and he fell to jesting
with me at once about the habits of the Sawles, as though I
were an ally. Deborah made up in masculinity what her brother
lacked, being heavily moustached and speaking from her shoes,
while Gillian, the younger sister, was all coy prettiness in spite
of her forty years, bedecked with rouge and ribbons, and with
a high thin laugh that pierced my eardrum like a sword.

"This dread war," said Deborah in bass tones, "has brought
us all together," which seemed to me a hollow sentiment,
as none of them were on speaking terms with one another,
and while Gillian praised my looks and my gown, I saw Will,
out of the tail of my eye, making a cheating move upon the
chequers board.

The air seemed purer somehow in the gatehouse than the
gallery, and after I had visited the apartments of Alice and Joan
and Elizabeth, and watched the romping of the children and
the kicking of the babies, I was thankful enough to retire to
my own chamber and blissful solitude. Matty brought me my
dinner—this being a privilege to which I clung—and was full
of gossip, as was her nature, about the servants in the house and
what they said of their masters. Jonathan, my brother-in-law,
was respected, feared, but not much loved. They were all easier
when he was from home. He kept an account of every penny

spent, and any servant wasting food or produce was instantly dismissed. Mary, my sister, was more liked, though she was said to be a tyrant in the stillroom. The young people were all in high favour, especially Alice, whose sweet face and temper would have endeared her to the devil himself, but there was much shaking of heads over her handsome husband Peter, who had a hot eye for a fine leg, as Matty put it, and was apt to put an arm round the kitchen girls if he had the chance. I could well believe this, having flung a pillow at Peter often enough myself for taking liberties.

"Master John and Mistress Joan are also liked," said Matty, "but they say Master John should stand up more to his father." Her words put me in mind of the afternoon, and I asked her what she knew of the apartment next to mine. "It is a lumber room, they tell me," she answered. "Mr. Rashleigh has the key, and has valuables shut away."

My curiosity was piqued, though, and I bade her search for a crack in the door. She put her face to the keyhole but saw nothing. I gave her a pair of scissors, both of us giggling like children, and she worked away at the panelling for ten minutes or so until she had scraped a wide enough crack at which to place one eye. She knelt before it for a moment or two, then turned to me in disappointment. "There's nothing there," she said. "It's a plain chamber, much the same as this, with a bed in one corner and hangings on the wall." I felt quite aggrieved, having hoped—in my idiotic romantic fashion—for a heap of treasure. I bade her hang a picture over the crack and turned to my dinner. But later, when Joan came to sit with me at sunset, and the shadows began to fall, she said suddenly, with a shiver, "You know, Honor, I slept once in this room when John had the ague, and I did not care for it."

"Why so?" I asked, drinking my wine.

"I thought I heard footsteps in the chamber next door."

I glanced at the picture over the crack, but it was well hidden. "What sort of footsteps?" I said.

She shook her head, puzzled. "Soft ones," she said, "like someone walks with slippered soles for fear he shall be heard."

"How long ago was this?" I asked.

"During the winter," she said. "I did not tell anyone."

"A servant perhaps," I suggested, "who had no business to be there."

"No," she said, "none of the servants have a key; no one has but my father-in-law, and he was from home then." She waited a moment, and then she said, glancing over her shoulder, "I believe it is a ghost."

"Why should a ghost walk at Menabilly?" I answered. "The house has not been built fifty years."

"People have died here, though," she said. "John's old grand-father and his uncle John." She watched me with bright eyes, and, knowing my Joan, I wagered there was more to come.

"So you, too, have heard the poison story," I said, drawing a bow at venture. "But I don't believe it," she said, "it would be wicked, horrible. He is too good and kind a man. But I do think it was a ghost that I heard, the ghost of the elder brother that they called Uncle John."

"Why should he pace the room with padded soles?" I asked.

She did not answer for a moment, and then, guiltily, she whispered, "They never speak of it—John made me promise not to tell—but he was mad, a hopeless idiot, and they used to keep him shut up in the chamber there."

This was something I had never heard before. I found it horrible.

"Are you certain?" I said.

"Oh, yes," she replied. There is a bit about it in old Mr. Rashleigh's will; John told me. Old Mr. Rashleigh, before he died, made my father-in-law promise to look after the elder brother, give him food and drink and shelter in the house. They say the chamber there was set aside for him, built in a special way; I don't exactly know. And then he died, you see, very suddenly of the smallpox. John and Alice and Elizabeth don't remember him; they were only babies."

"What a disagreeable tale," I said. "Give me some more wine, and let's forget it." After a while she went away, and Matty came to draw the curtains. I had no more visitors that night. But as the shadows lengthened and the owls began to hoot down in the warren, I found my thoughts returning to the idiot Uncle John, shut up in the chamber there, year after year, from the first building of the house, a prisoner of the mind, as I was of the body.

But in the morning I heard news that made me forget, for a while, this talk of footsteps in the night.

Eight

$\mathscr{T}$HE DAY BEING FINE, I VENTURED FORTH IN MY CHAIR
once more upon the causeway, returning to the house at
midday to find that a messenger had ridden to Menabilly during
my absence, bearing letters from Plymouth and elsewhere to
members of the household, and the family were now gathered
in the gallery discussing the latest information from the war.
Alice was seated in one of the long windows overlooking the
garden, reading aloud a lengthy epistle from her Peter. "Sir
John Digby has been wounded," she said, "and the siege is now
to be conducted by a new commander who has them all by the
ears at once. Poor Peter—this will mean an end to hawking
excursions and supper parties. They will have to wage the
war more seriously." She turned the page of scrawled writing,
shaking her head. "And who is to command them?" inquired
John, who once more was acting as attendant to my chair. "Sir
Richard Grenvile," answered Alice.

Mary was not in the gallery at the time, and since she was
the only person at Menabilly to know of the romance long
finished and forgotten, I was able to hear mention of his name
without embarrassment. For it is a strange truth, as I had by
then discovered, that we only become aware of hot discomfort
when others are made awkward for our sakes.

I knew, from something that Robin had let slip, that Richard was come into the West, his purpose being to raise troops for the King, so I understood, and to be placed now in command of the siege of Plymouth meant promotion. He had already become notorious, of course, for the manner in which he had hoodwinked Parliament and joined His Majesty. "And what" I heard myself saying, "does Peter think of his new commander?" Alice folded up her letter. "As a soldier, he admires him," she answered, "but I think he has not a great opinion of him as a man."

"I have heard," said John, "that he hasn't a scruple in the world, and once an injury is done to him he will never forget it or forgive."

"I believe," said Alice, that when in Ireland he inflicted great cruelty on the people—though some say it was no more than they deserved. But I fear he is very different from his brother."

It made strange hearing to have the lover who had held me once against his heart discussed in so calm and cool a fashion.

At this moment Will Sparke came up to us, also with a letter in his hand. "So Richard Grenvile is commanding now at Plymouth," he said. "I have the news here from my kinsman in Tavistock, who is with Prince Maurice. It seems the Prince thinks highly of his ability, but, my heaven—what a scoundrel."

I began to burn silently, my old love and loyalty rising to the surface.

"We were just talking of him," said John.

"You heard his first action on coming West, I suppose?" said Will Sparke, warming, like all his kind, to malicious gossip. "I had it direct from my kinsman at the time. Grenvile rode straight to Fitzford, his wife's property, turned out the caretakers, seized all the contents, had the agent flung into jail, and took all the money owed by the tenants to his wife for his own use."

"I thought," said Alice, "that he had been divorced from his wife."

"So he is divorced," replied Will. "He is not entitled to a penny from the property. But that is Richard Grenvile for you."

"I wonder," I said calmly, "what has happened to his children?"

"I can tell you that," said Will. "The daughter is with the mother in London—whether she has friends in Parliament or not I cannot say. But the lad was at Fitzford with his tutor when Grenvile seized the place, and by all accounts is with him now. They say the poor boy is in fear and trembling of his father, and small blame to him."

"No doubt," I said, "he was brought up to hate him by his mother."

"Any woman," retorted Will, "who had been as ill used as she, unhappy lady, would hardly paint her spouse in pretty colours."

Logic was with him, as it always was with the persons who maligned Richard, and presently I bade John carry me upstairs to my apartment. But the day that had started so well when I set forth upon the causeway turned sour on me, and I lay on my bed for the rest of it, telling Matty I would see no visitors.

For fifteen years the Honor that had been lay dead and buried, and here she was struggling beneath the surface once again at the mere mention of a name that was best forgotten. Richard in Germany, Richard in Ireland, was too remote a person to swim into my daily thoughts. When I thought of him or dreamt of him—which was often—it was always as he had been in the past. And now he must break into the present, a mere thirty miles away, and there would be constant talk of him, criticism, and discussion; I should be forced to hear his name bandied and besmirched, as Will Sparke had bandied it this morning. "You know," he had said, before I went upstairs, "the Roundheads call him

Skellum Grenvile and have put a price upon his head. The nickname suits him well, and even his own soldiers whisper it behind his back."

"And what does it signify?" I asked.

"Oh," he said. "I thought you were a German scholar, Mistress Harris, as well as learned in the Greek and Latin." He paused. "It means a vicious beast," he sniggered.

Oh, yes, there was much reason for me to lay moodily on my bed, with the memory of a young man smiling at me from the branches of an apple tree, and the humming of the bees in the blossom.

Fifteen years... he would be forty-four now, ten years older than myself. "Matty," I said, before she lit the candles, "bring me a mirror."

She glanced at me suspiciously, her long nose twitching.

"What do you want a mirror for?" she asked.

"God damn you, that's my business," I answered.

We snapped at one another continually, she and I, but it meant nothing. She brought me the mirror, and I examined my appearance as though seeing myself as a stranger would.

There were my two eyes, my nose, my mouth, much as they had always been, but I was fuller in the face now than I had been as a maid—sluggish from lying on my back, I told myself. There were little lines, too, beneath my eyes, lines that had grown there from pain when my legs hurt me. I had less colour than I had once. My hair was the best point, for this was Matty's special pride, and she would brush it for hours to make it glossy. I handed back the mirror to Matty with a sigh. "What do you make of it?" she asked.

"In ten years," I said, "I'll be an old woman."

She sniffed and began to fold my garments on a chair.

"I'll tell you one thing," she said, drawing in her underlip.

"What's that?"

"You're fairer now as a woman than you ever were as a prinking, blushing maid, and I'm not the only one that thinks it."

This was encouraging, and I had an immediate vision of a long train of suitors all tiptoeing up the stairs to pay me homage. A pretty fancy, but where the devil were they?

"You're like an old hen," I said to Matty, "who always thinks her poorest chick the loveliest. Go to bed."

I lay there for some time, thinking of Richard, wondering too about his little son, who must be a lad now of fourteen. Could it be true, as Will Sparke had said, that the boy went in fear of his father? Supposing we had wedded, Richard and I, and this had been our son. Would we have sported with him as a child, danced him upon our knees, gone down with him on all fours on the ground and played at tigers? Would he have come running to me with muddied hands, his hair about his face, laughing? Would he be auburn-haired like Richard?

Would we all three have ridden to the chase, and Richard have shown him how to sit straight in the saddle? Vain, idle supposition, drenched in sentiment, like buttercups by the dew on a wet morning. I was half asleep, muzzy with a dream, when I heard a movement in the next chamber. I raised my head front the pillow, thinking it might be Matty in the dressing room, but the sound came from the other side. I held my breath and waited. Yes, there it was again. A stealthy footstep padding to and fro. I remembered in a flash the tale that Joan had told me of the mad Rashleigh uncle confined in there for years. Was it his ghost, in truth, that stole there in the shadows? The night was pitch, for it was only quarter moon, and no glimmer came to me from either casement. The clock in the belfry struck one. The footsteps ceased, then proceeded once again, and for the first time, too, I was aware of a cold current of air coming to my apartment from the chamber beyond.

My own casements were closed, save the one that looked into

the inner court, and this was only open to a few inches; besides, the draught did not come from that direction. I remembered then that the closed-up door into the empty chamber did not meet the floor at its base but was raised two inches or so from the ground, for Matty had tried to look under it before she made the crack with the scissors.

It was from beneath this door that the current of air blew now—and to my certain knowledge there had never been a draught from there before. Something, then, had happened in the empty chamber next to mine to cause the current. The muffled tread continued, stealthy, soft, and with the sweat running down my face I thought of the ghost stories my brothers had recounted to me as a child, of how an earth-bound spirit would haunt the place he hated, bringing with him from the darker regions a whisper of chill dank air. One of the dogs barked from the stables, and this homely sound brought me to my senses. Was it not more likely that a living person was responsible for the cold current that swept beneath the door, and that the cause of it was the opening of the barred window that, like my western one, looked out on to the outer court? The ghost of poor idiot Uncle John would have kept me in my bed forever, but a living soul, treading furtively in the night hours in a locked chamber, was something to stir the burning curiosity of one who, it may be remembered, had from early childhood shown a propensity to eavesdrop where she was not wanted.

Secretly, stealthily, I reached out my hand to the flint that Matty from long custom left beside my bed, and lit my candle. My chair was also within reach. I pulled it close to me, and with the labour that years of practice had never mitigated, lowered myself into it. The footsteps ceased abruptly. So I am right, I thought in triumph. No ghost would hesitate at the sound of a creaking chair. I waited perhaps for as long as five minutes, and then the intruder must have recovered himself, for I heard the faint noise of the opening of a drawer. Softly I wheeled myself across the room. Whoever is there, I smiled grimly. is not aware that a cripple can be mobile, granted she has a resourceful brother with a talent for invention. I came abreast of the door and waited once again. The picture that Matty had hung over the crack was on a level with my eye. I blew out my candle, trusting to fortune to blunder my way back to bed when my curiosity was satisfied. Then, very softly, holding my breath, I lifted the picture from the nail and, framing my face with my hands for cover, I peered with one eye into the slit. The chamber was in half darkness, lit by a single candle on a bare table. I could not see to right or left—the crack was not large enough—but the table was in a direct line with my eye. A man was sitting at the table, his back turned to me. He was booted and spurred and wore a riding cloak about his shoulders. He had a pen in his hand and was writing on a long white slip of paper, consulting now and again another list propped up before him on the table. Here was flesh and blood indeed, and no ghost; the intruder was writing away as calmly as though he were a clerk on a copying stool. I watched him come to the end of the long slip of paper, and then he folded it and, going to the cabinet in the wall, opened the drawer with the same sound I had heard before. The light was murky, as I have said, and with his back turned to me and his hat upon his head, I could make little of him except that his riding cloak was a dark crimson. Then he moved out of my line of vision, taking the candle, and walked softly to the far corner of the room. I heard nothing after that and no further footsteps, and while I waited, puzzled, with my eye still to the crack, I became aware suddenly that the draught of air was no longer blowing beneath the door. Yet I had heard no sound of a closing window. I bent down from my chair, testing the bottom of the door with my hand, but no current came. The intruder, therefore, had by some action unperceived by me, cut off the draught, making his exit at the same time. He had left the chamber, as he had entered it, by some entrance other than the door that led into the corridor. I blundered back across my room in clumsy fashion, having first replaced the picture on its nail, and knocking into a table on the way, woke that light sleeper, Matty. "Have you lost your senses?" she scolded, "circling round your chamber in the pitch black?" And she lifted me like a child and dumped me in my bed.

"I had a nightmare," I lied, "and thought I heard footsteps. Is there anyone moving in the courtyard, Matty?"

She drew aside the curtain. "Not a soul," she grumbled, "not even a cat scratching on the cobbles. Everyone is asleep."

"You will think me mazed, I don't doubt," I answered, "but venture with your candle a moment into the passage and try the door of the locked apartment next to this."

"Mazed it is," she snapped. "This comes of looking into the mirror on a Friday night." In a moment she was back again. "The door is locked as it always is," she said, "and, judging by the dust upon the latch, it has not been opened for months, or more."

"No," I mused. "That is just what I supposed."

She stared at me, and shook her head.

"I'd best brew you a hot cordial," she said.

"I do not want a hot cordial," I answered.

"There's nothing like it for putting a stop to bad dreams," she said. She tucked in my blankets and after grumbling a moment or two, went back to her own room. But my mind was far too lively to find sleep for several hours. I kept trying to remember the formation of the house, seen from without, and what it was that struck me as peculiar the day before, when John had wheeled me in my chair towards the gatehouse. It was past four in the morning when the answer came to me. Menabilly was built foursquare around the courtyard, with clean, straight lines and no protruding wings. But at the northwest corner of the house, jutting from the wall outside the fastened chamber, was a buttress, running tall and straight from the roof down to the cobbles. Why in the name of heaven, when old John Rashleigh built his house in 1600, did he build the northwest corner with a buttress? And had it some connection with the fact that the apartment behind was designed for the special use of his idiot eldest son?

Some lunatics were harmless; some were not. But even the worst, the truly animal, were given air and exercise at certain periods of the day and would hardly be paraded through the corridors of the house itself. I smiled to myself in the darkness, for I had guessed, after three restless hours of tossing on my back, how the intruder had crept into the apartment next to mine without using the locked door into the passage. He had come and he had gone, as poor Uncle John had doubtless done nearly half a century before, by a hidden stairway in the buttress. But why he had come, and what was his business, I had yet to discover.

Nine

*I*T TURNED TO RAIN THE NEXT MORNING, AND I WAS UNABLE to take my usual airing in the grounds. But later in the day the fitful sun peeked through the low clouds and, wrapping my cloak about me, I announced to Matty my intention of going abroad.

John Rashleigh was out riding round the farms on the estate, with the steward Langdon, whose house it was I had observed beyond the bowling green. Thus I had not my faithful chair attendant. Joan came with me instead, and it was an easy enough matter to persuade her to wheel me first through the archway to the outer court, where I made pretence of looking up to admire my quarters in the gatehouse.

In reality, I was observing the formation of the buttress, which ran, as I thought it did, the whole length of the house on the northwest corner, immediately behind it being the barred chamber.

The width of the buttress was a little over four feet, so I judged, and, if it was hollow behind a false facade of stone, could easily contain a stair. There was, however, no outlet to the court; this was certain. I bade Joan wheel me to the base on pretence of touching the lichen, which already, after only fifty years, was forming on the stone, and I satisfied myself that the outside of the buttress, at any rate, was solid. If my supposition was correct, then there must be a stairway within the buttress leading underground, far beneath the foundations of the house, and a passage running some distance to an outlet in the grounds. Poor Uncle John. It was significant that there was no portrait of him in the gallery, alongside the rest of the family. If so much trouble was taken by his father that he should not be seen, he must have been an object of either fear or horror. We left the outer court and, traversing the warren, came by the path outside the steward's lodge. The door was open to the parlour, and Mrs. Langdon, the steward's wife, was standing in the entrance, a comfortable homely woman, who on being introduced to me insisted that I take a glass of milk. While she was absent, we glanced about the trim room and Joan, laughing, pointed to a bunch of keys that hung on a nail beside the door. "Old Langdon is like a jailer," she whispered. "As a rule he is never parted from that bunch but dangles them at his belt. John tells me he has a duplicate of each key belonging to my father-in-law."

"Has he been steward long?" I asked.

"Oh yes," said Joan. "He came here as a young man when the house was built. There is no corner of Menabilly that he does not know."

I wager, then, I thought to myself, that he knows too the secret of the buttress, if there is a secret. Joan, with a curiosity much like mine, was examining the labels on the keys.

"Summerhouse," she read, and with a mischievous smile at me, she slipped it from the bunch and dangled it before my eyes. "You expressed a wish to peep into the tower on the causeway, did you not?" she teased. At this moment Mrs. Langdon returned with the milk, and fearful of discovery, Joan, like a guilty child, reddened and concealed the key within her gown. We chatted for a few moments, while I drank my milk in haste and Joan gazed with great innocence at the ceiling. Then we bade the good woman farewell and turned into the gardens, through the gate in the high wall.

"Now you have done for yourself," I said. "How in the world will you return the key?"

Joan was laughing under her breath. "I'll give it to John," she said. "He must devise some tale or other to satisfy old Langdon. But, seeing that we have the key, Honor, it would be a pity not to make some use of it." She was an accomplice after my own heart, and a true godchild. "I make no promise," I murmured. "Wheel me along the causeway, and we will see which way the wind is blowing."

We crossed the gardens, passing the house as we did so, and waved to Alice at the window of her apartment above the gallery. I caught sight, too, of Temperance Sawle, peering like a witch from the side door, evidently in half a mind to risk the damp ground and join us. "I am the best off in my chair," I called to her. "The walks are wringing wet, and clouds coming up again from the Gribben."

She bolted like a rabbit within doors again, and I saw her pass into the gallery, while Joan, smothering her laughter, propelled me through the gate on to the causeway.

It was only when mounted thus some ten feet from the ground that the fine view of the sea could be obtained, for down on the level the sloping ground masked all sight of it. Menabilly, though built on a hill, lay therefore in a saucer, and I commented on the fact to Joan as she wheeled me towards the towered summerhouse at the far end of the causeway. "Yes," she said, "John has explained to me that the house was so built that no glimpse of it should be sighted from the sea. Old Mr. Rashleigh lived in great fear of pirates. But, if the truth be told, he was not above piracy himself, and in the old days, when he was alive, there were bales of silk and bars of silver, concealed somewhere within the house, stolen from the French and brought hither by his own ships, and then landed down at Pridmouth yonder."

In which case, I thought privately, a passage known to no one but himself, and perhaps his steward, would prove of great advantage.

But we had reached the summerhouse, and Joan, glancing first over her shoulder to see that no one came, produced her key, and turned it in the lock. "I must tell you," she confessed, "that there is nothing great to see. I have been here once or twice with my father-in-law, and it is nought but a rather musty room, the shelves lined with books and papers, and a fine view from the windows." She wheeled me through the door, and I glanced about me, half hoping, in a most childish manner, to find traces of piracy. But all was in order. The walls of the summerhouse were lined with books, save for the windows, which, even as she said, commanded the whole stretch of the bay to the Gribbin and to the east showed the steep coast road that led to Fowey. Anyone, on horse or on foot, approaching Menabilly from the east would be observed by a watcher at the window, likewise a vessel sailing close inshore. Old Mr. Rashleigh had shown great cunning as a builder.

The flagged floor was carpeted, save in one corner by my brother-in-law's writing table, where a strip of heavy matting served for his feet. It was in keeping with his particular character that the papers on his desk were neatly documented and filed in order. Joan left me in my chair to browse among the books, while she herself kept watch out on the causeway. There was nothing much to tempt my interest. Books of law, dry as dust, books of accountancy, and many volumes docketed as "County Affairs," no doubt filed when Jonathan was sheriff for the Duchy of Cornwall. On a lower shelf, near to his writing table, were volumes labelled "My Town House" and another

"Menabilly," while close behind these he had "Marriage Settlements" and "Wills." He was nothing if not methodical in his business. The volume marked "Wills" was nearest to me and surprisingly tempting to my hand. I looked over my shoulder and saw through the window that Joan, humming a tune, was busily engaged in picking posies for her children. I reached out my hand and took the volume. Page after page was covered in my brother-in-law's meticulously careful hand. I turned to the entries headed by the words "My father, John Rashleigh, born, 1554. Died, 6 May 1624," and folded close to this—perhaps it had slipped in by accident—was an account of a case brought to the Star Chamber in the year 1616 by one Charles Bennett against the above John Rashleigh. This Charles Bennett, I remembered, was father to Robert Bennett, our neighbour at Looe, who had spread the poison rumour. The case, had I time to peruse it, would have made good reading, for it was of a highly scandalous nature; Charles Bennett accused John Rashleigh of "leading a most incontinent course of life, lying with divers women, over forty-five in number, uttering blasphemies, etc., etc., and his wife dying through grief at his behaviour, she being a sober virtuous woman." I was somewhat surprised after this, glancing at the end, to find that John Rashleigh had been acquitted. What a lovely weapon, though, to hold over the head of my self-righteous brother-in-law when he made boast, as he sometimes did, of the high morals of his family. But I turned a page and came to the will I had been seeking. So old John Rashleigh had not done too badly for his relatives. Nick Sawle had got fifty pounds (which I dare say Temperance had snatched from him) and the Sparkes had benefited to the same extent. The poor of Fowey had some twenty pounds bestowed upon them. It is really most iniquitous, I told myself, that I should be prying thus into matters that concern me not at all, but I read on. All lands in

Cornwall, his house in Fowey, his house at Menabilly, and the residue of his estate to his second son Jonathan, his executor. And then the codicil at the end: "Thirty pounds annuity out of Fowey to the use of my eldest son John's maintenance, to be paid after the death of my second son Jonathan, who during his life will maintain him and allow him a chamber with meat, drink, and apparel." I caught a glimpse of Joan's shadow passing the window, and with a hurried, guilty movement I shut the volume and put it back upon the shelf.

There was no doubt then about the disability of poor Uncle John. I turned my chair from the desk, and as I did so the right wheel stuck against some obstruction on the ground beneath the heavy matting. I bent down from my chair to free the wheel, turning up the edge of the mat as I did so. I saw then that the obstruction was a ring in the flagstone, which, though flat to the ground and unnoticeable possibly to a foot treading upon it, had been enough to obstruct the smooth running of my chair.

I leant from my chair as far as I could, and seizing the ring with my two hands, succeeded in lifting the stone some three inches from the ground, before the weight of it caused me to drop it once again. But not before I had caught a glimpse of the sharp corner of a step descending into darkness. I replaced the mat just as my godchild came into the summerhouse.

"Well, Honor," she said, "have you seen all you have a mind to for the present?"

"I rather think I have," I answered, and in a few moments she had closed the door, turned the key once more in the lock, and we were bowling back along the causeway. She prattled away about this and that, but I paid but scant attention, for my mind was full of my latest discovery. It seemed fairly certain that there was a pit or tunnel underneath the flagstone in the summerhouse, and the placing of a mat on top of it and the position of the desk suggested that the hiding of it was deliberate. There was no rust about the ringbolt to show disuse, and the ease with which I, helpless in my chair, had lifted the stone a few inches proved to me that this was no cobwebby corner of concealment long forgotten. The flagstone had been lifted frequently and recently. I looked over my shoulder down the pathway to the beach, or Pridmouth Cove, as Joan had termed it. It was narrow and steep, flanked with stubby trees, and I thought how easy it would be for an incoming vessel, anchored in deep water, to send a boat ashore with some half dozen men, who could climb up the path to where it ended beneath the summerhouse on the causeway, and for a watcher at the window of the summerhouse to relieve the men of any burden they should bear upon their backs. Was this what old John Rashleigh had foreseen when he built his tower, and did bales of silk and bars of silver lie stacked beneath the flagstone some forty years before? It seemed very probable, but whether the step beneath the flagstone had any connection with my suspicions of the buttress it was difficult to say. One thing was certain. There was a secret entrance to Menabilly, through the chamber next to mine, and someone had passed that way only the night before, for I had seen him with my own eyes.

"You are silent, Honor," said Joan, breaking in upon my thoughts. "What are you thinking of?"

"I have just come to the opinion," I answered, "that I was somewhat rash to leave Lanrest, where each day was alike, and come amongst you all at Menabilly, where something different happens every day."

"I wish I thought as you did," she replied. "To me the days and weeks seem much the same, with the Sawles backbiting at the Sparkes, and the children fretful, and my dear John grousing all the while that he cannot go fighting with Peter and the rest."

We came to the end of the causeway, and were about to turn in through the gate into the walled gardens when her little son Jonathan, a child of barely three years, came running across the path to greet us. "Uncle Peter is come," he cried, "and another gentleman, and many soldiers. We have been stroking the horses."

I smiled up at his mother. "What did I tell you?" I said. "Not a day passes but there is some excitement at Menabilly."

I had no wish to run the gauntlet of the long windows in the gallery, where the company would be assembled, and bade Joan wheel me to the entrance in the front of the house, which was usually deserted at this time of the day, when no one was within the dining chamber. Once indoors, one of the servants could carry me to my apartment in the gatehouse, and later I could send for Peter, always a favourite with me, and have his news of Robin. We passed in then through the door, little Jonathan running in front, and at once we heard laughter and talk coming from the gallery. The wide arched door to the inner courtyard was open, and we could see some half dozen troopers with their horses watering at the well beneath the belfry. There was much bustle and clatter, a pleasant lively sound, and I saw one of the troopers look up to a casement in the attic and wave his hand in greeting to a blushing kitchen girl. He was a big, strong-looking fellow with a broad grin on his face, and then he turned and signalled to his companions to follow him, which they did, each one leading his horse away from the well and following him through the archway beneath my gatehouse to the outer courtyard and the stables.

It was when they turned thus and clattered through the court that I noticed how each fellow wore upon his shoulder a scarlet shield with three gold rests upon it. For a moment I thought my heart would stop beating, and I was seized with sudden panic.

"Find one of the servants quickly," I said to Joan. "I wish to be carried straightway to my room."

But it was too late. Even as she sent little Jonathan scampering hurriedly towards the servants' quarters, Peter Courtney came out into the hall, his arm about his Alice, in company with two or three brother officers. "Why, Honor," he cried. "This is a joy indeed. Knowing your habits, I feared to find you hiding in your apartment, with Matty standing like a dragon at the door. Gentlemen, I present to you Mistress Honor Harris, who has not the slightest desire to make your acquaintance." I could have slain him for his lack of discretion, but he was one of those gay lighthearted creatures with a love of jesting and poking fun, and no more true perception than a bumblebee. In a moment his friends were bowing before my chair and exchanging introductions, and Peter, still laughing and talking in his haphazard strident way, was pushing my chair through to the gallery. Alice, who made up in intuition all he lacked, would have stopped him had I caught her eye, but she was too glad to have a glimpse of him to do anything but smile and hold his arm. The gallery seemed full of people—Sawles, and Sparkes, and Rashleighs all chatting at the top of their voices, and at the far end by the window I caught sight of Mary in conversation with someone whose tall back and broad shoulders were painfully, almost terrifyingly familiar. Mary's expression, preoccupied and distrait, told me that she was at that moment wondering if I had returned from my promenade, for I saw her eyes search the gardens; and then she saw me, and her brow wrinkled in a well-known way and she began talking sixteen to the dozen. Her loss of composure gave me back my own. What in hell's name do I care, after fifteen years? I told myself. There is no need to swoon at an encounter. God knows I have breeding enough to be mistress of the situation, here in Mary's house at Menabilly, with nigh a score of people in the room.

Peter, impervious to any doubtful atmosphere, propelled me slowly towards the window, and out of the corner of my eye I saw my sister Mary, overcome by cowardice, do something that I dare swear I might have done myself had I been her, and that was to murmur a hasty excuse to her companion about summoning the servants to bring further refreshment before she fled from the gallery without looking once in my direction. Richard turned and saw me. And as he looked at me it was as if my whole heart moved over in my body and was mine no longer.

"Sir," said Peter, "I am pleased to present to you my dearly loved kinswoman, Mistress Honor Harris of Lanrest."

"My kinswoman also," said Richard, and then he bent forward and kissed my hand.

"Oh, is that so, sir?" said Peter vaguely, looking from one to the other of us. "I suppose all we Cornish families are in some way near related. Let me fill your glass, sir. Honor, will you drink with us?"

"I will," I answered. In truth, a glass of wine seemed to me my only salvation at the moment. While Peter filled the glasses I had my first long look at Richard. He had altered. There was no doubt of it. He had grown much broader, for one thing, not only in the body, but about the neck and shoulders. His face was somewhat heavier than it had been. There was a brown, weather-beaten air about him that was not there before, and lines beneath his eyes. It was after all, fifteen years. And then he turned to me, giving me my glass, and I saw that there was only one white streak in his auburn hair, high above the temple, and the eyes that looked at me were quite unchanged.

"Your health and fortune," he said quietly, and draining his glass, he held it out with mine to be refilled. I saw the little tell-tale pulse beating on his right temple, and I knew then that the encounter was as startling and as moving to him as it was to me.

"I did not know," he said, "that you were at Menabilly."

I saw Peter glance at him curiously, and I wondered if this was the first time he had ever seen his commanding officer show any sign of nervousness or strain. The hand that held the glass trembled very slightly, and the voice that spoke was hard, queerly abrupt.

"I came here a few days since from Lanrest," I answered, my voice perhaps as oddly flat as his. "My brothers said I must not live alone while the war continues."

"They showed wisdom," he replied. "Essex is moving westward all the time. It is very probable we shall see fighting once again this side of the Tamar." At this moment Peter's small daughters came running to his knees, shrieking with joy to see their father, and Peter, laughing an apology, was swept into family life upon the instant, taking one apiece upon his shoulder and moving down the gallery in triumph. Richard and I were thus left alone beside the window. I looked out on to the garden, noting the trim yew hedges and the smooth lawns, while a score of trivial observations ran insanely through my head.

"How green the grass is after the morning rain," and "It is something chilly for the time of year" were phrases I had never yet used in my life, even to a stranger, but they seemed, at that moment, to be what was needed to the occasion. Yet though they rose unbidden to my tongue, I did not frame them, but continued looking out upon the garden in silence, with Richard as dumb as myself. And then in a low voice, clipped and hard, he said:

"If I am silent you must forgive me. I had not thought, after fifteen years, to find you so damnably unchanged."

This streak back from the indifferent present to the intimate past was a new shock to be borne, but a curiously exciting one.

"Why damnably?" I said, watching him over the rim of my glass.

"I had become used, over a long period, to a very different picture," he said. "I thought of you as an invalid, wan and pale, a sort of shadow without substance, hedged about with doctors and attendants. And instead I find—this." He looked me then full in the face with a directness and a lack of reserve that I remembered well.

"I am sorry," I answered, "to disappoint you."

"You misinterpret me," he said. "I have not said I was disappointed. I am merely speechless." He drained his glass once more and put it back on the table. "I shall recover," he said, "in a moment or two. Where can we talk?"

"Talk?" I asked. "Why, we can talk here, I suppose, if you wish to."

"Amidst a host of babbling fools and screaming children—not on your life," he answered. "Have you not your own apartments?"

"I have," I replied with some small attempt at dignity, "but it would be considered somewhat odd if we retired there."

"You were not used to quibble at similar suggestions in the past," he said.

This was something of a blow beneath the belt, and I had no answer for him.

"I would have you remember," I said, with lameness, "that we have been strangers to one another for fifteen years."

"Do you think," he said, "that I forget it for a moment?"

At this juncture we were interrupted by Temperance Sawle, who with baleful eyes had been watching us from a distance and now moved within our orbit. "Sir Richard Grenvile, I believe," she said.

"Your servant, ma'am," replied Richard with a look that would have slain anyone less soul-absorbed than Temperance.

"The Evil One seeks you for his own," she announced. "Even at this moment I see his talons at your throat and his jaws open to devour you. Repent, repent, before it is too late."

"What the devil does she mean?" said Richard.

I shook my head, and pointed to the heavens, but Temperance, warming to her theme, continued:

"The mark of the Beast is on your forehead," she declared. "The men you lead are become as ravening wolves. You will all perish, every one of you, in the bottomless pit."

"Tell the old fool to go to hell," said Richard.

I offered Mistress Sawle a glass of wine, but she flinched as if it had been boiling oil. "There shall be a weeping and a gnashing of teeth," she continued.

"My God, you're right," said Richard, and, taking her by the shoulders, he twisted her round like a top, and walked her across the room to the fireplace and her husband.

"Keep this woman under control," he ordered, and there was an immediate silence, followed by a little flutter of embarrassed conversation. Peter Courtney, very red about the neck, hurried forward with a brimming decanter. "Some more wine, sir?" he said.

"Thank you, no, I've had about as much as I can stand," said Richard. I noticed the young officers, all with their backs turned, examining the portraits on the walls with amazing interest. Will Sparke was one of the little crowd about the fireplace, staring hard at the King's general, his mouth wide open.

"A good day for catching flies, sir," said Richard pleasantly.

A little ripple of laughter came from Joan, hastily suppressed as Richard turned his eyes upon her.

Will Sparke pressed forward. "I have a young kinsman under your command," he said, "an ensign of the Twenty-third Regiment of Foot."

"Very probably," said Richard. "I never speak to ensigns." He beckoned to John Rashleigh, who had returned but a few moments ago from his day's ride and was now hovering at the entrance to the gallery somewhat mudstained and splashed, bewildered by the unexpected company. "Hi, you," called

Richard, "Will you summon one of your fellow servants and carry Mistress Harris's chair to her apartment? She has had enough of the company downstairs."

"That is John Rashleigh, sir," whispered Peter hurriedly, "the son of the house, and your host in his father's absence."

"Ha! My apologies," said Richard, walking forward with a smile. "Your dress being somewhat in disorder, I mistook you for a menial. My own young officers lose their rank if they appear so before me. How is your father?"

"Well, sir, I believe," stammered John in great nervousness.

"I am delighted to hear it," said Richard. "Tell him so when you see him. And tell him, too, that now I am come into the West I propose to visit here very frequently—the course of the war permitting it."

"Yes, sir."

"You have accommodation for my officers, I suppose, and for a number of men out in the park, should we wish to bivouac at any time."

"Yes, indeed, sir."

"Excellent. And now I propose to dine upstairs with Mistress Harris, who is a close kinswoman of mine, a fact of which you may not be aware. What is the usual method with her chair?"

"We carry it, sir. It is quite a simple matter." John gave a nod to Peter, who, astonishingly subdued for him, came forward, and the pair of them seized an arm of my chair on either side.

"It would be an easier matter," said Richard, "if the occupant were bodily removed, and carried separately." And before I could protest he had placed his arms about me and had lifted me from the chair. "Lead on, gentlemen," commanded Richard.

The strange procession proceeded up the stairs, watched by the company in the gallery and by some of the servants, too, who, with their backs straight against the wall, and their eyes lowered, permitted us to pass. John and Peter tramped on ahead with the chair between them, step by step, both of them red about the neck; while I, with my head on Richard's shoulder, and my arms tight about him for fear of falling, thought the way seemed over long.

"I was in error just now," said Richard in my ear. "You have changed after all."

"In what way?" I asked.

"You are two stone heavier." he answered.

And so we came to my chamber in the gatehouse.

Ten

I CAN RECOLLECT THAT SUPPER AS IF IT WERE YESTERDAY. I lay on my bed with the pillows packed behind me, and Richard was seated on the end of it, with the low table in front of us both.

It might have been a day since we had parted, instead of fifteen years. When Matty came into the room bearing the platters, her mouth pursed and disapproving—for she had never understood how we came to lose one another, but imagined he had deserted me because of my crippled state—Richard burst out laughing on the instant, calling her "old go-between," which had been his nickname for her in those distant days, and asked her how many hearts she had broken since he saw her last. She was for replying to him shortly, but it was no use. He would have none of it and, taking the platters from her and putting them on the table, he soon had her reconciled—blushing from head to toe—while he poked fun at her broadening figure and the frizzed curl on her forehead. "There are some half dozen troopers in the court," he told her, "waiting to make your acquaintance. Go and prove to them that Cornish women are better than the frousts in Devon," and she went off, closing the door behind her, guessing no doubt that for the first time in fifteen years I had no need of her services. He fell to eating right away, for he was always a good trencherman, and soon cleared all that had been put before us, while I—still weak with the shock of seeing him—toyed with the wishbone of a chicken. He started walking about the chamber before he had finished, a habit I remembered well, with a great bone in one hand and a pie in the other, talking all the while about the defences at Plymouth, which his predecessor had allowed to become formidable instead of razing them to the ground on first setting siege to the place. "You'd hardly credit it, Honor," he said, "but there's that fat idiot Digby been sitting on his arse nine months before the walls of Plymouth, allowing the garrison to sortie as they please, fetch food and firewood and build up barricades, while he played cards with his junior officers. Thank God a bullet in his head will keep him to his bed a month or two and allow me to conduct the siege instead."

"And what do you propose to do?" I asked.

"My first two tasks were simple," he replied, "and should have been done last October. I threw up a new earthwork at Mount Batten, and the guns I have placed there so damage the shipping that endeavours to pass through the Sound that the garrison are hard put to it for supplies. Secondly, I have cut off their water power, and the mills within the city can no longer grind flour for the inhabitants. Give me a month or two to play with, and I'll have 'em starved." He took a great bite out of his pie, and winked at me.

"And the blockade by land, is that effective now?" I questioned.

"It will be when I've had time to organize it," he answered. "The trouble is that I've arrived to find that most of the officers in my command are worse than useless—I've sacked more than half of them already. I have a good fellow in charge at Saltash, who sent the rebels flying back to Plymouth with several fleas in their ears when they tried a sortie a week or two back—a

sharp engagement in which my nephew Jack—Bevil's eldest
boy, you remember him—did very well. Last week we sprang
a little surprise on one of their outposts close to Maudlyn.
We beat them out of their position there and took a hundred
prisoners. I rather think the gentlemen of Plymouth sleep not
entirely easy in their beds."

"Prisoners must be something of a problem," I said. "It is
hard enough to find forage in the country for your own men.
You are obliged to feed them, I suppose?"

"Feed them be damned," he answered. "I send the lot to
Lydford Castle, where they are hanged without trial for high
treason." He threw his drumstick out of the window and tore
the other from the carcase.

"But, Richard," I said, hesitating, "that is hardly justice, is
it? I mean—they are only fighting for what they believe to be
a better cause than ours."

"I don't give a fig for justice," he replied. "The method is
effective, and that's the only thing that matters."

"I am told the Parliament has put a price upon your head
already," I said. "I am told you are much feared and hated by
the rebels."

"What would you have them do, kiss my backside?" he
asked. He smiled and came and sat beside me on the bed.

"The war is too much with us; let us talk about ourselves,"
he said. "I had not wished for that but hoped to keep him busy
with his siege of Plymouth."

"Where are you living at the moment?" I parried. "In tents
about the fields?"

"What would I be doing in a tent," he mocked, "with the
best houses in Devon at my disposal? Nay, my headquarters
are at Buckland Abbey, which my grandfather sold to Francis
Drake half a century ago, and I do not mind telling you that I
live there very well. I have seized all the sheep and cattle upon

the estate, and the tenants pay their rents to me or else are hanged. They call me the Red Fox behind my back, and the women, I understand, use the name as a threat to their children when they misbehave, saying 'Grenvile is coming. The Red Fox will have you.'"

He laughed, as if this was a fine jest, but I was watching the line of his jaw, which was heavier than before, and the curve of his mouth that narrowed at the corners.

"It was not thus," I said softly, "that your brother Bevil's reputation spread throughout the West."

"No," he said, "and I have not a wife like Bevil had, nor a home I love, nor a great brood of happy children."

His voice was harsh suddenly and strangely bitter. I turned my face away and lay back on my pillows.

"Do you have your son with you at Buckland?" I asked quietly.

"My spawn?" he said. "Yes, he is somewhere about the place with his tutor."

"What is he like?"

"Dick? Oh, he's a little handful of a chap with mournful eyes. I call him 'whelp' and make him sing to me at supper. But there's no sign of Grenvile in him—he's the spit of his Goddamned mother."

The boy we would have played with, and taught, and loved... I felt suddenly sad and oddly depressed that his father should dismiss him with this careless shrug of a shoulder.

"It went wrong with you then, Richard, from the beginning?" I said.

"It did," he answered.

There was a long silence, for we had entered upon dangerous ground.

"Did you never try," I asked, "to make some life of happiness?"

"Happiness was not in question," he said. "That went with you, a factor you refused to recognize."

"I am sorry," I said

"So am I," he answered

The shadows were creeping across the floor. Soon Matty would come to light the candles.

"When you refused to see me that last time," he said, "I knew that nothing mattered any more but bare existence. You have heard the story of my marriage with much embellishment, no doubt, but the bones of it are true."

"Had you no affection for her?"

"None whatever. I wanted her money, that was all."

"Which you did not get."

"Not then. I have it now. And her property, and her son—whom I fathered in a moment of black insensibility. The girl is with her mother up in London. I shall get her, too, one day when she can be of use to me."

"You are very altered, Richard, from the man I loved."

"If I am so, you know the reason why."

The sun had gone from the windows; the chamber seemed bleak and bare. Every bit of those fifteen years was now between us. Suddenly he reached out his hand to mine and, taking it, held it against his lips. The touch I so well remembered was very hard to bear.

"Why, in the name of God," he said, rising to his feet, "were you and I marked down for such tragedy?"

"It is no use being angry," I said. "I gave that up long ago. At first, yes, but not now. Not for many years. Lying on my back has taught me some discipline—but not the kind you engender in your troops."

He came and stood beside my bed, looking down upon me.

"Has no one told you," he said, "that you are more lovely now than you were then?"

I smiled, thinking of Matty and the mirror.

"I think you flatter me," I answered, "or maybe I have more time now. I lie idle to play with paint and powder."

No doubt he thought me cool and at my ease, and had no knowledge that his tone of voice ripped wide the dusty years and sent them scattering.

"There is no part of you," he said, "that I do not now remember. You had a mole in the small of your back which gave you much distress. You thought it ugly—but I liked it well."

"Is it not time," I said, "that you went downstairs to join your officers? I heard one of them say you were to sleep this night at Grampound."

"There was a bruise on your left thigh," he said, "caused by that confounded branch that protruded halfway up the apple tree. I compared it to a dark-sized plum, and you were much offended."

"I can hear the horses in the courtyard," I said. "Your troopers are preparing for the journey. You will never reach your destination before morning."

"You lie there," he said, "so smug and so complacent on your bed, very certain of yourself now you are thirty-four. I tell you, Honor, I care not two straws for your civility."

And he knelt then at my bed with his arms about me, and the fifteen years went whistling down the wind.

"Are you still queasy when you eat roast swan?" he whispered.

He wiped away the silly childish tears that pricked my eyes and laughed at me and smoothed my hair.

"Beloved half-wit, with your Goddamned pride," he said, "do you understand now that you blighted both our lives?"

"I understood that at the time," I told him.

"Why then, in the name of heaven, did you do it?"

"Had I not done so, you would soon have hated me, as you hated Mary Howard."

"That is a lie, Honor."

"Perhaps. What does it matter? There is no reason now to harp back on the past."

There I agree with you. The past is over. But we have the future with us. My marriage is annulled; you know that, I suppose. I am free to wed again."

"Then do so, to another heiress."

"I have no need of an heiress now, with all the estates in Devon to my plunder. I have become a gentleman of fortune, to be looked upon with favour by the spinsters of the West."

"There are many you might choose from, all agog for husbands."

"In all probability. But I want one spinster only, and that yourself."

I put my two hands on his shoulders and stared straight at him. The auburn hair, the hazel eyes, the little pulse that beat in his right temple. He was not the only one with recollections. I had my memories, too, and could—had I the mind and lack of modesty—have reminded him of a patch of freckles that had been as much a matter for discussion as the mole upon my back.

"No, Richard."

"Why?"

"Because I will not have you wedded to a cripple."

"You will never change your mind?"

"Never."

"And if I carry you by force to Buckland?"

"Do so, if you will; I can't prevent you. But I shall still be a cripple." I leant back on my pillows, faint suddenly, and exhausted. It had not been a light thing to bear, this strain of seeing him, of beating down the years. Very gently he released me and smoothed my blankets, and when I asked for a glass of water he gave me one in silence. It was nearly dark, and the dock in the belfry had struck eight a long while since. I could hear the jingling of harness from the courtyard and the scraping sound of horses.

"I must ride to Grampound," he said at length.

"Yes," I said.

He stood for a moment looking down on to the court. The candles were lit now throughout the house. The west windows of the gallery were open, sending a beam of light into my chamber. There was a sound of music. Alice was playing her lute and Peter singing.

Richard came once more and knelt beside my bed.

"I understand," he said, "what you have tried so hard to tell me. There can never be between us what there was once. Is that it?"

"Yes," I said.

"I knew that all along, but it would make no difference," he said.

"It would," I said, "after a little while."

Peter had a young voice, clear and gay, and his song was happy. I thought how Alice would be looking at him over her lute.

"I shall always love you," said Richard, "and you will love me too. We cannot lose each other now, not since I have found you again. May I come and see you often, that we may be together?"

"Whenever you wish," I answered.

There came a burst of clapping from the gallery, and the voices of the officers and the rest of the company asking for more. Alice struck up a lively jiggling air upon her lute—a soldier's drinking song, much whistled at the moment by our men—and they one and all chimed in upon the chorus, with the troopers in the courtyard making echo to the song.

"Do you have as much pain now as when you were first hurt?" he said.

"Sometimes," I answered, "when the air is damp. Matty calls me her weatherglass."

"Can nothing be done for it?"

"She rubs my legs and my back with lotion that the doctors gave her, but it is of little use. You see, the bones were all smashed and twisted, and they cannot knit together."

"Will you show me, Honor?"

"It is not a pretty sight, Richard."

"I have seen worse in battle."

I pulled aside my blanket and let him look upon the crumpled limbs that he had once known whole and clean. He was thus the only person in the world to see me so, except Matty and the doctors. I put my hands over my eyes, for I did not care to see his face.

"There is no need for that," he said. "Whatever you suffer you shall share with me from this day forward." He bent then and kissed my ugly twisted legs and after a moment, covered me again with the blanket. "Will you promise," he said, "never to send me from you again?"

"I promise," I said.

"Farewell, then, sweetheart, and sleep sound this night." He stood for a moment, his figure carved clear against the beam of light from the windows opposite, and then turned and went away down the passage. Presently I heard them all come out into the courtyard and mount their horses; there was the sound of leave-taking and laughter, Richard's voice high above the others, telling John Rashleigh he would come again. Suddenly clipt and curt, he called an order to his men, and they went riding through the archway beneath the gatehouse where I lay, and I heard the sound of the hoofbeats echo across the park.

Eleven

*T*HAT RICHARD GRENVILE SHOULD BECOME SUDDENLY, within a few hours, part of my life again was a mental shock that for a day or two threw me out of balance. The first excitement over and the stimulation of his presence that evening fading away, reaction swung me to a low ebb. It was all too late. No good could come of it. Memory of what had been, nostalgia of the past coupled with sentiment, had stirred us both to passion for a moment; but reason came with daylight. There could never be a life for us together, only the doubtful pleasure of brief meetings which the hazards of war might at any time render quite impracticable. What then? For me a lifetime of lying on my back, waiting for a chance encounter, for a message, for a word of greeting; and for him, after a space, a nagging irritation that I existed in the background of his life, that he had not visited me for three months and must make some effort to do so, that I expected some message from him which he found difficult to send—in short, a friendship that would become as wearisome to him as it would be painful to me.

Although his physical presence, his ways, his tenderness—however momentary—had been enough to engender in me once again all the old love and yearning in my heart, cold criticism told me he had altered for the worse.

Faults that I had caught glimpses of in youth were now increased tenfold. His pride, his arrogance, his contempt for anyone's opinion but his own—these were more glaring than they had ever been. His knowledge of military matters was great, that I well believed, but I doubted if he would ever work in harmony with the other leaders, and his quick temper was such that he would have every royalist leader by the ears, and in the end give offence to His Majesty himself.

The callous attitude toward prisoners—dumped within Lydford Castle and hanged without trial—showed me that streak of cruelty I had always known was in his nature; and his contemptuous dismissal of his little son, who must, I felt sure, be baffled and bewildered at the sudden change in his existence, betrayed a deliberate want of understanding that was almost vile. That suffering and bitterness had turned him hard, I granted. Mine was the fault, perhaps; mine was the blame.

But the hardness had bitten into his nature now, and it was too late to alter it. Richard Grenvile at forty-four was what fate, and circumstance, and his own will had made him.

So I judged him without mercy, in those first days after our encounter, and was within half a mind of writing to him once again, putting an end to all further meetings. Then I remembered how he had knelt beside my bed, and I had shared with him my terrible disfigurement, and he, more tender than any father, more understanding than any brother, had kissed me and bade me sleep.

If he had this gentleness and intuition with me, a woman, how was it that he showed to others, even to his son, a character at once so proud and cruel, so deliberately disdainful?

I felt torn between two courses, lying there on my bed in the gatehouse. One was to see him no more, never, at any time. Leave him to carve his own future, as I had done before. And the other was to ignore the great probability of my own personal suffering, spurn my own weak body that would be tortured incessantly by his physical presence, and give to him wholeheartedly and without any reservation all the small wisdom I had learnt, all the love, all the understanding that might yet bring him some measure of peace.

This second course seemed to me more positive than the first, for if I renounced him now, as I had done before, it would be through cowardice, a sneaking fear of being hurt in more intolerable a fashion, if it were possible, than I had been fifteen years ago.

Strange how all arguments in solitude, sorted, sifted, and thrashed in the quietude of one's own chamber, shrivel to nothing when the subject of them is close once more instead of separated by distance. And so it was with Richard, for when he rode to Menabilly on his return from Grampound to Plymouth and, coming out on to the causeway to seek me, found me in my chair looking out towards the Gribben, and kissed my hand with all the old fire and love and ardour—haranguing me straightforth upon the gross inefficiency of every Cornishman he had so far encountered except those under his immediate command—I knew that we were bound together for all time, and I could not send him from me. His faults were my faults, his arrogance my burden, and he stood there, Richard Grenvile, what my tragedy had made him.

"I cannot stay long," he said to me. "I have word from Saltash that those damned rebels have made a sortie in my absence, effecting a landing at Cawsand and taking the fort at Inceworth. The sentries were asleep, of course, and if the enemy haven't shot them, I will. I'll have my army purged before I'm finished."

"And no one left to fight for you, Richard," I said.

"I'd sooner have hired mercenaries from Germany or France than own these soft-bellied fools," he answered. And he was gone in a flash, leaving me half happy, half bewildered, with an ache in my heart that I knew now was to be forever part of my existence.

That evening my brother-in-law, Jonathan Rashleigh, returned to Menabilly, having been some little while in Exeter on the King's affairs. He had come by way of Fowey, having spent, so he informed us, the last few days at his town house there on the quay, where he had found much business to transact and some loss amongst his shipping, for the Parliament had at this time command of the sea and seized every vessel they could find, and it was hard for any unarmed merchant ship to run the gauntlet.

Some feeling of constraint came upon the place at his return, of which even I, secure in my gatehouse, could not but be aware.

The servants were more prompt about their business, but less willing. The grandchildren, who had run about the passages in his absence, were closeted in their quarters with the doors well shut. The voices in the gallery were more subdued. It was indeed obvious that the master had returned. Alice, John, and Joan found their way more often to the gatehouse, as if it had become in some way a sanctuary. John looked harassed and preoccupied, and Joan whispered to me in confidence that his father found fault with his running of the estate and said he had no head for figures.

I could see that Joan was burning to inquire about my friendship with Richard Grenvile, which they must have thought strangely sudden, and I saw Alice look at me, though she said nothing, with a new warm glance of understanding. "I knew him well long ago, when I was eighteen," I told them, but to plunge back into the whole history was not my wish. I think Mary had given them a hint or two in private. She herself said little of the visit, beyond remarking he had grown much stouter, a true sisterly remark, and then she showed me the letter he had left for Jonathan, which ended with these words:

> I here conclude, praying you to present once more my best respects to your good wife, being truly glad she is yours, for a more likely good wife was in former time hardly to be found, and I wish my fortune had been as good—but patience is a virtue, and so I am your ready servant and kinsman, Richard Grenvile.

Patience is a virtue. I saw Mary glance at me as I read the lines.

"You do not intend, Honor," she said in a low voice, to take up with him again?"

"In what way, Mary?"

"Why, wed with him, to be blunt. This letter is somewhat significant."

"Rest easy, sister. I shall never marry Richard Grenvile or any man."

"I should not be comfortable, nor Jonathan either, if Sir Richard should come here and give an impression of intimacy. He may be a fine soldier, but his reputation is anything but that."

"I know, Mary."

"Jo writes from Radford that they say hard things of him in Devon."

"I can well believe it."

"I know it is not my business, but it would sadden me much, it would greatly grieve us all, if—if you bound yourself to him in some way."

"Being a cripple, Mary, makes one strangely free of bonds."

She looked at me doubtfully and then said no more, but I think the bitterness was lost on her.

Presently Jonathan himself came up to pay his respects to me. He hoped I was comfortable, that I had everything I needed and did not find the place too noisy after the quiet of Lanrest.

"And you sleep well, I trust, and are not disturbed at all?"

His manner, when he asked this, was somewhat odd, a trifle evasive, which was strange for him, who was so self-possessed a person.

"I am not a heavy sleeper," I told him. "A creaking board or a hooting owl is enough to waken me."

"I rather feared so," he said abruptly. "It was foolish of Mary to put you in this room, facing as it does a court on either side. You would have been better in the south front, next to our own apartments. Would you prefer this?"

"Indeed, no. I am very happy here."

I noticed that he stared hard at the picture on the door, hiding the crack, and once or twice seemed as if he would ask a question but could not bring himself to the point; then, after chat upon no subject in particular, he took his leave of me.

That night, between twelve and one, since I was wakeful, I sat up in bed to drink a glass of water. I did not light my candle, for the glass was within my reach. But as I replaced it on the table I became aware of a cold draught of air blowing beneath the door of the empty room. That same chill draught I had noticed once before. I waited, motionless, for the sound of footsteps, but none came. And then, faint and hesitating, came a little scratching sound upon the panel of the door where I had hung the picture. Someone, then, was in the empty room, clad in his stockinged feet, with his hands upon the door.

The sound continued for five minutes, certainly not longer, and then ceased as suddenly as it had started, and once again the telltale draught of air was cut in a trice and all was as before. A horrid suspicion formed then in my mind, which in the morning became certainty. When I was dressed and in my chair and Matty busy in the dressing room, I wheeled myself to the door and lifted the picture from the nail. It was as I thought. The crack had been filled in. I knew then that my presence in the gatehouse had been a blunder on the part of my sister, and that I caused annoyance to that unknown visitor who prowled by night in the adjoining chamber.

The secret was Jonathan Rashleigh's and not mine to know. Suspecting my prying eyes, he had given orders for my peephole to be covered. I pondered then upon the possibility, which had entered my head earlier, that Jonathan's elder brother had not died of the smallpox some twenty years before but was still alive—in some horrid state of preservation, blind and dumb—living in animal fashion in a lair beneath the buttress, and that the only person to know of this were my brother-in-law and his steward Langdon, and some stranger—a keeper possibly—clad in a crimson cloak.

If it were indeed so, and my sister Mary and her stepchildren were in ignorance of the fact, while I, a stranger, had stumbled upon it, then I knew I must make some excuse and return home to Lanrest, for to live day by day with a secret of this kind upon my conscience was something I could not do. It was too sinister, too horrible.

I wondered if I should confide my fears to Richard when he next came, or whether, in his ruthless fashion, he would immediately give orders to his men to break open the room and force the buttress, so bringing ruin, perhaps, to my brother-in-law and host.

Fortunately, the problem was solved for me in a very different way, which I will now disclose. It will be remembered that on the day of Richard's first visit my godchild Joan had mischievously borrowed the key of the summerhouse, belonging to the steward, and allowed me to explore the interior. The flurry and excitement of receiving visitors had put all thoughts of the key from her little scatterbrained head, and it was not until two days after my brother-in-law's return that she remembered the key's existence.

She came to me with it in her hands in great perturbation, for, she said, John was already so much out of favour with his father for some neglect on the estate that she was loath now to tell him of her theft of the key, for fear it should bring him into greater trouble. As for herself, she had not the courage to take the key back to Langdon's house and confess the foolery. What was she then to do?

"You mean," I said, "what am I to do? For you wish to absolve yourself of all responsibility, isn't that so?"

"You are so clever, Honor," she pleaded, "and I so ignorant. Let me leave the key with you and so forget it. Baby Mary has a cough, and poor John a touch of his ague. I really have so much on my mind."

"Very well, then," I answered, "we will see what can be done."

I had some idea of taking Matty into my confidence and weaving a tale by which Matty would visit Mrs. Langdon and say she had found the key thrown down on a path in the Warren, which would be plausible enough, and while I turned this over in my mind I dangled the key between my fingers. It was of medium size, not larger, in fact, than the one in my own door. I compared the two and found them very similar. A sudden thought then struck me and, wheeling my chair into the passage, I listened for a moment to discover who stirred about the house. It was a little before nine o'clock, with the servants all at their dinner and the rest of the household either talking in the gallery or already retired to their rooms for the night. The moment seemed well chosen for a very daring gamble, which might, or might not, prove nothing to me. I turned down the passage and halted outside the door of the locked chamber. I listened again, but no one stirred. Then very stealthily I pushed the key into the rusty lock. It fitted. It turned. And the door creaked open. I was so carried away for a moment by the success of my own scheme that I was nonplussed. I sat in my chair, uncertain what to do. But that there was a link between this chamber and the summerhouse now seemed definite, for the key turned both locks.

The chance to examine the room might never come again, and, for all my fear, I was devoured with horrid curiosity. I edged my chair within the room and, kindling my candle, for it was of course in darkness with the windows barred, I looked about me. The chamber was simple enough. Two windows, one to the north and the other to the west, both with iron bars across them. A bed in the far corner, a few pieces of heavy furniture, and the table and chair I had already seen from the crack. The walls were hung about with a heavy arras, rather old and worn in many parts. It was indeed a disappointing room, with little that seemed strange in its appointments. It had the faded, musty smell that always clings about disused apartments. I laid the candle on the table and wheeled myself to the corner that gave upon the buttress. This, too, had an arras hanging from the ceilings, which I lifted—and found nothing but bare stone behind it. I ran my hands over the surface but could find no join. The wall seemed smooth to my touch. But it was murky and I could not see, so I returned to the table to fetch my candle, first listening at the door to make certain that the servants were still at supper. It was while I waited there, with an eye to the passage that turned at right angles running beneath the belfry, that I felt a sudden breath of cold air on the back of my head.

I looked swiftly over my shoulder, and noticed that the arras on the wall beside the buttress was blowing to and fro, as though a cavity had opened, letting through a blast of air; and even as I watched I saw, to my great horror, a hand appear from behind a slit in the arras and lift it to one side. There was no time to wheel my chair into the passage, no time even to reach my hand out to the table and blow the candle. Someone came into the room with a crimson cloak about his shoulders and stood for a moment with the arras pushed aside and a great black hole in the wall behind him. He considered me a moment, and then spoke. "Close the door gently, Honor," he said, "and leave the candle. Since you are here, it is best that we should have an explanation and no further mischief."

He advanced into the room, letting the arras drop behind him, and I saw then that the man was my brother-in-law, Jonathan Rashleigh.

Twelve

J FELT LIKE A CHILD CAUGHT OUT IN SOME MISDEMEANOUR
and was hot with shame and sick embarrassment. If he,
then, was the stranger in the crimson cloak, walking his house
in the small hours, it was not for me to question it. To be
discovered thus, prying in his secrets, with the key not only of
this door but of his summerhouse as well, was surely something
he could never pardon.

"Forgive me," I said. "I have acted very ill."

He did not answer at once, but first made certain that the
door was closed. Then he lit further candles and, laying aside
his cloak, drew a chair up to the table.

"It was you," he said, "who made a crack there in the panel?
It was not there before you came to Menabilly."

His blunt question showed me what a shrewd grasp he had
of my gaping curiosity, and I confessed that I was indeed the
culprit. "I will not attempt to defend myself." I said. "I know
I had no right to tamper with your walls. There was some talk
of ghosts, otherwise I would not have done it. And one night
during last week I heard footsteps."

"Yes," he said. "I had not thought to find your chamber
occupied. I heard you stir and guessed then what had
happened. We are somewhat pushed for room, as you no

doubt realize, otherwise you would not have been put into the gatehouse."

He waited a moment and then, looking closely at me, he said, "You have understood, then, that there is a secret entry to this chamber."

"Yes."

"And the reason you are here this evening is that you wished to find whither it led?"

"I knew it must be within the buttress."

"How did you come upon that key?"

This was the very devil, but there was nothing for it but to tell him the whole story, putting the blame heavily upon myself and saying little of Joan's share in the matter. I said that I had looked about the summerhouse, and admired the view, but as to my peering at his books and his father's will and lifting the heavy mat and finding the flagstone—nay, he would have to put me on the rack before I confessed to that.

He listened in silence, regarding me coldly all the while, and I knew what an interfering fool he must consider me.

"And what do you make of it now you know that the nightly intruder is none other than myself?" he questioned.

Here was a stumbling block. For I could make nothing of it. And I did not dare voice that secret, very fearful supposition that I kept hidden at the back of my mind.

"I cannot tell, Jonathan," I answered, "except that you use this entry for some purpose of your own and that your family know nothing of it." At this he was silent, considering me slowly, and then after a long pause, he said to me: "John has some knowledge of the subject, but no one else, except my steward Langdon. Indeed, the success of the royal cause we have at heart would gravely suffer should the truth become known."

This last surprised me. I did not see that his family secrets could be of any concern to His Majesty. But I said nothing.

"Since you already know something of the truth," he said, "I will acquaint you further, desiring you first to keep all knowledge of it to yourself."

I promised after a moment's hesitation, being uncertain what dire secret I might now be asked to share.

"You know," he said, "that at the beginning of hostilities I, with certain other gentlemen, was appointed by His Majesty's Council to collect and receive the plate given to the royal cause in Cornwall and arrange for it to be taken to the mint at Truro and there melted down?"

"I knew you were Collector, Jonathan—no more than that."

"Last year another Mint was erected at Exeter, under the supervision of my kinsman, Sir Richard Vyvyan, hence my constant business with that city. You will appreciate, Honor, that to receive a great quantity of very valuable plate and be responsible for its safety until it reaches the Mint, is a heavy burden upon my shoulders."

"Yes, Jonathan."

"Spies abound, as you are well aware. Neighbours have long ears, and even a close friend can turn informer. If some member of the rebel army could but lay his hands upon the treasure that so frequently passes into my keeping, the Parliament would be ten times the richer and His Majesty ten times the poorer. Therefore, all cartage of the plate has to be done at night, when the roads are quiet. Also, it is necessary to have depots throughout the county, where the plate can be stored until the necessary transport can be arranged. You have followed me so far?"

"Yes, Jonathan, and with interest."

I found myself getting hot under the skin, not at the implied sarcasm of his words, but because his revelation was so very different from what I—with excess of imagination—had supposed.

"The buttress against the far corner of this room," he continued, "is hollow in the centre. A flight of narrow steps leads to a small room, built in the thickness of the wall and beneath the courtyard, where it is possible for a man to stand and sit, though it is but five feet square. This room is connected with a passage, or rather tunnel, which runs under the house and so beneath the causeway to an outlet in the summerhouse. It is in this small buttress room that I have been accustomed, during the past year, to hide the plate. You understand me?"

I nodded, gripped by his story and deeply interested.

"When the plate is brought to this depot, or taken away, we work by night, my steward, John Langdon, and I. The wagons wait down at Pridmouth, and we bring the plate from the buttress room, along the tunnel to the summerhouse, and so down to the cove in one of my handcarts, where it is placed in the wagons. The men who conduct the procession from here to Exeter are all trustworthy, but none of them, naturally, know whereabouts at Menabilly. I have kept the plate hidden. That is not their business. No one knows that but myself and Langdon, and now you, Honor, who—I regret to say—have really no right at all to share the secret."

I said nothing, for there was no possible defence.

"John knows the plate has been concealed in the house but has never inquired where. He is, as yet, ignorant of the room beneath the buttress, as well as the tunnel to the summerhouse."

Here I risked offence by interrupting him.

"It was providential," I said, "that Menabilly possessed so excellent a hiding place."

"Very providential," he agreed. "Had it not been so, I could hardly have set about the business. You wonder, no doubt, why the house should have been so constructed?"

I confessed to some small wonder on the subject.

"My father," he said briefly, "had certain—how shall I put it?—shipping transactions, which necessitated privacy. The tunnel was, therefore, useful in many ways."

In other words, I said to myself, your father, dear Jonathan, was nothing more or less than a pirate of the first order, whatever his standing and reputation in Fowey and the county.

"It happened, also," he said in a lower tone, "that my unfortunate elder brother was not in full possession of his faculties. This was his chamber from the time the house was built, in 1600, until his death, poor fellow, twenty-four years later. At times he was violent, hence the reason for the little cell beneath the buttress, where lack of air and close confinement soon rendered him unconscious and easy then to handle."

He spoke naturally and without restraint, but the picture that his words conjured up turned me sick. I saw the wretched, shivering maniac choking for air in the dark room beneath the buttress, with the four walls closing in upon him. And now this same room stacked with silver plate like a treasure house in a fairy-tale.

Jonathan must have seen my change of face, for he looked kindly at me and rose from his chair.

"I know," he said, "it is not a pretty story. It was a relief to me, I must admit, when the smallpox that carried off my father took my brother too. It was not a happy business, caring for him, with young children in the house. You have heard, no doubt, the malicious tales that Robert Bennett spread abroad?"

I mentioned vaguely that some rumour had come to my ears.

"He took the disease some five days after my father," said Jonathan. "Why he should have taken it, while my wife and I escaped, we shall never know. But so he did, and, becoming violent at the same time with one of his periodic fits, stood not a chance. It was over very quickly."

There were sounds now of the servants moving from the kitchens.

"You will return now to your apartment," he said, "and I will go back the way I came. You may give me John Langdon's key. If in future you hear me come to this apartment, you will understand what I am about. I keep accounts here of the plate temporarily in my possession, which I refer to from time to time. I need hardly tell you that not a word of what has this night passed between us must be spoken about to any other person."

"I give you my solemn promise, Jonathan."

"Good night then, Honor."

He helped me turn my chair into the passage and then, very softly, closed the door behind me. I got to my own room a few moments before Matty came upstairs to draw the curtains.

Thirteen

*A*LTHOUGH THERE WERE NEVER ANY TIES OF AFFECTION between me and my brother-in-law, I certainly held him in greater respect and regard after our encounter of that evening. I knew now that "the King's business" on which he travelled to and fro was no light matter, and it was small wonder he was often short-tempered with his family. Men with less sense of duty would long since have shelved the responsibility to other shoulders. I respected him, too, for having taken me into his confidence after my unwarrantable intrusion into his locked chamber. I was left only with a sneaking regret that he had not shown me the staircase in the buttress or the cell beneath it, but this would have been too much to expect. I had a vivid picture, though, of the flapping arras and the black gulf behind. Meanwhile, the progress of the war was causing each one of us no small concern. Our Western army was under the supreme command of the King's nephew, Prince Maurice, who was in great need of reinforcements, especially of cavalry, if he was ever to strike a decisive blow against the enemy. But the plan of the summer campaign appeared unsettled, and although Maurice's brother, Prince Rupert, endeavoured to persuade the King to send some two thousand horses into the West, there was the usual obstruction from the council, and the cavalry were not forthcoming. This, of course, we heard from Richard, who, fuming with impatience because he had as yet none of the guns that had been promised him, told us with grim candour that our Western army was, anyhow, worn with sickness and quite useless, and that Prince Maurice himself had but one bee in his bonnet, which was to sit before Lyme Regis, waiting for the place to open up to him. "If Essex and the rebel army choose to march west," said Richard, "there is nothing to stop him except a mob of sick men all lying on their backs and a handful of drunken generals. I can do nothing with my miserable two men and a boy squatting before Plymouth." Essex did choose to march west, and was in Weymouth and Bridport by the third week of June, and Prince Maurice, with great loss of prestige, retreated in haste to Exeter.

Here he found his aunt, the Queen, who had arrived in a litter from Bristol, being fearful of the approaching enemy, and it was here at Exeter that she gave birth to her youngest child, which did not lessen the responsibilities of Prince Maurice and his staff. He decided that the wisest course was to get her away to France as speedily as possible, and she set forth for Falmouth, very weak and nervous, two weeks after the baby had been born.

My brother-in-law Jonathan was among those who waited on her as she passed through Bodmin on her way south, and came back telling very pitiful tales of her appearance, for she was much worn and shaken by her ordeal. "She may have ill-advised His Majesty on many an occasion," said Jonathan, "but at least she is a woman, and I tremble to think of her fate if she fell into the hands of the rebels." It was a great relief to all the Royalists in Cornwall when she reached Falmouth without mishap and embarked for France.

But Essex and the rebel army were gathering in numbers all the while, and we felt it was but a matter of weeks before he passed through Dorset into Devon, with nothing but the Tamar then between him and Cornwall. The only one who viewed the approaching struggle with relish was Richard. "If we can but draw the beggar into Cornwall," he said, "a county of which he knows nothing and whose narrow lanes and high hedges would befog him completely, and then, with the King's and Rupert's army coming up in the rear and cutting off all retreat, we will have him surrounded and destroyed."

I remember him rubbing his hands gleefully and laughing at the prospect like a boy on holiday, but the idea did not much appeal to Jonathan and other gentlemen, who were dining at Menabilly on that day. "If we have fighting in Cornwall, the country will be devastated," said Francis Bassett, who with my brother-in-law was engaged at that time in trying to raise troops for the King's service and finding it mighty hard. The land is too poor to feed an army; we cannot do it. The fighting must be kept the other side of the Tamar, and we look to you and your troops, Grenvile, to engage the enemy in Devon and keep us from invasion."

"My good fool," said Richard—at which Francis Bassett coloured, and we all felt uncomfortable—"you are a country squire, and I respect your knowledge of cattle and pigs. But for God's sake leave the art of war to professional soldiers like myself. Our aim at present is to destroy the enemy, which we cannot do in Devon, where there is no hope of encirclement. Once across the Tamar, he will run his head into a noose. My only fear is that he will not do so but will use his superior cavalry on the open Devon moors against Maurice and his hopeless team of half-wits, in which case we shall have lost one of the greatest chances this war has yet produced."

"You are prepared, then," said Jonathan, "to see Cornwall laid waste, people homeless, and much sickness and suffering spread abroad? It does not appear to be a prospect of much comfort."

"Damn your comfort," said Richard. "It will do my fellow countrymen a world of good to see a spot of bloodshed. If you cannot suffer that for the King's cause, then we may as well treat with the enemy forthwith."

There was some atmosphere of strain in the dining chamber when he had spoken, and shortly afterwards my brother-in-law gave the host's signal for dispersal. It was an oddity I could not explain even to myself that since Richard had come back into my life, I could face company with greater equanimity than I had done before and had now formed the habit of eating downstairs rather than in my chamber. Solitude was no longer my one aim. After dining, since it was still light, he took a turn with me upon the causeway, making himself attendant to my chair.

"If Essex draws near to Tavistock," he said, "and I am forced to raise the siege of Plymouth and retreat, can I send the whelp to you?"

I was puzzled for a moment, thinking he alluded to his dog.

"What whelp?" I asked. "I did not know you possessed one."

"The Southwest makes you slow of brain," he said. "My spawn, I mean, my pup, my son and heir. Will you have him here under your wing and put some sense into his frightened head?"

"Why, yes, indeed, if you think he would be happy with me."

"I think he would be happier with you than with any other person in the world. My aunt Abbot at Hartland is too old, and Bevil's wife at Stowe is so slung about with her own brood that I do not care to ask her. Besides, she has never thought much of me."

"Have you spoken to Jonathan?"

"Yes, he is willing. But I wonder what you will make of Dick. He is a scrubby object."

"I will love him, Richard, because he is your son."

"I doubt that sometimes when I look at him. He has a shrinking, timid way with him, and his tutor tells me that he cries for a finger scratch. I would exchange him any day for young Joe Grenvile, a kinsman, whom I have as aide-de-camp at Buckland. He is up to any daring scheme, that lad, and a fellow after my own heart, like Bevil's eldest boy."

"Dick is barely turned fourteen," I said to him. "You must not expect too much. Give him a year or two to learn confidence."

"If he has taken after his mother, then I'll turn him off and let him starve," said Richard. "I won't have frog's spawn about me."

"Perhaps," I said, "your example does not greatly encourage him to take after yourself. Were I a child I would not want a red fox for a father."

"He is the wrong age for me," said Richard: "too big to dandle and too small to talk to. He is yours, Honor, from this day forward. I declare I will bring him over to you this day week."

And so it was arranged, with Jonathan's permission, that Dick Grenvile and his tutor, Herbert Ashley, should add to the numbers at Menabilly. I was strangely happy and excited the day they were expected and went with my sister Mary to inspect the room that had been put to their service beneath the clock tower.

I took pains with my toilet, wearing my blue gown that was my favourite and bidding Matty brush my hair for half the morning. And all the while I told myself what a sentimental fool I was to waste such time and trouble for a little lad who would not look at me. It was about one o'clock that I heard the horses trotting across the park, and I called in a fever to Matty to fetch the servants to carry me downstairs, for I wished to be in the garden when I greeted them, for I have a firm belief that it is always easier to become acquainted with anyone out of doors in the sun than to be shut fast within four walls.

I was seated, then, in the walled garden beneath the causeway when the gate opened and a lad came walking across the lawn towards me. He was taller than I had imagined, with the flaming Grenvile locks, and an impudent snub nose and a swagger about him that reminded me instantly of Richard. And then, as he spoke, I realized my mistake. "My name is Joe Grenvile," he said. "They have sent me from the house to bring you back. There has been a slight mishap. Poor Dick tumbled from his horse as we drew rein in the courtyard—the stones were somewhat slippery—and he has cut his head. They have taken him to your chamber, and your maid is washing off the blood."

This was very different from the picture I had painted, and I was at once distressed that the arrival should have gone awry.

"Is Sir Richard with you?" I asked as he wheeled me down the path. "Yes," said young Joe, "and in a great state of irritation, cursing poor Dick for incompetence, which made the little fellow worse. We have to leave again within the hour. Essex has reached Tiverton, you know, and Taunton Castle is also in the rebel's hands. Prince Maurice has withdrawn several units from our command, and there is to be a conference at Okehampton, which Sir Richard must attend. Ours are the only troops that are now left outside Plymouth."

"And you find all this greatly stirring, do you, Joe?" I asked.

"Yes, madam. I can hardly wait to have a crack at the enemy myself."

We turned in at the garden entrance and found Richard pacing up and down the hall. "You would hardly believe it possible," he said, "but the whelp must go and tumble from his horse, right on the very doorstep. Sometimes I think he has softening of the brain, to act in so boobish a fashion. What do you think of Joe?" He clapped the youngster on the shoulder, who looked up at him with pride and devotion. "We shall make a soldier of this chap, anyway," he said. "Go and draw me some ale, Joe, and a tankard for yourself. I'm as thirsty as a drowning man."

"What of Dick?" I asked. "Shall I not go to him?"

"Leave him to the women and his useless tutor," said Richard. "You'll soon have enough of him. I have one hour to spend at Menabilly, and I want you to myself." We went to the little anteroom beyond the gallery, and there he sat with me while he drank his ale and told me that Essex would be at Tavistock before the week was out.

"If he marches on Cornwall, then we have him trapped," said Richard, "and if the King will only follow fast enough on his heels, the game is ours. It will be unpleasant while it lasts, my sweetheart, but it will not be for long; that I can promise you."

"Shall we see fighting in this district?" I asked, with some misgiving.

"Impossible to answer. It depends on Essex, whether he strikes north or south. He will make for Liskeard and Bodmin, where we shall try to hold him. Pray for a dirty August, Honor, and they will be up to their eyes in mud. I must go. I sleep tonight in Launceston if I can make it." He put his tankard on the table and, first closing the door, knelt beside my chair. "Look after the little whelp," he said, "and teach him manners. If the worst should happen and there be fighting in the neighbourhood, hide him under your bed. Essex would take any son of mine as hostage. Do you love me still?"

"I love you always."

"Then cease listening for footsteps in the gallery and kiss me as though you meant it."

It was easy for him, no doubt, to hold me close for five minutes and have me in a turmoil with his love-making and then ride away to Launceston, his mind aflame with other matters; but for me, left with my hair and gown in disarray, and no method of escape and long hours stretching before me to think about it all, it was rather more disturbing. I had chosen the course, though—I had let him come back into my life, and I must put up with the fever he engendered in me which could never more be stilled.

So, calling to his aide-de-camp, he waved his hand to me and rode away to Launceston, where, I told myself with nagging jealousy, he and young Joe would in all probability dine over-well and find some momentary distraction before the more serious business of tomorrow, for I knew my Richard too well to believe he lived a life of austerity simply because he loved me.

I patted my curls and smoothed my lace collar, then pulled the bellrope for a servant, who, with the aid of another, bore me in my chair to my apartments. I did not pass through the front of the house, as was my custom, but through the back rooms beneath the belfry, and here in a passage I found Frank Penrose, my brother-in-law's cousin and dependant, engaged in earnest conversation with a young man of about his own age who had a sallow complexion and retreating chin and who appeared to be recounting the story of his life.

"This is Mr. Ashley, Mistress Honor," said Frank with the smarming manner peculiar to him. "He has left his charge resting in your apartment. Mr. Ashley is about to take refreshment with me below."

Mr. Ashley bowed and scraped his heels.

"Sir Richard informed me you are the boy's godmother, madam," he said, "and that I am to take my commands from you. It is, of course, rather irregular, but I will endeavour to adapt myself to the circumstances." You are a fool, I thought, and a prig, and I don't think I am going to like you, but aloud I said, "Please continue, Mr. Ashley, as you have been accustomed to at Buckland. I have no intention of interfering in any way, except to see that the boy is happy." I left them both bowing and scraping and ready to pull me to pieces as soon as my back was turned, and so was brought to the gatehouse. I met Matty coming forth with a basin of water, and strips of bandage on her arm.

"Is he much hurt?" I asked.

Her lips were drawn in the tight line that I knew meant disapproval of the whole proceeding.

"More frightened than anything else," she said, "He'll fall to pieces if you look at him."

The servants set me down in the room and withdrew, closing the door. He was sitting hunched up in a chair beside the hearth, a white shrimp of a boy with great dark eyes and tight black locks, his pallor worsened by the bandage on his head. He watched me, nervously biting his nails all the while.

"Are you better?" I said gently.

He stared at me for a moment, and then said, with a queer jerk of his head: "Has he gone?"

"Has who gone?" I asked.

"My father."

"Yes, he has ridden away to Launceston with your cousin." He considered this a moment.

"When will he be back?" he asked.

"He will not be back. He has to attend a meeting at Okehampton tomorrow or the following day. You are to stay here for the present. Did he not tell you who I am?"

"I think you must be Honor. He said I was to be with a lady who was beautiful. Why do you sit in that chair?"

"Because I cannot walk. I am a cripple."

"Does it hurt?"

"No, not very much. I am used to it. Does your head hurt you?"

He touched the bandage warily. "It bled," he said. "There is blood under the bandage."

"Never mind, it will soon heal."

"I will keep the bandage on or it will bleed afresh," he said. "You must tell the servant who washed it not to move the bandage."

"Very well," I said, "I will tell her."

I took a piece of tapestry and began to work on it so that he should not think I watched him and would grow accustomed to my presence.

"My mother used to work at tapestry," he said after a lengthy pause. "She worked a forest scene with stags running."

"That was pretty," I said.

"She made three covers for her chairs," he went on. "They were much admired at Fitzford. You never came to Fitzford, I believe?"

"No, Dick."

"My mother had many friends, but I did not hear her speak of you."

"I do not know your mother, Dick. I only know your father."

"Do you like him?" The question was suspicious, sharply put.

"Why do you ask?" I said, evading it.

"Because I don't. I hate him. I wish he would be killed in battle." The tone was savage, venomous. I stole a glance at him and saw him once more biting at the back of his hand.

"Why do you hate him?" I asked quietly.

"He is a devil, that's why. He tried to kill my mother. He tried to steal her house and money and then kill her."

"Why do you think that?"

"My mother told me."

"Do you love her very much?"

"I don't know. I think so. She was beautiful. More beautiful than you. She is in London now with my sister. I wish I could be with her."

"Perhaps," I said, "when the war is finished with, you will go back to her."

"I would run away," he said, "but for London being so far, and that I might get caught in the fighting. There is fighting everywhere. There is no talk of anything at Buckland but the fighting. I will tell you something."

"What is that?"

"Last week I saw a wounded man brought into the house upon a stretcher. There was blood upon him."

The way he said this puzzled me, his manner was so shrinking.

"Why," I asked, "are you so much afraid of blood?"

The colour flamed into his pale face.

"I did not say I was afraid," he answered quickly.

"No, but you do not like it." Neither do I. It is most unpleasant. But I am not fearful if I see it spilt."

"I cannot bear to see it spilt at all," he said after a moment. "I have always been thus, since I was a little child. It is not my fault."

"Perhaps you were frightened as a baby."

"That's what my mother brought me up to understand. She told me that when she had me in her arms once my father came into the room and quarrelled violently with her upon some matter, and that he struck her on the face, and she bled. The blood ran onto my hands. I cannot remember it, but that is how it was."

I began to feel very sick at heart and despondent but was careful that he should not notice it.

"We won't talk about it any more then, Dick, unless you want to. What shall we discuss instead?"

"Tell me what you did when you were my age, how you looked, and what you said, and had you brothers and sisters?"

And so I wove him a tale about the past, thus making him forget his own, while he sat watching me; and by the time that Matty came, bringing us refreshment, he had lost enough of his nervousness to chat with her, too, and make big eyes at the pasties, which soon disappeared, while I sat and looked at his little chiselled features, so unlike his father's, and the close black curls upon his head. Afterwards I read to him for a while, and he left his chair and came and curled on the floor beside my chair, like a small dog who would make friends in a strange house, and when I closed the book, he looked up at me and smiled—and the smile for the first time was Richard's smile and not his mother's.

Fourteen

ROM THAT DAY FORWARD DICK BECAME MY SHADOW. HE
arrived early with my breakfast, never my best moment
of the day, but because he was Richard's son I suffered him.
He then left to do his lessons with the sallow Mr. Ashley while
I made my toilet, and later in the morning came to walk beside
my chair upon the causeway.

He sat beside me in the dining chamber and brought a stool to
the gallery when I went there after dinner; seldom speaking, always
watchful, he hovered continually about me like a small phantom.

"Why do you not run and play in the gardens," I asked, "or
ask Mr. Ashley to take you down to Pridmouth? There are
fine shells there on the beach and, as the weather is warm, you
could swim if you had the mind. There's a young cob, too, in
the stables you could ride across the park."

"I would rather stay with you," he said.

And he was firm on this and would not be dissuaded. Even
Alice, who had the warmest way with children I ever saw,
failed with him, for he would shake his head and take his stool
behind my chair.

"He has certainly taken a fancy to you, madam," said the
tutor, relieved, I am sure, to find his charge so little trouble. "I
have found it very hard to interest him."

"He is your conquest," said Joan, "and you will never more be rid of him. Poor Honor. What a burden to the end of your days!"

But it did not worry me. If Dick was happy with me, that was all that mattered, and if I could bring some feeling of security to his poor lonely little heart and puzzled mind I should not feel my days were wasted. Meanwhile, the news worsened, and some five days after Dick's arrival word came from Fowey that Essex had reached Tavistock, and the siege of Plymouth had been raised, with Richard withdrawing his troops from Saltash, Mount Stampford, and Plympton, and retreating to the Tamar bridges.

That evening a council was held at Tywardreath amongst the gentry in the district, at which my brother-in-law presided, and one and all decided to muster what men and arms and ammunition they could, and ride to Launceston to help defend the county.

We were at once in a state of consternation, and the following morning saw the preparations for departure. All those on the estate who were able-bodied and fit to carry arms paraded before my brother-in-law with their horses, their kits packed on the saddles, and amongst them were the youngest of the house servants who could be spared and all the grooms. Jonathan, and his son-in-law, John Rashleigh of Coombe, and Oliver Sawle from Penrice—brother to old Nick Sawle—and many other gentlemen from round about Fowey and St. Austell gathered at Menabilly before setting forth, while my poor sister Mary went from one to the other with her face set in a smile I knew was sadly forced, handing them cake and fruit and pasties to cheer them on their way. John was left with many long instructions, which I could swear he would never carry in his head, and then we watched them set off across the park, a strange, pathetic little band full of ignorance and high courage, the tenants wielding their muskets as though they were hayforks, and with considerably more danger to themselves than to the enemy they might encounter. It was '43 all over again, with the rebels not thirty miles away, and although Richard might declare that Essex and his army were running into a trap, I was disloyal enough to wish they might keep out of it.

Those last days of July were clammy and warm. A sticky breeze blew from the southwest that threatened rain and never brought it, while a tumbled sea rolled past the Gribben white and gray. At Menabilly we made a pretence of continuing as though all were as usual, and nothing untoward likely to happen, and even forced a little gaiety when dining that we must wait upon ourselves, now that there were none but womenfolk to serve us. But for all this deception, intended to convey a sense of courage, we were tense and watchful—our ears always pricked for the rumble of cannon or the sound of horses. I can remember how we all sat beside the long table in the dining chamber, the portrait of His Majesty gazing calmly down upon us from the dark panelling above the open hearth, and how at the end of a strained, tedious meal Nick Sawle, who was the eldest amongst us, conquered his rheumatics and rose to his feet in great solemnity, saying, "It were well that in this time of stress and trouble we should give a toast unto His Majesty. Let us drink to our beloved King, and may God protect him and all who have gone forth from this house to fight for him."

They all then rose to their feet, too, except myself, and looked up at his portrait—those melancholy eyes, that small obstinate mouth—and I saw the tears run down Alice's cheeks as she thought of Peter, and sad resignation come to Mary's face, her thoughts with Jonathan. Yet none of them, gazing at the King's portrait, dreamed of blaming him for the trouble that had come upon them. God knows I had no sympathy for the rebels, who each one of them was out for feathering his own nest and building up a fortune, caring nothing for the common people whose lot they pretended would be bettered by their victory; but nor could I, in my heart, recognize the King as the fountain of all truth, but thought of him always as a stiff, proud man, small in intelligence as he was in stature, yet commanding by his grace of manner, his dignity, and his moral virtue a wild devotion in his followers that sprang from their warm hearts and not their reason.

We were a quiet, subdued party who sat in the long gallery that evening. Even the sharp tongue of Temperance Sawle was stilled, her thin features were pinched and anxious, while the Sparkes forewent their usual game of chequers and sat talking in low voices, Will, the rumour-monger, without much heart now for his hobby. "Have the rebels crossed the Tamar?" This was, I think, the thought in all our minds, and while Mary, Alice, and Joan worked at their tapestry, and I read in a soft voice to Dick, my brain was busy all the while reckoning the shortest distance that the enemy would take and whether they would cross by Saltash or by Gunnislake. John had left the dining chamber as soon as the King's health had been drunk, saying he could stand this waiting about no longer but must ride to Fowey for news. He returned about nine o'clock, saying that the town was well-nigh empty, with so many ridden to north to join the army, but those who were left were standing at their doors, glum and despondent, saying that word had come that Grenvile and his troops had been defeated at Newbridge below Gunnislake, while Essex and some ten thousand men were riding towards Launceston. I remember Will Sparke leaping to his feet at hearing this and breaking out into a tirade against Richard, his shrill voice sharp and nervous. "What have I been saying all along?" he cried. "When it comes to a test like this, the fellow is no commander. The pass at Gunnislake should be easy to defend, no matter the strength of the opponent, and here is Grenvile pulled out and in full retreat without having struck a blow to defend Cornwall. Heaven, what a contrast to his brother."

"It is only rumour, cousin Will," said John with an uncomfortable glance in my direction. "There was no one in Fowey able to swear to the truth of it."

"I tell you, everything is lost," said Will. "Cornwall will be ruined and overrun, even as Sir Francis Bassett said the other day. And if it is so, then Richard Grenvile will be to blame for it."

I watched young Dick swallow the words with eager eyes, and, pulling at my arm, he whispered, "What is it he says? What has happened?"

"John Rashleigh hears that the Earl of Essex has passed into Cornwall," I told him softly, "finding little opposition. We must wait until the tale is verified."

"Then my father has been slain in battle?"

"No, Dick, nothing has been said of that. Do you wish me to continue reading?"

"Yes, please, if you will do so."

And I went on with the tale, taking no notice of his biting of his hand, for my anxiety was such that I could have done the same myself. Anything might have happened during these past forty-eight hours. Richard left for slain upon the steep road down from Gunnislake and his men fled in all directions, or taken prisoner, perhaps, and at this moment being put to torture in Launceston Castle that he might betray the plan of battle. It was always my fault to let imagination do its worst, and although I guessed enough of Richard's strategy to know that a retreat on the Tamar bank was probably his intention from the first, in order to lure Essex into Cornwall, yet I longed to hear the opposite and that a victory had been gained that day and the rebels pushed back into Devon.

I slept but ill that night, for to be ignorant of the truth is, I shall always believe, the worst sort of mental torture, and for a powerless woman who cannot forget her fears in taking action, there is no remedy. The next day was as hot and airless as the one preceding, and when I came down after breakfast I wondered if I looked as haggard and careworn to the rest of the company as they looked to me. And still no news. Everything was strangely silent; even the jackdaws who usually clustered in the trees down in the warren had flown and settled elsewhere. Shortly before noon, when some of us were assembled in the dining chamber to take cold meat, Mary, coming from her sun parlour across the hall, cried, "There is a horseman riding through the park towards the house." Everyone began talking at once and pushing to the windows, and John, something white about the lips, went to the courtyard to receive whomever it should be.

The rider clattered into the inner court, with all of us watching from the windows, and though he was covered from head to foot with dust and had a great slash across his boot, I recognized him as young Joe Grenvile.

"I have a message for Mistress Harris," he said, flinging himself from his horse. My throat went dry, and my hands went wet. He is dead, I thought, for certain.

"But the battle? How goes the battle?" and "What of the rebels?" "What has happened?" Questions on all sides were put to him, with Nick Sawle on one side and Will Sparke on the other, so that he had to push his way through them to reach me in the hall.

"Essex will be in Bodmin by nightfall," he said briefly. "We have just had a brush above Lostwithiel with Lord Robartes and his brigade, who have now turned back to meet him. We ourselves are in hot retreat to Truro, where Sir Richard plans to raise more troops. I am come from the road but to bring this message to Mistress Harris."

"Essex at Bodmin?" A cry of alarm went up from all the company, and Temperance Sawle went straightway on her knees and called upon her Maker. But I was busy tearing open Richard's letter. I read:

> My sweet love, the hook is nicely baited, and the poor misguided fish gapes at it with his mouth wide open. He will be in Bodmin tonight, and most probably in Fowey tomorrow. His chief adviser in the business is that crass idiot, Jack Robartes, whose mansion at Lanhydrock I have just had infinite pleasure in pillaging. They will swallow the bait, hook, line, and sinker. We shall come up on them from Truro, and His Majesty, Maurice, and Ralph Hopton from the east. The King has already advanced as far as Tavistock, so the fish will be most prettily landed. Your immediate future at Menabilly being somewhat unpleasant, it will be best if you return the whelp to me, with his tutor. I have given Joe instructions on the matter. Keep to your chamber, my dear love, and have no fear. We will come to your succour as soon as may be. My respects to your sister and the company.
>
> Your devoted servant,
> Richard Grenvile

I placed the letter in my gown, and turned to Joe.

"Is the General well?" I asked.

"Never better," he grinned. "I have just left him eating roast pork on the road to Grampound, while his servant cleaned his boots. We seized a score of pigs from Lord Robartes's park, and a herd of sheep, and some twenty head of cattle—the troops are in high fettle. If you hear rumours of our losses at Newbridge, pay no attention to them; the higher the figure they are put at by the enemy, the better pleased will be Sir Richard."

I motioned then that I would like to speak with him apart, and he withdrew alone with me to the sun parlour.

"What is the plan for Dick?" I asked.

"Sir Richard thinks it best if the boy and Mr. Ashley embark by fishing boat for St. Mawes, if arrangements can be made with one of the fellows at Polkerris. They can keep close inshore, and once around the Dodman the passage will not be long. I have money here to pay the fishermen, and pay them well, for their trouble."

"When should they depart?"

"As soon as possible. I will see to it and go with them to the beach. Then I shall return to join Sir Richard and, with any luck, catch up with him on the Grampound–Truro road. The trouble is that the roads are already choked with people in headlong flight from Essex, all making for the West, and it will not be long now before the rebel cavalry reach the district."

"There is, then, no time to lose," I answered. "I will ask Mr. John Rashleigh to go with you to Polkerris; he will know the men there who are most likely to be trusted."

I called John to come to me, and hurriedly explained the plan, whereupon he set forth straightway to Polkerris with Joe Grenvile, while I sent word to Herbert Ashley that I wished to speak to him. He arrived looking very white about the gills, for rumour had run riot in the place that the Grenvile troops were flying in disorder with the rebels on their heels and the war was irrevocably lost. He looked much relieved when I told him that he and Dick were to depart upon the instant, by sea and not by road, and went immediately to pack their things, promising to be ready within the hour. The task then fell upon me to break the news to my shadow. He was standing by the side door, looking out on to the garden, and I beckoned him to my side.

"Dick," I said to him, "I want you to be brave and sensible. The neighbourhood is likely to be surrounded by the enemy before another day, and Menabilly will be seized. Your father thinks it better you should not be found here, and I have arranged, therefore, with Mr. Rashleigh, that you and your tutor should go by boat to St. Mawes, where you will be safe."

"Are you coming too?" he asked.

"No, Dick. This is a very sudden plan, made only for your-selves. I and the rest of the company will remain at Menabilly."

"Then so will I."

"No, Dick. You must let me judge for you. And it is best for you to go."

"Does it mean that I must join my father?"

"That I cannot tell. All I know is that the fishing boat is to take you to St. Mawes."

He said nothing but looked queerly sulky and strange, and after a moment or two went up to join his tutor.

I had a pain at the pit of my stomach all the while, for there is nothing so contagious as panic, and the atmosphere of sharp anxiety was rife in the air. In the gallery little groups of people were gathered, with strained eyes and drawn faces, and Alice's children, aware of tension, chose—poor dears—this moment to be fretful and were clinging to her skirts, crying bitterly.

"There is time yet to reach Truro if only we had convey-ance," I heard Will say, his face gray with fear, "but Jonathan took all the horses with him, and the farm wagons would be too slow. Where has John gone? Is it not possible for him to arrange in some manner that we be conducted to Truro?"

His sisters watched him with anxious eyes, and I saw Gillian whisper hurriedly to Deborah that none of their things were ready, and it would take her till evening to sort out what was necessary for travel. Then Nick Sawle, drawing himself up proudly, said in a loud voice, "My wife and I propose to stay at

Menabilly. If cowards care to clatter on the roads as fugitives, they are welcome to do so, but I find it a poor return to our Cousin Jonathan to desert his house like rats in a time of trouble."

My sister Mary looked towards me in distress. "What do you counsel, Honor?" she asked. "Should we set forth, or should we stay? Jonathan gave me no commands. He assured me that the enemy would not cross the Tamar, or, at the worst, be turned back after a few miles."

"My God," I said, "if you care to hide in the ditches with the driven cattle, then by all means go, but I swear you will fare worse upon the road than you are likely to do at home. Better to starve under your own roof than in the hedges."

"We have plenty of provisions," said Mary, snatching a ray of hope. "We are not likely to want for anything, unless the siege be long." She turned in consultation to her stepdaughters, who were all of them still occupied in calming the children, and I thought it wisest not to spread further consternation by telling her that once the rebels held the house they would make short work of her provisions.

The clock in the belfry had just struck three when Dick and his tutor came down ready for departure. The lad was still sulky and turned his head from me when I would say good-bye. This was better than the rebellious tears I had expected, and with a cheerful voice I wished him a speedy journey and assured him that a week or less would see the end of all our troubles. He did not answer, and I signed to Herbert Ashley to take his arm and to start walking across the park with Frank Penrose, who would conduct them to Polkerris, and there fall in with John Rashleigh and Joe Grenvile, who must by this time have matters well arranged.

Anxiety and strain had brought an aching back upon me, and I desired now nothing so much as to retire to the gatehouse and lie upon my bed. I sent for Matty, and she, with the help of Joan and Alice, carried me upstairs. The sun was coming strongly through my western casement and the room was hot and airless. I lay upon my bed sticky wet, wishing with all my heart that I were a man and could ride with Joe Grenvile on the road to Truro, instead of lying there, a woman and a cripple, waiting for the relentless tramp of enemy feet. I had been there but an hour, I suppose, snatching brief oblivion, when I heard once more the sound of a horse galloping across the park, and, calling to Matty, I inquired who it should be. She went to the casement and looked out.

"It's Mr. John," she said, "in great distress by his expression. Something has gone amiss." My heart sank at her words. Perhaps, after all, the fishermen at Polkerris could not be tempted to set sail. In a moment or two I heard his footstep on the stairs and he flung into my room, forgetting even to knock upon the door.

"We have lost Dick," he said. "He has vanished. He is nowhere to be found." He stood staring at me, the sweat pouring down his face, and I could see that his whole frame was trembling.

"What do you mean? What has happened?" I asked swiftly, raising myself in my bed.

"We were all assembled on the beach," he said, his breath coming quickly, "and the boat was launched. There was a little cuddy below deck, and with my own eyes I saw Dick descend to it, his bundle under his arm. There was no trouble to engage the boat, and the men—both of them stout fellows, well known to me—were willing. Just before they drew anchor we heard a clatter on the cobbles beside the cottages, and some lads came running down in great alarm to tell us that the first body of rebel horse had cut the road from Castledore to Tywardreath and that Polmear Hill was already blocked with troops. At this the men began to make sail, and young Joe Grenvile turned to me with a wink and said, 'It looks as if I must go by water too.' Before I could answer him, he had urged his horse into the sea and was making for the sand flats half a mile away to the westward. It was half tide, but he had reached them and turned in his saddle to wave to us within five and twenty minutes. He'll be on Gosmoor by now and halfway to St. Austell."

"But Dick?" I said. "You say you have lost Dick?"

"He was in the boat," he said stubbornly. "I swear he was in the boat, but we turned to listen to the lads and their tale of the troops at Tywardreath, and then with one accord we watched young Joe put his horse to the water and swim for it. By heaven, Honor, it was the boldest thing I have ever seen a youngster do, for the tide can run swiftly between Polkerris and the flats. And then Ashley, the tutor, looking about him, called for Dick but could not find him. We searched the vessel from stem to stern, but he wasn't there. He was not on the beach. He was not anywhere. For God's sake, Honor, what are we to do now?"

I felt as helpless as he did, and sick with anxiety, for here was I, having failed utterly in my trust, and the rebel troops were not two miles away.

"Where is the boat now?" I asked.

"Lying off the Gribben, waiting for a signal from me," said John, "with that useless tutor aboard, with no other thought in his mind but getting to St. Mawes. But even if we find the boy, Honor, I fear it will be too late."

"Search the cliffs in all directions," I said, "and the grounds, and the park and pasture. Was anything said to the lad upon the way?"

"I cannot say. I think not. I only heard Frank Penrose tell him that by nightfall he would be with his father."

So that was it, I thought. A moment's indiscretion, but enough to turn Dick from his journey and make him play truant like a child from school. I could do nothing in the search but bade John set forth once more with Frank Penrose, saying no word to anyone of what had happened. And, calling to Matty, I bade her take me to the causeway.

Fifteen

*O*NCE ON THE HIGH GROUND, I HAD AS GOOD A VIEW OF the surrounding country as I could wish, and I saw Frank Penrose and John Rashleigh strike out across the park to the beacon fields and then divide. All the while I had a fear in my heart that the boy had drowned himself and would be found with the rising tide floating face downwards in the wash below Polkerris cliffs. There was no sign of the boat, and I judged it to be to the westward beyond Polkerris and the Gribben.

Back and forth we went along the causeway, with Matty pushing my chair, and still no sign of a living soul, nothing but the cattle grazing on the farther hills and the ripple of a breeze blowing the corn upon the skyline.

Presently I sent Matty within doors for a cloak, for the breeze was freshening, and on her return she told me that stragglers were already pouring into the park from the roads, women, and children, and old men, all with makeshift bundles on their backs, begging for shelter, for the route was cut to Truro and the rebels were everywhere. My sister Mary was at her wit's end to know what to say to them, and many of them were already kindling fires down in the warren and making rough shelter for the night.

"As I came out just now," said Matty, "a litter borne by four horses came to rest in the courtyard, and a lady within demanded harbourage for herself and her young daughters. I heard the servant say they had been nine hours upon the road."

I thanked God in my heart that we had remained at Menabilly and not lost our heads like these other poor unfortunates.

"Go back, Matty," I said, "and see what you can do to help my sister. None of the servants have any sense left in their heads."

She had not been gone more than ten minutes before I saw two figures coming across the fields towards me. One of them, seeing me upon the causeway, waved his arm, while with the other he held fast to his companion.

It was John Rashleigh, and he had Dick with him.

When they reached me I saw the boy was dripping wet and scratched about the face and hands by brambles, but for once he was not bothered by the sight of blood but stared at me defiantly.

"I will not go," he said. "You cannot make me go."

John Rashleigh shook his head at me, and shrugged his shoulders in resignation. "It's no use, Honor," he said. "We shall have to keep him. There's a wash on the beaches now, and I've signalled to the boat to make sail and take the tutor across the bay to Mevagissey or Gorrau where he must make shift for himself. As for this lad, I found him halfway up the cliff, a mile from Polkerris—he had been waist-deep in water for the past three hours. God only knows what Sir Richard will say to the bungle we have made."

"Never mind Sir Richard, I will take care of him," I said, "when—and if—we ever clap eyes on him again. That boy must return to the house with me and be shifted into dry clothes before anything else is done with him."

Now the causeway at Menabilly is set high, as I have said, commanding a fine view both to east and west, and at this moment, I know not why, I turned my head towards the coast road that descended down to Pridmouth from Coombe and Fowey, and I saw, silhouetted on the skyline above the valley, a single horseman. In a moment he was joined by others who paused an instant on the hill and then, following their leader, plunged down the narrow roadway to the cove. John saw them, too, for our eyes met and we looked at one another long and silently, while Dick stood between us, his eyes downcast, his teeth chattering.

Richard in the old days was wont to tease me for my south-coast blood, so sluggish, he averred, compared with that which ran through his own north-coast veins, but I swear I thought, in the next few seconds, as rapidly as he had ever done or was likely yet to do.

"Have you your father's keys?" I said to John.

"Yes," he said.

"All of them?"

"All of them."

"On your person now?"

"Yes."

"Then open the door of the summerhouse."

He obeyed me without question—thank God his stern father had taught him discipline—and in an instant we stood at the threshold with the door flung open.

"Lift the mat from beneath the desk there," I said, "and raise the flagstone." He looked at me then in wonder but went without a word to do as I had bidden him. In a moment the mat was lifted and the flagstone, too, and the flight of steps betrayed to view. "Don't ask me any questions, John," I said. "There is no time. A passage runs underground from those steps to the house. Take Dick with you now, first replacing the flagstone above your heads, and crawl with him along the passage to the farther end. You will come then to a small room like a cell, and another flight of steps. At the top of the steps is a door that opens, I believe, from the passage end. But do not try to open it until I give you warning from the house."

I could read the sense of what I had said go slowly to his mind and a dawn of comprehension come into his eyes.

"The chamber next to yours?" he said. "My uncle John?"

"Yes," I said. "Give me the keys. Go quickly."

There was no trouble now with Dick. He had gathered from my manner that danger was deadly near and the time for truancy over. He bolted down into the hole like a frightened rabbit. I watched John settle the mat over the flagstone and, descending after Dick, he lowered the stone above his head and disappeared. The summerhouse was as it had been, empty and untouched. I leant over in my chair and turned the key in the lock and then put the keys inside my gown. I looked out to the eastward and saw that the skyline was empty. The troopers would have reached the cove by now and after they had watered their horses at the mill, would climb up the farther side and be at Menabilly within ten minutes. The sweat was running down my forehead clammy cold, and as I waited for Matty to fetch me—and God only knew how much longer she would be—I thought how I would give all I possessed in the world at that moment for one good swig of brandy.

Far out on the beacon hills I could see Frank Penrose still searching hopelessly for Dick, while in the meadows to the west one of the women from the farm went calling to the cows, all oblivious of the troopers who were riding up the lane.

And at that moment my godchild Joan came hurrying along the causeway to fetch me, her pretty face all strained and anxious, her soft dark hair blowing in the wind.

"They are coming," she said. "We have seen them from the windows. Scores of them, on horseback, riding now across the park."

Her breath caught in a sob, and she began running with me along the causeway, so that I, too, was caught in a sudden panic and could think of nothing but the wide door of Menabilly still open to enfold me. "I have searched everywhere for John," she faltered, "but I cannot find him. One of the servants said they saw him walking out towards the Gribben. Oh, Honor—the children—what will become of us? What is going to happen?"

I could hear shouting from the park, and out on the hard ground beyond the gates came the steady rhythmic beat of horses trotting; not the light clatter of a company, but line upon line of them, the relentless measure of a regiment, the jingle of harness, the thin alien sound of a bugle.

They were waiting for us by the windows of the gallery, Alice, Mary, the Sawles, the Sparkes, a little tremulous gathering of frightened people, united now in danger, and two other faces that I did not know, the peaky, startled faces of strange children with lace caps upon their heads and wide lace collars. I remembered then the unknown lady who had flung herself upon my sister's mercy, and as we turned into the hall, slamming the door behind us, I saw the horses that had drawn the litter still standing untended in the courtyard, save that the grooms had thrown blankets upon them, coloured white and crimson, and stamped at the corners with a dragon's head. A dragon's head... but even as my memory swung back into the past I heard her voice, cold and clear, rising above the others in the gallery: "If only it can be Lord Robartes, I can assure you all no harm will come to us. I have known him well these many years and am quite prepared to speak on your behalf."

"I forgot to tell you," whispered Joan. "She came with her two daughters scarce an hour ago. The road was held, and they could not pass St. Blazey. It is Mrs. Denys of Orley Court."

Her eyes swung round to me. Those same eyes, narrow, heavy-lidded, that I had seen often in my more troubled dreams, and her gold hair, golder than it had been in the past, for art had taken counsil with nature and outstripped it. She stared at the sight of me, and for a second I caught a flash of odd discomfort like a flicker in her eyes, and then she smiled her slow, false, well-remembered smile, and, stretching out her hands, she said, "Why, Honor this is indeed a pleasure. Mary did not tell me that you, too, were here at Menabilly."

I ignored the proffered hand, for a cripple in a chair can be as ill mannered as she pleases, and as I stared back at her in my own fashion, with suspicion and foreboding in my heart, we heard the horses ride into the courtyard and the bugles blow. Poor Temperance Sawle went down upon her knees, the children whimpered, and my sister Mary, with her arm about Joan and Alice, stood very white and still. Only Gartred watched with cool eyes, her hands playing gently with her girdle.

"Pray hard and pray fast, Mrs. Sawle," I said. "The vultures are gathering."

And, since there was no brandy in the room, I poured myself some water from a jug and raised my glass to Gartred.

Sixteen

*I*T WAS WILL SPARKE, I REMEMBER, WHO WENT TO UNBAR the door—though he had been the first to bolt it earlier—and as he did so he excused himself in his high-pitched shaking voice, saying, "It is useless to start by offending them. Our only hope lies in placating them."

We could see through the windows how the troopers dismounted, staring about them with confident, hard faces beneath their close-fitting skull helmets, and it seemed to me that one and all they looked the same, with their cropped heads and their drab brown leather jerkins, and this ruthless similarity was both startling and grim. There were more of them on the eastward side now, in the gardens, the horses' hoofs trampling the green lawns and the little yew trees as a first symbol of destruction, and all the while the thin, high note of the bugle sounded, like a huntsman summoning his hounds to slaughter. In a moment we heard their heavy footsteps in the house, clamping through the dining chamber and up the stairs, and into the gallery returned Will Sparke, a nervous smile on his face, which was drained of all colour. Behind him came three officers, the first a big, burly man with a long nose and heavy jaw, wearing a green sash about his waist. I recognized him at once as Lord Robartes, the owner of Lanhydrock, a big estate on the Bodmin road, who in former days had gone riding and hawking with my brother Kit, but was not much known to the rest of us. He was now our enemy and could dispose of us as he wished. "Where is the owner of the house?" he asked, and looked towards old Nick Sawle, who turned his back.

"My husband is from home," said Mary, coming forward, "and my stepson somewhere in the grounds."

"Is everyone living in the place assembled here?"

"All except the servants."

"You have no malignants in hiding?"

"None."

Lord Robartes turned to the staff officer at his side.

"Make a thorough search of the house and grounds," he said. "Break down any door you find locked and test the panelling for places of concealment. Give orders to the farm people to round up all sheep and cattle and other livestock, and place men in charge of them and the granaries. We will take over this gallery and all other rooms on the ground floor for our personal use. Troops to bivouac in the park."

"Very good, sir." The officer stood to attention and then departed about his business. Lord Robartes drew up a chair to the table and the remaining officer gave him paper and a quill.

"Now, madam," he said to Mary, "give me your full name and the name and occupation of each member of your household."

One by one he had us documented, looking at each victim keenly as though the very admission of name and age betrayed some sign of guilt. Only when he came to Gartred did his manner relax something of its hard suspicion. "A foolish time to journey, Mrs. Denys," he said. "You would have done better to remain at Orley Court."

"There are so many soldiery abroad of little discipline and small respect," said Gartred languidly. "It is not very pleasant for a widow with young daughters to live alone, as I do. I hoped by travelling south to escape the fighting."

"You thought wrong," he answered, "and, I am afraid, you must abide by the consequences of such an error. You will have to remain here in custody with Mrs. Rashleigh and her household."

Gartred bowed and did not answer. Lord Robartes rose to his feet. "When the apartments above have been searched you may go to them," he said, addressing Mary and the rest of us, "and I must request you to remain in them until further orders. Exercise once a day will be permitted in the garden here under close escort. You must prepare your food as, and how, you are able. We shall take command of the kitchens, and certain stores will be allotted to you. Your keys, madam."

I saw Mary falter and then, slowly and reluctantly, she unfastened the string from her girdle. "Can I not have entry there myself?" she asked.

"No, madam. The stores are no longer yours but the possession of the Parliament, like everything pertaining to this estate."

I thought of the jars of preserves upon Mary's shelves, the honeys, and the jams, and the salted pilchards in the larders, and the smoked hams, and the sides of salted mutton. I thought of the bread in the bakeries, the flour in the bins, the grain in the granaries, the young fruit setting in the orchards. And all the while I thought of this, the sound of heavy feet came tramping from above and out in the grounds came the bugle's cry.

"I thank you, madam. I must warn you, and the rest of the company, that any attempt at escape, any contravention of my orders, will be punished with extreme severity."

"What about milk for the children?" said Joan, her cheeks very flushed, her head high. "We must have milk, and butter, and eggs. My little son is delicate and inclined to croup."

"Certain stores will be given you daily, madam. I have already said so," said Lord Robartes. "If the children need more nourishment, you must do without yourselves. I have some five hundred men to quarter here, and their needs come before yours or your children's. Now you may go to your apartments."

This was the moment I had waited for and, catching Joan's eye, I summoned her to my side. "You must give up your apartment to Mrs. Denys," I murmured, "and come to me in the gatehouse. I shall move my bed into the adjoining chamber." Her lips framed a question, but I shook my head. She had sense enough to accept it, for all her agitation, and went at once to Mary with the proposition, who was so bewildered by the loss of her keys that her natural hospitality had deserted her.

"I beg of you to make no move because of me," said Gartred, smiling, her arms about her children. "May and Gertie and I can fit in anywhere. The house is something like a warren; I remember it of old."

I looked at her thoughtfully and remembered then how Kit had been at Oxford at the same time as my brother-in-law, when old Mr. Rashleigh was still alive, and that during the days of Jonathan's first marriage Kit had ridden over to Menabilly often from Lanrest.

"You have been here before then?" I said to Gartred, speaking to her for the first time since I had come into the gallery.

"Why, bless me, yes," she yawned. "Some five-and-twenty years ago Kit and I came for a harvest supper and lost ourselves about the passages." But at this moment Lord Robartes, who had been conferring with his officer, turned from the door.

"You will now, please," he said, "retire to your apartments."

We went out the farther door, where the servants were huddled like a flock of startled sheep, and Matty and two others seized the arms of my chair. Already the troopers were in the kitchens, in full command, and the round of beef that had been roasting for our dinner was being cut into great slices and served out amongst them, while down the stairs came three more of them two fellows and a non-commissioned officer, bearing loads of Mary's precious stores in their arms.

Another had a great pile of blankets and a rich embroidered cover that had been put aside until winter in the linen room.

"Oh, but they cannot have that," said Mary. "Where is an officer? I must speak to someone of authority."

"I have authority," replied the sergeant, "to remove all linen, blankets, and covers that we find. So keep a cool temper, lady, for you'll find no redress." They stared us coolly in the face, and one of them favoured Alice with a bold, familiar stare and then whispered something in the ear of his companion.

Oh, God, how I hated them upon the instant. I, who had regarded the war with irony and cynicism hitherto and a bitter shrug of the shoulder, was now filled with burning anger when it touched me close. Their muddied boots had trampled the floors, and upstairs wanton damage could at once be seen where they had thrust their pikes into the panelling and stripped the hangings from the walls. In Alice's apartments the presses had been overturned and the contents spilled upon the floor, and already a broken casement hung upon its hinge with the glass shattered. Alice's nurse was standing in the centre of the room crying and wringing her hands, for the troopers had carried off some of the children's bedding, and one clumsy oaf had trodden his heel upon the children's favourite doll and smashed its head to pieces. At the sight of this, their precious toy, the little girls burst into torrents of crying, and I knew then the idiot rage that surges within a man in wartime and compels him to commit murder. In the gardens the troopers were trampling down the formal beds, and with their horses had flattened the growing flowers, whose strewn petals lay crumpled now and muddied by the horses' hoofs.

I took one glance and then bade Matty and her companions bear me to my room. It had suffered like disturbance, with the bed tumbled and the stuffing ripped from the chairs for no rhyme or reason, and they had saved me the trouble of unlocking the barred chamber, for the door was broken in and pieces of planking strewn about the floor. The arras was torn in places, but the arras that hung before the buttress was still and undisturbed.

I thanked God in my heart for the cunning of old John Rashleigh and, desiring Matty to set me down beside the window, I looked out into the courtyard and saw the soldiers all gathered below, line upon line of them, with their horses tethered, and the tents gleaming white already in process of erection in the park, with the campfires burning, and the cattle lowing as they were driven by the soldiers to a pen, and all the while that Goddamned bugle blowing, high-pitched and insistent in a single key. I turned from the window and told Matty that Joan and her children would now be coming to the gatehouse, and I would remain here in the chamber that had been barred.

"The troopers have made short work of mystery," said Matty, looking about her, and at the broken door. "There was nothing put away here after all, then." I did not answer, and while she busied herself with moving my bed and my own belongings I wheeled myself to the cabinet and saw that Jonathan had taken the precaution of removing his papers before he went, leaving the cabinet bare.

When the two rooms were in order, and the servants had helped Matty to repair the door, thus giving me my privacy from Joan, I sent them from me to give assistance to Joan in making place for Gartred in the southern front. All was now quiet, save for the constant tramping of soldiers in the court below, and the comings and goings beneath me in the kitchens.

Very cautiously I drew near the northeast corner of my new apartment and lifted the arras. I ran my hands over the stone wall, as I had done that time before in the darkness when Jonathan had discovered me, and once again I could find no outlet, no division in the stone.

I realized then that the means for entry must be from without only, a great handicap to us who used it now, but no doubt cunningly intended by the builder of the house, who had no desire for his idiot elder son to come and go at pleasure. I knocked with my fists against the wall, but they sounded not at all. I called "John," in a low voice, expecting no answer; nor did I receive one.

This, then, was a new and hideous dilemma, for I had warned John not to attempt an entry to the chamber before I warned him, since I was confident at the time that I would be able to find the entrance from inside. This I could not do, and John and Dick were in the meantime waiting in the cell below the buttress for a signal from me. I placed my face against the wall, crying, "John… John… " as loudly as I dared, but I guessed, with failing heart, that the sound of my voice would never carry through the implacable stone. Hearing footsteps in the corridor, I let the arras fall and returned to the window, where I made a pretence of looking down into the court. I heard movement in my old apartment in the gatehouse, and a moment later a loud knocking on the door between. "Please enter," I called, and the roughly repaired door was pushed aside, tottering on its hinges, and Lord Robartes himself came into the room accompanied by one of his officers and Frank Penrose, with his arms bound tight behind him.

"I regret my sudden intrusion," said Lord Robartes, "but we have just found this man in the grounds. He volunteered information I find interesting, which you may add to, if you please."

I glanced at Frank Penrose, who, half frightened out of his wits, stared about him like a hare, passing his tongue over his lips.

I did not answer but waited for Lord Robartes to continue.

"It seems you have had living here, until today, the son of Skellum Grenvile," he said, watching me intently, "as well as his tutor. They were to have left by fishing boat for St. Mawes a few hours since. You were the boy's godmother and had the care of him, I understand. Where are they now?"

"Somewhere off the Dodman, I hope," I answered.

"I am told that as the boat set sail from Polkerris the boy could not be found," he replied, "and Penrose here and John Rashleigh went in search of him. My men have not yet come upon John Rashleigh or the boy. Do you know what has become of them?"

"I do not," I answered. "I only trust they are aboard the boat."

"You realize," he said harshly, "that there is a heavy price upon the head of Skellum Grenvile, and to harbour him or any of his family would count as treason to Parliament; The Earl of Essex has given me strict orders as to this."

"That being the case," I said, "you had better take Mrs. Denys into closer custody. She is Sir Richard's sister, as you no doubt know."

I had caught him off guard with this, and he looked at me nonplussed. Then he began tapping on the table in sudden irritation. "Mrs. Denys has, I understand, little or no friend-ship with her brother," he said stiffly. "Her late husband, Mr. Antony Denys, was known to be a good friend to Parliament and an opposer of Charles Stuart. Have you nothing further to tell me about your godson?"

"Nothing at all," I said, "except that I have every belief that he is upon that fishing boat, and with the wind in the right quarter he will be, by this time, nearly halfway to St. Mawes."

He turned his back on me at that and left the room, with the luckless Frank Penrose shuffling at his heels, and I realized, with relief, that the agent was ignorant as to Dick's whereabouts,

like everybody else in Menabilly, and for all he knew my tale
might be quite true and both Dick and John some ten miles out
at sea. Not one soul, then, in the place, knew the secret of the
buttress but myself, for Langdon, the steward, had accompanied
my brother-in-law to Launceston. This was a great advantage,
making betrayal an impossibility. But I still could not solve the
problem of how to get food and drink and reassurance to the
two fugitives I had myself imprisoned. And another fear began
to nag at me, with recollection of brother-in-law's words: "Lack
of air and close confinement soon rendered him unconscious
and easy to handle." Uncle John, gasping for breath in the little
cell beneath the buttress. How much air, then, came through to
the cell from the tunnel beyond? *Enough for how many hours?*

Once again, as earlier in the day, the sweat began to trickle
down my face, and half-unconsciously I wiped it away with my
hand. I felt myself defeated. There was no course for me to take.
A little bustle from the adjoining room and a child's cry told me
that Joan and her babies had come to my old apartment, and in
a moment she came through with little Mary whimpering in
her arms and small Jonathan clinging to her skirts.

"Why did you move, Honor dear?" she said. "There was no
need." And, like Matty, she gazed about the room in curiosity. "It
is very plain and bare," she added, "nothing valuable at all. I am
much relieved, for those brutes would have got it. Come back in
your own chamber, Honor, if you can bear with the babies."

"No," I said. "I am well enough."

"You look so tired and drawn," she said, "but I dare swear
I do the same. I feel I have aged ten years these last two hours.
What will they do to us?"

"Nothing," I said, "if we keep to our rooms."

"If only John would return," she said, tears rising to her eyes.
"Supposing he has had some skirmish on the road and has been
hurt? I cannot understand what can have become of him."

The children began to whimper, hearing the anxiety in her voice, and then Matty, who loved children, came and coaxed the baby and proceeded to undress her for her cot, while little Jonathan, with a small boy's sharp nervous way, began to plague us all with questions: Why did they come to their Aunt Honor's room? And who were all the soldiers? And how long would they stay?

The hours wore on with horrid dragging tedium, and the sun began to sink behind the trees at the far end of the park, while the air was thick with smoke from the fires lit by the troopers.

All the time there was tramping below, and orders called, and the pacing to and fro of horses, with the insistent bugle sometimes far distant in the park, echoed by a fellow bugle, and sometimes directly beneath the windows. The children were restless, turning continually in their cots and calling for either Matty or their mother, and when Joan was not hushing them she was gazing from my window, reporting fresh actions of destruction, her cheeks aflame with indignation. "They have rounded up all the cattle from the beef park and the beacon fields and driven them into the park here with a pen about them," she said, "and they are dividing up the steers now into another pen." Suddenly she gave a little cry of dismay. "They have slaughtered three of them," she said. "The men are quartering them already by the fires. Now they are driving the sheep." We could hear the anxious baaing of the ewes to the sturdy lambs and the lowing of the cattle. I thought of the five hundred men encamped there in the park, and the many hundreds more between us and Lostwithiel, and how they and their horses must be fed, but I said nothing. Joan shut the window, for the smoke from the campfires blew thick about the room, and the noise of the men shouting and calling orders made a vile and sickening clamour. The sun set in a dull crimson sky and the shadows lengthened.

About half past eight Matty brought us a small portion of a pie upon one plate, with a carafe of water. Her lips were grimly set.

"This for the two of you," she said. "Mrs. Rashleigh and Lady Courtney fare no better. Lady Courtney is making a little broth for the children's breakfast, in case they give us no eggs."

Joan ate my piece of pie as well as hers, for I had no appetite. I could think of one thing only, and that was that it was now nearly five hours since her husband and Richard's son had lain hidden in the buttress. Matty brought candles, and presently Alice and Mary came to say good night, poor Mary looking suddenly like an old woman from anxiety and shock, with great shadows under her eyes.

"They're axing the trees in the orchard," she said. "I saw them myself, sawing the branches and stripping the young fruit that has scarce formed. I sent down a message to Lord Robartes, but he returned no answer. The servants have been told by the soldiers that tomorrow they are going to cut the corn, strip all the barley from eighteen acres and the wheat from the Great Meadow. And it wants three weeks to harvest."

The tears began to course down her cheeks, and she turned to Joan.

"Why does John not come?" she said in useless reproach. "Why is he not here to stand up for his father's home?"

"If John was here he could do nothing," I said swiftly before Joan could lash back in anger. "Don't you understand, Mary, that this is war? This is what has been happening all over England, and we in Cornwall are having our first taste of it."

Even as I spoke there came a great burst of laughter from the courtyard and a tongue of flame shot up to the windows. The troopers were roasting an ox in the clearing above the warren, and because they were too idle to search for firewood they had broken down the doors from the dairy and the bakery and were piling them upon the fire.

"There must have been thirty officers or more at dinner in the gallery," said Alice quietly. "We saw them from our windows afterwards walk up and down the terrace before the house. One or two were Cornish—I remember meeting them before the war—but most of them were strangers."

"They say the Earl of Essex is in Fowey," said Joan, "and has set up his headquarters at Place. Whether it is true or not I do not know."

"The Treffrys will not suffer," said Mary bitterly. "They have too many relatives fighting for the rebels. You won't find Bridget has her stores pillaged, and her larders ransacked."

"Come to bed, Mother," said Alice gently. "Honor is right—it does no good to worry. We have been spared so happily until now. If my father and Peter are safe somewhere, with the King's army, nothing else can matter."

They went to their own apartments, and Joan to the children next door, while Matty—all oblivious of my own hidden fears—helped me undress for bed.

"There's one discovery I've made this night, anyway," she said grimly, as she brushed my hair.

"What is that, Matty?"

"Mrs. Denys hasn't lost her taste for gentlemen."

I said nothing, waiting for what would follow.

"You and the others and Mrs. Sawle and Mistress Sparke, had pie for your supper," she said, "but there was roast beef and burgundy taken up to Mrs. Denys and places set for two upon the tray. Her children were put together in the dressing room, and had a chicken between them."

I realized that Matty's partiality for eavesdropping and her nose for gossip might stand us in good stead in the immediate future.

"And who was the fortunate who dined with Mrs. Denys?" I asked.

"Lord Robartes himself," said Matty with sour triumph.

My first suspicion became a certainty. It was not mere chance that had so strangely brought Gartred to Menabilly after five-and-twenty years. She was here for a purpose.

"Lord Robartes is not an ill-looking man," I said. "I might invite him to share cold pie with me another evening."

Matty snorted and lifted me to bed. "I'd like to see Sir Richard's face if you did," she snapped.

"Sir Richard would not mind," I answered. "Not if there was something to be gained from it."

I feigned a lightness I was far from feeling, and when she had blown the candles and was gone I lay back in my bed with my nerves tense and strained. The flames outside my window died away, and slowly the shouting and the laughter ceased, and the tramping of feet, and the movement of the horses, and the calling bugles. I heard the clock in the belfry strike ten, then eleven, and then midnight. The people within the house were still and silent, and so was the alien enemy. At a quarter after midnight a dog howled in the far distance, and as though it were a signal I felt suddenly upon my cheek a current of cold chill air. I sat up in bed and waited. The draught continued, blowing straight from the torn arras on the wall. "John," I whispered, and "John," I whispered again. I heard a movement from behind the arras, like a scratching mouse. Slowly, stealthily, I saw the hand come from behind the arras, lifting it aside, and a figure step out, dropping on all fours and creeping to my bed. "It is I, Honor," I said, and the cold, froggy hand touched me, icy cold, and the hands clung to me and the dark figure climbed on to my bed, and lay trembling beside me.

It was Dick, the clothes still dank and chill upon him, and he began to weep, long and silently, from exhaustion and from fear.

I held him close, warming him as best I could, and when he was still I whispered, "Where is John?"

"In the little room," he said, "below the steps. We sat there waiting, hour after hour, and you did not come. I wanted to turn back, but Mr. Rashleigh would not let me." He began to sob again, and I drew the covers over his head.

"He has fainted, down there on the steps," he said. "He's lying there now, his head between his hands. I got hold of the long rope that hangs there above the steps and pulled at it, and the hinged stone gave way, and I came up into this room. I did not care. I could not stay there longer, Honor. It's black as pitch, and closer than a grave." He was still trembling, his head buried in my shoulder. I went on lying there, wondering what to do, whether to summon Joan and thus betray the secret to another, or wait until Dick was calmer and then send him back there with a candle to John's aid. And as I waited, my heart thumping, my ears strained to all sounds, I heard from without the tiptoe of a footstep in the passage, the noise of the latch of the door gently lifted and then let fall again as the door was seen to be fastened, and a moment's pause; then the footsteps tiptoeing gently away once more, and the soft, departing rustle of a gown. Someone had crept to the chamber in the stillness of the night, and that someone was a woman.

I went on lying there with my arms wrapped close about the sleeping boy and the clock in the belfry struck one, then two, then three....

Seventeen

As the first gray chinks of light came through the casement I roused Dick, who lay sleeping with his head upon my shoulder like a baby, and when he had blinked a moment and got his wits restored to him, I bade him light the candle and creep back again to the cell. The fear that gripped me was that lack of air had caused John to faint, and since he was by nature far from strong, anything might have happened. Never, in all the fifteen years I had been crippled, had I so needed the use of my legs as now, but I was helpless. In a few moments Dick was back again, his little ghost's face looking more pallid than ever in the gray morning light. "He is awake," he said, "but very ill, I think. Shaking all over and seeming not to know what has been happening. His head is burning hot, but his limbs are cold."

At least he was alive, and a wave of thankfulness swept over me. But from Dick's description I realized what had happened. The ague that was his legacy from birth had attacked John once again with its usual ferocity, and small wonder after more than ten hours crouching beneath the buttress. I made up my mind swiftly. I bade Dick bring the chair beside my bed, and with his assistance I lowered myself into it. Then I went to the door communicating with the gatehouse chamber and very gently called for Matty. Joan answered sleepily, and one of the children stirred.

"It is nothing," I said, "it is only Matty that I want." In a moment or two she came from the little dressing room, her round plain face yawning beneath her nightcap, and would have chided me for rising had I not placed my finger on my lips. The urgency of the situation was such that my promise to my brother-in-law must finally be broken, though little of it held as it was. And without Matty it would be impossible to act. She came in then, her eyes round with wonder when she saw Dick. "You love me, Matty, I believe," I said to her. "Now I ask you to prove that love as never before. This boy's safety and life is in our hands." She nodded, saying nothing.

"Dick and Mr. John have been hiding since last evening," I said. "There is a staircase and a little room built within the thickness of these walls. Mr. John is ill. I want you to go to him and bring him here. Dick will show you the way."

He pulled aside the arras, and now for the first time I saw how the entrance was effected. A block of stone, about four feet square, worked on a hinge, moved by a lever and a rope if pulled from beneath the narrow stair. This gave an opening just wide enough for a man to crawl through. When it was shut, the stone was so closely fitting that it was impossible to find it from within the chamber, nor could it be pushed open, for the lever held it. The little stairway, set inside the buttress, twisted steeply to the cell below, which had height enough for a man to stand upright. More I could not see, craning from my chair, save for a dark heap that must be John lying on the lower step.

There was something weird and fearful in the scene with the gray light of morning coming through the casement, and Matty, a fantastic figure in her night clothes and cap, edging her way through the gap in the buttress. As she disappeared with Dick I heard the first high call of the bugle from the park, and I

knew that for the rebel army the day had now begun. Soon the
soldiers within the house would also be astir, and we had little
time in hand. It was, I believe, some fifteen minutes before they
were all three within the chamber, though it seemed an hour,
and in those fifteen minutes the daylight had filled the room
and the troopers were moving in the courtyard down below.
John was quite conscious, thank God, and his mind lucid, but
he was trembling all over and in a high fever, fit for nothing but
his own bed and his wife's care. We took rapid consultation in
which I held firmly to one thing, and that was that no further
person, not even Joan his wife nor Mary his stepmother, should
be told how he had come into the house or that Dick was with
us still.

John's story, then, was to be that the fishing boat came in
to one of the coves beneath the Gribben, where he put Dick
aboard, and that on returning across the fields he had seen the
arrival of the troopers and hid until nightfall. But, his fever
coming upon him, he decided to return and therefore climbed
in by the lead piping and the creeper that ran along the south
front of the house outside his father's window. For corrobora-
tion of this John must go at once to his father's room, where his
stepmother was sleeping, and waken her, and win her acceptance of the story. And this immediately, before the household
were awake. It was like a nightmare to arrange, with Joan, his
wife, in the adjoining chamber through which he must pass
to gain the southern portion of the house. For if he went by
passage beneath the belfry he might risk encounter with the
servants or the troopers. Matty went first, and when there was
no question from Joan nor any movement from the children,
we judged them to be sleeping, and poor John, his body on
fire with fever, crept swiftly after her. I thought of the games
of hide-and-seek I had played with my brothers and sisters at
Lanrest as children, and how now that it was played in earnest

there was no excitement but a sickening strain that brought sweat to the forehead and a pain to the belly. When Matty returned and reported John in safety in his father's rooms, the first stage of the proceeding was completed. The next I had to break to Dick with great misgiving and an assumption of sternness and authority I was far from feeling. It was that he could remain with me in my apartment but must be prepared to stay, perhaps for long hours at a time, within the secret cell beneath the buttress, and must have a palliasse there to sleep upon, if need be, should there be visitors to my room.

He fell to crying at once, as I had expected, and beseeching me not to let him stay alone in the dark cell. He would go mad, he said—he could not stand it, he would rather die.

I was well-nigh desperate, now that the house was beginning to stir, and the children beginning to talk in the adjoining chamber.

"Very well, then," I said. "Open the door, Matty. Call the troopers. Tell them that Richard Grenvile's son is here and wishes to surrender himself to their mercy. They have sharp swords, and the pain will soon be over." God forgive me that I could find it in my heart so to terrify the lad, but it was his only salvation.

The mention of the swords, bringing the thought of blood, sent the colour draining from his face, as I knew it would, and he turned to me, his dark eyes desperate, and said, "Very well. I will do as you ask me." It is those same dark eyes that haunt me still and will always do so to the day I die.

I bade Matty take the mattress from my bed, and the stool beside the window, and some blankets, and bundle them through the open gap on to the stair. "When it is safe for you to come, I will let you know," I said. "But how can you," said Dick, "when the gap is closed?" Here I was forced back again into the old dilemma of the night before. I could have wept with strain and weariness, and looked at Matty in despair. "If you do not quite close the gap," she said, "but let it stay open three inches, Master Dick, with his ear put close to it, will hear your voice."

We tried it, and although I was not happy with the plan, it seemed the one solution. We found, too, that with a gap of two or three inches he could hear me strike with a stick upon the floor, once, twice, or thrice, which we arranged as signals. Thrice meant real danger, and then the stone must be pulled flush to the wall.

He had gone to his cell, with his mattress and his blankets and half a loaf that Matty had found for him, as the clock in the belfry struck six, and almost immediately little Jonathan from the adjoining room came pushing through the door, his toys under his arm, calling in loud tones for me to play with him. The day had started. When I look back now to the intolerable strain and anguish of that time, I wonder how in God's name I had the power to endure it. For I had to be on guard, not only against the rebels, but against my friends, too, and those I loved. Mary, Alice, and Joan must all three remain in ignorance of what was happening, and their visits to my chamber, which should have been a comfort and a consolation in this time of strain, merely added to my anxiety.

What I would have done without Matty I do not know. It was she, acting sentinel as she had done in the past, who kept them from the door when Dick was with me, and, poor lad, I had to have him often, for the best part of the day. Luckily, my crippled state served as a good excuse, for it was known that often in the past I had "bad days," and had to be alone, and this lie was now my only safeguard. John's story had been accepted as full truth, and since he was quite obviously ill and in high fever, he was allowed to remain in his father's rooms with Joan to care for him and was not removed to closer custody under guard. Severe questioning from Lord Robartes could not shake

John from his story, and thank heaven Robartes had too many other cares gathering fast upon his shoulders to worry any further about what had happened to Skellum Grenvile's son.

I remember Matty saying to me on that first day, Friday, the second of August: "How long will they be here, Miss Honor? When will the Royalist army come to relieve us?"

And I, thinking of Richard down at Truro and His Majesty already, so the rumour ran, entering Launceston, told her four days at the longest. But I was wrong. For four whole weeks the rebels were our masters.

It is nearly ten years since that August of '44, but every day of that agelong month is printed firm upon my memory.

The first week was hot and stifling, with a glazed blue sky and not a cloud upon it, and in my nostrils now I can recapture the smell of horseflesh, and the stink of sweating soldiery, borne upwards to my open casement from the fetid court below.

Day in, day out, came the jingle of harness, the clattering of hoofs, the march of tramping feet, and the grinding sound of wagon wheels, and ever insistent above the shouting of orders and the voices of the men, the bugle call hammering its single note.

The children, Alice's and Joan's, unused to being within doors at high summer, hung fretful from the windows, adding to the babel; and Alice, who had the care of all of them whilst Joan nursed John in the greater quietude of the south front, would take them from room to room to distract them. Imprisonment made cronies of us all, and no sooner had Alice and the brood departed than the Sparke sisters, who hitherto had preferred chequers to my company, would come inquiring for me with some wild rumour to unfold, gleaned from the frightened servants, of how the house was to be burnt down with all its inmates when Essex gave the order, but not till the women had been ravaged. I dare say I was the only woman in the house to be unmoved by such a threat, for God knows I could not be more bruised and broken than I was already. But for Deborah and Gillian it was another matter, and Deborah, whom I judged to be even safer from assault than I was myself, showed me with trembling hands the silver bodkin with which she would defend her honour. Their brother Will was become a sort of toady to the officers, thinking that by smiling and wishing them good morning he would win their favour and his safety, but as soon as their backs were turned he was whispering some slander about their persons and repeating snatches of conversation he had overheard, bits and pieces that were no use to anyone. Once or twice Nick Sawle came tapping slowly to my room, leaning on his two sticks, a look of lost bewilderment and muddled resentment in his eye because the rebels had not been flung from Menabilly within four-and-twenty hours of their arrival, and I was forced to listen to his theories that His Majesty must be now at Launceston, now at Liskeard, now back again at Exeter, suppositions that brought our release no nearer. While he argued, his poor wife, Temperance, stared at him dully, in a kind of trance, her religious eloquence pent up at last from shock and fear so that she could do no more than clutch her prayer book without quoting from it.

Once a day we were allowed within the garden for some thirty minutes, and I would leave Matty in my room on an excuse and had Alice push my chair while her nurse walked with the children. The poor gardens were laid waste already, with the yew trees broken and the flower beds trampled, and up and down the muddied paths we went, stared at by the sentries at the gate and by the officers gathered at the long windows in the gallery. Their appraising, hostile eyes burnt through our backs but must be endured for the sake of the fresh air we craved, and sometimes their laughter came to us. Their voices were hard and ugly, for they were mostly from London and the eastern counties, except the staff officers of Lord Robartes, and I never could abide the London twang, made doubly alien now through enmity. Never once did we see Gartred when we took our exercise, though her two daughters, reserved and unfriendly, played in the far corner of the garden, watching us and the children with blank eyes. They had neither of them inherited her beauty, but were brown-haired and heavy-looking, like their dead father, Antony Denys.

"I don't know what to make of it," said Alice in my ear. "She is supposed to be a prisoner like us, but she is not treated so. I have watched her from my window walk in the walled garden beneath the summerhouse, talking and smiling to Lord Robartes, and the servants say he dines with her most evenings."

"She only does what many other women do in wartime," I said, "and turns the stress of the day to her advantage."

"You mean she is for the Parliament?" asked Alice.

"Neither for the Parliament, nor for the King, but for Gartred Denys," I answered. "Do you not know the saying—to race with the hare and to run with the hounds? She will smile on Lord Robartes and sleep with him, too, if she has a mind, just as long as it suits her. He would let her leave tomorrow if she asked him."

"Why, then," said Alice, "does she not do so and return in safety to Orley Court?"

"That," I answered, "is what I would give a great deal to find out." And as we paced up and down, up and down, before the staring, hostile eyes of the London officers, I thought of the footstep I had heard at midnight in the passage, the soft hand on the latch, and the rustle of a gown. Why should Gartred, while the house slept, find her way to my apartment in the northeast corner of the building and try my door, unless she knew her way already? And granting that she knew her way, what, then, was her motive?

It was ten days before I had my answer.

On Sunday, August the eleventh, came the first break in the weather. The sun shone watery in a mackerel sky, and a bank of cloud gathered in the southwest. There had been much coming and going all the day, with fresh regiments of troopers riding to the park, bringing with them many carts of wounded, who were carried to the farm buildings before the house. Their cries of distress were very real and terrible and gave to us, who were their enemies, a sick dread and apprehension. The shouting and calling of orders was persistent on that day, and the bugle never ceased from dawn to sundown.

For the first time we were given soup only for our dinner and a portion of stale bread, and this, we were told, would be the best we could hope for from henceforward. No reason was given, but Matty, with her ears pricked, had hung about the kitchens with her tray under her arm and gleaned some gossip from the courtyard.

"There was a battle yesterday on Braddock Down," she said. "They've lost a lot of men." She spoke softly, for with our enemies about us we had grown to speak in whispers, our eyes upon the door.

I poured half my soup into Dick's bowl and watched him drink it greedily, running his tongue round the rim like a hungry dog. "The King is only three miles from Lostwithiel," she said. "He and Prince Maurice have joined forces and set up their headquarters at Boconnoc. Sir Richard has advanced with nigh a thousand men from Truro and is coming up on Bodmin from the west. 'Your fellows are trying to squeeze us dry,' said the trooper in the kitchen, 'like a bloody orange. But they won't do it.'"

"And what did you answer him?" I said to Matty.

She smiled grimly, and cut Dick the largest slice of bread.

"I told him I'd pray for him, when Sir Richard got him," she answered.

After eating, I sat in my chair looking out across the park and watched the clouds gather thick and fast. There were scarce a dozen bullocks left in the pen out of the fine herds there had been the week before, and only a small flock of sheep. The rest had all been slaughtered. These remaining few would be gone within the next eight-and-forty hours. Not a stem of corn remained in the far meadows. The whole had been cut and ground and the ricks pulled. The grass in the park was now bare earth where the horses had grazed upon it. Not a tree stood in the orchard beyond the warren. If Matty's tale was true, and the King and Richard were to east and west of Lostwithiel, then the Earl of Essex and ten thousand men were pent up in a narrow strip of land some nine miles long with no way of escape except the sea.

Ten thousand men with provisions getting low and only the bare land to live on, while three armies waited in their rear.

There was no laughter tonight from the courtyard, no shouting, and no chatter; only a blazing fire as they heaped the cut trees and kitchen benches upon it, the doors torn from the larder and the tables from the steward's room, and I could see their sullen faces lit by the leaping flames.

The sky darkened, and slowly, silently, the rain began to fall. And as I listened to it, remembering Richard's words, I heard the rustle of a gown and a tap upon my door.

Eighteen

$\mathcal{D}$ICK WAS GONE IN A FLASH TO HIS HIDING PLACE AND Matty cleared his bowl and platter. I sat still in my chair with my back to the arras and bade them enter who knocked upon the door.

It was Gartred. She was wearing, if I remember right, a gown of emerald green, and there were emeralds round her throat and in her ears. She stood a moment within the doorway, a half smile on her face. "The good Matty," she said, "always so devoted. What ease of mind a faithful servant brings."

I saw Matty sniff and rattle the plates upon her tray while her lips tightened in ominous fashion.

"Am I disturbing you, Honor?" said Gartred, that same smile still on her face. "The hour is possibly inconvenient; you go early, no doubt, to bed?"

All meaning is in the inflexion of the voice, and when rendered on paper words seem plain and harmless enough. I give the remarks as Gartred phrased them, but the veiled contempt, the mockery, the suggestion that because I was crippled I must be tucked down and in the dark by half past nine, this was in her voice and in her eyes as they swept over me.

"My going to bed depends upon my mood, as doubtless it does with you," I answered. "Also it depends upon my company."

"You must find the hours most horribly tedious," she said, "but then, no doubt, you are used to it by now. You have lived in custody so long that to be made prisoner is no new experience. I must confess I find it unamusing." She came closer in the room, looking about her, although I had given her no invitation.

"You have heard the news, I suppose?" she said.

"That the King is at Boconnoc and a skirmish was fought yesterday in which the rebels got the worst of it? Yes, I have heard that," I answered. The last of the fruit, picked before the rebels came, was standing on a platter in the window. Gartred took a fig and began to eat it, still looking about her in the room. Matty gave a snort of indignation that passed unnoticed and, taking her tray, went from the chamber with a glance at Gartred's back that would have slain her had it been perceived.

"If this business continues long," said Gartred, "we none of us here will find it very pleasant. The men are already in an ugly mood. Defeat may turn them into brutes."

"Very probably," I said.

She threw away the skin of her fig and took another.

"Richard is at Lanhydrock," she said. "Word came today through a captured prisoner. It is rather ironic that we have the owner of Lanhydrock in possession here. Richard will leave little of it for him by the time this campaign is settled, whichever way the battle goes. Jack Robartes is black as thunder."

"It is his own fault," I said, "for advising the Earl of Essex to come into Cornwall and run ten thousand men into a trap."

"So it is a trap," she said. "And my unscrupulous brother the baiter of it? I rather thought it must be."

I did not answer. I had said too much already, and Gartred was in quest of information. "Well, we shall see," she said, eating her fig with relish, "but if the process lasts much longer the rebels will turn cannibal. They have the country stripped already between here and Lostwithiel, and Fowey is without provisions. I shudder to think what Jack Robartes would do to Richard if he could get hold of him."

"The reverse equally holds good," I told her.

She laughed and squeezed the last drop of juice into her mouth.

"All men are idiots," she said, "and more especially in wartime. They lose all sense of values."

"It depends," I said, "upon the meaning of values."

"I value one thing only," she said. "My own security."

"In that case," I said, "you showed neglect of it when you travelled upon the road ten days ago."

She watched me under heavy lids and smiled.

"Your tongue hasn't blunted with the years," she said, "nor tribulation softened you. Tell me, do you still care for Richard?"

"That is my affair," I said.

"He is detested by his brother officers. I suppose you know that," she said, "and loathed equally in Cornwall as in Devon. In fact, the only creatures he can count his friends are sprigs of boys who daren't be rude to him. He has a little train of them nosing his shadow."

Oh God, I thought, you bloody woman, seizing upon the one insinuation in the world to make me mad. I watched her play with her rings.

"Poor Mary Howard," she said, "what she endured. You were spared intolerable indignities, you know, Honor, by not being his wife. I suppose Richard has made great play lately of loving you the same, and no doubt he does, in his curious vicious fashion. Rather a rare new pastime, a woman who can't respond."

She yawned and strolled over to the window. "His treatment of Dick is really most distressing," she said. "The poor boy adored his mother, and now I understand Richard intends to rear him as a freak just to spite her. What did you think of him when he was here?"

"He was young and sensitive, like many other children," I said.

"It was a wonder to me he was ever born at all," said Gartred, "when I think of the revolting story Mary told me. However, I will spare your feelings, if you still put Richard on a pedestal. I am glad, for the lad's sake, that Jack Robartes did not find him here at Menabilly. He has sworn an oath to hang any relative of Richard's."

"Except yourself," I said.

"Ah, I don't count," she answered. "Mrs. Denys of Orley Court is not the same as Gartred Grenvile." Once more she looked up at the walls and then again into the courtyard.

"This is the room, isn't it," she said, "where they used to keep the idiot? I can remember him mouthing down at Kit when we rode here five-and-twenty years ago."

"I have no idea," I said. "The subject is not discussed among the family."

"There was something odd about the formation of the house," she said carelessly. "I cannot recollect exactly what it was. Some cupboard, I believe, where they used to shut him up when he grew violent, so Kit told me. Have you discovered it?"

"There are no cupboards here," I said, "except the cabinet over yonder."

"I am so sorry," she said, "that my coming here forced you to give your room to Joan Rashleigh. I could so easily have made do with this one, which one of the servants told me was never used until you took it over."

"It was much simpler," I said, "to place you and your daughters in a larger room, where you can entertain visitors to dinner."

"You always did like servants' gossip, did you not?" she answered. "The hobby of all old maids. It whips their appetite to imagine what goes on behind closed doors."

"I don't know," I said. "I hardly think my broth tastes any better for picturing you hip to hip with Lord Robartes."

She looked down at me, her gown in her hands, and I wondered who had the greatest capacity for hatred, she or I.

"My being here," she said, "has at least spared you all, so far, from worse unpleasantness. I have known Jack Robartes for many years."

"Keep him busy, then," I said. "That's all we ask of you."

I was beginning to enjoy myself at last, and, realizing it, she turned towards the door. "I cannot guarantee," she said, "that his good temper will continue. He was in a filthy mood tonight at dinner when he heard of Richard at Lanhydrock and has gone off now to a conference at Fowey with Essex and the chiefs of staff."

"I look to you, then," I said, "to have him mellow by the morning." She stood with her hand on the door, her eyes sweeping the hangings on the wall. "If they lose the campaign," she said, "they will lose their tempers too. A defeated soldier is a dangerous animal. Jack Robartes will give orders to sack Menabilly, and destroy inside and without."

"Yes," I said. "We are all aware of that."

"Everything will be taken," she said, "clothes, jewels, furniture, food—and not much left of the inhabitants. He must be a curious man, your brother-in-law, Jonathan Rashleigh, to desert his home, knowing full well what must happen to it in the end."

I shrugged my shoulders. And then, as she left, she gave herself away. "Does he still act as collector for the Mint?" she said. Then for the first time I smiled, for I had my answer to the problem of her presence.

"I cannot tell you," I said. "I have no idea. But if you wait long enough for the house to be ransacked, you may come upon the plate you think he has concealed. Good night, Gartred."

She stared at me a moment, and then went from the room. At last I knew her business, and had I been less preoccupied with my own problem of concealing Dick, I might have guessed it sooner. Whoever won or lost the campaign in the West, it would not matter much to Gartred; she would see to it that she had a footing on the winning side. She could play the spy for both. Like Temperance Sawle, I was in a mood to quote the Scriptures and declaim, "Where the body lies, there will the eagles be gathered together." If there were pickings to be scavenged in the aftermath of battle, Gartred Denys would not stay at home in Orley Court. I remembered her grip upon the marriage settlement with Kit; I remembered that last feverish search for a lost trinket on the morning she left Lanrest, a widow; and I remembered too the rumours I had heard since she was widowed for the second time, how Orley Court was much burdened with debt and must be settled among her daughters when they came of age. Gartred had not yet found a third husband to her liking, but in the meantime she must live. The silver plate of Cornwall would be a prize indeed, could she lay hands on it.

This, then, was her motive, with suspicion already centred on my room. She did not know the secret of the buttress, but memory had reminded her that there was, within the walls of Menabilly, some such hiding place. And with sharp guesswork she had reached the conclusion that my brother-in-law would make a wartime use of it. That the hiding place might also conceal her nephew had, I was certain, never entered her head. Nor—and this was supposition on my part—was she working in partnership with Lord Robartes. She was playing her own game, and if the game was likely to be advanced by letting him make love to her, that was only by the way. It was far pleasanter to eat roast meat than watered broth; besides, she had a taste for burly men. But if she found she could not get what she wanted by playing a lone hand, then she would lay her cards upon the table and damn the consequences.

This, then, was what we had to fear, and no one in the house knew of it but myself. So Sunday, August the eleventh, came and went, and we woke next morning to another problematical week in which anything might happen, with the three Royalist armies squeezing the rebels tighter hour by hour, the strip of country left to them becoming daily more bare and devastated, and a steady, sweeping rain turning all the roads to mud.

Gone was the hot weather, the glazed sky, and the sun. No longer did the children hang from the windows, and listen to the bugles, and watch the troopers come and go. No more did we take our daily exercise before the windows of the gallery. A high blustering wind broke across the park, and from my tightly shut casement I could see the closed, dripping tents, the horses tethered line upon line beneath the trees at the far end, their heads disconsolate, while the men stood about in huddled, melancholy groups, their fires dead as soon as kindled. Many of the wounded died in the farm buildings. Mary saw the burial parties go forth at dawn, a silent, gray procession in the early morning mist, and we heard they took them to the Long Mead, the valley beneath the woods at Pridmouth.

No more wounded came to the farm buildings, and we guessed from this that the heavy weather had put a stop to fighting. But we heard also that His Majesty's army now held the east bank of the Fowey River, from St. Veep down to the fortress at Polruan, which commanded the harbour entrance. The rebels in Fowey were thus cut off from their shipping in the Channel and could receive no supplies by sea, except from such small boats as could land at Pridmouth or Polkerris or on the sand flats at Tywardreath, which the heavy run from the southwest now made impossible. There was little laughter or chatter now from the messroom in the gallery, so Alice said, and the officers, with grim faces, clamped back and forth from the dining chamber, which Lord Robartes had taken for his own use, while every now and then his voice would be raised in irritation and anger, as a messenger would ride through the pouring rain bearing some counterorder from the Earl of Essex in Lostwithiel or some fresh item of disaster. Whether Gartred moved about the house or not I do not know. Alice said she thought she kept to her own chamber. I saw little of Joan, for poor John's ague was still unabated, but Mary came from time to time to visit me, her face each day more drawn and agonized as she learnt of further devastation to the estate. More than three hundred of the sheep had already been slaughtered, thirty fatted bullocks, and sixty store bullocks. All the draught oxen taken, and all the farm horses, some forty of these in number. A dozen or so hogs were left out of the eighty there had been, and these would all be gone before the week was out. The last year's corn had vanished the first week of the rebel occupation, and now they had stripped the new, leaving no single blade to be harvested. There was nothing left, of course, of the farm wagons, or carts, or farming tools—these had all been taken. And the sheds where the winter fuel had been stored were as bare as the granaries. There was, in fact, so the servants in fear and trembling reported to Mary, scarcely anything remaining of the great estate that Jonathan Rashleigh had left in her keeping a fortnight since. The gardens spoilt, the orchards ruined, the timber felled, the livestock eaten. Whichever way the war in the West should go, my brother-in-law would be a bankrupt man. And they had not yet started upon the house or the inhabitants. Our feeding was already a sore problem. At midday we all gathered to the main meal of the day. This was served to us in Alice's apartment in the east wing, while John lay ill in his father's chamber, and there some twenty of us herded side by side, the children clamouring and fretful, while we dipped stale bread in the mess of watery soup provided, helped sometimes by swollen beans and cabbage. The children had their milk, but no more than two cupfuls for the day, and already I noticed a staring look about them, their eyes over-large in the pale faces, while their play had become listless, and they yawned often. Young Jonathan started his croup, bringing fresh anxiety to Joan, and Alice had to go below to the kitchen and beg for rhubarb sticks to broil for him—a favour which was only granted her because her gentle ways won sympathy from the trooper in charge. The old people suffered like the children and complained fretfully with the same misunderstanding of what war brings. Nick Sawle would stare long at his empty bowl when he had finished and mutter, "Disgraceful! Quite unpardonable!" under his beard, and look malevolently about him as though it were the fault of someone present, while Will Sparke, with sly cunning, would seat himself among the younger children and, under pretence of making friends, sneak crumbs from them when Alice and her nurse turned their backs. The women were less selfish, and Deborah, whom I had thought as great a freak in her own way as her brother was in his, showed great tenderness, on a sudden, for all those about her who seemed helpless, nor did her deep voice and incipient moustache discourage the smallest children.

It was solely with Matty's aid that I was able to feed Dick at all. By some means, fair or foul, which I did not inquire into, she had made an ally of the second scullion, to whom she pulled a long story about her ailing, crippled mistress, with the result that further soup was smuggled to my chamber beneath Matty's apron, and no one the wiser for it. It was this same scullion who fed us with rumours, too, and most of them disastrous to his own side, which made me wonder if a bribe would make him a deserter. At midweek we heard that Richard had seized Restormel Castle by Lostwithiel and that Lord Goring, who commanded the King's horse, held the bridge and the road below St. Blazey. Essex was now pinned up in our peninsula, some seven miles long and two broad, with ten thousand men to feed, and the guns from Polruan trained on Fowey Harbour. It could not last much longer. Either Essex and the rebels must be relieved by a further force marching to him from the East, or they must stand and make a fight of it. And we would sit, day after day, with cold hearts and empty bellies, staring out upon the sullen soldiery as they stood huddled in the rain outside their tents, while their leaders within the house held councils of despondency. Another Sunday came, and with it a whisper of alarm among the rebels that the country people were stealing forth at night and doing murder. Sentries were found strangled at their posts; men woke to find their comrades with cut throats; others would stagger to headquarters from the high road, their hands lopped from their wrists, their eyes blinded. The Cornish were rising.

On Tuesday, the twenty-seventh, there was no soup for our midday dinner, only half a dozen loaves amongst the twenty of us. On Wednesday one jugful of milk for the children, instead of three, and the milk much watered.

On Thursday Alice and Joan and Mary, and the two Sparke sisters and I, divided our bread amongst the children and made for ourselves a brew of herb tea with scalding water. We were not hungry. Desire for food left us when we saw the children tear at the stale bread and cram it in their mouths, then turn and ask for more, which we could not give to them. And all the while the southwest wind tore and blustered in the teeming sky, and the rebel bugle that had haunted us so long sounded across the park like a challenge of despair.

Nineteen

*O*N FRIDAY, THE THIRTIETH OF AUGUST, I LAY ALL DAY upon my bed, for to gather with the others now would be a farce, and in any case I had not the strength to do so. My cowardly soul forbade me watch the children beg and cry for their one crust of bread.

Matty brewed me a cup of tea, and it seemed wrong to swallow even that. Hunger had made me listless, and, heedless of danger, I let Dick come and lie upon his mattress by my bed while he knawed a bone that Matty had scavanged for him. His eyes looked larger than ever in his pale face, and his black curls were lank and lustreless. It seemed to me that in his hunger he grew more like his mother, and sometimes, looking down on him, I would fancy she had stepped into his place and it was Mary Howard I fed and sheltered from the enemy, and she who licked the bones with little pointed teeth and tore at the strips of flesh with small, eager paws.

Matty herself was hollow-eyed and sallow. Gone were the buxom hips and the apple cheeks. Whatever food she could purloin from her friend the scullion—and there was precious little now for the men themselves—she smuggled to Dick or to the children.

During the day, while I slipped from one racking dream into

another, with Dick curled at my feet like a puppy, Matty leaned up against the window, staring at the mist that had followed now upon the rain and hid the tents and horses from us.

The hoofbeats woke me shortly after two, and Matty, opening the window, peered down into the outer court and watched them pass under the gatehouse to the courtyard. Some dozen officers, she said, with an escort of troopers, and the leader, on a great black horse wearing a dark gray cloak. She slipped from the room to watch them descend from their horses in the inner court and came back to say that Lord Robartes had stood himself on the steps to receive them, and they had all passed into the dining chamber with sentries before the doors.

Even my tired brain seized the salient possibility that this was the last council to be held, and that the Earl of Essex had come to it in person. I pressed my hands over my eyes to still my aching head. "Go find your scullion," I said to Matty. "Do what you will to him, but make him talk." She nodded, tightening her lips, and before she went she brought another bone to Dick from some lair within her own small room and, luring him with it like a dog to his kennel, got him to his cell beneath the buttress.

Three, four, five, and it was already murky, the evening drawing in early because of the mist and rain, when I heard the horses pass beneath the archway once again and so out across the park. At half-past five Matty returned. What she had been doing those intervening hours I never asked her from that day to this, but she told me the scullion was without and wished to speak to me. She lit the candles, for I was in darkness, and as I raised myself upon my elbow I questioned her with my eyes, and she gave a jerk of her head towards the passage.

"If you give him money," she whispered, "he will do anything you ask him." I bade her fetch my purse, which she did, and then, going to the door, she beckoned him within.

He stood blinking in the dim light, a sheepish grin on his face, but that face, like ours, was lean and hungry.

I beckoned him to my bed, and he came near, with a furtive glance over his shoulder. I gave him a gold piece, which he pocketed instantly. "What news have you?" I asked.

He looked at Matty, and she nodded. He ran his tongue over his lips.

"'Tis only rumour," he said, "but it's what they're saying in the courtyard." He paused and looked again towards the door.

"The retreat begins tonight," he said. "There'll be five thousand of them marching through darkness to the beaches. You'll hear them if you listen. They'll come this way, down to Pridmouth and Polkerris. The boats will take them off when the wind eases."

"Horses can't embark in small boats," I said. "What will your generals do with their two thousand horse?"

He shook his head, and glanced at Matty. I gave him another gold piece.

"I had but a word with Sir William Balfour's groom," he said. "There's talk of breaking through the Royalist lines tonight when the foot retreat. I can't answer for the truth of it, nor could he."

"What will happen to you and the other cooks?" I asked.

"We'll go by sea, same as the rest," he said.

"Not likely," I said. "Listen to the wind."

It was soughing through the trees in the warren, and the rain spattered against my casement.

"I can tell you what will happen to you," I said. "The morning will come, and there won't be any boats to take you from the beaches. You will huddle there, in the driving wind and rain, with a thundering great southwest sea breaking down at Pridmouth and the country people coming down on you all from the cliffs with pitchforks in their hands. Cornish folk are not pleasant when they are hungry."

The man was silent, and passed his tongue over his lips once again.

"Why don't you desert?" I said. "Go off tonight before worse can happen to you. I can give you a note to a Royalist leader."

"That's what I told him," said Matty. "A word from you to Sir Richard Grenvile would see him through to our lines."

The man looked from one to the other of us, foolish, doubtful, greedy. I gave him a third gold piece. "If you break through to the King's Army," I said, "within an hour, and tell them there what you have just told me—about the horse trying to run for it before morning—they'll give you plenty more of these gold pieces, and a full supper into the bargain." He scratched his head, and looked again at Matty. "If the worst comes to the worst and you're held prisoner," I told him, "it would be better than having the bowels torn out of you by Cornishmen."

It was these last words that settled him. "I'll go," he said, "if you'll write a word for me."

I scribbled a few words to Richard, which were as like as not never to reach his hands (nor did they do so, I afterward discovered), and I bade the fellow find his way through the woods to Fowey if he could and in the growing darkness get a boat to Bodinnick, which was held by the Royalists, and there give warning of the rebel plan.

It would be too late, no doubt, to do much good, but it was at least a venture worth the trying. When he had gone, with Matty to speed him on his way, I lay back on my bed and listened to the rain, and as it fell I heard in the far distance, from the high road beyond the park, the tramp of marching feet. Hour after hour they sounded, tramp, tramp, without a pause, through the long hours of the night, with the bugle crying thin and clear above the moaning of the wind. When the morning broke, misty, and wet, and gray, they were still marching there upon the high road, bedraggled, damp, and dirty, hundred upon hundred straggling in broken lines across the park and making for the beaches.

Order was gone by midday on Saturday; discipline was broken, for as a watery sun gleamed through the scurrying clouds we heard the first sounds of gunfire from Lostwithiel, as Richard's army broke upon them from the rear. We sat at our windows, hunger at last forgotten, with the rain blowing in our weary faces, and all day long they trudged across the park, a hopeless tangle now of men and horses and wagons; voices yelling orders that were not once obeyed, men falling to the ground in weariness and refusing to move further, horses, carts, and the few cattle that remained, all jammed and bogged together in the sea of mud that once had been a park. The sound of the gunfire drew nearer, and the rattle of musket shots, and one of the servants, climbing to the belfry, reported that the high ground near Castledore was black with troops and smoke and flame, while down from the fields came little running figures, first a score, then fifty, then a hundred, then a hundred more, to join the swelling throng about the lanes and in the park.

And the rain went on, and the retreat continued.

At five o'clock word went round the house that we were every one of us to descend to the gallery. Even John, from his sickbed, must obey the order. The rest had little strength enough to drag their feet, and I found difficulty holding to my chair. Nothing had passed our lips now but weak herb tea for two whole days. Alice looked like a ghost, for I think she had denied herself entirely for the sake of her three little girls. Her sister Elizabeth was scarcely better, and her year-old baby in her arms was as still as a waxen doll. Before I left my chamber I saw that Dick was safe within his cell, and this time, in spite of protestations, I closed the stone that formed the entrance.

A strange band we were, huddled there together in the

gallery, with wan faces; the children strangely quiet, and an ominously heavy look about their hollow eyes. It was the first time I had seen John since that morning a month ago, and he seemed most wretchedly ill, his skin a dull yellow colour, and shaking still in every limb. He looked across at me as though to ask a question, and I nodded to him, summoning a smile.

We sat there waiting, no one with the heart or strength to speak. A little apart from us, near the centre window, sat Gartred with her daughters. They, too, were thinner and paler than before and, I think, had not tasted chicken now for many days, but compared to the poor Rashleigh and Courtney babies, they were not ill nourished.

I noticed that Gartred wore no jewels and was very plainly dressed, and somehow the sight of this gave me a strange foreboding. She took no notice of us, beyond a few words to Mary on her entrance, and, seated beside the little table in the window, she proceeded to play patience. She turned the cards with faces uppermost, considering them with great intentness. This, I thought, is the moment she has been waiting for for over thirty days.

Suddenly there was a tramping in the hall, and into the gallery came Lord Robartes, his boots splashed with mud, the rain running from his coat His staff officers stood beside him, and one and all wore faces grim and purposeful.

"Is everybody in the household here?" he called harshly.

Some sort of murmur rose from amongst us, which he took to be assent.

"Very well, then," he said, and, walking towards my sister Mary and her stepson John, he stood confronting them.

"It has come to my knowledge," he said, "that your malignant husband, madam, and your father, sir, have concealed upon the premises large quantities of silver, which should by right belong to Parliament. The time has ended for any trifling or protestation. Pressure is being brought to bear upon our armies at this moment, forcing us to a temporary withdrawal. The Parliament needs every ounce of silver in the land to bring this war to a successful conclusion. I ask you, madam, therefore, to tell me where the silver is concealed."

Mary, God bless her ignorance, turned up her bewildered face to him.

"I know nothing of any silver," she said, "except the few pieces of plate we have kept of our own, which you now possess, having my keys."

"I talk of great quantities, madam, stored in some place of hiding, until it can be transported by your husband to the Mint."

"My husband was collector for Cornwall, that is true, my lord. But he has never said a word to me about concealing it at Menabilly."

He turned from her to John.

"And you sir? No doubt your father told you all his affairs?"

"No," said John firmly. "I know nothing of my father's business, nor have I any knowledge of a hiding place. My father's only confidant is his steward, Langdon, who is with him at present. No one here at Menabilly can tell you anything at all."

For a moment Lord Robartes stared down at John, then, turning away, he called to his three officers. "Sack the house," he said briefly. "Strip the hangings and all furnishings. Destroy everything you find. Take all jewels, clothes, and valuables. Leave nothing of Menabilly but the bare walls."

At this poor John struggled to his feet, "You cannot do this," he said. "What authority has Parliament given you to commit such wanton damage? I protest, my lord, in the name of common decency and humanity." And my sister Mary, coming forward, threw herself upon her knees. "My Lord

Robartes," she said, "I swear to you by all I hold most dear that there is nothing concealed within my house. If it were so I would have known of it. I do implore you to show mercy to my home."

Lord Robartes stared down at her, his eyes hard.

"Madam," he said, "why should I show your house mercy, when none was shown to mine? Both victor and loser pay the penalty in civil war. Be thankful that I have heart enough to spare your lives." And with that he turned on his heel and went from us, taking his officers with him and leaving two sentries at the door.

Once again he mounted his horse in the courtyard and rode away, back to the useless rear-guard action that was being fought in the hedges and ditches up at Castledore, with the mizzle rain falling thick and fast. We heard the major he had left in charge snap forth an order to his men—and straightway they started tearing at the panelling in the dining chamber. We could hear the woodwork rip and the glass shatter as they smashed the mullioned windows. At this first warning of destruction Mary turned to John, the tears ravaging her face. "For God's sake," she said, "if you know of any hiding place, tell them of it, so that we save the house. I will take full blame upon myself when your father comes." John did not answer. He looked at me. And no one of the company there present saw the look save Gartred, who at that moment raised her head. I made no motion of my lips. I stared back at him, as hard and merciless as Lord Robartes. He waited a moment, then answered very slowly, "I know nought of any hiding place."

I think had the rebels gone about their work with shouts and merriment, or even drunken laughter, the destruction of the house would have been less hard to bear. But because they were defeated troops and knew it well, they had cold savage murder in their hearts, and did what they had to do in silence.

The door of the gallery was open, with the two sentries standing on guard beside it, and no voices were uplifted, no words spoken. There was only the sound of the ripping wood, the breaking of the furniture, the hacking to pieces of the great dining table, and the grunts of the men as they lifted their axes. The first thing that was thrown down to us across the hall, torn and split, was the portrait of the King, and even the muddied heel that had been ground upon the features, and the great crack across the mouth, had not distorted those melancholy eyes that stared up at us without complaint from the wrecked canvas.

We heard them climb the stairs and break into the south rooms, and as they tore down the door of Mary's chamber she began to weep, long and silently, and Alice took her in her arms and hushed her like a child. The rest of us did nothing but sat like spectres, inarticulate. Then Gartred looked towards me from her window. "You and I, Honor, being the only members of the company without a drop of Rashleigh blood, must pass the time somehow. Tell me, do you play piquet?"

"I haven't played it since your brother taught me, sixteen years ago," I answered.

"The odds are in my favour, then," she said. "Will you risk a *partie*?" As she spoke she smiled, shuffling her cards, and I guessed the double meaning she would bring to it

"Perhaps," I said, "there is more at stake than a few pieces of silver."

We heard them tramping overhead and the sound of the splitting axe, while the shivering glass from the casements fell to the terrace outside.

"You are afraid to match your cards against mine?" said Gartred.

"No," I said. "No, I am not afraid."

I pushed my chair towards her and sat opposite her at the

table. She handed the cards for me to cut and shuffle, and when I had done so, I returned them to her for the dealing, twelve apiece. There started then the strangest partie of piquet that I have ever played, before or since, for while Gartred risked a fortune I wagered for Richard's son, and no one knew it but myself. The rest of the company, dumb and apathetic, were too weak even to wonder at us, and if they did it was with shocked distaste and shuddering dislike that we—because we did not belong to Menabilly—could show ourselves so heartless.

"Five cards," called Gartred.

"What do they make?" I said.

"Making nine."

"Good."

"Five."

"A quart major, nine. Three knaves."

"Not good."

She led with the ace of hearts, to which I played the ten, and as she took the trick we heard the rebels wrenching the tapestry from the bedroom walls above. There was a dull smouldering smell, and a wisp of smoke blew past the windows of the gallery.

"They are setting fire," said John quietly, "to the stables and the farm buildings before the house."

"The rain will surely quench the flames," whispered Joan.

"They cannot burn fiercely, not in the rain."

One of the children began to wail, and I saw gruff Deborah take her on her knee and murmur to her. The smoke of the burning buildings was rank and bitter in the steady rain, and the sound of the axes overhead and the tramping of the men was as though they were felling trees in a thick forest, instead of breaking to pieces the great four-poster bed where Alice had borne her babies. They threw the glass mirror out on to the terrace, where it splintered to a thousand fragments, and with it came the broken candlesticks, the tall vases, and the tapestried chairs.

"Fifteen," said Gartred, leading the king of diamonds, and "Eighteen," I answered, trumping it with my ace.

Some of the rebels, with a sergeant in charge of them, came down the staircase, and they had with them all the clothing they had found in Jonathan's and Mary's bedroom, and her jewels, too, and combs, and the fine figured arras that had hung upon the walls. This they loaded in bundles upon the pack horses that waited in the courtyard. When they were fully laden a trooper led them through the archway, and two more took their places. Through the broken windows of the wrecked dining chamber, we could see the disordered rebel bands still straggling past the smouldering farm buildings towards the meadows and the beach, and as they gazed up at the house, grinning, their fellows at the house windows, warming to their work and growing reckless, shouted down to them with jeers and catcalls, throwing out the mattresses, the chairs, the tables, all they could lay hands upon which would make fodder for the flames that rose reluctantly in the slow drizzle from the blackened farm buildings.

There was one fellow making a bundle of all the clothing and the linen. Alice's wedding gown, and the little frocks she had embroidered for her children, and all Peter's rich apparel that she had kept with such care in her press till he should need it. The tramping ceased from overhead, and we heard them pass into the rooms beneath the belfry. Some fellow, in mockery, began to toll the bell, and the mournful clanging made a new sound in our ears, mingling with the shouting and yelling and rumble of wagon wheels that still came to us from the park, and the ever-increasing bark of cannon shot, now barely two miles distant.

"They will be in the gatehouse now," said Joan. "All your

books and your possessions, Honor, they will not spare them any more than ours." There was reproach in her voice, and disillusionment, that her favourite aunt and godmother should show no sign of grief. "My cousin Jonathan would never have permitted this," said Will Sparke, his voice high with hysteria. "Had there been plate concealed about the premises he would have given it, and willingly, rather than have his whole house robbed, and we, his relatives, lose everything." Still the bell tolled, and the ceilings shook with heavy, murderous feet, and down into the inner court now they threw the debris from the west part of the building—portraits, and benches, rugs and hangings, all piled on top of one another in hideous confusion—while those below discarded the less valuable and fed them to the flames.

"We started upon the third hand of the *partie*. A tierce to a king," called Gartred, and "Good," I replied, following her lead of spades. And all the while I knew that the rebels had now come to the last room of the house and were tearing down the arras before the buttress. I saw Mary raise her grief-stricken face and look toward us. "If you would say one word to the officer," she said to Gartred, "he might prevent the men from further damage. You are a friend of Lord Robartes and have some sway with him. Is there nothing you can do?"

"I could do much," said Gartred, "if I were permitted. But Honor tells me it is better for the house to fall about our ears. Fifteen, sixteen, seventeen, and eighteen. My trick, I fancy."

She wrote her score on the tablet by her side.

"Honor," said Mary, "you know that it will break Jonathan's heart to see his home laid desolate. All that he has toiled and lived for, and his father before him, for nearly fifty years. If Gartred can in some way save us and you are trying to prevent her, I can never forgive you, nor will Jonathan when he knows of it."

"Gartred can save no one, unless she likes to save herself," I answered, and began to deal for the fourth hand.

"Five cards," called Gartred.

"Equal," I answered.

"A quart to a king."

"A quart to a knave."

We were in our fifth and last game, each winning two apiece, when we heard them tramping down the stairs, with the major in the lead. The terrace and the courtyard were heaped high with wreckage, the loved possessions and treasures of nearly fifty years, even as Mary had said, and what had not been packed upon the horses was left now to destroy. They set fire to the remainder and watched it burn, the men leaning upon their axes and breathing hard now that the work was over. When the pile was well alight the major turned his back upon it and, coming into the gallery, clicked his heels and bowed derisively to John.

"The orders given my by Lord Robartes have been carried out with implicit fidelity," he announced. "There is nothing left within Menabilly house but yourselves, ladies and gentlemen, and the bare walls."

"And you found no silver hidden?" asked Mary.

"None, madam, but your own—now happily in our possession."

"Then this wanton damage, this wicked destruction, has been for nothing?"

"A brave blow has been struck for Parliament, madam, and that is all that we, her soldiers and her servants, need consider."

He bowed and left us, and in a moment we heard him call further orders, and horses were brought, and he mounted and rode away even as Lord Robartes had done an hour before. The flames licked the rubble in the courtyard, and save for their dull hissing and the patter of the rain, there was suddenly no other sound. A strange silence had fallen upon the place. Even the sentries stood no longer by the door. Will Sparke crept to the hall.

"They've gone," he said. "They've all ridden away. The house is bare, deserted."

I looked up at Gartred, and this time it was I who smiled, and I who spread my cards upon the table.

"Discard for carte blanche," I said softly and, adding ten thus to my score, I led her for the first time, and with my next hand drew three aces to her one, and gained the partie.

She rose then from the table without a word, save for one mock curtsy to me, and, calling her daughters to her, went upstairs. I sat alone, shuffling the cards as she had done, while out into the hall faltered the poor weak members of our company to gaze about them, stricken at the sight that met their eyes.

The panels ripped, the floors torn open, the windows shattered from their frames, and all the while the driving rain that had neither doors nor windows now to bar it, blew in upon their faces, soft and silent, with great flakes of charred timber and dull soot from the burning rubble in the courtyard. The last rebels had retreated to the beaches, save for the few who still made the stand at Castledore, and there was no trace of them left now at Menabilly but the devastation they had wrought and the black, churning slough that once was road and park. As I sat there listening, still shuffling the cards in my hands, I heard for the first time a new note above the cannon and the musket shot and the steady pattering rain. Not clamouring or insistent, like the bugle that had haunted me so long, but quick, triumphant, coming ever nearer, the sharp, brisk tattoo of the Royalist drums.

Twenty

$\mathcal{T}$HE REBEL ARMY CAPITULATED TO THE KING IN THE EARLY hours of Sunday morning. There was no escape by sea for the hundreds of men herded on the beaches. Only one fishing boat put forth from Fowey bound for Plymouth in the dim light before dawn, and she carried in her cabin the Lord General the Earl of Essex and his adviser, Lord Robartes. So much we learnt later, and we learnt, too, that Matty's scullion had proved faithful to his promise and borne his message to Sir Jacob Astley at Bodinnick on the Friday evening. But by the time word had reached His Majesty the outposts upon the road were warned, and the Parliament horse had success-fully broken through the Royalist lines and made good their escape to Saltash. So, by a lag in time, over two thousand rebel horse got clean away to fight another day, a serious mishap which was glossed over by our forces in the heat and excitement of the big surrender, and I think the only one of our commanders to go nearly hopping mad at the escape was Richard Grenvile.

It was, I think, most typical of his character, that when he sent a regiment of his foot to come to our succour on that Sunday morning, bringing us food from their own wagons, he did not come himself but forwarded me this brief message, stopping not to consider whether I lived or died, or whether his son was with me still:

> You will soon learn that my plan has only partially succeeded. The horse have got away, all owing to that besotted idiot Goring lying in a stupor at his headquarters, and permitting— you will scarcely credit it—the rebels to slip through his lines without as much as a musket shot at their backsides. May God preserve us from our own commanders. I go now in haste to Saltash in pursuit, but have little hope of overtaking the sods, if Goring, with his cavalry, has already failed.

First a soldier, last a lover, my Richard had no time to waste over a starving household and a crippled woman who had let a whole house be laid waste about her for the sake of the son he did not love. So it was not the father, after all, who carried the fainting lad into my chamber once again and laid him down, but poor sick John Rashleigh who, crawling for the second time into the tunnel beneath the summerhouse, found Dick unconscious in the buttress cell, tugged at the rope, and so opened the hinged stone into the room.

This was about nine o'clock on the Saturday night, after the house had been abandoned by the rebels, and we were all too weak to do much more than smile at the Royalist foot when they beat their drums under our gaping windows on the Sunday morning.

The first necessity was milk for the children and bread for ourselves, and later in the day, when we had regained a little measure of our strength and the soldiers had kindled a fire for us in the gallery—the only room left liveable—we heard once more the sound of horses, but this time heartening and welcome, for they were our own men coming home. I suppose I had been through a deal of strain those past four weeks, something harder than the others because of the secret I had guarded; and so, when it was over, I suffered a strange relapse, accentuated maybe by natural weakness, and had not the strength for several days to lift my head. The scenes of joy and reunion then were not for me. Alice had her Peter, Elizabeth her John of Coombe, Mary had her Jonathan, and there was kissing, and crying, and kissing again, and all the horrors of our past days to be described, and the desolation to be witnessed. But I had no shoulder on which to lean my head and no breast to weep upon. A truckle bed from the attic served me for support, this being one of the few things found that the rebels had not destroyed. I recollect that my brother-in-law bent over me when he returned and praised me for my courage, saying that John had told him everything and I had acted as he would have done himself, had he been home. But I did not want my brother-in-law. I wanted Richard. And Richard had gone to Saltash, chasing rebels. All the rejoicing came as an anticlimax. The bells pealing in Fowey Church, echoed by the bells at Tywardreath, and His Majesty summoning the gentlemen of the county to his headquarters at Boconnoc and thanking them for their support—he presented Jonathan with his own lace handkerchief and prayer book—and a sudden wild thanksgiving for deliverance and for victory seemed premature to me and strangely sour. Perhaps it was some fault in my own character, some cripple quality, but I turned my face to the wall and my heart was heavy. The war was not over, for all the triumphs in the West. Only Essex had been defeated, and his eight thousand men. There were many thousands in the North and East of England who had yet to show their heels. "And what is it all for?" I thought, "Why can they not make peace? Is it to continue thus, with the land laid waste, and houses devastated, until we are all grown old?"

Victory had a hollow sound, with our enemy Lord Robartes in command at Plymouth, still stubbornly defended, and there was something narrow and parochial in thinking the war over because Cornwall was now free. It was the second day of our release, when the menfolk had ridden off to Boconnoc to take leave of His Majesty, that I heard the sound of wheels in the outer court and preparation for departure and then those wheels creaking over the cobbles and disappearing through the park. I was too tired then to question it, but later in the day, when Matty came to me, I asked her who it was that went away from Menabilly in so confident a fashion. "Who else could it be," Matty answered, "but Mrs. Denys?" So Gartred, like a true gambler, had thought best to cut her losses and be quit of us.

"How did she find the transport?" I inquired.

Matty sniffed as she wrung out a piece of cloth to bathe my back. "There was a gentleman she knew, it seems, amongst the Royalist party who rode hither yesterday with Mr. Rashleigh. A Mr. Ambrose Manaton. And it's he who has provided her the escort for today."

I smiled in spite of myself. However much I hated Gartred, I had to bow to the fashion in which she landed on her feet in all and every circumstance.

"Did she see Dick," I asked, "before she left?"

"Aye," said Matty. "He went up to her at breakfast and saluted her. She stared at him, amazed—I watched her. And then she asked him, 'Did you come in the morning with the infantry?' And he grinned like a little imp and answered: 'I have been here all the time.'"

"Imprudent lad," I said. "What did she say to him?"

"She did not answer for a moment, Miss Honor, and then she smiled—you know her way—and said, 'I might have known it. You may tell your jailer you are not worth one bar of silver.'"

"And that was all?"

"That was all. She went soon after. She'll never come again to Menabilly." And Matty rubbed my sore back with her hard, familiar hands. But Matty was wrong, for Gartred did come again to Menabilly, as you shall hear, and the man who brought her was my own brother. But I run ahead of my story, for we are still in September '44.

That first week, while we recovered our strength, my brother-in-law and his steward set to work to find out what it would cost to make good the damage that had been wrought upon his house and his estate. The figure was collossal and beyond his means. I can see him now, seated in one corner of the gallery, reading from his great account book, every penny he had lost meticulously counted and entered in the margin. It would take months—nay, years—he said, to restore the house and bring back the estate to its original condition. While the war lasted no redress would be forthcoming. After the war, so he was told, the Crown would see that he was not the loser. I think Jonathan knew the value of such promises, and, like me, he thought the rejoicings in the West were premature. One day the rebels might return again, and next time the scales be turned.

In the meantime, all that could be done was to save what was left of the harvest—and that but one meadow of fourteen acres that the rebels had left uncut but the rain had well-nigh ruined.

Since his house in Fowey had been left bare in the same miserable fashion as Menabilly, his family, in their turn, were homeless, and the decision was now made amongst us to divide. The Sawles went to their brother at Penrice, and the Sparkes to other relatives at Tavistock. The Rashleighs themselves, with children, split up among near neighbours until a wing of Menabilly should be repaired. I was for returning to Lanrest until I learnt, with a sick heart, that the whole house had suffered a worse fate than Menabilly and was wrecked beyond hope of restoration.

There was nothing for it but to take shelter, for the time being, with my brother Jo at Radford, for although Plymouth was still held by Parliament, the surrounding country was safe in Royalist hands, and the subduing of the garrison and harbour was only, according to our optimists, a matter of three months at the most.

I would have preferred, had the choice been offered me, to live alone in one bare room at Menabilly than repair to Radford and the stiff household of my brother, but alas, I had become in a few summer months but another of the vast number of homeless people turned wanderer through war, and must swallow pride and be grateful for hospitality, from whatever direction it might come.

I might have gone to my sister Cecilia at Mothercombe, or my sister Bridget at Holberton, both of whom were pleasanter companions than my brother Jo, whose official position in the county of Devon had turned him somewhat cold and proud, but I chose Radford for the reason that it was close to Plymouth—and Richard was once more commander of the siege. What hopes I had of seeing him? God only knew, but I was sunk deep now in the mesh I had made for myself, and waiting for a word from him, or a visit of an hour had become my sole reason for existence.

"Why cannot you come with me to Buckland?" pleaded Dick, for the tutor, Herbert Ashley, had been sent to fetch him home. "I would be content at Buckland, and not mind my father, if you could come, too, and stand between us."

"Your father," I answered him, "has enough work on his hands without keeping house for a crippled woman."

"You are not crippled," declared the boy with passion. "You are only weak about the legs and so must sit confined to your chair. I would tend you and wait upon you, hour by hour with Matty, if you would but come with me to Buckland."

I smiled and ran my hand through his dark curls.

"You shall come and visit me at Radford," I said, "and tell me of your lessons. How you fence, and how you dance, and what progress you make in speaking French."

"It will not be the same," he said, "as living here with you in the house. Shall I tell you something? I like you best of all the people that I know—next to my own mother."

Ah well, it was an achievement to be second once again to Mary Howard. The next day he rode away in company with his tutor, turning back to wave to me all the way across the park, and I shed a useless, sentimental tear when he was gone from me.

What might have been—what could have been. These are the saddest phrases in our English tongue. And back again, pell-mell would come the fantasies; the baby I had never borne, the husband I would never hold. The sickly figures in an old maid's dream, so Gartred would have told me.

Yes, I was thirty-four, an old maid and a cripple; but sixteen years ago I had had my moment, which was with me still, vivid and enduring, and by God, I swear I was happier with my one lover than Gartred ever had been with her twenty.

So I set forth upon the road again and turned my back on Menabilly, little thinking that the final drama of the house must yet be played with blood and tears, and I kissed my dear Rashleighs one and all and vowed I would return to them as soon as they could have me.

Jonathan escorted me in my litter as far as Saltash, where Robin came to meet me. I was much shaken, not by the roughness of the journey, but by the sights I had witnessed on the road. The aftermath of war was not a pleasant sight to the beholder.

The country was laid waste, for one thing and that was the fault of the enemy. The corn ruined, the orchards devastated, the houses smoking. And in return for this the Cornish people had taken toll upon the rebel prisoners. There were many of them still lying in the ditches, with the dust and flies upon them. Some without hands and feet, some hanging downwards from the trees. And there were stragglers who had died upon the road in the last retreat, too faint to march from Cornwall—and these had been set upon and stripped of their clothing and left for the hungry dogs to lick.

I knew then, as I peered forth from the curtains of my litter, that war can make beasts of every one of us, and that the men and women of my own breed could act even worse in warfare than the men and women of the eastern counties. We had, each one of us, because of the civil war, streaked back two centuries in time and were become like those half savages of the fourteen hundreds who, during the Wars of the Roses, slit each other's throats without compunction.

At Saltash there were gibbets in the market square, with the bodies of rebel troopers hanging upon them scarcely cold, and as I turned my sickened eyes away from them I heard Jonathan inquire of a passing soldier what faults they had committed.

He grinned, a fine tall fellow, with the Grenvile shield on his shoulder. "No fault," he said, "except that they are rebels, and so must be hanged, like the dogs they are."

"Who gave the order, then?"

"Our general, of course, Sir Richard Grenvile."

Jonathan said nothing, but I saw that he looked grave, and I leant back upon my cushions, feeling, because it was Richard's doing and I loved him, that the fault was somehow mine and I was responsible. We halted there that night, and in the morning Robin came with an escort to conduct me across the Tamar, and so through the Royalist lines outside the Plymouth defences, round to Radford.

Robin looked well and bronzed, and I thought again with

cynicism how men, in spite of protestations about peace, are really bred to war and thrive upon it. He was not under Richard's command but was colonel of foot under Sir John Berkeley, in the army of Prince Maurice, and he told us that the King had decided not to make a determined and immediate assault upon Plymouth after all, but leave it to Grenvile to subdue by slow starvation, while he and Prince Maurice marched east out of Devon towards Somerset and Wiltshire, there to join forces with Prince Rupert and engage the Parliament forces which were still unsubdued. I thought to myself that Richard would reckon this bad strategy, for Plymouth was no pooping little town, but the finest harbour in all England next to Portsmouth, and for His Majesty to gain the garrison and have command also of the sea was of very great importance. Slow starvation had not conquered it before; why then should it do so now? What Richard needed for assault was guns and men. But I was a woman and not supposed to have knowledge of these matters. I watched Robin and Jonathan in conversation and caught a murmur of the word "Grenvile" and Robin say something about "harsh treatment of the prisoners" and "Irish methods not suiting Devon men, and I guessed that Richard was already getting up against the county. No doubt I would hear more of this at Radford."

No one hated cruelty more than I did, nor deplored the streak of it in Richard with greater sickness of heart, but as we travelled towards Radford, making a great circuit of the forts around Plymouth, I noticed with secret pride that the only men who carried themselves like soldiers were those who wore the Grenvile shields on their shoulders. Some of Goring's horse were quartered by St. Budeaux, and they were lolling about the village, drinking with the inhabitants, while a sentry squatted on a stool, his great mouth gaping in a yawn, his musket lying at his feet. From the nearby inn came a group of officers, laughing and very flushed, but the sentry did not leap to his feet when he observed them. Robin joined the officers a moment, exchanged greetings, and as we passed through the village he told me that the most flushed of the group was Lord Goring himself, a very good fellow, and a most excellent judge of horses.

"Does that make him a good commander?" I asked.

"He is full of courage," said Robin, "and will ride at anything. That is all that matters." And he proceeded to tell me about a race that had been run the day before, under the very noses of the rebels, and how Lord Goring's chestnut had beaten Lord Wentworth's roan by half a neck. "Is that how Prince Maurice's army conducts its war?" I asked. Robin laughed—he too thought it all very fine sport.

But the next post we passed was held by Grenvile men. And here there was a barrier across the road with armed sentries standing by it, and Robin had to show his piece of paper, signed by Sir John Berkeley, before we could pass through. An officer barked an order to the men, and they removed the barrier. There were perhaps a score of them standing by the postern, cleaning their equipment; they looked lean and tough, with an indefinable quality about them that stamped them Grenvile men. I would have known them on the instant had I not seen the scarlet pennant by the postern door, with the three golden rests staring from the centre, capped by a laughing gryphon.

We came at length by Plymstock to Radford and my brother's house, and as I was shown to my apartments looking north over the river towards the Cattwater and Plymouth, I thought of my eighteenth birthday long ago, and how Richard had sailed into the Sound with the Duke of Buckingham. It seemed a world ago, and I another woman. My brother was now a widower, for Elizabeth Champernowne had died a few years before the war in childbed, and my youngest brother

Percy, with his wife Phillipa, had come to live with him and look after Jo's son John, a child of seven, since they themselves were childless. I had never cared much for Radford, even as a girl, and now within its austere barrack precincts I found myself homesick, not so much for Lanrest and the days that were gone, but for my last few months at Menabilly. The danger I had known there and the tension I had shared had, in some strange fashion, rendered the place dear to me. The gatehouse between the courtyards, the long gallery, the causeway that looked out to the Gribben and the sea seemed to me now, in retrospect, my own possession, and even Temperance Sawle with her prayers and Will Sparke with his high-pitched voice were people for whom I felt affection because of the siege we had each of us endured. The fighting did not touch them here at Radford, for all its proximity to Plymouth, and the talk was of the discomfort they had to bear by living within military control.

Straight from a sacked house and starvation, I wondered that they should think themselves ill-used, with plenty of food upon the table, but no sooner had we sat down to dinner (I had not the face to demand it, the first evening, in my room) than Jo began to hold forth, with great heat, upon the dictatorial manners of the army. "His Majesty has thought fit," he said, "to confer upon Richard Grenvile the designation of General in the West. Very good. I have no word to say against the appointment. But when Grenvile trades upon the title to commandeer all the cattle within a radius of thirty miles or more to feed his army, and rides roughshod over the feelings of the county gentry with the one sentence, 'Military necessities come first,' it is time that we all protested."

If Jo remembered my old alliance with Richard, the excitement of the moment had made him conveniently forget it. Nor did he know that young Dick had been in my care at Menabilly the past weeks. Robin, too, full of his own commander,

Berkeley, was pleased to agree with Jo. "The trouble with Grenvile," said Robin, "is that he insists upon his fellows being paid. The men in his command are like hired mercenaries. No free quarter, no looting, no foraging as they please, and all this comes very hard upon the pockets of people like yourself, who must provide the money."

"Do you know," continued Jo, "that the commissioners of Devon have been obliged to allot him one thousand pounds a week for the maintenance of his troops? I tell you, it hits us very hard."

"It would hit you harder," I said, "if your house was burnt down by the Parliament."

They stared at me in surprise, and I saw young Phillipa look at me in wonder for my boldness. Woman's talk was not encouraged at Radford. "That my dear Honor," said Jo coldly, "is not likely to happen." And, turning his shoulder to me, he harped on about the outraged Devon gentry, and how this new-styled General in the West had coolly told them he had need of all their horses and their muskets in this siege of Plymouth, and if they did not give them to him voluntarily he would send a company of his soldiers to collect them.

"The fellow is entirely without scruples, no doubt of that," said Percy, "but in fairness to him I must say that all the country people tell me they would rather have Grenvile's men in their villages than Goring's. If Grenvile finds one of his own fellows looting, he is shot upon the instant. But Goring's men are quite out of control, and drunk from dawn to dusk."

"Oh, come," frowned Robin, "Goring and his cavalry are entitled to a little relaxation, now that the worst is over. No sense in keeping fellows standing to attention all day long."

"Robin is right," said Jo. "A certain amount of licence must be permitted to keep the men in heart. We shall never win the war otherwise."

"You are more likely to lose it," I said, "by letting them loll about the villages with their tunics all undone."

The statement was rendered the more unfortunate by a servant entering the room upon this instant and announcing Sir Richard Grenvile. He strode in, with his boots ringing on the stone flags, in that brisk way I knew so well, totally unconscious of himself or the effect he might produce, and with a cool nod to Jo, the master of the house, he came at once to me and kissed my hand.

"Why the devil," he said, "did you come here and not to Buckland?" That he at once put me at a disadvantage amongst my relatives did not worry him. I murmured something about my brother's invitation and attempted to introduce him to the company. He bowed to Phillipa but turned back immediately to me.

"You've lost that weight that so improved your person," he said. "You're as thin as a church mouse."

"So would you be," I answered, "if you'd been held prisoner by the rebels for four weeks."

"The whelp is asking for you all day long," said Richard. "He dins your praises in my ears till I am sick of them. I have him outside with Joseph. Hi, spawn!" He turned on his heels, bawling for his son. I think I never knew of any man, save Richard, who could in so brief a moment fill a room with his presence and become, as it were, the master of a house that was in no way his. Jo stood at his own table, his napkin in his hand, and Robin, too, and Percy, and they were like dumb servants waiting for the occasion, while Richard took command. Dick crept in cautiously, timid and scared as ever, his dark eyes lighting at the sight of me, and behind him strode young Joseph Grenvile, Richard's kinsman and aide-de-camp, his features and his colouring so like his general's as to make me wonder, and not for the first time, God forgive my prying mind, whether Richard had been purposely vague about the relationship between them and whether he was not as much his son as Dick was. Goddamn you, I thought, begetting sons about the countryside before I was even crippled. "Have you all dined?" said Richard, reaching for a plum. These lads and I could eat another dinner." Jo, with heightened colour and a flea in his ear, as the saying goes, called the servants to bring back the mutton. Dick squeezed himself beside me, like a small dog regaining his lost mistress, and while they ate Richard declaimed upon the ill advisability of the King having marched east without first seeing Plymouth was subdued.

"It's like talking to a brick wall, God bless him," said Richard, his mouth full of mutton. "He knows no more of warfare than this dead sheep I swallow." I saw my brothers look at one another in askance, that a general should dare to criticize his king. "I'll fight in his service until there's no breath left in my body," said Richard, "but it would make it so much simpler for the country if he would ask advice of soldiers. Put some food into your belly, spawn. Don't you want to grow as fine a man as Jo here?" I saw Dick glance under his eyes at Joseph with a flicker of jealousy. Jo, then, was the favourite, no doubt about that. What a world of difference between them, too, the one so broad-shouldered, big, and auburn-haired; the other little, with black hair and eyes. I wonder, I thought grudgingly, what buxom country girl was Joseph's mother, and if she still lived, and what had happened to her. But while I pondered the question, as jealous as young Dick, Richard continued talking. "It's that damned lawyer who's to blame," he said, "that fellow Hyde, an upstart from God knows what snivelling country town, and now jumped into favour as Chancellor of the Exchequer. His Majesty won't move a finger without asking his advice. I hear Rupert has all but chucked his hand in and returned to Germany. Depend upon it, it's fellows like this one who will lose the war for us."

"I have met Sir Edward Hyde," said my brother. "He seemed to me a very able man."

"Able my arse," said Richard. "Anyone who jiggles with the Treasury must be double-faced to start with. I've never met a lawyer yet who didn't line his own pockets before he fleeced his clients." He tapped young Joseph on the shoulder. "Give me some tobacco," he said. The youngster produced a pipe and pouch from his coat. "Yes, I hate the breed," said Richard, blowing a cloud of smoke across the table, "and nothing affords me greater pleasure than to see them trounced. There was a fellow called Braband, who acted as attorney for my wife against me in the Star Chamber in the year '33, a neighbour of yours, Harris, I believe?"

"Yes," said my brother coldly, "and a man of great integrity devoted to the King's cause in this war."

"Well, he'll never prove that now," said Richard. "I found him creeping about the Devon lanes disguised the other day and seized the occasion to arrest him as a spy. I've waited eleven years to catch that blackguard."

"What have you done to him, sir?" asked Robin.

"He was disposed of," said Richard, "in the usual fashion. No doubt he is doing comfortably in the next world."

I saw young Joseph hide his laughter in his wineglass, but my three brothers gazed steadfastly at their plates.

"I dare say," said my eldest brother slowly, "that I should be very ill advised if I attempted to address to you, General, a single word of criticism, but…"

"You would, sir," said Richard, "be extremely ill advised." And laying his hand a moment on Joseph's shoulder, he rose from the table. "Go on, lads, and get your horses. Honor, I will conduct you to your apartment. Good evening, gentlemen."

I felt that whatever reputation I might have for dignity in the eyes of my family was gone to the winds forever as he swept me to my room. Matty was sent packing to the kitchen, and he lay me on my bed and sat beside me.

"You had far better," he said, "return with me to Buckland. Your brothers are all asses. As for the Champeraownes, I have a couple of them on my staff, and both are useless. You remember Edward, the one they wanted you to marry? Dead from the neck upwards."

"And what would I do at Buckland," I said, "among a mass of soldiers. What would be thought of me?"

"You could look after the whelp," he said, "and minister to me in the evening. I get very tired of soldiers' company."

"There are plenty of women," I said, "who could give you satisfaction."

"I have not met any," he said.

"Bring them in from the hedgerows," I said, "and send them back again in the morning. It would be far less trouble than having me upon your hands from dawn till dusk."

"My God," he said, "if you think I want to bounce about with some fat female after a hard day's work sweating my guts out before the walls of Plymouth, you flatter my powers of resilience. Keep still, can't you, while I kiss you."

Below the window, in the drive, Jo and Dick paced the horses up and down. "Someone," I said, "will come into the room."

"Let them," he answered. "What the hell do I care?"

I wished that I could have the same contempt for my brother's house as he had. It was dark and by the time he left, and I felt as furtive as I had done at eighteen when slipping from the apple tree.

"I did not come to Radford," I said weakly, "to behave like this."

"I have a very poor opinion," he answered, "of whatever else you came for."

I thought of Jo and Robin, Percy and Phillipa, all sitting

in the hall below, and the two lads pacing their horses under the stars.

"You have placed me," I said, "in a most embarrassing position."

"Don't worry, sweetheart," he said. "I did that to you sixteen years ago." As he stood there laughing at me, with his hand upon the door, I had half a mind to throw my pillow at him.

"You and your double-faced attorneys," I said. "What about your own two faces? That boy out there—your precious Joseph—you told me he was your kinsman."

"So he is," he grinned.

"Who was his mother?"

"A dairymaid at Killigarth. A most obliging soul. Married now to a farmer and mother of his twelve sturdy children."

"When did you discover Joseph?"

"A year or so ago, on returning from Germany, and before I went to Ireland. The likeness was unmistakable. I took some cheeses and a bowl of cream off his mother, and she recalled the incident, laughing with me in her kitchen. She bore no malice. The boy was a fine boy. The least I could do was to take him off her hands. Now I wouldn't be without him for the world."

"It is the sort of tale," I said sulkily, "that leaves a sour taste in the mouth."

"In yours, perhaps," he said, "but not in mine. Don't be so mealymouthed, my loved one."

"You lived at Killigarth," I said, "when you were courting me."

"Goddamn it," he said, "I didn't ride to see you every day."

I heard them all in a moment laughing beneath my window and then mount their horses and gallop away down the avenue, and as I lay upon my bed, staring at the ceiling, I thought how the blossom of my apple tree, so long dazzling and fragrant white, had a little lost its sheen and was become, after all, a common apple tree; but that the realization of this, instead of driving me to torments as it would have done in the past, could now, because of my four-and-thirty years, be borne with equanimity.

Twenty-One

I WAS FULLY PREPARED THE FOLLOWING MORNING TO HAVE my brother call upon me at an early hour and inform me icily that he could not have his home treated as a bawdy house for soldiery. I knew so well the form of such a discourse. The honour of his position, the welfare of his young son, the delicate feelings of Phillipa, our sister-in-law, and although the times were strange and war had done odd things to conduct, certain standards of behaviour were necessary for people of our standing. I was, in fact, already planning to throw myself upon my sister Cecilia's mercy over at Mothercombe, and had my excuses already framed, when I heard the familiar sound of tramping feet; I bid Matty look from the window, and she told me that a company of infantry was marching up the drive, wearing the Grenvile shields. This, I felt, would add fuel to the flames that must already be burning in my brother's breast.

Curiosity, however, was too much for me, and instead of remaining in my apartment like a child who had misbehaved, I bade the servants carry me downstairs to the hall. Here I discovered my brother Jo in a heated argument with a fresh-faced young officer who declared coolly, and with no sign of perturbation, that his general, having decided that Radford was most excellently placed for keeping close observation on the enemy battery at Mount Batten, wished to commandeer certain rooms of the house for himself as a temporary headquarters, and would Mr. John Harris be good enough to show the officer a suite of rooms commanding a northwestern view?

Mr. Harris, added the officer, would be put to no inconvenience, as the general would be bringing his own servants, cooks, and provisions. "I must protest," I heard my brother say, "that this is a highly irregular proceeding. There are no facilities here for soldiers, I myself am hard-pressed with work about the county, and..."

"The general told me," said the young officer, cutting him short, "that he had a warrant from His Majesty authorizing him to take over any place of residence in Devon or Cornwall that should please him. He already has a headquarters at Buckland, Werrington, and Fitzford, and there the inhabitants were not permitted to remain but were forced to find room elsewhere. Of course, he does not propose to deal thus summarily with you, sir. May I see the rooms?"

My brother stared at him tight-lipped for a moment, then, turning on his heel, escorted him up the stairs which I had just descended. I was very careful to avoid his eye.

During the morning the company of foot proceeded to establish themselves in the north wing of the mansion and, watching from the long window in the hall, I saw the cooks and pantry boys stagger towards the kitchen entrance bearing plucked fowls, and ducks, and sides of bacon, besides crate after crate of wine. Phillipa sat at my side, stitching her sampler.

"The King's General," she said meekly, "believes in doing himself well. I have not seen such fare since the siege of Plymouth started. Where do you suppose he obtains all his supplies?"

I examined my nails, which were in need of trimming, and so did not have to look her in the face.

"From the many houses," I answered, "that he commandeers."

"But I thought," said Phillipa with maddening persistency, "that Percy told us Sir Richard never permitted his men to loot."

"Possibly," I said with great detachment, "Sir Richard looks upon ducks and burgundy as perquisites of war."

She went to her room soon after, and I was alone when my brother Jo came down the stairs.

"Well," he said grimly, "I suppose I have you to thank for this invasion."

"I know nothing about it," I answered.

"Nonsense. You planned it together last night."

"Indeed we did not."

"What were you doing, then, closeted with him in your chamber?"

"The time seemed to pass," I said, "in reviving old memories."

"I thought," he said after a moment's pause, "that your present condition, my dear Honor, would make talk of your former intimacy quite intolerable, and any renewal of it beyond question."

"So did I," I answered.

He looked down at me, his lips pursed.

"You were always shameless as a girl," he said. "We spoilt you most abominably, Robin, your sisters, and I. And now at thirty-four you behave like a dairymaid."

He could not have chosen an epithet, to my mind, more unfortunate.

"My behaviour last night," I said, "was very different from a dairymaid."

"I am glad to hear it. But the impression, upon us here below, was to the contrary. Sir Richard's reputation is notorious, and for him to remain within a closed apartment for nearly an hour and three quarters alone with a woman can conjure, to my mind, one thing and one thing only."

"To my mind," I answered, "it can conjure at least a dozen."

After that I knew I must be damned forever and was not surprised when he left me without further argument, except to express a wish that I might have some respect for his roof, though "ceiling" would have been the apter word, in my opinion.

I felt brazen and unrepentant all the day, and when Richard appeared that evening in tearing spirits, commanding dinner for two in the apartment his soldiers had prepared for him, I had a glow of wicked satisfaction that my relatives sat below in gloomy silence while I ate roast duck with the general overhead.

"Since you would not come to Buckland," he said, "I had perforce to come to you."

"It is always a mistake," I said, "to fall out with a woman's brothers."

"Your brother Robin has ridden off with Berkeley's horse to Tavistock," he answered, "and Percy I am sending on a delegation to the King. That leaves only Jo to be disposed of. It might be possible to get him over to the Queen in France."

He tied a knot in his handkerchief as a reminder.

"And how long," I asked, "will it take before Plymouth falls before you?" He shook his head, and looked dubious.

"They have the whole place strengthened," he said, "since our campaign in Cornwall, and that's the devil of it. Had His Majesty abided by my advice and tarried here a fortnight only with his army, we would have the place today. But no. He must listen to Hyde and march to Dorset, and here I am, back again where I was last Easter, with less than a thousand men to do the job."

"You'll never take it then," I asked, "by direct assault?"

"Not unless I can increase my force," he said, "by nearly another thousand. I'm already recruiting hard up and down the county. Rounding up deserters and enlisting new levies. But the fellows must be paid. They won't fight otherwise, and I don't blame 'em. Why the devil should they?"

"Where," I said, "did you get this burgundy?"

"From Lanhydrock," he answered. "I had no idea Jack Robartes had laid down so good a cellar. I've had every bottle of it removed to Buckland." He held his goblet to the candlelight and smiled.

"You know that Lord Robartes sacked Menabilly simply and solely because you had pillaged his estate?"

"He is an extremely dull-witted fellow."

"There is not a pin to choose between you, where pillaging is concerned. A Royalist does as much damage as a rebel. I suppose Dick told you that Gartred was one of us at Menabilly?"

"What was she after?"

"The Duchy silver plate."

"More power to her. I could do with some of it myself to pay my troops."

"She was very friendly with Lord Robartes."

"I have yet to meet a man that she dislikes."

"I think it very probable that she acts spy for Parliament."

"There you misjudge her. She would do anything to gain her own ends but that. You forget the old saying that of the three families in Cornwall, a Godolphin was never wanting in wit, a Trelawney in courage, or a Grenvile in loyalty. Gartred was born and bred a Grenvile, no matter if she beds with every fellow in the duchy."

A brother, I thought, will always hold a brief for a sister. Perhaps Robin at this moment was doing the same thing for me.

Richard had risen and was looking through the window towards the distant Cattwater and Plymouth.

"Tonight," he said quietly, "I've made a gambler's throw. It may come off. It may be hopeless. If it succeeds, Plymouth can be ours by daybreak."

"What do you mean?"

He continued looking through the window to where the lights of Plymouth flickered.

"I'm in touch with the second-in-command in the garrison," he said softly, "a certain Colonel Searle. There is a possibility that for the sum of three thousand pounds he will surrender the city. Before wasting further lives, I thought it worth my while to assay bribery."

I was silent. The prospect was hazardous and somehow smelt unclean.

"How have you set about it?" I asked at length.

"Young Jo slipped through the lines tonight at sunset," he answered, "and will, by now, be hidden in the town. He bears upon him my message to the colonel and a firm promise of three thousand pounds."

"I don't like it," I said. "No good will come of it."

"Maybe not," he said indifferently, "but at least it was worth trying. I don't relish the prospect of battering my head against the gates of Plymouth the whole winter."

I thought of young Jo and his impudent brown eyes.

"Supposing," I said slowly, "that they catch your Joseph?"

Richard smiled. "The lad," he answered, "is quite capable of looking after himself."

But I thought of Lord Robartes as I had seen him last, with muddied boots and the rain upon his shoulders, sour and surly in defeat, and I knew how much he must detest the name of Grenvile.

"I shall be rising early," said Richard, "before you are awake. If by midday you hear a salvo from every gun inside the garrison, you will know that I have entered Plymouth after one swift and very bloody battle." He took my face in his hands and kissed it and then bade me good night. But I found it hard to sleep. The excitement of his presence in the house had turned to anxiety and strain. I knew, with all the intuition in my body, that he had gambled wrong.

I heard him ride off with his staff about 5:30 in the morning, and then, dead tired, my brain chasing itself in circles, I fell into a heavy sleep.

When I awoke it was past ten o'clock. A gray day with a nip of autumn in the air. I had no wish for breakfast, nor even to get up, but stayed there in my bed. I heard the noises of the house, and the coming and going of the soldiers in their wing, and at twelve o'clock I raised myself upon my elbow and looked towards the river. Five past twelve. A quarter past. Half past twelve. There was no salvo from the guns. There was not even a musket shot. It rained at two, then cleared, then rained again. The day dragged on, dull, interminable. I had a sick feeling of suspense all the while. At five o'clock Matty brought me my dinner on a tray, which I picked at with faint appetite. I asked her if she had heard any news, but she said she knew of none. But later, when she had taken away my tray, and come to draw my curtains, her face was troubled.

"What is the matter?" I asked.

"It's what one of Sir Richard's men was saying down there to the sentry," she answered. "Some trouble today in Plymouth. One of their best young officers taken prisoner by Lord Robartes and condemned to death by council of war. Sir Richard has been endeavouring all day to ransom him but has not succeeded."

"Who is it?"

"I don't know."

"What will happen to the officer?"

"The soldier did not say."

I lay back again on my bed, my hands over my eyes to dim the candle. Foreboding never played me wrong, not when I was seized with it for a whole night and day. Maybe perception was a cripple quality. Later I heard the horses coming up the drive and the sentries standing to attention. Footsteps climbed the stairs, slowly, heavily, and passed along to the rooms in the northern wing. A door slammed, and there was silence. It was a long while that I waited there, lying on my back. Just before midnight I heard him walk along the passage, and his hand fumbled a moment on the latch of my door. The candles were blown, and it was darkness. The household slept. He came to my side and knelt before the bed. I put my hand on his head and held him close to me. He knelt thus for many moments without speaking.

"Tell me," I whispered, "if it will help you."

"They hanged him," he said, "above the gates of the town where we could see him. I sent a company to cut him down, but they were mown down by gunfire. They hanged him, before my eyes." Now that suspense was broken and the long day of strain behind me, I was aware of the feeling of detachment that possesses all of us when a crisis has been passed and the suffering is not one's own.

This was Richard's battle. I could not fight it for him. I could only hold him in the darkness.

"That rat Searle," he said, his voice broken, strangely unlike my Richard, "betrayed the scheme, and so they caught the lad. I went myself beneath the walls of the garrison to parley with Robartes. I offered him any terms of ransom or exchange. He gave me no answer. And while I stood there waiting, they strung him up above the gate..."

He could not continue. He lay his head upon me, and I held his hands that clutched so fiercely at the patchwork quilt upon the bed.

"Tomorrow," I said, "it might have been the same. A bullet through the head. A thrust from a pike. An unlucky stumble from his horse. This happens every day. An act of war. Look upon it in that way. Jo died in your service, as he would wish to do."

"No," he said, his voice muffled. "It was my fault. On me

the blame, now, tonight, for all eternity. An error in judgement. The wrong decision."

"Jo would forgive you. Jo would understand."

"I can't forgive myself. That's where the torture lies."

I thought then of all the things that I would want to bring before him. How he was not infallible and never had been, and that this stroke of fate was but a grim reminder of the fact. His own harsh measures to the enemy had been repaid, measure for measure. Cruelty begat cruelty; betrayal gave birth to treachery; the qualities that he had fostered in himself these past years were now recoiled upon him.

The men of Parliament had not forgotten his act of perfidy in the spring, when, feigning to be their friend, he had deserted to the King, bearing their secrets. They had not forgotten the executions without trial, the prisoners condemned to death in Lydford Castle, nor the long line of troopers hanging from the gibbets in the market square of Saltash. And Lord Robartes, with his home Lanhydrock ravaged and laid waste, his goods seized, had seen rough justice and revenge in taking the life of the messenger who bore an offer of bribery and corruption in his pocket.

It was the irony of the Devil, or Almighty God, that the messenger should have been no distant kinsman but Richard Grenvile's son. All this came before me in that moment when I held Richard in my arms. And now, I thought, we have come to a crisis in his life. The dividing of the ways. Either to learn from this single tragedy of a boy's death that cruelty was not the answer, that dishonesty dealt a returning blow, that accepting no other judgement but his own would in a space of time make every friend an enemy; or to learn nothing, to continue through the months and years deaf to all counsel, unscrupulous, embittered, the Skellum Grenvile with a price upon his head, the Red Fox who would be pointed

to for evermore as lacking chivalry, a hated contrast to his
well-beloved brother.

"Richard…" I whispered. "Richard, my dear and only
love…" But he rose to his feet; he went slowly to the window
and, pulling aside the curtains, stood there with the moonlight
on his hands that held the sword but his face in shadow.

"I shall avenge him," he said, "with every life I take. No
quarter any more. No pardons. Not one of them shall be
spared. From this moment I shall have one aim only in my
life, to kill rebels. And to do it as I wish I must have command
of the army; otherwise I fail. I will brook no dispute with my
equals; I will tolerate no orders from those senior to me. His
Majesty made me General in the West, and by God, I swear
that the whole world shall know it."

I knew then that his worse self possessed him, soul and body,
and that nothing that I could say or do could help him in the
future. Had we been man and wife, or truly lovers, I might,
through the close day-by-day intimacy, have learnt to soften
him; but Fate and circumstance had made me no more than a
shadow in his life, a phantom of what might have been. He had
come to me tonight because he needed me, but neither tears
nor protestations nor assurances of my love and tenderness to all
eternity would stay him now from the pursuit of the dim and
evil star that beckoned to him.

Twenty-Two

*R*ICHARD WAS CONSTANTLY AT RADFORD DURING THE SIX months that followed. Although his main headquarters were at Buckland, and he rode frequently through both Devon and Cornwall raising new recruits to his command, a company of his men was kept at my brother's house throughout, and his rooms always in preparation.

The reason given that watch must be kept upon the fortresses of Mount Batten and Mount Stamford was true enough, but I could tell from my brother's tightened lips, and Percy and Phillipa's determined discussion upon other matters when the general's name was mentioned, that my presence in the house was considered to be the reason for the somewhat singular choice of residence. And when Richard with his staff arrived to spend a night or two and I was bidden to a dinner tete-a-tete immediately upon his coming into the house, havoc at once was played with what shred of reputation might be left to me. The friendship was considered odd, unfortunate; I think had I thrown my cap over the mills and gone to live with him at Buckland, it might have been better for the lot of us. But this I steadfastly refused to do, and even now, in retrospect, I cannot give the reason, for it will not formulate in words. Always, at the back of my mind, was the fear that by sharing his life with too great intimacy, I would become a burden to him and the love we bore for one another slip to disenchantment. Here at Radford he could seek me out upon his visits, and being with me would bring him peace and relaxation, tonic and stimulation; whatever mood he would be in, weary or high-spirited, I could attune myself accordingly. But had I made myself persistently available, in some corner of his house, little by little he would have felt the tug of an invisible chain, the claim that a wife brings to bear upon a husband, and the lovely freedom that there was between us would exist no more. The knowledge of my crippled state, so happily glossed over and indeed forgotten when he came to me at Radford, would have nagged me, a perpetual reproach, had I lived beneath his roof at Buckland. The sense of helplessness, of ugly inferiority, would have worked like a maggot in my mind, and even when he was most gentle and most tender I should have thought, with some devil flash of intuition—"This is not what he is wanting."

That was my greatest fault; I lacked humility. Though sixteen years of discipline had taught me to accept crippledom and become resigned to it, I was too proud to share the stigma of it with my lover. Oh God, what I would have given to have walked with him and ridden, to move and turn before him, to have liveliness and grace.

Even a gypsy in the hedges, a beggar woman in the gutters, had more dignity than I. He would say to me, smiling over his wine: "Next week you shall come to me at Buckland. There is a chamber, high up in the tower, looking out across the valley to the hills. This was once my grandfather's, who fought in the *Revenge*, and when Drake purchased Buckland he used the chamber as his own and hung maps upon the wall. You could lie there, Honor, dreaming of the past and the Armada. And in the evening I would come to you and kneel beside your bed, and we would make believe that the apple tree at Lanrest was still in bloom and you eighteen."

I could see the room as he described it. And the window looking to the hills. And the tents of the soldiers below. And the pennant flying from the tower, scarlet and gold. I could see, too, the other Honor, walking by his side upon the terrace, who might have been his lady.

And I smiled at him, and shook my head. "No, Richard," I said, "I will not come to Buckland."

And so the autumn passed, and a new year came upon us once again. The whole of the West Country was held firmly for the King, save Plymouth, Lyme, and Taunton, which stubbornly defied all attempts at subjugation, and the two seaports, relieved constantly by the Parliament shipping, were still in no great danger of starvation. So long as these garrisons were unsubdued, the West could not be counted truly safe for His Majesty, and although the Royalist leaders were of good heart, and expressed great confidence, the people throughout the whole country were already sick and tired of war, which had brought them nothing but loss and high taxation. I believe it was the same for Parliament, and that troops deserted from the army every day. Men wanted to be home again upon their rightful business. The quarrel was not theirs. They had no wish to fight for King or Parliament. "A plague on both your houses!" was the common cry. In January, Richard became sheriff for Devon, and with this additional authority he could raise fresh troops and levies, but the way he set about it was never pleasing to the commissioners of the county. He rode roughshod over their feelings, demanding men and money as a right, and for the smallest pretext he would have a gentleman arrested and clapped into jail, until such time as a ransom would be paid.

This would not be hearsay from my brother, but frank admissions on the part of Richard himself. Always unscrupulous where money was concerned, now that he had an army to pay, any sense of caution flew to the winds. Again and again I would hear his justification: "The country is at war. I am a professional soldier, and I will not command men who are not paid. While I hold this appointment from His Majesty, I will undertake to feed, clothe, and arm the forces at my disposal, so that they hold themselves like men and warriors and do not roam the countryside, raping and looting and in rags, like the disorderly rabble under the so-called command of Berkeley, Goring, and the rest. To do this I must have money. And to get money I must demand it from the pockets of the merchants and the gentry of Cornwall and Devon." I think he became more hated by them every day, but by the common people more respected. His troops won such credit for high discipline that their fame spread far abroad to the eastern counties, and it was, I believe, because of this that the first seeds of jealousy began to sow themselves in the hearts and minds of his brother commanders. None of them were professionals like himself, but men of estate and fortune who, by their rank, had immediately, upon the outbreak of the war, been given high commands and expected to lead newly raised armies into battle. They were gentlemen of leisure, of no experience, and, though many of them were gallant and courageous, warfare to them consisted of a furious charge upon blood horses, dangerous and exciting, with more speed to it than a day's hawking, and when the fray was over, a return to their quarters to eat, and drink, and play cards, while the men they had led could fend for themselves. Let them loot the villages, and strip the poor inhabitants; it saved the leaders a vast amount of unpleasantness and the trouble that must come from organization. But it was irritating, I imagine, to hear how Grenvile's men were praised and how Grenvile's men were paid and fed and clothed; and Sir John Berkeley, who commanded the troops at Exeter and was forever hearing complaints from the common people about Lord Goring's cavalry and Lord Wentworth's foot, was glad enough, I imagine, to report to his supreme commander, Prince Maurice, that even if Grenvile's men were disciplined, the commissioners of Devon and Cornwall had no good word to say of Grenvile himself, and that in spite of all the fire-eating and hanging of rebel prisoners, Plymouth was still not taken.

In the despatches that passed between John Berkeley and Richard, which from time to time he quoted to me with a laugh, I could read the veiled hint that Berkeley at Exeter, with nothing much to do, would think it far preferable for himself and for the royal cause if he should change commands with Richard.

"They expect me," Richard would say, "to hurl my fellows at the defences without any regard for their lives, and having lost three quarters of them in one assault, recruit another five hundred the following week. Had I command of unlimited forces and of God's quantity of ammunition, a bombardment of three days would reduce Plymouth to ashes. But with the little I have at my disposal I cannot hope to reduce the garrison before the spring. In the meanwhile, I can keep the swine harassed night and day, which is more than Digby ever did."

His blockade of Plymouth was complete by land, but the rebels having command of the Sound, provisions and relief could be brought to them by sea, and this was the real secret of their success. All that Richard as commander of the siege could do was to wear out the defenders by constant surprise attack upon the outward positions, in the hope that in time they would, from very weariness, surrender.

It was a hopeless, gruelling task, and the only people to win glory and praise for their stout hearts were the men who were besieged within the city.

It was shortly after Christmas that Richard decided to send Dick to Normandy with his tutor, Herbert Ashley.

"It's no life for him at Buckland," he said. "Ever since Jo went I've had a guard to watch him day and night, and the thought of him so close to the enemy should they try a sally, becomes a constant anxiety. He can go to Caen or Rouen, and when the business is well over I shall send for him again."

"Would you never," I said with diffidence, "consider returning him to London, to his mother?"

He stared at me as though I had lost my senses.

"Let him go back to that bitch-faced hag," he said, astounded, "and become more of a little reptile than he is already? I would sooner send him this moment to Robartes and let him hang."

"He loves her," I said. "She is his mother."

"So does a pup snuggle to the cur that suckled him," he answered, "but soon forgets her smell once he is weaned. I have but one son, Honor, and if he can't be a credit to me and become the man I want, I have no use for him."

He changed the subject abruptly, and I was reminded once again how I had chosen to be friend, not wife, companion and not mistress, and to meddle with his child was not my business. So Dick rode to Radford to bid me good-bye, and put his arms about me, and said he loved me well. "If only," he said, "you could have come with me to Normandy."

"Perhaps," I said, "you will not remain there long. And anyway, it will be fresh and new to you, and you will make friends there and be happy."

"My father does not wish me to make friends," he said. "I heard him say as much to Mr. Ashley. He said that in Caen there were few English, therefore it would be better to go there than to Rouen, and that I was to speak to no one and go nowhere without Mr. Ashley's knowledge or permission. I know what it is. He is afraid that I might fall in with some person who should be friendly to my mother."

I had no answer to this argument, for I felt it to be true. "I shall not know you," I said, summoning a smile, "the next time that I lay eyes upon you. I know how boys grow once they are turned fifteen. I saw it with my brother Percy. You will be a young man, with lovelocks on your shoulders and a turn for poetry in six months' time."

"Fine poetry I shall write," he sulked, "conversing in French day by day with Mr. Ashley."

If I were in truth his stepmother, I thought, I could prevent this; and if I were in truth his stepmother, he would have hated me. So whichever way I looked upon the matter, there was no solution to Dick's problem. He had to face the future, like his father. And so Dick and the timid, unconvincing Herbert Ashley set sail for Normandy the last day of December, taking with them a bill in exchange for twenty pounds, which was all that the General in the West could spare them, Dick taking, besides, my love and blessing, which would not help at all. And while they rocked upon the Channel between Falmouth and Saint Malo, Richard launched an attack upon Plymouth which this time, so he promised, would not fail. I can see him now, in his room in that north block at Radford, poring over his map of the Plymouth defences. When I asked to look at it he tossed it to me with a laugh, saying no woman could make head or tail of his marks and crosses.

And he was right, for never had I seen a chart more scribbled upon with dots and scratches. But even my unpractised eye could note that the network of defences was formidable indeed, for before the town and the garrison could be attacked a chain of outer forts or "works," as he termed them, had first to be breached. He came and stood beside me and with his pen pointed to the scarlet crosses on the map.

"There are four works here to the north, in line abreast," he said, "the Pennycomequick, the Maudlyn, the Holiwell, and the Lipson forts. I propose to seize them all. Once established there, we shall turn the guns against the garrison itself. My main strength will fall upon the Maudlyn works, the others being more in the nature of a feint to draw their fire." He was in high spirits, as always before a big engagement, and suddenly, folding his map, he said to me: "You have never seen my fellows, have you, in their full war paint prior to a battle? Would you like to do so?"

I smiled. "Do you propose to make me your aide-de-camp?"

"No, I am going to take you round the posts."

It was three o'clock, a cold, fine afternoon in January. One of the wagons was fitted as a litter for my person, and with Richard riding at my side, we set forth to view his army.

It was a sight that even now, when all is over and done with and the Siege of Plymouth a forgotten thing except for the official records in the archives of the town, I can call before me with wonder and with pride. The main body of his army was drawn up in the fields behind the little parish of Egg Buckland (not to be confused with the Buckland Monachorum, where Richard had his headquarters) and since there had been no warning of our coming, the men were not summoned to parade, but were going about their business in preparation for the attack ahead.

The first signal that the general had come in person was a springing to attention of the guards before the camp, and straightway there came a roll upon the drums from within, followed by a second more distant, and then a third, and then a fourth, so that in the space of a few moments, so it seemed to me, the air around me rang with a tattoo, as the drums of every company sounded the alert. And swiftly, unfolding in the crisp cold air, the scarlet pennant broke from the pole head, with the golden rests staring from the centre.

Two officers approached and, saluting with their swords, stood before us. This Richard acknowledged with a half gesture

THE KING'S GENERAL

of his hand, and then my chair was lifted from the wagon, and with a stalwart young corporal to propel me, we proceeded round the camp.

I can smell now the wood smoke from the fires as the blue rings rose into the air, and I can see the men bending over their washtubs, or kneeling before the cooking pots, straightening themselves with a jerk as we approached, and standing to attention like steel rods. The foot were quartered separately from the horse, and these we inspected first, great brawny fellows of five foot ten or more, for Richard had disdain for little men and would not recruit them. They had a bronzed, clean look about them, the result, so Richard said, of living in the open. "No billeting in cottages amongst the village folk for Grenvile troops," he said. "The result is always the same, slackness and loss of discipline."

I had fresh in my mind a picture of the rebel regiment who had taken Menabilly. Although they had worn a formidable air upon first sight, with their close helmets and uniform jerkins, they had soon lost their sheen, and as the weeks wore on they became dirty-looking and rough, and with the threat of defeat had one and all reverted to a London mob in panic.

Richard's men had another stamp upon them, and though they were drawn mostly from the farms and moors of Cornwall and of Devon, rustic in speech and origin, they had become knit, in the few months of his command, into a professional body of soldiers, quick of thought and swift of limb, with an admiration for their leader that showed at once in the upward tilt of their heads as he addressed them and the flash of pride in their eyes. A strange review. I in my chair, a hooded cloak about my shoulders, and Richard walking by my side; the campfires burning, the white frost gleaming on the clipped turf, the drums beating their tattoo as we approached each different company.

The horse were drawn up on the farther field, and we watched them being groomed and watered for the night, fine sleek animals—many of them seized from rebel estates, as I was fully aware—and they stamped on the hard ground, the harness jingling, their breath rising in the cold air like the smoke did from the fires.

The sun was setting, fiery red, beyond the Tamar into Cornwall, and as it sank beyond the hills it threw a last dull, sullen glow upon the forts of Plymouth to the south of us.

We could see the tiny figures of the rebel sentries, like black dots, upon the outer defences, and I wondered how many of the Grenvile men about me would make themselves a sacrifice to the spitting thunder of the rebel guns. Lastly, as evening fell, we visited the forward posts, and here there was no more cleaning of equipment, no grooming of horses, but men stripped bare for battle, silent, motionless, and we talked in whispers, for we were scarce two hundred yards from the enemy defences. The silence was grim, uncanny. The assault force seemed dim figures in the gathering darkness, for they had blackened their faces to make themselves less visible, and I could make out nothing of them but white eyes gleaming and the show of teeth when they smiled.

Their breastplates were discarded for a night attack, and in their hands they carried pikes, steely sharp. I felt the edge of one of them and shuddered.

At the last post we visited the men were not so prompt to challenge us as hitherto, and I heard Richard administer a sharp reproof to the young officer in charge. The colonel of the regiment of foot, in command of the post, came forth to excuse himself, and I saw that it was my old suitor of the past, Jo's brother-in-law, Edward Champernowne. He bowed to me somewhat stiffly, and then, turning to Richard, I heard him stammer several attempts at explanation, and the two withdrew to a little distance. On his return Richard was silent, and we straightway turned back towards my wagon and the escort, and I knew that the review was finished.

"You must return alone to Radford," he said. "I will send the escort with you. There will be no danger."

"And the coming battle?" I asked. "Are you confident, and pleased?"

He paused a moment before replying. "Yes," he answered, "yes, I am hopeful. The plan is sound, and there is nothing wanting in the men. If only my seconds were more dependable." He jerked his head toward the post from which we had just lately come. "Your old lover, Edward Champernowne," he said, "I sometimes think he would do better to command a squad of ducks. He has a flickering reason when his long nose is glued upon a map ten miles from the enemy, but give him a piece of work to do upon the field a hundred yards away and he is lost."

"Can you not replace him with some other?" I questioned.

"Not at this juncture," he said. "I have to risk him now."

He kissed my hand and smiled, and it was not until he had turned his back on me and vanished that I remembered I had never asked him whether the reason for his not returning with me to Radford was because he proposed to lead the assault in person.

I jogged back in the wagon to my brother's house, my spirits sinking. Shortly before daybreak next morning, the attack began. The first we heard of it at Radford was the echo of the guns across the Cattwater, whether from within the garrison or from the outer defences we could not tell, but by midday we had the news that three of the works had been seized and held by the Royalist troops, and the most formidable of the forts, the Maudlyn, stormed by the commanding general in person. The guns were turned, and the men of Plymouth felt for the first time their own fire fall upon the walls of the city. I could see nothing from my window but a pall of smoke hanging like a curtain in the sky, and now and again, the wind being northerly, I thought I heard the sound of distant shouting from the besieged within the garrison.

At three o'clock, with barely three hours of daylight left, the news was not so good. The rebels had counterattacked, and two of the forts had been recaptured. The fate of Plymouth now depended upon the rebels gaining back the ground they had lost and driving the Royalists from their foothold all along the line, and most especially from the Maudlyn Works. I watched the setting sun, as I had done the day before, and I thought of all those, both rebel men and Royalist, whose lives had been held forfeit within these past four-and-twenty hours. We dined in the hall at half past five, with my brother Jo seated at the head of his table as was his custom, and Phillipa at his right hand, and his little motherless son, young John, upon his left. We ate in silence, none of us having much heart for conversation, while the battle only a few miles away hung thus in the balance. We were nearly finished when my brother Percy, who had ridden down to Plymouth to get news, came bursting in upon us.

"The rebels have gained the day," he said grimly, "and driven off Grenvile with the loss of three hundred men. They stormed the fort on all sides and finally recaptured it barely an hour ago. It seems that Grenvile's covering troops, who should have come to his support and turned the scale to success, failed to reach him. A tremendous blunder on the part of someone."

"No doubt the fault of the general himself," said Jo drily, "in having too much confidence."

"They say down in Plymstock that the officer responsible has been shot by Grenvile for contravention of orders," said Percy, "and is lying now in his tent with a bullet through his head. Who it is they could not tell me, but we shall hear anon."

I could think of nothing but those three hundred men who were lying now upon their faces under the stars, and I was filled with a great war-sickness, a loathing for guns and pikes and blood and battle cries. The brave fellows who had smiled at me the night before, so strong, so young and confident, were now carrion for the seagulls who swooped and dived in Plymouth Sound, and it was Richard, my Richard, who had led them to their death. I could not blame him. He had only, by attacking, done his duty. He was a soldier...

As I turned away to call a servant for my chair, a young secretary employed by my elder brother on the Devon Commission came into the room, much agitated, with a request to speak to him.

"What is the matter?" said Jo tersely. "There is no one but my family present."

"Colonel Champernowne lies at Egg Buckland mortally wounded," said the secretary. "He was not hurt in battle but pistolled by the general himself on returning to headquarters."

There was a moment of great silence. Jo rose slowly from his chair, very white and tense, and I saw him turn round and look at me, as did my brother Percy. In a moment of perception I knew what they were thinking. Jo's brother-in-law, Edward Champernowne, had been my suitor seventeen years before, and they both saw, in this sudden terrible dispute after the heat of battle, no military cause but some private jealous wrangle, the settling of a feud.

"This," said my elder brother slowly, "is the beginning of the end for Richard Grenvile."

His words fell upon my ear cold as steel, and calling softly to the servant, I bade him take me to my room.

The next day I left for Mothercombe, to my sister Cecilia, for to remain under my brother's roof one moment longer would have been impossible. The vendetta had begun.

My eldest brother, with the vast family of Champernowne

behind him, and supported by the leading families in the county of Devon, most of them members of the commission, pressed for the removal of Sir Richard Grenvile from his position as sheriff and commander of the King's forces in the West. Richard retaliated by turning my brother out of Radford and using the house and estate as a jumping ground for a fresh assault upon Plymouth.

Snowed up in Mothercombe with the Pollexefens, I knew little of what was happening, and Cecilia, with consummate tact and delicacy, avoided the subject. I myself had had no word from Richard since the night I had bidden him good-bye before the battle, and now that he was engaged in a struggle with foe and former friends as well, I thought it best to keep silent. He knew my whereabouts, for I had sent word of it, and should he want me he would come to me.

The thaw burst at the end of March, and we had the first tidings of the outside world for many weeks.

The peace moves between King and Parliament had come to nothing, for the Treaty of Uxbridge had failed, and the war, it seemed, was to be carried on more ruthlessly than ever.

The Parliament, we heard, was forming a new model army, likely to sweep all before it, in the opinion of the judges, while His Majesty had sent forth an edict to his enemies, saying that unless the rebels repented, their end must be damnation, ruin, and infamy. The young Prince of Wales, it seemed, was now to bear the title of supreme commander of all the forces in the West, and was gone to Bristol, but since he was a lad of only fifteen years or so, the real authority would be vested in his advisory council, at the head of whom was Hyde, the Chancellor of the Exchequer.

I remember John Pollexefen shaking his head as he heard the news. "There will be nothing but wrangles now between the Prince's council and the generals," he said. "Each will countermand the orders of the other. Lawyers and soldiers never agree. And while they wrangle, the King's cause will suffer. I do not like it."

I thought of Richard and how he had once vouchsafed the same opinion. "What is happening at Plymouth?" asked my sister. "Stalemate," said her husband. "A token force of less than a thousand men left to blockade the garrison, and Grenvile with the remainder gone to join Goring in Somerset and lay siege to Taunton. The spring campaign has started."

Soon a year would have come and gone since I had left Lanrest for Menabilly. The snow melted down in the Devon valley where Cecilia had her home, and the crocus and daffodil appeared. I made no plans. I sat and waited. Someone brought a rumour that there was great disaffection in the High Command, and that Grenvile, Goring, and Berkeley were all at loggerheads.

March turned to April. The golden gorse was in full bloom. And on Easter Day a horseman came riding down the valley, wearing the Grenvile badge. He asked at once for Mistress Harris and, saluting gravely, handed me a letter.

"What is it?" I asked before I broke the seal. "Has something happened?" My throat felt dry and strange, and my hands trembled. "The General has been gravely wounded," replied the soldier, "in a battle before Wellington House, at Taunton. They fear for his life." I tore open the letter, and read Richard's shaky scrawl.

> Dear heart, this is the very devil. I am like to lose my leg, if not my life, with a great gaping hole in my thigh below the groin. I know now what you suffer. Come teach me patience. I love you.

I folded the letter and, turning to the messenger, asked him where the General lay.

"They were bringing him from Taunton down to Exeter when I left," he answered. "His Majesty had dispatched his own chirurgeon to attend upon Sir Richard. He was very weak and bade me ride without delay to bring you this."

I looked at Cecilia, who was standing by the window. "Would you summon Matty to pack my clothes," I said, "and ask John if he would arrange for a litter and for horses? I am going to Exeter."

Twenty-Three

WE TOOK THE SOUTHERN ROUTE TO EXETER, AND AT EVERY halt upon the journey I thought to hear the news of Richard's death.

Totnes, Newton Abbot, Ashburton, each delay seemed longer than the last, and when at length after six days I reached the capital of Devon and saw the great cathedral rising high above the city and the river, it seemed to me I had been weeks upon the road.

Richard still lived. This was my first inquiry and the only thing that mattered. He was lodging at the hostelry in the cathedral square, where I immediately repaired. He had taken the whole building for his personal use and had a sentry before the door.

When I gave my name a young officer immediately appeared from within, and something ruddy about his colouring and familiar in his bearing made me pause a moment before addressing him correctly. Then his courteous smile gave me the clue.

"You are Jack Grenvile, Bevil's boy," I said, and he reminded me of how he had come once with his father to Lanrest in the days before the war. I remembered, too, how I had washed him as a baby on that memorable visit to Stowe in '28, but this I did not tell him.

"My uncle will be most heartily glad to see you," he said as I was lifted from my litter. "He has talked of little else since writing to you. He has sent at least ten women flying from his side since coming here, swearing they were rough and did not know their business, nor how to dress his wound. 'Matty shall do it,' he said, 'while Honor talks to me.'" I saw Matty colour up with pleasure at these words and assume at once an air of authority before the corporal who shouldered our trunks.

"And how is he?" I asked as I was set down within the great inn parlour, which had been, judging by the long table in the centre, turned into a messroom for the general's staff.

"Better these last three days than hitherto," replied his nephew, "but at first we thought to lose him. Directly he was wounded I applied to the Prince of Wales to wait on him, and I attended him here from Taunton. Now he declares he will not send me back. Nor have I any wish to go."

"Your uncle," I said, "likes to have a Grenvile by his side."

"I know one thing," said the young man. "He finds fellows of my age better company than his contemporaries, which I take as a great compliment." At this moment Richard's servant came down the stairs, saying the General wished to see Mistress Harris upon the instant. I went first to my room, where Matty washed me and changed my gown, and then with Jack Grenvile to escort me, I went along the corridor in my wheeled chair to Richard's room.

It looked out upon the cobbled square, and as we entered the great bell from the cathedral chimed four o'clock.

"God confound that blasted bell," said a familiar voice, sounding stronger than I had dared to hope, from the dark curtained bed in the far corner. "A dozen times I have asked the mayor of this damned city to have it silenced, and nothing has been done. Harry, for God's sake, make a note of it."

"Sir," answered hurriedly a tall youth at the foot of the bed, scribbling a word upon his tablets.

"And move these pillows, can't you? Not that way, you clumsy lout; behind my head, thus. Where the devil is Jack? Jack is the only lad who knows how I like them placed."

"Here I am, Uncle," said his nephew, "but you will not need me now. I have brought you someone with gentler hands than I."

He pushed my chair towards the bed, smiling, and I saw Richard's hand reach out to pull back the curtains.

"Ah!" he said, sighing deeply. "You have come at last." He was deathly white. And his eyes had grown larger, perhaps in contrast to the pallor of his face. His auburn locks were clipped short, giving him a strangely youthful look. For the first time I noticed in him a resemblance to Dick. I took his hand and held it.

"I did not wait," I said, "once I had read your letter."

He turned to the two lads standing at the foot of the bed, his nephew and the one he had named Harry.

"Get out, both of you," he said, "and if that damned chirurgeon shows his face, tell him to go to the devil."

"Sir," they replied, clicking their heels, and I could swear that as they left the room young Jack Grenvile winked an eye at his companion.

Richard lifted my hand to his lips and then cradled it beside his cheek. "This is a good jest," he said, "on the part of the Almighty. You and I both smitten in the thigh."

"Does it pain you much?" I asked.

"Pain me? My God, splinters from a cannonball, striking below the groin burn something fiercer than a woman's kiss. Of course it pains me."

"Who has seen the wound?"

"Every chirurgeon in the army, and each one makes more mess of it than his fellow."

I called for Matty, who was waiting outside the door, and she came in at once with a basin of warm water and bandages and towels.

"Good day to you, mutton-face," said Richard. "How many corporals have you bedded with en route?"

"No time to bed with anyone," snapped Matty, "carried at the rate we were, with Miss Honor delaying only to sleep a few snatched hours every night. Now we've come here to be insulted."

"I'll not insult you, unless you tie my bandages too tight."

"Come, then," she said. "Let's see what they have done to you."

She unfolded the bandages with expert fingers and exposed the wound. It was deep, in truth, the splinters having penetrated the bone and lodged there. With every probe of her fingers he winced and groaned, calling her every name under the sun, which did not worry her.

"It's clean, that's one thing," she said. "I fully expected to find it gangrenous. But you'll have some of those splinters to the end of your days, unless you let them take your leg off."

"They'll not do that," he answered. "I'd rather keep the splinters and bear the pain."

"It will give you an excuse, at any rate, for your bad temper," she replied. She washed the wound and dressed it once again, and all the while he held my hand as Dick might do. Then she finished, and he thumbed his finger to his nose as she left the room.

"Over three months," he said, "since I have seen you. Are the Pollexefens as unpleasant as the rest of your family?"

"My family were not unpleasant till you made them so."

"They disliked me from the first. Now they pursue their dislike across the county. You know the commissioners of Devon are in Exeter at this moment, with a list of complaints a mile long to launch at me?"

"I did not know."

"It's all a plot hatched by your brother. Three members of the Prince's council are to come down from Bristol and discuss the business with the commissioners; and as soon as I am fit enough to move I am to go before them. Jack Berkeley, commanding here at Exeter, is up to his neck in the intrigue."

"And what exactly is the intrigue?"

"Why, to have me shifted from my command, of course, and for Berkeley to take my place."

"Would you mind so very much? The blockade of Plymouth has not brought you much satisfaction."

"Jack Berkeley is welcome to Plymouth. But I'm not going to lie down and accept some secondary command, dished out to me by the Prince's council while I hold authority from His Majesty himself."

"His Majesty," I said, "appears by all accounts to have his own troubles. Who is this General Cromwell we hear so much about?"

"Another Goddamned Puritan with a mission," said Richard. "They say he talks with the Almighty every evening, but I think it far more likely that he drinks. He's a good soldier, though. So is Fairfax. Their new model army will make mincemeat of our disorganized rabble."

"And, knowing this, you choose to quarrel with your friends?"

"They are not my friends. They are a set of low, backbiting blackguards. And I have told them all so to their faces."

It was useless to argue with him. And his wound had made him more sensitive on every point. I asked if he had news of Dick, and he showed me a stilted letter from the tutor, as well as copies of instructions that he had sent to Herbert Ashley.

There was nothing very friendly or encouraging amongst them. I caught a glimpse of the words, "for his education I desire he may constantly and diligently be kept to the learning of the French tongue; reading, writing, and arithmetic, also riding, fencing, and dancing. All this I shall expect of him, which if he follow according to my desire for his own good, he shall not want anything. But if I understand that he neglects in any kind what I have herein commanded him to do, truly I will neither allow him a penny to maintain him, nor look on him again as my son." I folded the instructions and put them back into the case, which he locked and kept beside him.

"Do you think," I said, "to win his affection in that way?"

"I don't ask for his affection," he said. "I ask for his obedience."

"You were not harsh thus with Jo. Nor are you so unrelenting to your nephew Jack."

"Jo was one in a million, and Jack has some likeness to him. That lad fought at Lansdown like a tiger when poor Bevil fell. And he was but fifteen, as Dick is now. All these lads I have affection for because they hold themselves like men. But Dick, my son and heir, shudders when I speak to him and whimpers at the sight of blood. It does not make for pride in his father."

An argument. A blow. A baby's cry. And fifteen years of poison seeping through a child's blood. There was no panacea that I could think of to staunch the flood of resentment. Time and distance might bring a measure of healing that close contact only served to wound. Once again Richard kissed my hand. "Never mind young Dick," he said. "It is not he who has a dozen splinters through his thigh."

No man, I think, was ever a worse patient than Richard Grenvile, and no nurse more impervious to his threats and groans and curses than was Matty. My role, if less exacting, called for great equanimity of temperament. Being a woman, I did not have his spurs hurled at my head, as did his luckless officers, but I suffered many a bitter accusation because my name was Harris, and he liked to taunt me, too, because I had been born and bred in southeast Cornwall, where the women all were hags and scolds, so he averred, and the men cowards and deserters. "Nothing good came out of Cornwall yet," he said, "save from the north coast." And seeing that this failed to rouse me, he sought by other means to make me rankle, a strange and unprofitable pastime for a sick man, but one I could understand in full measure, for I had often wished so to indulge myself some seventeen years before, but had never the courage of my moods.

He kept his bed for some five weeks, and then, by the end of May, was sufficiently recovered to walk in his chamber with a stick and at the same time curse his harassed staff for idleness.

The feathers flew when he first came downstairs, for all the world like a turkey fight, and I never saw high-ranking officers more red about the ears than the colonels and the majors he addressed that May morning. They looked at the door with longing eyes, like schoolboys, with but one thought in their mind, to win freedom from his lashing tongue, or so I judged from their expressions. But when, after I had taken my airing in the square, I conversed with them, sympathy on the tip of my tongue, they one and all remarked upon the excellence of the general's health and spirits.

"It does one good," said a colonel of foot, "to see the general himself again. I hardly dared to hope for it, a month since."

"Do you bear no malice, then," I said, "for his words to you this morning?"

"Malice?" said the colonel, looking puzzled. "Why should I bear malice? The general was merely taking exercise."

The ways of professional soldiers were beyond me.

"It is a splendid sign," said Richard's nephew Jack, "when my uncle gives vent to frowns and curses. It mostly means he is well pleased. But see him smile and speak with courtesy, and you may well reckon that the luckless receiver of his favours is halfway to the guardroom. I once saw him curse a fellow for fifteen minutes without respite and that evening promote him to the rank of captain. The next day he received a prisoner, a country squire, I think, from Barnstaple, who owed him money, and my uncle plied him with wine, and smiles, and favours. He was hanging from a tree at Buckland two hours afterwards."

I remember asking Richard if these tales were true. He laughed. "It pleases my staff," he said, "to weave a legend about my person." But he did not deny them.

Meanwhile, the Prince's council had come to Exeter to have discussion with the Devon commissioners and to hear the complaints they had to make against Sir Richard Grenvile. It was unfortunate, I felt, that the head of the Prince's council was that same Sir Edward Hyde whom Richard had described to me at Radford as a jumped-up lawyer. I think the remark had been repeated to him, for when he arrived at the hostelry to call upon Richard, accompanied by Lords Culpepper and Capel, I thought his manner very cold and formal, and I could see he bore little cordiality towards the general who had so scornfully dubbed him upstart. I was presented to them and immediately withdrew. What they thought of me I neither knew nor cared. It would be but another scandalous tale to spread, that Sir Richard Grenvile had a crippled mistress.

What, in truth, transpired behind those closed doors I never discovered. As soon as the three members of the Prince's council tried to speak they would be drowned by Richard, with a tirade of accusations against the governor of the city, Sir John Berkeley, who, so he avowed, had done nothing for nine months now but put obstructions in his path. As to the commissioners of Devon, they were traitors, one and all, and tried to keep their money in their pockets rather than pay the army that defended them.

"Let Berkeley take over Plymouth, if he so desires it," Richard declared. (This he told me afterwards.) "God knows it troubles me to be confined to blocking up a place when there is likely to be action in the field. Give me power to raise men in Cornwall and in Devon, without fear of obstruction, and I will place an army at the disposal of the Prince of Wales that will be a match for Cromwell's Puritans." Whereupon he formally handed over his resignation as commander of the Siege of Plymouth and sent the lords of the council packing off back to Bristol to receive the Prince's authority sanctioning him to a new command. "I handled them," he said to me gleefully, "with silken gloves. Let Jack Berkeley stew at Plymouth, and good luck to him." And he drank a bottle and a half of burgundy at supper, which played havoc with his wound next morning.

I have forgotten how many days we waited for the royal warrant to arrive, confirming him in the appointment to raise troops, but it must have been ten days or more. At last Richard declared that he would not kick his heels waiting for a piece of paper that few people would take the trouble to read, and he proceeded to raise recruits for the new army. His staff were dispatched about the countryside rounding up the men who had been idle or had deserted and gone home during his illness. All were promised pay and clothing. And as sheriff of Devon (for this post he had not resigned with his command) Richard ordered his old enemies, the commissioners, to raise fresh money for the purpose. I guessed this would bring a hornet's nest about his ears again, but I was only a woman, and it was not my business.

I sat one day beside my window, looking out onto the cathedral, and I saw Sir John Berkeley, who had not yet gone to Plymouth, ride away from the hostelry looking like a thundercloud. There had been a stormy meeting down below and, according to young Jack, Sir John had got the worst of it.

"I yield to no man," said Richard's nephew, "in my admiration for my uncle. He has the better of his opponents every time. But I wish he would guard his tongue."

"What," I asked wearily, "are they disputing now?"

"It is always the same story," said Jack. "My uncle says that as sheriff of the county he can compel the commissioners to pay his troops. Sir John declares the contrary. That it is to him, as governor of the city and commander before Plymouth, to whom the money should be paid. They'll fight a duel about it before they have finished." Shortly afterwards Richard came to my room, white with passion. "My God," he said, "I cannot stand this hopeless mess an instant longer. I shall ride at once to Bristol to see the Prince. When in doubt, go to the highest authority. That has always been my rule. Unless I can get satisfaction out of His Highness I shall chuck the whole affair."

"You are not well enough to ride," I said.

"I can't help that. I won't stay here and have that hopeless nincompoop Jack Berkeley obstruct every move I make. He is hand in glove with your blasted brother, that's the trouble."

"You began the trouble," I said, "by making an enemy of my brother. All this has come about because you shot Edward Champernowne."

"What would you have had me do, promote the sod?" he stormed. "A weak-bellied rat who caused the death of three hundred of my finest troops because he was too lily-livered to face the rebel guns and come to my support. Shooting was too good for him. A hundred years ago he would have been drawn and quartered."

The next day he left for Barastaple, where the Prince of Wales had gone to escape the plague at Bristol, and I was thankful that he took his nephew Jack as aide-de-camp. He had three men to hoist him into the saddle and he still looked most damnably unwell. He smiled up at me as I leant from my window in the hostelry, and saluted with his sword. "Have no fear," he said, "I'll return within a fortnight. Keep well. Be happy."

But he never did return, and that was the end of my sojourn as a nurse and comforter at Exeter. On the eighteenth of June the King and Prince Rupert were heavily defeated by General Cromwell at Naseby, and the rebel army, under the supreme command of General Fairfax, was marching once again towards the West. The whole of the Royalist strategy had now to be changed to meet this new menace, and while rumours ran rife that Fairfax was coming upon Taunton, I had a message from Richard to say that he had been ordered by the Prince of Wales to besiege Lyme and had the commission of field marshal in his pocket.

"I will send for you," he said, "when I have fixed my headquarters. In the meantime, rest where you are. I think it very likely that we shall all of us, before the summer is out, be on the run again." This news was hardly pleasant hearing, and I bethought me of the relentless marching feet that I had heard a year ago at Menabilly. Was the whole horror of invasion to be endured once again? I did as he bade me and stayed at Exeter. I had no home, and one roof was as good to me now as another. If I lacked humility, I also had no pride. I was nothing more nor less, by this time, than a camp follower. A pursuivant of the drum.

On the last day of June, Jack Grenvile came for me with a troop of horse to bear my litter. Matty and I were already packed and ready. We had been waiting since the message a fortnight before.

"Where are we bound?" I said gaily, "for Lyme or London?"

"For neither," he said grimly. "For a tumbled-down residence in Ottery St. Mary. The general has thrown up his commission."

He could tell me little of what had happened, except that the bulk of the new forces that had been assigned to Richard's new command, and were to rendezvous at Tiverton, had suddenly been withdrawn by the orders of the Prince's council and diverted to the defence of Barastaple, without a word of explanation to the general. We came to Ottery St. Mary, a sleepy Devon village where the inhabitants stared at the strange equipage that drew up before the manor house as though the world were suddenly grown crazy, in which they showed good reason. In the meadows behind the village were drawn Richard's own horse and foot that had followed him from the beginning. Richard himself was seated in the dining chamber of his headquarters, his wounded leg propped upon a chair before him.

"Greetings," he said maliciously, "from one cripple to another. Let us retire to bed and see who has the greatest talent for invention."

"If that," I said, "is your mood, we will discuss it presently. At the moment I am tired, hungry, and thirsty. But would you care to tell me what the devil you are doing in Ottery St. Mary?"

"I am become a free man," he answered, smiling, "beholden to neither man nor beast. Let them fight the new model army in their own fashion. If they won't give me the troops, I do not propose to ride alone with Nephew Jack against Fairfax and some twenty thousand men."

"I thought," I said, "that you were become field marshal."

"An empty honour," he said, "signifying nothing. I have returned the commission to the Prince of Wales in an empty envelope, desiring him to place it up a certain portion of his person. What shall we drink for supper, hock or burgundy?"

Twenty-Four

$\mathcal{T}$HAT WAS, I THINK, THE MOST FANTASTIC FORTNIGHT I have ever known. Richard, with no command and no commission, lived like a royal prince in the humble village of Ottery St. Mary, the people for miles around bringing their produce to the camp, their corn, their cattle, in the firm belief that he was the supreme commander of His Majesty's troops from Lyme to Land's End. For payment he referred them graciously to the commissioners of Devon. The first Sunday after his arrival he caused an edict to be read in the church of Ottery St. Mary, and other churches in the neighbouring parishes, desiring that all those persons who had been plundered by the Governor of Exeter, Sir John Berkeley, when quartering troops upon them, should bring to him, Sir Richard Grenvile, the King's General in the West, an account of their losses, and he would see that they were righted.

The humble village folk, thinking that a saviour had come to dwell amongst them, came on foot from a distance of twenty miles or more, each one bearing in his hands a list of crimes and excesses committed, according to them, by Lord Goring's troopers and Sir John Berkeley's men, and I can see Richard now, standing in the village place before the church, distributing largesse in princely fashion, from a sum of money he had discovered behind a panel in his headquarters, a house belonging to an unfortunate squire with vague Parliamentary tendencies, whom Richard had immediately arrested. On the Wednesday, being fine, he held a review of his troops—the sight being free to the villagers—and the drums sounded, and the church bells pealed, and in the evening bonfires were lit and a great supper was served at the headquarters to the officers, at which I presided like a queen.

"We may as well be merry," said Richard, "while the money lasts."

I thought of that letter to the Prince of Wales, which must by now have reached the Prince's council, and I pictured the Chancellor of the Exchequer, Edward Hyde, opening the paper before the assembly. I thought also of Sir John Berkeley and what he would say when he heard about the edict in the churches, and it seemed to me that my rash and indiscreet lover would be wiser if he struck his camp and hid in the mists of Dartmoor, for he could not bluff the world much longer in Ottery St. Mary.

The bluff was superb while it lasted, and since the Parliamentary squire whom we had superseded kept a well-stocked cellar, we soon had every bottle sampled, and Richard drank perdition to the supporters of both Parliament and Crown.

"What will you do," I asked, "if the council sends for you?"

"Exactly nothing," he answered, "unless I have a letter, in his own handwriting, from the Prince of Wales himself."

And with a smile that his nephew would call ominous, he opened yet another bottle.

"If we continue thus," I said, turning my glass down upon the table, "you will become as great a sot as Goring."

"Goring cannot stand after five glasses," said Richard. "I can drill a whole division after twelve."

And rising from the table, he called to the orderly who stood without the door. "Summon Sir John Grenvile," he said. In a moment Jack appeared, also a little flushed and gay about the eyes.

"My compliments," said Richard, "to Colonels Roscarrick and Arundell. I wish the troops to be paraded on the green. I intend to drill them."

His nephew did not flicker an eyelid, but I saw his lips quiver.

"Sir," he said, "it is past eight o'clock. The men have been dismissed to their quarters."

"I am well aware of the fact," replied his uncle. "It was for the purpose of rousing them that drums were first bestowed upon the army. My compliments to Colonels Roscarrock and Arundell."

Jack clicked his heels and left the room. Richard walked slowly and very solemnly towards the chair where lay his sling and sword. He proceeded to buckle them about his waist.

"The sling," I said softly, "is upside down."

He bowed gravely in acknowledgement and made the necessary adjustment. And from without the drums began to beat, sharp and alert, in the gathering twilight.

I was, I must confess, only a trifle less dazed about the head than I had been on that memorable occasion long before, when I had indulged too heavily in burgundy and swan. This time, and it was my only safeguard, I had my chair to sit in and I can remember, through a sort of haze, being propelled towards the village green with the drums sounding in my ears and the soldiers running from all directions to form lines upon the grass sward. Villagers leant from their casements, and I remember one old fellow in a nightcap shrieking out that Fairfax was come upon them and they would all be murdered in their beds.

It was, I dare swear, the one and only occasion in the annals of His Majesty's army when two regiments have been drawn up and drilled by their commanding general in the dusk after too good a dinner.

"My God," I heard Jack Grenvile choke behind me, whether in laughter or emotion I never discovered, "this is magnificent. This will live for ever." And when the drums were silent I heard Richard's voice, loud and clear, ring out across the village green.

It was a fitting climax to a crazy fourteen days...

At breakfast the next morning a messenger came riding to the door of the headquarters with the news that Bridgwater had been stormed and captured by Fairfax and his rebel forces, the Prince's council had fled to Launceston, and the Prince of Wales bade Sir Richard Grenvile depart instantly with what troops he had and come to him in Cornwall.

"Is the message a request or a command?" asked my general.

"A command, sir," replied the officer, handing him a document, "not from the council, but from the Prince himself."

Once again the drums were sounded, but this time for the march, and as the long line of troops wound their way through the village and on to the highway to Okehampton I wondered how many years would pass before the people of Ottery St. Mary would forget Sir Richard Grenvile and his men. We followed, Matty and I, within a day or two, with an escort to our litter and orders to proceed to Werrington Park, near Launceston, which was yet another property that Richard had seized without a scruple from the owner of Buckland Monachorum, Francis Drake. We arrived to find Richard in fair spirits, restored to the Prince's favour after a very awkward three hours before the council. It might have been more awkward had not the council been in so immediate a need of his services.

"And what has been decided?" I asked.

"Goring is to go north to intercept the rebels," he said, "while I remain in Cornwall and endeavour to raise a force of some three thousand foot. It would have been better if they had sent me to deal with Fairfax, as Goring is certain to make a hash of it."

"There is no one but you," I said, "who can raise troops in Cornwall. Men will rally to a Grenvile, but none other. Be thankful that the council sent for you at all, after your impudence."

"They cannot afford," said Richard, "to do without me. And anyway, I don't give a fig for the council and that snake Hyde. I am only doing this business to oblige the Prince. He's a lad after my own heart. If His Majesty continues to haver as he does at present, with no coherent plan of strategy, I am not at all sure that the best move would not be to hold all Cornwall for the Prince, live within it like a fortress, and let the rest of England go to blazes."

"You have only to phrase that a little differently," I said, "and a malicious friend who wished you ill would call it treason."

"Treason be damned," he said. "It is but sound common sense. No man has greater loyalty to His Majesty than I, but he does more to wreck his own cause than any who serve under him."

While Matty and I remained at Werrington, Richard travelled the length and breadth of Cornwall recruiting troops for the Prince's army. It was no easy business. The last invasion had been enough for Cornishmen. Men wished only to be left alone to tend their land and business. Money was as hard to raise as it had been in Devon, and with some misgiving I watched Richard use the same highhanded measures with the commissioners of the duchy as he had with those of the sister county. Those who might have yielded with some grace to tact gave way grudgingly to pressure, and Richard, during that summer and early autumn of 1645, made as many enemies amongst the Cornish landowners as he had done in Devon.

On the north coast men rallied to his call because of his link with Stowe, the very name of Grenvile sounding like a clarion. They came to him from beyond the border, even from Appledore and Bideford, and down the length of that storm-bound Atlantic coast from Hartland Point to Padstowe. They were his best recruits. Clear-eyed, long-limbed, wearing with pride the scarlet shield with the three gold rests upon their shoulders. Men from Bude and Stratton and Tintagel, men from Boscastle and Camelford. And with great cunning Richard introduced his prince as Duke of Cornwall, who had come into the West to save them from the savage rebel hordes beyond the Tamar.

But farther south he met with rebuffs. Danger seemed more remote to people west of Truro, and even the fall of Bristol to Fairfax and the Parliament, which came like a clap of doom on the tenth of September, failed to rouse them from their lethargy.

"Truro, Helston, and St. Ives," said Richard, "are the three most rotten towns in Cornwall," and he rode down, I remember, with some six hundred horse to quell a rising of the townsfolk, who had protested against a levy he had raised the week before.

He hanged at least three men, while the remainder were either fined or imprisoned. He took the opportunity, too, of visiting the castle at St. Mawes and severely reprimanded its commander, Major Bonython, because he had failed to pay the soldiers under his command within the garrison.

"Whomever I find halfhearted in the Prince's cause must change his tune or suffer disciplinary action," declared Richard. "Whoever fails to pay his men shall contribute from his own pocket, and whoever shows one flicker of disloyalty to me as commander, or to the Prince I serve, shall answer for it with his life."

I heard him say this myself in the market place at Launceston before a great crowd assembled there, the last day of September, and while his own men cheered so that the echo came ringing back to us from the walls of the houses, I saw few smiles upon the faces of the townsfolk gathered there.

"You forget," I said that night to him at Werrington, "that Cornishmen are independent, and love freedom better than their fellows."

"I remember one thing," he answered with that thin, bitter smile of his I knew too well, "that Cornishmen are cowards and love their comfort better than their King."

As autumn drew on I began to wonder if either freedom or comfort would belong to any of us by the end of the year.

Chard, Crediton, Lyme, and finally Tiverton fell before Fairfax in October, and Lord Goring had done nothing to stop them. Many of his men deserted and came flocking to join Richard's army, having greater faith in him as a commander. This led to further jealousy, further recriminations, and it looked as though Richard would fall as foul with Goring as he had done with Sir John Berkeley three months earlier. There was constant fault-finding, too, by the Prince's council in Launceston, and scarcely a day would pass without some interfering measure from the Chancellor, Edward Hyde.

"If they would but leave me alone," stormed Richard, "to recruit my army and to train my troops, instead of flooding my headquarters day by day with dispatches written by lawyers with smudged fingers who have never so much as smelt gunpowder, there would be greater likelihood of my being able to withstand Fairfax when he comes."

Money was getting scarce again, and the equipping of the army for winter another nightmare for my general.

Boots and stockings were worn through and hard to replace, while the most vital necessity of all, ammunition, was very low in stock, the chief reason for this being that the Royalist magazine for the western forces had been captured at the beginning of the autumn by the rebels when they took Bristol, and all that Richard had at his disposal were the small reserves at Bodmin and Truro.

Then suddenly, without any warning, Lord Goring threw up his command and went to France, giving as the reason that his health had cracked and he could no longer shoulder any responsibility.

"The rats," said Richard slowly, "are beginning, one by one, to desert the sinking ship." Goring took several of his best officers with him, and the command in Devon was given to Lord Wentworth, an officer with little experience, whose ideas of discipline were even worse than Goring's. He immediately went into winter quarters at Bovey Tracey and declared that nothing could be done against the enemy until the spring. It was it this moment, I think, that the Prince's council first lost heart and realized the full magnitude of what might happen. They were fighting a losing cause. Preparations were made to move from Launceston and go further west to Truro. This, said Richard grimly when he told me, could mean but one thing. They wanted to be near Falmouth so that when the crisis came the Prince of Wales and the leaders of the council could take ship to France. It was then I asked him bluntly what he wished to do. "Hold a line," he answered, "from Bristol Channel to the Tamar and keep Cornwall for the Prince. It can bed one. There is no other answer."

"And His Majesty?"

Richard did not answer for a moment. He was standing, I remember well, with his back turned to the blazing log fire and his hands behind his back. He had grown more worn and lined during the past few months, the result of the endless anxieties that pressed upon him, and the silver streak that ran through his auburn locks had broadened above his brow. The raw November weather nipped his wounded leg, and I guessed, with my experience, what he must suffer. "There is no hope for His Majesty," he said at length, "unless he can come to agreement with the Scots and raise an army from them. If he fails, his cause is doomed."

Forty-three, '44, '45, and, approaching us, '46. For over three years men had fought and suffered and died for that proud, stiff little man and his rigid principles, and I thought of the picture that had hung in the dining chamber at Menabilly, which had afterwards been torn and trampled by the rebels. Would his end be as inglorious as the fate that befell his picture? Everything seemed doubtful, suddenly, and grim and hopeless. "Richard," I said, and he caught the inflexion in my voice and came beside me. "Would you, too," I asked, "leave the sinking ship?"

"Not," he said, "if there is any chance of holding Cornwall for the Prince."

"But if the Prince should sail for France," I persisted, "and the whole of Cornwall be overrun—what then?"

"I would follow him," he answered, "and raise a French army of fifty thousand men and land again in Cornwall."

He came and knelt beside me, and I held his face between my hands.

"We have been happy in our strange way, you and I," I said.

"My camp follower," he said. "My trailer of the drum."

"You know that I am given up as lost to all perdition by good persons," I said. "My family have cast me off and do not speak of me. Even my dear Robin is ashamed of his sister. I had a letter from him this very morning. He is serving with Sir John Digby before Plymouth. He implores me to leave you and return to the Rashleighs at Menabilly."

"Do you want to go?"

"No. Not if you still need me."

"I shall always need you. I shall never part with you again. But if Fairfax comes you would be safer in Menabilly than in Launceston."

"That is what was said to me last time, and you know what happened."

"Yes, you suffered for four weeks, and the experience made a woman of you." He looked down at me in his cruel, mocking way, and I remembered how he had never thanked me yet for succouring his son. "Next time it might be for four years," I said, "and I think I would be white-haired at the end of it."

"I shall take you with me if I lose my battle," he said. "When the crisis comes and Fairfax crosses the Tamar I will send you and Matty to Menabilly. If we win the day, so far so good. If we lose and I know the cause is lost, then I will come riding to you at your Rashleighs', and we will get a fishing boat from Polkerris and sail across the Channel to Saint-Malo, and find Dick."

"Do you promise?"

"Yes, sweetheart, I promise."

And when he had reassured me and held me close I was somewhat comforted, yet always, nagging at my mind, was the reminder that I was not only a woman but a cripple and would make a sorry burden to a fugitive. The next day the Prince's council summoned him to Truro and asked him there, before the whole assembly, what advice he could give them for the defence of Cornwall against the enemy and how the safety of the Prince of Wales could be best assured.

He did not answer them at once, but the next day, in his lodgings, he composed a letter to the Secretary-at-War and gave full details of the plan, so far only breathed to me in confidence, of what he believed imperative to be done. He showed me the draft of it on his return, and much of what he proposed filled me with misgiving, not because of its impracticability, but because the kernel of it was so likely to be misconstrued. He proposed, in short, to make a treaty with the Parliament, by which Cornwall would become separate from the remainder of the country and be ruled by the Prince of Wales, as Duke of the Duchy. The duchy would contain its own army, its own fortifications, and control its own shipping. In return the Cornish would give a guarantee not to attack the forces of the Parliament. Thus gaining a respite, the people of Cornwall, and especially the Western army, would become so strong that in the space of a year or more they would be in ripe condition to give effective aid unto His Majesty. (This last, it may be realized, was not to be one of the clauses in the treaty.) Failing an agreement with Parliament, then Richard advised that a line be held from Barastaple to the English Channel and ditches dug from the north coast to the Tamar, so that the whole of Cornwall become virtually an island. On this riverbank would be the first line of defence, and all the bridges would be destroyed. This line, he averred, could be held for an indefinite period and any attempt at an invasion be immediately repulsed. When he had finished his report and sent it to the council, he returned to me at Werrington to await an answer. Five days, a week, and no reply. And then at last a cold message from the Chancellor and the Secretary-at-War, to say that the plan had been considered but had not found approval. The Prince's council would thus consider other measures and acquaint Sir Richard Grenvile when his services would be required.

"So," said Richard, throwing the letter onto my lap, "a smack in the eye for Grenvile and a warning not to rise above his station. The council prefer to lose the war in their own fashion. Let them do so. Time is getting short, and if I judge Fairfax rightly, neither snow nor hail nor frost will hamper him in Devon. It would be wise, my Honor, if you sent word of warning to Mary Rashleigh and told her that you would spend Christmas with her."

The sands were running out I could tell it by his easy manner, his shrugging of his shoulders.

"And you?" I said with that old sick twist of foreboding in my heart.

"I will come later," he said, "and we will see the new year in together in that room above the gatehouse."

And so on the third morning of December, I set forth once again, after eighteen months, for my brother-in-law's house of Menabilly.

Twenty-Five

M Y SECOND COMING WAS VERY DIFFERENT FROM MY first. Then it had been spring, with the golden gorse in bloom and young John Rashleigh coming to meet me on the highway before the park. War had not touched the neighbour-hood, and in the park were cattle grazing, and flocks of sheep with their young lambs, and the last of the blossom falling from the fruit trees in the orchards. Now it was December, a biting wind cutting across the hills and valleys, and no young laughing cavalier came out to greet me. As we turned in at the park gates I saw at once that the walls were still tumbled and had not been repaired since the destruction wrought there by the rebels. Where the acres dipped to the sea above Polkerris a labourer with a team of oxen ploughed a single narrow enclosure, but about it to east and west the land was left uncultivated. Where should be rich brown ploughland was left to thistle. A few lean cattle grazed within the park, and even now, after a full year or more had come and gone, I noticed the great bare patches of grassland where the rebel tents had stood, and the blackened roots of the trees they had felled for firewood. As we climbed the hill towards the house I could see the reassuring curl of smoke rise from the chimneys and could hear the barking of the stable dogs, and I wondered, with a strange feeling of sadness and regret, whether I should be as welcome now as I had been eighteen months before. Once again my litter passed into the outer court and, glancing up at my old apartment in the gatehouse, I saw that it was shuttered and untenanted, even as the barred room beside it, and that the whole west wing wore the same forlorn appearance. Mary had warned me in her letter that only the eastern portion of the house had as yet been put in order, and they were living in some half a dozen rooms, for which they had found hangings and the bare necessities of furniture. Once more into the inner court, with a glance upward at the belfry and the tall weather vane, and then— reminiscent of my former visit—came my sister Mary out upon the steps, and I noticed with a shock that her hair had gone quite white. Yet she greeted me with her same grave smile and gentle kiss, and I was taken straightway to the gallery, where I found my dear Alice strung about as always with her mob of babies, and the newest of the brood, just turned twelve months, clutching at her knee in her first steps. This was now all our party. The Sawles had returned to Penrice, and the Sparkes to Devon, and my goddaughter Joan, with John and the children, were living in the Rashleigh town house at Fowey. My brother-in-law, it seemed, was somewhere about the grounds, and at once, as they plied me with refreshment, I had to hear all the news of the past year, of how Jonathan had not yet received one penny piece from the Crown to help him in the restoration of his property, and whatever had been done he had done himself, with the aid of his servants and tenants.

"Cornwall is become totally impoverished," said my sister sadly, "and everyone dissatisfied. The harvest of this summer could not make up for all we lost last year, and each man with an estate to foster says the same. Unless the war ends swiftly we shall all be ruined."

"It may end swiftly," I answered, "but not as you would wish it."

I saw Mary glance quickly at Alice, and Alice made as though to say something and then desisted. And I realized that as yet no mention had been made of Richard, my relationship to him being something that the Rashleighs possibly preferred should be ignored. I had not been questioned once about the past twelve months.

"They say, who know about these things," said Mary, "that His Majesty is very hopeful, and will soon send an army to the West to help us drive Fairfax out of Devon."

"His Majesty is too preoccupied in keeping his own troops together in the Midlands," I answered, "to concern himself about the West."

"You do not think," said Alice anxiously, "that Cornwall is likely to suffer invasion once again?"

"I do not see how we can avoid it."

"But—we have plenty of troops, have we not?" said Mary, still shying from mention of their general. "I know we have been taxed hard enough to provide for them."

"Troops without boots or stockings make poor fighters," I said, "especially if they have no powder for their muskets."

"Jonathan says everything has been mismanaged," said Mary. "There is no supreme authority in the West to take command. The Prince's council say one thing—the commanders say another. I, for my part, understand nothing of it. I only wish it were well over."

I could tell from their expressions, even Alice's, usually so fair and generous, that Sir Richard Grenvile had been as badly blamed at Menabilly as elsewhere for his highhanded ways and indiscretions, and that unless I broached his name now, there would be an uneasy silence on the subject for the whole duration of my visit. Not one of them would take the first step, and there would be an awkward barrier between us all, making for discomfort. "Perhaps," I said, "having dwelt with Richard

Grenvile for the past eight months, ever since he was wounded, I am prejudiced in his favour. I know he has many faults, but he is the best soldier that we have in the whole of His Majesty's army. The Prince's council would do well to listen to his advice on military matters, if on nothing else."

Neither of them said anything for a moment, and then Alice, colouring a little, said, "Peter is with your brother Robin, you know, under Sir John Digby, before Plymouth. He told us, when he was last here, that Sir Richard constantly sent orders to Sir John, which he has no right to do."

"What sort of orders, good or bad?" I asked.

"I hardly think the orders themselves were points of dispute," said Alice. "They were possibly quite necessary. But the very fact that he gave them to Sir John, who is not a subordinate, caused irritation."

At this juncture my brother-in-law came to the gallery and the discussion broke, but I wondered, with a heavy heart, how many friends were now left to my Richard, who had at first sworn fealty to his leadership. After I had been at Menabilly a few days my brother-in-law himself put the case more bluntly. There was no discreet avoidance, on his part, of Richard's name. He asked me straight out if he had recovered from his wound, as he had heard report from Truro that on the last visit to the council the general had looked far from well and very tired.

"I think he is tired," I said, "and unwell. And the present situation gives him little cause for confidence or good spirits."

"He has done himself irreparable harm here in Cornwall," said my brother-in-law, "by commanding assistance rather than requesting it."

"Hard times require hard measures," I said. "It is no moment to go cap in hand for money to pay troops, when the enemy is in the next county."

"He would have won far better response had he gone about his business with courtesy and an understanding of the general poverty of all of us. The whole duchy would have rallied to his side had he but half the understanding that was his brother Bevil's."

And to this I could give no answer, for I knew it to be true…

The weather was cold and dreary, and I spent much of my time within my chamber, which was the same that Gartred had been given eighteen months before. It had suffered little in the general damage, for which, I suppose, thanks had to be rendered to her. It was a pleasant room with one window to the gardens, still shorn of their glory, and the new grass seeds that had been sown very clipped yet and thin, and two windows to the south, from where I could see the causeway sloping to rising ground and the view upon the Bay. I was content enough, yet strangely empty, for it comes hard to be alone again after eight months in company with the man you love. I had shared his troubles and misfortunes and his follies too. His moods were become familiar, loved, and understood. The cruel quip, the swift malicious answer to a question, and the sudden fleeting tenderness, so unaccountable, so warming, that would change him in one moment from a ruthless soldier to a lover.

When I was with him the days were momentous and full; now they had all the chill drabness of December, when as I took my breakfast the candles must be lit, and for my brief outing on the causeway I must be wrapped in cloak and coverture. The fall of the year, always to me a moment of regret, was now become a period of tension and foreboding.

At Christmas came John and Joan from Fowey, and Peter Courtney, given a few days' grace from Sir John Digby in the watch on Plymouth, and we all made merry for the children's sake and maybe for our own as well. Fairfax was forgotten, and Cromwell, too, the doughty second-in-command who led his men to battle, so we were told, with a prayer upon his lips. We roasted chestnuts before the two fires in the gallery and burnt our fingers snatching sugar plums from the flames, and I remember, too, an old blind harper who was given shelter for the night on Christmas Eve and came and played to us in the soft candlelight. Since the wars there were many such wanderers upon the road, calling no home their own, straggling from village to village, receiving curses more often than silver pieces. Maybe the season had made Jonathan more generous, for this old fellow was not turned away, and I can see him now in his threadbare jerkin and torn hose, with a black shade over his eyes, sitting in the far corner of the gallery, his nimble fingers drumming the strings of his harp, his quivering old voice strangely sweet and true. I asked Jonathan if he were not afraid of thieves in these difficult times, and, shaking his head, he gestured grimly to the faded tapestries on the panels, and the worn chairs. "I have nothing left of value," he said. "You yourself saw it all destroyed a year since." And then, with a half-smile and a lowered voice, "Even the secret chamber and the tunnel contain nothing now but rats and cobwebs."

I shuddered, thinking suddenly of all I had been through when Dick had hidden there, and I turned with relief to the sight of Peter Courtney playing leapfrog with his children, the sound of their merry laughter rising above the melancholy strains of the harper's lament. The servants came to fasten the shutters, and for a moment my brother-in-law stood before the window, looking out upon the lead sky, so soon to darken, and together we watched the first pale snowflakes fall. "The gulls are flying inland," he said. "We shall have a hard winter." There was something ominous in his words, harmless in themselves, that rang like a premonition of disaster. Even as he spoke the wind began to rise, echoing in the chimneys, and circling above the gardens wheeled the crying gulls which came so seldom from their ledges in the cliffs, and with them the scattered flocks of redwing from the north, birds of passage seeking sanctuary.

Next morning we woke to a white world, strangely still, and a sunless sky teeming with further snow to come, while clear and compelling through the silence came the Christmas bells from the church at Tywardreath.

I thought of Richard, alone with his staff at Werrington, and I feared that he would never keep his promise now, with the weather broken and snowdrifts maybe ten feet deep upon the Bodmin moors.

But he did come, at midday on the ninth of January, when for four and twenty hours a thaw had made a slush of the frozen snow, and the road from Launceston to Bodmin was just passable to an intrepid horseman. He brought Jack Grenvile with him, and Jack's younger brother Bunny, a youngster of about the age of Dick, with a pugnacious jaw and merry eyes, who had spent Christmas with his uncle and now never left his side, vowing he would not return to Stowe again to his mother and his tutor, but would join the army and kill rebels. As I watched Richard tweak his ear and laugh and jest with him, I felt a pang of sorrow in my heart for Dick, lonely and unloved, save for that dreary Herbert Ashley, across the sea in Normandy, and I wondered if it must always be that Richard should show himself so considerate and kind to other lads, winning their devotion, and remain a stranger to his own son.

My brother-in-law, who had known Bevil well, bade welcome Bevil's boys, and after a first fleeting moment of constraint, for the visit was unexpected, he welcomed Richard, too, with courtesy. Richard looked better, I thought—the hard weather suited him—and after five minutes his was the only voice we heard in the long gallery, a sort of hush coming upon the Rashleigh family with his presence, and my conscience told me that his coming had put an end to their festivity. Peter Courtney, the jester-in-chief, was stricken dumb upon the instant, and I saw him frown to Alice to chide their eldest little girl, who, unafraid, ventured to Richard's side and pulled his sash.

None of them were natural any more because of the general, and, glancing at my sister Mary, I saw the well-known frown upon her face as she wondered about her larder and what fare she could provide, and I guessed, too, that she was puzzling as to which apartment could be given to him, for we were all crammed into one wing as it was. "You are on your way to Truro, I suppose?" she said to him, thinking he would be gone by morning. "No," he answered. "I thought, while the hard weather lasted, I might bide with you a week at Menabilly and shoot duck instead of rebels."

I saw her dart a look of consternation at Jonathan, and there was a silence that Richard found not at all unusual, as he was unused to other voices but his own, and he continued cursing, with great heartiness, the irritating slowness of the Cornish people. "On the north coast," he said, "where these lads and myself were born and bred, response is swift and sudden, as it should be. But the duchy falls to pieces south of Bodmin, and the men become like snails." The fact that the Rashleighs had been born in southeast Cornwall did not worry him at all. "I could never," he continued, "have resided long at Killigarth. Give a fellow a command at Polperro or at Looe on Christmas Day, and with a slice of luck it will be obeyed by midsummer."

Jonathan Rashleigh, who owned land in both places, stared steadily before him. "But whistle a fellow overnight at Stratton," said Richard, "or from Morwenstowe, or Bude, and he is at your side by morning. I tell you frankly that had I none other but Atlantic men in my army I would face Fairfax tomorrow with composure. But the first sight of cold steel the rats from Truro and beyond will turn and run."

"I think you underestimate your fellow countrymen and mine," said Jonathan quietly.

"Not a bit of it; I know them all too well."

If, I considered, the conversation of the week was to continue in this strain, the atmosphere of Menabilly would be far from easy. But Jack Grenvile, with a discretion born of long practice, tapped his uncle on the shoulder. "Look, sir," he said. "There are your duck." Pointing to the sky above the garden, still gray and heavy with unfallen snow, he showed the teal in flight, heading to the Gribben. Richard was at once a boy again, laughing, jesting, clapping his hands upon his nephew's shoulders, and in a moment the men of the household fell under the spell of his change of mood, and John and Peter, and even my brother-in-law, were making for the shore. We women wrapped ourselves in cloaks and went out upon the causeway to watch the sport, and it seemed to me that the years had rolled away, as I saw Richard, with Peter's goshawk on his wrist, turn to laugh at me. The boys were running across the thistle park to the long mead in the Pridmouth Valley, shouting and calling to one another, and the dogs were barking.

The snow still lay upon the fields, and the cattle in the beef park nosed hungrily for fodder. The flocks of lapwing, growing tame and bold, wheeled screaming round our heads. For a brief moment the sun came from the white sky and shone upon us, and the world was dazzling. "This," I thought, "is an interlude, lasting a single second. I have my Richard, Alice has her Peter, Joan her John. Nothing can touch us for today. There is no war. The enemy are not in Devon, waiting for the word to march."

In retrospect, the events of '44 seemed but an evil dream that could never be repeated, and as I looked across the valley to the farther hill and saw the coast road winding down the fields of Tregares and Culver Close to the beach at Pridmouth, I remembered the troopers who had appeared there on the skyline on that fateful August day. Surely Richard was mistaken. They could not come again. There was a shouting from the valley, and up from the marshes rose the duck, with the hawks above them, circling, and I suddenly shivered for no reason. Then the sun went blank, and a cat's paw rippled the sea, while a great shadow passed across the Gribben Hill. Something fell upon my cheek, soft and clammy white. It was snowing once again.

That night we made a circle by the fire in the gallery, while Jonathan and Mary retired early to their room.

The blind harper had departed with the new year, so there was none to make music for us save Alice and her lute, and Peter with his singing, while the two Grenvile brothers, Jack and Bunny, whistled softly together, a schoolboy trick learned from their father Bevil long ago, when the great house at Stowe had rung with singing and with music. John heaped logs upon the fire and blew the candles, and the flames lit the long room from end to end, shining on the panelling and on the faces of us, one and all, as we sat around the hearth.

I can see Alice as she was that night fingering her lute, looking up adoringly at her Peter, who was to prove, alas, so faithless in the years to come, while he, with his constraint before his general melting with the firelight and the late hour, threw back his head and sang to us:

And wilt thou leave me thus?
Say nay, say nay, for shame.
To save thee from the blame
Of all my grief and grame,
And wilt thou leave me thus?
Say nay! Say nay!

I saw Joan and John hold hands and smile; John, with his dear, honest face, who would never be unfaithful and a deserter to his Joan, as Peter would to Alice, but was destined to slip away from her for all that, to the land from which no one of us returns, in barely six years' time.

> And wilt thou leave me thus,
> And have no more pity
> Of him that loveth thee?
> Alas! thy cruelty.
> And wilt thou leave me thus?
> Say nay! Say nay!

Plaintive and gentle were Alice's fingers upon the lute, and Jack and Bunny, cupping their mouths with their hands, whistled softly to her lead. I stole a glance at Richard. He was staring into the flames, his wounded leg propped on a stool before him. The flickering firelight cast shadows on his features, distorting them to a grimace, and I could not tell whether he smiled or wept.

"You used to sing that once, long ago," I whispered, but if he heard me he made no move; he only waited for the last verse of Peter's song. Then he laid aside his pipe, blowing a long ribbon of smoke into the air, and reached across the circle for Alice's lute.

"We are all lovers here, are we not?" he said. "Each in our own fashion, except for these sprigs of boys." He smiled maliciously and began to drum the strings of the lute:

> Your most beautiful bride who with garlands
>   is crowned
> And kills with each glance as she treads on the
>   ground,
> Whose lightness and brightness doth shine in
>   such splendour,

That none but the stars
Are thought fit to attend her,
Though now she be pleasant and sweet to the
sense,
Will be damnably mouldy a hundred years
hence.

He paused, cocking an eye at them, and I saw Alice shrink back in her chair, glancing uncertainly at Peter. Joan was picking at her gown, biting her lips. Oh God, I thought, why do you break the spell? Why do you hurt them? They are none of them much more than children.

Then why should we turmoil in cares and in
fears,
Turn all our tranquil'ty to sighs and to tears?
Let's eat, drink, and play till the worms do
corrupt us,
'Tis certain, Post Mortem,
Nulla voluptas,
For health, wealth, and beauty, wit, learning
and sense,
Must all come to nothing a hundred years
hence.

He rippled a final chord upon the strings and, rising to his feet, handed the lute to Alice with a bow.

"Your turn again, Lady Courtney," he said. "Or would you prefer to play at spillikins?"

Someone—Peter, I think it was—forced a laugh, and then John rose to light the candles. Joan leant forward and raked apart the fire, so that the logs no longer burnt a flame. They flickered dully and went dark. The spell was broken.

"It is snowing still," said Jack Grenvile, opening a shutter. "Let us hope it falls twenty foot in depth in Devon and stifles Fairfax and his merry men."

"It will more likely stifle Wentworth," said Richard, "sitting on his arse in Bovey Tracey."

"Why does everyone stand up?" asked young Bunny. "Is there to be no more music?" But no one answered. The war was upon us once again, the fear, the doubt, the nagging insecurity, and all the quiet had vanished from the evening.

Twenty-Six

I SLEPT UNEASILY THAT NIGHT, PASSING FROM ONE TROUBLED dream into another, and at one moment I thought to hear the sound of horses' hoofs riding across the park. Yet my windows faced east, and I told myself it was but fancy, and the wind stirring in the snow-laden trees. But when Matty came to me with breakfast she bore a note in her hands from Richard, and I learnt that my fancy was in truth reality, and that he and the two Grenviles and Peter Courtney had all ridden from the house shortly after daybreak.

A messenger had come to Menabilly with the news that Cromwell had made a night attack on Lord Wentworth in Bovey Tracey and, finding the Royalist army asleep, had captured four hundred of the horse, while the remainder of the foot who had not been captured had fled to Tavistock in complete disorder and confusion. "Wentworth has been caught napping," Richard had scribbled on a torn sheet of paper, "which is exactly what I feared would happen. What might have been a small reverse is likely to turn into disaster, if a general order is given to retreat. I propose riding forthwith to the Prince's council, and offering my services. Unless they appoint a supreme commander to take over Wentworth's rabble, we shall have Fairfax and Cromwell across the Tamar."

Mary need not have worried after all. Sir Richard Grenvile had passed but a single night under her roof, and not the week that she had dreaded... I rose that morning with a heavy heart and, going downstairs to the gallery, found Alice in tears, for she knew that Peter would be foremost in the fighting when the moment came. My brother-in-law looked grave and departed at midday, also bound for Launceston, to discover what help might be needed from the landowners and gentry in the event of invasion. John, with Frank Penrose, set forth to warn the tenants on the estate that once again their services might be needed, and the day was wretchedly reminiscent of that other day in August, nearly eighteen months before. But now it was not midsummer, but midwinter. And there was no strong Cornish army to lure the rebels into a trap, with another Royalist army marching in the rear.

Our men stood alone—with His Majesty three hundred miles away or more, and General Fairfax was a very different leader from the Earl of Essex. He would walk into no trap, but if he came would cross the Tamar with a certainty.

In the afternoon Elizabeth from Coombe came to join us, her husband having gone, and told us that the rumour ran in Fowey that the siege of Plymouth had been raised, and Digby's troops, along with Wentworth's, were retreating fast to the Tamar bridges.

We sat before the smouldering fire in the gallery, a little group of wretched women, and I stared at that same branch of ash that had burnt so brightly the preceding night, when our men were with us, and was now a blackened log amongst the ashes.

We had faced invasion before, had endured the brief horrors of enemy occupation, but we had never known defeat. Alice and Mary were talking of the children, the necessity this time of husbanding supplies beneath the floorboards of the rooms, as though a siege was all that was before us. But I said nothing, only stared into the fire. And I wondered who would suffer most, the men who died swiftly in battle, or those who would remain to face imprisonment and torture. I knew then that I would rather Richard fought and died than stayed to fall into the hands of Parliament. It did not bear much thinking what they would do to Skellum Grenvile if they caught him.

"The King will march west, of course," Elizabeth was saying. "He could not leave Cornwall in the lurch. They say he is raising a great body of men in Oxfordshire this moment. When the thaw breaks..."

"Our defences will withstand the rebels," Joan said. "John was talking to a man in Tywardreath. Much has been accomplished since last time. They say we have a new musket—with a longer barrel—I do not know exactly, but the rebels will not face it, so John says..."

"They have no money," said Mary. "Jonathan tells me the Parliament is desperate for money. In London the people are starving. They have no bread. The Parliament are bound to seek terms from the King, for they will be unable to continue the war. When the spring comes..."

I wanted to put my fingers in my ears and muffle the sound of their voices. On and on, one against the other, the old false tales that had been told so often. It cannot go on... They must give in... They are worse off than we... When the thaw breaks, when the spring comes... And suddenly I saw Elizabeth look towards me. She had less reserve than Alice, and I did not know her so well. "What does Sir Richard Grenvile say?" she asked. "You must hear everything of what goes on. Will he attack and drive the rebels back to Dorset?"

Her ignorance and theirs was so supreme that I had not the heart nor the will to enlighten her.

"Attack?" I said. "With what forces do you suggest that he attack?"

"Why, with those at his disposal," she answered. "We have many able-bodied men in Cornwall."

I thought of the sullen bands I had seen sulking in the square at Launceston and the handful of brawny fellows in the fields below Werrington, wearing the Grenvile shield on their shoulders.

"A little force of pressed men," I said, "and volunteers, against some fifty thousand trained soldiers?"

"But man for man we are superior," urged Elizabeth. "Everyone says that. The rebels are well equipped, no doubt, but when our fellows meet them face to face in fair fight, in open country..."

"Have you not heard," I said softly, "of Cromwell and the new model army? Do you not realize, that never, in England, until now, has there been raised an army like it?"

They stared at me, nonplussed, and Elizabeth, shrugging her shoulders, said I had greatly altered since the year before and was now become defeatist. "If we all talked in that fashion," she said, "we would have been beaten long ago. I suppose you have caught it from Sir Richard. I do not wonder that he is unpopular."

Alice looked embarrassed, and I saw Mary nudge Elizabeth with her foot.

"Don't worry," I said. "I know his faults far better than you all. But I think if the council of the Prince would only listen to him this time, we might save Cornwall from invasion."

That evening, on going to my room, I looked out on the weather, and saw that the night was clear and the stars were shining. There would be no more snow, not yet awhile. I called Matty to me and told her my resolve. This was to follow Richard back to Werrington, if transport could be gotten for me at Tywardreath, and to set forth at noon the following day, passing the night at Bodmin, and so to Werrington the day after. By doing this I would disobey his last instructions, but I had, in my heart, a premonition that unless I saw him now I would never see him more. What I thought, what I feared, I cannot tell. But it came to me that he might fall in battle and that by following him I would be with him at the last.

The next morning was fine, as I expected, and I rose early and went down to breakfast and informed the Rashleigh family of my plan. They one and all begged me to remain, saying it was folly to travel the roads at such a season, but I was firm; and at length John Rashleigh, dear, faithful friend, arranged matters for me and accompanied me as far as Bodmin.

It was bitter cold upon the moors, and I had little stomach for my journey as, with Matty at my side, I left the hostelry at Bodmin at daybreak. The long road to Launceston stretched before us, bleak and dreary, with great snowdrifts on either side of us, and one false step of our horses would send the litter to destruction. Although we were wrapped about with blankets, the nipping, nagging wind penetrated the curtains, freezing our faces, and when we halted at Five Lanes for hot soup and wine to warm us, I had half a mind to go no farther but find lodging for the night at Altarnum. The man at the inn put an end to my hesitation. "We have had soldiers here these past two days," he said, "deserters from the army before Plymouth. Some of Sir John Digby's men. They were making for their homes in west Cornwall. They were not going to stay on the Tamar banks to be butchered, so they told me."

"What news had they?" I asked, my heart heavy.

"Nothing good," he answered. "Confusion everywhere. Orders, and counterorders. Sir Richard Grenvile was down on Tamar-side, inspecting bridges, giving instructions to blow them when the need arose, and a colonel of foot refused to take the order, saying he would obey none other than Sir John Digby. What is to become of us if the generals start fighting amongst themselves?"

I felt sick and turned away. There would be no biding for me this night at Altarnum. I must reach Werrington by nightfall.

On then, across the snow-covered moors, wind-swept and desolate, and every now and then we would pass straggling figures making for the west, their apparel proclaiming to the world that once they were King's men, but now deserters. They were blue from cold and hunger, and yet they wore a brazen, sullen look, as though they cared no longer what became of them, and some of them shouted as we passed, "To hell with the war. We're going home," and shook their fists at my litter, jeering, "You're driving to the devil."

The short winter afternoon soon closed in, and by the time we came to Launceston and turned out of the town to St. Stephens it was grown pitch-dark and snowing once again. An hour or so later I would have been snow-bound on the road, with nothing but waste moorland on either side of me. At last we came to Werrington, which I had not thought to see again, and when the startled sentry at the gates recognized me and let the horses pass through the park, I thought that even he, a Grenvile man, had lost his look of certainty and pride and would become, granted ill fortune, no better than the deserters on the road.

We drew up into the cobbled court, and an officer came forth whose face was new to me. His expression was blank when I gave him my name, and he told me that the general was in conference and could not be disturbed. I thought that Jack might help me and asked, therefore, if Sir John Grenvile or his brother Mr. Bernard could see Mistress Honor Harris on a matter of great urgency.

"Sir John is no longer with the general," answered the officer. "The Prince of Wales recalled him to his entourage yesterday. And Bernard Grenvile has returned to Stowe. I am the general's aide-de-camp at present." This was not hopeful, for he did not know me, and as I watched the figures of the soldiers passing backwards and forwards in the hall within the house and heard the tattoo of a drum in the far distance, I thought how ill-timed and crazy was my visit, for what could they do with me, a woman and a cripple, in this moment of great stress and urgency?

I heard a murmur of voices. "They are coming out now," said the officer. "The conference is over." I caught sight of Colonel Roscarrock, whom I knew well, a loyal friend of Richard's, and in desperation I leant from my litter and called to him. He came to my side at once, in great astonishment, but at once, with true courtesy, covered his consternation and gave orders for me to be carried into the house. "Ask me no questions," I said. "I have come at a bad moment, I can guess that. Can I see him?" He hesitated for a fraction of a minute. "Why, of course," he said, "he will want to see you. But I must warn you, things are not going well for him. We are all concerned..." He broke off in confusion, looking most desperately embarrassed and unhappy.

"Please," I said, avoiding his eyes, "please tell him I am here." He went at once into the room that Richard used as his own and where we had sat together, night after night, for over seven months. He stayed a moment, and then came for me. My chair had been lifted from the litter, and he took me to the room, then closed the door. Richard was standing by the table. His face was hard, set in the firm lines that I knew well. I could tell that of all things in the world I was, at that moment, farthest from his thoughts.

"What the devil," he said wearily, "are you doing here?"

It was not the welcome that I yearned for but was that which I deserved.

"I am sorry," I said. "I could not rest once you were gone. If anything is going to happen—which I know it must—I want to share it with you. The danger, I mean. And the aftermath."

He laughed shortly and tossed a paper onto my lap.

"There'll be no danger," he said, "not for you, or me. Perhaps, after all, it is as well you came. We can travel west together."

"What do you mean?" I said.

"That letter, you can read it," he, said. "It is a copy of a message I have just sent to the Prince's council, resigning from His Majesty's Army. They will have it in an hour's time."

I did not answer for a moment. I sat quite cold and still.

"What do you mean?" I asked at length. "What has happened?" He went to the fire and stood with his hands behind his back. "I went to them," he said, "as soon as I returned from Menabilly. I told them that if they wished to save Cornwall and the Prince they must appoint a supreme commander. Men are deserting in hundreds, discipline is non-existent. This would be the only hope, the last and final chance. They thanked me. They said they would consider the matter. I went away. I rode next morning to Gunnislake and Callington. I inspected the defences. There I commanded a certain colonel of foot to blow a bridge when need arose. He disputed my authority, saying his orders were to the contrary. Would you like to know his name?"

I said nothing. Some inner sense had told me.

"It was your brother, Robin Harris," he said. "He even dared to bring your name into a military matter. 'I cannot take orders from a man,' he said, 'who has ruined the life and reputation of my sister. Sir John Digby is my commander, and Sir John has bidden me to leave this bridge intact.'"

Richard stared at me an instant, and then began to pace up and down the strip of carpet by the fire.

"You would hardly credit it," he said, "such lunacy, such gross incompetence. It matters not that he is your brother, that he drags a private quarrel into the King's business. But to leave the bridge for Fairfax, to have the impertinence to tell me, a Grenvile, that John Digby knows his business best..."

I could see Robin, very red about the neck, with beating heart and swelling anger, thinking, dear damned idiot, that by defying his commander he was somehow defending me and downing, in some bewildering hothead fashion, the seducer of his sister.

"What then?" I asked. "Did you see Digby?"

"No," he answered. "What would be the use, if he defied me, as your brother did? I returned here to Launceston to take my commission from the council as supreme commander, and thus show my powers to the whole army, and be damned to them."

"And you have the commission?"

He leant to the table and, seizing a small piece of parchment, held it before my eyes. "The council of the Prince," he read, "appoints Lord Hopton in supreme command of His Majesty's forces in the West and desires that Sir Richard Grenvile should serve under him as lieutenant general of the foot."

He read slowly, with deadly emphasis and scorn, and then tore the document to tiny shreds and threw the pieces in the fire. "That is my answer to them," he said. "They may do as they please. Tomorrow you and I will return to shoot duck at Menabilly." He pulled the bell beside the fire, and his new aide-de-camp appeared. "Bid the servants bring some supper," he said. "Mistress Harris has travelled long, and has not dined."

When the officer had gone I put out my hand to Richard.

"You can't do this," I said. "You must do as they tell you."

He turned round on me in anger. "Must?" he said. "There is no must. Do you think that I shall truckle to that damned lawyer at this juncture? It is he who is at the bottom of this, he who is to blame. I can see him, with his bland attorney's manner, talking to the members of the council. 'This man is dangerous,' he says to them, 'this soldier, this Grenvile. If we give him the supreme command he will take precedence of us and send us about our business. We will give Hopton the command. Hopton will not dare to disobey. And when the enemy cross the Tamar, Hopton will withstand them just long enough for us to slip across to Guernsey with the Prince.' That is how the lawyer talks; that is what he has in mind. The traitor, the damned disloyal coward."

He faced me, white with anger.

"But, Richard," I persisted, "don't you understand, my love, my dear, that it is you they will call disloyal at this moment? To refuse to serve under another man, with the enemy in Devon? It is you who will be pointed at, reviled? You, and not Hyde?"

He would not listen; he brushed me away with his hand.

"This is not a question of pride, but concerns my honour," he said. "They do not trust me. Therefore, I resign. Now for God's sake let us dine and say no more. Tell me, was it snowing still at Menabilly?"

I failed him that last evening. Failed him miserably. I made no effort once to enter in his mood, that switched now so suddenly from black anger to forced jollity. I wanted to talk about the future, about what he proposed to do, but he would have none of it. I asked what his officers thought, what Colonel Roscarrock had said, and colonels Arundell, and Fortiscue. Did they, too, uphold him in his grave, unorthodox decision? But he would not speak of it. He bade the servants open another bottle of wine, and with a smile he drained it all, as he had done seven months before at Ottery St. Mary. It was nearly midnight when the new aide-de-camp knocked upon the door, bearing a letter in his hand.

Richard took it and read the message, then with a laugh threw it in the fire. "A summons from the council," he said, "to appear before them at ten tomorrow in the Castle Court at Launceston. Perchance they plan some simple ceremony and will dub me Earl. That is the customary reward for soldiers who have failed."

"Will you go?" I asked.

"I shall go," he said, "and then proceed with you to Menabilly."

"You will not relent?" I asked. "Not swallow your pride, or honour, as you call it, and consent to do as they demand of you?"

He looked at me a moment and he did not smile.

"No," he said slowly. "I shall not relent."

I went to bed, to my old room next to his and left the door open between our chambers, should he be restless and wish to come to me. But at past three in the morning I heard his footstep on the stair.

I slept one hour, perhaps, or two. I do not remember. It was still snowing when I woke, and dull and gray. I bade Matty dress me in great haste and sent word to Richard, asking if he would see me.

He came instead to my room and with great tenderness told me to stay abed, at any rate until he should return from Launceston.

"I will be gone an hour," he said; "two at the utmost. I shall but delay to tell the council what I think of them and then come back to breakfast with you. My anger is all spent. This morning I feel free and light of heart. It is an odd sensation, you know, to be at long last without responsibility." He kissed my two hands and then went away. I heard the sound of the horses trotting away across the park. There was a single drum and then silence. Nothing but the footsteps of the sentry pacing up and down before the house. I went and sat in my chair beside the window, with a rug under my knees. It was snowing steadily. There would be a white carpet on the Castle Green at Launceston. Here at Werrington the world was desolate.

The deer stood huddled under the trees down by the river. At midday Matty brought me meat, but I did not fancy it. I went on sitting at the window, gazing out across the park, and presently the snow had covered all trace of the horses, and the soft white flakes began to freeze upon the glass of the casement, clouding my view. It must have been past three when I heard the sentry standing to attention, and once again the muffled tattoo of a drum. Some horses were coming to the house by the northern entrance, and because my window did not face that way I could not see them. I waited. Richard might not come at once; there would be many matters to see to in that room downstairs. At a quarter to four there came a knock upon my door, and a servant demanded in a hushed tone if Colonel Roscarrock could wait on Mistress Harris. I told him certainly, and sat there with my hands clasped on my lap, filled with that apprehension that I knew too well.

He came and stood before the door, disaster written plainly on his face.

"Tell me," I said. "I would know the worst at once."

"They have arrested him," he said slowly, "on a charge of disloyalty to the Prince and to His Majesty. They seized him there before us, his staff, and all his officers."

"Where have they imprisoned him?"

"There in Launceston Castle. The governor and an escort of men were waiting to take him. I rode to his side and begged him to give fight. His staff, his command, the whole army, I told him, would stand by him if he would but give the word. But he refused. 'The Prince,' he said, 'must be obeyed.' He smiled at us there on the Castle Green, and bade us be of good cheer. Then he handed his sword to the governor, and they look him away."

"Nothing else?" I asked. "No other word, no message of farewell?"

"Nothing else," he said, "except he bade me take good care of you and see you safely to your sister."

I sat quite still, my heart numb, all feeling and all passion spent.

"This is the end," said Colonel Roscarrock. "There is no other man in the army fit to lead us but Richard Grenvile. When Fairfax chooses to strike he will find no opposition. This is the end."

Yes, I thought. This is the end. Many had fought and died, and all in vain. The bridges would not be blown now; the roads would not be guarded, nor the defences held. When Fairfax gave the word to march the word would be obeyed, and his troops would cross the Tamar, never to depart. The end of liberty in Cornwall, for many months, for many years, perhaps for generations. And Richard Grenvile, who might have saved his country, was now a prisoner, of his own side, in Launceston Castle.

"If we had only time," Colonel Roscarrock was saying, "we could have a petition signed by every man and woman in the duchy asking for his release. We could send messengers, in some way, to His Majesty himself, imploring pardon, insisting that the sentence of the council is unjust. If we had only time..." If we had only time, when the thaw broke, when the spring came. But it was that day, the nineteenth of January, and the snow was falling still.

Twenty-Seven

M Y FIRST ACTION WAS TO LEAVE WERRINGTON, WHICH I did that evening before Sir Charles Trevannion, on Lord Hopton's staff, came to take over for his commander. I no longer had any claim to be there, and I had no wish to embarrass Charles Trevannion, who had known my father well. I went therefore to the hostelry in Broad Street, Launceston, near to the castle; and Colonel Roscarrock, after he had installed me there, took a letter for me to the governor, requesting an interview with Richard for the following morning. He returned at nine o'clock with a courteous but firm refusal. No one, said the governor, was to be permitted to see Sir Richard Grenvile, by strict order of the Prince's council. "We intend," said Colonel Roscarrock to me, "to send a deputation to the prince himself at Truro. Jack Grenvile, I know, will speak for his uncle, and many more besides. Already, since the news has gone abroad, the troops are murmuring and have been confined to their quarters for twenty-four hours, in consequence. I can tell by what the Governor said that rioting is feared." There was no more I could ask him to do that day—I had already trespassed too greatly on his time already—so I bade him a good night and went to bed, to pass a wretched night, wondering all the while in what dungeon they had lodged Richard, or if he had been given lodging according to his rank.

The next day, the twentieth, driving sleet came to dispel the snow, and I think, because of this, and because of my unhappiness, I have never hated any place so much as Launceston. The very name sounded like a jail. Just before noon Colonel Roscarrock called on me with the news that there were proclamations everywhere about the town that Sir Richard Grenvile had been cashiered from every regiment he had commanded and was dismissed from His Majesty's army—and all without court-martial.

"It cannot be done," he said with vehemence. "It is against every military code and tradition. There will be a mutiny in all ranks at such gross injustice. We are to hold a meeting of protest today, and I will let you know, directly it is over, what is decided." Meetings and conferences, somehow I had no faith in them. Yet how I cursed my impotence, sitting in my hired room above the cobbled street in Launceston.

Matty, too, fed me with tales of optimism. "There is no other talk about the town," she said, "but Sir Richard's imprisonment. Those who grumbled at his severity before are now clamouring for his release. This afternoon a thousand people went before the castle and shouted for the governor. He is bound to let him go, unless he wants the castle burnt about his ears."

"The governor is only acting under orders," I said. "He can do nothing. It is to Sir Edward Hyde and the council that they should direct their appeals."

"They say in the town," she answered, "that the council have gone back to Truro, so fearful they are of mutiny."

That evening, when darkness fell, I could hear the tramping of many feet in the market square, and distant shouting, while flares and torches were tossed into the sky. Some were thrown at the windows of the Town Hall, and the landlord of my hostelry, fearing for his own, barred the shutters early, and the doors.

"They've put a double guard at the castle," he told Matty, "and the troops are still confined to their quarters."

How typical it was, I thought with bitterness, that now, in his adversity, my Richard should become so popular a figure. Fear was the whip that drove the people on. They had no faith in Lord Hopton or any other commander. Only a Grenvile, they believed, could keep the enemy from crossing the Tamar.

When Colonel Roscarrock came at last to see me, I could tell from his weary countenance that nothing much had been accomplished. "The general has sent word to us," he said, "that he will be no party to release by force. He asks for a court-martial, and a chance to defend himself before the Prince, and to be heard. As to us and to his army, he bids us serve under Lord Hopton."

Why, in God's name, I wondered, could he not do the same himself but twelve hours since?

"So there will be no mutiny?" I said. "No storming of the castle?"

"Not by the army," said Colonel Roscarrock in dejection. "We have taken an oath to remain loyal to Lord Hopton. You have heard the latest news?"

"No?"

"Dartmouth has fallen. The governor, Sir Hugh Pollard, and over a thousand men are taken prisoner. Fairfax has a line across Devon now from north to south."

This would be no time, then, to hold courts-martial.

"What orders have you," I asked wearily, "from your new commander?"

"None as yet. He is at Stratton, you know, in the process of taking over and assembling his command. We expect to hear nothing for a day or two. Therefore I am at your disposal. And I think—forgive me—there is little purpose in your remaining here at Launceston." Poor Colonel Roscarrock. He felt me to be a burden, and small blame to him. But the thought of leaving Richard a prisoner in Launceston Castle was more than I could bear.

"Perhaps," I said, "if I saw the governor myself?" But he gave me little hope. The governor, he said, was not the type of man to melt before a woman. "I will go again," he assured me, "tomorrow morning, and ascertain at least that the general's health is good and that he lacks for nothing." And with that assurance he left me to pass another lonely night, but in the morning I woke to the sound of distant drums and then heard the clattering of horses and troopers pass my window, and I wondered whether orders had come from Lord Hopton at Stratton during the night and the army was on the march again. I sent Matty below for news, and the landlord told her that the troops had been on the move since before daybreak. "All the horse," he said, "had ridden away north already."

I had just finished breakfast when a runner brought me a hurried word, full of apology, from Colonel Roscarrock, saying that he had received orders to proceed at once to Stratton, as Lord Hopton intended marching north to Torrington, and that if I had any friend or relative in the district it would be best for me to go to them immediately. I had no friend or relative, nor would I seek them if I had, and summoning the landlord, I told him to have me carried to Launceston Castle, for I wished to see the governor. I set forth, therefore, well wrapped against the weather, with Matty walking by my side and four fellows bearing my litter, and when I came to the castle gate I demanded to see the captain of the guard. He came from his room, unshaven, buckling his sword, and I thought how Richard would have dealt with him.

"I would be grateful," I said to him, "if you could give a message from me to the governor."

"The governor sees no one," he said at once, "without a written appointment."

"I have a letter here in my hands," I said. "Perhaps it could be given to him."

He turned it over, looking doubtful, and then looked at me again. "What exactly, madam, is your business?" he asked.

He looked not unkindly, for all his blotched appearance, and I took a chance. "I have come," I said, "to inquire after Sir Richard Grenvile." At this he handed back my letter.

"I regret, madam," he said, "but you have come on a useless errand. Sir Richard is no longer here."

Panic seized me on the instant, and I pictured a sudden, secret execution. "What do you mean?" I asked, "no longer here?"

"He left this morning under escort for St. Michael's Mount," replied the captain of the guard. "Some of his men broke from their quarters last night and demonstrated here before the castle. The governor judged it best to remove him from Launceston." At once the captain of the guard, the castle walls, the frowning battlements, lost all significance. Richard was no more imprisoned there. "Thank you," I said. "Good day." And I saw the officer stare after me, and then return to his room beneath the gate.

St. Michael's Mount... Some seventy miles away, in the western toe of Cornwall. At least he was far removed from Fairfax, but how in the world was I to reach him there? I returned to the hostelry, with only one thought in my head now, and that to get from Launceston as soon as possible.

As I entered the door the landlord came to meet me, and said that an officer had called to inquire for me and was even now waiting my return. I thought it must be Colonel Roscarrock, and went at once to see—and found instead my brother Robin. "Thank God," he said, "I have sight of you at last. As soon as I had news of Sir Richard's arrest, Sir John gave me leave of absence to ride to Werrington. They told me at the house you had been gone two days."

I was not sure whether I was glad to see him. It seemed to me, at this moment, that no man was my friend, unless he was friend to Richard also. "Why have you come?" I said coolly. "What is your purpose?"

"To take you back to Mary," he said. "You cannot possibly stay here."

"Perhaps," I answered, "I have no wish to go."

"That is neither here nor there," he said stubbornly. "The entire army is in process of reorganizing, and you cannot remain in Launceston without protection. I myself have orders to join Sir John Digby at Truro, where he has gone with a force to protect the prince in the event of invasion. My idea is to leave you at Menabilly on my way thither."

I thought rapidly. Truro was the headquarters of the council, and if I went there, too, there was a chance, faint yet not impossible, that I could have an audience with the prince himself.

"Very well," I said to Robin, shrugging my shoulders. "I will come with you, but on one condition. And that is that you do not leave me at Menabilly but let me come with you all the way to Truro."

He looked at me doubtfully. "What," he said, "is to be gained by that?"

"Nothing gained, nor lost," I answered, "only for old time's sake, do what I demand."

At that he came and took my hand and held it a minute.

"Honor," he said, his blue eyes full upon my face, "I want you to believe me when I say that no action of mine had any bearing on his arrest. The whole army is appalled. Sir John himself, who had many a bitter dispute with him, has written to the council, appealing for his swift release. He is needed at this moment more than any other man in Cornwall."

"Why," I said bitterly, "did you not think of it before? Why did you refuse to obey his orders about the bridge?"

Robin looked startled for a moment, and then discomforted.

"I lost my temper," he admitted. "We were all rankled that day, and Sir John, the best of men, had given me my orders. You don't understand, Honor, what it has meant to me, and Jo, and all your family, to have your name a byword in the county. Ever since you left Radford last spring to go to Exeter people have hinted, and whispered, and even dared to say aloud the foulest things."

"Is it so foul," I said, "to love a man and go to him when he lies wounded?"

"Why are you not married to him, then?" said Robin. "If you had been, in God's conscience you would have earned the right now to share in his disgrace. But to follow from camp to camp, like a loose woman. I tell you what they say, Honor, in Devon. That he well earns his name of Skellum to trifle thus with a woman who is crippled."

Yes, I thought, they would say that in Devon...

"If I am not Lady Grenvile," I said, "it is because I do not choose to be so."

"You have no pride then, no feeling for your name?"

"My name is Honor, and I do not hold it tarnished," I answered him.

"This is the finish. You know that?" he said, after a moment's pause. "In spite of a petition signed by all our names, I hardly think the council will agree to his release. Not unless they receive some counter-order from His Majesty."

"And His Majesty," I said, "has other fish to fry. Yes, Robin, I understand. And what will be the outcome?"

"Imprisonment at His Majesty's pleasure, with a pardon, possibly, at the end of the war."

"And what if the war does not go the way we wish, but the rebels gain Cornwall for the Parliament?"

Robin hesitated, so I gave the answer for him.

"Sir Richard Grenvile is handed over, a prisoner, to General Fairfax," I said, "and sentenced to death as a criminal of war." I pleaded fatigue then and went to my room, and slept easily for the first time for many nights, for no other reason but because I was bound for Truro, which was some thirty miles distant from St. Michael's Mount… The snow of the preceding days had wrought havoc on the road, and we were obliged to go a longer route, by the coast, for the moors were now impassable. Thus, with many halts and delays, it was well over a week before we came to Truro, only to discover that the council was now removed to Pendennis Castle, at the mouth of the Fal, and Sir John Digby and his forces were now also within the garrison.

Robin found me and Matty a lodging at Penryn and went at once to wait on his commander, bearing a letter from me to Jack Grenvile, whom I believed to be in close attendance on the Prince. The following day Jack rode to see me—and I felt as though years had passed since I had last set eyes upon a Grenvile, yet it was barely three weeks since he, and Richard, and young Bunny had ridden all three to Menabilly. I nearly wept when he came into the room.

"Have no fear," he said at once. "My uncle is in good heart and sturdy health. I have received messages from him from the Mount, and he bade me write you not to be anxious for him. It is rather he who is likely to be anxious on your part, for he believes you with your sister, Mrs. Rashleigh."

I determined then to take young Jack into my confidence.

"Tell me first," I said, "what is the opinion on the war?"

He made a face, and shrugged his shoulders. "You see we are at Pendennis," he said quietly. "That in itself is ominous. There is a frigate at anchor in the roads, fully manned and provisioned, with orders to set sail for the Scillies when the word is given. The prince himself will never give the word—he is all for fighting to the last—but the council lacks his courage. Sir Edward Hyde will have the last word, not the Prince of Wales."

"How long, then, have we till the word be given?"

"Hopton and the army have marched to Torrington," answered Jack, "and there is a hope—but I fear a faint one—that by attacking first, Hopton will take the initiative and force a decision. He is a brave fellow but lacks my uncle's power, and the troops care nothing for him. If he fails at Torrington and Fairfax wins the day—then you may expect that frigate to set sail."

"And your uncle?"

"He will remain, I fear, at the Mount. He has no other choice. But Fairfax is a soldier and a gentleman. He will receive fair treatment." This was no answer for me. However much a soldier and a gentleman Fairfax himself might be, his duty was to Parliament, and Parliament had decreed in '43 that Richard Grenvile was a traitor.

"Jack," I said, "would you do something for me, for your uncle's sake?"

"Anything in the world," he answered, "for the pair of you."

Ah, bless you, I thought, true son of Bevil.

"Get me an audience with the Prince of Wales," I said to him.

He whistled and scratched his cheek, a very Grenvile gesture.

"I'll do my best, I swear it," he said, "but it may take time and patience, and I cannot promise you success. He is so hemmed about with members of the council and dares do nothing but what he is told to do by Sir Edward Hyde. I tell you, Honor, he's led a dog's life until now. First his mother, and now the Chancellor. When he does come of age and can act for himself, I'll wager he'll set the stars on fire."

"Make up some story," I urged. "You are his age and a close companion. You know what would move him. I give you full licence."

He smiled—his father's smile. "As to that," he said, "he has only to hear your story and how you followed my uncle to Exeter to be on tenterhooks to look at you. Nothing pleases him better than a love affair. But Sir Edward Hyde—he's the danger."

He left me, with an earnest promise to do all he could, and with that I was forced to be content. Then came a period of waiting that seemed like centuries but was, in all reality, little longer than a fortnight. During this time Robin came several times to visit me, imploring me to leave Penryn and return to Menabilly. Jonathan Rashleigh, he said, would come himself to fetch me, would I but say the word.

"I must warn you, in confidence," he said, "that the council have little expectation of Hopton's withstanding Fairfax. The prince, with his personal household, will sail for Scilly. The rest of us within the garrison will hold Pendennis until we are burnt out of it. Let the whole rebel army come. We will not surrender."

Dear Robin. As you said that, with your blue eyes blazing and your jaw set, I forgave you for your enmity for Richard and the silly, useless harm you did in disobeying him.

Death or glory, I reflected. That was the way my Richard might have chosen. And here was I, plotting one thing only, that he should steal away like a thief in the night.

"I will go back to Menabilly," I said slowly, "when the Prince of Wales sets sail for the Scillies."

"By then," said Robin, "I shall not be able to assist you. I shall be inside the garrison at Pendennis, with our guns turned east upon Penryn."

"Your guns will not frighten me," I said, "any more than Fairfax's horse thundering across the moors from the Tamar. It will look well in after years, in the annals of the Harris family, to say that Honor died in the last stand in '46."

Brave words, spoken in hardihood, ringing so little true...

On the fourteenth of February, the feast of St. Valentine, that patron saint of lovers, I had a message from Jack Grenvile. The wording was vague, and purposely omitted names.

"The snake is gone to Truro," he said, "and my friend and I will be able to receive you for a brief space this afternoon. I will send an escort for you. Say nothing of the matter to your brother."

I went alone, without Matty, deeming in a matter of such delicacy it were better to have no confidante at all.

True to his word, the escort came, and Jack himself awaited me at the entrance to the castle. No haggling this time with a captain of the guard. But a swift word to the sentry, and we were through the arch and within the precincts of the garrison before a single soul, save the sentry, was a whit the wiser.

The thought occurred to me that this perhaps was not the first time Jack Grenvile had smuggled a woman into the fortress. Such swift handling came possibly from long experience. Two servants in the Prince's livery came to carry me, and after passing up some stairs (which I told myself were back ones and suitable to my person) I was brought to a small room within a tower and placed upon a couch. I would have relished the experience were not the matter upon which I sought an audience so deadly serious. There was wine and fruit at my elbow, and a posy of fresh flowers, and His Highness, I thought, for all his mother, has gained something by inheriting French blood.

I was left for a few moments to refresh myself, and then the door opened again, and Jack stood aside to let a youngster of about his own age pass before him. He was far from handsome, more like a gypsy than a prince, with his black locks and swarthy skin, but the instant he smiled I loved him better than all the famous portraits of his father that my generation had known for thirty years. "Have my servants looked after you?" he said at once. "Given you all you want? This is garrison fare, you know; you must excuse it." And as he spoke I felt his bold eyes look me up and down in cool, appraising fashion, as though I were a maid and not fifteen years his senior. "Come, Jack," he said, "present me to your kinswoman," and I wondered what the devil of a story Jack had spun.

We ate and drank, and all the while he talked he stared, and I wondered if his boy's imagination was running riot on the thought of his notorious and rebellious general making love to me, a cripple. "I have no claim to trespass on your time, sir," I said at length, "but Sir Richard, Jack's uncle, is my dear friend, and has been so now over a span of years. His faults are many, and I have not come to dispute them. But his loyalty to yourself has never, I believe, been the issue in question."

"I don't doubt it," said the prince, "but you know how it was. He got up against the council, and Sir Edward in particular. I like him immensely myself, but personal feeling cannot count in these matters. There was no choice but to sign that warrant for his arrest."

"Sir Richard did very wrong not to serve under Lord Hopton," I said. "His worse fault is his temper, and much, I think, had gone wrong that day to kindle it. Given reflection, he would have acted otherwise."

"He made no attempt, you know, sir," cut in Jack, "to resist arrest. The whole staff would have gone to his aid had he given them the word. That I have on good authority. But he told all of them he wished to abide by your Highness's command."

The prince rose to his feet and paced up and down the room.

"It's a wretched affair all round," he said. "Grenvile is the one fellow who might have saved Cornwall, and all the while Hopton fights a hopeless battle up in Torrington. I can't do anything about it, you know. That's the devil of it. I shall be whisked away myself before I know what is happening."

"There is one thing you can do, sir, if you will forgive my saying so," I said.

"What then?"

"Send word to the Mount that when you and the council sail for the Scillies Sir Richard Grenvile shall be permitted to escape at the same time and commandeer a fishing boat for France."

The Prince of Wales stared at me a moment, and then that same smile I had remarked upon his face before lit his whole ugly countenance. "Sir Richard Grenvile is most fortunate," he said, "to have so *fidèle* an ally as yourself. If I am ever in his shoes and find myself a fugitive, I hope I can rely on half so good a friend."

He glanced across at Jack. "You can arrange that, can't you?" he said. "I will write a letter to Sir Arthur Bassett at the Mount, and you can take it there and see your uncle at the same time. I don't suggest we ask for his company in the frigate when we sail, because I hardly think the ship would bear his weight alongside Sir Edward Hyde." The two lads laughed, for all the world like a pair of schoolboys caught in mischief. Then the prince turned and, coming to the couch, bent low and kissed my hand.

"Have no fear," he said. "I will arrange it. Sir Richard shall be free the instant we sail for the Scillies. And when I return—for I shall return, you know, one day—I shall hope to see you, and him also, at Whitehall." He bowed and went, forgetting me, I dare say, forevermore, but leaving with me an impression of black eyes and gypsy features that I have not forgotten to this day…

Jack escorted me to the castle entrance once again. "He will remember his promise," he said. "That I swear to you. I have never known him go back on his word. Tomorrow I shall ride with that letter to the Mount."

I returned to Penryn, worn out and utterly exhausted now that my mission was fulfilled. I wanted nothing but my bed and silence. Matty received me with sour looks and the grim pursed mouth that spelt disapproval. "You have wanted to be ill for weeks," she said. "Now that we are here, in a strange lodging, with no comforts, you decide to do so. Very well, I'll not answer for the consequences."

"No one asks you to," I said, turning my face to the wall. "For God's sake, if I want to, let me sleep, or die."

Two days later Lord Hopton was defeated outside Torrington, and the whole Western army in full retreat across the Tamar. It concerned me little, lying in that lodging at Penryn with a high fever. On the twenty-fifth of February Fairfax had marched and taken Launceston, and on the second of March had crossed the moors to Bodmin.

That night the Prince of Wales, with his council, set sail in the frigate *Phoenix*—and the war in the west was over...

The day Lord Hopton signed the treaty in Truro with General Fairfax, my brother-in-law, Jonathan Rashleigh, by permission of the Parliament, came down to Penryn to fetch me back to Menabilly. The streets were lined with soldiers, not ours, but theirs, and the whole route from Truro to St. Austell bore signs of surrender and defeat. I sat with stony face, looking out of the curtains of my litter, while Jonathan Rashleigh rode by my side, his shoulders bowed, his face set in deep, grim lines.

We did not converse. We had no words to say. We crossed St. Blazey's bridge and Jonathan handed his pass to the rebel sentry at the post, who stared at us with insolence and then jerked his head and let us pass. They were everywhere. In the road, in the cottage doors at Tywardreath, at the barrier, at the foot of Polmear hill. This was our future then, forevermore, to ask, in deep humility, if we might travel our own roads. That it should be so worried me no longer, for my days of journeying were over. I was returning to Menabilly to be no longer a camp follower, no longer a lady of the drum, but plain Honor Harris, a cripple on her back. And it did not matter to me, I did not care. For Richard Grenvile had escaped to France.

Twenty-Eight

*D*EFEAT, AND THE AFTERMATH OF WAR... NOT PLEASANT for the losers. God knows that we endure it still and I write in the autumn of 1653—but in the year '46 we were new to defeat and had not yet begun to learn our lesson. It was, I think, the loss of freedom that hit the Cornish hardest. We had been used, for generations, to minding our own affairs, and each man living after his fashion. Landlords were fair and usually well liked, with tenant and labourer living in amity together. We had our local disagreements, as every man with his neighbour, and our family feuds, but no body of persons had ever before interfered with our way of living, nor given us commands. Now all was changed. Our orders came to us from Whitehall, and a Cornish County Committee, way up in London, sat in judgement upon us. We could no longer pass our own measures and decide by local consultation what was suited to each town and village. The County Committee made our decisions for us.

Their first action was to demand a weekly payment from the people of Cornwall to the revenue, and this weekly assessment was rated so high that it was impossible to find the money, for the ravages of war had stripped the country bare. Their next move was to sequester the estate of every landlord who had fought for the King. Because the County Committee had not the time nor the persons to administer these estates, the owners were allowed to dwell there, if they so desired, but pay to the Committee, month by month, the full and total value of the property. This crippling injunction was made the harder because the estates were assessed at the value they had held before the war, and now that most of them were fallen into ruin through the fighting, it would take generations before the land gave a return once more.

A host of petty officials who were paid fixed salaries by the Parliament, and were the only men at these times to have their pockets well lined, came down from Whitehall to collect the sums due to the County Committee; and these agents were found in every town and borough, forming themselves in their turns into committees and subcommittees, so that no man could buy as little as a loaf of bread without first going cap in hand to one of these fellows and signing his name to a piece of paper. Besides these civil employees of the Parliament, we had the military to contend with, and whosoever should wish to pass from one village to another must first have a pass from the officer in charge, and then his motives questioned, his family history gone into, detail for detail, and as likely as not he would find himself arrested for delinquency at the end of it.

I truly believe that Cornwall was, in the first summer of '46, the most wretched county in the kingdom. The harvest was bad, another bitter blow to landlord and labourer alike, and the price of wheat immediately rose to fantastic prices. The price of tin, on the contrary, fell low, and many mines closed down on this account. Poverty and sickness were rife by the autumn, and our old enemy the plague appeared, killing great numbers in St. Ives and in the western districts. Another burden was the care of the many wounded and disabled soldiers, who, half naked and half starved, roamed the villages begging for charity. There was no single man or woman or little child who benefited, in any way, by this new handling of affairs by Parliament, and the only ones to live well were those Whitehall agents, who poked their noses into our affairs from dawn till dusk, and their wealthy masters, the big Parliamentary landlords. We had grumbled in the old days at the high taxes of the King, but the taxes were intermittent. Now they were continuous. Salt, meat, starch, lead, iron—all came under the control of Parliament, and the poor man had to pay accordingly.

What happened upcountry I cannot say—I speak for Cornwall. No news came to us much beyond the Tamar. If living was hard, leisure was equally restricted. The Puritans had the upper hand of us. No man must be seen out of doors upon a Sunday, unless he were bound for church. Dancing was forbidden—not that many had the heart to dance, but young-sters have light hearts and lighter feet—and any game of chance or village festival was frowned upon. Gaiety meant licence, and licence spelt the abomination of the Lord. I often thought how Temperance Sawle would have rejoiced in the brave new world, for all her Royalist traditions, but poor Temperance fell an early victim to the plague.

The one glory of that most dismal year of '46 was the gallant, though, alas, so useless, holding of Pendennis Castle for the King through five long months of siege. The rest of us were long conquered and subdued, caught fast in the meshes of Whitehall, while Pendennis still defied the enemy. Their commander was Jack Arundell, who had been in the old days a close friend as well as kinsman to the Grenviles, and Sir John Digby was his second-in-command. My own brother Robin was made a major-general under him. It gave us, I think, some last measure of pride in our defeat that this little body of men, with no hope of rescue and scarce a boatload of provisions, should fly the King's flag from March the second until August the seventeenth, and that even then they wished to blow themselves and the whole garrison to eternity rather than surrender. But starvation and sickness had made weaklings of the men, and for their sakes only did Jack Arundell haul down his flag. Even the enemy respected their courage, and the garrison were permitted to march out, so Robin told us afterwards, with the full honours of war, drums beating, colours flying, trumpets sounding… Yes, we have had our moments, here in Cornwall… When they surrendered, though, our last hopes vanished, and there was nothing now to do but sigh and look into the black well of the future.

My brother-in-law, Jonathan Rashleigh, like the rest of the Royalist landlords, had his lands sequestered by the County Committee and was told, when he went down to Truro in June, that he must pay a fine of some one thousand and eighty pounds to the Committee before he could redeem them. His losses, after the '44 campaign, were already above eight thousand, but there was nothing for it but to bow his head to the victors and agree to pay the ransom during the years to come. He might have quitted the country and gone to France, as many of our neighbours did, but the ties of his own soil were too strong, and in July, broken and dispirited, he took the National Covenant, by which he vowed never again to take arms against the Parliament. This bitter blow to his pride, self-inflicted though it was, did not satisfy the committee, and shortly afterwards he was summoned to London and ordered to remain there, nor to return to Cornwall until his full fine was paid. So yet another home was broken, and we at Menabilly tasted the full flavour of defeat. He left us, one day in September, when the last of the poor harvest had been gathered in, looking a good ten years older than his five-and-fifty years, and I knew then, watching his eyes, how loss of freedom can so blight the human soul that a man cares no longer if he lives or dies.

It remained for Mary, my poor sister, and John, his son, so to husband his estate that the debt could month by month be paid, but we well knew that it might take years, even the remainder of his life. His last words to me, before he went to London, were kind and deeply generous. "Menabilly is your home," he said, "for as long a time as you should so desire it. We are, one and all, sufferers in this misfortune. Guard your sister for me, share her troubles. And help John, I pray you. You have a wiser head than all I leave behind."

A wiser head... I doubted it. It needed a pettifogging mind, with every low lawyer's trick at the finger's end, to break even with the County Committee and the paid agents of the Parliament. There was none to help us. My brother Robin, after the surrender of Pendennis, had gone to Radford to my brother Jo, who was in much the same straits as ourselves, while Peter Courtney, loathing inactivity, left the West Country altogether, and the next we heard from him was that he had gone abroad to join the Prince of Wales. Many young men followed this example—living was good at the French court. I think, had they loved their homes better, they would have stayed behind and shared the burdens of defeat with their womenfolk.

Alice never spoke a word of blame, but I think her heart broke when we heard that he had gone... It was strange, at first, to watch John and Frank Penrose work in the fields side by side with the tenants, for every hand was needed if the land was to be tilled entirely and yield a full return. Even our womenfolk went out at harvesting, Mary herself, and Alice and Elizabeth, while the children, thinking it fine sport, helped to carry the corn. Left to ourselves, we would have soon grown reconciled and even well content with our labours, but the Parliament agents were forever coming to spy upon us, to question us on this and that, to count the sheep and cattle, to reckon, it almost seemed, each ear of corn, and nothing must be gathered, nothing spent, nothing distributed amongst ourselves, but all laid before the smug, well-satisfied officials in Fowey town, who held their licence from the Parliament. The Parliament... The Parliament... From day to day the word rang in our ears. The Parliament decrees that produce shall be brought to market only upon a Tuesday... The Parliament has ordered that all fairs shall henceforth be discontinued... The Parliament warns every inhabitant within the above-prescribed area that no one, save by permission, shall walk abroad one hour after sunset... The Parliament warns each householder that every dwelling will be searched each week for concealed firearms, weapons, and ammunition, from this day forward, and any holder of the same shall be immediately imprisoned...

"The Parliament," said John Rashleigh wearily, "decrees that no man may breathe God's air, save by a special licence, and then one hour in every other day. My God, Honor, no man can stand this long."

"You forget," I said, "that Cornwall is only one portion of the kingdom. The whole of England, before long, will suffer the same fate."

"They will not, they cannot, endure it," he said.

"What is their alternative? The King is virtually a prisoner. The party with the most money and the strongest army rules the country. For those who share their views life is doubtless very pleasant."

"No one can share their views and call his soul their own."

"There you are wrong. It is merely a matter of being accommodating and shaking hands with the right people. Lord Robartes lives in great comfort at Lanhydrock. The Treffrys—being related to Hugh Peters and Jack Trefusis—live very well at Place. If you chose to follow their example and truckle to the Parliament, doubtless you would find life here at Menabilly so much the easier."

He stared at me suspiciously. "Would you have me go to them and fawn, while my father lives a pauper up in London, watched every moment of his day? I would sooner die."

I knew he would sooner die, and loved him for it. Dear John, you might have had more years beside your Joan and be alive today, had you spared yourself and your poor health in those first few months of aftermath... I watched him toil, and the women, too, and there was little I could do to help but figure the accounts, an unpaid clerk with smudgy fingers, and tot up the debts we owed on quarter days. I did not suffer as the Rashleighs did, pride being, I believe, a quality long lost to me, and I was sad only in their sadness. To see Alice gazing wistfully from a window brought a pain to my heart, and when Mary read a letter from her Jonathan, deep shadows beneath her eyes, I think I hated the Parliament every whit as much as they did.

But that first year of defeat was, in some queer fashion, quiet and peaceful to me who bore no burden on my shoulders. Danger was no more. Armies were disbanded. The strain of war was lifted. The man I loved was safe across the sea, in France, and then in Italy, in the company of his son, and now and then I would have word of him, from some foreign city, in good heart and spirits, and missing me, it would seem, not at all. He talked of going to fight the Turks with great enthusiasm, as if, I thought with a shrug of my shoulder, he had not had enough of fighting after three hard years of civil war. "Doubtless," he wrote, "you find your days monotonous in Cornwall." Doubtless I did. To women who have known close siege and stern privation, monotony can be a pleasant thing... A wanderer for so many months, it was restful to find a home at last and to share it with people whom I loved, even if we were all companions in defeat. God bless the Rashleighs, who permitted me those months at Menabilly. The house was bare and shorn of its former glory, but at least I had a room to call my own. The Parliament could strip the place of its possessions, take the sheep and cattle, glean the harvest, but they could not take from me, nor from the Rashleighs, the beauty that we looked on every day. The devastation of the gardens was forgotten when the primroses came in spring, and the young green-budded trees. We, the defeated, could still listen to the birds on a May morning, and watch the clumsy cuckoo wing his way to the little wood beside the Gribbin Hill. The Gribbin Hill... I watched it, from my chair upon the causeway, in every mood from winter to midsummer. I have seen the shadows creep on an autumn afternoon from the deep Pridmouth Valley to the summit of the hill, and there stay a moment, waiting on the sun.

I have seen, too, the white sea mists of early summer turn the hill to fantasy, so that it becomes, in a single second, a ghost land of enchantment, with no sound coming but the wash of breakers on the hidden beach, where, at high noon, the children gather cowrie shells. Dark moods, too, of bleak November, when the rain sweeps in a curtain from the southwest. But quietest of all, the evenings of late summer, when the sun has set, and the moon has not yet risen, but the dew is heavy in the long grass.

The sea is very white and still, without a breath upon it, and only a single thread of wash upon the covered Cannis Rock. The jackdaws fly homeward to their nests in the warren. The sheep crop the short turf, before they, too, rub together beneath the stone wall by the winnowing place. Dusk comes slowly to the Gribbin Hill, the woods turn black, and suddenly, with stealthy pad, a fox creeps from the trees in the thistle park and stands watching me, his ears pricked... Then his brush twitches and he is gone, for here is Matty tapping along the causeway to bring me home; and another day is over. Yes, Richard, there is comfort in monotony...

I return to Menabilly to find all have gone to bed and the candles extinguished in the gallery. Matty carries me upstairs, and as she brushes my hair and ties the curling rags I think I am almost happy. A year has come and gone, and though we are defeated, we live, we still survive. I am lonely, yes, but that has been my portion since I turned eighteen. And loneliness has compensations. Better to live inwardly alone than together in constant fear. And as I think thus, my curl rag in my hand, I see Matty's round face looking at me from the mirror opposite.

"There were strange rumours in Fowey today," she says quietly.

"What rumours, Matty? There are always rumours."

She moistens a rag with her tongue, then whips it round a curl. "Our men are creeping back," she murmurs, "first one, then two, then three. Those who fled to France a year ago."

I rub some lotion on my hands and face.

"Why should they return? They can do nothing."

"Not alone, but if they band together, in secret, one with another..."

I sit still, my hands in my lap, and suddenly I remember a phrase in the last letter that came from Italy.

"You may hear from me," he said, "before the summer closes, by a different route." I thought him to mean he was going to fight the Turks.

"Do they mention names?" I say to Matty, and for the first time for many months a little seed of anxiety and fear springs to my heart. She does not answer for a moment; she is busy with a curl. Then at last she speaks, her voice low and hushed.

"They talk of a great leader," she says, "landing in secret at Plymouth from the Continent. He wore a dark wig, they said, to disguise his colouring. But they did not mention names..."

A bat brushes itself against my windows, lost and frightened, and close to the house an owl shrieks in warning. And it seemed to me, that moment, that the bat was no airey mouse of midsummer, but the scared symbol of all hunted things.

Twenty-Nine

RUMOURS. ALWAYS RUMOURS. NEVER ANYTHING OF certainty. This was our portion during the winter of '47 to '48. So strict was the Parliamentary hold on news that nothing but the bare official statements were given to us down in Cornwall, and these had no value, being simply what Whitehall thought good for us to know.

So the whispers started, handed from one to the other, and when the whispers came to us fifth-hand we had to sift the welter of extravagance to find the seed of truth. The Royalists were arming. This was the firm base of all the allegations. Weapons were being smuggled into the country from France, and places of concealment were found for them. Gentlemen were meeting in one another's houses. The labourers were conversing together in the field. A fellow at a street corner would beckon to another, for the purpose, it would seem, of discussing market prices; there would be a question, a swift answer, and then the two would separate, but information had been passed, and another link forged.

Outside the parish church of Tywardreath would stand a Parliamentary soldier leaning on his musket, while the busybody agent who had beneath his arm a fold of documents listing each member of the parish and his private affairs gave him good morning; and while he did so, the old sexton, with his back turned, prepared a new grave, not for a corpse this time, but for weapons. They could have told a tale, those burial grounds of Cornwall. Cold steel beneath the green turf and the daisies, locked muskets in the dark family vaults. Let a fellow climb to repair his cottage roof against the rains of winter, and he will pause an instant, and glance over his shoulder, and, thrusting his hand under the thatch, feel for the sharp edge of a sword. These would be Matty's tales. Mary would come to me with a letter from Jonathan in London. "Fighting is likely to start again at any moment," would be his guarded words. "Discontent is rife, even here, against our masters. Many Londoners who fought in opposition to the King would swear loyalty to him now. I can say no more than this. Bid John have a care whom he meets and where he goes. Remember, I am bound to my oath. If we meddle in these matters, he and I will answer for it with our lives."

Mary would fold the letter anxiously and place it in her gown. "What does it mean?" she would say. "What matters does he refer to?" And to this there could be one answer only. The Royalists were rising. Names that had not been spoken for two years were now whispered by cautious tongues. Trelawney... Trevannion...

Arundell... Bassett... Grenvile. Yes, above all, Grenvile.

He had been seen at Stowe, said one. Nay, that was false; it was not Stowe, but at his sister's house near Bideford. The Isle of Wight, said another. The Red Fox was gone to Carisbrooke to take secret council of the King. He had not come to the West Country. He had been seen in Scotland. He had been spoken to in Ireland. Sir Richard Grenvile was returned. Sir Richard Grenvile was in Cornwall...

I made myself deaf to these tales. For once too often, in my life, I had had a bellyful of rumours. Yet it was strange no letter came any more from Italy, or from France...

John Rashleigh kept silent on these matters. His father had bidden him not to meddle, but to work, night and day at the husbanding of the estate, so that the groaning debt to Parliament be paid. But I could guess his thoughts. If there were in truth a rising and the prince landed, and Cornwall was freed once more, there would be no debt to pay. If the Trelawneys were a party to the plan, and the Trevannions also, and all those in the county who swore loyalty to the King, in secret, then was it not something like cowardice, something like shame, for a Rashleigh to remain outside the company? Poor John. He was often restless and sharp-tempered, those first weeks of spring, after ploughing was done. And Joan was not with us to encourage him, for her twin boys, born the year before, were sickly, and she was with them and the elder children, at Mothercombe in Devon. Then Jonathan fell ill up in London, and though he asked permission of the Parliament to return to Cornwall, they would not grant it, so he sent for Mary and she went to him. Alice was the next to leave. Peter wrote to her from France, desiring that she should take the children to Trethurfe, his home, which was—so he had heard—in sad state of repair, and would she go there, now spring was at hand, and see what could be done. She went the first day of March, and it suddenly became strangely quiet at Menabilly. I had been used so long to children's voices, that now to be without them, and the sound of Alice's voice calling to them, and the rustle of Mary's gown, made me more solitary than usual, even a little sad. There was no one but John now for company, and I wondered what we should make of it together, he and I, through the long evenings.

"I have half a mind," he said to me, the third day we sat together, "to leave Menabilly in your care and go to Mothercombe."

"I'll tell no tales of you if you do," I said to him.

"I do not like to go against my father's wishes," he admitted, "but it's over six months now since I have seen Joan and the children, and not a word comes to us here of what is passing in the country. Only that the war has broken out again. Fighting in places as far apart as Wales and the Eastern Counties. I tell you, Honor, I am sick of inactivity. For very little I would take horse and ride to Wales."

"No need to ride to Wales," I said quietly, "when there is likely to be a rising in your own county."

He glanced at the half-open door of the gallery. A queer, instinctive move, unnecessary when the few servants that we had could all be trusted. Yet since we had been ruled by Parliament this gesture would be force of habit. "Have you heard anything?" he said guardedly. "Some word of truth, I mean, not idle rumour?"

"Nothing," I answered, "beyond what you hear yourself."

"I thought perhaps Sir Richard..." he began, but I shook my head.

"Since last year," I said, "rumour has it that he has been hiding in the country. I've had no message."

He sighed, and glanced once more towards the door.

"If only," he said, "I could be certain what to do. If there should be a rising and I took no part in it, how lacking in loyalty to the King I would seem, and what dishonour it would be to the name of Rashleigh."

"If there should be a rising and it failed," I said, "how damp your prison walls, how uneasy your head upon your shoulders."

He smiled, for all his earnestness. "Trust a woman," he said, "to damp a fellow's ardour."

"Trust a woman," I replied, "to keep war out of her home."

"Do you wish to sit down indefinitely, then, under the rule of Parliament?" he asked.

"Not so. But spit in their faces, before the time is ripe, and we shall find ourselves one and all under their feet forever."

Once again he sighed, rumpling his hair and looking dubious.

"Get yourself permission," I said, "and go to Mothercombe. It's your wife you need and not a rising. But I warn you, once you are in Devon, you may not find it so easy to return."

This warning had been repeated often during the past weeks. Those who had gone into Devon or to Somerset upon their lawful business, bearing a permit from the local Parliamentary official, would find great delay upon the homeward journey, much scrutiny and questioning, and this would be followed by a search for documents or weapons, and possibly a night or more under arrest. We, the defeated, were not the only ones to hear the rumours...

The sheriff of Cornwall at this time was a neighbour, Sir Thomas Herle of Prideaux, near St. Blazey, who, though firm for Parliament, was a just and fair man. He had done all he could to mitigate the heavy fine placed upon the Rashleigh estate, through respect for my brother-in-law, but Whitehall was too strong for his local powers. It was he now, in kindness, who granted John Rashleigh permission to visit his wife at Mothercombe in Devon; so it happened, this fateful spring, that I was, of all our party, the only one remaining at Menabilly. A woman and a cripple—it was not likely that such a one could foster, all alone, a grim rebellion. The Rashleighs had taken the oath. Menabilly was now above suspicion. And though the garrison at Fowey and other harbours on the coast were strengthened, and more troops quartered in the towns and villages, our little neck of land seemed undisturbed. The sheep grazed on the Gribben Hill. The cattle browsed in the beef park. The wheat was sown in eighteen acres. And smoke from a single fire—my own—rose from the Menabilly chimneys. Even the steward's house was desolate, now old John Langdon had been gathered to his fathers, for with the crushing burden on the estate his place had not been filled. His keys, once so important and mysterious, were now in my keeping, and the summerhouse, so sacred to my brother-in-law, had become my routine shelter on a windy afternoon. I had no wish these days to pry into the Rashleigh papers. Most of the books were gone, stored in the house, or packed and sent after him to London. The desk was bare and empty. Cobwebs hung from the walls. Green patches of mould showed upon the ceiling. But the torn matting on the floor still hid the flagstone with the iron ring... I saw a rat once creep from his corner and stare at me a moment with beady, unwinking eyes. A great black spider spun a web from a broken pane of glass in the east window, while ivy, spreading from the ground, thrust a tendril to the sill. A few years more, I thought, and nature would take toll of it all. The stones of the summerhouse would crumble, the nettles force themselves through the floor, and no one would remember the flagstone with the ring upon it, nor the flight of steps, and the earthy, mouldering tunnel. Well, it had served its purpose. Those days would not return.

I looked out towards the sea one day in March, and watched the shadows darken, for an instant, the pale ripple of the water beyond Pridmouth. The clock in the belfry struck four o'clock. Matty had gone to Fowey and should be back by now. I heard a footstep on the path beneath the causeway and called, thinking it was one of the farm labourers returning home who could bear a message for me to the house. The footsteps ceased, but there came no word in answer.

I called again, and this time I heard a rustle in the under-growth. My friend, the fox, perhaps, was out on his prowl. Then I saw a hand fasten to the sill and cling there for an instant, gripping for support. But the walls of the summerhouse were smooth, giving no foothold, and in a second the hand had slipped and was gone.

Someone was playing spy upon me... If one of the long-nosed Parliamentary agents who spent their days scaring the wits out of the simple country people wished to try the game on me, he would receive short measure.

"If anyone wishes to speak with Mr. Rashleigh, he is from home," I called loudly. "There is no one but myself in charge at Menabilly. Mistress Honor Harris, at your service."

I waited a moment, my eye still on the window, and then a shadow falling suddenly upon my right shoulder told me there was someone at the door. I whipped round in an instant, my hands on the wheels of my chair, and saw the figure of a man, small and slight, clad in plain dark clothes like a London clerk, with a hat pulled low over his face. He stood watching me, his hand upon the lintel of the door.

"Who are you?" I said. "What do you want?" There was something in his manner which struck a chord... The way he hesitated, standing on one foot, then bit his thumbnail. I groped for the answer, my heart beating, when he whipped his hat from his close black curls, and I saw him smile, tremulous at first, uncertain, until he saw me smile and stretch my arms towards him.

"Dick..." I whispered. He came and knelt by me at once, covering my hand with kisses.

I forgot the intervening years and had in my arms a little frightened boy who gnawed a bone and swore he was a dog and I his mistress. And then, raising his head, I saw he was a boy no longer, but a young man, with hair upon his lip and curls no longer riotous but sleek and close. His voice was low and soft, a man's voice.

"Four years," I said. "Have you grown thus in four small years?"

"I shall be eighteen in two months' time," he answered, smiling. "Have you forgotten? You wrote the first year for my birthday, but never since."

"Writing has not been possible, Dick, these past two years."

I could not take my eyes from him, he was so grown, so altered. Yet that way of watching with dark eyes, wary and suspicious, was the same, and the trick of gnawing at his hand.

"Tell me quickly," I said, "before they come to fetch me from the house, what you are doing here, and why."

He looked at me doubtfully. "I am the first to come, then?" he asked. "My father is not here?"

My heart leapt, but whether in excitement or in fear, I could not tell. In a flash of intuition it seemed that I knew everything. The waiting of the past few months was over. It was all to begin afresh... It was to start again...

"No one is here," I answered, "but yourself. Even the Rashleighs are from home."

"Yes, we knew that," he said. "That is why Menabilly has been chosen."

"Chosen for what?" I asked.

He did not answer. He started his old trick of gnawing at his hand. "They will tell you," he said, blinking his eyelids, "when they come."

"Who are they?" I asked.

"My father, first," he answered, with his eye upon the door, "and Peter Courtney another, and Ambrose Manaton of Trecarrel, and your own brother Robin, and of course my Aunt Gartred."

Gartred... At this I felt like someone who has been ill over-long, or withdrawn from the world, leading another life. There had been rumours enough, God knows, in southeast Cornwall, to stun the senses, but none so formidable as fell now upon my ears.

"I think it best," I said slowly, "if you tell me what has happened since you came to England."

He rose then from his knees and, dusting the dirt from his clothes with a fastidious hand, swept a place upon the windowsill to sit. "We left Italy last autumn," he said, "and came first of all to London. My father was disguised as a Dutch merchant, and I as his secretary. Since then we have travelled England from south to north, outwardly as foreign men of business, secretly as agents for the Prince. At Christmas we crossed the Tamar into Cornwall and went first of all to Stowe. My aunt is dead, you know, and no one was there but the steward, and my cousin Bunny, and the others. My father made himself known to the steward, and since then many secret meetings have been held throughout the county. From Stowe it is but a step to Bideford and Orley Court. There were found my aunt Gartred, who, having fallen out with her Parliamentary friends, was hot to join us, and your brother Robin also."

Truly the world had passed me by at Menabilly. The Parliament had one grace to its credit, that the stoppage of news stopped gossip also.

"I did not know," I said, "that my brother Robin lived at Bideford."

Dick shrugged his shoulders. "He and my aunt are very thick," he answered. "I understand your brother has made himself her bailiff. She owns land, does she not, that belonged to your eldest brother who is dead?"

Yes, they could have met again that way. The ground upon which Lanrest had stood, the fields below the Mill at Lametton. Why should I blame Robin, grown weary and idle in defeat?

"And so?" I asked.

"And so the plans matured, the clans gathered. They are all in it, you know, from east to west, the length and breadth of Cornwall. The Trelawneys, the Trevannions, the Bassetts, the Arundells. And now the time draws near. The muskets are being loaded and the swords sharpened. You will have a front seat at the slaughter."

There was a strange note of bitterness in his soft voice, and I saw him clench his hands upon the sill.

"And you?" I asked. "Are you not excited at the prospect? Are you not happy to be one of them?"

He did not answer for a moment, and when he did I saw his eyes look large and black in his pale face, even as they had done as a boy four years before.

"I tell you one thing, Honor," he said passionately. "I would give all I possess in the world, which is precious little, to be out of it."

The force with which he spoke shocked me for an instant, but I took care that he should not guess it.

"Why so?" I asked. "Have you no faith that they will succeed?"

"Faith?" he said wearily. "I have no faith in anything. I begged him to let me stay in Italy, where I was content, after my own fashion, but he would not let me. I found that I could paint, Honor. I wished to make painting my trade. I had friends, too, fellows of my age, for whom I felt affection. But no. Painting was womanish, a pastime fit for foreigners. My friends were womanish, too, and would degrade me. If I wished to live, if I hoped to have a penny to my name, I must follow him, do his bidding, ape his ways, grow like my Grenvile cousins. God in heaven, how I have come to loathe the very name of Grenvile!"

Eighteen, but he had not changed. Eighteen, but he was still fourteen. This was the little boy who had sobbed his hatred of his father.

"And your mother?" I asked gently.

He shrugged his shoulders. "Yes, I have seen her," he said listlessly, "but it's too late now to make amends. She cares nothing for me. She has other interests. Four years ago she would have loved me still. Not now. It's too late. His fault. Always his fault."

"Perhaps," I said, "when—when this present business is concluded, you will be free. I will speak for you. I will ask that you may return to Italy, to your painting, to your friends."

He picked at the fringe of his coat with his long slim hands—too long, I thought, too finely slim for a Grenvile.

"There will be fighting," he said slowly, "men killing one another for no purpose, save to spill blood. Always to spill blood…"

It was growing dim in the summerhouse, and still I had heard no more about their plans. The fear that I read in his eyes found an echo in my heart, and the old strain and anxiety was with me once again. "When did you leave Bideford?" I asked.

"Two days ago," he answered. "Those were my orders. We were to proceed separately, each by a different route. Lady Courtney has gone to Trethurfe, I presume?"

"She went at the beginning of the month."

"So Peter intended. It was part of the ruse, you see, for emptying the house. Peter has been in Cornwall and amongst us since before Christmas."

Another prey for Gartred? A second bailiff to attend on Orley Court? And Alice here, with wan cheeks, and chin upon her hand, at an open window… Richard did not choose his serviteurs for kindness.

"Mrs. Rashleigh was inveigled up to London for the same purpose," said Dick. "The scheme has been cunningly planned, like all schemes of my father's. And the last cast of all, to rid the house of John, was quite in keeping with his character."

"John went of his own accord," I answered, "to see his wife at Mothercombe in Devon."

"Aye, but he had a message first," said Dick, "a scrap of paper, passed to him in Fowey, saying that his wife was overfond of a neighbour, living in her father's house. I know, because I saw my father pen the letter, laughing as he did so, with aunt Gartred at his back."

I was silent at that. Goddamn them both, I thought, for cruelty. And I knew Richard's answer, even as I accused him in my thoughts. "Any means to secure the end that I desire."

Well, what was to come was no affair of mine. The house was empty. Let them make of it a place of assignation. I could not stop them. Let Menabilly become, in one brief hour, the headquarters of the Royalist rising. Whether they succeeded or failed was not my business. "Did your father," I said, "send any word to me? Did he know that I was here?"

Dick stared at me blankly for a moment, as though I were in truth the half-wit I now believed myself to be.

"Why, yes, of course," he said. "That is why he picked on Menabilly rather than on Caerhayes. There was no woman at Caerhayes to give him comfort."

"Does your father," I said, "still need comfort after two long years in Italy?"

"It depends," he answered, "what you intend by comfort. I never saw my father hold converse with Italian women. It might have made him better-tempered if he had."

I saw Richard, in my mind's eye, pen in hand, with a map of Cornwall spread on a table before him. And dotted upon the map were the houses by the coast that offered sanctuary. Trelawne... too deeply wooded. Penrice... not close enough to the sea. Caerhayes... yes, good landing ground for troops, but not a single Miss Trevannion. Menabilly... with a beach, and a hiding place, and an old love into the bargain, who had shared his life before and might be induced, even now, after long silence, to smile on him a moment after supper. And the pen would make a circle round the name of Menabilly. So I was become cynic in defeat. The rule of Parliament had taught me a lesson. But as I sat there, watching Dick and thinking how little he resembled his father, I knew that all my anger was but a piece of bluff deceiving no one, not even my harder self, and that there was nothing I wanted in the world so much as to play hostess once more to Richard, by candlelight, and to live again that life of strain and folly, anguish and enchantment.

Thirty

*I*T FELL ON ME TO WARN THE SERVANTS, I SUMMONED each one to my chamber in turn. "We are entering upon dangerous days," I said to them. "Things will pass here at Menabilly which you will not see and will not hear. Visitors will come and go. Ask no questions. Seek no answer. I believe you are, one and all, faithful subjects of His Majesty?"

This was sworn upon the Book of Common Prayer.

"One incautious word that leaves this house," I said, "and your master up in London will lose his life, and ourselves also, in all probability. That is all I have to say. See that there is clean linen on the beds, and sufficient food for guests. But be deaf and dumb and blind to those who come here."

It was on Matty's advice that I took them thus into my confidence. "Each one can be trusted," she said, "but a word of faith from you will bind them together, and not all the agents in the West Country will make them blab."

The household had lived sparsely since the siege of '44, and there were few comforts for our prospective visitors. No hangings to the walls, no carpets on the floors in the upper chambers. Straw mattresses in place of beds. They must make what shift they could, and be grateful.

Peter Courtney was the first to come. No secrecy for him. He flaunted openly his pretended return from France, dining with the Treffrys at Place upon the way and loudly announcing desire to see his children. Gone to Trethurfe? But all his belongings were at Menabilly. Alice had misunderstood his letter...

Nothing wan or pale about Peter. He wore a velvet coat that must have cost a fortune. Poor Alice and her dowry...

"You might," I said to him, "have sent her a whisper of your safe return. She would have kept it secret."

He shrugged a careless shoulder. "A wife can be a cursed appendage in times like these," he said, "when a man must live from day to day, from hand to mouth. To tell the truth, Honor, I am so plagued with debts that one glimpse of her reproachful eyes would drive me crazy."

"You look well on it," I said. "I doubt if your conscience worries you unduly." He winked, his tongue in his cheek, and I thought how the looks that I had once admired were coarsened now with licence and good living. Too much French wine, too little exercise.

"And what are your plans," I asked, "when Parliament is overthrown?"

Once again he shrugged his shoulders. "I shall never settle at Trethurfe," he said. "Alice can live there if she pleases. As for myself, why, war has made me restless."

He whistled under his breath and strolled towards the window. The aftermath of war, the legacy of losing it. Another marriage in the melting pot...

The next to come was Bunny Grenvile. Bunny, at seventeen, already head and shoulders taller than his cousin Dick. Bunny with snub nose and freckles. Bunny with eager, questing eyes, and a map of the coast under his arm. "Where are the beaches? Where are the landing places? No, I want no refreshment; I have work to do. I want to see the ground." And he was off to the Gribben, a hound to scent, another budding soldier, like his brother Jack.

"You see," said Dick cynically, his black eyes fastened on me, "how all Grenvile men but me are bred with a nose for blood? You despise me, don't you, because I do not go with him?"

"No, Dick," I answered gently.

"Ah, but you will in time. Bunny will win your affection, as he has won my father's. Bunny has courage. Bunny has guts. Poor Dick has neither. He is only fit for painting, like a woman."

He threw himself on his back upon the couch, staring upward at the ceiling. And this, too, I thought, has to be contended with. The demon jealousy, sapping his strength. The wish to excel, the wish to shine before his father. His father whom he pretended to detest. Our third arrival was Mr. Ambrose Manaton. A long familiar name to me, for my family of Harris had for generations past had lawsuits with the Manatons, respecting that same property of theirs, Trecarrel. What it was all about I could not say, but I know my father never spoke to any of them. There was an Ambrose Manaton who stood for Parliament before the war at Launceston. This man was his son. He was, I suppose, a few years older than Peter Courtney, some four-and-thirty years. Sleek and suave, with a certain latent charm. He wore his own fair hair, curling to his shoulders. Thinking it best spoken and so dismissed forever, I plunged into the family dispute as soon as I set eyes on him. "Our families," I said, "have waged a private war for generations. Something to do with property. Since I am the youngest daughter, you are safe with me. I can lay claim to nothing."

"I could not refuse so fair a pleader if you did," he answered.

I considered him thoughtfully as he kissed my hand. Too ready with his compliment, too easy with his smile. What exactly, I wondered, was his part in this campaign? I had not heard of him ever as a soldier. Money? Property? Those lands at Trecarrel and at Southill that my father could not claim? Richard had no doubt assessed the value. A Royalist rising cannot be conducted without funds. Did Ambrose Manaton, then, hold the purse? I wondered what had induced him to risk his life and fortune. He gave me the clue a moment afterwards.

"Mrs. Denys has not yet arrived?"

"Not yet. You know her well?"

"We found ourselves near neighbours in north Cornwall and north Devon." The tone was easy, the smile confident. Oh, Richard, my love of little scruple. So Gartred was the bait to catch the tiger.

What in the name of thunder had been going on all these long winter months at Bideford? I could imagine, with Gartred playing hostess. Well, I was hostess now at Menabilly. And the straw mattresses upstairs would be hard cheer after the feather beds of Orley Court. "My brother, Major General Harris, acts as bailiff to Mrs. Denys, so I understand?"

"Why, yes, something of the sort," said Ambrose Manaton. He studied the toe of his boot. His voice was a shade overcasual.

"Have you seen your brother lately?" he asked.

"Not for two years. Not since Pendennis fell."

"You will see a change in him then. His nerves have gone to pieces. The result of the siege, no doubt."

Robin never had a nerve in his body. Robin rode to battle with a falcon on his wrist. If Robin was changed, it was not the fault of five months' siege...

They came together shortly before dark. I was alone in the gallery to receive them. The rule of Parliament had fallen light on Gartred. She was, I think, a little fuller in the bosom, but it became her well. And, chancing fate, she had let nature do its damndest with her hair, which was no longer gleaming gold, but streaked with silver white, making her look more lovely and more frail.

She tossed her cloak to Robin as she came into the room, proclaiming in that first careless gesture all that I cared to know of their relationship. The years slipped backward in a flash, and she was a bride of twenty-three, already tired of Kit, her slave and bondsman, who had not the strength of will to play the master.

It might have been Kit once again, standing there in the gallery at Menabilly, with a dog's look of adoration in his eyes.

But Ambrose Manaton was right. There was not only adoration in Robin's eyes. There was strain too, doubt, anxiety. And the heavy jowls and puffy cheeks betrayed the easy drinker. Defeat and Gartred had taken toll, then, of my brother.

"We seem fated, you and I, to come together at moments of great crisis," I said to Gartred. "Do you still play piquet?"

I saw Robin look from one to the other of us, mystified, but Gartred smiled, drawing off her lace gloves.

"Piquet is out of fashion," she answered. "Dice is a later craze, but must be done in secret, since all games of chance are frowned upon by Parliament."

"I shall not join you, then," I said. "You will have to play with Robin or with Ambrose Manaton."

Her glance at me was swift, but I let it pass over my head.

"I have at least the consolation," she said, "of knowing that for once we shall not play in opposition. We are all partners on a winning side."

"Are we?" I said. It was only four years since she had come here as a spy for Lord Robartes.

"If you doubt my loyalty," said Gartred, "you must tell Richard when he comes. But it is rather late to make amends. I know all the secrets." She smiled again, and as I looked at her I felt like a knight of old saluting his opponent before combat.

"I have put you," I said, "in the long chamber overhead, which Alice has with her children when she is home."

"Thank you," she said.

"Robin is on your left," I said, "and Ambrose Manaton upon your right, at the small bedroom at the stairs' head. With two strong men to guard you, I think it hardly likely you'll be nervous."

She gave not a flicker of the eyelid but, turning to Robin, gave him some commands about her baggage. He went at once to obey her, like a servant.

"It has been fortunate for you," I said, "that the menfolk of my breed have proved accommodating."

"It would be more fortunate still," she answered, "if they could be at the same time less possessive."

"A family failing," I replied, "like the motto of our house, 'What we have, we hold.'"

She looked at me a moment thoughtfully. "It is a strange power," she said, "this magnetism that you have for Richard. I give you full credit."

I bowed to her from my chair. "Give me no credit, Gartred," I answered. "Menabilly is but a name upon a map that will do as well as any other. An empty house, a nearby shore."

"And a secret hiding place into the bargain," she said shrewdly.

But now it was my time to smile.

"The Mint had the silver long ago," I said, "and what was left has gone to swell the Parliament exchequer. What are you playing for this time, Gartred?"

She did not answer for a moment, but I saw her cat's eyes watching Robin's shadow in the hall.

"My daughters are grown up," she said. "Orley Court becomes a burden. Perhaps I would like a third husband and security."

Which my brother could not give her, I thought, but which a man some fifteen years younger than herself, with lands and

fortune, might be pleased to do. Mrs. Harris... Mrs. Denys...
Mrs. Manaton? "You broke one man in my family," I said.
"Take care that you do not seek to break another."

"You think you can prevent me?"

"Not I. You may do as you please. I only give you warning."

"Warning of what?"

"You will never play fast and loose with Robin, as you did
with Kit. Robin would be capable of murder."

She stared at me a moment, uncomprehending. And then
my brother came into the room.

I thought that night of the Royalist rising which had planned
to kindle Cornwall from east to west, while all the time there
was enough material for explosive purposes gathered beneath
the roof of Menabilly to set light to the whole country.

We made strange company for dinner. Gartred, her silver
hair bejewelled, at the head of the table, and those two men on
either side of her, my brother with hand ever reaching to the
decanter, his eyes feasting on her face, while Ambrose Manaton,
cool and self-possessed, kept up a flow of conversation in her
right ear, excluding Robin, about the corrupt practices of
Parliament that made me suspect he must have a share in it,
from knowing so much detail. On my left sat Peter Courtney,
who from time to time caught Gartred's eye and smiled in
knowing fashion. But as he did the same to the serving maid
who passed his place, and to me when I chanced to glance his
way, I guessed it to be habit rather than conspiracy. I knew
my Peter. Dick glowered in the centre, throwing black looks
towards his cousin opposite, as he rattled on about the letters he
had received from his brother Jack, who was grown so high in
favour with the Prince of Wales in France that they were never
parted. And as I looked at each in turn, seeing they were served
with food and wine, playing the hostess in this house that was
not mine, frowned upon, no doubt, by the ghost of old John

Rashleigh, I thought, with some misgiving that, had Richard sought his hardest in the county, he could not have found six people more likely to fall out and disagree than those who sat around the table now.

Gartred, his sister, had never wished him well. Robin, my brother, had disobeyed his orders in the past. Peter Courtney was one of those who had muttered at his leadership. Dick, his son, feared and hated him. Ambrose Manaton was an unknown quantity, and Bunny, his nephew, a pawn who could read a map. Were these to be the leaders of the rising? If so, God help poor Cornwall and the Prince of Wales.

"My uncle," Bunny was saying, arranging the salt cellars in the fashion of a fort, "never forgets an injury. He told me once, if a man does him an ill turn he will serve him with a worse one."

He went on to describe some battle of the past, to which no one listened, I think, except Peter, who did so from good nature, but the words Bunny had spoken so lightly, without thinking, rang strangely in my head. "My uncle never forgets an injury."

He must have been injured by all of us, at one time or other, seated at the table now at Menabilly. What a time to choose to pay old scores, Richard, my lover, mocking and malevolent. The eve of a rising, and these six people in it to the hilt.

There was something symbolic in the empty chair beside me.

Then we fell silent, for the door suddenly opened and he stood there, watching us, his hat upon his head, his long cloak hanging from his shoulders. Gone was the auburn hair I loved so well, and the curled wig that fell below his ears gave him a dark, satanic look that matched his smile.

"What a bunch of prizes," he said, "for the sheriff of the duchy if he chose to call. Each one of you a traitor."

They stared at him, blankly, even Gartred, for once, slow

to follow his swift mind. But I saw Dick start and gnaw his fingernails. Then Richard tossed his hat and cloak to the waiting servant in the hall and came to the empty chair at my right side.

"Have you been waiting long?" he said to me.

"Two years and three months," I answered him.

He filled the glass from the decanter at his side.

"In January '46," he said to the company, "I broke a promise to our hostess here. I left her one morning at Werrington, saying I would be back again to breakfast with her. Unfortunately, the Prince of Wales willed otherwise. And I breakfasted instead in Launceston Castle. I propose to make amends for this tomorrow."

He lifted his glass, draining it in one measure, then put out his hand to mine, and held it on the table.

"Thank God," he said, "for a woman who does not give a damn for punctuality."

Thirty-One

*I*T WAS LIKE WERRINGTON ONCE MORE. THE OLD ROUTINE. The old haphazard sharing of our days and nights. He would burst into my chamber as I breakfasted, my toilet undone, my hair in curl rags, while he paced about the room, talking incessantly, touching my brushes, my combs, my bracelets on the table, cursing all the while at some delay in the plans he was proposing. Trevannion was too slow. Trelawney the elder too cautious. And those who were to lead the insurrection farther west had none of them big names; they were all small fry, lacking the right qualities for leadership. "Grose of St. Buryan, Maddern of Penzance, Keigwin of Mousehole," said Richard, "none of them held a higher rank than captain in '46 and have never led troops into action. But we have to use them now. It is a case of *faute de mieux*. The trouble is that I can't be in fifty places at the same time."

Like Werrington once more. A log fire in the dining chamber. A heap of papers scattered on the table, and a large map in the centre. Richard seated in his chair, with Bunny, instead of Jack, at his elbow. The red crosses on the beaches where the invading troops should land. Crinnis... Pentewan... Veryan... The beacons on the headlands to warn the ships at sea. The Gribben... The Dodman... The Nare... My brother

Robin standing by the door, where Roscarrick would have stood. And Peter Courtney, riding into the courtyard, bearing messages from Jonathan Trelawney.

"What news from Talland?"

"All well. They will wait upon our signal. Looe can easily be held. There will be no opposition there to matter."

The messages sifted, one by one. like all defeated peoples, those who had crumbled first in '46 were now the most eager to rebel.

Helston... Penzance... St. Ives... The confidence was supreme. Grenvile, as commander in chief, had but to give the word.

I sat in my chair by the fireside, listening to it all, and I was no longer in the dining chamber at Menabilly, but back at Werrington, at Ottery St. Mary, at Exeter... The same problems, the same arguments, the same doubtings of the commanders, the same swift decisions. Richard's pen pointing to the Scillies. "This will be the main base for the prince's army. No trouble about seizing the islands. Your brother Jack can do it with two men and a boy." And Bunny, grinning, nodded his auburn head.

"Then the main landings to be where we have our strongest hold. A line between here and Falmouth, I should fancy, with St. Mawes the main objective. Hopton has sent me obstructive messages from Guernsey, tearing my proposals to pieces. He can swallow them, for all I care. If he would have his way he would send a driblet here, a driblet there, some score of pissing landings scattered round the whole of Cornwall, in order, so he says, to confuse the enemy. Confuse, my arse. One big punch at a given centre, with us here holding it in strength, and Hopton can land his whole army in four-and-twenty hours..."

The big conferences would be held at night. It was easier then to move about the roads. The Trelawneys from Trelawne,

Sir Charles Trevannion from Caerhayes, the Arundells from Trerice, Sir Arthur Bassett from Tehidy. I would lie in my chamber overhead and hear the drone of voices from the drawing room below and always that clear tone of Richard's, overtopping them all. Was it certain that the French would play? This was the universal doubt, expressed by the whole assembly, that Richard would brush impatiently aside. "Goddamn the French. What the hell does it matter if they don't? We can do without them. Never a Frenchman yet but was not a liability to his own side."

"But," murmured Sir Charles Trevannion, "if we at least had the promise of their support and a token force to assist the Prince in landing, the moral effect upon Parliament would be as valuable as ten divisions put against them."

"Don't you believe it," said Richard. "The French hate fighting on any soil but their own. Show a frog an English pike, and he will show you his backside. Leave the French alone. We won't need them once we hold the Scillies and the Cornish forts. The Mount... Pendennis... St. Mawes... Bunny, where are my notes giving the present disposition of the enemy troops? Now, gentlemen..."

And so it would continue. Midnight, one, two, three o'clock. What hour they went, and what hour he came to bed, I would not know, for exhaustion would lay claim on me long since.

Robin, who had proved his worth in those five weeks at Pendennis, had much responsibility upon his shoulders. The episode of the bridge had been forgotten. Or had it? I would wonder sometimes, when I watched Richard's eyes upon him. Saw him smile for no reason. Saw him tap his pen upon his chin.

"Have you the latest news from Helston?"

"Here, sir. To hand."

"I shall want you to act as deputy for me tomorrow at

Penrose. You can be away two nights; no more. I must have the exact number of men they can put upon the roads between Helston and Penryn."

"Sir… " And I would see Robin hesitate a moment, his eyes drift towards the door leading to the gallery, where Gartred's laugh would suddenly ring loud and clear. Later, his flushed face and bloodshot eye told its own tale.

"Come, Robin," Richard would say curtly after supper, "we must burn the midnight candle once again. Peter has brought me messages in cypher from Penzance, and you are my expert. If I can do with four hours' sleep, so can the rest of you."

Richard, Robin, Peter, Bunny crowded round the table in the dining room, with Dick standing sentinel at the door, watching them wearily, resentfully. Ambrose Manaton standing by the fire, consulting a great sheaf of figures. "All right, Ambrose," Richard would say, "I shan't need your assistance over this problem. Go and talk high finance to the women in the gallery."

And Ambrose Manaton, smiling, bowing his thanks. Walking from the room with a shade too much confidence, humming under his breath.

"Will you be late?" I said to Richard. "H'm… H'm…" he answered absently. "Fetch me that file of papers, Bunny." Then of a sudden, looking up at Dick, "Stand straight, can't you? Don't slop over your feet," he said harshly.

Dick's black eyes blinking, his slim hands clutching at his coat. He would open the door for me to pass through in my chair, and all I could do to give him confidence was to smile and touch his hand. No gallery for me. Three makes poor company. But upstairs to my chamber, knowing that the voices underneath would drone for four hours more. An hour, perhaps, would pass, while I read on my bed, and then the swish of a skirt upon the landing as Gartred passed into her room. Silence.

Then that tell-tale creaking stair. The soft closing of a door. But beneath me in the dining room the voices would drone on till after midnight.

One evening, when the conference broke early and Richard sat with me awhile before retiring, I told him bluntly what I heard.

He laughed, trimming his finger-nails by the open window.

"Have you turned prude, sweetheart, in your midde years?" he said.

"Prudery be damned," I answered. "But my brother hopes to marry her. I know it, from his hints and shy allusions about rebuilding the property at Lanrest."

"Then hope will fail him," replied Richard. "Gartred will never throw herself away upon a penniless soldier. She has other fish to fry, and small blame to her."

"You mean," I asked, "the fish she is in the process of frying at this moment?"

"Why, yes, I suppose so," he answered with a shrug. "Ambrose has a pretty inheritance from his Trefusis mother, besides what he will come into when his father dies. Gartred would be a fool if she let him slip from her."

How calmly the Grenviles seized fortunes for themselves.

"What exactly," I asked, "does he contribute to your present business?" He cocked an eye at me, and grinned.

"Don't poke your snub nose into my affairs," he said. "I know what I'm about. I'll tell you one thing, though: we'd have difficulty in paying for this affair without him."

"So I thought," I answered

"Taking me all round," he said, "I'm a pretty cunning fellow."

"If you call it cunning," I said, "to play one member of your staff against another. For my part, I would call it knavery."

"Good generalship," he said

"Gerrymandering," I answered.

"A *ruse-de-guerre*," he countered.

"Pawky politics," I argued.

"Ah, well," he said, "if the manoeuvre serves my purpose it matters not how many lives be broken in the process."

"Take care they're broken afterwards, and not before," I said.

He came and sat beside me on the bed.

"I think you mislike me much, now my hair is black," he suggested.

"It becomes your beauty, but not your disposition."

"Dark foxes leave no trail behind them."

"Red ones are more lovable."

"When the whole future of a country is at stake, emotions are thrown overboard."

"Emotions, but not honour."

"Is that a pun upon your name?"

"If you like to take it so."

He took my hands in his and pressed them backwards on the pillow, smiling. "Your resistance was stronger at eighteen," he said.

"And your approach more subtle."

"It had to be, in that confounded apple tree."

He laid his head upon my shoulder, and turned my face to his.

"I can swear in Italian now as well as Spanish," he said to me.

"Turkish also?"

"A word or two. The bare necessities."

He settled himself against me in contentment One eye drooped. The other regarded me malevolently from the pillow.

"There was a woman I encountered once in Naples..."

"With whom you passed an hour?"

"Three, to be exact."

"Tell the tale to Peter," I yawned. "It doesn't interest me."

He lifted his hands to my hair and took the curlers from it.

"If you placed these rags upon you in the day, it would be

more to your advantage and to mine," he mused. "Where was I, though? Ah, yes, the Neapolitan."

"Let her sleep, Richard, and me also."

"I only wished to tell you her remark to me on leaving. 'So it is true, what I have always heard,' she said to me, 'that Cornishmen are famed for one thing only, which is wrestling.' 'Signorina,' I replied, 'there is a lady waiting for me in Cornwall who would give me credit for something else besides.'" He stretched and yawned, and, propping himself on his elbow, blew the candle. "But there," he said, "these southern women were as dull as milk. My vulpine methods were too much for them."

The nights passed thus, and the days as I have described them. Little by little the plans fell into line, the schemes were tabulated. The final message came from the Prince in France that the French fleet had been put at his disposal, and an army, under the command of Lord Hopton, would land in force in Cornwall, while the Prince with Sir John Grenvile, seized the Scillies. The landing was to coincide with the insurrection of the Royalists under Sir Richard Grenvile, who would take and hold the key points in the duchy.

Saturday, the thirteenth of May, was the date chosen for the Cornish rising... The daffodils had bloomed, the blossom was all blown, and the first hot days of summer came without warning on the first of May. The sea below the Gribben was glassy calm. The sky deep blue, without a single cloud. The labourers worked in the fields, and the fishing boats put to sea from Gorran and Polperro. In Fowey all was quiet. The townsfolk went about their business, the Parliamentary agents scribbled their roll upon roll of useless records to be filed in dusty piles up in Whitehall, and the sentries at the castle stared yawning out to sea. I sat out on the causeway, watching the young lambs, and thinking, as the hot sun shone upon my bare

head, how in a bare week now the whole peaceful countryside
would be in an uproar once again. Men shouting, fighting,
dying... The sheep scattered, the cattle driven, the people
running homeless on the roads. Gunfire once again, the rattle
of musketry. The galloping of horses, the tramp of marching
feet. Wounded men, dragging themselves into the hedges,
there to die untended. The young corn trampled, the cottage
thatch in flames. All the old anxiety, the old strain and terror.
The enemy are advancing. The enemy are in retreat. Hopton
has landed in force. Hopton has been repulsed. The Cornish
are triumphant. The Cornish have been driven back. Rumours,
counter-rumours. The bloody stench of war...

The planning was all over now, and the long wait had begun.
A week of nerves, sitting at Menabilly with our eyes upon the
dock. Richard, in high spirits as always before battle, played
bowls with Bunny in the little walled green beside the steward's
empty lodge. Peter, in sudden realization of his flabby stomach
muscles, rode furiously up and down the sands at Par to reduce
his weight. Robin was very silent. He took long walks alone
down in the woods, and on returning went first to the dining
room, where the wine decanter stood. I would find him there
sometimes, glass in hand, brooding; and when I questioned him
he would answer me evasively, his eyes strangely watchful, like
a dog listening for the footstep of a stranger. Gartred, usually
so cool and indifferent when she had the whip hand in a love
affair, showed herself, for the first time, less certain and less sure.
Whether it was because Ambrose Manaton was fifteen years her
junior, and the possibility of marriage with him hung upon a
thread, I do not know, but a new carelessness had come upon
her which was, to my mind, the symbol of a losing touch. That
she was heavily in debt at Orley Court I knew for certain.
Richard had told me as much. Youth lay behind her. And a
future without a third husband to support her would be hard

going, once her beauty went. A dowager, living in retirement with her married daughters, dependent on the charity of a son-in-law? What an end for Gartred Grenvile! So she became careless. She smiled too openly at Ambrose Manaton. She put her hand on his at the dining table. She watched him over the rim of her glass with the same greed I had noticed years before, when, peeping through her chamber door, I had seen her stuff the trinkets in her gown. And Ambrose Manaton, flattered, confident, raised his glass to her in return.

"Send her away," I said to Richard. "God knows she has caused ill feeling enough already. What possible use can she be to you now, here at Menabilly?"

"If Gartred went, Ambrose would follow her," he answered "I can't afford to lose my treasurer. You don't know the fellow as I do. He's as slippery as an eel, and as close-fisted as a Jew. Once back with her in Bideford, and he might pull out of the business altogether."

"Then send Robin packing. He will be no use to you, anyway, if he continues drinking in this manner."

"Nonsense. Drink in his case is stimulation. The only way to ginger him. When the day comes I'll ply him so full of brandy that he will take St. Mawes' Castle single-handed."

"I don't enjoy watching my brother go to pieces."

"He isn't here for your enjoyment. He is here because he is of use to me, and one of the few officers that I know who doesn't lose his head in battle. The more rattled he becomes here at Menabilly, the better he will fight outside it."

He watched me balefully, blowing a cloud of smoke into the air.

"My God," I said, "have you no pity at all?"

"None," he said, "where military matters are concerned."

"You can sit here quite contentedly, with your sister behaving like a whore upstairs, holding one string of Manaton's purse and you the other, while my brother, who loves her, drinks himself to death and breaks his heart?"

"To hell with his heart. His sword is all I care about, and his ability to wield it."

And, leaning from the window in the gallery, he whistled his nephew Bunny to a game of bowls. I watched them both, jesting with one another like a pair of schoolboys without a care, casting their coats upon the short green turf. "Goddamn the Grenviles one and all," I said, my nerves in ribbons. As I spoke, thinking myself alone, I felt a slim hand touch me on the shoulder and heard a boy's voice whisper in my ear: "That's what my mother said, eighteen years ago."

And there was Dick behind me, his black eyes glowing in his pale face, gazing out across the lawn towards his father and young Bunny.

Thirty-Two

THURSDAY THE ELEVENTH OF MAY DAWNED AS HOT AND sticky as as its predecessors. Eight-and-forty hours to go before the torch of war was lit once more in Cornwall. Even Richard was on edge that morning, when word came from a messenger at noon to say that spies had reported a meeting a few days since at Saltash, between the Parliamentary commander in the West, Sir Hardress Waller, and several of the Parliamentary gentlemen, and instructions had been given to double the guards at the chief towns throughout the duchy. Some members of the Cornish County Committee had gone themselves to Helston to see if all was quiet

"One false move now," said Richard quietly, "and all our plans will have been made in vain."

We were gathered in the dining room, I well remember, save only Gartred, who was in her chamber, and I can see now the drawn, anxious faces of the men as they gazed in silence at their leader. Robin, heavy, brooding; Peter, tapping his hand upon his knee; Bunny, with knitted brows; and Dick, as ever, gnawing at his hand.

"The one thing I have feared all along," said Richard. "Those fellows in the West can't hold their tongues. like ill-trained redhawks, too keen to sight the quarry. I warned

Keigwin and Grose to stay this last week within doors, as we
have done, and hold no conferences. No doubt they have been
out upon the roads, and whispers have the speed of lightning."
He stood by the window, his hands behind his back. We were
all, I believe, a little sick with apprehension. I saw Ambrose
Manaton rub his hands nervously together, his usual calm
composure momentarily lost to him.

"If anything should go wrong," he ventured hesitating,
"what arrangements can be made for our own security?"

Richard threw him a contemptuous glance. "None," he said
briefly. He returned to the table and gathered up his papers.

"You have your orders, one and all," he said. "You know
what you have to do. Let us rid ourselves of all this junk then,
useless to us once the battle starts."

He began to throw the maps and documents into the fire,
while the others still stared at him, uncertain.

"Come," said Richard. "You look, the whole damned lot of
you, like a flock of crows before a funeral. On Saturday we make
a bid for freedom. If any man is afraid let him say so now, and I'll
put a halter round his neck for treason to the Prince of Wales."

Not one of us made answer. Richard turned to Robin. "I
want you to ride to Trelawne," he said, "and tell Jonathan
Trelawney and his son that the rendezvous for the thirteenth
is changed. They and Sir Arthur Bassett must join Sir Charles
Trevannion at Caerhayes. Tell them to go tonight, skirting the
high roads, and accompany them there."

"Sir," said Robin slowly, rising to his feet, and I think I
was the only one who saw the flicker of his glance at Ambrose
Manaton. As for myself, a weight was lifted from me. With
Robin gone from the house, I, his sister, might safely breathe
again. Let Gartred and her new lover make what they could of
the few hours remaining. I did not care a jot, so long as Robin
was not there to listen to them.

"Bunny," said his uncle, "you have the boat at Pridmouth standing by in readiness?"

"Sir," said Bunny, his gray eyes dancing. He was, I think, the only one who still believed he played at soldiers.

"Then we shall rendezvous also at Caerhayes," said Richard, "at daybreak on the thirteenth. You can sail to Gorran tomorrow and give my last directions about the beacon on the Dodman. A few hours on salt water in this weather will be good practice for your stomach." He smiled at the lad, who answered it with boyish adoration, and I saw Dick lower his head and trace imaginary lines upon the table with slow, hesitating hand.

"Peter?" said Richard.

Alice's husband leapt to his feet, drawn from some pleasant reverie of French wine and women to the harsh reality of the world about him. "My orders, sir?"

"Go to Caerhayes and warn Trevannion that the plans are changed. Tell him the Trelawneys and Bassett will be joining him. Then return here to Menabilly in the morning. And a word of warning, Peter."

"What is that, sir?"

"Don't go a-Courtneying on the way there. There is not a woman worth it from Tywardreath to Dodman."

Peter turned pink, for all his bravado, but nerved himself to answer, "Sir" with great punctility.

He and Robin left the room together, followed by Bunny and by Ambrose Manaton. Richard yawned and stretched his arms above his head, and then, wandering to the hearth, stirred the black embers of his papers in the ashes.

"Have you no commands for me?" said Dick slowly.

"Why, yes," said Richard, without turning his head, "Alice Courtney's daughters must have left some dolls behind them. Go search in the attics and fashion them new dresses."

Dick did not answer. But he went, I think, a little whiter than before and, turning on his heel, left the room.

"One day," I said, "you will provoke him once too often."

"That is my intention," answered Richard.

"Does it please you, then, to see him writhe in torment?"

"I hope to see him stand up to me at last, not take it lying down, like a coward."

"Sometimes," I said, "I think that after twenty years I know even less about you than I did when I was eighteen."

"Very probably."

"No father in the world would act as harshly to his son as you do to your Dick."

"I only act harshly because I wish to purge his mother's whore blood from his veins."

"You will more likely kindle it."

He shrugged his shoulders, and we fell silent a moment, listening to the sound of the horses' hoofs echoing across the park as Robin and Peter rode to their separate destinations.

"I saw my daughter up in London, when I lay concealed there for a while," said Richard suddenly.

Foolishly, a pang of jealousy shot through my heart, and I answered like a wasp. "Freckled, I suppose? A prancing miss?"

"Nay. Rather studious and quiet. Dependable. She put me in mind of my mother. 'Bess,' I said to her, 'will you look after me in my declining years?' 'Why, yes,' she answered, 'if you send for me.' I think she cares as little for that bitch as I do."

"Daughters," I said, "are never favourites with their mothers. Especially when they come to be of age. How old is she?"

"Near seventeen," he said, "with all that natural bloom upon her that young people have..." He stared absently before him. This moment, I thought with great lucidity and calm above the anguish, is in a sense our moment of farewell, our parting of the ways, but he does not know it. Now his daughter is of age he will not need me.

"Heigh-ho," he said. "I think I start to feel my eight-and-forty years. My leg hurts damnably today, and no excuse for it, with the sun blazing in the sky."

"Suspense," I said, "and all that goes along with it."

"When this campaign is over," he said, "and we hold all Cornwall for the Prince of Wales, I'll say good-bye to soldiering. I'll build a palace on the north coast, near to Stowe, and live in quiet retirement, like a gentleman."

"Not you," I said. "You'd quarrel with all your neighbours."

"I'd have no neighbours," he answered, "save my own Grenvile clan. My God, we'd make a clean sweep of the duchy. Jack, and Bunny, and I. D'you think the Prince would make me Earl of Launceston?" He lay his hand upon my head an instant and then was gone, whistling for Bunny, and I sat there alone in the empty dining room, despondent, oddly sad...

That evening we all went early to our beds, with the thunder that would not come still heavy in the air. Richard had taken Jonathan Rashleigh's chamber for his own, with Dick and Bunny in the dressing rooms between.

Now Peter and Robin had gone, the one to Caerhayes, the other to Trelawne, I thought, with cynicism, that Ambrose Manaton and Gartred could indulge their separate talents for invention until the morning, should the spirit move them.

A single door between their chambers, and I the only neighbour, at the head of the stairs. I heard Gartred come first, and Ambrose follow her—then all was silent on the landing. Ah, well, I thought, wrapping my shawl around me, thank God I can grow old with some complacency. White hairs could come, and lines, and crow's feet, and they would not worry me. I did not have to struggle for a third husband, not having had a first. But it was hard to sleep, with the full moon creeping to my window.

I could not hear the clock in the belfry from my present chamber, as I used to in the gatehouse, but it must have been near midnight, or just after, when I woke suddenly from the light sleep into which I had fallen, it seemed, but a few moments earlier, with a fancy that I had heard someone moving in the dining room below. Yes, there it was distinctly. The furtive sound of one who blundered his way in darkness and bumped into a table or a chair. I raised myself in my bed and listened. All was silent once again. But I was not easy. I put my hand out to my chair and dragged it to me, then listened once again, sudden, unmistakable, came the stealthy tread of a footstep on the creaking telltale stair. Some intuition, subconscious, perhaps, from early in the day, warned me of disaster. I lowered myself into my chair, and without waiting to light my candle—nor was there need with the moon casting a white beam on the carpet—I propelled myself across the room and turned the handle of my door.

"Who is there?" I whispered.

There was no answer, and, coming to the landing, I looked down upon the stair and saw a dark figure crouching there, his back against the wall, the moonlight gleaming on the naked sword in his hand. He stood in stockinged feet, his shirt sleeves rolled above his elbow, my brother Robin, with murder in his eyes. He said nothing to me, only waited to see what I would do.

"Two years ago," I said softly, "you disobeyed an order given you by your commander because of a private quarrel. That was in January '46. Do you intend to do the same in May of '48?"

He crept close and stood on the top stair beside me, breathing strangely. I could smell the brandy on his breath.

"I have disobeyed no one," he said. "I gave my message. I parted with the Trelawneys at the top of Polmear Hill."

"Richard bade you accompany them to Caerhayes," I said.

"No need to do so, Trelawney told me; two horsemen pass more easily than three. Let me by, Honor."

"No, Robin. Not yet. Give me first your sword."

He did not answer. He stood staring at me, looking, with his tumbled hair and troubled eyes, so like the ghost of our dead brother Kit that I trembled, even as his hands did on his sword. "You cannot fool me," he said, "neither you, nor Richard Grenvile. This business was but a pretext to send me from the house so that they could be together."

He looked forward to the landing and the closed door of the room beyond the stairs.

"Go to bed, Robin," I said, "or come and sit with me in my chamber. Let me talk to you awhile."

"No," he said. "This is my moment They will be together now. If you try to prevent me, I shall hurt you also."

He brushed past my chair and made across the landing, tiptoeing, furtive, in his stockinged feet, and whether he was drunk or mad I could not tell. I knew only the purpose in his eyes.

"For God's sake, Robin," I said, "do not go into that room. Reason with them in the morning, if you must, but not now, not at this hour."

For answer he turned the handle, a smile upon his lips both horrible and strange, and I wheeled then, sobbing, and went back into my room and hammered loudly to the dressing rooms where Dick and Bunny slept.

"Call Richard," I said. "Bid him come quickly, now, this instant. And you, too, both of you. There is no time to lose."

A startled voice—Bunny's, I believe—made answer, and I heard him clamber from his bed. But I had turned again and crossed my room towards the landing, where all was silent still and undisturbed. Nothing but the moonlight shining strong into the eastern windows. And then there came that sound for which I waited, piercing the silence with its shrill intensity. Not an oath, not a man's voice raised in anger, but the shocking horror of a woman's scream.

Thirty-Three

*A*CROSS THE LANDING, THROUGH AMBROSE MANATON'S empty room, to Gartred's chamber beyond. The wheels of my chair turning slowly, for all my labour. And all the while calling, "Richard... Richard... " with a note in my voice I did not recognize.

Oh, God, that fight there in the moonlight, the cold white light pouring into the unshuttered windows, and Gartred with a crimson gash upon her face clinging to the hangings of the bed. Ambrose Manaton, his silken nightshirt stained with blood, warding off with his bare hands the desperate blows that Robin aimed at him, until, with a despairing cry, he reached the sword that lay among his heap of clothes upon a chair. Their bare feet padded on the boards, their breath came quick and short, and they seemed, the two of them, like phantom figures, lunging, thrusting, now in moonlight and now in shadow, with no word uttered. "Richard... " I called again, for this was murder, here before my eyes, with the two men between me and the bed where Gartred crouched, her hands to her face, the blood running down between her fingers.

He came at last, half-clad, carrying his sword, with Dick and Bunny at his heels bearing candles. "An end to this, you

Goddamned idiots," he shouted, forcing himself between them, his own sword shivering their blades, and there was Robin, his right wrist hanging limp, with Richard holding him, and Ambrose Manaton back against the farther wall, with Bunny by his side.

They stared at one another, Robin and Ambrose Manaton, like animals in battle, chests heaving, eyes bloodshot, and suddenly Robin, seeing Gartred's face, realized what his work had done. He opened his mouth to speak, but no words came. He trembled, powerless to move or utter, and Richard pushed him to a chair and held him there. "Call Matty," said Richard to me. "Get water, bandages."

Once more I turned to the landing, but already the household were astir, the frightened servants gathering in the hail below, the candles lit. "Go back to bed," said Richard harshly. "No one of you is needed save Mistress Honor's woman. There has been a trifling accident, but no harm done." I heard them shuffle, whisper, retire to their own quarters, and here was Matty, staunch, dependable, seizing the situation in a glance and fetching bowls of water, strips of clean linen. The room was lit now by some half dozen candles. The phantom scene was done; the grim reality was with us still.

Those tumbled clothes upon the floor, Gartred's and his. Manaton leaning upon Bunny's arm, staunching the cuts he had received, his fair curls lank and damp with sweat. Robin upon a chair, his head buried in his hands, all passion spent. Richard standing by his side, grim and purposeful. And one and all we looked at Gartred on the bed with that great gash upon her face from her right eyebrow to her chin. It was then, for the first time, that I noticed Dick.

His face was ashen white, his eyes transfixed in horror, and suddenly he reeled and fell as the blood that stained the clean white linen spread and trickled onto Matty's hand.

Richard made no move. He said to Bunny, between clenched teeth, his eyes averted from his son's limp body, "Carry the spawn to his bed and leave him." Bunny obeyed, and as I watched him stagger from the room, his cousin in his arms, I thought with cold and deadly weariness, "This is the end. This is finality."

Someone brought brandy. Bunny, I suppose, on his return. We had our measure, all of us. Robin drinking slow and deep, his hands shaking as he held his glass. Ambrose Manaton, quick and nervous, the colour that had gone soon coming to his face again. Then Gartred, moaning faintly with her head on Matty's shoulder, her silver hair still horribly bespattered with her blood.

"I do not propose," said Richard slowly, "to hold an inquest. What has been, has been. We are on the eve of deadly matters, with the whole future of a kingdom now at stake. This is no time for any man to seek private vengeance in a quarrel. When men have sworn an oath to my command, I demand obedience."

Not one of them made answer. Robin gazed, limp and shattered, at the floor.

"We will snatch," said Richard, "what hours of sleep we can until the morning. I will remain with Ambrose in his room and Bunny, stay with Robin. In the morning you will go together to Caerhayes, where I shall join you. Can I ask you, Matty, to remain here with Mrs. Denys?"

"Yes, Sir Richard," said Matty steadily.

"How is her pulse? Has she lost much blood?"

"She is well enough now, Sir Richard. The bandages are firm. Sleep and rest will work wonders by the morning."

"No danger to her life?"

"No, Sir Richard. The cut was jagged, but not deep. The only damage done is to her beauty." Matty's lips twitched in the way I knew, and I wondered how much she guessed of what had happened.

Ambrose Manaton did not look towards the bed. The woman who lay upon it might have been a stranger. This is their finish too, I thought. Gartred will never become Mrs. Manaton and own Trecarrel.

I turned my eyes from Gartred, white and still, and felt Richard's hands upon my chair. "You," he said quietly, "have had enough for one night to contend with." He took me to my room and, lifting me from my chair, laid me down upon my bed.

"Will you sleep?" he said. "I think not," I answered.

"Rest easy. We shall be gone so soon. A few hours more and it will be over. War makes a good substitute for private quarrels."

"I wonder…"

He left me and went back to Ambrose Manaton, not, I reflected, for love to share his slumbers, but to make sure his treasurer did not slip from him in the few remaining hours left to us before daylight. Bunny had gone with Robin to his room, and this also, I surmised, was a precaution. Remorse and brandy have driven stronger men than Robin to their suicide.

What hope of sleep had any of us? There was the full moon, high now in the heavens, and you, I thought, shining there in the hushed gardens with your pale cold face above the shadows, have witnessed strange things this night at Menabilly. We Harrises and Grenviles had paid ill return for Rashleigh hospitality….

The hours slipped by, and I suddenly remembered Dick, who slept in the dressing room next door to me, alone. Poor lad, faint at the sight of blood as he had been in the past, was he now lying wakeful like me, with shame upon his conscience? I thought I heard him stir and I wondered if dreams haunted him as they did me, and if I wished for company. "Dick… " I called softly. "Dick… " I called again, but there was no answer. Later a little breeze rising from the sea made a draught come to my room from the open window, and playing with the latch upon the door, shook it free, so that it swung to and fro, banging every instant like a loosened shutter.

He must sleep deep, then, if it did not waken him.

The moon went, and the morning light stole in and cleared the shadows, and still the door between our two rooms creaked and closed and creaked again, making a nagging accompaniment to my uneasy slumbers. Maddened at last, I climbed to my chair to shut it, and as my hand fastened on the latch I saw through the crack of the door that Dick's bed was empty. He was not in the room….

Numb and exhausted, I stumbled to my bed. He has gone to find Bunny, I thought. He has gone to Bunny and to Robin. But before me was the picture of his white anguished face, and sleep, when it did come, could not banish the memory.

Next morning, when I woke to find the broad sun streaming in my room, the scenes of the hours before held a nightmare quality. I longed for them to dissipate, as nightmares do, but when Matty bore my breakfast I knew them to be true.

"Yes, Mrs. Denys had some sleep," she answered to my query, "and will, to my mind, be little worse for her adventure until she lifts her bandage." Matty, with a sniff, had small pity in her bosom.

"Will the gash not heal in time?" I asked.

"Aye, it will heal," she said, "but she'll bear the scar there for her lifetime. She'll find it hard to trade her beauty now." She spoke with a certain relish, as though the events of the preceding night had wiped away a legion of old scores.

"Mrs. Denys," said Matty, "has got what she deserved."

Had she? Was this a chessboard move, long planned by the Almighty, or were we one and all just fools to fortune? I knew one thing, since I had seen the gash on Gartred's face, I hated her no longer....

"Were all the gentlemen at breakfast?" I said suddenly.

"I believe so."

"And Master Dick as well?"

"Yes. He came somewhat later than the others, but I saw him in the dining room an hour ago."

A wave of relief came to me, for no reason except that he was safely in the house. "Help me to dress," I said to Matty.

Friday, the twelfth of May. A hazard might have made it the thirteenth. Some sense of delicacy kept me from Gartred's chamber. Now that her beauty was marred, she and I would now hold equal ground, and I had no wish to press the matter home. Other women might have gone to her, feigning commiseration, but with triumph in their hearts, but Honor Harris was not one of them. I sent messages by Matty that she should ask for what she wanted, and left her to her thoughts. I found Robin in the gallery, standing moodily beside the window, his right arm in a sling. He turned his head at my approach, then looked away again in silence.

"I thought you had departed with Bunny to Caerhayes," I said to him.

"We wait for Peter Courtney," he answered dully. "He has not yet returned."

"Does your wrist pain you?" I asked gently.

He shook his head, and went on staring from the window.

"When the shouting is over, and the turmoil done," I said, "we will keep house together, you and I, as we did once at Lanrest."

Still he did not answer, but I saw the tears start in his eyes.

"We have loved the Grenviles long enough," I said, "each in our separate fashion. The time has come when they must learn to live without us."

"They have done that," he said, his voice low, "for nearly thirty years. It is we who are dependent upon them."

These were the last words we ever held upon the subject, Robin and I, from that day unto this. Reserve has kept us silent, though we have lived together for five years...

The door opened, and Richard came into the gallery, Bunny at his shoulder like a shadow.

"I cannot understand it," he said, pacing the floor in irritation. "Here it is nearly noon and no sign yet of Peter. If he left Caerhayes at daybreak, he should have been here long ago. I suppose, like every other fool, he has thought best to ignore my orders."

The barb was lost on Robin, who was too far gone in misery to mind. "If you permit me," he said humbly, "I can ride in search of him. He may have stayed to breakfast with the Sawles at Penrice."

"He is more likely behind a haystack with a wench," said Richard. "My God, I will have eunuchs on my staff, next time I go to war. Go then, if you like, but keep a watch upon the roads. I have heard reports of troops riding through St. Blazey. The rumour may be false, and yet..." He broke off in the middle of his speech and resumed his pacing of the room. Presently we heard Robin mount his horse and ride away. The hours wore on; the clock in the belfry struck twelve, and later one. The servants brought cold meat and ale, and we helped ourselves, haphazard, all of us with little appetite, our ears strained for sound. At half-past one there was a footfall on the stairs, slow and laboured, and I noticed Ambrose Manaton glance subconsciously to the chamber overhead, then draw back against the window. The handle of the door was turned, and Gartred stood before us, dressed for travel, one side of her face shrouded with a veil, a cloak around her shoulders. No one spoke as she stood there like a spectre. "I wish," she said at length, "to return to Orley Court. Conveyance must be found for me."

"You ask for the impossible," said Richard shortly, "and no one knows it better now than you. In a few hours the roads will be impassable."

"I'll take my chance of that," she said. "If I fall fighting with the rabble, I think I shall not greatly care. I have done what you asked me to do. My part is played."

Her eyes were upon Richard all the while and never once on Ambrose Manaton. Richard and Gartred.... Robin and I... Which sister had the most to forgive, the most to pay for? God knows I had no answer.

"I am sorry," said Richard briefly. "I cannot help you. You must stay here until arrangements can be made. We have more serious matters on our hands than the transport of a sick widow."

Bunny was the first to catch the sound of the horse's hoofs galloping across the park. He went to the small mullioned window that gave on to the inner court and threw it wide; and as we waited, tense, expectant, the sound drew closer, and suddenly the rider and his horse came through the arch beneath the gatehouse, and there was Peter Courtney, dust covered and dishevelled, his hat gone, his dark curls straggling on his shoulders. He flung the reins to a startled waiting groom and came straightway to the gallery.

"For God's sake, save yourselves! We are betrayed," he said.

I think I did not show the same fear and horror on my face as they did, for although my heart went cold and dead within me, I knew with wretched certainty that this was the thing I had waited for all day. Peter looked from one to the other of us, and his breath came quick. "They have all been seized," he said. "Jonathan Trelawney, his son, Charles Trevannion, Arthur Bassett, and the rest. At ten this morning they came riding to the house, the sheriff, Sir Thomas Herle, and a whole company of soldiers. We made a fight for it, but there were more than thirty of them. I leapt from an upper window, by Almighty Providence escaping with no worse than a wrenched ankle. I got the first horse to hand and put spurs to him without mercy. Had I not known the by-lanes as I know my own hand, I could not have reached you now. There are soldiers everywhere. The bridge at St. Blazey blocked and guarded. Guards on Polmear Hill."

He looked around the gallery, as though in search of someone. "Robin gone?" he asked. "I thought so. It was he, then, I saw, when I was skirting the sands, engaged in fighting with five of the enemy or more. I dared not go to his assistance. My first duty was to you. What now? Can we save ourselves?"

We all turned now to look at our commander. He stood before us, calm and cool, giving no outward sign that all he had striven for lay crushed and broken. "Did you see their colours?" he asked swiftly. "What troops were they? Of whose command?"

"Some were from Bodmin, sir," said Peter, "the rest advance guards of Sir Hardress Waller's. There were line upon line of them, stretching down the road towards St. Austell. This is no chance encounter, sir. The enemy are in strength."

Richard nodded, turning quick to Bunny. "Go to Pridmouth," he said. "Make sail instantly. Set a course due south until you come in contact with the first outlying vessel of the French fleet. They will be cruising eastward of the Scillies by this time tomorrow evening. Ask for Lord Hopton's ship. Give him this message." He scribbled rapidly upon a piece of paper.

"Do you bid them come?" said Ambrose Manaton. "Can they get to us in time?" He was white to the lips, his hands clenched tight.

"Why, no," said Richard, folding his scrap of paper, "I bid them alter course and sail for France again. There will be no rising. The Prince of Wales does not land this month in Cornwall." He gave the paper to his nephew. "Good chance, my Bunny," he said smiling. "Give greetings to your brother Jack, and with a spice of luck you will find the Scillies fall to you like a plum a little later in the summer. But the Prince must say good-bye to Cornwall for the present."

"And you, Uncle?" said Bunny. "Will you not come with me? It is madness to delay if the house is likely to be surrounded?"

"I'll join you in my own time," said Richard. "For this once, I ask that my orders be obeyed."

Bunny stared at him an instant, then turned and went, his head high, bidding none of us farewell.

"But what are we to do? Where are we to go?" said Ambrose Manaton. "Oh God, what a fool I have been to let myself be led into this business. Are the roads all watched?" He turned to Peter, who stood shrugging his shoulders, watching his commander.

"Who is to blame? Who is the traitor? That is what I want to know," said Ambrose Manaton, all composure gone, a new note of suspicion in his voice. "None but ourselves knew the change in rendezvous. How did the sheriff time his moment with such devilish accuracy that he could seize every leader worth a curse?"

"Does it matter," said Richard gently, "who the traitor was once the deed is done?"

"Matter?" said Ambrose Manaton. "Good God, you take it coolly. Trevannion, the Trelawneys, the Arundells, and Bassetts, all of them in the sheriff's hands, and you ask does it matter who betrayed them? Here are we, ruined men, likely to be arrested within the hour, and you stand there like a fox and smile at me."

"My enemies call me fox, but not my friends," said Richard softly. He turned to Peter. "Tell the fellows to saddle a horse for Mr. Manaton," he said, "and for you also. I guarantee no safe conduct for the pair of you, but at least you have a sporting chance, as hares do from a pack of hounds."

"You will not come with us, sir?"

"No. I will not come with you."

Peter hesitated, looking first at him and then at me.

"It will go ill with you, sir, if they should find you."

"I am well aware of that."

"The sheriff, Sir Thomas Herle, suspects your presence here in Cornwall. His first challenge, when he came before Caerhayes and called Trevannion, was, 'Have you Sir Richard Grenvile here in hiding? If so, produce him, and you shall go free.'"

"A pity, for their sakes, I was not there."

"He said that a messenger had left a note at his house at Prideaux early before dawn, warning him that the whole party, yourself included, would be gathered later at Caerhayes. Some wretch had seen you, sir, and with devilish intuition guessed your plans."

"Some wretch indeed," said Richard smiling still, "who thought it sport to try the Judas touch. Let us forget him."

Was it his nephew Jack who, long ago at Exeter said once to me, "Beware my uncle when you see him smile…"

Then Ambrose Manaton came forward, his finger stabbing at the air. "It is you," he said to Richard, "you who are the traitor, you who have betrayed us. From first to last, from beginning to the end, you knew it would end thus. The French fleet never were to come to our aid; there never was to be a rising. This is your revenge for that arrest four years ago at Launceston. Oh God, what perfidy…" He stood before him, trembling, a high note of hysteria in his voice, and I saw Peter fall back a pace, the colour draining from his face, bewilderment, then horror, coming to his eyes.

Richard watched them, never moving, then slowly pointed to the door. The horses had been brought to the courtyard, and we heard the jingle of the harness.

"Put back the clock," I whispered savagely. "Make it four years ago, and Gartred acting spy for Lord Robartes. Let her take the blame. Fix the crime on her. She is the one who will emerge from this unscathed, for all her spoilt beauty." I looked towards her and saw, to my wonder, that she was looking at me also. Her scarf had slipped, showing the vivid wound upon her cheek. The sight of it and the memory of the night before filled me, not with anger or with pity, but despair. She went on looking at me, and I saw her smile.

"It's no use," she said. "I know what you are thinking. Poor Honor, I have cheated you again. Gartred has the perfect alibi."

The horses were galloping from the courtyard. I saw Ambrose Manaton go first, his hat pulled low, his cloak bellying, and Peter follow him, with one brief glance towards our windows.

The clock in the belfry struck two. A pigeon, dazzling white against the sky, fluttered to the court below. Gartred lay back against the couch, the smile on her lips a strange contrast to the gash upon her face. Richard stood by the window, his hands behind his back. And Dick, who had never moved once in all the past half hour, waited, like a dumb thing, in his corner.

"Do the three Grenviles," I said slowly, "wish to take council alone amongst themselves?"

Thirty-Four

ICHARD WENT ON STANDING BY THE WINDOW. NOW that the horses were gone, and the sound of their galloping had died away, it was strangely hushed and still within the house. The sun blazed down upon the gardens; the pigeons pricked the grass seeds on the lawn. It was the hottest hour of a warm summer day, when bumble bees go humming in the limes, and the young birds fall silent. When Richard spoke he kept his back turned to us, and his voice was soft and low.

"My grandfather," he said, "was named Richard also. He came of a long line of Grenviles who sought to serve their country and their king. Enemies he had in plenty, friends as well. It was my misfortune and my loss that he died in battle nine years before my birth. But I remember, as a lad, asking for tales of him and looking up at that great portrait which hung in the long gallery at Stowe. He was stern, they said, and hard, and rarely smiled, so I have heard tell, but his eyes that looked down upon me from the portrait were hawk's eyes, fearless and far-seeing. There were many great names in those days: Drake, Raleigh, Sydney—and Grenvile was of their company. He fell, mortally wounded, you may remember, on the decks of his own ship, called the *Revenge*. He fought alone with the Spanish fleet about him, and when they asked him to surrender he went on fighting still, with masts gone, sails gone, the decks torn beneath his feet. The Grenvile of that day had courage and preferred to have his vessel blown to pieces rather than sell his life for silver to the pirate hordes of Spain." He fell silent a moment, watching the pigeons on the lawn, and then he went on talking, with his hands behind his back. "My Uncle John," he said, "explored the Indies with Sir Francis Drake. He was a man of courage too. They were no weaklings, those young men who braved the winter storms of the Atlantic in search of savage lands beyond the seas. Their ships were frail, they were tossed week after week at the mercy of wind and sea, but some salt tang in their blood kept them undaunted. He was killed there, in the Indies, was my Uncle John, and my father, who loved him well, built a shrine to him at Stowe." There was no sound from anyone of us in the gallery. Gartred lay on the couch, her hands behind her head, and Dick stood motionless in his dark corner.

"There was a saying, born about this time," continued Richard, "that no Grenvile was ever wanting in loyalty to his king. We were bred to it, my brothers and I. Gartred too, I think, will well remember those evenings in my father's room at Stowe when he, though he was not a fighting man—for he lived in days of peace—read to us from an old volume with great clasps about it of the wars of the past, and how our forebears fought in them."

A gull wheeled overhead above the gardens, his wings white against the dark blue sky, and I remembered of a sudden the kittiwakes at Stowe, riding the rough Atlantic beneath Richard's home.

"My brother Bevil," said Richard, "was a man who loved his family and his home. He was not bred to war. He desired, in his brief life, nothing so much as to rear his children with his wife's care, and live at peace amongst his neighbours. When war came he knew what it would mean, and did not turn his back upon it. Wrangling he detested, bloodshed he abhorred, but because he bore the name of Grenvile he knew, in 1642, where his duty lay. He wrote a letter at that time to our friend and neighbour, John Trelawney, who has this day been arrested, as you know, and because I believe that letter to be the finest thing my brother ever penned I asked Trelawney for a copy of it. I have it. with me now. Shall I read it to you?"

We did not answer. He felt in his pocket slowly for a paper and, holding it before the window, read aloud.

> I cannot contain myself within my doors when the King of England's standard waves in the field upon so just occasion, the cause being such as must make all those that die in it little inferior to martyrs. And for mine own part I desire to acquire an honest name or an honourable grave. I never loved life or ease so much as to shun such an occasion, which if I should, I were unworthy of the profession I have held, or to succeed those ancestors of mine who have so many of them, in several ages, sacrificed their lives for their country.

Richard folded the letter again, and put it once more into his pocket. "My brother Bevil died at Lansdowne," he said, "leading his men to battle, and his young son Jack, a lad of but fifteen, straightway mounted his father's horse and charged the enemy. That youngster who has just left us, Bunny, ran from his tutor last autumn, playing truant, that he might place himself at my disposal and hold a sword for this cause we all hold dear. I have no brief for myself. I am a soldier. My faults are many and my virtues few. But no quarrel, no dispute, no petty act of vengeance has ever turned me, or will turn me now, from loyalty to my country and my King. In the long and often bloody history of the Grenviles, not one of them until this day has proved a traitor."

His voice had sunk now, deadly quiet. The pigeons had flown from the lawns. The bees had hummed their way below the thistle park.

"One day," said Richard, "we may hope that His Majesty will be restored to his throne, or if not he, then the Prince of Wales instead. In that proud day, should any of us live to see it, the name of Grenvile will be held in honour, not only here in Cornwall, but in all England too. I am judge enough of character, for all my other failings, to know that my nephew Jack will prove himself as great a man of peace as he has been a youth of war, nor will young Bunny ever lag behind. They can tell their sons in the years to come, 'We Grenviles fought to bring about the restoration of our King,' and their names will rank in that great book at Stowe my father read to us, beside that of my grandfather Richard who fought in the *Revenge*." He paused a moment, then spoke lower still.

"I care not," he said, "if my name be written in that book in smaller characters. 'He was a soldier,' they may say. 'The King's general in the West.' Let that be my epitaph. But there will be no other Richard in that book at Stowe. For the King's general died without a son." A long silence followed his last words. He went on standing at the window, and I sat still in my chair, my hands folded on my lap. Soon now it would come, I thought, the outburst, the angry, frightened words, or the torrent of wild weeping. For eighteen years the storm had been pent up, and the full tide of emotion could not wait longer now. This is our fault, I whispered to myself, not his. Had Richard been more forgiving, had I been less proud, had our hearts been filled with love and not hatred, had we been blessed with greater

understanding… Too late. Full twenty years too late. And now
the little scapegoat of our sins went bleeding to his doom…

But the cry I waited for was never uttered. Nor did the tears
fall. Instead, he came out from his corner and stood alone an
instant in the centre of the room. The fear was gone now from
the dark eyes, and the slim hands did not tremble. He looked
older than he had done hitherto, older and wiser. As though,
while his father had been speaking, a whole span of years had
passed him by.

Yet when he spoke, his voice was a boy's voice, young and
simple. "What must I do?" he said. "Will you do it for me, or
must I kill myself?"

It was Gartred who moved first. Gartred, my lifelong foe
and enemy. She rose from her couch, pulling the veil about her
face, and came up to my chair. She put her hands upon it, and,
still with no word spoken, she wheeled me from the room. We
went out into the garden under the sun, our backs turned to
the house, and we said no words to one another, for there were
none to say. But neither she nor I, nor any man or woman,
alive or dead, will ever know what was said there in the long
gallery at Menabilly by Richard Grenvile to his only son.

That evening the insurrection broke out in the West. There
had been no way to warn the Royalists of Helston and Penzance
that the leaders in the east had been arrested, and the prospective
rising was now doomed to failure. They struck at the appointed
hour, as had been planned, and found themselves faced, not
with the startled troops they had expected, but the strong
forces, fully prepared and armed, that came riding posthaste
into Cornwall for the purpose. No French fleet beyond the
Scillies came coasting to Land's End and the Lizard. There was
no landing of twenty thousand men upon the beaches beneath
Dodman and the Nare. And the leaders who should have come
riding to the West were shackled, wrist to wrist, in the garrison

at Plymouth. No Trelawney, no Arundell, no Trevannion, no Bassett. What was to have been the torch to light all England was no more than a sudden quivering flame, spurting to nothing, spluttering for a single moment in the damp Cornish air. A few shops looted at Penzance… a smattering of houses pillaged at Mullion… a wild unruly charge upon Goonhilly Down, with no man knowing whither he rode or wherefore he was fighting… and then the last hopeless, desperate stand at Mawgan Creek, with the Parliamentary troops driving the ill-led Royalists to destruction, down over the rocks and stones to the deep Helford River.

The rebellion of '48. The last time men shall ever fight, please God, upon our Cornish soil. It lasted but a week, but for those who died and suffered it lasted for eternity. The battles were west of Truro, so we at Menabilly smelt no powder. But every road and every lane was guarded, and not even the servants ventured out of doors. That first evening a company of soldiers, under the command of Colonel Robert Bennett, our old neighbour near to Looe, rode to Menabilly and made a perfunctory search throughout the house. He found no one present but myself and Gartred. He little knew that had he come ten minutes earlier he would have found the greatest prize of all.

I can see Richard now, his arms folded, seated in the dining chamber with the empty chairs about him, deaf to all my pleading. "When they come," he said, "they shall take me as I am. Mine is the blame. I am the man for whom my friends now suffer. Very well, then. Let them do their worst upon me, and by surrendering my person I may yet save Cornwall from destruction."

Gartred, with all her old cool composure back again, shrugged her shoulders in disdain. "Is it not a little late now in the day to play the martyr?" she suggested. "What good will your surrender do at this juncture? You flatter yourself, poor Richard, if you think the mere holding of a Grenvile will spare the rest from imprisonment and death. I hate these last-minute gestures, these sublime salutes. Show yourself a man and escape, the pair of you, as Bunny did." She did not look towards Dick. Nor did I. But he sat there, silent as ever, at his father's side.

"We shall maker fine figures on the scaffold, Dick and I," said Richard. "My neck is somewhat thicker, I know, than his, and may need two blows from the axe instead of one."

"You may not have the pleasure, nor the parade, of a martyr's execution," said Gartred, yawning, "but instead a knotted rope in a dank dungeon. Not the usual finish for a Grenvile."

"It would be better," said Richard quietly, "if these two Grenviles did die in obscurity."

There was a pause, and then Dick spoke, for the first time since that unforgettable moment in the gallery.

"How do we stand," he said jerkily, "with the Rashleighs? If my father and I are found here by the enemy, will it be possible to prove to them that the Rashleighs are innocent in the matter?"

I seized upon his words for all the world like a drowning woman. "You have not thought of that," I said to Richard. "You have not considered for one moment what will become of them. Who will ever believe that Jonathan Rashleigh and John, too, were not party also to your plan? Their absence from Menabilly is no proof. They will be dragged into the matter, and my sister Mary also. Poor Alice at Trethurfe, Joan at Mothercombe, a legion of young children. They will all of them, from Jonathan in London to the baby on Joan's knee, suffer imprisonment, and maybe death into the bargain, if you are taken here."

It was at this moment that a servant came into the room, much agitated, his hands clasped before him. "I think it best to tell you," he said, "that a lad has come running across the park to say the troopers are gathered at the top of Polmear Hill. Some have gone down towards Polkerris. The rest are making for Tregaminion and the park gates."

"Thank you," said Richard, bowing. "I am much obliged to you for your discretion." The servant left the room, hoping, I dare say, to feign sickness in his quarters when the troopers came.

Richard rose slowly to his feet and looked at me.

"So you fear for your Rashleighs?" he said "And because of them you have no wish to throw me to the wolves? Very well, then. For this once I will prove accommodating. Where is the famous hiding place that four years ago proved so beneficial to us all?"

I saw Dick flinch and look away from me towards his father. "Dick knows," I answered. "Would you condescend to share it with him?"

"A hunted rat," said Richard, "has no choice. He must take the companion that is thrust upon him."

Whether the place was rank with cobwebs, mould, or mildew, I neither knew nor cared. At least it would give concealment while the troopers came. And no one, not even Gartred, knew the secret.

"Do you remember," I said to Dick, "where the passage led? I warn you, no one has been there for four years."

He nodded, deathly pale. And I wondered what bug of fear had seized him now, when but an hour ago he had offered himself, like a little lamb, for slaughter.

"Go then," I said, "and take your father. Now, this instant, while there is still time."

He came then to me, his newfound courage wavering, looking so like the little boy who loved me once that my heart went out to him. "The rope," he said, "the rope upon the hinge. What if it has frayed now, with disuse, and the hinge rusted?"

"It will not matter," I said, "you will not need to use it now. I shall not be waiting for you in the chamber overhead."

He stared at me, lost for a moment, dull, uncomprehending, and I verily believe that for one brief second he thought himself a child again. Then Richard broke the spell with his hard, clear voice.

"Well?" he said. "If it must be done, this is the moment. There is no other method of escape."

Dick went on staring at me, and there came into his eyes a strange new look I had not seen before. Why did he stare at me thus, or was it not me he stared at but some other, some ghost of a dead past that tapped him on the shoulder?

"Yes," he said slowly. "If it must be done, this is the moment." He turned to his father, opening first the door of the dining room. "Will you follow me, sir?" he said to Richard.

Richard paused a moment on the threshold. He looked first at Gartred, then back at me again. "When the hounds are in full cry," he said, "and the coverts guarded, the Red Fox goes to earth."

He smiled, holding my eyes for a single second, and was gone after Dick, on to the causeway... Gartred watched them disappear, then shrugged her shoulders. "I thought," she said, "the hiding place was in the house. Near your old apartment in the gatehouse."

"Did you?" I said.

"I wasted hours, four years ago, searching in the passages, tiptoeing outside your door," she said.

There was a mirror hanging on the wall beside the window. She went to it and stared, pulling her veil aside. The deep crimson gash ran from her eyebrow to her chin, jagged, irregular, and the smooth contour of her face was gone forever.

I watched her eyes, and she saw me watching them through the misty glass of the little mirror.

"I could have stopped you," she said, "from falling with your horse to the ravine. You knew that, didn't you?"

"Yes," I said.

"You called to me, asking for the way, and I did not answer you."

"You did not," I said.

"It has taken a long time to call it quits," she said to me. She came away then from the mirror and, taking from her sack the little pack of cards I well remembered, sat down by the table, close to my wheeled chair. She dealt the cards face downwards on the table. "We will play patience, you and I, until the troopers come," said Gartred Grenvile.

Thirty-Five

I DOUBT, IF COLONEL BENNETT HAD SEARCHED ALL Cornwall, whether he could have found a quieter couple, when he came, than the two women playing cards in the dining hall at Menabilly. One with a great scar upon her face and silver hair, the other a hopeless cripple. Yes, there had been guests with us until today, we admitted it. Mr. Rashleigh's son-in-law, Sir Peter Courtney, and my own brother, Robin Harris. No, we knew nothing of their movements. They came and went as they pleased. Mr. Trelawney had called once, we understood, but we had not seen him. Why was I left alone at Menabilly by the Rashleighs? From necessity, and not from choice. Perhaps you have forgotten, Colonel Bennett, that my home at Lanrest was burnt down four years ago, by your orders, someone told me once. A strange action for a neighbour. And why was Mrs. Denys from Orley Court near Bideford a guest of mine at the present season? Well, she was once my sister-in-law, and we had long been friends… Yes, it was true my name had been connected with Sir Richard Grenvile in the past. There are gossips in the West country as well as at Whitehall. No, Mrs. Denys had never been very friendly with her brother. No, we had no knowledge of his movements. We believed him to be in Naples. Yes, search the house, from the cellars to the attics;

search the grounds. Here are the keys. Do what you will. We have no power to stop you. Menabilly is no property of ours. We are merely guests, in the absence of Mr. Rashleigh...

"Well, you appear to speak the truth, Mistress Harris," he said to me on the conclusion of his visit (he had called me Honor once, when we were neighbours near to Looe), "but the fact that your brother and Sir Peter Courtney are implicated in the rising which is now breaking out at Helston and Penzance, renders this house suspect. I shall leave a guard behind me, and I rather think, when Sir Hardress Waller comes into the district, he will make a more thorough search of the premises than I have had time to do today. Meanwhile—" He broke off abruptly, his eyes drifting, as if in curiosity, back to Gartred.

"Pardon my indelicacy, madam," he said, "but that cut is recent?"

"An accident," said Gartred, shrugging, "a clumsy movement and some broken glass."

"Surely—not self-inflicted?"

"What else would you suggest?"

"It has more the appearance of a sword cut, forgive my rudeness. Were you a man, I would say you had fought a duel and received the hurt from an opponent."

"I am not a man, Colonel Bennett. If you doubt me, why not come upstairs, to my chamber and let me prove it to you?" Robert Bennett was a Puritan. He stepped back a pace, colouring to his ears. "I thank you, madam," he said stiffly. "My eyes are sufficient evidence."

"If promotion came by gallantry," said Gartred, "you would still be in the ranks. I can think of no other officer in Cornwall, or in Devon either, who would decline to walk upstairs with Gartred Denys." She made as though to deal the cards again, but Colonel Bennett made a motion of his hands.

"I am sorry," he said shortly, "but whether you are Mrs.

Denys or Mrs. Harris these days does not greatly matter. What does matter is that your maiden name was Grenvile."

"And so?" said Gartred, shuffling her cards.

"And so I must ask you to come with me and accept an escort down to Truro. There you will be held, pending an investigation, and when the roads are quieter you will have leave to depart to Orley Court."

Gartred dropped her cards into her sack and rose slowly to her feet. "As you will," she said, shrugging her shoulders. "You have some conveyance, I presume? I have no dress for riding."

"You will have every comfort, madam."

He turned then to me. "You are permitted to remain here until I receive further orders from Sir Hardress Waller. These may be forthcoming in the morning. But I must ask you to be in readiness to move upon the instant, should the order come. You understand?"

"Yes," I answered. "Yes, I understand."

"Very good, then. I will leave a guard before the house, with instructions to shoot on sight, should his suspicions be in any way aroused. Good evening. You are ready, Mrs. Denys?"

"Yes, I am ready." Gartred turned to me and touched me lightly on the shoulder. "I am sorry," she said, "to cut my visit short. Remember me to the Rashleighs when you see them. And tell Jonathan what I said about the gardens. If he wishes to plant flowering shrubs, he must first rid himself of foxes…"

"Not so easy," I answered. "They are hard to catch. Especially when the go underground."

"Smoke them out," she said. "It is the only way. Do it by night; they leave less scent behind them. Good-bye, Honor."

"Good-bye, Gartred." She went, throwing her veil back from her face to show the vivid scar, and I have not seen her from that day to this.

I heard the troopers ride away from the courtyard and out across the park. Before the two entrance doors stood sentries, with muskets at their sides. And a sentry stood also at the outer gate, and by the steps leading to the causeway. I sat watching them, then pulled the bellrope by the hearth for Matty.

"Ask them," I said, "if Colonel Bennett left permission for me to take exercise in my chair within the grounds."

She was back in a moment with the message that I feared.

"He is sorry," she answered, "but Colonel Bennett gave strict orders that you were not to leave the house."

I looked at Matty, and she looked at me.

The thoughts chased round my head in wild confusion. "What hour is it?" I asked.

"Near five o'clock," she answered.

"Four hours of daylight still," I said.

"Yes," she answered.

From the window of the dining hall I could see the sentry pacing up and down before the gates of the south garden. Now and then he paused to look about him and to chat with his fellow at the causeway steps. The sun, high in the southwest, shone down upon their muskets.

"Take me upstairs, Matty," I said slowly.

"To your own chamber?"

"No, Matty. To my old room beyond the gatehouse."

I had not been there in all the past two yean of my stay at Menabilly. The west wing was still bare, untouched. Desolate and stripped as when the rebels had come pillaging in '44. The hangings were gone from the walls. The room had neither bed, nor chair, nor table. One shutter hung limp from the farther window, giving a faint creak of light. The room had a dead, fusty smell, and in the far corner lay the bleached bones of a rat. The west wing was very silent. Very still. No sound came from the deserted kitchens underneath.

"Go to the stone," I whispered. "Put your hands against it."

Matty did so, kneeling on the floor. She pressed against the square stone by the buttress, but it did not move.

"No good," she murmured. "It is hard fixed. Have you forgotten that it only opened from the other side?"

Had I forgotten? It was the one thing that I remembered. "Smoke them out," said Gartred. "It is the only way." Yes, but she did not understand. She thought they were hidden somewhere in the woods. Not behind stone walls three feet thick.

"Fetch wood and paper," I said to Matty. "Kindle a fire. Not in the chimney, but here, against the wall."

There was a chance, a faint one, God knew well, that the smoke would penetrate the cracks in the stone and make a signal. They might not be there, though. They might be crouching in the tunnel at the farther end, beneath the summerhouse.

How slow she was, good Matty, faithful Matty, fetching the dried grass and the twigs. How carefully she blew the fire, how methodically she added twig to twig. "Hurry," I said. "More wood, more flame."

"Patience," she whispered. "It will go in its own time."

In its own time. Not my time. Not Richard's time...

The room was filled with smoke. It seeped into our eyes, our hair; it clung about the windows. But whether it seeped into the stones we could not tell. Matty went to the window and opened the crack two inches farther. I held a long stick in my hands, poking helplessly at the slow sizzling fire, pushing the sticks against the buttress wall. "There are four horsemen riding across the park," said Matty suddenly, "troopers like those who came just now."

My hands were wet with sweat. I threw away my useless stick and rubbed my eyes, stung and red with smoke. I think I was nearer panic at that moment than any other in my eight-and-thirty-years.

"Oh, God," I whispered. "What are we to do?"

Matty closed the window gently. She stamped upon the embers of the fire. "Come back to your chamber," she said. "Later tonight I will try here once again. But we must not be found here now." She carried me in her broad arms from the dark musty room, through the gatehouse, to the corridor beyond, and down to my own chamber in the eastern wing. She lay me on my bed, bringing water for my face and hands. We heard the troopers ride into the courtyard, and then the sound of footsteps below. Impervious to man or situation, the clock beneath the belfry struck six, hammering its silly leaden notes with mechanical precision. Matty brushed the soot from my hair and changed my gown, and when she finished there came a tap upon the door. A servant with frightened face whispered that Mistress Harris was wanted down below. They put me in my chair and carried me downstairs. There had been four troopers, Matty said, riding across the park, but only three stood here, in the side hall, looking out across the gardens. They cast a curious glance upon me as Matty and the servant put me down inside the door of the dining hall. The fourth man stood by the fireplace, leaning upon a stick. And it was not another trooper like themselves, but my brother-in-law, Jonathan Rashleigh.

For a moment I was too stunned to speak. Then relief, bewilderment, and something of utter helplessness swept over me, and I began to cry. He took my hand and held it, saying nothing. In a minute or two I had recovered and, looking up at him, I saw what the years had done. Two, was it, he had been away in London? It might be twenty. He was, I believe, at that time but fifty-eight. He looked seventy. His hair was gone quite white; his shoulders, once so broad, were shrunk and drooping. His very eyes seemed sunk deep in his skull. "What has happened?" I asked. "Why have you come back?"

"The debt is paid," he said, and even his voice was an old man's voice, slow and weary. "The debt is paid; the fine is now wiped out. I am free to come to Cornwall once again."

"You have chosen an ill moment to return," I answered.

"So they have warned me," he said slowly.

He looked at me, and I knew, I think, in that moment, that he had been, after all, a party to the plan. That all the guests who had crept like robbers to his house had come with his connivance, and that he, a prisoner in London, had risked his life because of them.

"You came by road?" I asked him.

"Nay, by ship," he answered. "My own ship, the *Frances*, which plies between Fowey and the Continent, you may remember."

"Yes, I remember."

"Her merchandise has helped to pay my debt. She fetched me from Gravesend a week ago, when the County Committee gave me leave to go from London and return to Fowey. We came to harbour but a few hours since."

"Is Mary with you?"

"No. She went ashore at Plymouth to see Joan at Mothercombe. The guards at Plymouth told us that a rising was feared in Cornwall and troops were gone in strength to quell it. I made all haste to come to Fowey, fearing for your safety."

"You knew then that John was not here? You knew I was—alone?"

"I knew you were—alone."

We both fell silent, our eyes upon the door.

"They have arrested Robin," I said softly, "and Peter also, I fear."

"Yes," he said. "So my guards tell me."

"No suspicion can fall upon yourself?"

"Not yet," he answered strangely.

I saw him look towards the window, where the broad back of the sentry blocked the view. Then slowly, from his pocket, he drew a folded paper, which when he opened it I saw that it was a poster, such as they stick upon the walls for wanted men. He read it to me:

"Anyone who has harboured at any time, or seeks to barbour in the future, the malignant known as Richard Grenvile, shall, upon discovery, be arrested for high treason, his lands sequestered finally and forever, and his family imprisoned."

He folded the paper once again. "This," he said, "is posted upon every wall in every town in Cornwall."

For a moment I did not speak, and then I said, "They have searched this house already. Two hours ago. They found nothing."

"They will come again," he answered, "in the morning."

He went back to the hearth and stood in deep thought, leaning on his stick. "My ship the *Frances*," he said slowly, "anchors in Fowey only for the night. Tomorrow, on the first tide, she sails for Holland."

"For Holland?"

"She carries a light cargo as far as Flushing. The master of the vessel is an honest man, faithful to any trust that I might lay upon him. Already in his charge is a young woman, whom I thought fit to call my kinswoman. Had matters been other than they are, she might have landed with me, here in Fowey. But fate and circumstance decided otherwise. Therefore, she will proceed to Flushing also, in my ship, the *Frances*."

"I don't see," I said, after a moment's hesitation, "what this young woman has to do with me. Let her go to Holland by all means."

"She would be easier in mind," said Jonathan Rashleigh, "if she had her father with her."

I was still too blind to understand his meaning, until he felt in his breast pocket for a note, which he handed to me. I opened it and read the few words scribbled in an unformed youthful hand. "If you still need a daughter in your declining years," ran the message, "she waits for you, on board the good ship *Frances*. Holland, they say, is healthier than England. Will you try the climate with me? My mother christened me Elizabeth, but I prefer to sign myself your daughter Bess."

I said nothing for a little while, but held the note there in my hands. I could have asked a hundred questions, had I the time—or inclination. Woman's questions, such as my sister Mary might have answered, and perhaps understood. Was she pretty? Was she kind? Had she his eyes, his mouth, his auburn hair? Would she understand his lonely moods? Would she laugh with him when his moods were gay? But none of them mattered, or were appropriate to the moment. Since I should never see her, it was not my affair.

"You have given me this note," I said to Jonathan, "in the hope that I can pass it to her father?"

"Yes," he answered.

Once again he looked at the broad back of the sentry by the window.

"I have told you that the *Frances* leaves Fowey on the early tide," he said. "A boat will put off to Pridmouth, as they go from harbour, to lift lobster pots dropped between the shore and the Cannis Rock. It would be a simple matter to pick up a passenger in the half-light of morning."

"A simple matter," I answered, "if the passenger is there."

"It is your business," he said, "to see then that he is."

He guessed that Richard was concealed within the buttress; so much I could tell from his eyes and the look he fastened now upon me. "The sentries," I said, "keep a watch upon the causeway."

"At this end only," he said softly. "Not at the other."

"The risk is very great," I said, "even by night, even by early morning."

"I know that," he answered, "but I think the person of whom we speak will dare that risk."

Once again he drew the poster from his pocket. "If you should deliver the note," he said quietly, "you could give him this as well." I took the poster in silence, and placed it in my gown.

"There is one other thing that I would have you do," he said to me.

"What is that!"

"Destroy all trace of what has been. The men who will come tomorrow have keener noses than the troops who came today. They are scent hounds, trained to the business."

"They can find nothing from within," I answered. "You know that. Your father had the cunning of all time when he built his buttress."

"But from without," he said, "the secret is less sure. I give you leave to finish the work begun by the Parliament in '44. I shall not seek to use the summerhouse again."

I guessed his meaning as he stood there watching me, leaning on his stick.

"Timber burns fiercely in dry weather," he said to me, "and rubble makes a pile, and the nettles and the thistles grow apace in midsummer. There will be no need to clear those nettles in my lifetime, nor in John's either."

"Why do you not stay," I whispered, "and do this work yourself."

But even as I spoke the door of the dining hall was opened and the leader of the three troopers waiting in the hall entered the room. "I am sorry, sir," he said, "but you have already had fifteen minutes of the ten allotted to you. I cannot go against my orders. Will you please make your farewell now, and return with me to Fowey?"

I stared at him blankly, my heart sinking in my breast again.

"I thought Mr. Rashleigh was a free agent once again?"

"The times being troublesome, my dear Honor," said Jonathan quietly, "the gentlemen in authority deem it best that I should remain at present under surveillance, if not exactly custody. I am to spend the night, therefore, in my town house at Fowey. I regret if I did not make myself more clear." He turned to the trooper. "I am grateful to you," he said, "for allowing me this interview with my sister-in-law. She suffers from poor health, and we have all been anxious for her." And without another word, he went from me and I was left there, with the note in my hand and the poster in my gown, and the lives of not only Richard and his son, but those of the whole family of Rashleigh, depending upon my wits and my sagacity.

I waited for Matty, but she did not come to me, and, impatient at last, I rang the bell beside the hearth. The startled servant who came running at the sound told me that Matty was not to be found; he had sought for her in the kitchen, in her bedroom, but she had not answered. "No matter," I said, and made a pretence of taking up a book and turning the pages.

"Will you dine now, madam?" he said to me. "It is nearly seven. Long past your usual hour."

"Why, yes," I said, "if you care to bring it," feigning intensity upon my book, yet all the while counting the hours to darkness, and wondering with an anxious heart what had become of Matty. I ate my meat and drank my wine, tasting them not at all, and as I sat there in the dark panelled dining hall with the portrait of old John Rashleigh and his wife frowning down upon me, I watched the shadows lengthen and the murky evening creep on, and the great banked clouds of evening steal across the sky.

It was close on nine o'clock when I heard the door open with a creak. Turning in my chair, I saw Matty standing there, her gown stained green and brown with bracken and with earth. She put her finger to her lips, and I said nothing. She came across the room and closed the shutters. As she folded the last one into place, she spoke softly over her shoulder. "He is not ill-looking, the sentry on the causeway."

"No?"

"He knows my cousin's wife at Liskeard."

"Introductions have been made on less than that."

She fastened the hasp of the shutter and drew the heavy curtain. "It was somewhat damp in thistle park," she said.

"So I perceive," I answered.

"But he found a sheltered place beneath a bush, where we could talk about my cousin's wife... While he was looking for it I waited in the summerhouse."

"That," I said, "was understandable."

The curtains were now all drawn before the shutters, and the dining hall in darkness. Matty came and stood beside my chair. "I lifted the flagstone," she said. "I left a letter on the steps. I said, if the rope be still in place upon the hinge, would they open the stone entrance in the buttress tonight at twelve o'clock. We would be waiting for them."

I felt for her strong comforting hand and held it between mine.

"I pray they find it," she said slowly. "There must have been a fall of earth since the tunnel was last used. The place smelt of the tomb..."

We clung to one another in the darkness, and as I listened I could hear the steady thumping of her heart.

Thirty-Six

I LAY UPON MY BED UPSTAIRS FROM HALF PAST NINE UNTIL A quarter before twelve. When Matty came to rouse me the house was deadly still. The servants had gone to their beds in the attics, and the sentries were at their posts about the grounds. I could hear one of them pacing the walk beneath my window. The treacherous moon, never an ally to a fugitive, rose slowly above the trees in thistle park. We lit no candles. Matty crept to the door and listened. Then she lifted me in her arms, and trod the long, twisting corridor to the empty gatehouse. How bare were the rooms, how silently accusing, and there was no moonlight here on the western side to throw a beam of light upon the floor.

Inside the room that was our destination the ashes of our poor fire, kindled that afternoon, flickering feebly still, and the smoke hung in clouds about the ceiling. We sat down beside the wall in the far corner and waited. It was uncannily still. The stillness of a place that has not known a footstep or a voice for many years. The quietude of a long-forgotten prison where no sunlight ever penetrates, where all seasons seem alike.

Winter, summer, spring, and autumn, would all come and go but never here, never in this room. Here was eternal night. And I thought, sitting there beside the cold wall of the buttress, that this must be the darkness that so frightened the poor idiot Uncle John when he lay here, long ago, in the first building of the house. Perhaps he lay upon this very spot on which I sat, his hands feeling the air, his wide eyes searching...

Then I felt Matty touch me on the shoulder, and as she did so the stone behind me moved. There came, upon my back, the current of cold air I well remembered, and now, turning, I could see the yawning gulf and the narrow flight of steps behind, and could hear the creaking of the rope upon its rusty hinge.

Although it was the sound I wanted most in all the world to hear, it struck a note of horror, like a summons from the grave.

Now Matty lit her candle, and throwing the beam onto the steps, I saw him standing there, earth upon his face, his hands, his shoulders, giving him, in that weird, unnatural light, the features of a corpse new-risen from his grave. He smiled, and the smile had in it something grim and terrible.

"I feared," he said, "you would not come. A few hours more, and it would have been too late."

"What do you mean?" I asked.

"No air," he said. "There is only room here from the tunnel for a dog to crawl. I have no great opinion of your Rashleigh builder."

I leant forward, peering down the steps, and there was Dick, huddled at the bottom, his face as ghostly as his father's.

"It was not thus," I said, "four years ago."

"Come," said Richard. "I will show you. A jailer should have knowledge of the cell where she puts her prisoners."

He took me in his arms and, crawling sideways, dragged me through the little stone entrance to the steps and down to the cell below. I saw it for the first time, and the last, that secret room beneath the buttress. Six foot high, four square, it was no larger than a closet; and the stone walls, clammy cold with years, icy to my touch. There was a little stool in the corner, and by its side an empty trencher, with a wooden spoon. Cobwebs and mould were thick upon them, and I thought of the last meal that had been eaten there, a quarter of a century before, by idiot Uncle John. Above the stool hung the rope, near frayed, upon its rusty hinge, and beyond this the opening of the tunnel, a round black hole about eighteen inches high, through which a man must crawl and wriggle if he wished to reach the farther end. "I don't understand," I said shuddering. "It could not have been thus before. Jonathan would never have used it, had it been so."

"There has been a fall of earth and stones," said Richard, "from the foundations of the house. It blocks the tunnel save for a small space through which we burrowed. I think, when the tunnel was used before, the way was cleared regularly with pick and spade. Now that it has not been used for several years, Nature has claimed it for her own again. My enemies can find me a new name. Henceforth I will be badger, and not fox."

I saw Dick's white face watching me. What is he telling me, I wondered, with his dark eyes? What is he trying to say?

"Take me back," I said to Richard. "I have to talk to you."

He carried me to the room above, and it seemed to me, as I sat their breathing deep, that the bare boards and smoky ceiling were paradise compared to the black hole from which we had come. Had I in truth forced Dick to lie there, hour after hour, as a lad four years ago? Was it because of this that his eyes accused me now? God forgive me, but I thought to save his life. We sat there, by the light of a single candle, Richard, and Dick, and I, while Matty kept watch upon the door.

"Jonathan Rashleigh has returned," I said.

Dick threw me a questioning glance, but Richard answered nothing.

"The fine is paid," I said. "The County Committee have allowed him to come home. He will be able to live in

Cornwall, henceforth, a free man, unencumbered, if he does nothing more to rouse the suspicions of the Parliament."

"That is well for him," said Richard. "I wish him good fortune."

"Jonathan Rashleigh is a man of peace," I said, "who, though he loves his King, loves his home better. He has endured two years of suffering and privatoin. I think he has earned repose now, and he had but one desire, to live amongst his family, in his own house, without anxiety."

"The desire," said Richard, "of almost every man."

"His desire will not be granted," I said, "if it should be proved he was a party to the rising."

Richard glanced at me, than shrugged his shoulders.

"That is something that the Parliament would find difficult to lay upon him," he said. "Rashleigh has been two years in London."

For answer, I took the bill from my gown and, spreading it on the floor, put the candlestick upon it. I read it aloud, as my brother-in-law had read it to me that afternoon:

"'Anyone who has harboured at any time, or seeks to harbour in the future, the malignant known as Richard Grenvile, shall, upon discovery, be arrested for high treason, his lands sequestered finally and for ever, and his family imprisoned.'"

I waited a moment, and then I said, "They will come in the morning, Jonathan said, to search again."

A blob of grease from the candle fell upon the paper, and the edges curled. Richard placed it on the flame, and the paper caught and burnt, wisping to nothing in his hands, then fell and scattered.

"You see?" said Richard to his son. "life is like that. A flicker, and a spark, and then it is over. No trace remains."

It seemed to me that Dick looked at his father as a dumb dog gazes at his master. Tell me, said his eyes, what you are asking me to do?

"Ah, well," said Richard with a sigh, "there's nothing for it but to run our necks into cold steel. A dreary finish. A scrap upon the road, some dozen men upon us, handcuffs and rope, and then the march through the streets of London, jeered at by the mob. Are you ready, Dick? Yours was the master hand that brought us to this pass. I trust you profit by it now."

He rose to his feet and stretched his arms above his head. "At least," he said, "they keep a sharp axe in Whitehall. I have watched the executioner do justice before now. A little crabbed fellow, he was, last time I saw him, but with biceps in his arms like cannon balls. He only takes a single stroke." He paused a moment, thoughtful. "But," he said slowly, "the blood makes a pretty mess upon the straw."

I saw Dick grip his ankle with his hand, and I turned like a fury on the man I loved. "Will you be silent?" I said. "Hasn't he suffered enough these eighteen years?"

Richard stared down at me, one eyebrow lifted.

"What?" he said smiling. "Do you turn against me too?"

For answer, I threw him the note I was clutching in my hand. It was smeared by now, and scarcely legible.

"There is no need for your fox's head to lie upon the block," I said to him. "Read that and change your tune."

He bent low to the candle, and I saw his eye change in a strange manner as he read, from black malevolence to wonder.

"I've bred a Grenvile after all," he answered softly.

"The *Frances* leaves Fowey on the morning tide," I said. "She is bound for Flushing and has room for passengers. The master can be trusted. The voyage will be swift."

"And how," asked Richard, "do the passengers go aboard?"

"A boat, in quest of lobsters and not foxes, will call at Pridmouth," I said lightly, "as the vessel sails from harbour. The passengers will be waiting for it. I suggest that they conceal themselves for the remainder of the night till dawn on the

cowrie beach near to the Gribben Hill, and when the boat
creeps to its post, in the early morning light, a signal will bring
it to the shore."

"It would seem," said Richard, "that nothing could be
more easy."

"You agree, then, to this method of escape? Adieu to your
fine heroics of surrender?" I think he had forgotten them
already, for his eyes were travelling beyond my head to plans
and schemes in which I played no part. "From Holland to
France," he murmured, "and, once there, to see the Prince.
A new plan of campaign better than this last. A landing,
perchance, in Ireland, and from Ireland to Scotland..." His eyes
fell back upon the note screwed up in his hand. "My mother
christened me Elizabeth," he read, "but I prefer to sign myself
your daughter Bess."

He whistled under his breath and tossed the note to Dick.
The boy read it, then handed it back in silence to his father.

"Well?" said Richard. "Shall I like your sister?"

"I think, sir," said Dick slowly, "you will like her very well."

"It took courage, did it not," pursued his father, "to leave
her home, find herself a ship, and be prepared to land alone in
Holland without friends or fortune?"

"Yes," I said, "it took courage, and something else besides."

"What was that?"

"Faith in the man she is proud to call her father. Confidence
that he will not desert her, should she prove unworthy."

They stared at one another, Richard and his son, brooding,
watchful, as though between them both was some dark secret
understanding that I, a woman, could not hope to share. Then
Richard put the note into his pocket and turned, hesitating, to
the entrance in the buttress. "Do we go," he said, "the same
way by which we came?"

"The house is guarded," I said. "It is your only chance."

"And when the watchdogs come tomorrow," he said, "and seek to sniff our tracks, how will you deal with them."

"As Jonathan Rashleigh suggested," I replied. "Dry timber in midsummer burns easily, and fast. I think the family of Rashleigh will not use their summerhouse again."

"And the entrance here?"

"The stone cannot be forced. Not from this side. See the rope there and the hinge."

We peered, all three of us, into the murky depths. And Dick, of a sudden, reached out to the rope and pulled upon it, and the hinge also. He gave three tugs, and then they broke, useless forever.

"There," he said, smiling oddly. "No one will ever force the stone again, once you have closed it from this side."

"One day," said Richard, "a Rashleigh will come and pull the buttress down. What shall we leave them for legacy?" His eyes wandered to the bones in the corner. "The skeleton of a rat," he said. And with a smile, he threw it down the stair.

"Go first, Dick," he said. "I will follow you."

Dick put his hand out to me, and I held it for a moment.

"Be brave," I said. "The journey will be swift. Once safe in Holland you will make good friends."

He did not answer. He gazed at me with his great dark eyes, then turned to the little stair.

I was alone with Richard. We had had several partings, he and I. Each time I told myself it was the last. Each time we had found one another once again. "How long this time?" I said.

"Two years," he said. "Perhaps eternity."

He took my face in his hands and kissed me long.

"When I come back," he said, "we'll build that house at Stowe. You shall sink your pride at last and become a Grenvile."

I smiled, and shook my head.

"Be happy with your daughter," I said to him.

He paused at the entrance to the buttress.

"I tell you one thing," he said. "Once out in Holland, I'll put pen to paper and write the truth about the Civil War. My God, I'll flay my fellow generals and show them for the sods they are. Perhaps, when I have done so the Prince of Wales will take the hint and make me at last supreme commander of his forces."

"He is more likely," I said, "to degrade you to the ranks."

He climbed through the entrance and knelt upon the stair, where Dick waited for him.

"I'll do your destruction for you," he said. "Watch from your chamber in the eastern wing, and you will see the Rashleigh summerhouse make its last bow to Cornwall, and the Grenviles also."

"Beware the sentry," I said. "He stands below the causeway."

"Do you love me still, Honor?"

"For my sins, Richard."

"Are they many?"

"You know them all."

And as he waited there, his hand upon the stone, I made my last request.

"You know why Dick betrayed you to the enemy?"

"I think so."

"Not from resentment, not from revenge. But because he saw the blood on Gartred's cheek…"

He stared at me thoughtfully, and I whispered, "Forgive him, for my sake, if not for your own."

"I have forgiven him," he said slowly, "but the Grenviles are strangely fashioned. I think you will find that he cannot forgive himself." I saw them both, father and son, standing upon the stair, with the little cell below, and then Richard pushed the stone flush against the buttress wall, and it was closed for ever. I waited there beside it for a moment, and then I called for Matty.

"It's all over," I said. "Finished now, and done with."

She came across the room and lifted me in her arms.

"No one," I said to her, "will ever hide in the buttress cell again." I put my hand on to my cheek. It was wet. I did not know I had been crying. "Take me to my room," I said to Matty.

I sat there, by the far window, looking out across the gardens. The moon was high now, not white as last night, but with a yellow rim about it. Clouds had gathered in the evening and were banking curled and dark against the sky. The sentry had left the causeway steps and was leaning against the hatch door of the farm buildings opposite, watching the windows of the house. He did not see me sitting there, in the darkness, with my chin upon my hand.

Hours long, it seemed, I waited there, staring to the east, with Matty crouching at my side, and at length I saw a little spurt of flame rise above the trees in thistle park. The wind was westerly, blowing the smoke away, and the sentry down below, leaning against the barn, could not see it from where he stood.

Now, I said to myself, it will burn steadily till morning, and when daylight comes they will say poachers have lit a bonfire in the night that spread, catching the summerhouse alight, and someone from the estate here must go, cap in hand, with apologies for carelessness, to Jonathan Rashleigh in his house at Fowey. Now, I said also, two figures wend their way across the cowrie beach and wait there, in the shelter of the cliff. They are safe; they are together. I can go to bed and sleep and so forget them. And yet I went on sitting there, beside my bedroom window, looking out upon the lawns, and I did not see the moon, nor the trees, nor the thin column of smoke rising into the air, but all the while Dick's eyes, looking up at me, for the last time, as Richard closed the stone in the buttress wall.

Thirty-Seven

A T NINE IN THE MORNING CAME A LINE OF TROOPERS riding through the park. They dismounted in the courtyard, and the officer in charge, a colonel from the staff of Sir Hardress Waller at Saltash, sent word up to me that I must dress and descend immediately and be ready to accompany him to Fowey. I was dressed already, and when the servants carried me downstairs I saw the troopers he had brought prising the panelling in the long gallery. The watchdogs had arrived...

"This house was sacked once already," I said to the officer, "and it has taken my brother-in-law four years to make what small repairs he could. Must this work begin again?"

"I am sorry," said the officer, "but the Parliament can afford to take no chances with a man like Richard Grenvile."

"You think to find him here?"

"There are a score of houses in Cornwall where he might be hidden," he replied. "Menabilly is but one of them. This being so, I am compelled to search the house, rather too thoroughly for the comfort of those who dwell beneath its roof. I am afraid that Menabilly will not be habitable for some little while... Therefore, I must ask you to come with me to Fowey."

I looked about me, at the place that had been my home now for two years. I had seen it sacked before. I had no wish to witness the sight again. "I am ready," I said to the officer.

As I was placed in the litter, with Matty at my side, I heard the old sound I well remembered of axes tearing the floorboards, of swords ripping the wood, and another jester, like his predecessor in '44, had already climbed up to the belfry and hung cross-legged from the beam, the rope between his hands, swinging the great bell from side to side. It tolled us from the gatehouse, tolled us from the outer court. This, I thought to myself in premonition, is my farewell to Menabilly. I shall not live here again.

"We will go by the coast," said the officer, "looking in the window of my litter. The highway is choked with troops, bound for Helston and Penzance."

"Do you need so many," I asked, "to quell but a little rising?"

"The rising will be over in a day or so," he answered, "but the troops have come to stay. There will be no more insurrections in Cornwall, east or west, from this day forward." And as he spoke the Menabilly bell swung backwards, forwards, in a mournful knell, echoing his words.

I looked up from the path beneath the causeway, and the summerhouse that had stood there yesterday, a little tower with its long windows, was now charred rubble, a heap of sticks and stones.

"By whose orders," called the officer, "was that fire kindled?" I heard him take counsel of his men, and they climbed to the causeway to investigate the pile, while Matty and I waited in the litter. In a few moments the officer returned.

"What building stood there?" he asked me. "I can make nothing of it from the mess. But the fire is recent, and smoulders still."

"A summerhouse," I said, "My sister, Mrs. Rashleigh, loved it well. We sat there often when she was home. This will vex her sorely. Colonel Bennett, when he came here yesterday, gave orders, I believe, for its destruction."

"Colonel Bennett," said the officer, frowning, "had no authority without permission of the sheriff, Sir Thomas Herle."

I shrugged my shoulders. "He may have had permission. I cannot tell you. But he is a member of the County Committee, and therefore can do much as he pleases."

"The County Committee takes too much upon itself," said the officer. "One day they will have trouble with us in the Army." He mounted his horse in high ill temper and shouted an order to his men. A civil war within a civil war. Did no faction ever keep the peace among themselves? Let the Army and the Parliament quarrel as they pleased; it would help our cause in the end, in the long run... And as I turned and looked for the last time at the smouldering pile upon the causeway, and the tall trees in thistle park, I thought of the words that had been whispered two years ago in '46: When the snow melts, when the thaw breaks, when the spring comes.

We descended the steep path to Pridmouth. The tide was low, the Cannis Rock showed big and clear, and on the far horizon was the black smudge of a sail. The millstream gurgled out upon the stones and ran sharply to the beach, and from the marsh at the farther end a swan rose suddenly, thrashing his way across the water, and, circling in the air a moment, winged his way out to the sea. We climbed the farther hill, past Coombe Manor, where the Rashleigh cousins lived, and so down to my brother-in-law's town house on Fowey quay. The first thing I looked for was a ship at anchor in the Rashleigh roads, but none was there. The harbour water was still and gray, and no vessels but little fishing craft anchored at Polruan. The people on the quayside watched with curiosity as I was lifted from my litter and taken to the house. My brother-in-law was waiting for me in the parlour. The room was dark panelled, like the dining hall at Menabilly, the great windows looking out upon the quay. On the ledge stood the model of a ship—the same ship that his father had built and commissioned forty years before, to sail with Drake against the Armada. She too was named the *Frances*.

"I regret," said the officer, "that for a day or so, until the trouble in the West has quietened down, it will be necessary to keep a watch upon this house. I must ask you, sir, and this lady here, to stay within your doors."

"I understand," said Jonathan. "I have been so long accustomed to surveillance that a few more days of it will not hurt me now."

The officer withdrew, and I saw a sentry take up his position outside the window, as his fellow had done the night before at Menabilly.

"I have news of Robin," said my brother-in-law. "He is detained in Plymouth, but I think they can fasten little upon him. When this matter has blown over he will be released, on condition that he takes the oath of allegiance to the Parliament, as I was forced to do."

"And then?" I said.

"Why, then he can become his own master and settle down to peace and quietude. I have a little house in Tywardreath that would suit him well, and you too, Honor, if you should wish to share it with him. That is... if you have no other plan."

"No," I said. "No, I have no other plan."

He rose from his chair and walked slowly to the window, looking out upon the quay. An old man, white-haired and bent, leaning heavily upon his stick. The sound of the gulls came to us as they wheeled and dived above the harbour.

"The *Frances* sailed at five this morning," he said slowly.

I did not answer.

The fishing lad who went to lift his pots pulled first into

Pridmouth for his passenger. He found him waiting on the beach, as he expected. "He looked tired and wan," the lad said, "but otherwise little the worse for his ordeal."

"One passenger?" I said.

"Why, yes, there was but one," said Jonathan, staring at me. "Is anything the matter? You looked wisht and strange."

I went on listening to the gulls above the harbour, and now there were children's voices also, laughing and crying, as they played upon the steps of the quay.

"There is nothing the matter," I said. "What else have you to tell me?"

He went to his desk in the far corner and, opening a drawer, took out a length of rope, with a rusted hinge upon it.

"As the passenger was put aboard the vessel," said my brother-in-law, "he gave the fisher-lad this piece of rope and bade him hand it, on his return, to Mr. Rashleigh. The lad brought it to me as I breakfasted just now. There was a piece of paper wrapped about it, with these words written on the face: 'Tell Honor that the least of the Grenviles chose his own method of escape.'"

He handed me the little scrap of paper.

"What does it mean?" he asked. "Do you understand it?"

For a long while I did not answer. I sat there with the paper in my hands, and I saw once more the ashes of the summerhouse blocking forevermore the secret tunnel, and I saw too the silent cell, like a dark tomb, in the thick buttress wall.

"Yes, Jonathan," I said, "I understand."

He looked at me a moment and then went to the table and put the rope and hinge back in the drawer.

"Well," he said, "it's over now, praise heaven. The danger and the strain. There is nothing more that we can do."

"No," I answered. "Nothing more that we can do."

He fetched two glasses from the sideboard, and filled them

with wine from the decanter. Then he handed one to me. "Drink this," he said kindly, his hand upon my arm. "You have been through great anxiety." He took his glass, and lifted it to the ship that had carried his father to the Armada.

"To the other *Frances*?" he said, "and to the King's General in the West. May he find sanctuary and happiness in Holland."

I drank the toast in silence, then put the glass back upon the table. "You have not finished it," he said. "That spells ill luck to him whom we have toasted."

I took the glass again, and this time I held it up against the light so that the wine shone clear and red.

"Did you ever hear," I said, "those words that Bevil Grenvile wrote to John Trelawney?"

"What words were those?"

Once more we were assembled, four-and-twenty hours ago, in the long gallery at Menabilly. Richard at the window, Gartred on the couch, and Dick, in his dark corner, with his eyes upon his father. "And for mine own part," I quoted slowly, "I desire to acquire an honest name or an honourable grave. I never loved my life or ease so much as to shun such an occasion, which, if I should, I were unworthy of the profession I have held, or to succeed those ancestors of mine who have so many of them, in several ages, sacrificed their lives for their country."

I drank my wine then to the dregs and gave the glass to Jonathan.

"Great words," said my brother-in-law, "and the Grenviles were all great men. As long as the name endures we shall be proud of them in Cornwall. But Bevil was the finest of them. He showed great courage at the last."

"The least of them," I said, "showed great courage also."

"Which one was that?" he asked.

"Only a boy," I said, "whose name will never now be

written in the great book at Stowe, nor his grave be found in the little churchyard at Kilkhampton."

"You are crying," said Jonathan slowly. "This time has been hard and long for you. There is a bed prepared for you above. Let Matty take you to it. Come now, take heart. The worst is over. The best is yet to be. One day the King will come into his Own again; one day your Richard will return."

I looked up at the model of the ship upon the ledge and across the masts to the blue harbour water. The fishing boats were making sail, and the gulls flew above them, crying, white wings against the sky.

"One day," I said, "when the snow melts, when the thaw breaks, when the spring comes…"

What Happened to the People in the Story

SIR RICHARD GRENVILE. The King's General never returned to England again. He bought a house in Holland, where he lived with his daughter Elizabeth, until his death in 1659, just a year before the Restoration. He offered his services to the Prince of Wales in exile (afterwards Charles II), but they were not accepted, due to the ill feeling between himself and Sir Edward Hyde, later Earl of Clarendon. The exact date of his death is uncertain, but he is said to have died in Ghent, lonely and embittered, with these words only for his epitaph: "Sir Richard Grenvile, the King's General in the West."

SIR JOHN GRENVILE (JACK). BERNARD GRENVILE (BUNNY). These two brothers were largely instrumental in bringing about the restoration of Charles II in 1660. They both married, lived happily, and were in high favour with the King. John was created Earl of Bath.

GARTRED DENYS. She never married again, but left Orley Court and went to live with one of her married daughters, Lady Hampson, at Taplow, where she died at the ripe age of eighty-five.

JONATHAN RASHLEIGH. Suffered further imprisonment for debt at the hands of Parliament, but lived to see the Restoration. He died in 1675, a year after his wife, Mary.

JOHN RASHLEIGH. He died in 1651, aged only thirty, in Devon, when on the road home to Menabilly, after a visit to London about his father's business. His widow Joan lived in Fowey until her death in 1668, aged forty-eight. Her son Jonathan succeeded to his grandfather's estate at Menabilly.

SIR PETER COURTNEY. He deserted his wife, ran hopelessly into debt, married a second time, and died in 1670.

ALICE COURTNEY. Lived the remainder of her life at Menabilly, and died there in 1659, aged forty. There is a tablet to her memory in the church at Tywardreath.

AMBROSE MANATON. Little is known about him, except that he was M.P. for Camelford in 1668. His estate, Trecarrel, fell into decay.

ROBIN AND HONOR HARRIS. The brother and sister lived in retirement at Tywardreath, in a house provided for them by Jonathan Rashleigh. Honor died on the seventeenth day of November 1653, and Robin in June 1655. Thus they never lived to see the Restoration. The tablet to their memory in the church runs thus:

In memory of Robert Harris, sometime Major-General of His Majesty's forces before Plymouth, who was buried here under the 29th day of June 1655. And of Honor Harris, his sister, who was likewise here underneath buried, the 17th day of November, in the year of our Lord 1653. Loyal and stout; thy Crime this—this thy praise, Thou'rt here with Honour laid—thought without Bayes.

Postscript

In the year 1824, Mr. William Rashleigh, of Menabilly, in the parish of Tywardreath in Cornwall, had certain alterations made to his house, in the course of which the outer courtyard was removed, and blocked in to form kitchens and a larder. The architect, summoned to do the work, noticed that the buttress against the northwest corner of the house served no useful purpose, and he told the masons to demolish it. This they proceeded to do, and on knocking away several of the stones they came upon a stair, leading to a small room or cell, at the base of the buttress. Here they found the skeleton of a young man seated on a stool, a trencher at his feet, and the skeleton was dressed in the clothes of a cavalier, as worn during the period of the Civil War. Mr. William Rashleigh, when he was told of the discovery, gave orders for the remains to be buried with great reverence in the churchyard at Tywardreath. And because he and his family were greatly shocked at the discovery, he ordered the masons to brick up the secret room that no one in the household should come upon it in future. The alterations of the house continued, the courtyard was blocked in, a larder built against the buttress, and the exact whereabouts of the cell remained forever a secret held by Mr. Rashleigh and his architect. When he consulted family records,

Mr. Rashleigh learnt that certain members of the Grenvile family had hidden at Menabilly before the rising of 1648, and he surmised that one of them had taken refuge in the secret room and had been forgotten. This tradition has been handed down to the present day.

—Daphne du Maurier

About the Author

Daughter of the famous actor-manager Sir Gerald du Maurier, **Daphne du Maurier** was educated at home in London, and then in Paris, before writing her first novel, *The Loving Spirit*, in 1931. Three others, and a frank biography of her father, followed before *Rebecca*, in 1938, made her to her surprise one of the most popular authors of the day. Nearly all her fifteen novels have been bestsellers, and several of her works became successful films, notably *Rebecca*, starring Laurence Olivier, and the short stories *The Birds and Don't Look Now*. She also wrote biographies of Branwell Bronte and her own Victorian family, two volumes of autobiography, and Vanishing Cornwall, an eloquent evocation of her beloved countryside that is such a strong feature of her fiction.

Daphne du Maurier, who was married to Lieutenant-General Sir Frederick Browning, KCVO, DSO, was made a DBE in 1969. When she died in 1989, Margaret Forster wrote in tribute: "No other popular writer has so triumphantly defied classification… She satisfied all the questionable criteria of popular fiction, and yet satisfied, too, the exacting requirements of 'real literature,' something very few novelists ever do."

Das Buch

Thomas Quasthoff ist einer der erfolgreichsten und ungewöhnlichsten Sänger der Gegenwart. Obwohl die Musikhochschule Hannover dem contergangeschädigten Bariton mit der Begründung, er könne nicht Klavier spielen, ein Gesangsstudium verwehrte, stand sein Berufswunsch fest. Heute werden seine CD-Veröffentlichungen regelmäßig von der internationalen Fachpresse ausgezeichnet, hat er mehrere Wettbewerbe und hochangesehene Preise gewonnen und eine Gesangsprofessur inne. In der glatten und glamourösen Welt der klassischen Musik ist Quasthoff dabei nicht nur optisch eine auffällige Erscheinung, sondern auch, weil der Jazz-Fan die Grenzen von U- und E-Musik immer wieder durchschreitet. In seinen Erinnerungen erzählt er von seinen großen internationalen Erfolgen, von Konzertatmosphäre, Reisen und Plattenaufnahmen, aber auch von seinem Handicap, den Kämpfen, die seine Eltern und er mit den Behörden führen mussten, und der erfahrenen Ausgrenzung.

Der Autor

Thomas Quasthoff, geboren 1959, studierte Jura und arbeitete in einer Sparkasse sowie beim NDR, bevor er seine Sängerkarriere begann, in deren Verlauf er zahlreiche Auszeichnungen erhielt, darunter zwei Grammys. Seit 2004 ist er Professor an der »Hanns Eisler«-Hochschule für Musik in Berlin. Er lebt in Hannover.
Michael Quasthoff, Jahrgang 1957, ist Autor und Publizist und lebt in Hannover.

Von Thomas und Michael Quasthoff ist außerdem erschienen:

Ach, hört mit Furcht und Grauen

Thomas Quasthoff

Die Stimme

Autobiografie

Aufgezeichnet von Michael Quasthoff

List Taschenbuch

Besuchen Sie uns im Internet:
www.list-taschenbuch.de

Ungekürzte Ausgabe im List Taschenbuch
List ist ein Verlag der Ullstein Buchverlage GmbH, Berlin
1. Auflage Januar 2006
6. Auflage 2010
© Ullstein Buchverlage GmbH, Berlin 2004 / Ullstein Verlag
Umschlaggestaltung und Konzeption: RME – Roland Eschlbeck und
Kornelia Bunkofer
(unter Verwendung einer Vorlage von Jorge Schmidt, München)
Titelabbildung: Kasskara, Berlin
Satz: ew print & medien service, Würzburg
Gesetzt aus der Palatino
Papier: Munken Print von Arctic Paper Munkedals AB, Schweden
Druck und Bindearbeiten: CPI – Clausen & Bosse, Leck
Printed in Germany
ISBN 978-3-548-60580-7

Inhalt

Südstadt

Hannovers Südstadt, Februar, die Gastwirtschaft Taverne. Die Bierstube mit Speisebetrieb ist gut gefüllt. Am Tresen parlieren die Wirte Armin und Gerrit mit Stammgästen, gerahmt von der Weihnachtsdeko, die hier bis Ostern an den Wänden kleben wird. Hinten rechts am Stammtisch hocken die Brüder Quasthoff, vor sich wuchtige Mettwurstbrote und zwei Gläser Bier. Michael, der große, kaut. Thomas, der kleine, spricht:

TQ: »... und dann sage ich, warum soll ich meine Autobiografie schreiben. Mir geht's doch gut. Ich bin kein berühmter Alkoholiker, ich hab mir mein Geld nicht ergaunert, ich schlafe nicht mit prominenten Damen und ans Sterben denk ich eigentlich auch noch nicht.«

MQ (nimmt einen großen Schluck Bier): »Nicht?«

TQ: »Definitiv nicht.«

MQ: »Dann bestellen wir noch zwei.« (Er winkt Richtung Tresen.) »Armin, Gerrit, bitte noch zwei Pils.«

TQ: »Jedenfalls hat sich die Literaturagentin nicht beirren lassen und insistiert, das Leben von berühmten Leuten wäre immer interessant, und ich sei ja ein sehr berühmter Sänger ...«

MQ: »Stimmt. Aber die meisten Promis schreiben ihre Autobiografie, weil sie nicht mehr berühmt sind.«

TQ: »Hab ich ja auch gesagt. Aber sie sagt, meine Geschichte ist etwas ganz Besonderes ...«

MQ: »Das Argument würde ich tatsächlich gelten lassen. Conterganopfer, dem die Musikhochschule das Studium verwehrt, singt sich aus dem Streckverband zum

Grammy hoch. Super Story, alles drin: schwere Kindheit, Kampf gegen die Krake Bürokratie, Drama, Liebe, Wahnsinn. Am Ende Triumph in Amerika, dem Land der unbegrenzten Möglichkeiten. Die Republik kann Erfolgsgeschichten brauchen.«

Gerrit, ein hünenhafter Exilholländer, bringt zwei frische Biere.

Gerrit: »Bittesssehr, die Herrren.«

MQ: »Besten Dank, Gerrit. Hör mal, Tommi soll seine Biografie schreiben. Würdest du die gerne lesen?«

Gerrit: »Na klaaarrr, isss doch irrre interrrressant. Die Gesssichten von der Sssingerei, den Reisssen, von berühmten Dirigenten und sssönen Tenören. (Im Weggehen.) Ach, herrrlich.«

MQ: »Da hast du's.«

TQ: »Selbst wenn ich wollte, hätte ich gar keine Zeit, ein Buch zu schreiben.«

MQ: »Das machen die wenigsten Prominenten selber. Die erzählen alles einem Ghostwriter, und der schreibt es dann auf.«

TQ: »Und was kommt dabei heraus? Halbwahrheiten und geschönter Edelkitsch.«

MQ: »›Erlaubt ist, was gefällt.‹«

TQ: »Komm mir nicht mit Goethe.«

MQ: »Dann eben mit Herrn Frisch: ›Wahrheit lässt sich nicht zeigen, nur erfinden.‹«

TQ: »Dann schreib du das Buch, im Erfinden bist du ja Profi.«

MQ: »Ich bestelle lieber noch ein Pils.« (Er hält sein Glas hoch.) »Willst du auch noch eins?«

TQ: »Bitte.«

MQ: »Armin, Gerrit, zwei …«

Dietrich zur Nedden: »Drei bitte.«

Zur Nedden, stadtbekannter Publizist und Spezi der

Brüder, klopft auf den Tisch und lässt sich auf die Sitzbank plumpsen.

DZN: »Na, was gibt's Neues?«

TQ (grinst): »Micha schreibt mein Leben auf. Ein Verlag will daraus ein Buch machen.«

MQ: »Quatsch mit Soße.«

DZN: »Wieso? Ist nicht die schlechteste Idee. Tommi hat viel zu erzählen und meistens ist es urkomisch. Da gibt es bestimmt einige Leute, die das mit Kusshand lesen. Außerdem werdet ihr es ja nicht umsonst machen.«

MQ: »Das hört die Publizistengilde gern.«

DZN: »Es ist sowieso besser, wenn ihr selbst schreibt. Tommi hat doch schon zwei Angebote von Verlagen abgelehnt. Spätestens nach dem dritten Grammy fragt euch keiner mehr, sondern lässt einfach schreiben. Und du weißt nicht, wer sich dann durch dein Leben wühlt.«

TQ: »Da ist was dran. Ich darf gar nicht dran denken, was für ein Blödsinn über mich schon in der Zeitung stand.«

MQ (trinkt sein Glas leer und atmet tief durch): »Nur mal angenommen, wir schreiben das Buch wirklich, dann machen wir es richtig. Das heißt, realistisch. Das sind wir schon Mama und Vater schuldig.«

TQ: »Genau. Keine Gefangenen. Jeder kriegt, was er verdient. Im Guten wie im Schlechten.«

DZN: »Na, das kann ja heiter werden.«

MQ: »Sehr heiter. Aber ich kenne welche, die werden nichts zu lachen haben.«

DZN: »Wenn es keine Promis sind, ändert halt die Namen.«

TQ: »Deinen?«

DZN: »Bloß nicht. Ich bin ein durch und durch integrer Charakter. Das soll die Welt ruhig wissen.«

MQ: »Wo er Recht hat, hat er Recht. Darum spendiert Didi auch noch eine Runde.«

DZN: »Überredet.« (Er hebt den Arm.)

Wirt Armin (zeigt ihm drei Finger): »Ich hab's gesehen. Komme sofort.«

MQ: »Und womit sollen wir anfangen?«

TQ: »Wie wäre es mit meinem ersten Auftritt 1996 in New York. Da bist du doch mitgefahren. Weißt du noch, wie viel Spaß wir hatten? Wir sind zum Cape Cod gefahren. Wir haben Felicitas getroffen, die im Goethe-Institut von Boston gerade eine Lesung hatte …«

MQ: »… der verrückte Tony war dabei …«

DZN: »… nicht zu vergessen dein Renatchen.«

MQ: »Stimmt. Schön war's. Vor allem wie der merkwürdige Mensch von deiner Konzertagentur in der Bar …«

TQ: »So könnten wir es machen.«

MQ: »Dann kommt dein Martyrium in der Gipsschale, die Jahre im Annastift, Schule …«

TQ: »… die ersten Gesangsstunden.«

MQ: »… nicht zu vergessen Vaters Gesangseinlage bei Peter Frankenfeld …«

TQ: »ARD-Wettbewerb, Grammy, Oper, ein paar Wahrheiten über den Musikbetrieb, die schönsten Reiseabenteuer. Fertig.«

DZN: »Na also. Das Buch schreibt sich doch von allein.«

MQ: »Nach vier großen Pils geht alles wie von selbst.«

Wirt Armin (stellt das Tablett ab): »So ist es. Bitte sehr die Herren. Drei frische Fünf-Minuten-Biere. Wohl bekomms.«

MQ (brummt): »Der Wahn ist kurz, die Reue lang.«

TQ: »Schiller.«

DZN: »*Die Glocke.*« (Er hebt das Glas.) »Wir sehen uns auf der Buchmesse.«

You did it in New York,
you did it everywhere

»Brrroigh«, dröhnt der Presslufthammer. »Brrroigh, brrroigh.« Wenn er Pause hat, brummt die Heizung, und vom Columbus Circle steigt das automobile Grundrauschen bis in den fünften Stock des Mayflower Hotels. Irgendwo schrillen Polizeisirenen. New York ist eine laute Stadt. Auch um ein Uhr morgens. Jetzt macht es wieder »Brrroigh«. Im Nebenzimmer gibt es einen Rumms und jemand flucht. Oder kam das von der Straße, wo ein Trupp Bauarbeiter seit drei Stunden das Pflaster und meine Nerven traktiert? Ich hoffe, man zahlt ihnen für diese Gemeinheit anständige Nachtzuschläge.

Ich rutsche von der viel zu weichen Matratze und schalte den Fernseher an. Durch die Nachrichten schwebt Raumfahrtpionier John Glenn, mit achtzig Jahren auf seiner letzten Mission im All – zapp – »the mysterious prostitute murderer in Newark. Seventeen victims since 1994« – zapp – ein dicker Mann in grüner Schürze kippt »rich molasse based sauce« über eine Riesenportion »pork ribs«. »Spicy, but not spicy enough«, jubelt der Dicke und hält die angeblich beste Knoblauchpaste der Welt in die Kamera – zapp – auf dem History Channel jagt General Patton Rommels Afrikacorps durch die libysche Wüste. Geschieht den ollen Nazis immer wieder recht. In Libyen explodieren jetzt Granaten. Geräuschlos, denn vor dem Fenster arbeitet wieder der Presslufthammer. »Brrroigh, brrrrroigh, brrroigh.« Zerrüttet schalte ich die Kiste aus und tigere durchs Zimmer. Das kann ja heiter werden. Morgen steht in der Avery Fisher Hall Gustav Mahlers *Des Knaben Wunderhorn* auf dem Programm, mein lang ersehntes Debüt mit den New Yorker Philharmonikern. Die Baritonpartien sind hoch und nicht ganz einfach. Eigentlich brauche ich einen klaren Kopf und viel Schlaf. Doch daran ist heute wohl nicht mehr zu denken. Eher an ein Beruhigungstonikum. Ich rufe meinen Bruder Michael an, der mit Freundin Renate drei Zimmer weiter garantiert auch nicht schlafen kann. Gott sei Dank sind die beiden für ein spätes Bier immer zu haben. Und für jeden Blödsinn.

Renate höre ich schon auf dem Flur. Mit einer Variante des Neil-Young-Klassikers *Ohio*. »Sleepless, helpless, sleepless«, flötet sie und steckt grinsend ihren roten Schopf durch die Tür.

»… keine Ruhe Tag und Nacht, nichts, was mir Vergnügen macht«, kontere ich mit Don Giovanni.

»Auf Wolfgang Amadeus und den DGB, der zu Hause die Nachtruhe der Arbeiterklasse garantiert«, brummt Micha und knackt drei Flaschen Adams Pils. Das lässt den New Yorker Bautrupp natürlich unbeeindruckt, der das Erdreich jetzt mit einer horribel wummernden Benzinwalze plättet. Wir stehen am Fenster, trinken schweigend unser Bier und sehen auf den Central Park, dessen Laubdach vor den illuminierten Betonquadern von Midtown Manhattan gähnt wie ein riesiges schwarzes Loch.

Ich gähne auch. »Wie spät ist es?«

»Kurz nach drei«, sagt Renate und streicht mir mitfühlend über den Kopf. Micha holt noch mal Bier. Er hält die Flasche gegen den fahlen Mond und deklamiert: »Du bist die Ruh, der Friede mild, die Sehnsucht du, und was sie stillt.«

»Rückert«, sage ich.

»Treffer«, nickt Renate.

»Prost«, sagt Micha mit versteinerter Miene. Im nächsten Augenblick müssen wir loslachen. Es geht doch nichts über eine solide humanistische Halb- und Herzensbildung. Wir sind ein gutes Team.

»Iiiiiiiiiiiiiiiiiiiiiiiiiiiieeeeeeeeeeh.« Am nächsten Morgen lärmt nicht mehr der Presslufthammer, sondern »Mr. Quasthoff takes his voice for a drive«, wie das mexikanische Zimmermädchen, das die für meine Waschungen unerlässliche Fußbank bringt, mit bezauberndem Lächeln anmerkt. Außerdem ist die Redewendung physiologisch erstaunlich korrekt. Denn bei der Lauterzeugung werden die vorn im Kehlkopf festgewachsenen, hinten mit zwei beweglichen Knorpelpyramiden angedockten Stimmbänder durch motorische Kontraktion der Ränder dazu gebracht, unterschiedlich lange und starke Luftströme in Schallwellen zu verwandeln, die dann konzentrisch durch die Resonanzräume, sprich Brustkorb, Mundhöhle und Nase, nach draußen strömen. »Iiiiiiiiiiiiiiiiiiieeeeeeeh.« Das klingt nicht schön, lockert aber sehr effektiv die Stimmbänder. Trotz der kurzen Nacht bin ich hochzufrieden: die Stimme sitzt. Nun ja, vielleicht fehlt es noch an jener »saugenden Unheimlichkeit«, die der Kritiker der *Berliner Zeitung* Peter Uehling bei meinen Konzerten so schmerzlich vermisst. Aber die wird sich spätestens bei der Premierenfeier einstellen. Nach einer ausgiebigen Dusche rücke ich die Fußbank vor das Waschbecken, steige hinauf und mustere grimassierend mein Spiegelbild. »Verkrüppelte Arme und Beine und eigentlich überhaupt keinen Grund zum Lachen«, hat ein Boulevardblatt das Ergebnis einmal zusammengefasst. Ich sehe das ganz anders. Da steht ein ein Meter zweiunddreißig großer Konzertsänger, ohne

Kniegelenke, ohne Arme und Oberschenkel, mit nur vier Fingern an der rechten und dreien an der linken Hand. Er hat Geheimratsecken auf dem blonden Dickschädel, ein paar Pfunde zuviel um die Hüften und beste Laune. Das Einzige, was ihm fehlt, ist eine Rasur.

Eine halbe Stunde später sitzen wir beim Frühstück im Carnegie Deli, Ecke Seventh Avenue und 55th Street. Das Bistro ist legendär. Weil es in mindestens zwei Woody-Allen-Filmen auftaucht, weil man hier das beste koschere Pastrami-Sandwich der Stadt serviert und wegen der Leinenservietten, die der Geschäftsführer an prominente Stammgäste wie Kinky Friedman und seinen Kumpel Ratso verteilt, während sich die Laufkundschaft Papier in den Kragen stopfen muss. Das behauptet jedenfalls Kinky, der die Geschichte in jedem seiner zehn Kriminalromane mindestens einmal auftischt. Und man darf sie ihm ruhig glauben. Der begnadete Fabulierer ist nämlich nicht nur der Lieblingsautor so unterschiedlich determinierter Charaktere wie Bill Clinton und Wiglaf Droste, sondern als Bandleader der Texas Jewboys auch verantwortlich für den wahrhaftigsten Countrysong aller Zeiten: *They Ain't Makin' Jews Like Jesus Anymore.*

Uns legt man natürlich Papierservietten neben die Teller. »Allesquatsch. Jedä kriegt hie Babierservettn«, mulmt es aus meinem Bruder, dem ein mächtiger Pastrami-Brocken in der Backe steckt.

Renate sieht auf die Uhr. »Für die Prominenz ist es wohl auch noch ein bisschen früh.«

»Wetten, nicht«, unkt Micha und peilt mit der Gabel Richtung Tresen. Was da energisch heranpömpst, ist zwar nicht Kinky Friedman, trägt aber immerhin einen Hut, dessen Format jeden echten Texaner vor Neid erblassen ließe. Die Enormität ist allerdings lila wie das Kleid, in dem eine vornehme ältere Dame steckt. In der rechten Hand hält sie einen Kugelschreiber, die linke umklammert ein Notizbuch. Ihre Stimme hat etwas von einer rostigen Klingel.

»Oh, you are the fabulous singer. Nice to meet you. Please, give me an autograph.« Passend zum Outfit der Dame laufe ich erst zartrosa an, dann tue ich ihr den Gefallen. Auf die Frage, woher sie mich kenne, stellt sich heraus, dass sie mein Gesicht auf CBS gesehen hat und in der *New York Times* eine lobende Vorabgeschichte des gefürchteten Kritikerzaren Anthony Tommassini erschienen ist. Karten für heute Abend hat sie auch.

»Naturally! We know you in this town, honey«, schrillt es zum Abschied durch das Lokal. Dann stöckelt sie wieder an ihren Tisch.

Nett, denke ich, nur ein bisschen überkandidelt, die gute Frau. Aber als wir auf dem Rückweg zum Mayflower einen kleinen Schlenker durch den Central Park machen, muss ich noch ein halbes Dutzend Autogramme geben. Nein, man hält mich auch hier nicht für Danny de Vito. Die Leute möchten tatsächlich meinen Namenszug auf hastig hervorgekramten Einkaufszetteln, Zeitungsrändern und Kinoprogrammen lesen. Es ist unglaublich, wie offen und freundlich die gemeinhin als Raubeine verschrienen New Yorker sind. Und musikverrückt. Alle wünschen mir »good luck« für das Konzert. Ich kann es brauchen.

Normalerweise leide ich kaum unter Lampenfieber. Auftritte in den USA sind auch nichts Neues für mich. Ich habe in Washington und Seattle gesungen, in Chicago, Portland und Boston; in Eugene, Oregon, bin ich regelmäßig Gast beim Bach-Festival meines Mentors und Freundes Helmuth Rilling. Nur ein Gastspiel in New York ließ sich bisher nie realisieren. Dass ich nun an der Upper West Side logiere und in wenigen Stunden in einem der schönsten Konzertsäle der Welt auftreten werde, noch dazu mit der New York Philharmonic, bringt meinen Kreislauf doch ein bisschen ins Schlingern. Oder es liegt wieder mal am Hotelaufzug! Normalgewachsene müssen nämlich wissen: Fahrstühle sind für Menschen meines Formats einerseits unumgänglich, andererseits, wenn sie voll sind (und sie sind meistens voll), eine grobe Zumutung. Unter der Gürtellinie sozusagen. Erschwerend kommt hinzu, dass im Mayflower vorrangig Touristen wohnen, deren Ehrgeiz sich darauf zu beschränken scheint, die halbe Stadt leer zu kaufen. Ich glaube, es spielt überhaupt keine Rolle, was da so alles in den Boutiquen der Madison Avenue, bei Bloomingdale's, Saks oder Macy's zusammengerafft wird – das meiste gibt es schließlich auch in Osaka, Lyon und Düsseldorf – viel wichtiger ist der feine und möglichst fett gedruckte Schriftzug auf der Verpackung, damit er daheim als Ausweis rastloser Hipness und globaler Kreditwürdigkeit beneidet werden kann.

Drei Dutzend dieser Jäger und Sammler drängeln jetzt in den Aufzug. Eine mittlere Stampede ist nichts dagegen, und nur unter resolutem Einsatz meiner Stentorstimme ergattere ich ebenfalls ein Plätzchen. Während die Kabine langsam aufwärts zuckelt, geht es mit mir steil bergab. Die Luft ist zum Schneiden, die Enge ein klarer Fall für die Menschenrechtskommission. Verkeilt zwischen zwei Zentnern Taschen, Kartons und Plastiktüten, bedrängt von ausladenden Hinterteilen, Hosenbeinen und nylonbeschichteten Damenschenkeln, fühle ich mich schon im zweiten Stock wie zerlaufener Chester auf lauwarmem Schinkentoast. Wie gesagt, ich muss in den fünften.

Im Hotelzimmer angekommen, falle ich aufs Bett und zähle »7 … 8 … 9 … aus«. Technischer K.o. Ich nehme zwei Aspirin und versuche, das Elend mit einem Ross-Thomas-Schmöker zu vertreiben, den Renate mir gestern von einem Streifzug durchs Village mitgebracht hat. Er hat den passenden Titel *Der Tod wirft gelbe Schatten* und fängt mit dem Satz an: »Es begann, wie das Ende der Welt beginnen wird: mit Telefonklingeln um drei Uhr morgens.« »Immerhin ist erst Mittag«, schießt es mir tröstlich durch den Kopf, dann wirkt das Aspirin. Ich falle ins Reich der Träume. Da ist es ruhig und angenehm. Zumindest gibt es kein Telefon, womit sich auch der Weltuntergang erledigt hat. Und siehe da: nach zwei Stunden Tiefschlaf ist das Gröbste überstanden. Ich fühle mich besser. Der Restposten Nervosität wird unter dem Rubrum »kreative Anspannung« verbucht und mit professioneller Routine gedämpft.

Das ist im Musikerfach nicht anders als beim Klettern. Bevor es losgeht, überprüft man akribisch die Ausrüstung: Muss der Frack noch mal gebügelt werden? Ist das Einstecktuch bündig gefaltet? Passt heute eher der weiße oder der schwarze Rolli? Glänzen die Lackschuhe? Wo sind die schwarzen Socken und wo der verflixte Kamm? Dann schreitet man im Geist noch mal die Partitur ab, um sich schwierige Grate, Schründe und Überhänge einzuprägen. Zum Schluss braucht es eine Stärkung. Nicht gerade »sechs Spiegeleier mit heißem Kakao«, wie sie Anderl Heckmair verputzte, ehe er sein Bündel schnürte und durch die Eigernordwand stieg. Eher etwas leicht Verdauliches, das nicht wie Steinbruch im Magen liegt und aufs Zwerchfell drückt. In meinem Fall reichen da immer ein paar Kekse, die mit Wasser oder Saft hinuntergespült werden. Es folgt die wichtigste Vorbereitungsphase: das Einsingen. Ich stelle mich dabei noch einmal unter die heiße Dusche, weil es für meine Stimme nichts Besseres gibt als tröpfchensatte, schwüle Luft. Das vokale Stretching nimmt je nach anstehendem Repertoire eine halbe bis Dreiviertelstunde in Anspruch. Wenn man höhere Partien wie eben Mahlers *Wunderhorn*-Lieder zu singen hat, dauert es ein bisschen länger.

Pünktlich um vier kommt Brüderchen Micha und hilft beim Anlegen der Berufskleidung. Das ist nicht unbedingt nötig – ich komme auch ganz gut allein zurecht –, vereinfacht aber die Prozedur. Weil er im Gegensatz zu mir bequem unter Tische, Schränke und Kommoden kriechen kann, wohin sich Kamm, Schuhanzieher oder Strümpfe nur allzu gerne zurückziehen. Vorzugsweise kurz vor Konzertbeginn. Das ist das berüchtigte »Immer verschwinden die Dinge, wenn man sie am dringendsten braucht«-Axiom. Welches tückische Weltgesetz dahinter steckt, habe ich nie herausgefunden. Die Wissenschaft leider auch nicht. Wahrscheinlich werden alle diesbezüglichen Bemühungen von Lobbyisten der Textil- und Kurzwarenbranche im Keim erstickt.

»Hab eine!« Mein Bruder wedelt triumphierend mit einer Socke, als Linda Marder anruft. Linda ist blond, patent, ungefähr so alt wie ich, ein wirklich feiner Kerl und meine New Yorker Agentin. Zusammen mit ihrem Kollegen Charles Cumella sitzt sie in einem kleinen Büro in der 96th Street und regelt für mich die Geschäfte zwischen Boston und San Francisco. Die beiden kümmern sich um gute, das heißt künstlerisch interessante Engagements und – was viel wichtiger ist – sie lehnen schlechte ab; sie koordinieren die Pressearbeit, handeln Verträge aus und achten auf anständige Bezahlung. Wenn die Agentur Lieder-Tourneen quer durch den Kontinent organisiert, finden sie nicht nur die am wenigsten strapaziösen Flugverbindungen, sie buchen die Hotels auch so, dass der Auftrittsort für mich schnell und bequem zu erreichen ist. Kurz gesagt, Linda und Charles sorgen dafür, dass es mir gut geht und mich niemand übers Ohr haut. Und darin sind sie erstklassig, oder wie man hier sagt: they do a very good job.

Linda erinnert mich an die Bitte der New York Philharmonic, den wichtigsten Sponsoren nach dem Konzert für ein so genanntes »ten minutes smile« zur Verfügung zu stehen. Ein klassischer Euphemismus, hinter dem sich in Wahrheit ein uramerikanischer Triathlon verbirgt. Übung 1: dreißig Minuten Händeschütteln, Übung 2: vierzig Minuten Smalltalk. Am Schluss wartet der Dinner-Parcours samt Spargelhürden, Ochsen am Spieß und einer Schwadron gesottener Hummer. Aber die Teilnahme ist Ehrensache. In den USA bekommen Kultureinrichtungen wie die New Yorker Philharmonie, Kunstmuseen oder die großen Theater am Broadway keinen einzigen Cent aus öffentlichen Kassen. Sie leben ausschließlich von Sponsoren, Spenden und Eintrittsgeldern. Das heißt, ohne den Goodwill privater Geldgeber könnte das Konzert heute Abend gar nicht stattfinden. Ich werde also hingehen und hoffentlich ein paar interessante Menschen treffen.

»Das wirst du«, versichert Linda. »Übrigens, die Fisher Hall ist seit Wochen ausverkauft.«

»Wow«, sage ich und imaginiere den mit dreitausend Leuten gefüllten Saal. Vor so einer gewaltigen Kulisse habe ich noch nie gesungen.

»Bist du nervös?«

»Nicht mehr. Ich bin einfach nur froh, dass ich hier auftreten darf.«

»Sehr gut, Tommi, das ist die richtige Einstellung!«

Micha hat inzwischen den zweiten Socken ausgegraben. Ich warte, bis auch der Schuhanzieher auftaucht, gleite in die Lackslipper, dann mache ich mich auf den Weg zur Fisher Hall. Es sind nur fünfzehn Minuten Fuß-marsch und ich gehe vor dem Konzert gerne ein paar Schritte. In diesem Fall die Central West hinauf, bis »San Remo« und »El Dorado« auftauchen, die Zwillingstürme der Century-Apartments. Im San Remo logierten früher Stars wie die Monroe und Groucho Marx, ihre Nachmieter heißen Diane Keaton und Dustin Hoffman. Biegt man zwei Straßen weiter links ab in die 64th, öffnet sich nach kurzer Zeit die Häuserschlucht und gibt den Blick frei auf einen der großartigsten Tempelbezirke der säkularisierten Moderne: das Lincoln Center for the Performing Arts.

Fünf Millionen Kunstjünger pilgern jährlich auf das sechs Hektar große Areal, wo in vier Theatern und zwei Konzertsälen das Beste aus Klassik und Jazz, Tanz und Schauspiel geboten wird. Herzstück ist die »Met«, das Metropolitan Opera House. Mit seinen fassadenfüllenden Rundbogenfenstern sieht es tatsächlich aus wie eine Bauhaus-Version des Athener Parthenon. Nebenan im New York State Theatre residiert das City Ballet, die Avery Fisher Hall ist Heimstatt der Philharmoniker. Man mag kaum glauben, dass hier in den vierziger Jahren des vergangenen Jahrhunderts noch Gangs wie die »Jets« und die »Sharks« die Szenerie beherrschten, deren blutige Fehden Leonard Bernstein in der *West Side Story* verewigt hat. Nur zwei Dekaden später, im Mai 1959, war das Gang-Land Geschichte. Bernstein hob den Dirigentenstab, der Julliard-Chor schmetterte »Hallelujah« und Präsident Eisenhower stieß seine Schaufel in den planierten Slum-boden. Das Lincoln Center war geboren.

Am Künstlereingang der Fisher Hall schenkt mir der Portier ein erstauntes Nicken. Es ist erst fünf, ich bin früh dran. »Du bist immer und überall zu früh dran«, würde mein Bruder spotten. Ich kenne die Litanei: »Zu früh auf dem Bahnsteig, zu früh am Flughafen, zu früh im Restaurant und sogar zu früh beim Zahnarzt. Wenn du so weitermachst, wird dich Freund Hein zur Strafe weit vor der Zeit in die Grube fahren lassen.« Aber als Profi und bekennender Phänomenologe nenne ich das »rechtzeitig da sein« die einzig wirksame Strategie gegen die Unwägbarkeit des Lebens. Das mag zwar manchmal aussehen wie ein »langer, träger Fluss«, aber allein mit dem »Prinzip Hoffnung« lässt der sich nicht befahren. Nicht nur deshalb sind mir Unpünktlichkeit und Trödelei suspekt. Noch schlimmer finde ich, mich über Gebühr abhetzen zu müssen. Brüderchen dagegen ist der typische »Auf den letzten Drücker«-Mann. Ein heiterer Solipsist, der glaubt, alle Welt hätte nichts Besseres zu tun, als auf ihn zu warten. Man kann sich denken, dass dieser mentale Frontverlauf im Vorfeld gemeinsamer Reisen Dramolette von shakespearescher Wuchtigkeit gebiert. Genauso ist es auch. Ich sitze auf heißen Kohlen, mahne zehnmal zum Aufbruch und trete vor Wut gegen jeden erreichbaren Eimer, während Micha die nächste Zigarette aus der Packung angelt, seelenruhig die *Süddeutsche* liest und mich einen neurotischen Hektiker nennt. Mit der Nummer könnten wir auftreten.

An einem anderen Sketch arbeitete ich seit zwei Tagen mit Bühnenarbeiter Jim. Er geht so:

Jim: »Hi, little big man.«

Quasthoff: »Hi, big belly.«

Jim: »Everything's okay with Gustav Mahler?«

Quasthoff: »Yes! He rests in peace. I hope he's still resting after the concert.«

»Ha ha ha.« Jims kugelrunder Bauch wackelt auch dieses Mal wie Pudding, sein sonniges Keckern scheppert spielend bis unter die Decke. Man kann sagen, was man will, die Akustik der Fisher Hall ist brillant.

Ich bin hinunter zur Bühne gegangen, um vor dem Konzert noch einmal meinen Arbeitsplatz zu inspizieren. Die Gestaltungsvorschriften hält ein Memo fest, das meine Agentur an jeden Veranstalter schickt. »Thomas Quasthoff benötigt für das Konzert: ein Podest, circa ein mal ein Meter, vierzig bis fünfzig Zentimeter hoch (entspricht etwa einem Dirigentenpodest ohne Geländer) mit zwei Stufen, einen Stuhl (wenn möglich höhenverstellbar), ein Holznotenpult.«

Die Requisitenliste ist weder Extravaganz noch Allüre, sondern meiner Behinderung geschuldet. Zum einen fällt es mir sehr schwer, ein längeres Konzert im Stehen durchzuhalten (mehrstündige Passionen schaffen auch »normale« Kollegen nur mit Sitzpausen). Zum anderen sind bei geistlichen oder orchestralen Werken immer mehrere Solisten gleichzeitig im Einsatz, die sich im Stile einer Fußballelf neben dem Dirigenten formieren. Würde mich das Podest nicht auf Augenhöhe bringen, müsste der Maestro schon das Sichtfeld eines Uhus haben, um seine Kommandos punktgenau an den von schrankgroßen Tenören und barocken Altistinnen umstellten Sängerknirps zu bringen. Im Gegenzug wäre ich ständig gezwungen, den Taktgeber hinter dem Rücken meiner Kollegen anzupeilen. Ich würde schwanken wie ein Rohr im Wind, was dem ästhetischen Eindruck nicht gerade förderlich wäre respektive manchen Zuschauer auf die Idee bringen könnte, der Mann sei nicht ganz nüchtern. Also heißt das Rechenexempel: Fünfzig Zentimeter Podest + ein Meter Stuhl + siebzig Zentimeter sitzender Bariton = sehen und gesehen werden. Das Pult wiederum erspart mir das Halten der gewichtigen Notenbücher und erleichtert das Umblättern. Aus Holz soll es sein, weil diese Variante den Gravitationskräften zuverlässiger Paroli bietet als seine blechernen Vettern.

Die Standfestigkeit aller Beteiligten gehört schließlich zu den Grundvoraussetzungen einer gelungenen Aufführung. Wer als junger Lied-Interpret jahrelang durch Schulaulen und zugige Kleinstadtsäle gezogen ist, kann das beurteilen. Damals war ich ganze Abende lang damit beschäftigt, auf wackeligen Apfelsinenkisten die Balance zu halten und aufzupassen, dass der vom Veranstalter zwecks Zuschussakquise mit Engelszungen zur Teilnahme genötigte und nun in Reihe eins selig vor sich hin schnarchende Kulturdezernent nicht durch einen kippenden Blechnotenständer aufgeschreckt, wenn nicht gar vom Bariton persönlich erschlagen wird. Gesungen habe ich dann auch noch. Aber fragt lieber nicht, wie.

Dazu ist es im Wennigser Musikclub Zombie gar nicht erst gekommen. Ich trat damals mit einer Soulband auf. Außer mir hatte man auch den Keyboarder auf einem fragwürdigen Sperrholzpodest abgestellt. Gleich nach dem Instrumental-Intro brach die Konstruktion mit gewaltigem Karacho zusammen. Wir überlebten, das E-Piano und die Gesangsanlage leider nicht. Der Rest der Band versuchte zu retten, was zu retten war, aber als nach zwei weiteren Stücken auch der Bassverstärker den Geist aufgab, war das Konzert beendet. Und was hatte man davon? Unkosten, Pfiffe, Prellungen und eine Beule am Kopf im Kartoffelkloßformat. So hart kann das Musikbiz sein. Aber das gehört in ein anderes Kapitel.

Hier und jetzt wird es nämlich höchste Zeit für den Auftritt von Tony Shalit. Und da klopft es auch schon an der Garderobentür. Herein tänzelt ein eleganter Endfünfziger. Sein verschmitztes, scharf geschnittenes Profil ragt sonnenbraun aus dem Hemdkragen, das eisgraue Haar liegt schütter über der hohen Stirn. Mit einer lässigen Bewegung verschwindet die Sonnenbrille in der Brusttasche seines Sportjacketts. Tony breitet die Arme aus und steht einen Augenblick da wie David Letterman, der gleich einen Spitzenwitz abfeuern wird. Dann fällt er mir doch lieber um den Hals und strahlt dabei, als habe er gerade für drei Wochen Sonnenschein, wahlweise Nicole Kidman gepachtet. Prompt bekomme ich einen feuchten Kuss auf die Wange.

»Hallo, Sweetheart, wie gähts!«

»Alles bestens.«

»All right. Du wirst heut Abend guuht sain, du wirst formidabel sain.«

»Hmm.«

»Du wirst New York schwindelik singän.«

»Hmm.«

»Don't say ›hmm‹, say ›yes‹!« Tony ist aufgesprungen und stelzt euphorisiert wie ein balzender Marabu von Wand zu Wand. »The best Orchestra der Welt mit de bästä Singer der Welt. Das wird History schraiben.«

»Tony, come on.«

»I talked about it with Colin Davis. I said to him …«

»Tony, setz dich hin!!!« Ich will lieber nicht wissen, was er Davis alles erzählt hat. Sir Colin ist nämlich nicht nur Chef der Londoner Symphoniker, einer der größten Mozart-, Sibelius- und Berlioz-Interpreten und Ritter seiner Majestät Elizabeth II., zufällig wird er heute Abend auch die New Yorker Philharmoniker dirigieren. Mir wäre es ziemlich peinlich, wenn er Mr. Quasthoff und seinem Herold noch vor dem Konzert einen Napoleonkomplex unterstellt. Tony, der sich schnaufend in den Sessel fallen lässt, ist das herzlich wurst. Er hat in der Musikgemeinde zwischen Bayreuth und Sidney einen soliden Ruf als Quartalsexzentriker, Bonvivant und freier Radikaler. Und immer das letzte Wort.

»I know, es wird wundebaa.«

»Schaun wir mal.«

»What means ›sch-a-u-n‹? You have to stroke my ears, not my eyes.«

»Oh, Lord!«

»Yes, here I am!«

So geht das seit zehn Jahren. Gemeinsam schipperten wir 1993 auf einem Luxus-Kreuzfahrtschiff durchs Mittelmeer. Tony als Passagier. Ich gehörte zur Abteilung »Kulturelles Begleitprogramm«. Zusammen mit Berühmtheiten wie dem Geiger Vladimir Spivakov, dem Cello-Gott Mstislaw Rostropowitsch und seiner Gattin, der gefeierten Operndiva Galina Wischnewskaja. Es war meine erste Seereise und mein erster Ausflug in die Welt der Hundert-Dollar-Trinkgelder. Ich fand vieles sehr sonderbar. Zum Beispiel, dass man sich am Tag sieben Mal umziehen kann, oder die Nouvelle Cuisine, also die Kunst, auf fünf Gänge zu strecken, was bei uns zu Hause auf einen Teller passt. Die Aussicht, neben den Heroen der Branche musikalisch bestehen zu müssen, machte die Sache nicht besser. Ich lief herum wie Falschgeld. Tony rettete mich. Er hörte mein erstes Konzert, fand es »magnificent« und nahm mich unter seine Fittiche. Tony duzte den Kapitän, er duzte die Stars und er duzte die Kellner, und alle duzten gern zurück. Er bestellte die richtigen Weine, war vorlaut und charmant, intelligent und witzig und zu jeder Tages- und Nachtzeit der allseits akzeptierte »Master of Ceremony«. Wie er das machte? Anfangs dachte ich, es läge an seinen Essgewohnheiten: Zum Frühstück nahm er einen Joint mit Tee, mittags einen Joint mit Fisch, abends bestellte er zum Marihuana Salat. Aber ich lag falsch. Im Kreis der mitreisenden Macht- und Erfolgsmenschen, die gewöhnlich schon zum Kaffee Martinis kippten, war Tony etwas ganz Besonderes. Ein freier Geist, der das (bisweilen ins Hochkomisch-Spleenige lappende) Unkonventionelle nicht um seiner selbst willen kultiviert, sondern

Eigensinn, Unabhängigkeit und Toleranz für elementare Menschenrechte hält. Natürlich muss man sich diese Haltung leisten können. Tony kann. Von Haus aus Anwalt für Internationales Recht machte er ein Vermögen, indem er australischen Firmen mit ein paar Kniffen Zugang zum US-Markt verschaffte. Mit fünfzig beschloss er, Arbeit Arbeit sein zu lassen und sich nur noch der Familie, einigen Hobbys, vor allem aber der Obsession seines Lebens zu widmen: der Musik. Wenn er also nicht gerade im Indischen Ozean segelt, Kunst und wertvolle Bücher kauft oder mit dem Hubschrauber mal eben frischen Kaviar besorgt, folgt er rund um den Globus den Routen der Sänger und Dirigenten wie Ahab dem weißen Wal.

In den letzten Jahren habe vor allem ich von seiner Besessenheit profitiert. Seit besagter Kreuzfahrt sind wir Freunde fürs Leben, und so oft er kann, begleitet mich Tony auf meinen Tourneen. Das ist immer die Garantie für eine Menge Spaß. Ich kann mich jedenfalls an keine Reise erinnern, wo nicht irgendetwas Verrücktes passiert wäre. Unter anderem, weil Tony bei jeder passenden und unpassenden Gelegenheit zu erschöpfenden Exkursionen durch die Musikgeschichte neigt. Meist beginnen sie bei Monteverdi und enden mit dem Satz »Ich weiß einfach nicht, was dieser Schönberg wollte«. Das mag in einem Museumscafé angehen, vor der Fleischtheke eines deutschen Supermarktes kann es den Blutdruck in ungeahnte Höhen treiben. Vor allem in der Schlange hinter ihm. »Sülze«, trompetet es dann gerne oder: »Geh nach Haus und frag noch mal.« Nun ist Tony zwar ein geschliffener Weltmann und Erzromantiker, den die ersten Töne der *Tannhäuser*-Ouvertüre zu Tränen rühren können. Andererseits stammt er aus New York, wo die Jungs schon im Kindergarten lernen, dass man eine Verbalinjurie niemals unbeantwortet lässt. Also dreht sich Tony um, macht ein Gesicht wie Robert De Niro in *Kap der Angst* und bellt, dass »Krauts«, die zwei Weltkriege angezettelt und obendrein verloren haben, sich besser nie mehr in fremde Angelegenheiten mischen sollten. Ist das einmal klargestellt, kann man ihn seelenruhig ein halbes Pfund »bloody Roastbeef« bestellen und, sein verschrecktes Publikum keines Blickes würdigend, zur Kasse marschieren sehen. So ist Freund Tony, ein unerschrockenes Unikat, mit einem Herzen aus Gold, den man in einer Welt, die immer mehr den Produkten der Firma Playmobil ähnelt, eigentlich unter Artenschutz stellen sollte.

Aber er muss sich langsam auf den Weg machen. Aus dem Lautsprecher über meiner Garderobentür hallt ein Gong und zeigt an, dass das Konzert in zwanzig Minuten beginnen wird. Ich begleite Tony ein Stück, um vom Balkon im Foyer den Einzug des New Yorker Publikums zu verfolgen. Für jemanden, der aus Old Europe kommt, ist das ein lehrreiches Schauspiel. Was sofort ins Auge springt, ist das Fehlen jener idealisch raunenden Beflissenheit, die heimische Bühnenhäuser seit Goethens und Schillers Tagen umflort. Stattdessen freut man sich an der lockeren Atmosphäre, an der Selbstverständlichkeit, mit der die Amerikaner ihre Kulturtempel – ja, ich schreibe es ruhig hin – benutzen. Man sieht Menschen aller Hautfarben, aller Alters- und Einkommensklassen, bloß lassen sich Letztere anders als bei uns nicht auf Anhieb unterscheiden. Natürlich gibt es auch hier das standesbewusste Defilee von Maßanzügen, Schmuckständern und Designerroben. Doch das Gros der Besucher watet in Jeans und Turnschuhen durch die knöcheltiefe Auslegeware. Manche schleppen Einkaufstüten, andere beißen ungezwungen in Thunfischburger, wieder andere sitzen in komfortablen Sofaecken und lesen. Wobei die Herren der Schöpfung nicht etwa das Programmheft studieren, sondern den Sportteil der *Post*, der heute vermeldet, dass die Kufencracks der Rangers gegen Boston wieder einmal auf verlorenem Posten gestanden haben. Da dürfte nachher *Der Schildwache Nachtlied* (»Ich kann und mag nicht fröhlich sein«) so recht den Nerv des Auditoriums treffen.

Diese grunddemokratische und sehr sympathische Hemdsärmeligkeit hat auch ihre Kehrseite. Es kann zum Beispiel passieren, dass gegen Ende einer nicht gar so fesselnden Vorführung der halbe Saal aufspringt und zum Ausgang strebt. Die letzten Takte versinken in einer Kakophonie aus Kleiderraascheln, Stuhlgeklapper und quengliger Drängelei, obwohl der Dirigent das Orchester zu einem trotzigen, aber hilflosen Forte zwingt. Das sei völlig okay, sagte mir mal ein Pizzabäcker aus Seattle. Er zahle pro Jahr fünftausend steuerlich absetzbare Dollar in die Opernkasse. Damit habe er sich als »Donor« einen Platz auf der Messingplatte im Foyer erworben genauso wie das Recht, sein Auto vor dem zu erwartenden Stau aus der Tiefgarage zu holen. Es ist eben alles eine Mentalitätsfrage. Mir persönlich erscheint die Angewohnheit des Homo americanus, die klassischen Künste nicht höher zu hängen als andere Formen intelligenter Unterhaltung, sei es der Film oder Basketball, trotz manchmal unschöner Nebenwirkungen als echte zivilisatorische Errungenschaft. Zumal Qualität und Berufsauffassung der Künstler nicht darunter leiden. Eher ist das Gegenteil der Fall.

Zurück im Backstage-Bereich, registriere ich, dass selbst die Asse der New Yorker Philharmonie gespannt sind wie Rennpferde vor dem Start. Durch die Flure zieht eine Wolke aus Tonleitern, Melodiefetzen, Akkorden, vermischt mit den Aromen von Haargel, Parfüm, Schweiß und Kolophonium. Die Musiker spielen ihre Instrumente warm, lockern Lippen und Finger, wandern herum oder stehen grüppchenweise beisammen. Gerade hat es zum zweiten Mal gegongt, der Countdown läuft – noch zehn Minuten. Es wird an letzten Zigaretten gezogen, hier ein Kleid, da eine Fliege zurechtgezupft, man verteilt Küsschen und spuckt dem Kollegen nach altem Theaterbrauch über die Schulter.

»See you«, ruft mir eine Klarinette zu, dann muss das Orchester auf die Bühne.

Colin Davis eröffnet den Abend mit der *König Lear*-Ouvertüre von Hector Berlioz und Frank Martins *Petite Symphonie Concertante*. Die Mahler-Lieder stehen erst nach der Pause auf dem Programm. Ich kann also noch eine Weile in meiner Garderobe sitzen, ein paar Stimmübungen machen und das Konzert nebenbei via Lautsprecher und TV-Monitor verfolgen. Doch als die ersten Noten durch die Halle schweben, starre ich fasziniert auf den Schirm. Die Tonqualität der Übertragung ist nicht die allerbeste, aber man ahnt, es muss wunderbar klingen. Nach einer Weile will ich es genau wissen und pirsche zum rechten Seiteneingang der Bühne.

Durch die schmale Öffnung sehe ich das Schlagwerk, kompakte Männer, die ihre Sticks wuchtig und präzise auf die Felle schmettern, ich sehe Frisuren und Geigenbögen fliegen, und ich sehe Sir Colin, der das romantisch brodelnde *Lear*-Vorspiel mit ruhiger, konzentrierter Gestik zur Klimax bringt. Er dirigiert einen nahezu perfekten Klangkörper: austrainiert, gesegnet mit hochsensiblen Nervenbahnen und spannkräftigen Muskeln, getrieben von einem Kraftzentrum, das irgendwo in der Mitte zwischen Oboen, Violinen und Bratschen pulsen muss. Denn von dort, vermeint das Ohr, entspringt ein mächtiger Energiestrom, der die Musiker jederzeit bis in die Fingerspitzen elektrisiert. Frank Martin hat einmal gesagt, gute Musik wirke wie »ein Organismus«. Die New Yorker Philharmoniker klingen, als gehöre der einem begnadeten Tänzer. So leichtfüßig federt das Orchester über den von Berlioz in prä-mahlerschem Farbreichtum ausgerollten Klangteppich, so traumwandlerisch sicher folgen die Instrumentengruppen noch den subtilsten thematischen Verschiebungen der *Petite Symphonie*.

Mir war klar, dass die Philharmoniker großartig sind, schließlich proben wir seit drei Tagen. Dass sie, wenn es darauf ankommt, noch zwei Klassen besser spielen können, hätte ich einfach nicht für möglich gehalten. Inger Dam-Jensen, meine dänische Kollegin, zeigt sich ähnlich beeindruckt, als wir uns nach der Pause zum Einmarsch in die Halle formieren. Normalerweise lässt man ja der Dame den Vortritt. Ich nicht. Zumindest nicht auf der Bühne. Das alte Fahrstuhlproblem! Inger ist eine groß gewachsene schlanke Blondine, ich bin ein Meter zweiunddreißig. Auf diesem Niveau hinter ihr herzutraben sähe ein wenig kurios aus. Wir könnten dem Komikerduo Pat und Patachon Konkurrenz machen – um ein Beispiel aus dem dänischen Kulturkreis zu wählen. Mir fällt auch sofort Oskarchen ein, Günter Grassens Wachstum verweigernder Blechtrommler. Der Kleine stiefelt fünfhundert Seiten lang ständig und überall vorneweg. Ein Bild aus dem Militärischen, aus der Welt der Paraden, wird der beschlagene Leser sagen. Das glaube ich nicht. Ich glaube, es handelt sich hier um ein ehernes Gesetz im Reich der Ästhetik, ähnlich dem goldenen Schnitt. Wer sich noch an die *Lucky Luke*-Comics erinnert, an den Cowboy, der schneller schießt als sein Schatten, und an seine ewigen Widersacher, die Dalton-Brüder, weiß, was ich meine. Das Quartett tritt Lucky stets stufenförmig gestaffelt entgegen, steht mithin in der Prärie wie einer von Nebukadnezars Zikkurat-Türmen. Man kann auch sagen wie ein Treppenwitz. Vorne der gnomische Joe Dalton, hinten der tumbe

Lulatsch Averell. Auf altägyptischen Darstellungen, die bekanntlich alles im Profil abbilden, regiert dasselbe Prinzip: der, die oder das Kleine gehört einfach *vor* das Große. In unserem speziellen Fall trifft die Redewendung »Alter kommt vor Schönheit« den Kern der Sache aber ebenso gut.

In dieser Reihenfolge queren Inger und ich nun die Orchesterfront. Der Moment, in dem man aus dem Backstage-Dämmer auf die Bühne tritt, hat für mich immer wieder etwas Magisches. Es ist heiß und blendend hell da draußen. Die Scheinwerfer zaubern funkelnde Reflexe auf das Blech und auf das blank polierte Holz der Streichinstrumente, gleichzeitig spannt das gleißende Bühnenlicht einen dunklen Vorhang vor die Sitzreihen. Man spürt die raunende Menge mehr, als dass man irgendetwas erkennen kann. Nach ein, zwei Schritten schäumt aus dem Nichts plötzlich Beifall auf, wie ein erster Brecher, den Wind und aufkommende Flut an ein nächtliches Gestade werfen. Die Phonstärke nimmt noch zu, als Sir Colin das Podium besteigt und lächelnd das graue Lockenhaupt neigt. Doch kaum hat er dem Publikum den Rücken zugedreht, umfängt den freundlichen Gentleman die Aura des allgewaltigen Imperators. »Er stellt sich auf; er räuspert sich; er hebt den Stab: alle verstummen und erstarren«, schreibt Elias Canetti in seiner epochalen Studie *Masse und Macht* über den Dirigenten, und er weiß auch, warum es nur so und nicht anders funktionieren kann: »Da während der Aufführung die Welt aus nichts anderem bestehen soll als aus dem Werk, ist er (der Dirigent) genau so lange der Herrscher der Welt.«

Sir Colin hat inzwischen den Stab gesenkt und das Orchester begonnen, die Partitur Schicht um Schicht zu gewaltigem Marsch- und Schlachtenlärm zu türmen. Mit entsprechender Verve schleudert die Schildwache, in diesem Fall also meine Wenigkeit, die erste Strophe des *Nachtliedes* ins Parkett: »Ich kann und mag nicht fröhlich sein! / Wenn alle Leute schlafen, / So muss ich wachen, / muss traurig sein.« Inger versucht mir einzuflüstern, für Depressionen gebe es gar keinen Grund, »im Rosengarten, / im grünen Klee« warte ja die Jungfer auf ihren Soldaten. Außerdem bliebe noch Gottes Segen, auf den man sich auch »im Feld« verlassen könne, jedenfalls »wer's glauben tut«. Dabei gleitet ihr lieblich lockender Sopran über eine schwebende Kadenz aus Dur-Dreiklängen, die Mahler am Ende ins Zwielichtige, genau genommen in einen e-Moll-Akkord kippen lässt. Da merkt die arme Schildwache, das zart erotisierte Naturidyll ist nichts als Traum und Gaukelei. Außerdem findet der Mann, Gottvertrauen sei hier fehl am Platz: »Er ist ein König! / Er ist ein Kaiser! / Er führt den Krieg.«

Die Philharmoniker setzen das Trauerspiel so inspiriert in Szene, unsere Stimmen harmonieren so prächtig, dass schon am Ende des ersten Liedes Applaus von den Balkonen rieselt. Eine Todsünde unter traditionsbewussten Klassik-Aficionados. Der Respekt vor dem Kunstwerk gebietet: Man hat gefälligst zu warten, bis der Zyklus zu Ende ist. Seit wann diese Regel gilt und wer sie aufgestellt hat, weiß ich nicht. Tatsache ist, sie wird öfter gebrochen, als man denkt. Und ehrlich gesagt, finde ich das auch nicht tragisch. Manchmal sogar herzerfrischend komisch, wie ein Vorfall beweist, der sich, wenn ich mich richtig erinnere, in Chicago ereignet hat.

Einige Kollegen und ich waren, begleitet vom Freiburger Barockorchester, mit Mozart-Liedern auf Tournee. Ich sang gerade die Arie des Leporello »Schöne Donna, dies genaue Register« aus *Don Giovanni*. Am Ende der Partie gibt es eine große Fermate, das heißt, ein Ton muss ziemlich lange auf gleicher Höhe gehalten werden. In diese

Fermate brüllte jemand aus dem Publikum sehr laut »Bravo«. Ich brüllte, ohne die Stimme abzusetzen, zurück: »Too early!« Dann sang ich weiter, allerdings waren die letzten Akkorde des Stückes nicht mehr zu vernehmen, weil sich das Publikum vor Lachen krümmte.

So weit kommt es heute Abend nicht. Trotzdem wird es immer schöner. Denn zum Glück für uns Sänger und zur großen Freude des Publikums hat Colin Davis beschlossen, alle Lieder, die dialogisch aufgebaut sind, auch tatsächlich im Duett vortragen zu lassen. Das ist zwar vom Komponisten so nicht vorgesehen, aber durchaus im Sinne der beiden *Wunderhorn*-Herausgeber Clemens Brentano und Achim von Arnim. Als die verschwägerten Dichterfreunde 1805 den ersten Band ihrer altdeutschen Gedicht- und Liedersammlung vorlegten, handelte es sich ja nur bedingt um originäre Volkspoesie. Sie hatten ihr Material bearbeitet, das heißt, wenn es der Dramaturgie diente, nach Gutdünken Reime geglättet, Verse gestrichen oder ganze Strophen hinzugefügt. Dem *Lied des Verfolgten im Turm* implantierten sie kurzerhand eine Mädchenrolle. Man kann die Nähte sehen. Und hören. Die beiden Textblöcke ergeben kein homogenes Ganzes, sondern sind eigentlich zwei Monologe und wie Parallelhandlungen im Film montiert.

Szene 1: Im Kerker. Durch die Gitterstäbe fällt fahl ein Streifen Sonnenlicht. Die Kamera zoomt auf das ausgezehrte Gesicht des Gefangenen. Er wirkt gefasst. Er wird nicht zu Kreuze kriechen. Er wird seinem Schicksal trotzen, indem er allem Liebes- und Glücksverlangen entsagt und die platonischen Freuden der inneren Emigration beschwört. Der Gefangene erhebt sich von der Pritsche, ballt die Fäuste und singt: »Die Gedanken sind frei, / Wer kann sie erraten? / Sie rauschen vorbei / Wie nächtliche Schatten. / Kein Mensch kann sie wissen, / Kein Jäger sie schießen. / Es bleibet dabei / Die Gedanken sind frei.« Szene 2 zeigt das Mädchen. Sie hockt, den Kopf in die Hände gestützt, auf der Treppe vor dem Gemäuer und will das alles nicht wahrhaben. Über ihr Bäckchen rinnt eine Träne, während sie die verlorene Zweisamkeit imaginiert: »Im Sommer ist gut lustig sein, / Auf hohen, wilden Heiden. / Dort findet man grün' Plätzelein. / Mein herzverliebtes Schätzelein, / Von dir mag ich nicht scheiden.« So geht es weiter in wechselnden Gegenschnitten, bis der Gefangene ein letztes Machtwort spricht: »Und weil du so klagst, / Der Lieb ich entsage … es bleibet dabei, die Gedanken sind frei.« Die Kamera fliegt durch das Kerkerfenster, das Mädchen als Häuflein Elend tief unter sich zurücklassend, dem Horizont entgegen. Abspann.

»Eine Art Kurz-*Fidelio* für Gesangsvereine«, hat ein Witzbold das Werk etwas abschätzig, aber durchaus treffend tituliert. Wie überhaupt das Dramatisch-Szenische die Basis aller *Wunderhorn*-Lieder ist. Antonius von Padua »geht zu den Flüssen und predigt den Fischen«; *Der Tambourgesell* sitzt in der Todeszelle; das *Rheinlegendchen* wird während eines Spaziergangs ausgesponnen; *Das irdische Leben* und *Verlorene Müh'* schildern Szenen aus dem bäuerlichen Milieu; in *Trost im Unglück* liefern sich Husar und Mädchen ein neckisches Abschiedsgeplänkel; das *Lob des hohen Verstands* verhandelt den Sängerwettstreit zwischen Kuckuck und Nachtigall, den der Kritiker, natürlich ein ausgemacht dummer Esel, zugunsten des Kuckucks entscheidet. Alles spielt in sorgsam ausgeleuchteten Kulissen. Die Sujets ermöglichen Mahler eine größtmögliche kompositorische Variationsbreite auf engstem Raum. Allein in *Wo die schönen Trompeten blasen*, der Ballade vom toten Soldaten, der nachts aus dem Grab steigt, um die Geliebte in sein »Haus, von grünem Rasen« zu holen, hat er nacheinander untergebracht: elegische Trompetenquinten, die brachiale Marschrhythmen eskortieren; einen D-Dur-Satz im Dreivierteltakt; eine Kantilene in Ges-Dur; weitere Trompeten in Dur, die aber zum Schluss ins Mollige tauchen. Andernorts wimmelt es von Kuriosa wie falschen Bässen, von Sextenparallelen zwischen Dur-Episoden, von Dezimen-Sprüngen über Sechzehntelstakkati in düsterem Moll. Im *Revelge*, hat Habakuk Traber beobachtet, schreibe den Akkorden gleich gar »keine Regel mehr vor, wie sie zu stehen und zu gehen haben«. Kein Wunder, dass dabei mit Schlagzeug, Bläsern und Flöten auch der ganze militärische Lärmapparat außer Rand und Band gerät, wenn der gefallene Tambour die Leichen seiner Kameraden zusammentrommelt, in die Schlacht führt und hernach stolz vor »Schätzeleins Haus« strammstehen lässt. »Morgens stehen da die Gebeine / In Reih' und Glied, sie steh'n wie Leichensteine / Die Trommel steht voran / Dass sie ihn sehen kann. / Trallali, trallalei, trallalera.« Das Lied endet hier gnädig mit Paukenschlägen und ätzenden Trompetenclustern. Ich möchte mir jedenfalls nicht ausmalen, welch ein Gesicht das »Schätzelein« beim Anblick der Zombieversammlung gemacht hat. Zumindest dürfte sie so verblüfft gewesen sein wie der Musik-Schriftsteller Ernst Decsey, als er Mahler einmal auf das höchst wirkungsvolle, aber »merkwürdige Weiter- und Umbilden einer Dominante« ansprach. Der Komponist beschied ihn bündig: »Ach was! Dominante! Nehmen Sie die Sachen so naiv, wie sie gemeint sind.« Was zeigt, dass man das Theoretisieren nicht übertreiben sollte.

Ich höre auch schon auf. Musikwissenschaft kann das Faszinosum der *Wunderhorn*-Lieder sowieso nur unzureichend erklären. Preisen wir einfach Mahlers Genie, der es fertig gebracht hat, dem anarchisch-naiven Volkston der Textvorlagen ein modernes, noch immer gültiges Weltgefühl aufzuprägen. Durch den Zyklus zieht sich je-

nes ausweglose »So-« beziehungsweise »Geworfensein«
des spätbürgerlichen Individuums, an dem sich kluge
Köpfe von Heidegger bis Derrida bändeweise abgearbei-
tet und letztlich doch die Zähne ausgebissen haben. So
viel Einsamkeit, Verzweiflung und schmerzhafte Schönheit liegt in Mahlers Musik, so viel Grimm, Trotz und
Spott im Angesicht des zum Fürchten sinnleeren Weltge-
brumms, dass sie uns bis heute im Innersten berührt.

»It was so wonderful!«
     »Unbelievable!«
     »Hey, man, great job!«
     »That was music, that was sound!«
     »You are the best!«
     »No, you are the best!«
Hinter der Bühne ist das große Schulterklopfen ausge-
brochen. Die beiden Sänger werfen mit Komplimenten,
die Violinen werfen zurück. Celli beglückwünschen Klarinetten, Posaunen herzen Bässe. Jeder hat ein Lächeln im
Gesicht und ein paar Verwandte, Freunde oder Bekannte
einbestellt, die sich hochgradig enthusiasmiert und die
Könnerschaft ihrer Lieben preisend ebenfalls ins Getüm-
mel stürzen. Es ist ein einziges Tohuwabohu, aber ich finde es wunderbar. Verschwitzt, die Adern geschwollen
vom Adrenalin, rapportiere ich Micha und Renate erste
Eindrücke: »Fantastisch … wie Inger die Koloraturen im
Liedlein … Colin Davis hat den Triolenteil … die Pianissi-
mi der Philharmoniker … super, einfach super gelaufen …
Durst … muss unbedingt was trinken … ach, schön, dass
ihr da seid …« Ich rede wie ein Sturzbach, aber jetzt sind
die Schleusen auf, jetzt muss alles raus, sonst platze ich.
Sieben Mal sind wir abgetreten, sieben Mal haben sie uns
wieder herausgeklatscht, sieben Mal musste Sir Colin das
Orchester von den Sitzen holen, umrauscht von stehen-

den Ovationen, die er selbst mit britischer Noblesse, das heißt unter leichtem Einknicken des Oberkörpers, entgegennahm.

Tony dagegen ringt um Fassung. Er hat meinem Debüt in seiner Heimatstadt wahrscheinlich weit nervöser entgegengefiebert als Muhammad Ali dem erstem WM-Fight gegen Sonny Liston. Jetzt ist es vorbei und Tony schwer gerührt. Was man daran merkt, dass ihm anders als Ali tatsächlich einmal die Worte fehlen. Er hat in meiner Garderobe gewartet und drückt mich fest an die Brust. Seine Augen schimmern feucht. Viel Zeit fürs Sentiment bleibt allerdings nicht. Denn auch hier geht es drunter und drüber. Musiker kommen und verschwinden, Journalisten schneien herein, Markus Sievers, ein Vertreter meiner deutschen Agentur, verteilt Visitenkarten wie andere Leute Skatblätter, und ich staune über wildfremde Menschen, die mir erst den erigierten Daumen, dann ein Programm zum Signieren vor die Nase halten. Und die meisten hätten gerne einen Drink. Gerade noch rechtzeitig tauchen Linda Marder und Charles Cumella auf. Die Guten schleppen einen voluminösen Präsentkorb, den ich mir nicht etwa heute Abend verdient habe, sondern vor vier Tagen an meinem Geburtstag. Der essbare Inhalt reicht für eine Polarexpedition, die Getränke nicht. Sie werden sofort requiriert. Das Bier ist für Micha, der die Gelegenheit nutzt, ausgerechnet dem Weintrinker Charles eine Debatte zum Thema »Der globale Freihandel und das deutsche Reinheitsgebot« aufzunötigen. Der Champagner ist für alle da.

»Mach doch mal einer 'ne Flasche auf!«, rufe ich fidel in die Runde.

Das lässt sich Tony nicht zweimal sagen. Den Triumphmarsch aus *Aida* pfeifend, knallt er zwei Korken gegen die Decke und verteilt die edle Flüssigkeit auf eine

Großpackung Partybecher. Dann schlägt er die Hacken zusammen, salutiert und hebt den Plastikkelch: »Cheers!«

So könnte es weitergehen. Darf es aber nicht. Morgen ist wieder Vorstellung, und nachher steht noch ein Premieren-Dinner auf dem Programm. Nicht zu vergessen das »ten minutes smile«. Die Sponsoren warten schon im Empfangsraum des Foyers. Begleitet von herzlichem Beifall werden Inger, Sir Colin und ich hereingeführt und gut sichtbar neben das Büffet gestellt. Es gibt eine kurze Begrüßung, ein paar Worte des Dankes an die Mäzene, dann formiert man sich zum Triptychon gepflegter Geselligkeit. Mit klarer Arbeitsteilung: einer redet, einer kaut, der Künstler lächelt. Aber Linda hatte Recht. Die New Yorker sind ebenso unterhaltsame wie ökonomische Smalltalker.

Ein Bibliothekar schafft es in zehn Minuten von der Wiener Hofoper über Schostakowitschs *Stalingrader Sinfonie*, Kafkas *Amerika* und Bob Dylans christliche Periode bis zur 23rd Street ins berühmte Boheme-Hotel Chelsea, das zum letzten Mal 1978 Schlagzeilen machte, als Punk-Bassist Sid Vicious im dritten Stock seine Freundin niederstach. Nach zwanzig weiteren Minuten haben mich zwei Ärztinnen auf den aktuellen Stand der Lewinsky-Affäre gebracht. Ich kenne Details aus John Carpenters neuestem Vampir-Movie, die ich niemals wissen wollte, und sämtliche Anekdoten über Jesse Ventura, den Ex-Profi-Catcher, der bei den Gouverneurswahlen in Minnesota gerade Demokraten und Republikaner souverän auf die Matte gelegt hat. Als die Rede auf Basketball kommt, auf das ehrwürdige Team der New York Niks, muss ich den Damen leider einen Korb geben. Meine Beine schmerzen, ich kann nicht mehr stehen.

Eine halbe Stunde später sitzen wir in einem der berühmten Restaurants von Chinatown.

»Oliginal Canton and Szechuan Cuisine!«, hatte der Maître erklärt und mit undurchdringlichem Lächeln hinzugefügt: »You have to tly oul legional specials.«

Renate, der in einer Garküche zu Taipeh nach ähnlichen Empfehlungen ein toter Hund begegnet ist, plädiert für Chop Suey: Gemüseragout. Mir knurrt der Magen. Das heißt, ich bin an weiteren Details nicht interessiert und ordere ein sensationell klingendes und, wie ich hoffe, auch sensationell nahrhaftes Menü, das man mir ungefähr mit »Dreizehn Köstlichkeiten aus dem Lotosgarten der siebten Konkubine des erhabenen Kaisers Soundso« übersetzt. Ich werde nicht enttäuscht. Alsbald huschen flinke Kellner heran und arrangieren Schälchen, Näpfe und Tiegel über dem Kerzenrost zu einem herrlich duftenden Ensemble. Einer bringt Krebse und schwarze Bohnen, ein anderer eingelegte Schweine-, Fisch- und Rinderbällchen, der dritte Sojasprossen, Karotten und Lauch in bunter Tunke. Dass die gelben Männer den Serviervorgang mit der mantraartig repetierten Warnung »vely hot« oder »vely peppely« garnieren, sollte mich allerdings stutzig machen. Tut es aber nicht. Andere schon. Inger, ihr Gatte, das Ehepaar Davis, Linda und Charles, Renate, Micha, Tony, Markus und das Trio aus dem Pressestab des Orchesters haben die Nahrungsaufnahme unterbrochen. Sie mustern mich mit dem nüchternen Interesse von Chemikern, die ihren Laborratten ein neues Toxikum verabreichen. Mir ist das zu dumm, man hat schließlich seinen Stolz. Entschlossen angle ich ein Stück Rind aus der grünlich schimmernden Soße und beiße hinein.

»Pass auf, heiß und scharf«, zischt Micha.

Ja, ja, jetzt weiß ich es auch, höre mich aber todesverachtend hecheln: »Chehr gut, ehlich.«

Cool bleiben heißt die Devise, obwohl ich am liebsten Feuer spucken würde, wie Genosse Drache, der glubschäugig und manisch grinsend von der Tapete grüßt. Hoffentlich sehe ich nicht auch so aus. Oder so wie mein Freund Bernhard, nachdem ihm in einem Hamburger Thai-Imbiss eine besonders teuflische Abart der Okra-Schote zwischen die Zähne geraten war. Sein Gesicht verlor die Farbe, dann setzte eine Art Leichenstarre ein. Außerdem konnte er drei Stunden lang nicht sprechen.

Mir läuft zwar der Schweiß aus allen Poren, ansonsten ist die Fassade wohl halbwegs intakt. Zumindest scheinen meine Mitesser keine Sterbeszene mehr zu erwarten, wie ein Blick in die Runde lehrt. Sie haben sich längst wieder ihren Tellern zugewandt oder machen Konversation. Nur Sir Colin kommt nicht zum Essen. Er sitzt neben Tony, und Tony ist bei seinem Lieblingsthema. »Schubert«, bröselt es dem Maestro ins süß-saure Hühnerklein, »Schumann … Brahms … Wagner … the genius of romantic music. But can you explain what Schönberg's idea was?«

Ob Colin Davis eine zufrieden stellende Antwort parat hat, ist mir entgangen. Ich bin vollauf mit der Koordination der Löscharbeiten beschäftigt.

»Kein Wasser, nichts Kaltes, Weißbrot«, hat Renate, die erfahrene Asienreisende, verfügt und kannenweise grünen Tee bestellt, den ich vorsichtig Schluck für Schluck in den wunden Schlund sickern lasse. Dabei bleibe ich auch, als wir den Abend in kleinerem Kreis im Tavern on the Green beschließen. Die Bar am Central Park ist nicht gerade ein Hort der Gemütlichkeit. Das Interieur sieht aus wie direkt dem *Fegefeuer der Eitelkeiten*, Tom Wolfes genial bösem Abgesang auf die Yuppie-Dekade, entsprungen: prächtig und kalt. Nichts als Chrom, Spiegelwände und zu grelles Licht. Grell sind auch die Preise. Aber zum einen ist es auf der Upper West Side nicht ganz einfach, nach dreiundzwanzig Uhr ein Lokal zu finden, wo man trinken *und* rauchen darf – auf dieser Kombination hat die EU-Fraktion unseres Häufleins bestanden –, zum anderen war Agenturmann Markus partout nicht davon abzubringen, holpernd wie gernegroß in die Novembernacht zu endreimen: »Los, wir gehen da jetzt rein, zur Feier des Tages lade ich euch ein.«

Nun, das war *vor* der Tür. Drinnen transpiriert er nach einer Stunde fast so heftig wie ich vorhin im Restaurant. Sein Kopf leuchtet tomatenrot am Tresen, während er das Portmonee umgräbt und mit dem Personal die Rechnung diskutiert. Am Tisch diskutieren wir amüsiert, ob wir ihn auslösen oder zum Abwaschen dalassen sollen. Mein Bruder, der befeuert von geistigen Getränken gerne grundsätzlich wird, zitiert Heiner Müller: »Der Mensch ein Dreck, sein Leben ein Gelächter.« Er ist für Abwaschen. Am Ende können wir ihn natürlich doch auf Kants kategorischen Imperativ verpflichten, der bekanntlich nur die schlichte Volksweisheit paraphrasiert: »Was du nicht willst, das man dir tu, das füg auch keinem andern zu.« Generös zahlt Micha für Renate und mich gleich mit. Was ihn aber nicht hindert, mir auf dem Heimweg mehrmals und eindringlich ins Ohr zu raunen: »Die Vernunft gebiert Ungeheuer, hörst du? Ungeheuer! Da wächst nichts Gutes draus.«

Das ist eben die Dialektik der Aufklärung. Aber solange mich Horkheimer und Adorno nicht bis in den Schlaf verfolgen, soll mir alles recht sein. Und der große Sandmann hat diesmal ein Einsehen. Kein Alb, kein Bautrupp stört meine Nachtruhe, kein Staubsauger kann mich wecken. Ich schlafe tief und fest durch bis Mittag.

Als ich aufwache, liegt auf dem Nachttisch ein Gruß von Renate und Micha. »Wandern heute durch die Museen. Sehen uns später. Mach dir einen schönen Tag. PS: Unbedingt in die Zeitung schauen!« Ich beschließe, es ruhig angehen zu lassen und im Hotel zu frühstücken. Probleme dürfte es nicht geben, die Jäger und Sammler sind längst wieder auf der Pirsch. Im Speisesaal herrscht folgerichtig Flaute. Sehr schön. Ich mache es mir in einer Ecke bequem, ordere Eier mit Schinken, Toast und viel Kaffee und lasse mir die Morgenblätter bringen. Als in den Feuilletons mein Name fett gedruckt unter dem von Sir Colin auftaucht, pumpert mein Herz un poco presto. Die ausführlichen Kritiken erscheinen zwar erst morgen, aber an den kurzen Anreißern lässt sich meist schon die Tendenz ablesen. Also gut. Einmal tief Luft holen und durch. Dann gaaanz langsam Ausatmen. Alles ist gut. Um nicht zu sagen, besser geht nicht. Man lobt Colin Davis, man lobt die Philharmoniker, man lobt das Gesamtkunstwerk in höchsten Tönen. Vor allem aber lobt man »the little German singer with the big voice«. Sogar der unbestechliche Mr. Tommassini ist entzückt. Er schreibt in der *Times*, man freue sich darauf, »the marvelous Bariton« Thomas Quasthoff jetzt öfter in New York zu hören.

»No, thanks«, ich trinke lieber keinen Kaffee mehr. Kurz darauf erscheint der Kellner erneut und legt das Telefon neben den Orangensaft. Linda ist dran.

»Good morning, Tommi. Hast du schon einen Blick in die Zeitungen geworfen?«

»Gerade eben.«

»Und? Ist das nicht fantastisch? Alle sind hin und weg von deiner Stimme. Morgen wirst du in ganz Amerika ein berühmter Sänger sein.«

»Super, komme ich dann in die Jay-Leno-Show?«

»Du wirst noch ganz andere Sachen machen. Du kannst dir aussuchen, wo du auftreten möchtest, mit wem du auftreten möchtest und mit welchem Programm. Die Fisher Hall hat schon angerufen und nach Terminen für einen Liederabend gefragt. Tommi, du hast es geschafft. Bei uns sagt man: You did it in New York, you did it everywhere. Wer sich hier durchsetzt, der braucht sich keine Sorgen mehr zu machen. Wir werden jede Menge Arbeit bekommen.«

Linda meint gewöhnlich, was sie sagt, und weiß, was sie tut. Trotzdem sollte ich den Ober um eine kräftige Kopfnuss bitten, nur um zu prüfen, ob das alles wirklich wahr ist. Seufzend lasse ich mich in die Polster sinken. Vor dem Fenster im milchigen Novemberlicht läuft die übliche Drei-Uhr-Vorstellung: Jogger, die verbissen übers Pflaster stampfen, dicke Schulkinder in Sneakers groß wie Schuhschachteln, zwei Obdachlose dösend vor ihrer Höhle aus Kartons, Geschäftsleute, die mit wehenden Mantelschößen aus den feinen Broadway-Restaurants in die Bürotürme der Midtown streben. Ein Trupp schwarzer Straßenkehrer schlendert lachend in den Park und am Zeitungskiosk langweilen sich die Fahrer der Taxicabs. Männer aus der Ukraine und dem Jemen, aus Pakistan, Nigeria oder Gabun. Männer auf der Suche nach dem Glück, das sie genauso selten finden wie die Straßennamen auf den Planquadraten ihrer Citymaps. Mir dagegen scheint es gerade nachzurennen. Vielleicht habe ich deshalb in letzter Zeit öfter noch als sonst das Gefühl, Akteur in einem Film zu sein. Nein, nicht im sprichwörtlich falschen. Es ist eigentlich ein heiteres Werk, aber auch ein wenig surreal, so als hieße der Regisseur, sagen wir, nicht Billy Wilder, sondern Luis Buñuel. Ich mag Buñuel, und ich mag diese schwerelose, im Wortsinn leicht verrückte Stimmung.

Sie liegt irgendwie schon in der Luft, als wir in Hamburg die Amerikareise antreten. Mir schwirrt durch den Kopf, dass ich innerhalb von drei Wochen die beiden bedeutendsten Konzerte meines Lebens singen und mit den besten Orchestern der USA auf der Bühne stehen werde. Genau das habe ich immer gewollt, und ich weiß, dass ich es kann. Für mich bedeutet es sozusagen die erste Champions-League-Teilnahme, nachdem ich, um in der Fußballsprache zu bleiben, bisher um die UEFA-Cup-Plätze gespielt und ein paar nationale Pokale gewonnen habe. Einen davon, den Echo-Klassik '98, hat man mir tags zuvor in der Hamburger Musikhalle überreicht. Es handelt sich um den Preis der Deutschen Phonoakademie in der Kategorie »Bester Sänger«. Das ist eine schöne Sache. Die Trophäe weniger. Das pfundschwere und konkurrenzlos hässliche Stück Alteisen lagert glücklicherweise im Auto meiner Eltern, die gestern Abend stolz im Saal saßen und ihre Sprösslinge nun an der Passkontrolle verabschieden. Mutter wie immer mit praktischen Ratschlägen:

»Kommt man nicht unter die Räder, macht keinen Blödsinn, und die schmutzige Wäsche von Thomas lasst ihr nicht im Hotel waschen, das mach ich lieber selbst.«

Mein Vater mit entscheidenden letzten Fragen:

»Jungs, habt ihr die Reisepässe?«

»Türlich!«

»Und eure Bordkarten?«

»Klar!«

»Guckt lieber noch mal nach. Micha ist doch so 'n alter Schussel.«

»Keine Sorge, Papa, alles da.«

»Na hoffentlich! Dann macht's mal gut und ruft gleich an, wenn ihr heil angekommen seid!«

»Sonst ruft der Arzt an!«

»Du bist und bleibst ein Dämelack.«

»Du bist der Beste.«

»So, nu is Schluss. Tschüs, meine Lieben.«

»Tschüs, tschüs!« Alle küssen sich und gehen ab.

Hoch über dem Flugfeld spannt sich ein azurblaues Laken mit Zirrusmuster und Sonnenfleck. Golden ist der Oktober, und die Quasthoff-Brüder sind in Ferienstimmung. Es kommt nämlich nicht oft vor, dass Micha Zeit herausschlagen kann, um mich auf einer Konzertreise zu begleiten. Und diese hier ist besonders schön, weil zwischen den Auftritten in Boston und New York fast vierzehn Tage Freizeit liegen. Außerdem haben die Veranstalter zweimal Businessclass bezahlt, was keineswegs selbstverständlich, aber bei langen Flügen ein wahrer Segen ist. Wir sitzen also recht kommod, lassen uns von den Stewardessen betütern, führen Männergespräche (Fußball lokal, Fußball national, Fußball international, Musik) und markieren im Reiseführer das Touristenprogramm vom New Yorker Jazzclub Birdland bis zum »Whale watching« in Cape Cod.

Die erste Etappe ist Boston. Seiji Ozawa hat mich eingeladen, mit seinem Boston Symphony Orchestra Mahlers *Das Lied von der Erde* aufzuführen. Ich kenne den kleinen energischen Mann mit der charakteristischen Löwenmähne aus Matsumoto in Japan. Dort hat er das Saito-Kinen-Festival ins Leben gerufen, wo ich 1997 unter seiner Leitung die *Matthäus-Passion* singen durfte. Es war eine beeindruckende Erfahrung. Seiji Ozawa ist nicht nur ein einfühlsamer, hochintelligenter Musiker, sondern einer jener raren Großmeister, denen es stets aufs Neue gelingt, neben Struktur und Klangspektrum auch die spirituelle Dimension eines Werkes auszuleuchten.

Und wie ein gutes Omen offenbart sich uns der Spirit von Boston auch gleich mit einer Art chorischer Massen-Performance. In der Kapitale des Kennedy-Clans nähert sich nämlich der Gouverneurswahlkampf dem Siedepunkt. Beim ersten Stadtrundgang geraten wir downtown am Quincy Market mitten zwischen die Fronten. Rechts vor dem Säulengang der Markthalle steht ein adrett kostümiertes Bürger-Bataillon, gegenüber paradiert ein eher bunt gemischtes Völkchen. Die Kombattanten beplänkeln sich im Stil vormoderner Feldschlachten. Das heißt, alle brüllen wie am Spieß. Was sie brüllen, ist auf hunderten vorgestanzter Schilder zu lesen, mit denen man drohend wider die feindlichen Reihen fuchtelt. Auf den blauen steht »Hershburger«, auf den roten »Celluzzi«. Aus dem blauen Block ragen noch zwei weitere Parolen. Eine wird postuliert von Frauen, deren Aufzug keinen Zweifel an ihrer Profession lässt. Sie tragen schwarze Capes und spitze schwarze Hüte, haben ihre Gesichter mit Lippen- und Kajalstift in ein expressionistisches Inferno verwandelt und sehen insgesamt aus wie Cousinen der Disney-Hexe Gundel Gaukelei. Genau das sind sie auch: »The witches minority votes Hershburger (Die Hexenminderheit wählt Hershburger)« schreien die Damen. In diesem Sinne erheben auch die Abgesandten der Schwulen-und-Lesben-Vereinigung Massachusetts lauthals ihre Stimmen, denn »Celluzzi is Hitler«.

»Celluzzi muss der Republikaner sein«, bemerkt Micha trocken. Fasziniert betrachten wir den politischen Schreikampf und mögen für diesmal nicht entscheiden, ob Amerika es wirklich besser hat.

»Not better«, sagt Tony, dem ich die Geschichte am nächsten Tag erzähle. »But for us, die meiste Politicians sind Großmäuler or langweilige Opportunists. Wenn wir müssen uns schon beschäftigen mit diese Typen, wir wollen wenigstens haben ain bischn Spaß.«

Das wiederum hat auch für Urnengänger aus Old Europe etwas zwingend Logisches.

Tony ist aus New York herübergeflogen und begleitet mich in die Boston Symphony Hall zur ersten Probe. Unterwegs schwärmt er von Ben Heppner: »One of the best tenors on earth.« Heppner wird im *Lied von der Erde* mein Partner sein. Ich besitze Schallplatten von ihm, habe den Kanadier aber noch nie getroffen. Jetzt stehe ich in meiner Garderobe, um mich einzusingen, als nebenan jemand beginnt, rasende Bebop-Läufe in ein Klavier zu donnern. Da ich selbst ein großer Jazzfan und von Natur aus neugierig bin, gehe ich nachsehen, wer der Virtuose ist. Ich klopfe zweimal laut, drinnen echot eine gewaltige Stimme:

»Come in!« Das Instrument wird von einem eleganten Hünen bearbeitet. Auf seinem Kopf sitzt ein Borsalino, um seine Schultern windet sich ein Seidenschal.

»Hello, my name is Thomas Quasthoff. I am a singer from Germany. I don't want to disturb you, but I hear someone playing funky like Victor Chestnut.«

»That would be nice. He's my favourite pianist«, brummt es aus dem schweren Mann. »I am just Ben Heppner.«

Heppner gilt in der Welt der Klassik als herausragende Größe. Mit Victor Chestnut könnten in Deutschland die wenigsten Kollegen etwas anfangen, weil hierzulande immer noch akademischer Dünkel am Grenzzaun zwischen E- und U-Musik Patrouille geht. In Amerika sind die Musiker meistens in mehreren Genres zu Hause. Wie Swing-König Benny Goodman, der die Klarinettenkonzerte von Mozart und Weber mit der gleichen Könnerschaft spielte wie *Lullaby in Rhythm* oder *Stompin' at the Savoy*. Ähnliche Kunststücke bringen auch meine Freunde Jeffrey Kahane und Rick Todd fertig. Rick, der sein Waldhorn singen lassen kann wie Miles Davis die Trompete, liegen die Jazzkritiker zu Füßen, was seinem Ruf als herausragender Orchestermusiker keinen Abbruch tut.

Dass auch Ben Heppners Ruhm mehr als verdient ist, demonstriert er eine Viertelstunde später live. »Mit voller

Kraft« hat Mahler über den Gesangspart des *Trinkliedes vom Jammer der Erde* geschrieben. Ich habe selten einen Tenor gehört, der dem einleitenden wuchtigen Allegro der Hornfanfare solche Strahlkraft entgegensetzt. »Schon winkt der Wein im goldnen Pokale« jubiliert Heppner und verwandelt die Verse des chinesischen Dichters Li Tai Po in ein funkelndes Plädoyer zugunsten des dionysischen Daseinsprinzips. Denn da der Mensch außerstande ist, Erkenntnisse über Sinn und Zweck des Lebens zu gewinnen, gibt es kein richtiges Leben im falschen, mithin auch nicht den geringsten Anlass, dass »die Freude welkt« oder die »Gärten der Seele wüst liegen«. Drum »nehmt den Wein, Genossen! Jetzt ist es Zeit, Genossen! / Leert eure goldnen Becher zu Grund / Dunkel ist das Leben, dunkel ist der Tod.« Es klingt großartig.

Am Aufführungstag ist Ben Heppner noch besser in Form und die Bostoner Symphoniker spielen einfach überirdisch. Getragen von dieser inspirierten Atmosphäre, bleibt meiner Stimme gar nichts anderes übrig, als gleichfalls schwerelos durch die Partitur zu segeln. Großen Anteil daran hat Seiji Ozawa, der die verästelten Motiv- und Themenfolgen der zwischen Todesahnung und Lebensbejahung oszillierenden *Erde*-Lieder mit feinstem Pinsel ausmalt. In *Abschied* fügt er schließlich alles zu einem ergreifenden symphonischen Tableau der Erlösungssehnsucht. Am Schluss des Liedes schwebt das Leitmotiv in Gestalt einer unaufgelösten Dissonanz hauchzart in der Luft, und ich lasse mein »Ewig ... ewig ...« darüber hinwehen. Als die Musik sich endgültig ins quasi Transzendente auflöst, ist es minutenlang still im Saal. Dann bricht ein Beifallssturm los, der selbst für die erfolgsverwöhnte Boston Symphony nicht alltäglich ist. Wie oft wir abgehen und wieder zurück auf die Bühne müssen, kann ich nicht mehr sagen. Ich erinnere nur noch, dass mir eine

Oboe kopfschüttelnd zuruft: »My goodness, the auditorium looks like a rodeo.«

Da sich die Kritiker von der Euphorie anstecken lassen und dazu beitragen, dass es nach der nächsten Aufführung genauso aussieht, schwebe ich auf Wolke sieben. Und wie das so ist, wenn man einen Lauf hat, passieren ganz nebenbei die schönsten Sachen. Eines Morgens steht plötzlich mein alter Spezi Steve Scharf in der Hotelhalle. Stevie spielt Geige im Los Angeles Chamber Orchestra. Wir musizieren fast jedes Jahr zusammen beim Bach-Festival in Oregon. Er hat sich am anderen Ende des Kontinents mal eben ins Flugzeug gesetzt, nur um sich das Mahler-Konzert anzuhören. Na ja, genau genommen führte ihn sein erster Weg noch vor dem Frühstück ins Foxborough-Stadion.

Die Heimstatt der Boston Red Sox ist für Baseball-Maniacs von ähnlich sakraler Bedeutung wie die Kaaba in Mekka für den gläubigen Moslem. Leider war Foxborough geschlossen, aber Mr. Scharf hat die Kultstätte dreimal umrundet und sein Team, die San Francisco 49ers, zehrt, wie er glaubhaft versichert, bis heute davon.

Am selben Tag stellt sich heraus, dass auch Felicitas Hoppe in Boston ist. Zumindest avisiert der Veranstaltungskalender einen Abend mit der *Aspekte*-Literaturpreisträgerin. Sie soll im Goethe-Institut aus ihrem wunderbaren Reiseroman *Pigafetta* lesen. Wir sind seit langem befreundet, und wenn der Termin kein Druckfehler ist, muss man sich selbstverständlich treffen. Schnell wird die Goethe-Nummer herausgesucht und nach ein, zwei Durchstellereien haben wir Feli am Telefon.

»Die Quasthoff-Brüder. Na, sagt mal, das ist eine echte Überraschung. Was macht ihr denn hier?«

»Ich singe, Micha ruft an den richtigen Stellen ›Bravo‹ und ›Da capo‹.«

»Und das klappt?«

»Wie am Schnürchen.«

»Dann leih ihn mir heute mal aus.«

Das brauche ich gar nicht. Für Micha ist der Besuch der Lesung Ehrensache.

Als er in der deutschen Dichter-und-Denker-Dependance auftaucht – ich habe noch eine Vorstellung und muss passen –, gibt es ein großes Hallo, das nach Lesungs- und Konzertende in großer Runde seine feuchtfröhliche Fortsetzung findet.

»Man hat mich bei Goethens begrüßt wie einen Promi«, staunt mein Bruder noch nach dem dritten Bier. Feli kann das erklären. Als der Institutsleiter fragte, wen er auf die Gästeliste setzen soll, hatte sie scherzend geantwortet: »Die Quasthoff-Brothers. Die treten zurzeit auch in Boston auf. Der eine singt, der andere ruft an den richtigen Stellen ›Bravo‹.« Seitdem hält uns der gute Mann, dem der Name wohl vage durch den Kopf spukte, für ein berühmtes Comedy-Duo.

Die nächsten Tage habe ich gespeichert wie ein kostbares Fotoalbum. Da ist ein ausgelassenes Abendessen, an dessen Ende Seiji Ozawa Micha lachend fragt: »Is your brother always so crazy?« Und da ist der Ausflug nach Cape Cod, das Dahingleiten auf dem Highway 93 unter strahlendem Himmel, der Indian Summer, der in psyche- delischen Rot- und Gelbtönen am Seitenfenster vorbei- rauscht, und Feli, die auf der Rückbank durch eine ge- rollte Landkarte Loewe-Balladen tutet. Da sind die bunt gestrichenen Holzhäuser und Cranberry-Felder von Rhode Island, die waldumkränzten Marschwiesen und Dünenstreifen hinter dem Kanal, der Cape Cod vom Fest- land trennt. Und endlich in Provincetown der herrliche Ozean und jede Menge Wind.

Woge auf Woge rauscht in schaumgekröntem Hock-
ney-Blau an den Strand, während sich unsereiner wie ein
schiefer Pfahl im 45-Grad-Winkel gegen die Böen stemmt.
Ein anderes Bild zeigt die weit geschwungene Bucht von
Plymouth, wo 1620 die ersten Puritaner an Land gingen.
Links liegt ein Modell der *Mayflower* vor Anker, in der
Mitte springt der verrückte Tony um einen tempelbe-
schirmten Gedenkstein und verkündet feixend, dieser
scheußliche Granitblock müsste eigentlich ein Riesen-
Donut sein.

Dann sehe ich uns in New York auf dem JFK-Flughafen
herumlungern, besorgt und hundemüde, weil Renates
Flug vier Stunden Verspätung hat. Drei Stunden später
stehen wir alle in der Knitting Factory und sind vor Begeisterung schier aus dem Häuschen, weil Steven Bernsteins Quintett »Sex Mob featuring John Medeski« in
Topform »John Barry's Music from James Bond Films«
performt. Ich sehe uns auf das Empire State Building
klettern und durch Little Odessa schlendern, wo die Häu-
serblocks fast in den Ozean fallen. Ich sehe uns im Museum of Modern Art die abstrakten Farbtafeln Mark Roth-
kos bewundern. Und ich sehe, wie Renate das Brüderpaar
kameragerecht vor der Carnegie Hall aufbaut. Dabei höre
ich mich mit Gerhard Schröder rufen: »Ich will da rein«.
Das mit Abstand schönste Erinnerungsbild stammt jedoch
aus dem Birdland. Wir feiern hinein in meinen neunund-
dreißigsten Geburtstag. Micha hat in dem legendären
Jazzclub einen Tisch gemietet. Auf der Bühne drängelt
sich eine dreißigköpfige New Yorker Allstar-Band und
pfeffert messerscharfe Riffs in den Saal, unten wippen
Füße und die Köpfe wackeln immer verwegener im afro-
kubanischen Rhythmusgewitter. Schlag zwölf unterbricht
die Band ihr Programm, das Personal gratuliert mit einer
Magnum-Flasche Champagner, Renate hat eine Geburts-

tagstorte und Wunderkerzen herbeigezaubert, und alle lassen mich hochleben.

Heute haben natürlich auch die Fisher-Hall-Konzerte, die für meine Karriere so wichtig waren, einen Ehrenplatz im Amerika-Album. Immer wenn ich es aufschlage, muss ich an meine Eltern denken, daran, dass diese Karriere ohne ihre Liebe, ohne ihr Vertrauen und ohne ihre jahrelange Unterstützung gar nicht möglich gewesen wäre; aber auch daran, wie viel es ihnen bedeutet, mich erfolgreich und auf eigenen Füßen, vor allem aber glücklich im Leben stehen zu sehen. Denn dass es so kommen würde, ist keineswegs abzusehen, als meine Mutter am 9. November 1959 im Hildesheimer Bernwardskrankenhaus eines von zwölftausend verkrüppelten Contergankindern zur Welt bringt.

Innerste Blues

Rechts, links, rechts, links, rechts, links metronomt mein Kopf auf dem Laken. Ich liege halb nackt da, Hüfte und Beine festgeklemmt in einem Streckverband aus Gips. Über die Beinschalen laufen Lederriemen, die links am Bettgestell, rechts am Metallgitter festgeschnallt sind. Das Bett steht in einem großen Raum mit fünfzehn anderen Betten. Die Betten sind weiß und leer. Es stinkt nach billigem Waschpulver, Sagrotan und Urin. Ich will es nicht riechen. Nein, ich rieche es nicht. Rechts, links, rechts, links: immer weiter taktelt der Kopf. Seit einer Stunde? Seit zwei Stunden? Ich spüre meine Beine nicht, nicht die schweißgetränkte Stelle, dort wo das Haar über das Laken rollt, und nicht die Schwären am wund gelegenen Gesäß. Ich spüre gar nichts. Nur die Pupillen springen. Rechts an die Gitterstäbe, links an das Fensterkreuz, rechts an die Gitterstäbe, links an das Fensterkreuz. Schön ist das, leicht geht das. Und in dieses tranceartige Dahinschwingen des Schädels, in diesen rhythmischen Dämmer dringt irgendwann nichts als Musik. Sie kommt vom Spielplatz draußen im Hof, schwappt aus den Räumen des Internates oder aus einem Radio im Schwesternzimmer. Eins, zwei, eins, zwei, eins, zwei. Glücklich formen meine Lippen Tonfolgen, Kinderlieder, Schlagerfetzen: »Heitschi bummbeitschi bummbumm, Heitschi bumbeitschi bummbumm.«

Das ist ein Song von Lolita. So nennt sich merkwürdigerweise eine sehr erwachsene Dame, die eine schöne Altstimme besitzt und Anfang der sechziger Jahre ein paar

Hits in den bundesdeutschen Charts unterbringt. Meine Mutter liebt ihre Platten. Meine Mutter heißt Brigitte. Unter der Woche steht sie zwei-, dreimal hinter einer dicken Glasscheibe, die den Besucherraum vom inneren Klinikbereich trennt. Wenn sie kommt, schiebt eine Schwester mein Bett vor die Scheibe. Ich sehe Mamas schmales blasses Gesicht, ihr Lächeln und wie sie die Handflächen gegen die Glasplatte legt. Manchmal sagt sie etwas, aber ich kann nicht verstehen, was. Manchmal muss sie weinen. Dann legt mein Vater Hans den Arm um ihre Schultern und drückt selbst eine Träne weg. Manchmal steht auch Micha da und macht Grimassen. Er quetscht am Glas die Nase platt, faltet mit beiden Händen das Gesicht zusammen, zieht ein Augenlid herunter und den Mund nach oben. Er sieht gruselig aus. Wie Charles Laughton alias Quasimodo, der auf dem Sims von Notre-Dame die Zigeunerin Esmeralda über den Buckel stemmt und »Asylrecht« brüllt. Vor Schreck fange ich ebenfalls an zu brüllen. Dafür bekommt Micha von Vater einen Klaps auf die Backe und mimt den sterbenden Schwan. Ich muss lachen, Micha muss lachen, Vater grinst. Da lacht auch Mama und gibt meinem Bruder einen Kuss. Familienfreuden!

Nach einer halben Stunde werde ich zurückgeschoben in den großen kahlen Saal. Ich bin wieder allein. Allein mit meinem gelben Teddybär und dem Radio im Schwesternzimmer. »Liebeskummer lohnt sich nicht, my Darling. / Schade um die Tränen in der Nacht«, trällert die blonde Siv Malmquist, und ich trällere mit. Und wieder beginnt mein Kopf zu rollen – rechts, links, rechts, links, rechts, links.

»Sie haben ein sehr musikalisches Kind«, sagen die Schwestern beim nächsten Besuch zu meiner Mutter. Mama nickt stumm und blickt mich mit großen Augen an.

»Wann kann der Junge denn endlich nach Hause?«, fragt Vater. Die Schwestern zucken mit den Schultern.

Eineinhalb Jahre geht das so. Eineinhalb Jahre liege ich in Hannover im orthopädischen Rehabilitationszentrum Annastift und sehe meine Familie nur durch diese Trennscheibe. »Wegen der Infektionsgefahr muss jeder Körperkontakt vermieden werden«, erklärt man meinen Eltern. Ich kriege trotzdem alles, was im Angebot ist: Masern, Windpocken, Mumps und ein Dutzend Mal die Grippe. Ich bin eigentlich immer krank. Den Ärzten macht das nichts. Ich bleibe in Quarantäne oder besser gesagt: unter Beobachtung. So ein Conterganfall ist eben neu, medizinisch gesehen hochinteressant und man weiß ja nie.

Was man zu diesem Zeitpunkt ganz genau weiß, ist, dass meiner Mutter das Beruhigungsmittel Contergan nie hätte verschrieben werden dürfen. Als sie die Pillen im Frühjahr 1959 schluckt, kursiert beim Hersteller Grünenthal, dessen Werbestrategen bevorzugt Schwangere im Visier haben (»garantiert ohne Nebenwirkungen«), längst der Verdacht auf fetale Hirn- und Nervenschäden, verursacht durch den Wirkstoff Thalidomid. Ein Jahr später weist ein Hamburger Arzt erstmals den Zusammenhang von Conterganeinnahme und Missbildungen bei Neugeborenen nach. Dennoch lässt Grünenthal jeden juristisch verfolgen, der behauptet, Contergan sei schädlich. 1962 ist die Beweislast erdrückend, es kommt zum Prozess. Grünenthal muss das nur unzureichend getestete Mittel vom Markt nehmen und findet die Opfer mit niedrigen fünfstelligen Summen ab. Die Kosten setzte Grünenthal von der Steuer ab.

Gegen den Beschluss des Bundesgesundheitsministeriums, Medikamente künftig auf derartige Risiken zu prüfen, legt die Firma mithilfe des Pharmaverbandes erfolgreich ihr Veto ein. »Wir sind nicht der Meinung, dass die bisherigen Erfahrungen eine Änderung des Gesetzes in diesem Punkt erfordern«, steht schwarz auf weiß in der Begründung. Wie die Industrie so etwas deichselt, zeigt sich Anfang der siebziger Jahre. Als die sozialliberale Regierung sich erneut an einer Novellierung des Arzneimittelgesetzes versucht, droht die Pharma-Lobby, »dass wir alle uns zu Gebote stehenden Möglichkeiten der Einflussnahme ausschöpfen«. Details sind einem Dossier zu entnehmen, das man im Schweizer Banksafe des FDP-Mannes Hans-Otto Scholl, seines Zeichens Hauptgeschäftsführer des Bundesverbandes der Pharmazeutischen Industrie, findet. Es enthält Zahlen und ein dickes Namensregister, darunter Bonner Prominenz wie Alfred Dregger oder Martin Bangemann und hohe Funktionsträger des Gesundheitswesens. Alle kassierten Wahlkampfspenden oder Schmiergelder, um dafür zu sorgen, das neue Arzneimittelgesetz zu entschärfen. Bis heute wird Contergan unter anderem Namen von Lizenznehmern in Brasilien und den USA vertrieben.

An den verheerenden Folgen hat sich nichts geändert. Contergan oder Thalidomid wirkt besonders aggressiv während der ersten drei Schwangerschaftsmonate. In dieser Zeit bildet der Embryo das Skelett und alle Organe aus. Die Art der Deformationen hängt von Zeitpunkt und Dauer der Einnahme ab. Zwischen dem 21. und dem 22. Tag der Schwangerschaft führt Thalidomid zu Missbildungen der Ohrmuscheln und ruft Hirnnervenschäden hervor. Zwischen 24. und 29. Schwangerschaftstag verursacht der Wirkstoff Phokomelie, die so genannte Robbengliedrigkeit. Das Phänomen heißt so, weil die langen Röhrenknochen von Armen und Beinen nicht vollständig entwickelt sind, so dass Hände und Füße flossenartig am

Schulter- bzw. Hüftgelenk andocken. Vom 30. bis zum 36. Tag bilden sich Verkrüppelungen der Hände und anorektale Stenosen (Verengung von After und Mastdarm) aus. An derartigen organischen Schäden sterben allein in Westdeutschland rund fünftausend Contergankinder, fast die Hälfte aller Geschädigten. Ein weiteres Drittel trägt bleibende Hirnschäden davon.

Nach eineinhalb Jahren sind die Experten im Annastift sicher: Der kleine Quasthoff hat noch mal Glück gehabt. Sein Kopf funktioniert einwandfrei, dito der Stoffwechsel. Er sieht nur aus wie eine kleine Robbe mit verkrüppelten Händen und Füßen, die nicht nach vorne stehen, sondern bei der Geburt im 90-Grad-Winkel nach hinten gebogen sind. »Laufen wird er nie können«, sagt Professor Hauberg, der Klinikleiter, »aber mit der Gipsschale lässt sich das wenigstens optisch korrigieren.«

Ich darf nach Hause. Das Bündel Mensch, das sie meiner Mutter zum Abtransport in die Arme legen, ist drei Jahre alt und wiegt fünf Kilo. Mit Gipsschale zehn. Das unförmige Ding gibt es gratis dazu. Samt einer Portion guter Ratschläge. Einer lautet: »Kopf hoch, auch an so einem Kind kann man viel Freude haben.«

»Goldig«, ruft Oma Else.

»Was für ein Süßer«, ruft Tante Frida.

»Aber dünn wie 'n Zahnstocher.« Oma Lieschen, schwer und rund wie ein Eichenfass, schüttelt fassungslos das graue Haupt. Wenn sich das rüstige Trio über sein Bettchen beugt und den blonden Haarschopf streichelt, strahlt der Bub wie ein Honigkuchenpferd. Bis sie ihm den nächsten Schokoladenkanten in den Mund schieben. Dann grunzt er behaglich, sabbert und stammelt »Lade«, was Nachschub meint.

»Ein kluges Kind«, frohlockt Oma Else.

»Bitte stopft ihn nicht so mit Süßigkeiten voll«, fleht Mama.

Tante Frida ist pikiert: »In der Anstalt hat er so was Feines ja nich jekriecht.«

Eine Stunde später spucke ich Mama die Nudeln auf die Schürze und heule und schreie wie am Spieß. Nicht zum ersten Mal an diesem Tag. Und nicht zum letzten Mal. Ich habe diese Art Protestkultur im Annastift zu nervenzerfetzender Meisterschaft entwickelt.

»Komm, du kleine Heulboje«, brummt Vater und legt den krähenden Nachwuchs in der Sofaecke vor dem Radio ab, um wenigstens am Sonntag in Ruhe zu frühstücken. Es läuft der NDR-Seemannstrost *Zwischen Hamburg und Tahiti.* Gisela aus Aurich grüßt Obermaat Heinz Klüwer, auf der *Senator II* unterwegs in der Malaiischen See. Dann schmachtet Freddy Quinn *Junge, komm bald wieder.* Das kann ich bald auswendig und rolle meinen Kopf in leichter Dünung über die Sofapolster. Rechts, links, rechts, links, rechts, links. Spielt das Radio den *Lachenden Vagabunden*, einen anderen Chartbreaker dieser Jahre, ist es mit der Ruhe schnell wieder vorbei. Und der Titel wird oft gespielt.

»Sie sollten das Lied verbieten«, murmelt Mama automatenhaft wie der Römer Cato sein »Carthaginem esse delendam«. Denn nach dem Refrain fällt Interpret Fred Bertelmann regelmäßig in ein derartig perverses Gegacker, dass der Song eigentlich »Der lachende Unhold« heißen müsste.

Und schon brülle ich wieder los. Ich schreie morgens und ich schreie abends. Ich heule, weil ich achtzehn Monate in der Gipsschale verbracht habe und es nicht gewohnt bin, herumgetragen zu werden; ich heule, wenn man mich wieder in das steife Korsett schnallt, weil es auf dem Arm von Mama und Papa eigentlich doch viel schöner ist. Ich schreie und heule, sobald fremde Menschen die Wohnung bevölkern, wenn Micha mir nicht sein rotes Feuerwehrauto überlässt und wenn ich nachts die Gipsschale voll gepinkelt habe. Ich pinkele jede Nacht die Gipsschale voll.

Mama nimmt es hin, Mama nimmt vieles hin. Dass mich die Nachbarn im Hausflur anstarren wie ein Gespenst, dass ihr Leute beim Edeka nachrufen, »den haste wohl im Suff gezeugt«, dass man in der Bischofsstadt Hildesheim Kreuze schlägt, wenn sie mich im Park spazieren fährt. Mama hat das Contergan geschluckt. Mama quält sich mit Vorwürfen: sie ist schuld, dass ich behindert bin. Vater sagt, dass das Blödsinn ist, Mama weiß, dass er Recht hat. Einerseits. Andererseits scheuert Mama jede Nacht klaglos die Gipsschale sauber. Dann trägt sie mich in das große Ehebett, buckt meinen Kopf an ihre Brust und weint still in die Kissen.

Vater kann das Elend irgendwann nicht mehr mit ansehen. Eines Abends stapft er quer über die Straße zum alten Bergner. Bergner, ein sehniger Kraftmensch mit Händen wie Kohleschaufeln und einem Herz aus Gold, betreibt Hildesheims einzige Pferdeschlachterei. Die beiden sind Männer vom Land und gewohnt, Probleme auf rustikal-pragmatische Art zu lösen. Als Vater heimkommt, hat er ein paar Bier intus, über seinem Arm baumelt ein ausgekochter Pferdedarm. Er bahnt sich den Weg ins Schlafzimmer. Mama ist entsetzt: »Hänschen, das willst du doch dem Kind nicht …«

»Doch. Meinen inkontinenten Großvater haben wir genau so trockengelegt.«

Unbeirrt stülpt er mir den Naturkatheder über den Harnausgang, hängt das andere Ende in einen Nachttopf auf dem Fußboden und betrachtet sein Werk.

»Es singen die Wasser vom Schlafe noch fort / vom Tage vom heute gewesenen Tage«, mörikt er fröhlich. »Aber heute nicht.«

Dann legt er sich hin und schläft den Schlaf der Gerechten. Mama auch. Zum ersten Mal seit Wochen.

Das ist die Nacht, in der ich still- und trockengelegt werde. Ein familienhistorisch bedeutsames Datum. Es folgt ein Wochenende, an dem Micha und ich meine Eltern kaum zu Gesicht bekommen. Sie verschanzen sich in der Wohnstube. Sie hocken in der Küche. Sie reden. Stundenlang. Wir sitzen im Kinderzimmer und lauschen bange. Es wird laut, Türen knallen und Tränen fließen. Sie streiten, sie halten sich in den Armen, streiten wieder. Aber am Ende ist alles gut. Es ist wie ein reinigendes Gewitter. Von nun an wird es aufwärts gehen. Oder besser gesagt: vorwärts. Meine Eltern haben beschlossen, auf die Bedenken der Ärzte zu pfeifen, Behinderung Behinderung sein zu lassen und ihrem Jüngsten endlich den aufrechten Gang und damit den ersten Schritt zur vollkommenen Menschwerdung beizubringen. Dazu dient ein weiteres Mitbringsel aus dem Annastift.

Um mich wenigstens ab und an in die Senkrechte zu bringen, wurde in der orthopädischen Werkstatt eine Abart der Gipsschale konstruiert, der Schienenschellenapparat. Die klobige Prothese besteht, wie der Name sagt, aus Metallschienen, die an Hüfte und Beinen entlanglaufen und mit Lederriemen und Stahlschellen festgezurrt werden. Die Fußauflage ist etwa dreißig Zentimeter über dem Boden angebracht. Sobald man mich hineinmontiert, erreiche ich eine meinem Alter angemessene Größe. Das ist schön und gut für den Kreislauf, der endlich mal richtig Schwung holen kann. Manchmal aber auch ein bisschen viel für einen, der sein Leben bis dato im oblomowschen Sinne, also eher im Sitzen und Liegen gefristet hat.

Einmal aufgerichtet, wird mir oft schwindelig wie einer Landratte, die man vom Boden der Tatsachen stante pede in den Mastkorb einer Brigg versetzt. Immerhin bleiben mir andere Symptome der Seekrankheit erspart, weil das Monstrum jede Bewegung unmöglich macht. Ich hänge so hilflos im Geschirr wie die letzten französischen Ritter in ihrer Rüstung, als die Engländer bei Azincourt zum Angriff blasen. Immerhin behandelt man mich besser als Henri V. seine Widersacher. Im Annastift werde ich bevorzugt dekorativ an die Wand gelehnt oder an Orten platziert, wo ich, sollte es mich umwerfen, wenig Sachschaden anrichten kann.

Natürlich wirft es mich öfter um. Da mir Arme zum Abstützen fehlen, schlage ich jedes Mal lang hin wie ein Besenstiel, und auf meiner Stirn wachsen Beulen groß wie Hühnereier.

»Ne Bonje wie Kruppstahl«, kommentiert Onkel Herbert anerkennend die Signaturen meines ersten heimatlichen Absturzes. Mamas angeheirateter Cousin weiß, wovon er spricht. Dem alten Sozialdemokraten hat die SA mal ein Bierseidel über die Glatze gezogen. Die Narben sitzen tief. »Keene Lebensart der Faschist, det war sein Erfolgsressept. De EsssPD hat imma mit Anstand zurückjekloppt, mit de Fäuste, nur ab un an mal mit 'n Stuhlbeen. Un wat hat's jenütz? Jarnüscht!« Bei diesem Thema, weiß Vater, braucht Onkelchen schnell einen Doppelkorn, sonst müssen wir uns die Geschichte der Arbeiterbewegung von Lassalle bis zum Godesberger Programm anhören.

»Herbertchen, denk an dein Herz«, mahnt Cousine Elsie mit strengem Blick auf das randvolle Glas.

»Keene Bange, Mäuseken, det schlägt nur für dir«, spricht Herbert und schluckt den Weizenbrand auf ex weg.

Mein Vater bannt die Sturzgefahr schließlich durch ein brusthohes Holzgestell, das er eigenhändig im Keller zusammenzimmert. Ich kann mich daran festhalten und es fängt mich auf, wenn ich das Gleichgewicht verliere. So gesichert ist es nicht weit bis zum nächsten, das heißt meinem ersten Schritt. Mama hat nämlich herausgefunden, dass man mir ein wenig Beinfreiheit verschaffen kann, wenn sie an der Prothese in Hüfthöhe zwei Schellen offen lässt.

Seitdem läuft in der Küche täglich folgender Feldversuch: Auf dem Tisch steht ein großer Teller mit Süßigkeiten. Zwei Meter entfernt hat sie das Holzgestell aufgebaut. Mama hievt mich samt Schienenschellenapparat hinein, tritt an den Tisch und nimmt ein Stück Schokolade in die Hand.

»Lade«, strahlt der Proband.

»Genau«, sagt Mama, »leckere süße Vollmilchorange, die beste Schokolade der Welt.«

Dem Probanden läuft das Wasser im Mund zusammen, er wartet auf die Fütterung. Aber die bleibt aus. Stattdessen legt Mama die Leckerei zurück auf den Teller, breitet die Arme aus und flötet: »Komm, mein Kleiner, komm, setz schön ein Bein vor das andere und hol sie dir.«

Diese Niedertracht beruht auf dem berühmten Experiment des russischen Psychologen Iwan Petrowitsch Pawlow. 1904 hält er seinen Hunden wochenlang einen Napf dicht, aber unerreichbar vor die Nasen, klingelt mit einem Glöckchen und sieht mitleidlos mit an, wie ihnen der Speichel von den Lefzen tropft. Als Pawlow feststellt, der Reflex funktioniert auch ohne Napf, nur auf das Glöckchenzeichen hin, hat er die Konditionierung entdeckt und bekommt den Nobelpreis.

Ich bekomme erst mal gar nichts. Ich mache keinen Schritt. Ich sehe das überhaupt nicht ein. Vage ahnend, dass Mutter und Sohn hier am Rubikon stehen, dass das Grundrecht auf Vertilgung von Vollmilchorangenschokolade zum Geschacher erniedrigt wird, dass mithin die Wolfsgesetze des Kapitalismus erste dunkle Schatten auf das Reich bedingungsloser Elternliebe werfen, verweigert mein kindliches Gemüt jede Kooperation.

»Mmmmh, schmeckt das gut!« Mama zerkaut genüsslich ein Stück Schokolade. Sie zerkaut einen Keks.

»Nur drei kleine Schritte. Komm, du kannst das, es ist ganz leicht.«

Als sie das nächste Stück Vollmilchorange zwischen ihren Lippen verschwinden lässt, beginnt es in mir zu arbeiten. Mama langt noch mal zu und blickt mich traurig an.

»Oh, Tommi, sieh mal, gleich ist alles alle.«

Sie kaut, sie schluckt, ihre Hand kreist wieder über dem Teller. Dann hat sie mich. Oder um mit Galilei zu reden: Er bewegt sich doch. Ich setze das rechte Bein vor, die Scharniere der Prothese ächzen, ich ziehe das linke nach, das Holzgestell beginnt über das Steingut des Küchenbodens zu schaben, noch mal das rechte Bein nach vorn, noch mal das linke, und schon bin ich da. Es geht wirklich ganz leicht. Mama strahlt wie ein Kronleuchter. Sie herzt und küsst mich, schiebt mir die Belohnung in den Mund und sagt: »Sehr schön, mein Schätzchen, das machen wir gleich noch mal.«

Ich liebe Schokolade, und ich lerne schnell. Bald schaffe ich es ohne das stützende Holzgerüst bis zum Küchentisch, nach einer Woche geht es sogar ohne Schokolade. Herr Pawlow hat seinen Nobelpreis zweifellos verdient. Wir fahren nach Hannover ins Annastift, um Professor Hauberg das Kunststück vorzuführen. Der Orthopäde lehnt mit verschränkten Armen am Fenster seines Büros und kaut am Bügel seiner Hornbrille, als ich seinen Schienenschellenapparat unbeholfen, aber so zielstrebig wie unfallfrei um die lederne Sitzgruppe wuchte.

»Erstaunlich, das ist wirklich ganz erstaunlich!« Hauberg schüttelt erst den Kopf, dann wendet er sich an meine Eltern: »Das hätte ich nie für möglich gehalten. Das haben Sie sehr gut gemacht.« Er ist tatsächlich ein bisschen gerührt. Aber auch ein zupackender und hilfsbereiter Mensch. Er drückt auf eine Klingel, lässt sich einen Zeichenblock bringen und wirft ein paar schnelle, präzise Striche aufs Papier. Zwei Monate später habe ich eine neue, leichtere Prothese. Und einen neuen Trainer.

Vater hat die Schuhe aus- und den Bauch eingezogen. Seine Hände liegen an der Hosennaht, das Kinn strebt an die Decke. Er steht im Schlafzimmer auf dem Bett, als warte er darauf, dass ihm jemand das Bundesverdienstkreuz an die Jacke heftet. Ich stehe davor und warte, dass er endlich umfällt. Vater lässt sich nicht lumpen.

»Aaachtung!«, ruft er, »aufgepasst!« Und schon schrägt sein Körper im Stil einer Bahnschranke der Matratze entgegen, gewinnt an Fahrt, wird schneller, wird rasend schnell. Doch kurz vor dem Aufprall dreht er den rechten Arm und fängt den Sturz mit der Schulter ab. Leider verdirbt ihm der elastische Federkern den bis dato tadellosen Auftritt. Vater verliert das Gleichgewicht und landet mit einem halben Überschlag auf dem Fußboden. Als er sich wieder aufrappelt, hält er sich ächzend das Knie, ignoriert mein Grinsen und sagt: »Den Schlussteil kannste vergessen, mein Junge, aber das Prinzip ist klar, oder?«

Dann bin ich dran. Vater schnallt mir die neue Prothese um, dann hebt er mich auf das Bett. Ich muss die Übung wiederholen. Stehen, fallen, abrollen. Stehen, fallen, abrollen. Immer wieder. Jeden Tag eine halbe Stunde.

»Bis du das im Schlaf kannst«, sagt Vater. Als ich es im

Schlaf kann, verordnet er mir dieselbe Trainingseinheit ohne Prothese. Der Erfolg ist verblüffend. An meinem vierten Geburtstag wird die Gipsschale feierlich zerbrochen und ich schnüre durch die Wohnung wie ein junger Dachs. Nicht unfall-, aber weitgehend beulenfrei!

Das Terrain hält sich in überschaubaren Grenzen. Drei Zimmer, Küche, Bad, zweiter Stock, in der Arneckenstraße 10, ein graues Haus in der grauen Innenstadt von Hildesheim. Aber drinnen, zwischen Nierentisch, Gummibaum und furnierter Schrankwand ist es kommod und niemals langweilig.

Mein Lieblingsplatz befindet sich im Wohnzimmer vor der Musiktruhe. Das Blaupunkt-Modell besitzt einen integrierten Plattenspieler, der zehn Singles stapeln kann. Ist ein Song abgelaufen, schwingt der Tonarm zurück und die nächste Platte fällt mit einem sanften Plopp auf den Teller. Ist der ganze Stapel durchgenudelt, brauche ich nur die Zauberformel »Mutti, wechseln!« zu rufen. Prompt erscheint die gute Fee, öffnet ein Fach unter dem Radio, wo die Platten säuberlich nach Alphabet geordnet in grünen und braunen Kunststoffmappen lagern, und steckt ein weiteres Singlesandwich auf den Plattenhalter. Mama wartet, den Kopf leicht geneigt und die Hände in die Hüften gestemmt, bis die Nadel die ersten Töne aus dem knisternden Vinyl kratzt. Dann slowfoxt sie fröhlich pfeifend zurück in die Küche. Unter der Woche, wenn Vater im Landgericht und Micha in der Schule sitzt, mögen wir's nämlich leicht. Das Bert Kaempfert Orchester schnulzt *Spanish Eyes*, Peter Alexander glaubt, dass an seiner präsenilen Demenz nur *Die Beine von Dolores* schuld sind, Conny Froboess packt die Badehose ein und der sonore Bass von Bruce Low zieht als *Wandering Star* über die Wüste Arizonas.

Am Wochenende hat Vater die Programmhoheit. Dann wird der Gemütsbalsam der Wirtschaftswunderjahre mit Perlen aus dem klassischen Fundus angereichert: Josef Metternich singt Verdi, Hans Hotter Beethoven, Josef Greindl die Balladen von Carl Loewe und der stimmgewaltige Kurt Böhme brummt sich durch das komische Rollenfach der deutschen Oper. Böhmes Glanzpartie ist das Borstenvieh-Couplet des Zsupán aus Johann Straußens *Zigeunerbaron*. Vaters auch. Wenn es das Wetter erlaubt, steht er sonntags gern mal auf dem Balkon, räuspert seinen Generalbass und schmettert die Arie in den Morgenhimmel.

Sehr zum Leidwesen von Herrn und Frau Kurbjuweit aus dem ersten Stock. Herr Kurbjuweit ist Kriegsinvalide, Frau Kurbjuweit war bei der Reichsbahn. Nun kompensiert das Duo die Ödnis auf dem frühverrenteten Abstellgleis, indem sie der Hausgemeinschaft als Blockwart (er) und audiophober Kinderschreck (beide) auf den Wecker fallen. Für die Quasthoff-Sprösslinge dagegen ist Vaters Performance jedes Mal ein Heidenspaß. Uns gefällt vor allem der Text. Er geht so: »Das Schreiben und das Lesen ist nie mein Fach gewesen, / denn schon von Kindesbeinen befasst ich mich mit Schweinen, / auch war ich nie ein Dichter, Potzdonnerwetter, Paraplui, / nur immer Schweinezüchter, poetisch war ich nie!« Anfangs hallt das Agrarier-Credo nur risoluto pomposo über den Hinterhof. Sobald aber Geschirrklappern und unterdrücktes Fluchen signalisieren, dass auch die Kurbjuweits ihre Frühstückseier an die frische Luft getragen haben, legt Vater eine Schippe drauf und molto furioso los. »Ja, mein idealer Lebenszweck ist Borstenvieh, ist Schweinespeck, / mein idealer Lebenszweck ist Borstenvieh, ist Schweinespeck, / ist Borstenvieh und Schweinespeck.«

Hier folgt meistens eine Kunstpause, und Vater fängt

leise an zu zählen. Spätestens bei drei schiebt Kurbjuweit seinen Hohlkopf, der immer glüht wie ein Produkt der Firma Osram, über die Geranienkästen und beginnt zu zetern: »Am Sonntag ist das keine Ruhestörung, sondern eine kriminelle Handlung!«

Was der Familienchor durch die Wiederholung des Refrains souverän zu kontern pflegt, allerdings mit einer kleinen Variante: »Hört her, wer steht da unter Schock, das Borstenvieh im ersten Stock / hört her, wer steht da unter Schock, das Borstenvieh im ersten Stock, / das Borstenvieh im ersten Stock.«

Zugegeben, es gibt subtilere Späße. Und Mama ist das manchmal ein bisschen peinlich. Aber auf grobe Klötze gehören grobe Keile. Die Kunstbanausen verdienen es schlicht nicht besser. Vater singt nämlich nicht nur gern und laut. Er singt auch sehr schön. Genauer gesagt, kann er eine fast komplette Gesangsausbildung vorweisen. Er musste sie abbrechen, weil mein Großvater Fritz seit 1939 tot und Oma Lieschen wie die meisten Witwen nach dem Krieg arm wie eine Kirchenmaus war. Was sie in täglicher Fron zusammenrackerte, langte kaum für das Essen, geschweige denn für das Musikstudium an der Hochschule in Braunschweig. Ein entfernter Verwandter, der Vaters Begabung erkannte, bot sich an, die Kosten zu übernehmen. Leider ging dem Mäzen kurz vor dem krönenden Abschluss das Lebenslicht und meinem alten Herrn damit das Geld aus. Immerhin reichte der Bühnenschliff, um sich in den Varietés und Gemeindesälen des Harzer Vorlandes, wo damals auch Größen wie Hans Albers und Ilse Werner ihren Ufa-Ruhm versilberten, als Sänger, Conferencier und Komiker ein paar D-Mark oder, sofern die nagelneue Währung nicht verfügbar war, eine Wochenration Schwarzgebrannten zu verdienen. Er wurde aus Zuckerrüben gemacht und im Dreieck Bockenem, Seesen,

Salzgitter legen Veteranen bis heute großen Wert auf die Feststellung, der Konsum sei um einiges gefährlicher gewesen als die Herstellung.

Bei einem dieser Gastspiele hat Vater dann einem bildhübschen Mädchen namens Brigitte Fellberg erstmals und gleich ziemlich tief in die Augen geschaut. Sie wohnte im Nachbardorf, arbeitete in Hildesheim als Sekretärin und blickte interessiert zurück. Das war der Anfang vom Ende seiner jungen Künstlerlaufbahn. Emil Fellberg, der Schwiegervater in spe, stellte ihn kurz und bündig vor die Alternative: »Wähle, Sohn, meine Tochter oder das Tingeltangel.«

Opa Emil meinte es ernst. Nachdem er die ruinösen Tollheiten der Hitlerei, Mord und Totschlag an zwei Fronten, den Sprung aus einem russischen Gefangenzug und einen Rückmarsch durch halb Europa überstanden hatte, war der zähe Preuße nicht gewillt, das Schicksal seiner Tochter in die Hände eines windigen Theaterschlemihls zu legen. Da musste etwas Solides her. Vater befragte sein Herz, bedachte die kargen abendlichen D-Mark-Gagen und die leberstrapazierende Ersatzwährung und kam schnell zu dem Schluss, dass ihm ein Branchenwechsel in allen Belangen gut tun würde. Er schwor Hoch- und Kleinkunst ab und trat die gehobene Justizlaufbahn an. 1954, im Jahr des Wunders von Bern, gab er seiner Brigitte das Jawort. Wie beide glaubhaft versichern, hat Vater es nie bereut. Er ist auch niemals rückfällig geworden. Na ja, fast nie. Aber das eine Mal hat ihm keiner übel genommen. Im Gegenteil. Seitdem besitzen die Quasthoffs nämlich einen Fernseher.

Danke, Peter Frankenfeld. Die Anschaffung wird 1964 getätigt, als der NDR Vater einlädt, bei *Toi, toi, toi* aufzutreten, einer Talentshow, die Frankenfeld, der Quiz-

und Humor-Grande des bundesrepublikanischen TV-Neolithikums, moderiert. Wie sich herausstellt, hat Michas Patenonkel Albert der Redaktion heimlich ein Tonband mit Gesangsproben seines Freundes Hans zugespielt. Nun trifft die frohe Botschaft ein, Vater habe sich binnen dreier Tage in Hamburg einzufinden, um an der Livesendung teilzunehmen. Der fällt zunächst aus allen Wolken und ist sauer. Auf Kumpel Albert, auf Frankenfeld und auf Mama, die gegen einen Ausflug in die Hansestadt eigentlich nichts einzuwenden hätte. Ausgerechnet Brigitte Fellberg. Hat er nicht auf Betreiben dieser Dame eine steile Karriere an den Nagel gehängt und verbringt seine Tage statt als umschwärmter Starbariton an der Scala als karg besoldeter Amtsinspektor im Landgericht? Nicht, dass er sich beschweren will. Aber Vater macht keine halben Sachen, Vater ist jetzt Beamter, und ein Beamter muss nicht ins Fernsehen. Basta.

»Sei doch nicht so stur«, sagt Mama.

»Nein, Puttchen, das kommt gar nicht in Frage. Wir bleiben zu Hause.« Da lächelt Mama. Wenn ihr Hänschen sie zärtlich Puttchen nennt, ist das letzte Wort noch nicht gesprochen.

»Du brauchst gar nicht so zu grinsen. Ich singe nicht.«

Zwei Tage später spazieren die beiden um den Michel und in der Arneckenstraße wird ein Fernsehgerät angeliefert. Großmutter Else hat den zentnerschweren Apparat spendiert. Jetzt dirigiert sie die Packer lautstark durch die Wohnstube.

»Vorsicht, meine Herren, da steht 'ne Schrankwand! Machen Se mir bloß nischt kaputt, ich bin hier nämlich bloß die Oma und auf Besuch.«

Großmutter Lieschen berserkert derweil seit morgens um sieben in der Küche. Eigentlich darf sie da gar nicht rein. Die Küche ist tabu, sagt Mama. Besonders für Lieschen. Das kann man verstehen. Oma ist professionelle Köchin und der festen Überzeugung, ihre Schwiegertochter kann es nicht. Jedenfalls kocht sie nicht halb so nahrhaft, wie es sein sollte, sagt Oma. Eine Ansicht, die ihr weder durch Mamas virtuose Saucenkreationen, ihre luftigen Soufflees noch durch unsere zufriedenen Bäuerchen auszutreiben ist. Lieschen hat ihr Handwerk zur Hochzeit wilhelminischer Kalorienbombenproduktion gelernt. Ihr passt die ganze Richtung nicht. Weshalb sie die Quasthoffschen Männer ständig dem Hungertode nahe wähnt. Wenn die beiden am Herd stehen, herrscht kalter Krieg:

»Noch 'n Stück Butter«, mosert Lieschen in die Töpfe, »da gehört Schmalz dran.« Oder: »Das ist keine Mehlschwitze, das ist Wassersuppe.«

Mama hat jahrelang eisern geschwiegen, bis ihr doch mal der Kragen platzt und die Küche zum Schwiegermuttersperrgebiet erklärt wird. Aber heute ist die verbotene Zone unbewacht und Lieschen in ihrem Element. Mit bloßen muskulösen Armen walkt sie Cellischen Butterkuchen über ein Blech, selcht einen Schweinebraten und schmiert »für zwischendurch« noch ein paar Wurstbemmen. Auf dem Herd gurgelt eine Rindersuppe, in der die Fettaugen eindeutig Oberwasser haben.

»Wen hast du denn alles eingeladen?«, fragt Oma Else konsterniert.

»Wieso eingeladen? Niemand. Meine Enkel müssen doch mal was Anständiges zwischen die Zähne kriegen.«

Als Vaters großer Auftritt naht, dräut auf dem Wohnzimmertisch ein herrlich duftendes Mittelgebirge aus Fett und reinem Kohlenhydrat. Doch ans Essen denkt jetzt niemand. Es ist ja alles so aufregend. Die Großmütter haben den Enkeln zum x-ten Mal die Scheitel gerade und sich selbst festlich angezogen. Lieschens voluminöse Gestalt thront schon seit einer halben Stunde wie in Stein gemeißelt vor der blinden Bildröhre, Oma Else sucht den Einschaltknopf, dann ihre Brille, dann wieder den Einschaltknopf. Sie findet ihn gerade noch rechtzeitig.

»Da ist Papa«, kräht Micha. Tatsächlich erscheinen auf dem Schirm zwei winzige Männer. Einer sieht aus wie Vater, der andere wie ein Vertreter für großkarierte Herrenkonfektion.

»Ist das der Kulenkampff?«, flüstert Oma Else.

»Nein, das ist Peter Frankenfeld«, sagt Lieschen kühl wie eine Regierungssprecherin. Dabei könnte sie platzen, so stolz ist sie auf ihren Filius. Frankenfeld sagt gerade:

»… sehr schön, mein Lieber, Sie haben die Gattin mitgebracht. Grüße, gnä' Frau.« Er verneigt sich vage Richtung Saalpublikum und fährt fort: »Und nun möchten wir natürlich wissen, was Sie noch so tun. Außer singen, meine ich.«

»Ich bin Justizbeamter.«

»Ah, ein Staatsdiener, da bleibt ja viel Zeit zum Üben, hahaha. Nichts für ungut, kleiner Scherz von mir. Und was werden wir jetzt hören?«

»Lortzing, *Zar und Zimmermann*. Die Antritts-Arie des Bürgermeisters van Bett: *Oh, sancta justitia! Ich möchte rasen.*«

»Oh ha. Na, wir hoffen mal, dass Ihr Amtsleiter nicht vor dem Fernseher sitzt. Hahaha, noch ein kleiner Scherz. Aber jetzt geht's medias in res, wie der olle Lateiner sagt. Bitte, Herr Kapellmeister. Bühne frei für Hans Quasthoff aus dem schönen Hildesheim mit *Oh, sancta justitia*. Toi, toi, toi.«

Vater schlägt sich prächtig und wird bei seiner Rückkehr nicht nur von der Lokalzeitung wie ein Held gefeiert. Überhaupt entpuppt sich Großmutters Idee mit dem Fernseher als rundherum tolle Sache. Neben *Lassie, Rin Tin Tin* und *Fury* beschert mir der Apparat eine weitere einschneidende Begegnung mit der klassischen Vortrags-kunst. Diesmal ist es ein Schock. Genauer gesagt, der gefeierte lyrische Tenor und Trümmerfrauenschwarm Rudolf Schock. Er materialisiert sich an einem Samstag im *Blauen Bock*. Für die Jüngeren unter uns sei angemerkt, dass es sich dabei um eine Sendung des Hessischen Rund-funks handelt. Das Konzept ist denkbar einfach: der Na-me ist Programm. Kujoniert von einem zwergnasehaften Brabbelkopf namens Heinz Schenk, von Lia Wöhr, die alle nur »Frau Wittin« rufen, und Reno Nonsens, einem trauri-gen Komiker, dem sich die kulturelle Wüstenei der Ade-nauer-Ära furchentief zwischen die bernhardinerhaften Backenlappen gegraben hat, trinkt eine Menge Volk vor laufender Kamera eine Menge Äppelwoi und durch-schunkelt den deutschen Liederkranz. Dieses Bembel-paradies bildet bis in die frühen Siebziger einen Grund-pfeiler des zwangsunionierten Familienlebens. Man hat es mithin im Kreise seiner Lieben ohne Murren auszuhalten, sonst bekommt man nachfolgend die Sportschau und das Abendbrot gestrichen.

Schicksalsergeben kauere ich also Samstagnachmittag neben Micha in der Sofaecke. Wir zerkauen eine Prinzen-rolle und sehen mit an, wie – flankiert von Schenk, »Frau Wittin« und den schalen Witzchen des Herrn Nonsens – der alternde Kammersänger Rudolf Schock unter großem Hallo vor das Blaue-Bock-Orchester geführt wird, um dortselbst Schuberts *Heideröslein* zum Vortrag zu bringen. So weit ist alles gut. Aber nun kommt, was mir bis heute unvergesslich und eine heilsame Lehre geblieben ist. Denn kaum setzt Schock an, seinen Tenor auf das erste der vier präliminierenden gestrichenen Hs zu hieven, be-ginnen dem Vortragskünstler die Züge auf unheimliche Weise zu verrutschen. Über dem klagend aufgerissenen Mund schieben sich die Wangen zu gewaltigen von roten

Adern durchzogenen Wülsten zusammen, welche wiederum in Tateinheit mit der akkordeonös gefalteten Stirnpartie die Sehorgane in die Zange nehmen und zwar dergestalt, dass sie aus den Höhlen quellen wie ein prall gefüllter Fahrradschlauch aus einem unsachgemäß repariertem Gummimantel. Gleichzeitig nehme ich an den Ohren ein Zucken wahr, Schocks blonde Brauen heben und senken sich wie in schwerem Seegang, so dass, weil angetrieben von denselben Muskelgruppen, auch der Haaransatz, ja die ganze Frisur auf dem Schädel herumruckt und -zuckt, als massiere ihm eine unsichtbare Pranke von hinterwärts die Kopfhaut. Obendrein starrt der Sänger jetzt rollenden Auges abwechselnd zum Orchesterchef und heraus aus dem Empfangsgerät in unsere gute Stube. Wie es scheint, mir direkt ins Gesicht. Fassungslos sehe ich mich um. Vater saugt seelenruhig an seiner Pfeife, Mama stippt Bienenstich in den Tee, und Oma Else hat nicht eine Masche fallen lassen. Nur Micha bemerkt ebenfalls, dass hier nicht nur eine ästhetische Grenze überschritten, sondern auch jener dämonische Abgrund einen Spalt weit aufgerissen worden ist, von dem H. P. Lovecraft behauptet hat, er sei die Generalstabskarte des Universums. Entsetzt hält sich Micha die Ohren zu. Dabei ist noch kein einziger Ton zu hören gewesen.

Obwohl auch Schocks folgenden Vortrag etwas latent Hybrides durchweht, bringt der alte Haudegen das Lied ganz passabel zu Ende und wird mit rauschendem Beifall verabschiedet. Ich betone das auf ausdrücklichen Wunsch meiner lieben Mutter. Sie mag den Schock. Sie hat ihn in seinen großen Zeiten zweimal auf der Bühne erlebt, und ich habe ihr den obigen Abschnitt zur Begutachtung vorgelegt. Mama findet, ich übertreibe maßlos, so schlimm wäre das mit der Grimassiererei nie und nimmer gewesen. Der Schock habe halt Ausdruck. Aber ich glaube,

Erwachsene sehen so etwas nicht. Weil sie es nicht sehen wollen. Erwachsene schalten instinktiv auf stur, wenn der ganz alltägliche Wahnsinn an der Pforte klingelt. Das ist auch sehr gesund, es gibt einfach zu viel davon. Kinder wissen das noch nicht. Kinder sehen den Phänomenen offen ins Gesicht. Und was sie sehen, sei es pure Schönheit oder das nackte Grauen, prägt sich ihnen überdeutlich ein wie unter einem Vergrößerungsglas. Ich jedenfalls erinnere mich genau, dass die Quasthoff-Brüder, als der Schock vorbei ist, tagelang damit beschäftigt sind, die mimischen Kapriolen des Kammersängers vor dem Spiegel nachzustellen, und sich dabei schieflachen.

Kurz darauf ist erst mal Schluss mit lustig. Ich werde sechs Jahre alt. Meine Eltern möchten, dass ich dieselbe Schule besuche wie Micha. Sie liegt nur drei Straßen von unserer Wohnung entfernt, so dass ich sie bequem zu Fuß erreichen kann. Sie machen einen Termin beim Direktor. Sie schildern ihm meinen Fall, betonen, ich sei ein ganz normaler Junge, sogar ein ausgesprochen heller Kopf und musikalisch hoch begabt. Nur eben körperlich eingeschränkt.

»Der Bruder ist ja auch da und wird sich kümmern«, sagt Mama. »Die beiden sind ein Herz und eine Seele.«

»Sicher, sicher«, lächelt der Herr Direktor, »ich verstehe. Füllen Sie mal dies Formular aus, Sie kriegen dann Bescheid.« Er liegt zwei Tage später in der Post.

»Sehr geehrter Herr Quasthoff, leider muss ich Ihnen mitteilen, dass wir Ihren Sohn Thomas nicht aufnehmen können. Ein Kind mit diesem Maß an Behinderungen muss jeden Pädagogen und damit den gesamten Lehrbetrieb zwangsläufig überfordern.«

Vater schreibt wütend zurück, er habe den Eindruck,

dazu brauche es seinen Sohn gar nicht. Mama sagt, Vater soll sich nicht aufregen, vielleicht ist der Mann nur ein außergewöhnlich borniertes Exemplar. Borniert – und der Regelfall. Das merken sie im nächsten Schulleiterbüro. Im übernächsten ebenso. Man weist ihnen höflich, aber bestimmt die Tür. Sie versuchen es in anderen Stadtteilen, sie klappern die Volksschulen der Vororte ab. Sie rennen von Pontius zu Pilatus. Bald kennen sie jedes Lehrerzimmer im Landkreis Hildesheim. Vater macht eine Eingabe beim Schulamt, er wendet sich an den Kultusminister. Die Antwort ist immer die gleiche: Krüppel sind nicht erwünscht, Krüppel gehören in eine Sonderschule.

Mangels Alternativen lande ich wieder im Annastift. Es gibt dort keine Tagesschule, nur ein angeschlossenes Behinderteninternat. Vater hat mir erklärt, was das ist, ein Internat. Ein Ort, wo Kinder gemeinsam wohnen, wo sie Schreiben und Lesen und viele neue Freunde kennen lernen. Ich habe verstanden. Ich muss weg von zu Hause, wie damals, als ich anderthalb Jahre in der Gipsschale lag. Ich will nicht ins Internat.

»Mama, warum kann ich nicht hier bleiben?«

»Du bist jetzt ein großer Junge und musst zur Schule gehen.«

»Micha muss auch zur Schule.«

»Ja, Schätzchen, aber du bist etwas ganz Besonderes. Du gehst auf eine besondere Schule.«

»Ins Internat!«

»Ja, aber sieh mal, es sind doch nur fünf Tage, und am Wochenende bist du schon wieder zu Hause.«

»Mama, warum bin ich was ganz Besonderes?«

»Ach Tommilein«, Mama seufzt und drückt mich fest an sich. »Weil wir stolz auf dich sind und dich sehr lieb haben.«

»Ich hab euch auch lieb.«

»Ich weiß, mein Liebling. Aber jetzt schlaf. Wir müssen morgen früh raus.«

Am nächsten Morgen bringt mich Mama nach Hannover ins Annastift. »Bis Samstag hältst du durch. Sei schön brav und lass es dir gut gehen«, hat sie gesagt.

Dann sehe ich unseren klapprigen VW Variant über den Kiesweg davonrollen. Mir ist hundeelend. Aber ich bin ein besonderer Junge, ich bin ein großer Junge, also will ich versuchen, mich auch so zu benehmen. Die erste Woche ist noch nicht halb herum, da ahne ich, dass das allen guten Vorsätzen zum Trotz eine ziemlich harte Nuss werden wird.

Eine Schwester in blauem Kattunkittel hat mich auf eine Krankenstation gebracht und mir ein Zimmer zugewiesen. Das Quartier kommt mir nur allzu bekannt vor. Es riecht nach billigem Waschpulver, Sagrotan und Urin. An den Wänden stehen fünfzehn Betten. Diesmal jedoch ist nur eines leer.

Meine neuen Kameraden sind Conterganfälle wie ich, spastisch gelähmt oder Muskelschwundpatienten; es gibt auch einige demente Kinder, es gibt Mongoloide, Epileptiker und Autisten.

Der Direktor des Internats sitzt selbst im Rollstuhl. Er heißt Bläsig und hält vor der ersten Schulstunde eine Rede. Er sagt, der Herrgott hat behinderte und nichtbehinderte Menschen gemacht und jedem seinen Platz in der Welt zugewiesen; er sagt, dass unser Platz jetzt hier im Annastift ist und dass wir lernen sollen, uns nützlich zu machen. Er spricht von den Freuden des Nützlichseins, von Demut und Gehorsam, welche die Erlangung dieser Freuden erst möglich machen, und er spricht von der Dankbarkeit, die wir für jede der demnächst verabreichten Wohltaten empfinden müssen. Zur Einstimmung rieselt ein Choral vom Band. Dann werden wir auf die Klassen verteilt.

In der 1b wartet Fräulein Neddermeyer. Sie ist jung, sympathisch und gesegnet mit Güte und wahrer Engelsgeduld. Aber das nützt ihr nichts. Denn man hat ihr zwei Mal Contergan, vier Mal Muskelschwund und fünf Spastiker vor die Nase gesetzt. Eine dem stringenten Lehrbetrieb eher hinderliche Mischung. Die Spastiker sind nicht dumm, aber etwas langsam, weil ihr Nerven- und Sprachzentrum durch krampfartige Blockaden beeinträchtigt wird. Sobald Fräulein Neddermeyer versucht, ihnen die Mysterien des Dezimalsystems zu entschlüsseln, bohrt der Rest der Klasse gelangweilt in der Nase. Das sind die guten Tage. An schlechten Tagen toben wir herum, spielen Fangen und tun so, als wäre die Neddermeyer gar nicht vorhanden. Passt sie das Tempo uns Contergankindern an, ramentern die Spastiker in den Bänken, weil sie nur Bahnhof verstehen. Oft werden sie dabei aus der Bahn geworfen, entweder durch ihre chronischen motorischen Störungen oder von einem epileptischen Anfall. Mit anderen Worten: Die 1b stellt vorrangig lebende Bilder einer sonderpädagogischen Sackgasse.

Nachmittags auf dem Zimmer findet die Freakshow ihre Fortsetzung. Nur in größerer Besetzung. Die Spastiker wühlen jetzt in einer am Fenster lieblos aufgeschütteten Halde Legosteine, die Autisten streifen kopfwackelnd durch ein Paralleluniversum, die Epileptiker sind die Epileptiker und spucken ab und an mit zuckenden Gliedern Schaum, die Dementen sind unberechenbar, während das Contergan mit dem Muskelschwund um die Hackordnung rangelt. Da muss eine halbe Portion sehen, wo sie bleibt. Ich lege mir schnell ein ziemlich großes Mundwerk zu und wappne mich mit einem Panzer aus Gleichmut. Es gibt ja keine Ruhe, keinen Rückzugsraum, keine Minute

Privatheit. Dem Gros meiner Kameraden macht das wenig aus. Sie kennen nichts anderes. Ihre Eltern haben dem gesunden deutschen Volksempfinden Tribut gezollt und den missratenen Nachwuchs gleich nach der Geburt im Annastift zur lebenslangen Verwahrung eingelagert. Es gibt auch eine Lagerkommandantin: Stationsvorsteherin Müller. Wir nennen sie nur Frau Mahlzahn, weil sie genauso böse, verschlagen und rachsüchtig ist wie der Drache in Michael Endes Klassiker *Jim Knopf und Lukas der Lokomotivführer*, aus dem mir Vater am Wochenende immer vorliest. Allerdings besteht ein entscheidender Unterschied zwischen Poesie und Wirklichkeit: Im Buch verwandelt sich Frau Mahlzahn zum guten Schluss in einen sanften weisen Drachen. Eine Metamorphose, die im Falle der Stationsvorsteherin jenseits aller Vorstellungskraft liegt.

Die Müller ist eine ausgemachte Sadistin. Und wie alle Sadisten hasst sie Menschen, die widersprechen, die vor ihr nicht gleich zu Kreuze kriechen. Frau Mahlzahn hat mich gefressen. Vom ersten Tag an.

»Das macht man nicht«, protestiere ich, als sie meinen Bettnachbarn Peter wegen einer verschütteten Tasse Tee ohrfeigt. Spastiker verschütten nämlich immer etwas, das steht quasi auf ihrer Festplatte, sie können einfach nichts dafür.

»Ich mache noch ganz andere Sachen«, sagt Frau Mahlzahn und sperrt mich in die Besenkammer. Sie nimmt mir mein Tonband weg, weil es zu laut ist, konfisziert Süßigkeiten, weil sie angeblich ungesund sind, sie verbietet mir, mit Mama zu telefonieren. Sie sagt, du brauchst nicht zu petzen, deine Mutter ist weit weg, ich werde dir die Renitenz schon austreiben.

Und eins muss man ihr lassen, sie legt sich mächtig ins Zeug. Ihr Disziplinierungskatalog besteht aus purer Gemeinheit. An der Tagesordnung sind vierundzwanzig Stunden ohne Essen und das Gurgeln mit Salzwasser, eine Prozedur, die so lange fortgeführt werden muss, bis einem die Lake vollständig in den Magen gelaufen ist. Wen sie richtig auf dem Kieker hat, den lässt sie abends im Bett festschnallen. Anschließend wird der Delinquent aus dem Zimmer gerollt und die ganze Nacht allein auf dem hell erleuchteten Flur abgestellt. Droht einer der seltenen Kontrollgänge des Oberarztes, verschwindet man samt Bett in einem Kabuff, wo gebrauchte Urinflaschen auf die Reinigung warten. Im Winter hat Frau Mahlzahn auch eine Variante ohne Licht im Repertoire. Ich habe mehrmals zitternd vor Angst und Kälte im Dunkeln gelegen und jede einzelne Minute bis zum Morgen gezählt. Um sicherzugehen, dass sich der Tortur niemand durch Übermüdung entziehen kann, weist der alte Drachen Schwestern, Nachtwächter und Putzfrauen an, das wehrlose Opfer mit Vorhaltungen oder Drohungen zu piesacken. So weit erniedrigt sich nicht jeder. Aber einen findet die Müller gewöhnlich immer, dem die Sorge um den Arbeitsplatz näher liegt als ein bisschen Mitgefühl. Notfalls besorgt sie die Drecksarbeit höchstpersönlich.

Leider garantieren auch sanktionsfreie Tage keinesfalls eine ruhige Nacht. Viele der geistig Behinderten werden regelmäßig von Schreikrämpfen geschüttelt, einige schaffen es nie bis auf die Toilette. Von Panikattacken getrieben, klettern sie aus ihren Betten und beschmieren sich und andere mit Kot. Eine Notklingel gibt es nicht, es hapert an Personal. Das ändert sich erst, als die Frühschicht eines der Muskelschwundkinder beim Wecken leblos in seinem Bett findet. Der Junge heißt Tim und ist mein bester Freund. Man holt die Müller. Sie untersucht Tim kurz und professionell, dann zieht sie ihm ein Laken über den Kopf. Zwei Pfleger fahren ihn hinaus.

»Was ist denn los mit Tim?«, frage ich irritiert.

»Er ist gestorben«, sagt die Stationsvorsteherin lapidar. Ich weiß, dass Tim sehr krank ist, aber das Wort »gestorben« habe ich noch nie gehört.

»Kriegt Tim jetzt neue Medizin?«

»Die braucht er nicht, er ist tot, er kommt nicht wieder.«

»Wieso kommt Tim nicht wieder?«

»Frag nicht so dumm. Steh auf und geh dich waschen. In zehn Minuten gibt's Frühstück.«

»Jawohl, Frau Mahlzahn.«

»Du frecher Rotzlöffel …« Soll sie toben. Trinke ich statt Kakao eben Salzwasser.

Die Müller kann mich schon lange nicht mehr einschüchtern. Ich lebe seit zwei Jahren im Internat und habe einfach schon zu oft auf dem Flur geschlafen. Meine Resistenz verdanke ich aber in erster Linie Mutter und Vater. Sie treiben der Müller die schlimmsten Exzesse aus, indem sie ihr mit einer Klage drohen. Sie beschweren sich so lange bei der Internatsleitung, bis wir schließlich in Vierbettzimmer verlegt werden. Und sie versäumen es nicht ein einziges Mal, mich am Wochenende nach Hause zu holen. Pünktlich wie die Maurer stehen die beiden Samstagmittag, Schlag zwölf Uhr, vor dem Internat, Vater schmeißt meinen Ranzen in den Kofferraum, und dann geht es mit Karacho über den Messeschnellweg nach Hildesheim und – sofern das Wetter mitspielt – in die Badeanstalt oder mit Micha zum Spielen auf die verwilderten Bunkeranlagen neben der Ziegelei. Oft packt Mama Tim und Peter oder ein, zwei andere Freunde gleich mit ins Auto. Die armen Würmer kriegen die eigene Familie höchstens mal zu Weihnachten oder am Geburtstag zu sehen. Vater spendiert jedes Mal ein großes Eis mit Sahne und Karten fürs Kino. Wohlig lassen wir uns in die Dunkelheit fallen und von den Bildern an all die magischen Orte tragen, wo das Böse immer kleinlich und finster und das Gute edel, clever und unbezwingbar ist. Wo Typen wie Tarzan wohnen, der mit Elefanten sprechen kann, oder Olli und Stan, die ihrem Kontaktbereichsbeamten ungestraft eine Torte an die Birne werfen dürfen. Wir werden bleich, als der alte Fischer den kleinen Pinocchio um ein Haar in die brutzelnde Pfanne haut, wir lachen über Fuzzy, den dämlichsten Cowboy westlich des Pecos, und zappeln aufgeregt in den Sitzen, wenn Winnetou und Old Shatterhand den schuftigen Ölprinzen durch Jugoslawiens Berge jagen. Zu Hause jagen die tapferen Annastiftler dann Comanchero Micha durch die Wohnung, bis er gutmütig kapituliert. Zur Belohnung stellt Mama dampfenden Kakao und Kartoffelsalat auf den Tisch, und wir spielen *Mensch ärgere dich nicht*. Abends kriecht die Rasselbande todmüde in den Quelle-Wigwam von Häuptling »Tommi-drei-Finger«, den Vater vom einzigen, leider eher kläglichen Lottogewinn seines Lebens bestellt und im Kinderzimmer aufgebaut hat.

Natürlich rauscht das Wochenende viel zu schnell vorbei. Die Rückfahrt nach Hannover gleicht meistens einem traurigen Stummfilm, der Abschied ist ein verheultes Melodram. Als Tim stirbt und Mama sagt, dass mein Freund jetzt im Himmel auf einer weichen Wolke sitzt und mit kleinen Engeln spielt, wäre ich am liebsten auch tot, anstatt Woche für Woche mit dem Drachen Mahlzahn zu kämpfen. Ich habe die Nase gestrichen voll. Meinen Eltern geht es ähnlich. Sie hätten mich längst aus dem Internat geholt, wenn sich doch bloß eine normale Schule finden ließe, die mich haben will. Aber sie geben nicht auf. Sie halten es mit Goethe: »Wir hoffen immer, und in allen Dingen ist besser hoffen als verzweifeln.«

Dann kommt das Jahr 1967: der Sommer der Liebe, die APO und das kilometerlange Gitarrensolo. Das graue Bonner Neobiedermeier wird durchgelüftet und zartrosa angestrichen. Habermas fordert einen »Strukturwandel der Öffentlichkeit«, Marcuse »nonrepressive, entsublimierte Verhältnisse«, und die Jugend gibt sich alle Mühe, »den Horizont einer beschränkten Sphäre« (Karl Marx) zu erweitern. Als das mühsamer ist als erwartet, verweigert sie bis auf weiteres jeden Friseurbesuch. Zwar wird damit vorerst nur der deutsche Sprachschatz um die Vokabel »Gammler« bereichert, aber die frische Brise streift selbst das erzkatholische Hildesheim. Unter anderem weht sie Herrn Scholz auf den Direktorensessel der Brauhausschule. Herr Scholz, hört Vater, ist ein freier, dem Fortschritt verpflichteter Geist. Sofort lässt er sich einen Termin geben. Zwei Stunden später weiß er, Direktor Scholz hat obendrein Zivilcourage, und köpft mit Mama eine Flasche Herva mit Mosel. Die Brauhausschule will mich tatsächlich aufnehmen. Sie wird eine der ersten öffentlichen Lehranstalten in Deutschland sein, die ein behindertes Kind unterrichten.

Die gute Nachricht löst nicht überall Begeisterung aus. Im Annastift votiert man strikt gegen den Wechsel. Institutsleiter Bläsig türmt jede argumentative und bürokratische Hürde auf, die ihm einfällt. Ob er dabei um sein Betreuungsmonopol fürchtet oder wirklich glaubt, ein Krüppel käme nicht zurecht in der normalen Welt? Ich kann es nicht sagen. Vielleicht muss ein Behinderter so denken, der das Herrenmenschentum der Nazis überlebt und gesehen hat, mit welcher Chuzpe die Deutschen kurz darauf schon wieder die Ellbogen ausfahren, um sich in Ludwig Erhards nivellierter Mittelstandsgesellschaft nach oben zu drängeln. Ich bin dem Annastift durchaus dankbar, denn ich habe dort auch angenehme Zeiten verbracht.

Es gibt ja nicht nur die Müller und ihre Schergen, es gibt das nette Fräulein Neddermeyer und großartige Physiotherapeuten, die mir helfen, die Widrigkeiten des Alltags zu meistern. Ohne ihre Anleitung hätte ich nie gelernt, mich alleine anzuziehen, Messer und Gabel zu gebrauchen, mir ein Buch aus dem Regal zu holen, allein aufs Klo zu gehen. Sie haben mir das Zeichnen beigebracht und sind verantwortlich, dass ich heute nicht auf einen Betreuer angewiesen bin. Nur auf andere Erfahrungen hätte ich eben gerne verzichtet.

Bläsigs Invektiven können meine Eltern nicht umstimmen. Als wir ein letztes Mal sein Büro betreten, um meine Papiere abzuholen, wünscht er mir Glück, dann sieht er Vater verkniffen an und sagt: »Eines muss Ihnen klar sein: Wenn es schief geht, nehmen wir Thomas nicht wieder auf.«

Es geht nicht schief. Ich muss in der Brauhausschule zwar eine Menge Stoff nachholen, aber ich bin nicht auf den Kopf gefallen. Und ich bin dem Internat entronnen, ich bin endlich frei. Daher geht es mir wie Hundert-Meter-Mann Ben Johnson: Ich bin gedopt bis unter die Haarspitzen. Allerdings nur auf Naturbasis. Durch meine Adern rauscht reines Adrenalin, so dass mir ein bisschen Büffelei nichts ausmacht. Wenn es allzu schwierig wird, helfen mir Micha und Mama bei den Schularbeiten, und nach kurzer Zeit schaffe ich das Pensum der vierten Klasse ohne Probleme. Auch mit meinen neuen Mitschülern komme ich prima klar. Natürlich ist ein armloser Zwerg, der auf Prothesen über den Schulhof stelzt, ein ungewohnter Anblick und provoziert in den ersten Wochen unschöne Hänseleien. Doch mit meiner großen Klappe verschaffe ich mir schnell Respekt. Nun bewährt sich, dass meine Eltern von Anfang an keine falschen Rücksichten genommen haben, den kleinen Krüppel nicht versteckt, sondern genauso behandelt haben wie den großen Micha. Schon als ich vier war, haben sie die Brüder mit zwei Mark und guten Wünschen zum Bäcker, zum Kinderfest oder zum Friseur geschickt. Blöde Gaffer gibt es überall, fiese Bemerkungen auch – und sie tun immer weh. Aber wenn ich nach Hause komme und mich beklage, hat Vater die Anfälle von Selbstmitleid stets im Keim erstickt:

»Jungchen, die Welt ist vor allem roh und dumm. Und das meiste, was auf ihr rumtrampelt, auch. Aber vergiss nie: Du könntest blind oder taubstumm sein, dann wärst du viel schlechter dran. Noch schlechter geht es nur den Dummen, weil sie nicht merken, mit wie viel Blödheit sie geschlagen sind.«

Da hat er natürlich Recht. Nur manchmal hilft einem auch die stringenteste Hermeneutik nicht weiter.

Zum Beispiel an diesem strahlenden Sonntag im August. Ich bin unterwegs mit meinem Laufrad. Es hat drei Räder, ist feuerrot und mein ganzer Stolz. Als ich das Gefährt um eine Häuserecke bugsiere, taucht direkt vor meiner Nase ein Junge auf. Zum Bremsen ist es viel zu spät, zum Ausweichen fehlt der Platz. Und schon ist es passiert. Ich und mein Vorderrad rollen ihm über den Schuh. Der ziemlich große Junge schnauzt: »Ey, pass auf, du Zwerg!«

Es klingt, als sei ihm obendrein noch etwas Furchtbares über die Leber gelaufen. Ich murmle eine matte Entschuldigung und will nur eins: weg. Doch der Junge hat etwas dagegen und stellt mir ein Bein in den Weg. Was aber nur dazu führt, dass jetzt auch sein zweiter Schuh – und zwar mit Schmackes – überfahren wird. Rumms, habe ich eine Hand im Gesicht.

»Merk dir das, Zwerg Nase«, sagt der große Junge. Das ist eine reichlich dumme Bemerkung, die ich einfach ignorieren sollte. Schließlich hat Vater mir beigebracht, dass Dumme arm dran sind und Nachsicht verdienen. Andererseits gibt es nur einen, der mich ungestraft Zwerg nennen darf, und das ist mein Bruder. Also sage ich: »Bin kein Zwerg, Blödmann.« Zack, schlägt die nächste Ohrfeige ein. Dann noch eine. Ich verliere das Gleichgewicht und knalle samt Rad aufs Pflaster. Das Nächste, was ich sehe, ist Blut. Aber es ist nicht meins. Es gehört dem Blödmann, der plötzlich neben mir liegt und von Micha mit beiden Fäusten bearbeitet wird. Mama hat ihn genau im richtigen Moment losgeschickt, um mich zum Abendbrot zu holen. Jetzt sitzt er rittlings auf dem Blödmann und brüllt:

»Los, sag, ›ich bin eine feige Arschgeige‹.«

»If bin eine feige Afgeige«, schnieft der Blödmann und spuckt zwei Zähne in sein Taschentuch, ehe er wie ein geprügelter Hund von dannen zieht.

Die Quasthoff-Brüder ziehen im Triumphmarsch nach Hause.

»Was ist denn mit dir passiert«, ruft Mama bestürzt und begutachtet die Platzwunde auf meiner Stirn. Micha erzählt, ich sei vom Rad gefallen, was immerhin die halbe Wahrheit ist. Mama hasst Keilereien, und sie hasst Geflunker. Aber es kommt doch alles heraus. Wir sitzen gerade beim Essen, da klingelt es an der Tür. Es ist der Blödmann mit seinem Vater.

»Sehen Sie sich meinen Sohn an«, raunzt Vater Blödmann. »Und sehen Sie sich das an.« Er öffnet die rechte Handfläche. Mein Vater mustert den zerbeulten Knaben, er mustert zwei blutverschmierte Schneidezähne.

»Dafür ist eine Ihrer Gören verantwortlich. Ich werde Ihnen eine Anzeige ins Haus schicken und eine gepfefferte Schmerzensgeld-Rechnung«, bellt der alte Blödmann.

»So, so«, brummt Vater, »nur immer hübsch langsam mit den jungen Pferden.« Er ruft uns an die Tür und fragt, ob wir ihn bitte schön mal aufklären könnten, was hier los ist. Ich schildere ihm den Hergang. Vater nickt. Dann kratzt er sich am Kinn und sagt ganz ruhig: »Ich werde Ihren Sohn nicht anzeigen. Wie es aussieht, hat er gekriegt, was er verdient. Aber Sie und dieses Würstchen sollten schleunigst verschwinden. Sonst könnte das hier gleich ein ganz unschönes Nachspiel geben.«

Sie fliegen förmlich die Treppe hinunter.

Ein Nachspiel gibt es trotzdem. Am nächsten Tag enden die Sommerferien. Micha kommt in die fünfte Klasse und muss seine Schulpflicht nun im Gymnasium Andreanum absitzen. Als er einrückt, sind die Blödmänner schon da. Der eine steht auf dem Schulhof und kaut mit schmerzverzerrtem Gesicht ein Pausenbrot, der andere stellt sich als sein neuer Latein- und Klassenlehrer vor. Auch das noch, schießt es Micha durch den Kopf, da kann ich ja gleich einpacken. Vater sagt: »Setz dich auf den Hosenboden, dann kann er dir nichts.« Kann er doch. Der alte Blödmann piesackt meinen Bruder bis zur Quinta nach Strich und Faden.

»Male partum male dilabuntur. Alles Quatsch mit Soße«, flucht Micha, wenn er nach Schulschluss mal wieder eine Ordnungsstrafe abbrummen muss und das Mittagessen versäumt. Sich mit Fünfern und Sechsern für die Abreibung seines Sprösslings zu rächen, hat der alte Blödmann dann aber doch nicht fertig gebracht, dafür hat Micha zu viel Grips. Ein großer Freund des Lateinischen ist aus ihm allerdings nicht mehr geworden.

Ich wechsele zwei Jahre später ebenfalls zum Andreanum. Das ehrwürdige Institut – die erste urkundliche Erwähnung datiert aus dem Jahr 1216 – residiert in einem schmucklosen Neubau aus Waschbeton, kompensiert diesen Umstand aber durch seine exponierte Lage am Hagentorwall, hochherrlich über der Stadt. An der Nordflanke grünt der Liebesgrund, im Westen begrenzen die mächtigen Quader von St. Michaelis die Immobilie, südwärts, gerahmt vom düsteren Waldband des Galgenberges, leuchtet der Bernward-Dom, Turm der Christenheit und Hüter des tausendjährigen Rosenstocks. Ich sage nur: Weltkulturerbe!

Entsprechend hält das Kollegium auf Tradition und versteht sich als humanistisches Bollwerk wider den wankelmütigen Zeitgeist. Hier wirken Geistesriesen wie Studienrat Lichter, der seit Willy Brandts Kanzlerwahl die Neuerscheinungen der Reihe rororo aktuell nach Wörtern wie »Marxismus« und »sozialistisch« durchforsten lässt, um uns die Statistik anschließend mit nie erlahmendem Furor und kruder Semantik um die Ohren zu hauen: »Meine Damen und Herren, das sind keine Sachbücher, das ist Moskaus fünfte Kolonne.«

Die Herren Stolp und Wirschner, hauptberuflich Altphilologe beziehungsweise Erd- und Gemeinschaftskundler, haben sich durch praktische Anwendungen der Evolutionstheorie einen gewissen Ruf erworben. Vor allem Wirschners Feldversuche sind so berüchtigt wie legendär. Zu Beginn eines neuen Schuljahres federt er in eine Klasse – sagen wir in die Prima –, mustert grienend das Operationsfeld und umreißt die Zielvorgabe: »Bauer, Maschmann, Brunkhorst, euch will ich in der Oberprima nicht mehr sehen, und ich werde euch nicht mehr sehen.«

Dieses so genannte »unnatürliche Selektionsprinzip« funktioniert leider öfter, als uns lieb ist. Mathematiker Schaffrath dagegen hängt der Irrlehre an, Mädchen könnten nicht rechnen, weshalb auch die brillantesten Dreisatz-Deuterinnen nie über ein »Befriedigend« hinauskommen, während unsereiner, der bei den Damen mühsam abspicken muss, es wenigstens zeitweise auf ein glattes »Gut« bringt. Andere Kollegen leiden unter schwerster Affekt-Inkontinenz, oder sie bereichern das Pädagogen-

Panoptikum durch Eigenheiten, die dem Typus »sonderbarer Kauz« völlig neue Seiten abgewinnen.

Da ist zum Beispiel Dr. Florettiner. Der Germanist und konkrete Experimentaldichter führt sich gern mal mit der Bemerkung »Ich bin nicht schizophren« ein. Oder er verschanzt sich ganze Stunden lang hinter der *Frankfurter Allgemeinen Zeitung* und wartet, was passiert. Florettiner nennt das interaktiven Unterricht. Aber es passiert nie etwas. Wir sind ja froh, wenn uns einer mal in Ruhe Schiffeversenken oder Autoquartett spielen lässt. Manche vermuten jedoch, das mit der Interaktivität sei nur ein Vorwand. In Wahrheit kontrolliere Florettiner, ob das *FAZ*-Feuilleton endlich eines seiner Experimentalgedichte abgedruckt hat, die er in Zehnerpacken an Reich-Ranicki schickt. Es stände aber wohl nie eins drin. Deshalb ärgere er sich schwarz und bliebe verbittert hinter der Zeitung hocken. Später wird Florettiner tatsächlich schwermütig und in ein Spital gesperrt. Bei Herrn Schmalbach, der seine depressiven Phasen ebenfalls unter strenger ärztlicher Aufsicht verbringen muss, ist es grad umgekehrt. Sobald der Frühling und das Manische durchbrechen, lehrt er uns alte Sprachen und macht das tipptopp, es sei denn, man hat seinen Lehrkörper wieder einmal überreichlich sediert. Dann bettet er das Haupt aufs Pult und schnarcht durch bis zum Pausengong. Auf diese Art hat es Schmalbach zwar nie zu einer Beförderung gebracht, aber er ist die beliebteste Abituraufsicht in der Geschichte des Gymnasiums.

Den nicht verhaltensauffälligen Teil des Kollegiums eingerechnet, bietet das Andreanum jungen Menschen also genügend Stoff, um tatsächlich etwas für das Leben zu lernen. Ich nehme das Angebot dankend an. Ich singe im Schulchor und in der assoziierten Michaelis-Kantorei, ich sammle gute Noten en gros, sogar in Sport, weil ich eine neue Schwimmtechnik irgendwo zwischen Delfin und Dackel kreiere, mit der ich mir erst das Frei-, dann das Fahrtenschwimmerabzeichen erstrampele, ich treffe in meiner Klasse alte Freunde aus der Volksschule und finde jede Menge neue. Kurz gesagt: Anfang der siebziger Jahre könnte die Welt nicht schöner sein. Oder wie Funny van Dannen in melancholischer Rückschau reimen wird: »Die Welt war jung und Deutschland ein Wort / und Squash war noch gar kein Sport / der Urlaub machte richtig Spaß / und im Fernsehen gab es *Wünsch Dir was*.«

Das gucken wir natürlich in Farbe. Genauso wie die Mondlandung und die ebenso unvergessliche Fußball-europameisterschaft, als der immer wieder unwiderstehlich aus der Tiefe des Raumes vorstürmende Günter Netzer eine schwerelos kombinierende DFB-Elf zum Titel führt.

Der Fernseher steht jetzt in der Göttingstraße 5. Der Umzug in Hildesheims Süden hat mir nicht nur ein eigenes Zimmer beschert, sondern auch eine Menge Auslauf an der frischen Luft. Nicht weit entfernt von unserem neuen Domizil bummelt das Flüsschen Innerste durch die Johanniswiesen. Das von Baumgruppen und dichtem Buschwerk durchsetzte Überlaufbecken ersetzt uns je nach Bedarf den Wilden Westen, das Amazonasdelta und Flints Schatzinsel, vor allem aber die berühmten Fußballarenen dieser Welt. Maracana, Wembley, San Siro oder die Anfield Road. Auf einem höher gelegenen Abschnitt gibt es nämlich einen Bolzplatz mit Handballtoren, die – welch ein Luxus – Pfosten aus Holz und Netze aus Maschendraht haben.

Wenn Micha und ich mittags nach Hause kommen, wird schnell der Schulkram erledigt, der Ball aufgepumpt, dann geht es hinaus, um die siegreichen Schlachten von Benfica Lissabon oder Bayern München nachzustellen. Micha schwärmt für den portugiesischen Wunderstürmer Eusébio, ich bin den Bayern verfallen, seit ich sie zum ersten Mal live gesehen habe. Es war im Niedersachsenstadion, ich war zehn Jahre alt, und die Mannen des Kaisers (der damals noch gar nicht Kaiser, sondern nur der Knorr-Suppenkasper war) verloren 0:1 gegen Hannover 96. Aber am Ende der Saison standen sie in der Tabelle ganz oben. Ich kann die Meisterelf 1968/69 jederzeit im Schlaf hersagen. Bitte:

Maier
Schmidt Brenninger Ohlhauser Schwarzenbeck
Olk Beckenbauer Pumm
Roth Müller Starek

Auf der Johanniswiese bin ich natürlich Gerd Müller, weil der genauso kompakt und nicht viel größer ist als ich. Außerdem muss ich nicht so viel laufen, sondern brauche nur im Strafraum herumzulungern und die Kugel ins Tor zu hauen. Wenn sie denn mal vorbeikommt. Unser Kumpel Kuno zum Beispiel gibt nie ab. Kuno, ein Bayern-Maniac wie ich, gibt immer nur den »Bulle« Roth.

»Jürgen ist frei«, ruft Karsten.

»Spiel links rüber«, dirigiert Micha.

Kuno ist das egal. Mit dem Ruf: »Der Bulle gibt nicht ab«, trommelt er rechts die Linie herunter und hämmert das Leder Richtung Tor. Zwei Sekunden später kann man ein kollektives Stöhnen und den Torwart maulen hören: »Klasse, Kuno, den darfste selber wieder rausholen.«

Im Gegensatz zu Franz »Bulle« Roth, der mit seinen wuchtigen Alleingängen bekanntlich nicht nur das Europapokal-Endspiel gegen die Glasgow Rangers (1:0) entschieden hat, ist Kunos Trefferquote verheerend. Zur Strafe steht er wieder mal bis zu den Knien in der Innerste und angelt mit der Luftpumpe den Ball aus der Strömung.

Doch es kommt eine Zeit, da hat Kuno nachmittags plötzlich andere Termine. Auch Christian und Uwe erscheinen nur noch sporadisch. Fragt man Kuno, was denn so wichtig wäre, dass er nicht zum Kicken kommen kann, wird herumgedruckst und irgendetwas von »Gartenarbeit bei Mahlbaums« gemurmelt: »Kennste doch, die Moni Mahlbaum geht bei euch in die 7b.« Bei meinen Schulfreunden zeigen sich ähnliche Symptome. Meine Kreuzritterburg, sonst ein ausdauernd belagertes Objekt der Begierde, hat erheblich an Strahlkraft verloren, selbst Mamas Frankfurter Kranz scheint keinen mehr hinter dem Ofen hervor und in die Göttingstraße zu locken. Ich versteh die Welt nicht mehr. Bis ich Bernhard eines Tages Hand in Hand mit der dürren und viel zu langen Iris, mit »Fahnenstange« Iris, aus der Eisdiele spazieren sehe. Jetzt dämmert mir auch, warum Christian neuerdings ein unerklärliches Interesse für Hermann Hesse entwickelt und Regina bekniet, ihm doch mal *Narziss und Goldmund* zu leihen, er habe gehört, das sei »ein hammermäßiger Schmöker«. Als sich dann auch noch Christian nicht entblödet, nach dem Sport Suses kaputtes Fahrrad durch die halbe Stadt nach Hause zu schieben, obwohl er zwei Blocks neben der Turnhalle wohnt, fällt es mir wie Schuppen von den Augen: Mädchen! Die gehen mit Mädchen!

Nicht, dass ich es ihnen nicht gönnen würde. Sollen sie doch, wenn's Spaß macht. Ich weiß nur nicht, was man mit den kapriziösen Trinen quatschen oder machen soll. Okay, ich weiß es schon, Mama hat mir das mit dem Küssen und dem Kuscheln und dem Kinderkriegen in groben Zügen erläutert. Aber was, verdammt noch mal, ist daran besser als Fußball oder Ritterburgen? Der Haken ist nur: Ich erwische mich immer öfter dabei, wie ich im Flur vor dem großen Spiegel stehe und denke: Mit dir wird nie ein Mädchen Händchen haltend in die Eisdiele gehen. Du hast gar keine Hände. Richtige Beine auch nicht. Du hast nur zwei Strünke, und die sind so kurz, dass du nicht mal über ein Fahrrad gucken, geschweige denn so ein Ding für ein Mädchen durch die halbe Stadt schieben kannst. Du hast dir was vorgemacht, du bist nicht wie die anderen, du bist hässlich, du bist zu klein, du bist ein verkrüppelter Gnom.

Ich habe den Blues. Und er wird mit jedem Jahr schlimmer. In der Schule sehe ich nicht mehr an die Tafel, ich beobachte verstohlen die Jungs und ich beobachte die Mädchen. Sie tragen jetzt komische Hosen mit breiten Aufschlägen, Felljacken und Stiefel mit hohen Hacken und kurze Röcke, die einen ganz kirre machen. Ich bemerke die interessierten Blicke, all die kleinen Gesten, die von Bank zu Bank huschen, ich bemerke, wie sie in den Pausen umeinander schleichen, scheinbar gleichgültig, vertieft in Debatten über die letzte Schulsprecherwahl, die aktuellen Hits von T. Rex und Slade oder über die neuesten Anschläge der Rote Armee Fraktion, und dabei aber jede Bewegung des anderen Geschlechts aufmerksam registrieren. Ich erahne das Spielchen der Hormone und Botenstoffe, aber ich habe das Gefühl, ich darf nicht mitmachen. Das Schlimmste ist, dass ich mich nicht mal beschweren kann. Alle sind nett zu Tommi, alle kümmern sich, alle wollen, dass es Tommi gut geht.

»Na, Tommi, alles roger?« Klar, bei Tommi ist immer alles roger. Macht Tommi nicht ständig Witze? Kippen nicht alle vor Lachen vom Stuhl, wenn er den Wirschner, das zynische alte Aas, parodiert? Ist Tommi etwa nicht der unbestrittene Klassenclown?

Trotzdem hat er den Blues. Brüderchen auch. Zumindest hat Micha die passenden Platten. »I ain't trustin' nobody, I'm afraid of myself, / I cannot shun the devil, he stays right by my side, / There is no way to cheat, I am so dissatisfied«, so kann man den alten Peg Leg Howell an verregneten Nachmittagen aus seinem Zimmer heulen hören. Dann hockt Micha selbstvergessen vor dem Dual-Plattenspieler und schrummt auf seiner Neckermann-Gitarre die Akkorde nach. Ich setze mich auf den Fußboden und höre zu. Ich verstehe den Text nur bruchstückhaft, aber Peg Legs todtrauriges Wimmern spricht mir aus der Seele. Ich würde gerne wissen, ob Micha auch schon mit einem Mädchen geht. Aber darüber redet er nicht. Er redet in letzter Zeit überhaupt wenig. Dafür verweigert er den Gang zum Friseur und hat neben das Eusébio-Poster Bilder von John Fogerty und Che Guevara gepinnt. Statt dem *Kicker* liest er jetzt Bücher, die *Der Fremde* heißen und *Der Pfahl im Fleisch.*

»Den sollte mal einer wieder auf den Teppich holen«, sagt Vater.

»Lass ihn doch, das ist die Pubertät«, sagt Mama. Sie merkt auch, dass mit mir etwas nicht in Ordnung ist.

»Mein Kleiner, was hast du denn?«, fragt sie mich jeden zweiten Tag. Ich kann es ihr nicht sagen, obwohl ich ihr bisher alles sagen konnte. Aber diesmal weiß ich einfach nicht, was ich sagen soll. Ich könnte ihr Peg Legs *Low Down Rounder Blues* vorspielen.

»Hörst du, Mama, mir geht's mindestens so schlecht wie dem alten Neger, der da singt.« Besser könnte ich es nicht ausdrücken. Aber das hätte keinen Zweck. Mama kann kein Englisch, und sie hört Bert Kaempfert, keine Negermusik.

Aber ich habe immer noch den Blues. Ich vernachlässige die Schule, ich mache keine Hausaufgaben mehr, ich verhaue Mathe- und Chemiearbeiten. Meinen Eltern gaukele ich gekonnt den Musterschüler vor. Nur Micha weiß Bescheid. Er meint, das sei doch keine große Sache, das kann jedem mal passieren, das kannst du Mama und Vater ruhig sagen. Aber für mich ist es schlimm. Sehr schlimm sogar. Weil meine Eltern so darum gekämpft haben, dass ihr behindertes Kind auf eine normale Schule gehen kann. Weil sie wahrscheinlich enttäuscht wären, weil ich versagt und gelogen habe. Weil sie mich vielleicht nicht mehr lieb haben und vom Andreanum nehmen, um mich lebenslang in ein Heim zu stecken, wie das andere Eltern mit ihren Krüppelkindern machen.

»Quatsch mit Soße.« Micha tippt sich an die Stirn. »Du spinnst.«

Aber das macht die Sache nicht besser. Ich habe Angst, ich habe ein schlechtes Gewissen, ich habe keinen Appetit mehr. Ich will nicht mehr zur Schule gehen. Ich will nicht wieder in ein Heim. »I got stones in my passway, and my road is dark as night«, wie der Bluesmann Robert Johnson sagen würde. Ich würde am liebsten weglaufen. Und genau das mache ich auch.

An einem bitterkalten Novembermittag nutze ich einen Einkaufsgang von Mama und marschiere los, nur mit einer leichten Jacke auf der Schulter, weil der Winteranorak für mich unerreichbar hoch an der Garderobe hängt. Ich wandere ein Stück an der großen Ausfallstraße entlang, dann biege ich in einen Forstweg, der sich westwärts durch den Hildesheimer Wald fünf Kilometer hinauf zum Blaupunkt-Werk zieht. Nieselregen hat die Kleidung schon nach wenigen Metern durchweicht, der Wind fährt mir eisig in die Knochen. Als ich oben ankomme, ist es längst stockfinster. Halb erfroren, hungrig und todmüde schleppe ich mich auf der anderen Seite hinunter bis in das Kaff Neuhof. Kurz vor der Siedlung sinke ich kraftlos in den Straßengraben.

Zu Hause ist inzwischen der Teufel los. Mama ist krank vor Sorge. Sie hat angenommen, ich sei mit Micha auf dem Fußballplatz. Doch er kommt allein zurück. Sie alarmiert Vater, der im Amt sofort alles stehen und liegen lässt. Er versucht Mama zu beruhigen, breitet eine Landkarte aus und macht einen Plan. Micha soll mit dem Rad die Stadt abfahren. Vater und Mama setzen sich ins Auto und suchen systematisch, in konzentrischen Kreisen die Umgebung ab. Als sie gegen Mitternacht auf Neuhof zufahren, steht ein Krankenwagen am Straßenrand. Ein alter Mann hat mich gefunden und das Rote Kreuz und die Polizei informiert. Ich kann nur noch sagen: »Ich warte auf meine Mutti.« Dann bin ich in Ohnmacht gefallen.

Man bringt mich sofort ins städtische Krankenhaus. Mama und Vater bringt man auf die Wache. Sie müssen sich üble Fragen gefallen lassen. Warum ist der Junge weggelaufen? Hat er Angst vor Ihnen? Haben Sie das Kind geschlagen? Schlagen Sie den Jungen regelmäßig? Haben Sie das Kind misshandelt? Mama bekommt einen Nervenzusammenbruch und muss mit einer Spritze beruhigt werden. Mein Vater sagt: »Wenn morgen in der *Bild*-Zeitung steht, ›Grausame Eltern setzen Contergankind aus‹, hänge ich mich auf.«

Gott sei Dank behandelt mich in der städtischen Klinik ein Chefarzt, der unsere Familie sehr gut kennt. Er ruft die Wache an und erklärt den Beamten, wie absurd solche Vorwürfe sind.

Als ich am nächsten Tag hustend und leicht fiebrig nach Hause komme und Micha berichtet, was für einen Aufruhr mein Ausflug verursacht hat, möchte ich vor Scham im Boden versinken. Aber keiner will etwas von Entschuldigungen wissen. Und ich höre nicht ein einziges böses Wort. Im Gegenteil. Mama kocht mein Lieblingsessen, einen Nudelauflauf, Micha, der sich bei der Suche selbst eine schwere Grippe eingefangen hat, verliert absichtlich viermal hintereinander beim Mühlespielen, und Vater erzählt, dass er in der Schule selbst auch ein paar Fünfen geschrieben und niemand ihm dafür den Kopf abgerissen hat. Außerdem verspricht er, sich für mich um einen Gesangslehrer zu bemühen. Er zwinkert mir zu: »Damit es meinem kleinen Pflaumenaugust in Zukunft nie mehr so langweilig wird, dass er Gewaltmärsche unternehmen muss, die uns alle fast ins Grab bringen.«

Das Leben ist eine Bühne

»Alle Kunst ist gänzlich nutzlos«, heißt es in Oscar Wildes *Dorian Gray*. Ich persönlich kann nur sagen, hier irrt der Dichter. Mir hat sich ihr Mehrwert schon früh erschlossen. Die Erkenntnis vom evident Sinnhaften, ja, glücksakkumulierend Segensreichen aller künstlerischen Betätigung hängt zusammen mit dem Erwerb eines Bandgerätes der Marke Uher.

Das HiFi-Wunderwerk wird angeschafft, um den Hochzeitstag meiner Eltern auf der Höhe der Zeit – man schreibt das Jahr 1965 – und letztlich auch symbolisch zu feiern. Die Maschine ist nämlich mit zwei Tonspuren ausgerüstet, die man zusammenmischen, nach vollzogener Legierung aber nicht mehr trennen kann. Ich sehe Vater am Vorabend des Jubiläums die Treppe hinaufstapfen, das heißt, eigentlich sehe ich nur seine Beine und acht Finger. Rumpf und Kopf schnaufen hinter der voluminösen Verpackung her wie eine überheizte Dampflokomotive, ehe Gewicht und Vortrieb des Paketes den damals noch gertenschlanken Mann durch den Flur ins Wohnzimmer trudeln lassen. Ächzend bugsiert er den Karton auf den Teppich und wischt sich den Schweiß von der Stirn. Der Rest der Familie staunt Bauklötze.

»Überraschung«, grient Vater. Mehr kann man ihm nicht entlocken, obwohl wir vor Neugier platzen und echte Schwierigkeiten haben, uns auf Mr. Ed, den Helden unserer Lieblingsfernsehserie, zu konzentrieren. Mr. Ed ist ein sprechendes Pferd und ebenfalls vom Glauben an die Nützlichkeit der Kunst beseelt. Auf die verblüffte

Feststellung seiner Umwelt: »Sie können ja reden«, antwortet der Gaul stets mit dem schönen Satz: »Wenn Sie mir 'nen Schnaps geben, singe ich auch.«

Das muss mich schwer beeindruckt haben. Denn Quasthoff junior wird sich seinen ersten öffentlichen Auftritt ebenfalls in Naturalien vergüten lassen. Nicht mit Hochprozentigem, schließlich bin ich, als es so weit ist, erst zarte sechs. Ein Alter, das meinen Bruder seinerzeit keineswegs gehindert hat, sich an Oma Elses Eierlikörvorräten zu vergreifen. Aber das ist eine andere Geschichte, und ich erwähne sie hier nur, weil mich dieses legendäre, durch jahrelanges Repetieren im Familienkreis ins immer Spektakulärere wuchernde Desaster bis heute zum maßvollen Umgang mit Alkohol gemahnt.

Zurück zur Kunst, zu Mr. Ed und den Mysterien der Zweispurtechnik. Nach dem Frühstück hat Vater das Gerät aus dem Karton geschält und in die Schrankwand implantiert. Dort schimmert es jetzt matt metallic, flankiert von Gustav Freytags *Soll und Haben* und Friedrich Gerstäckers *Flusspiraten*. Micha guckt ein wenig skeptisch, als ahne er, dass es hier mit reiner Anschauung nicht getan sein wird. Alle anderen sind begeistert. Mama zückt sofort ein Staubtuch und befeudelt das imposante Möbelstück, Vater ist die nächste Stunde nicht ansprechbar. Er hockt im Schneidersitz vor seinem neuen Spielzeug, zieht Kabel, befingert die Knöpfe, während seine Lippen tonlos die Bedienungsanweisung herunterbeten. Dann müssen wir antreten zum Homerecording.

»Ach, du grüne Neune«, Micha hat es ja gewusst.

»Ruhe bitte«, schnarrt Vater, schon ganz der gewiefte Herr Produzent. Dann sagt er: »Achtung Aufnahme«, stülpt sich Kopfhörer über die Ohren und drückt Mama ein Mikrofon in die Hand. Als wär es eine zu heiße Brühwurst, hält sie das Ding mit spitzen Fingern auf Distanz.

»Komm, Puttchen, sing mal was hinein!«

»Was denn?«

»Wie wär's mit *That's Amore*.«

»Ich bin doch nicht Dean Martin.«

»Ich weiß, mein Schatz. Ich weiß. Sing einfach irgend-was.«

Mama haucht tapfer *Drei Chinesen mit dem Kontrabass*.

»Das war schon sehr schön«, lügt Vater mit professio-nellem Feingefühl.

»Wir sollten mal *Im Frühtau zu Berge* probieren – alle zusammen!« Vater bugsiert den Nachwuchs neben Mama in die Sofaecke. Er rückt das Mikrofon auf dem Tisch zu-recht. Er drückt die Zweispurtaste. Die Sitzgruppe hält den Atem an.

»Take 1. Eins, zwei drei, vier …« Mutter flötet los, ich setze eine saubere Quarte drüber. Nur Micha nölt in den Bässen herum, als ob er das Lied noch nie gehört hat. Da-bei singt er eigentlich ganz manierlich. Der Produzent kann es nicht fassen. Er haut auf die Stopp-Taste.

»Meine Lieben, etwas mehr Engagement bitte. Micha, konzentrier dich! *Im Frühtau zu Berge* – Take 2 …« Das Er-gebnis ist immer noch niederschmetternd. Der Produzent zieht ein Gesicht wie Dieter Bohlen beim Superstar-Casting. Mama hat ganz plötzlich in der Küche zu tun, Micha hat die Nase voll und verschwindet kopfschüttelnd im Kinderzimmer.

So beginnen Solokarrieren.

»Auch gut«, brummt Vater, »wozu hat das Ding denn Playback.«

Er will es jetzt wissen. Zielsicher fischt er unseren ak-tuellen Favoriten, die »Best of«-Collection des Golden Gate Quartetts, aus dem Regal und legt sie auf den Plat-tenteller. Ich beherrsche alle Songs im Schlaf, zur Not auch rückwärts. Vater geht es genauso. Wir können von den smarten Vokalarrangements einfach nicht genug bekommen, was leider dazu geführt hat, dass ein gewisser Materialabrieb nicht zu überhören ist. Während der Tonarm also unter beachtlichem Knispeln und Knuspern über die Rillen fräst, materialisiert sich in erlesener Vierstimmigkeit der Südstaatenklassiker *Swing Low, Sweet Chariot* und wird über den elektromagnetischen Tonkopf auf die erste Bandspur geleitet. Auf Spur zwo lässt mich Vater die Solostimme kopieren. Zusammengemischt klingt das tatsächlich, als wäre Tommi das fünfte Mitglied der weltberühmten schwarzen Soul- und Gospel-Gruppe. Ein kleines Wunder im Zeitalter der technischen Reproduzierbarkeit.

»Papa, das bin ich«, verkünde ich stolz.

»Jawohl, mein Sohn!« Endlich strahlt der Produzent wie Berry Gordy nach dem fünften Nummer-eins-Hit der Supremes.

Wir nehmen noch ein paar Schlager und Arien auf, bis Mama uns zum Essen ruft. Vater tätschelt mir die Wangen:

»Das wird heute Nachmittag alle aus den Puschen hauen.«

Heute Nachmittag ist Besuchszeit im Hause Quasthoff. Mama hat den Esstisch aus- und die Schondecken von der Sitzgarnitur abgezogen. Auf Sofa und Sesseln, Stühlen und Klapphockern verteilen sich die Omas Else und Lieschen, Onkel Herbert und sein Mäuseken, unsere Paten – der dicke Albert und der dünne Bertold nebst Gattinnen – und ein paar Freunde der Familie. Man hat Kaffee und Guglhupf vernichtet, Cracker und Fischli nachgestopft, etliche Flaschen Weißburgunder geleert und mit Schnäpsen abgelöscht. Die Stimmung ist aufgeräumt, tendiert jedoch partiell ins wohlig Matte. Vater nutzt die Gunst der Stunde, klopft an sein Glas und bittet um Gehör. Doch statt die erwartete Rede vom Stapel zu lassen, tritt er an die Schrankwand, dreht lässig am Einschaltknopf der Uher und zieht den Volumenregler nach oben.

Ein schweres Gewitter hätte kaum mehr Effekt gemacht. Aus den Boxen dröhnt in ohrenbetäubender Lautstärke *Ich liebe nur dich allein*, das Duett zwischen Dichter Rudolf und Mimi aus Puccinis *La Bohème*. Noch lauter dröhnt Vaters voluminöser Bass, der zwei Oktaven unter Rudi durch den Tenorpart pflügt. Live und unplugged, schließlich ist es sein Hochzeitstag. Die Gäste applaudieren, Mamas Teint überzieht ein süßes Rosé, Oma Lieschen rutscht vor Schreck das Gebiss vom Gaumen.

»Nu los, Hänschen, schwenk dein Puttchen mal 'n bisken rum«, bellt Herbert in die Hundert-Watt-Wand. Aber dafür ist das Wohnzimmer viel zu voll und die Nummer viel zu schnell vorbei. Stattdessen gospelt unser *Swing Low*-Remix fünfstimmig aus den Boxen. Das Publikum ist baff.

»Mensch, det Orjan kenn ik ooch.«

»Das ist Thomas!«

»Glaub ich nich.«

»Klar isser det!«

»Sehr richtig«, nickt Vater und beginnt, die Finessen des Uher-Zweispursystems anzupreisen. Doch er kommt nicht weit.

»Tommi soll uns das mal selber vorsingen!«

»Ein Ständchen! Ein Ständchen, das ist sehr gut.«

»Au ja, wo isser denn, der kleine Caruso?«, kreischt Tante Liselotte, deren Stimme bei vermehrtem Adrenalinausstoß unschön ins Hysterische kippt.

Der Kleine ist nicht Caruso, sondern Buffalo Bill und sitzt im Kinderzimmer, wo Fort Laramie gegen Michas Hartplastik-Apachen verteidigt werden muss. Mama wird losgeschickt, um die Auftrittsbedingungen auszuhandeln. Unglücklicherweise platzt sie mitten in eine Konterattacke. Buffalo ist unabkömmlich.

»Wir spielen!«, poche ich auf die Errungenschaften der Reformpädagogik. Sie dürfen laut Familienvertrag nur in Krisenfällen – mutwillig eingeschlagene Fensterscheiben, Türschlösser-Verkleben mit gebrauchtem Kaugummi, das Deponieren von Silvesterknallern in Nachbars Briefkasten – außer Kraft gesetzt werden. Eine Versammlung angeheiterter, im Unterhaltungsbereich unterversorgter Erwachsener ist kein Krisenfall. Fort Laramie ist ein Krisenfall. Mitgehen und singen hieße Kapitulation, hieße, den teuflischen Indsmen kampflos die Wallstatt zu überlassen. Aber ein Buffalo Bill kapituliert nicht. Niemals. Er lässt kapitulieren. Mama ist taktisch weitaus flexibler. Sie appelliert jetzt an meine Eitelkeit. Man wäre ganz begeistert von Vaters Aufnahmen und mit einer Gesangseinlage würde ich allen eine große Freude machen.

»Mir nicht«, trotzt Micha. Ungerührt zieht er den Belagerungsgürtel enger.

Da erinnere ich mich an Mr. Ed, das singende Pferd, und an die drei Prinzenrollen, die Mama zwecks kontrollierter Zuteilung unerreichbar im obersten Fach des Küchenschrankes verwahrt. Die Quasthoff-Brüder sterben für das runde Schokogebäck aus dem Hause de Beukelaer.

»Tommi singt was, wenn er Prinz-Kekse kriegt!«, lautet mein Angebot.

Dass Mama die Süßigkeiten am Ende anstandslos herausrückt, liegt vor allem an Vaters perfektem Timing. Profi bleibt eben Profi. Nachdem ich unter großem Gejohle der Festgemeinde Aufstellung genommen habe, beginnt er Gounods *Ave Maria* abzuspulen, jene wundervolle Kantate, die das erste C-Dur-Präludium aus Bachs Wohltemperiertem Klavier paraphrasiert und verdientermaßen seit hundertfünfzig Jahren den christlich-abendländischen Festkalender untermalt: molto animato, molto arioso und vor allem molto molto mesto. Solche Feinheiten sind dem jugendlichen Debütanten herzlich egal – ich singe das Stück einfach gern –, aber ihre Wirkung verblüfft immer wieder. Kaum ist die Eingangszeile »Gegrüßet seist du, Maria, voll der Gnade« verklungen, lecken rundherum die Tränensäcke. Dass ich mit Jerome Kerns *Ol' Man River* gleich das nächste Prachtexemplar einer musikalischen Trauerweide in Angriff nehme, macht die Sache nicht besser.

»Es iss so schön, es iss zum Heulen«, hört man Tante Liselotte klagemauern, während Onkel Bertold diskret Tempo-Taschentücher herumreicht. Damit der Nachmittag nicht gänzlich ins Mollige abgleitet, hat der Produzent natürlich noch ein Ass im Ärmel, beziehungsweise auf der Spule. Band ab – und schon schmettern Vater und Sohn die unverwüstlichen Verse:

»Wie oft schon hab ich am Rhein gedacht:
Kinder, wie wäre das schön,
wenn überraschend so ganz über Nacht,
zu mir ein Zauberer käm.
Er hält seinen Zauberstab dann einfach über mich,
mit Hokus und Pokus und so,
und eins, zwei, drei wär ich ein munterer Fisch
und schwämme im Rhein irgendwo.«

Dass das zwischen Bayer AG und Ciba-Geigy ein eher bedenkliches Ansinnen ist, kann Willy Schneiders Spirituosenhymne nichts anhaben. Als wir den Refrain ansteuern, singt und schunkelt der Gästechor im Dreiviertel-takt:

»Wenn das Wasser im Rhein gold'ner Wein wär,
dann möchte ich so gern ein Fischlein sein.
Ei, was könnte ich dann saufen,
brauchte keinen Wein zu kaufen,
denn das Fass vom Vater Rhein wird niemals leer.«

Ich weiß nicht, ob der deutsche Winzerfachverband Herrn Schneider jemals gedankt hat. Verdient hätte er mindestens die lebenslange Ehrenmitgliedschaft, inklusive freie Verkostung bis an den Grabesrand. Heißt es doch in der zweiten Strophe:

»Wär ich aber den Rheinwein mal leid,
schwämme zur Mosel ich hin
und bliebe dort dann für längere Zeit,
weil ich ein Weinkenner bin.
Doch wollt ich so gerne woanders noch sein,
drum macht ich 'ne Spritztour zur Ahr
und fände mich schließlich am Rhein wieder ein,
weil das ja der Ausgangspunkt war.«

Ich bevorzuge mittlerweile einen kräftigen Rioja, aber der Song zählt heute noch zu meinen Favoriten. Genauso wie das *Ave Maria* und *Ol' Man River*. Der Hit aus Jerome Kerns Musical *Show Boat* hat auf meinen Lied-Tourneen einen Stammplatz bei den Zugaben.

Und das wird nach der gefeierten Hochzeitstag-Gala zielstrebig ausgebaut. Bis dato habe ich ja immer nur zu meinem Vergnügen gesungen, für meine Eltern, oder ich habe Omas Geburtstag mit einem Ständchen garniert. Aber nun macht die Kunde, Quasthoffs Filius ist nicht einfach nur behindert, sondern obendrein ein begabter Vokalist, im weiteren Bekanntenkreis schnell die Runde. Jeder, der uns besucht, möchte eine Exklusiv-Vorstellung. Und fast jeder bekommt sie. Man braucht mich nicht mal mehr lange zu bitten. Viel zu süß schmecken Beifall, Lob und Schokoriegel, die das Publikum freigiebig über dem Dreikäsehoch ausschüttet.

Meine Eltern sehen das anfangs mit gemischten Gefühlen. Aber weil sie merken, wie ihr Sprössling, der unter der Woche im Internat regelmäßig in schwarzer Melancholie versinkt, aufblüht, sobald er Musik machen kann, lassen sie ihn gewähren. Jedenfalls solange ihm der frische Ruhm nicht zu Kopf steigt. Der Punkt ist zum ersten Mal erreicht, als ich im Lauf eines Samstagvormittags erst dem Briefträger, dann dem Schornsteinfeger ohne Vorwarnung entgegenkrähe: »Ich bin der Tommi. Soll ich was singen?«

»So geht es nicht«, befindet Mama und bittet am Abend auch Vater um eine Klarstellung. Vater nickt. Er schleift mich ins Kinderzimmer, knallt die Tür zu und stellt klar, dass es so wirklich nicht geht.

»Hast du das verstanden?«

»Jawohl.«

»Na hoffentlich.« Aber er muss schon wieder grinsen. Tief drinnen ist Vater nämlich stolz wie Oskar, dass seine Künstler-Gene auf fruchtbaren Boden gefallen sind. Damit sie ordnungsgemäß keimen, darf ich sogar die kostbare Uher mit ins Annastift nehmen. Außerdem habe ich jeden Monat drei frisch bespielte Bänder im Gepäck. Eins mit den aktuellen Produktionen der Schlager- und Easy-Listening-Branche, das ist von Mama, auf Band Nummer zwei sind die wertvollsten Perlen der klassischen Musik gespeichert, das dritte hat Micha mit Komikern bestückt. Mir ist alles gleich lieb, Haydn, Mozart, Hans Moser, Herb Alpert, die Beatles, Karl Valentin oder Insterburg & Co, Hauptsache, ich kann mich für ein paar Stunden vom Strafplaneten Müller-Mahlzahn hinwegträumen. Gemäß der immer noch gültigen Schopenhauer-Maxime: Das »Ansich des Lebens« ist »stets Leid und teils jämmerlich …, dasselbe hingegen als Vorstellung, rein angeschaut oder durch die Kunst wiederholt, ist frei von Qual«. Ich glaube, dem singenden Homunkulus ist das damals längst bewusst, und er ahnt – zwar vage noch und instinktiv –, dass für ihn unter den gegebenen Umständen ein Platz oben auf der Bühne allemal besser ist als ein Dauerabonnement im Parkett. Weshalb die elterlichen Ermahnungen meinen Offensivdrang in geordnete Bahnen lenken, aber nicht wirklich bremsen können.

Bald habe ich heraus, dass sich Effekt und Ertrag meiner Privataufführungen durch zielgruppenoptimierte Präsentation um ein Vielfaches steigern lassen. Die Erleuchtung wird mir auf dem Mahlumer Friedhof zuteil, wo mein Großvater Emil begraben liegt. Es ist ein warmer Frühlingstag. Ich sitze in der Kinderkarre, Oma Else kniet in den Rabatten und traktiert das Unkraut mit dem Klappspaten. Ein sanfter Wind durchkämmt die Bäume, in der Hecke zirpen Rotkehlchen und Fink. In meinem Kopf zirpt ein Lied: *Die Tiroler sind lustig, die Tiroler sind froh.* Ich weiß nicht, wie es da hineingekommen ist, ich weiß nur, das Lied muss wieder heraus. Laut und mit Schmackes.

Oma findet das gar nicht komisch: »Mein lieber Junge, ich höre dich immer gerne singen, aber das passt nicht hierher, hier schlafen die Leute.«

»Dann singe ich *Müde bin ich, geh zur Ruh.*« Oma ist ausmanövriert. Sie nimmt es mit amüsierter Gelassenheit.

»Na, denn mach mal, wenn du die Gosche partout nicht halten kannst!«

Ausgezahlt hat sich das aber erst auf dem Rückweg, vor dem Konsum. Dort lauert, abwechselnd an einer Juno Gold und an einer Halbliterflasche Wolters nuckelnd, Alt-bauer Hinke auf Gesellschaft. Strahlend wedelt er uns mit seiner Lodenkappe heran.

»Aaah, die Else un ihr'n lütten Domas. Na, Bengel, dich hev we jor lang nich sehn«, spricht's und lässt die Landmannspranke über meine Backe raspeln.

Hermann Hinke bildet mit Oma und zwei weiteren Witwen eine Rommé-Runde, die regelmäßig in ihrer Stube tagt. Als sie ihm die Friedhofsgeschichte erzählt, will er sich ausschütten vor Lachen und drückt mir – »for din Sparswin« – ein Fünfzigpfennigstück in die Hand. Später hat er mich noch großzügiger entlohnt. Wenn sich meine Mahlumbesuche mit den Sitzungen des Rommé-Quartetts überschneiden, bittet er mich manchmal, den zweiten großen Willy-Schneider-Evergreen abzusingen: *Man müsste noch mal zwanzig sein, und so verliebt wie damals.* Dazu verteilt der rüstige Charmeur Handküsse, Eierlikör und halbseidene Komplimente, was das rund zweihundertzwanzig Jahre alte Witwentrio jedes Mal in kichernde Backfische verwandelt und mir ein glattes Markstück einbringt.

Noch größere Erfolge ernte ich bei Mutters Kaffeekränzchen. Das verdanke ich dem singenden Seitenscheitel Heintje, Hollands später Rache für Schlieffenplan und Blitzkrieg. Die Damen gehen nie, ohne mindestens eine originalgetreue Kopie seines Monsterhits *Mama* serviert zu bekommen. Ich bekomme dafür die besten Sahnestücke ausgehändigt und allmählich ein wenig Speck auf die Hüften. Meine Mama will nicht, dass ich allzu dick werde, wegen meiner schwachen Hüftgelenke, außerdem findet sie das Lied ziemlich dämlich, aber was soll sie machen? Die Kaffeetanten rauswerfen? Dazu hat sich Mama, soweit ich mich erinnere, nur einmal hinreißen lassen. Es trifft eine gewisse Frau Benedikt, die ihrer Begeisterung mit folgenden Worten Ausdruck verleiht: »Ihr Sohn singt ganz wunderbar, nur angucken kann man ihn dabei nicht.«

Also muss Mama leiden, bis Heintjes Stimmbruch dem Spuk ein Ende macht. Abnehmen tue ich trotzdem nicht. Als wir drei Sommer hintereinander in Waging am See, im tiefsten Bayern, Urlaub machen, wird mir der kehlkopftechnisch saubere Vortrag alpenländischen Liedgutes regelmäßig mit Gratisbrause und doppeltem Nachtisch vergolten. Meine Spezialität ist der *Erzherzog-Johann-Jodler* (»Wo i geh und steh, tuat mir mai Herz so weh, jolohodrio, jolohojodriö«), den ich begleitet von einem Zitherspieler sogar einmal im Rahmen einer Aufführung des Waginger Trachtenvereins zum Besten geben darf. Ähnlich war es in Norderney, wo wir vorher unsere Ferien verbrachten. Da habe ich natürlich nicht gejodelt, sondern mir die Extraportionen mit Freddy Quinns MatrosenNummern verdient.

Aber ich kann auch Rock 'n' Roll. Für eine schmissige Version von *Marmor, Stein und Eisen bricht* belohnt mich Margret, das liebreizende Töchterlein von Onkel Herbert und Tante Elsi, mit einem dicken Kuss. Danach redet Micha drei Tage lang kein Wort mehr mit mir. Mama sagt, ich soll ihm nicht böse sein, er sei bis über beide Ohren verliebt. Ich glaube, sie hat Recht. Jedes Mal, wenn die wirklich sehr schöne Margret mit meinem Bruder spricht, wird er rot wie ein gesottener Hummer und wirft eine Vase um. Aber er weiß seine Eifersucht durchaus zu dosieren. Sobald Margrets fescher Gatte Helmut mit dem Opel Admiral vorfährt, um uns auf eine Spritztour einzuladen, hat Micha nur noch Augen für den ultramarinblauen Straßenkreuzer. Mit Margret und Helmut nimmt es zur Überraschung der Verwandtschaft (»ein ideales Paar«, »ein Traumpaar«) dann leider viel zu früh ein tragisches Ende. Helmut wird drei Jahre später von Margret verlassen und trägt den größten Teil seines Millionen-erbes in die Spielbank. Den Rest legt er in Wodka an. Als Geld und Alkohol zur Neige gehen, setzt er den Admiral mit 180 Sachen an einen Baum und stirbt. Kurz darauf stürzt die schöne Margret auf der ersten Klettertour, die sie mit ihrem neuen Freund, einem passionierten Berg-steiger, unternimmt, nahe der Ortlergruppe in eine tiefe Schlucht und bricht sich das Genick.

Auch Herr Pape sieht wie ein Bergsteiger aus. Aber er ist keiner. Herr Pape trägt Knickerbocker, Rucksack und genagelte Stiefel aus reiner Bequemlichkeit und vorwie-gend in der flachen Hildesheimer Börde spazieren. Aus dem gleichen Grund transportiert er seine Aktentasche auch nicht wie der Rest der Welt per Hand am dafür vor-gesehenen Griff, sondern hat sie um den Bauch ge-schnallt.

Herr Pape wird uns Buben als Jugendfreund und Kol-lege meines Vaters vorgestellt. Er sei ein bisschen seltsam, raunt Mama und lässt ihren Zeigefinger an der Schläfe ro-tieren. Herr Pape selbst führt sich als Naturapostel, Jünger des Anthroposophen Steiner und Radikalvegetarier ein. Wenn er bei uns am Tisch sitzt – und er tut das eine Zeit lang ziemlich oft –, stehen zermürbende Vorträge über Seelenwanderung und das Sein im Geistigen, über Kneippkuren und Eisbäder, wahlweise über Ernährungs- und Stoffwechselfragen auf dem Speiseplan. Die wich-tigsten Leitsätze verabreicht Pape gern auch in gereimter Form: »Den Bissen kauen hundertmal, erspart dem Darm so manche Qual.«

Man kann sich ausrechnen, wie lange es dauert, bis er eine simple Stulle eingespeichelt hat. Beliebt macht sich Herr Pape damit nicht. Erschwerend hinzu kommt seine Angewohnheit, nach dem Essen ein zerfleddertes Exem-plar des roten *Mundorgel*-Heftchens hervorzukramen

(»Beweg' dich oder singe laut, schnell wird die Nahrung abgebaut«). Ist ihm eine erbauungs-, sprich verdauungsfördernde Komposition ins Auge gefallen, hebt er an, dieselbe mit erbarmungswürdig dünnem Stimmchen vorzutragen. Nach einer Weile hält Pape inne, senkt den Kopf und fixiert mich über den Rand seiner Kassenbrille: »Das kennst du doch bestimmt, mein Kleiner?« Verzweifelt sehe ich Mama an, sie schüttelt resolut den Kopf. Vater indes sehe ich milde nicken. Da Höflichkeit eine Gabe der Weisen ist, sage ich ja und habe es im nächsten Augenblick bereut. Denn nun gilt es, begleitet von Papes inbrünstigem Gewimmer, Stück für Stück den Fundus der Wandervogelbewegung abzusingen. Es ist grausam. Mama starrt zähneknirschend an die Decke, Micha liegt krumm vor Lachen halb unter dem Tisch. Was mich besonders verbittert: Am Ende hat Pape nicht einmal Schokolade dabei, sondern überreicht mir einen natursauren, wahrscheinlich seit Kriegsende in seinen Knickerbockern klebenden Zitronendrops.

Wir ertragen das alles, weil Vater auf mildernde Umstände plädiert und die Ehehölle des Pape in Gestalt eines tyrannisch veranlagten und zu schwerster Hypochondrie neigenden Weibes mit breughelscher Palette ausmalt. Außerdem habe er ein Leberleiden und immer Hunger. Kochen kann die Xanthippe also auch nicht. Der Mann darf wiederkommen, wir sind ja keine Unmenschen. Mit unserer Geduld ist es allerdings jäh vorbei, als sich herausstellt, Papes Vegetarismus fußt recht eigentlich auf dem Diktat seines hypochondrischen Hausdrachens und ist nur sehr theoretischer Natur. Entsetzt müssen wir mit ansehen, wie sich die Konditionierung des Zwangsasketen von Mahlzeit zu Mahlzeit in geradezu unheimlichem, man kann auch sagen unverschämtem Tempo lockert. Schinken, Koteletts, Corned Beef, ganze Speckseiten verschwinden hinter seinen kariösen Palisaden, als gäbe es kein Morgen, von Mamas Gulasch nimmt er dreimal nach, von den köstlichen Aufläufen bleiben selbst meinen Eltern nur Kinderportionen, er kleistert ungeniert halbe Sülzfleischdosen auf sein Brötchen und schlägt furchtbare Schneisen in Vaters Wintervorrat an Eichsfelder Mettwürsten. Pape frisst uns die Haare von Kopf.

»Er oder wir«, sagt der Familienrat. Vater wirft einen Blick in die geplünderte Speisekammer, schüttelt traurig den Kopf und setzt die Verköstigung aus. Pape hat es nicht krumm genommen. Im Gegenteil. Mamas Halbpension muss ihm vorgekommen sein wie ein Ausflug ins Paradies. Nach einer Schamfrist von einer Woche hat er bei Vater angefragt, »ob die Brigitte mir nicht wenigstens ab und an ein Stullenpaket ...« Klar kann sie, und hat sie auch gemacht, mindestens dreimal die Woche, die gute Seele.

Heinz Otto Graf, ein anderer Freund der Familie, spielt die Solobratsche im Orchester des Norddeutschen Rundfunks. Ihm habe ich immer sehr gerne vorgesungen, denn er hat aufmerksam zugehört. Im Gegensatz zu diversen von Vater kontaktierten Gesangslehrern, die gleich den Hörer auflegen, wenn meine Behinderung zur Sprache kommt. Um Rat gefragt, wie man meine Begabung fördern könne, sagt Graf, unser Mann sei Sebastian Peschko, da müsse ich mich vorstellen, dann würde sich bestimmt die eine oder andere Möglichkeit ergeben. Man solle aber nichts überstürzen, sondern lieber noch ein Jahr warten, bis meine Stimme ausgereifter sei.

Professor Sebastian Peschko ist Vater natürlich ein Begriff. Bevor Peschko die Leitung der NDR-Abteilung »Kammermusik und Lied« übernahm, hat er als Pianist reüssiert und Größen wie Grace Bumbry, Hermann Prey, Nicolai Gedda oder Anneliese Rothenberger begleitet.

Weil ich meine Technik inzwischen im Schulchor des Andreanums und in der Michaelis-Kantorei vervollkommne, macht sich Vater nach Ablauf eines Jahres zuversichtlich auf den Weg nach Hannover, um Peschko zu bitten, mir ein Vorsingen zu gewähren. Dass der Mann vor Begeisterung an die Decke springt, kann man nicht gerade sagen. Kaum hat Vater sein Anliegen vorgebracht, steht er schon wieder auf dem Flur. Schuld ist wiederum der singende Seitenscheitel. Die bunten Storys vom Goldkehlchen Heintje, der es mit einer einzigen Single zum Film- und Fernsehstar bringt, seine Erzeuger aus der Knechtschaft entfremdeter Arbeit befreit und zu sorgenfreien Verwesern eines Windmühlen- und Streichelzoo-Imperiums macht, sind Manna für alle Zukurzgekommenen. Deutschlands Erziehungsberechtigte fallen in einen Goldrausch.

»Alle drei Tage wird uns ein neues Wunderkind angedient«, erläutert Peschkos Sekretärin die reservierte Haltung ihres Chefs. Ein Phänomen, das sich in den achtziger Jahren wiederholt, als von Ehrgeiz zerfressene Bundesbürger ihren Nachwuchs, sofern er halbwegs geradeaus laufen kann, auf den Tennisplatz prügeln, in der Hoffnung, eine zweite Steffi oder ein neues Bobbele zu formen.

»Mein Sohn hat wirklich Talent«, insistiert Vater. »Ich komme wieder.«

Und das ist keine leere Drohung. Nach zwei Dutzend Brief- und Telefonattacken hat er den »Lied«-Chef weich gekocht und tatsächlich einen Termin für mich herausgeschlagen. Wir treffen ihn im Kleinen Sendesaal des Funkhauses.

Peschko, ein stattlicher Mensch mit weißem Haar, hoher Stirn und würdevollen Zügen, gibt sich förmlich und höchst reserviert.

»Ich habe nur fünf Minuten Zeit«, wiederholt er ungefähr zehn Minuten lang. Eine weitere Viertelstunde sinniert der Professor über die Untiefen des Musikbetriebes und ästhetische Grenzwerte im öffentlichen Raum.

»Wir möchten doch nur, dass Sie unserem Sohn fünf Minuten zuhören«, fällt ihm Mama gereizt ins Wort. Peschko lässt nicht locker.

»Warum wollen Sie ihm das alles antun? Haben Sie je darüber nachgedacht, wie das Publikum auf so einen Schwerbehinderten reagiert?«

»Ich fange gerade damit an«, sagt Mama mit tonloser Stimme. Sie ist kreidebleich.

Als Peschko merkt, dass auch Vater gleich der Kragen platzt, stoppt er seinen Vortrag und wird zum ersten Mal verbindlich: »Verzeihen Sie, ich wollte nicht unhöflich sein. Ich wollte Ihnen nur sagen, was Ihren Sohn da draußen erwartet.« Er fuchtelt mit dem Arm vage Richtung Westen, wo hinter der schallgedämmten Wand der Maschsee träge in der Mittagssonne liegt. »Aber jetzt soll Thomas zeigen, was er kann.«

Ich habe mir auch lange genug die Prothesen in den Bauch gestanden. Froh, dass die Präliminarien endlich beendet sind, lasse ich mich von Vater die vier Stufen hinauf zur Bühne hieven und singe Brechts *Mackie Messer*-Song, schön durch die Nase wie der *Dreigroschen*-Dichter himself auf unserer alten Amiga-LP. Ich singe den Gitte-Schlager *Ich will 'nen Cowboy als Mann*, ich singe das *Ave Maria*. Peschko sitzt in der ersten Stuhlreihe, reglos, mit geschlossenen Augen, den Kopf auf die rechte Faust gestützt. Sieht aus, als ob er schläft. Aber er schläft nicht. Nach jedem Stück klappt er die Augendeckel hoch und sagt: »Das war sehr gut, mach nur weiter.« Anscheinend hat er doch ein bisschen Zeit. So viel Zeit, dass ich fast mein gesamtes Repertoire an den Mann bringen kann.

Ich singe Opernarien und Gospels, ich imitiere Jürgen von Manger und Theo Lingen, ich jodele und gebe Louis Armstrong, den swingenden Halskatarrh. Am Ende fällt mir nur noch Bill Ramseys *Zuckerpuppe aus der Bauchtanztruppe* ein. Da ist längst eine Stunde herum. Peschko lässt es gut sein und schüttelt den Eltern aufgeräumt die Hände:

»Vergessen Sie alles, was ich vorhin gesagt habe. Ich freue mich, dass Sie gekommen sind. Der kleine Bursche hat wirklich famose Anlagen. Ich werde mir etwas einfallen lassen und mich so bald wie möglich bei Ihnen melden.«

Peschko hält Wort. Zwei Wochen später hat er für mich das nächste Vorsingen arrangiert.

Es findet im Dörfchen Arnum bei Hannover statt, im Haus einer aufstrebenden Sopranistin, die von Peschko des Öfteren am Flügel begleitet wird. Als Vater am Gartentor des flachen Bungalows klingelt, erscheint eine aparte junge Dame in der Tür.

»Sie müssen die Quasthoffs sein. Ich bin Charlotte Lehmann, kommen Sie bitte herein.« Hinter ihr ragt ein hagerer Schädel in den Flur, der samt Hakennase, grauem Stoppelbewuchs und ledrigem Halsansatz an Karl Mays Trapper Geierschnabel erinnert. Er gehört dem Gatten Ernst Huber-Contwig, seines Zeichens Orchesterleiter in Santiago de Chile, Musikwissenschaftler und streitbarer Vorkämpfer der Avantgarde. Entsprechend regiert drinnen der funktionale Chic der klassischen Moderne: Glas, Metall und schwarzes Leder. Der Hausherr serviert Säfte, man tauscht Freundlichkeiten und Kurzbiografien aus, dann kommt der Augenblick der Wahrheit. Frau Lehmann setzt sich an den Flügel, lockert die Finger und lässt mich Aufstellung nehmen.

»Was möchtest du singen?«

»*Una furtiva lacrima* aus dem *Liebestrank.*«

Huber-Contwigs rechte Augenbraue rutscht einen Zentimeter nach oben. Gaetano Donizetti schrieb die sentimentale Romanze für den Tölpel Nemorino, der sie just in dem Moment vorträgt, da ihm dämmert, dass er das Herz der angebeteten Adina schon lange, im Grunde seit der Ouvertüre, im Sack hat und man sich die zwei Akte währenden Kapriolen um das Wunderelixier eigentlich hätte schenken können. Es gibt Leute, die Donizetti für einen verkitschten Fließbandkomponisten halten. »Sein Talent ist groß«, spottete Heinrich Heine, »aber noch größer ist seine Fruchtbarkeit, worin er nur den Karnickeln nachsteht.« Ehrlich gesagt, ich hätte mich auch lieber mit Mozart eingeführt. Doch Vater dekretiert unbeirrt: »Die Arie ist klasse. Reiner Belcanto, die perfekte Schmachteplatte für deinen Knabensopran.«

Ganz falsch hat er damit wohl nicht gelegen. Als Frau Lehmann den Schlussakkord setzt, nickt der Avantgardist anerkennend. Aber entscheidend ist das Urteil meiner Begleiterin:

»An deiner Stimme ist etwas, das mich reizt, ich würde sehr gerne mit dir arbeiten.«

Von da an bin ich einmal in der Woche nach Arnum gefahren. Mal bringt mich Mama, mal nehme ich ein Taxi. Ich lege zwanzig Mark auf den Küchentisch, bekomme eine Stunde Unterricht und eine Lektion für zu Hause zum Nacharbeiten. Frau Lehmann ist eine erfahrene Lehrerin, trotzdem dürfte es nicht immer ganz einfach gewesen sein, mit mir zu arbeiten. Ich bin mit vierzehn Jahren ziemlich jung für einen Gesangsschüler, mithin noch ein rechter Kindskopf, dem es oft an der nötigen Ernsthaftigkeit mangelt. Aber sie hat das von Anfang an sehr einfühlsam und geschickt gemacht. Sie hat zum Beispiel gleich gemerkt, dass man mir das präzise Regelwerk der Musik als großen Abenteuerspielplatz verkaufen muss, denn porös geworden durch die Tyrannei im Annastift reagiere ich auf Druck und Zwangsmaßnahmen allergisch und mit allen Symptomen des geborenen Cholerikers, als da sind: erhöhte Blutdruckwerte, scharlachrotes Anlaufen des Schädels, rasant anschwellende Phonstärke der Argumentationsketten.

»He is nu mal 'nen sturen Bock«, wie Oma Lieschen zu sagen pflegt, wenn mir die Richtlinienkompetenz meiner Eltern wieder mal partout nicht einleuchten will. Bei Frau Lehmann kommt das so gut wie nie vor. Dafür ist alles, was ich lerne, viel zu interessant. Zum Beispiel das richtige Atmen. Die meisten machen es sich dabei ja viel zu einfach.

»Im Atemholen sind zweierlei Gnaden:
Die Luft einziehen, sich ihrer entladen,
Jenes bedrängt, dieses erfrischt,
So wunderbar ist das Leben gemischt.
Du danke Gott, wenn er dich presst,
Und danke ihm, wenn er dich wieder entlässt.«

So wie Goethe habe ich es bisher auch gehalten. Von der Lehmann erfahre ich nun, was man beim Atmen alles falsch machen kann. Man kann zu kurz atmen oder zu unruhig, zu hoch oder zu flach atmen, und bitte nie nur aus dem Bauch. Weitaus gesünder ist da schon die Zwerchfell-Flankenatmung. Aber im Idealfall sollte der Mensch und vor allem der Sänger immer eine kombinierte Atemform, die gelöste Vollatmung anstreben. Das ist die Basis. Von hier aus gilt es, sich um die hohe Schule, die so genannte Stütze, zu bemühen. Die Stütze beruht auf dem kontrollierten Wechselspiel von tiefgestelltem Zwerchfell und gehobener Brustmuskulatur. Sie ist die Voraussetzung für eine ausgefeilte Technik, ohne die sich Luft nicht in Klang, Materie nicht in Geist verwandeln lässt.

»Piano singen«, trichtert mir Frau Lehmann ein, »heißt ja nicht, mit halber Kraft zu singen, sondern die volle Stimme durch Konzentration auf eine feinere Tonbildung zu justieren.«

Doch vor dem Gesang kommt erst einmal das richtige Sprechen. Und auch das ist eine Kunst für sich. Oder hatten Sie, verehrter Leser, beim Feilschen um die letzte Gehaltserhöhung stets im Hinterkopf, dass das »e« im Deutschen fünf Vokalfarben hat? Es gibt ein kurzes offenes »e« (Herz und Schmerz, Geld regiert die Welt), ein halb geschlossenes »e« (Weg, Steg, legen, lesen), ein geschlossenes »e« (Elend der Ehe, Teer im Meer), ein tonloses »e« (Treue, Freude, Wonne, Sonne) und das stumme »e« (Vieh, Poesie, Gier nach Bier). Auch über die Abgründe, die zwischen vorderem und hinterem »ch« liegen, habe ich mir bisher nie den Kopf zerbrochen. Dabei sind sie mindestens so breit wie der Grand Canyon. Das korrekte vordere »ch« ist ein Reibelaut und setzt eine geöffnete Stimmritze voraus, denn sie darf keinesfalls tönend mitschwingen. Des Weiteren hat die Zunge gehoben, das Zäpfchen gesenkt zu sein, während die Stellung des Kehlkopfes durch den jeweils vorausgehenden Vokal bestimmt wird. Sagt man »ich«, steht er hoch, rutscht einem ein überrashtes »Huch« heraus, steht er tief. Beim hinteren »ch«, einer Spezies aus der Klasse der Verschlusslaute, ist alles noch viel komplizierter.

Da unser Alphabet insgesamt sechsundzwanzig Buchstaben zuzüglich fünf Doppellauten kennt, die gerade von der singenden Zunft individuell betreut, sprich artikuliert werden wollen, öffnet sich ein weites Übungsfeld. Anfänger sollten allerdings darauf achten, dass sie ihre Trainingseinheiten in gut gedämmten Räumen und möglichst ohne Zeugen hinter sich bringen.

Für Micha, der im Zimmer neben mir haust, sind meine Exerzitien eine harte Prüfung. Denn Frau Lehmann legt anfangs vor allem Wert auf die technische Grundausbildung. Also verschwinde ich nach der Schule in meiner Klause, nehme die Grundstellung ein (»come una stàtua« – wie eine Statue: aufgerichteter Brustkorb, die Füße leicht gespreizt, jedoch nicht breiter als der Schultergürtel) und beginne mit dem stoßweisen, kontinuierlich schneller werdenden Ein- und Ausatmen. Diese Übung heißt Tiefhecheln. Mein Bruder mäkelt, es klingt eher wie ein asthmakranker Bernhardiner beim Besteigen des Matterhorns. Micha mag auch nicht einsehen, warum man Lautgedichte folgender Machart fünfzehn Mal hintereinander durch die Wohnung brüllen muss:

Barrrbarrraaa saaß naaah am Abhannng,
Sprrrrach gaaarrrr sangbaarrrr – zaaaghaft
lanngsaaam;
Mannhaft kaaam alsdann am Waldrrrand
Aaabrrraahaaam aa Sanctaaa Claarrraa!

oder

Arrrmer Mann, errmaaaahne Arrrmin:
Wer Macht verrrmeeehrrrrt,
Derrr minderrrr' mancherrr Mutteeerrr Müüüh' –
Verrrrmeeehrrr' verrrrmess'nerrrr Männerrrr Muuut!

Nicht weniger zermürbend sind Sprachübungen, die mit wechselndem Artikulationsansatz, aber immer laut, im Maschinengewehrtempo und mehrmals am Tag repetiert werden müssen.

Ta – da – ga / ga – da – ta / da – ta – ga / la – da – la.
Ta – da – ga / ga – da – ta / da – ta – ga / la – da – la.
Ta – da – ga / ga – da – ta / da – ta – ga / la – da – la.

So geht das sechs Monate lang. Dann bläst Micha zur Gegenoffensive. Beziehungsweise in eine C-Klarinette, die er auf dem Schrottplatz gefunden hat. Es ist ein altes, schäbiges Instrument. Die Klappen decken nicht, das Holz ist zerkratzt, das Mundstück zerkaut wie ein alter Pfeifenstiel. Man bringt nicht viel mehr heraus als ein kläglich dürres, aber durchdringendes Fiepen.

»Zum Gotterbarmen«, flucht Vater.

»Nicht zum Aushalten«, jammert Mama.

Micha macht das nichts. Er legt die *Live At The Village Vanguard*-LP der John Coltrane Band auf den Plattenteller, hält das Instrument in Hab-Acht-Stellung und wartet. Auf den Opener *Naima*, auf den Beginn meiner Sprachübungen und auf Opa Schneiderath, den alten Stalingrad-Kämpfer aus dem Souterrain. Wir haben unseren Einsatz, wenn Pharoah Sanders' Saxophon mit kreischendem Obertoninferno in Coltranes majestätische Melodiebögen fräst. Wir sind ein denkwürdiges Trio. Micha fiept sich die Seele aus dem Leib, ich rattere im Nebenzimmer vor mich hin (»Ta – da – ga / ga – da – ta / da – ta – ga / la – da – la«), während Schneiderath das Treppenhaus zusammenbrüllt. Und zwar mit den Worten: »Wir sind hier nicht bei den Hottentotten.« Er brüllt das mehrmals und mit schwellendem Diskant. Meistens bemerken wir ihn erst, wenn er seinen Armstumpf viertelstundenweise auf die Klingel drückt oder wenn Poli und Zisti unsere Haustür im Stile Cozy Powells mit dem Gummiknüppel bearbeiteten. Die Anzeige wegen Ruhestörung wird Micha gutgeschrieben und am Abend von Vater routiniert mit einer Kopfnuss quittiert. Dann schließt er die Klarinette für eine Woche weg. Ich darf weiter singen und lerne, die Welt ist oft ungerecht. Micha hat sich davon nicht beirren lassen. In den Ferien montiert er bei Bosch-Blaupunkt Zündkerzen in Doppelschicht, bis er sich ein Saxophon leisten kann. Vier Jahre später stehen wir auf der Bühne des Jazzclubs Hannover und spielen Charlie Parkers *Au Privave*. Unisono, fehlerfrei und zur vollen Zufriedenheit des Publikums.

Bis dahin ist allerdings noch ein gutes Stück Weg zurückzulegen. Die Quasthoff-Brüder marschieren zunächst einmal musikalisch sauber getrennt, als meine Eltern in Barienrode, einem Vorort von Hildesheim, stolze Besitzer einer Doppelhaushälfte werden. Micha und sein Saxophon finden Asyl im Keller. Dort ist Vaters Sammlung seltener Kornbrände eingelagert, und es gibt eine kleine Sauna, die sich wegen der Holzverschalung prima als Übungsraum eignet. Natürlich nur in ungeheiztem Zustand. Ich ziehe in den ersten Stock. Das Wohnzimmer, der bevorzugte Aufenthaltsraum der Eltern, befindet sich im Parterre, und ich bewundere heute noch, mit welcher Engelsgeduld sie das Spektakel ertragen haben. Von unten werden sie mit den exzentrischen Klängen der Free-Jazz-Bewegung beglückt, während ich mich immer rasanter und voluminöser durch die Tonleitern hangele. Frau Lehmanns akribischer Stimmaufbau trägt nämlich schnell die schönsten Früchte. Bald beherrsche ich auch schwierige Intervallsprünge wie den vertrackten Tritonus oder übermäßige Quinten und Quarten, und je besser ich verstehe, was physiologisch beim Singen passiert, desto näher rückt der Tag, an dem sich das Tor zum Reich der Musik wirklich öffnet. Da Charlotte Lehmanns Herz dem Liedgesang gehört, mache ich gleich zu Beginn die Bekanntschaft der Herren Loewe, Schubert, Schumann,

Brahms und Wolf, mit *Nöck* und *Erlkönig*, *Mondnacht*, *Parole* und *Mignon*, mit all den wunderbaren Liedern und den großen Zyklen der Romantik, die mein Sängerleben bis heute bestimmen. Von mir aus könnte es ewig so weitergehen. Tut es aber leider nicht.

In der Schule werde ich unsanft daran erinnert, dass Kunst die bitteren Realitäten bestenfalls veredeln, aber niemals verdrängen kann. Besonders hart, weil völlig unvorbereitet, trifft mich eine Geschichte, die sich im Schulchor zuträgt. Ich bin Mitglied seit der sechsten Klasse und habe immer mit Begeisterung am Notenpult gestanden. Nicht nur wegen der Musik. Der Schulchor ist anders als ein Sportplatz oder der Fetenkeller ein Ort, an dem ich das Gefühl habe, als Gleicher unter Gleichen anzutreten, wo es keine Rolle spielt, ob jemand groß oder klein, schön oder hässlich, normal oder behindert ist, was zählt, ist allein die Stimme. Das ändert sich nicht einmal während der Pubertät, als mich mit einsetzendem Bartwuchs auch der große Blues befällt.

Eines Tages höre ich zufällig, wie zwei Mädchen über eine bevorstehende Probenfreizeit reden, die Chor und Schulorchester zwei Wochen lang ins finnische Rovaniemi führen wird. Ich bin völlig aus dem Häuschen vor Glück. Zum ersten Mal kann ich ohne meine Eltern verreisen – und dann gleich bis ans Nordkap, wo die Lappen, die Indianer Europas, wohnen und ihre Rentiere unter dem Polarlicht zwischen unendlichen Wäldern und glitzernden Seen umhertreiben.

Schnurstracks eile ich zu Chorleiter Rabe, um mich nach den Einzelheiten zu erkundigen. Was man bezahlen und um wie viel Taschengeld ich meine Eltern bitten muss, ob man einen Reisepass braucht, wann es denn losgeht und so weiter und so fort. Rabe wird kreideweiß, druckst minutenlang herum, dann eröffnet er mir: »Wir fahren übermorgen, aber mit deiner Teilnahme gibt es Schwierigkeiten.«

»Warum denn?«

»Das hat mit der Versicherung zu tun«, sagt Rabe einsilbig, klemmt seine Jutetasche unter den Arm und macht sich eilends davon. Ich verstehe nur Bahnhof, merke aber, wie ein dicker Kloß meinen Hals blockiert. Verstört wende ich mich an Herrn Jörgensen, den Orchesterchef. Er ist ebenfalls platt.

»Versicherung? Blödsinn. Wir haben nur überlegt, du brauchst ein bisschen Hilfe beim Gepäck oder beim Anziehen. Rabe wollte die Sache schon vor Wochen mit deinen Eltern besprechen. Hat er sich nicht bei euch gemeldet?«

Hat er nicht. Wahrscheinlich hat er sich nicht getraut. Weitere Recherchen ergeben nämlich, dass er im Chor nachgefragt hat, wer bereit wäre, mir, falls nötig, ein wenig unter die Arme zu greifen. Aber in der versammelten halben Hundertschaft gibt es niemanden, der sich einen Krüppel ans Bein binden mag. Am wenigsten der Pädagoge Rabe. Also hat er beschlossen, das Problem zu ignorieren beziehungsweise einfach zu Hause zu lassen. Als der nette Herr Jörgensen anbietet, sich um eine Last-Minute-Lösung zu bemühen, winke ich ab. Ich fühle mich zutiefst gedemütigt. Ich weiß nur nicht, was mich mehr verletzt: die Feig- und Schuftigkeit des Luther- und Bach-Verehrers Rabe, der samt Pottschnitt, Vollbart und moralinsaurer Schmierigkeit über den Schulhof gockelt wie der Gestalt gewordene Kirchentag, aber nichts weiter ist als ein falscher Fuffziger. Oder die mangelnde Solidarität meiner Mitschüler, die mir kein Sterbenswörtchen von der Reise gesagt haben, von denen sich viele meine Freunde nennen und die obendrein wissen müssten, dass ich mit den meisten Dingen ganz gut allein klarkomme.

Von diesem Tiefschlag habe ich mich lange nicht erholt. Das Chorsingen ist mir gründlich verleidet, in der Schule verliere ich jeden Antrieb. Meine Leistungen sinken ins Bodenlose. Das ist nichts Neues. Aber dieses Mal trifft es selbst Fächer wie Deutsch, Geschichte und Musik, die ich früher ohne viel Aufwand bewältigt habe. Prompt muss ich die elfte Klasse wiederholen, was meine Motivation endgültig unter Normalnull treibt.

Das Einzige, was mich einigermaßen im Gleichgewicht hält, sind die Gesangsstunden bei Frau Lehmann und meine Familie. Vater, wie ich vom Stamm der Choleriker, reißt es zwar ab und an in einen verzweifelten Wutanfall. Aber für gewöhnlich zeichnen die Eltern die Fünfer und Sechser stoisch ab, zählen jeden Morgen vor dem Spiegel still ihre Sorgenfalten und fahnden nach geeigneten Nachhilfelehrern. Micha hingegen benimmt sich weniger wie ein Bruder, sondern wie ein guter Freund. Wir hocken ganze Nachmittage im Keller, quatschen über Gott (»seit langem verschollen, wahrscheinlich tot«) und die Erwachsenenwelt (»ein Sanierungsfall«) und hören Platten. Er leiht mir Bücher von Arno Schmidt, Camus oder Sartre und impft mir jene Portion existenzialistischen Snobismus ein, die einen pubertierenden Teenager befähigt, dem »Leviathan« (Schmidt), dem »Sein und dem Nichts« (Sartre), »dem Sinnlosen« (Camus), kurz: der Indolenz der Mitwelt erstmals bewusst und mit Würde ins Auge zu blicken.

Manchmal begleite ich ihn, wenn er mit seinen Freunden Musik macht, und sie lassen mich ein paar Chorusse singen. Oder wir gehen montags über die Brücke am Innerstewehr zur Bischofsmühle, wo die Jazzer auftreten. Der Eintritt kostet für drei Sets nur fünf Mark. Das ist in den späten siebziger Jahren der Wert von Ben Webster, Mal Waldron, Gary Bartz oder Gunter Hampel. Über dem Tresen des Clubs hängt eine Fotografie von Elvin Jones.

Der schwarze Drummer aus John Coltranes berühmtem Quartett trägt ein weißes T-Shirt und grinst über beide Backen. Wahrscheinlich weil er nicht weiß, was auf seinem T-Shirt steht. Ein Gönner des Jazzclubs, im Hauptberuf Betreiber eines Geschäftes für Malereibedarf, hat es bedrucken lassen. Die Inschrift lautete: »Mein Pinsel ist der größte.« So viel zur Political Correctness in der Hildesheimer Börde.

1977 ist aber auch das erst einmal vorbei. Micha muss im Kreiskrankenhaus Peine seinen Zivildienst antreten und zieht aus. Was folgt, ist die *Bleierne Zeit*, wie der Titel eines Films von Margarethe von Trotta die mentale Großwetterlage bündig zusammenfasst. Im Privaten genauso wie im großen Ganzen. Hier Schleyer-Mord, Rasterfahndung, Mogadischu, Stammheim – Deutscher Herbst, zwölf Monate lang, da schleppt sich Tommi Quasthoff quasi lobotomisiert dem Abitur entgegen. Die letzten beiden Schuljahre werden zum Großteil in der Undergrounddestille Hippetuk abgesessen. Das Antiestablishment süffelt eklig süßen Persico weg, flucht wider das Schweinesystem und nickt dumpf, wenn Bob Marley *I Shot the Sheriff* singt. Die Räumlichkeiten gehören dem Hildesheimer Bischof, der sie an ein stadtbekanntes Anarchistenkollektiv vermietet hat. Man sieht, ich bin nicht der Einzige, der etwas aus der Spur geraten ist. Während *Emma*, die erste Zeitschrift von Frauen für Frauen, Furore macht, fühlen sich Deutschlands Männer am Ende der Dekade ganz allgemein auf den »objektiven Faktor Subjektivität« (Rudolf zur Lippe) und postmaterialistische *Männerphantasien* (Klaus Theweleit) zurückgeworfen. Sie treiben dahin zwischen Wein, Weib und Fußballplatz und fühlen sich »unglücklich, neurotisch und allein« (Fritz Zorn, Volker Elis Pilgrim u. v. a.). Nur nicht der hannoversche

Nachwuchssozi Gerhard Schröder. Er wird 1977 zum Juso-Vorsitzenden gewählt und bedankt sich bei den Genossen mit den schönen Worten: »Ihr habt mich gewählt, ihr seid selber schuld.« Im selben Jahr kräht Johnny Rotten »Never mind the Bollocks, here's the Sex Pistols« und der Punkrock beginnt seinen Siegeszug um die Welt.

In Hildesheim bekommt man davon aber nicht viel mit. Im Hause Quasthoff schon gar nicht. Da hat man ganz andere Sorgen. Der Familienrat tagt und zerbricht sich die Köpfe über die Zukunft des Juniors. Meine Stimme hat sich inzwischen auf so hohem Niveau eingependelt, dass man die professionelle Singerei durchaus ins Auge fassen kann. Und ich möchte auch gar nichts anderes machen. Meine Eltern wälzen Bedenken. Was ist, wenn ich die Stimme verliere, beispielsweise durch einen Unfall? Womit soll ich dann meinen Lebensunterhalt bestreiten? Klassische Alternativen wie Taxifahrer oder Postbote sind mir ja verschlossen. Was ist, wenn die Leute einen behinderten Künstler tatsächlich nicht akzeptieren?

»Wie wäre es mit einem Rundfunk- oder Opernchor«, schlägt Mama vor.

»Dafür ist Tommi fast schon zu gut«, sagt Vater. Frau Lehmann ist der gleichen Meinung und empfiehlt ein Studium an der Musikhochschule Hannover. Dann könnte sie mich auch weiter unterrichten.

»Gut«, sagt Mama, »versuchen wir's.«

Ich schreibe eine Bewerbung, höre aber wochenlang nichts. Als die Immatrikulationsfrist fast abgelaufen ist, greift Vater zum Telefon. Er lässt sich mit dem Büro des Präsidenten verbinden und weder von der Sekretärin noch von Professor Jakobi persönlich abwimmeln. Zwei Tage später hockt er wieder einmal stundenlang in einem Vorzimmer, um die Talente seines Sohnes anzupreisen. Und wie immer ist das Gespräch beendet, sobald Vater meine Conterganbehinderung erwähnt. Da können auch die wärmsten Empfehlungen meiner Gesangslehrerin nichts ausrichten. Hochschulchef Jakobi erweist sich als blasierter Knochen mit den Manieren eines elbischen Junkers. Er zeigt nicht die geringste Lust, sich auf Diskussionen, geschweige denn auf ein Vorsingen einzulassen.

»Guter Mann, die deutsche Studienordnung setzt für ein Gesangsstudium zwingend die Beherrschung mindestens eines Instruments, nämlich des Klaviers, voraus ...«

»... ich habe doch schon erklärt, er ist ein Contergankind mit verstümmelten ...«

»... und wenn ich Sie richtig verstanden habe, ist Ihr Sohn dazu – warum auch immer – nicht in der Lage. Darum wird er hier nicht aufgenommen, und das sage ich Ihnen gleich, anderswo auch nicht. Auf Wiedersehen.«

Vater muss sich nicht nur wie ein dummer Junge abbügeln lassen. Als er versucht, mich bei einem Gesangsprofessor wenigstens als Hospitant unterzubringen, torpediert das Jakobi per Dienstanweisung. Er gönnt mir nicht mal den Status eines Gasthörers. Vater verbittert der Hochmut dieses Prachtexemplars von Musikfunktionär heute noch, was ich ihm nicht verdenken kann. Denn dass Jakobis dünkelhafte Pedanterie im Grunde ein Glücksfall ist, dass meine Stimme durch das intensive Privatstudium bei Frau Lehmann weit solider aufgebaut wird als im akademischen Routinebetrieb üblich und ich es nach vielen Umwegen doch noch zum erfolgreichen Berufssänger bringe, kann niemand ahnen. Damals bedeutet die Ablehnung eine mittlere Katastrophe, die Beerdigung meines Lebenstraums. Ich nehme zwar weiter Unterricht, muss mir aber einen anderen Broterwerb suchen.

Meine Wahl fällt auf die Juristerei. Das ist ein sehr praktisches Fach. Es hat keinen Numerus clausus und bietet vielfältige berufliche Perspektiven, außerdem kann man es in Hannover belegen, wo Micha inzwischen Germanistik studiert. Dass mein Bruder in derselben Stadt wohnt, beruhigt mich genauso wie meine Eltern, schließlich habe ich mich noch nie alleine durchgeschlagen, und wenn ich daran denke, was mich erwartet, wird mir schon etwas mulmig. Wie sich herausstellt, nicht ganz zu Unrecht.

Die Uni hat mir einen Platz im Studentenwohnheim zugewiesen. Es liegt im Ortsteil Kirchrode direkt neben der Medizinischen Hochschule. Mama liefert mich dort am Vorabend des Semesterbeginns mit ein paar Habseligkeiten ab. Als das Betongebirge hinter der letzten Kreiselausfahrt auftaucht, will ich gleich wieder nach Hause. Drinnen befällt mich derselbe Impuls. Nur dringlicher. Die Zimmer sind möblierte Schuhkartons, die Korridorfluchten haben kafkaeske Ausmaße, und aus der Teeküche starren zwei bleiche Grottenolme, die aussehen wie das sinistre Hotelpersonal aus *Barton Fink*, dem surrealen Alptraum-Thriller der Coen-Brüder. In den ersten Nächten habe ich den Schlüssel zweimal herumgedreht. Tagsüber wirken sie weniger bedrohlich. Da treffen die Adjektive streberhaft und stoffelig wesentlich besser. Einem der Olme begegne ich am nächsten Tag in der Bibliothek und bitte ihn, mir ein Buch aus der obersten Reihe des Regals zu reichen. Er schaut mich völlig entgeistert an und zischt: »Du siehst doch, dass ich arbeite.« Andere Kommilitonen sind auch nicht höflicher. In der Mensa bin ich fast verhungert, weil ich nicht an den Tresen heranreiche, wo man sich die Essenmarken abholen muss. Es findet sich einfach niemand, der mir behilflich ist. Nach einer Woche beschränken sich meine Sozialkontakte immer noch auf die Besuche von Micha. Während der Seminare und Vorlesungen wird mitgeschrieben und geschwiegen, es sei denn, der Dozent hat eine Frage. Anschließend verschwinden die Grottenolme in ihren Löchern und kommen erst wieder ans Licht, wenn Teutonia, Saxonia oder eine andere schlagende Verbindung zum Komasaufen ruft. Ich brauche drei Wochen, dann weiß ich, Jura ist nichts für einen musisch disponierten Menschen meines Schlages. Womit ich mir stattdessen die Brötchen verdienen soll, fällt mir leider auch nicht ein. Also studiere ich weiter. Sechs Semester lang, vier davon sogar ernsthaft. Ich besitze heute noch alle Scheine. Als ich mich exmatrikuliere, verstehen die Professoren gar nicht, warum ich aufhören will. Müssen sie auch nicht. Meine innere Uhr signalisiert, es reicht.

Ich kann auch nicht sagen, dass es drei verlorene Jahre gewesen sind. Ich habe keinen juristischen Abschluss, aber das Studium hat mir etwas viel Wertvolleres eingebracht: die Chance, mich von meinen Eltern abzunabeln. Ich war nie ein Muttersöhnchen, darauf haben die beiden auch stets großen Wert gelegt. Aber durch meine Behinderung ist zwischen uns eine fast symbiotische Beziehung entstanden, ohne die ich es niemals geschafft hätte, all die Schwierigkeiten im Annastift und in der Schulzeit zu überwinden. Dabei bleibt es nicht aus, dass man sich über Gebühr an gewisse Serviceleistungen gewöhnt. In Hannover ist plötzlich keine Mama mehr da, die mich tröstet, wenn es mir schlecht geht, oder mir einen Topf Nudeln hinstellt, sobald ich Hunger habe. Und wenn ich etwas brauche, kann ich nicht einfach nach Vater rufen, sondern muss mich selbst darum kümmern. Das ist anstrengend, stärkt aber das Selbstbewusstsein ungemein. In Hannover habe ich meine Angst vor Menschenansammlungen überwunden und mich zur Rushhour todesverachtend in den Supermarkt gestürzt, ich habe mich erstmals getraut, allein in eine Kneipe oder ins Kino zu gehen, ich bin in Jazz- und Rockclubs aufgetreten, oft zusammen mit Micha, aber immer öfter auch ohne ihn, ich habe Musiker und Künstler der unterschiedlichsten Genres kennen gelernt und dadurch meinen musikalischen Horizont entscheidend erweitert. Aber davon soll im nächsten Kapitel ausführlich die Rede sein. An dieser Stelle reicht es festzuhalten: Der kleine Quasthoff ist am Ende seiner Studienzeit ziemlich erwachsen geworden, und er hat einen Entschluss gefasst: Eines Tages wird er mit dem Singen sein Geld verdienen, komme, was da wolle.

»Dann musst du den Beruf auch ernst nehmen«, grantelt Frau Lehmann, als sie von meinen musikalischen Eskapaden Wind bekommt. Sie ist nicht gerade begeistert und liest mir gehörig die Leviten. Die Quintessenz der Standpauke lautet: »Du wirst dir damit deine Stimme ruinieren.«

In dasselbe Horn stößt Gatte Huber-Contwig. Seit der Maestro aus Chile zurück ist, bekomme ich von ihm Nachhilfestunden in Musiktheorie, Musikpsychologie und Musiksoziologie. Zum Nulltarif. Das sei nur theoretischer Kitt, der meine Gesangslektionen auf ein solides Fundament stellt, sagt er bescheiden. Und weil das so gut klappt, hat Huber-Contwig kurz darauf auch den Posten eines Korrepetitors inne, das heißt, er sitzt am Flügel und ackert sich mit mir durch die Orchesterpartituren der Opernliteratur.

Als in den achtziger Jahren die ersten Konzertangebote ins Haus kommen, bin ich also bestens präpariert und überhaupt nicht nervös. Ganz anders Mama und Vater. Bei meiner Premiere im Glashaus zu Bordenau sitzen die beiden paralysiert in einer der hinteren Reihen und warten auf meinen Auftritt wie auf ein Strafgericht. Mama ist schon den ganzen Tag übel vor lauter Aufregung. Morgens hockt sie wie ein Häufchen Elend am Küchentisch und will gar nicht mitfahren. Dicke Tränen rinnen ihr über das Gesicht.

»Mama, warum weinst du denn?«

Sie nimmt mich fest in den Arm und schluchzt: »Ach, Tommi, ich freue mich so für dich.« Aber das ist nur die halbe Wahrheit. Mama wird gepeinigt von der Vorstellung, das Publikum könnte bei meinem Anblick pfeifen oder, noch schlimmer, in hämisches Gelächter ausbrechen.

»Das hätte ich mir niemals verziehen, niemals!«, gesteht sie mir nach der Vorstellung und muss schon wieder weinen.

Dieses Mal sind es Freudentränen. Das Publikum hat zwar getuschelt und ziemlich blöd aus der Wäsche geguckt. Aber das ist kein Wunder. So etwas wie mich haben sie einfach noch nie auf der Konzertbühne stehen sehen. Einen liliputanergroßen Knirps ohne Arme, der mit roboterhaften Bewegungen vor dem Pult herumruckt, weil seine verwachsenen Beine zwischen Beinschienen klemmen, die Ritter Kuno alle Ehre gemacht hätten. Sobald ich jedoch meinen Bariton durch Carl Loewes majestätische Ballade *Prinz Eugen* rollen lasse, herrscht Ruhe im Auditorium, die schnell in Verblüffung und am Ende in helle Begeisterung umschlägt. Es ist wie mit dem Zauberer im Varieté. Keiner mag glauben, dass in dem kleinen Zylinder so viele Karnickel wohnen. Meiner Kleinheit traut eben keiner das Stimmvolumen zu.

Deshalb kommt es am Beginn meiner Laufbahn auch immer wieder zu Missverständnissen wie in Braunschweig. Kaum habe ich in Begleitung meiner Eltern den Konzertsaal betreten, segelt der Dirigent mit wehenden Frackschößen und freigelegten Zahnreihen direkt auf Vater zu.

»Mein lieber Herr Quasthoff, Sie glauben gar nicht, wie

ich mich freue, dass Sie heute bei uns den *Elias* singen.« Vater lacht.

»Nee, ich singe nicht, aber mein Sohn hier.« Der Dirigent blickt nach unten und ringt um Fassung.

»Ah, der Sohn, so, so, selbstverständlich, ehem, freut mich auch, freut mich sehr.« Im Abgehen höre ich ihn kopfschüttelnd sinnieren: »Der Chor, das große Orchester und dieser kleine Mensch, vielleicht sollten wir ein Mikrofon bereit …«

Dann kommt die Generalprobe. Kurz bevor Chor und Orchester zum ersten Mal zusammen mit der Solostimme einsetzen, fuchtelt der Dirigent aufgeregt in meine Richtung und ruft: »Fortissimo, fortissimo.«

Das kann er haben. Ich gebe weit mehr Gas, als die Partitur fordert, und lasse die Stimme röhren, als wär es kein Stück von Mendelssohn, sondern Wagners Walküre, der Gottvater Wotan mal wieder zeigt, wo Thors Hammer hängt. Vor Schreck fällt dem guten Mann der Taktstock aus der Hand.

»Recht so?«, frage ich. Er nickt stumm und hat sich nie wieder in meinen Gesangspart gemischt.

Kurz darauf soll ich im Bückeburger Schloss Mendelssohns *Paulus* singen. Der Orchesterleiter, ein Kantor, hat an meiner Gestalt nichts auszusetzen. Dafür kann er das Stück nicht dirigieren. Er stochert orientierungslos in der Luft herum, verschleppt die Tempi, unterbricht, sucht in den Noten, zählt falsch an, stochert, schleppt und unterbricht wieder.

Gott sei Dank ist es nur die Generalprobe, andererseits dauert sie nun schon neun Stunden. Damit wir am Tag der Aufführung rechtzeitig nach Hause kommen, beschließt das Ensemble, den sehr dicken Mann einfach zu ignorieren und *Paulus* per Autopilot auf Kurs zu halten.

Das geht auch gut, bis ihm – sei es seiner groben Motorik geschuldet oder einer überreichen Brotzeit – die Hosenträger reißen. Unglücklicherweise haben sie nicht nur die Beinkleider, sondern auch die Restwürde des Maestros zusammengehalten. Nun steht er da, mit der linken Hand die rutschende Textilie an der Freilegung peinlicher Körperregionen hindernd, während seine Rechte bemüht ist, gleichzeitig die musikalische Ordnung aufrecht- und seine Gesichtzüge vom Entgleisen abzuhalten. Ein Bild des Jammers, umbrandet von tosendem Gelächter.

So geht es jahrelang über Land durch Kirchen, Schulaulen und Gemeindesäle, und ich will nicht verhehlen, dass man dabei oft genug selbst eine komische Figur gemacht hat. Beispiele gefällig? Kein Problem: In Springe den Text vergessen, in Wolfenbüttel die Noten, in Clausthal-Zellerfeld zu spät gekommen und in Stade gar nicht angekommen, stattdessen hinter Hamburg falsch abgebogen und in Brake vor einer verschlossenen Kirche im eiskalten Wind gestanden, Grippe bekommen und deshalb in Oldenburg absagen müssen. Solche Geschichten kann jeder Musiker erzählen. Aber peu à peu werden die Hallen größer und die Gagen höher, in den Garderoben funktioniert die Heizung, und meine Stimme entwickelt sich zu einem geschmeidigen Bariton, der auch vor tieferen Tenorlagen oder dem Bassregister nicht kapituliert.

Frau Lehmann registriert es mit Genugtuung und findet, es wäre an der Zeit, mich bei Gelegenheit einmal mit der Konkurrenz zu messen. 1984 ist es so weit. Mein Name prangt beim alljährlichen Wettbewerb des »Vereins deutscher Musikerzieher und konzertierender Künstler« (VDMK) auf der Startliste. Ich singe eine Mozart-Arie und bekomme den Walter-Kaminski-Gedächtnis-Preis »in

Höhe« des ersten Preises. Aber Frau Lehmann ist nicht zufrieden. Sie ist wütend.

»Von wegen Kaminski. Du hast den ersten Preis verdient und hättest ihn auch bekommen, wenn du eingeschriebener Musikstudent wärst.«

Mir sind intrigante Musikpädagogen und ihre subtilen Machtspielchen herzlich egal. Mit stolzgeschwellter Brust posiere ich für die Fotografen. Nachdenklich werde ich erst, als ich zwei Jahre später nochmals teilnehme. Obwohl ich nach Meinung aller Juroren der Beste bin, bekomme ich nur einen zweiten Preis, der erste wird gar nicht vergeben.

»Wo gibt's denn so was«, maule ich.

Diesmal lächelt Frau Lehmann und sagt: »Das ist normal. Freu dich einfach, du hast ja gewonnen.«

Mache ich auch. Trotzdem wird mir das Wettbewerbswesen ein ewiges Rätsel bleiben. Als ich 1987 beim Mozart-Preis-Singen in Würzburg antrete, darf ich mich dann tatsächlich Erster Preisträger nennen. Dafür gibt es hier keinen zweiten Platz, aber mehrere dritte. Sag ich doch: meschugge.

Leider kann ich mir für die schönen Urkunden gar nichts und für das Preisgeld nur sehr wenig kaufen. Da auch Sieger essen müssen, entschließe ich mich, eine Banklehre bei der Kreissparkasse Hildesheim anzufangen. Der Direktor kennt meinen Vater, ist ein Klassik-Fan und hat mir den Job angeboten. Man behandelt mich dort sehr zuvorkommend. Nach der Prüfung, die ich mit Ach und Krach bestehe, lande ich in der Werbeabteilung, wo alle sitzen, die von Finanzen wenig, aber vom Sprücheklopfen eine Menge verstehen. Was nicht heißt, dass in dem fidelen Haufen keine großen Karrieren reifen können. Herbert Schmalstieg beispielsweise hat in der Werbeabteilung der Hannoverschen Kreissparkasse angefangen und die dort reichlich anfallende Freizeit in die Politik investiert. Der Sozialdemokrat ist mittlerweile nicht nur Oberbürgermeister der Leinestadt, sondern darf sich dienstältestes Stadtoberhaupt der Weltgeschichte nennen. Ein wahrer Leuchtturm seiner Zunft.

Beim NDR verdiene ich mir ein kleines Zubrot. Den Kontakt stellt ein Kameramann her, den ich im Leine-Domizil, Hannovers legendärem Musikclub, kennen lerne. Ich bin dort anlässlich des berüchtigten »Spontanmukkens« aufgetreten, einer Art Session, deren höherer Sinn darin liegt, dass die Platzhirsche der Szene dem Nachwuchs zeigen, was eine Harke ist. Weshalb sich die Darbietungen häufig in virtuoser Daddelei erschöpfen. Ich habe Glück und stehe mit einer tollen Soulband auf der Bühne.

In der Pause spricht mich der NDR-Mann an: »Gute Stimme. Hast du es mal mit Off-Sprechen versucht?«

»Nö, ich weiß gar nicht, was das ist.«

»Das lernst du schnell, gib mir mal deine Telefonnummer.«

Eine Woche später sitze ich am Rudolf-von-Bennigsen-Ufer in einem kleinen Studio des Funkhauses und lese einen Probetext.

»Gekauft«, sagt Chefsprecher Achim Gertz. »Willkommen im Team.«

Ich werde anfangs nach Stunden bezahlt, später erhalte ich einen Vertrag über eine halbe Stelle und kann in der Sparkasse kündigen. Wir arbeiten mit zehn Kollegen rund um die Uhr für alle Redaktionen. Der Job macht Spaß, ist abwechslungsreich, und es gibt jede Menge zu tun. Ganz nebenbei füllt man auch die Lücken in der Allgemeinbildung auf. Ich spreche wissenschaftliche Texte, lese Gedichte und Geschichten von Brecht bis Zuckmayer. Ich darf sogar Musiksendungen moderieren und – einsamer Höhepunkt meiner Rundfunklaufbahn – neben Will Quadflieg und Hans Paetsch in Hörspielen mitspielen.

Dann kommt der Tag, an dem ich meine erste Nachrichtensendung zu lesen habe. Es wird ein schwarzer Tag. Schuld ist die letzte Meldung vor dem Wetterbericht. Es geht um einen Unfall. Der Sachverhalt ist hochkomplex und von Redakteur Hellmann mit akribischer Detailfreude niedergelegt worden. Ein Lastwagenfahrer hat eine vierundachtzigjährige Frau überfahren. Nicht einmal, sondern dreimal. Das heißt, er hat sie einmal überrollt, dann hat er gebremst, weil er dachte, halt, da war doch was. Aber anstatt nachzusehen, setzt er zurück und malträtiert die arme Frau zum zweiten Mal. Wäre der Dummkopf diesmal ausgestiegen, hätte man das Schlimmste noch verhüten können. Das tut er aber nicht, sondern schaut nur aus dem Fenster. Da das Unfallopfer zu allem Unglück im toten Winkel liegt, kurbelt er das Fenster seelenruhig wieder hoch, gibt Gas und der Sache damit die finale Wendung, indem er sein vierachsiges Gespann zum dritten Mal, nun aber in ganzer Länge, über die Frau hinwegbrummen lässt. Das ist natürlich eine sehr traurige Geschichte. Und ich habe nie verstanden, warum den Redakteur Hellmann, der mit mir im Studio sitzt, ausgerechnet jetzt ein irrer Lachanfall heimsucht. Tatsache ist, er kann die Attacke einfach nicht unterdrücken, er kann gar nicht mehr aufhören zu lachen. Und das hat eine höchst ansteckende Wirkung. Die Inkubationszeit ist kurz. Noch vor dem Wetterbericht kann ich ebenfalls nicht mehr an mich halten und sacke prustend zusammen. Stöhnend entringt sich mir das Unwort »Scheiße«.

Man hört es laut und deutlich von Helmstedt bis Osnabrück, von Flensburg bis Holzminden. Dafür erteilt mir Achim Gertz zu Recht die erste strenge Rüge. Die erste offizielle Abmahnung folgt am nächsten Tag. Hellmann und ich haben wieder gemeinsam Dienst in der Morgensendung. Als Hellmann eine Meldung über Kanzler Helmut Kohl verliest, reitet mich der Racheteufel. Am Ende knödele ich, die Stimme Kohls imitierend: »Stimmt ja überhaupt nich'.« Darauf brüllt nicht nur Hellmann, sondern auch die gesamte Technik vor Lachen – und wahrscheinlich wieder halb Norddeutschland. Immerhin kassierte Hellman diesmal ebenfalls einen Tadel.

Ich habe mich danach kräftig am Riemen gerissen und in den nächsten Jahren lediglich handelsübliche Versprecher wie »In Haiti wurde der Militärpunsch niedergeschlagen« oder »Morgen ist im Westen mit leichter Bevölkerungszunahme zu rechnen« produziert.

Da ich im Funkhaus nur eine halbe Stelle bekleide, habe ich die Möglichkeit, das Gros meiner Energie auf den Gesang zu fokussieren. Nach einer Unterrichtsstunde im Februar 1988 bestätigt mir Frau Lehmann, dass sich die Mühe lohnt. Sie klappt den Klavierdeckel zu, dreht sich auf dem Hocker, bis sie mir ins Gesicht sehen kann, und strahlt mich an.

»Hättest du Lust, im September am ARD-Wettbewerb teilzunehmen?«

Ich bin sprachlos. Der »Internationale Musikwettbewerb der Rundfunkanstalten der Bundesrepublik Deutschland« ist weltweit eines der bedeutendsten Foren für junge Musiker. Für Nachwuchssänger sogar das Maß aller Dinge. In der Satzung heißt es drohend: »Die Anforderungen sind hoch und die Preise nur für außerordentliche Leistungen gedacht.« Klar will ich hinfahren, keine Frage, aber mir fällt ein, das geht gar nicht, im Funkhaus herrscht Urlaubsstopp.

Gott sei Dank habe ich einen verständnisvollen Chef. Achim Gertz räumt den Stein souverän aus dem Weg:

»Ich nehme das auf meine Kappe, du fährst.« Ich werde ihm ewig dankbar sein und verabschiede mich mit den Worten: »Keine Sorge, ich bin in drei Tagen zurück.«

Da habe ich allerdings ein bisschen zu viel versprochen. Ich werde den armen Herrn Gertz immer wieder vertrösten müssen: »Sorry, bin in der nächsten Runde.«

Bis es so weit ist, gibt es aber noch jede Menge zu erledigen. Zum Beispiel das Anmeldeformular ausfüllen, einen Scheck mit hundert Mark Anmeldegebühr nach München schicken und – für den unwahrscheinlichen Fall, dass ich es tatsächlich in die Endrunde schaffen sollte – neue Lackschuhe kaufen und einen zweiten schwarzen Anzug machen lassen. Das Dringlichste ist die Zusammenstellung meines Wettbewerbsprogramms. In der Sparte »Konzertgesang« verlangt die Jury »achtzehn Lieder, sechs Arien aus Oratorien beziehungsweise Konzertarien oder im Konzertrepertoire gebräuchliche Arien aus vorklassischen Opern«, die jeder Teilnehmer auf Abruf auswendig parat zu haben hat. Sie sollen aus verschiedenen Stilepochen stammen und mindestens drei Sprachen umfassen. Als das geschafft ist, bespreche ich mit Frau Lehmann die Pianistenfrage. Unsere Wahl fällt auf meinen Freund Peter Müller, mit dem ich auch schon einige Konzerte gegeben habe. Und dann heißt es natürlich üben, üben, üben.

Wie es die Teilnahmebedingungen besagen, reisen wir am 4. September, zwei Tage vor Beginn des Wettbewerbes, an. Vom Hauptbahnhof geht es per Taxi Richtung Viktualienmarkt, wo uns die Organisationsleitung ein nettes kleines Hotel zugewiesen hat. Eigentlich sollten wir gleich in die Betten sinken, um für die kommenden Aufgaben gerüstet zu sein, aber Peter und ich sind aufgedreht wie Brummkreisel. Der Portier weiß Abhilfe.

»Wenns aussi kimmt, biegts glei links eini, dann biegts

rechts eini, wiada links eini, dann stehts praktisch vorm Augustiner. Da hockts euch nei.«

In dem altehrwürdigen Braukeller gönnen wir uns jeder eine Maß – das hilft. Ich schlafe traumlos durch bis acht. Nach einem kräftigen Frühstück brechen wir auf zum Funkhaus des Bayerischen Rundfunks. Im Foyer sieht es aus, als tage ein überdimensionierter internationaler Frühschoppen. 229 Kandidaten aus 31 Ländern reden und wuseln durcheinander, die Sänger nippen an Kaltgetränken, Geiger und Hornisten hocken stullenkauend neben Instrumentenkoffern, wieder andere recken vor einer Pinnwand die Hälse, an der auf langen Listen Namen und Prüfungstermine für die erste Wettbewerbsrunde verzeichnet sind. Ich singe erst am nächsten Tag, muss mich aber heute noch persönlich anmelden, sonst kann ich gleich wieder nach Hause fahren. Im Sekretariat begrüßt uns Organisationleiterin Renate Ronnefeld. Sie weist uns einen Übungsraum zu, erläutert den Weg zur Essenausgabe und wünscht uns viel Glück. Das können wir brauchen.

Um die ausgelobten 28 000 Mark Preisgeld streiten nicht weniger als 62 Vokalisten. Ich bin der Einzige, der keine reguläre Ausbildung durchlaufen hat, und werde anfangs nicht ganz ernst genommen. Weder von der zehnköpfigen Jury noch von meinen Kollegen. Ich glaube, genau das ist letztlich der Schlüssel zum Erfolg gewesen. Peter und ich sind so froh, überhaupt teilnehmen zu dürfen, dass wir, als es endlich losgeht, überhaupt keinen Druck verspüren. Die Vorkämpfe finden im großen Sendesaal des BR statt. Jeder Teilnehmer kennt die Atmosphäre in einem voll besetzten Saal. Aber dieser hier ist fast leer. Vereinzelte Zuschauer, meist Journalisten oder die Konkurrenz, verlieren sich in dem weiten Rund. Das Einzige, was man wahrnimmt, sind die Juroren, die gepanzert mit unbewegten Mienen wie eine geschlossene Phalanx aus dem Gestühl ragen. Für viele wird da schon der Gang bis zur Bühne zum Spießrutenlauf. Es sind nur fünfzig Meter, aber mit jedem Schritt legt sich ein weiterer Zentner auf die Schulterblätter, und wenn man oben ankommt, zittern nicht nur die Knie, sondern auch die Stimmbänder.

Ich habe vor meinem ersten Auftritt zwar auch ein wenig Lampenfieber, aber das ist gesund und spätestens vorbei, als Peter mich umarmt und sagt: »Egal was rauskommt, lass uns reingehen und einfach schöne Musik machen.«

Eine weitere tragende Säule für mein Selbstbewusstsein ist Frau Lehmann, die vor jeder Runde extra aus Würzburg – sie hat an der dortigen Universität einen Lehrauftrag – oder aus Hannover anreist. So kann eigentlich nichts schief gehen.

Schon nach dem ersten Durchgang merke ich, wie sich die Atmosphäre ändert. Die Sänger sind alle ausnehmend freundlich, die Presse interessiert sich für mich, und die Mitglieder der Jury lächeln mir aufmunternd zu. Frau Lehmann lächelt auch. »Die hast du schwer beeindruckt.«

Nach drei Wochen habe ich drei Runden überstanden und bin einer von sechs Kandidaten, die zur entscheidenden Orchesterprüfung im Herkulessaal antreten dürfen. Zusammen mit der koreanischen Sopranistin Kyung-Shin Park, der deutschen Altistin Ursula Kunz, der Opernsopranistin Livia Ághová aus Bratislava und den beiden Tenören Robert Swensen und Martin Rudzinski aus den USA und Polen. Ich singe die Arie *Mache dich mein Herze rein* aus der Matthäus-Passion und Mendelssohn-Bartholdys *Gott sei mir gnädig*. Wer immer da oben zuständig ist, er muss mich erhört haben.

Das Publikum klatscht sich die Finger wund, die Jury

verleiht mir den Hauptpreis im Wert von 12 000 Mark, und die Kritiker überschlagen sich vor Begeisterung. Einer bescheinigt meinem Vortrag »bedrückende Intensität«, selten sei man »einem Künstler so unerbittlich ausgeliefert«. Die *Münchner Abendzeitung* zitiert das Jury-Mitglied Miguel Lerin-Vilardell: »Der Mann ist für mich ein Genie. Er hat etwas, das man in der Musik nur sehr selten findet: Charisma.« Selbst die nüchterne *Süddeutsche Zeitung* veröffentlicht nach den beiden Abschlusskonzerten der Preisträger, die ich mit Schubert- und Mussorgski-Liedern bestreite, eine hymnische Bilanz:

»An Eindringlichkeit konnte es kein Solist mit Thomas Quasthoff aufnehmen. Sein Ernst wie sein Humor teilen sich mit, als sei Singen das Einfachste von der Welt. Zwischen Emotion, Intelligenz und vokalen Fähigkeiten gibt es keine Brüche. Hochgreifend lässt sich sagen: Seit Jessye Norman hat es im Fach Gesang keine vergleichbare Entdeckung mehr gegeben.«

Nun, das ist alles ein bisschen viel für den kleinen Provinzsänger. Er taucht mit seinem Pianisten erst einmal ab. Nur meine alte Münchner Freundin Rosi stöbert uns auf. Sie hat einfach den richtigen Mann gefragt: »Wennst aussi kimmst, glei links eini, dann biegst rechts eini, wiada links eini, dann stehst praktisch vorm Augustiner. Da hockens seit drei Toag, die Saubuam.«

Ich glaube, Peter und ich sind eine ganze Woche lang mehr oder weniger beduselt gewesen. Denn auch zu Hause steht alles Kopf. Meine Eltern sind überglücklich und spendieren dem Duo ein üppiges Mahl im Hotel Rose, dem ersten Haus am Platz. Erwin Schütterle, Konzertveranstalter, Wirt und hannoversches Original, gibt in seiner Schenke Kanapee für uns ein großes Fest, und ich habe plötzlich jede Menge neue Freunde, für die ein Gutteil des Preisgeldes in Freibier investiert werden muss.

Schlagartig nüchtern werde ich erst, als die Boulevard-Presse in Hildesheim einfällt und jeden, der mich nur mal von weitem gesehen hat, ausquetscht wie eine Fuhre Rieslingtrauben. Innerhalb von zwei Tagen entstehen all die Klischees, mit denen man bei *Bild*, *Frau im Spiegel* oder der *Neuen Post* bis heute Artikel über mich zusammenrührt. Neben der Behindertennummer (»Ein junger Mann betritt die Bühne, klein, missgestaltet …«), das Tränenbad (»unten im Publikum greifen selbst Männer verstohlen zum Taschentuch«) und Schundromanprosa über die arme Mutter (»in ihren Augen steht die Liebe eines ganzen Lebens«). Obendrein machen bald die aberwitzigsten Geschichten die Runde. Ich sei ausgebildeter Rettungsschwimmer oder trainiere für die Fahrprüfung sind noch die harmlosesten Varianten. Außerdem werde ich von Artikel zu Artikel immer kleiner, zum Schluss bin ich auf ein Meter zwanzig geschrumpft (Bildunterschrift: »Thomas Quasthoff neben Sopranistin Mechthild Bach. Er steht auf einer Kiste.«). Die *Bunte* schießt den Vogel ab. Unter der etwas legasthenischen Überschrift »Contergan, Fall 1600: Singt sich zur Weltspitze hoch« resümiert ein Anonymus: Er singt, »als ob Gott einen Betriebsunfall wieder gutmachen wollte«.

Doch solche Lästerlichkeiten lässt der Herr nicht ungestraft. Als ich im November wieder nach München fahre, um mit Peter im Herkulessaal die *Winterreise* aufzuführen, gibt es die ersten Dämpfer für das frisch gebackene Top-Genie. Die *tz* zieht zwar noch Vergleiche mit den Größen Hans Hotter und Heinrich Schlusnus, dem bedeutenden Liedersänger der zwanziger und dreißiger Jahre, doch in der *Abendzeitung* wird das Fehlen »jeglicher Dramatik« vermerkt. Einen schmerzhaften Uppercut landet Joachim Kaiser, der verehrte Kritikerpapst von der *Süddeutschen*. »Ihm fehlen Ausdruckskraft, Passion, Wildheit«, vor allem mangele es an »Gestaltungskraft«. Immerhin schreibt er am Schluss: »Quasthoff mogelt nicht. Er singt angenehm unprätentiös, bescheiden. Wo ihm nichts einfällt, wo er nichts Besonderes fühlt, da macht er auch nichts. Mit fremden Expressionsfedern will er sich nicht schmücken. Er singt offen und ehrlich.«

Natürlich hat mich das im ersten Moment ein wenig geärgert. Dann habe ich mir gedacht: Gestern war ich eine Probe des Herrn, heute bringt mich der große Kaiser wieder auf Normalmaß. Darauf lässt sich doch aufbauen.

Ich brauche nur Musik, Musik, Musik

»Fremd bin ich eingezogen, / fremd zieh ich wieder aus«, murmelt der junge Mann und stiehlt sich aus dem Haus davon in die kalte Nacht. »Das Mädchen sprach von Liebe, / die Mutter gar von Eh', / nun ist die Welt so trübe, / der Weg gehüllt in Schnee.« Zügige Achtel geben das Marschtempo vor, die Tonart schwebt drei Strophen lang in Moll und kippt nur einmal kurz ins Dur, wenn dem Enttäuschten das Bild der Verflossenen aufscheint: »Will dich im Traum nicht stören, / wär schad um deine Ruh, / sollst meinen Tritt nicht hören, / sacht, sacht die Türe zu! / Schreib im Vorübergehen / ans Tor dir: gute Nacht, / damit du mögest sehen, / an dich hab ich gedacht.« Am Ende des Liedes wird der letzte Vers in Moll wiederholt und der Kragen hochgeschlagen. Denn fürderhin bläst dem Jüngling ein eisiger Wind ins Gesicht, die Tränen gefrieren auf seiner Wange, während seine Schritte ziellos über den frostigen Boden knirschen. Die Liebe ist wie die Blumen am Wegesrand zu trauriger Erinnerung erstarrt.

An einem Herbsttag des Jahres 1827 lässt Franz Schubert seinen Freunden bestellen: »Komme heute zu Schober. Ich werde euch einen Zyklus schauerlicher Lieder vorsingen. Ich bin begierig zu sehen, was ihr dazu sagt. Sie haben mich mehr angegriffen, als dieses je bei anderen Liedern der Fall war.«

Als alle versammelt sind, setzt sich der Komponist ans Klavier und singt »mit bewegter Stimme die ganze *Winterreise* durch«, wie Joseph von Spaun berichtet. Der vierundzwanzigteilige Zyklus basiert auf »Gedichten aus den hinterlassenen Papieren eines reisenden Waldhornisten«. Verfasser ist der Dessauer Bibliothekar und Hofrat Wilhelm Müller, wie Schubert und Büchner einer der vielen Frühvollendeten dieser Epoche. Müller stammt aus ärmlichen Verhältnissen, studiert Sprachwissenschaften in Berlin und meldet sich 1813 freiwillig zur preußischen Infanterie, um Napoleon aufs Haupt zu schlagen. Danach macht er sich im Kreise der Romantiker um Ludwig Tieck, Achim von Arnim und Baron de la Motte Fouqué schnell einen Namen als freiheitsbewegter Lyriker, dessen Talent selbst Heinrich Heine beeindruckt. Zurück in Dessau, korrespondiert er mit Goethe, Ludwig Uhland, Justinius Kerner und Carl Maria von Weber. Einmal rettet er den Dichter Friedrich Rückert vor dem Ertrinken. Als Müller 1827, ein Jahr vor Schubert, stirbt, ist er gerade dreiunddreißig und hinterlässt neben fünf Bänden Lyrik zahlreiche Erzählungen, Essays und Kritiken, eine Übersetzung von Marlowes *Doktor Faustus* und eine zehnbändige *Bibliothek Deutscher Dichter des 17. Jahrhunderts.* Eine heute kaum mehr vorstellbare Leistung. Vier Jahre zuvor hat Schubert schon einmal einen seiner Zyklen – *Die schöne Müllerin* – vertont. Die Sujets der beiden Werke sind wesensverwandt. Sie ranken sich um den in der Romantik oft und gern vorgeführten Typus des einsamen Wanderers, der – unverstanden von den Frauen, der Familie, am besten von der ganzen Gesellschaft – seine Gefühlswelt in der Natur gespiegelt findet. Ist es in der *Schönen Müllerin* ein heftig sprudelnder Bach, der den Burschen einer hübschen Mühlenerbin zuführt, seine Liebesschwüre, später seine finsteren Klagen untermalt, um den Verschmähten schließlich in den Selbstmord zu treiben, bildet in der *Winterreise* eine frostklirrende Ödnis die Kulisse für das verharschte Innenleben des Protagonisten. Der Unterschied liegt zum einen in der Erzählstruktur der Vorlagen, zum anderen in Schuberts kompositorischem Zugriff auf Müllers elegante, mit sanfter Ironie getränkte Verse. Die *Winterreise* entbehrt wirklicher Handlung und entwickelt den Sog eines inneren Monologs (obwohl der offiziell erst achtzig Jahre später von Hugo von Hofmannsthal erfunden wird), *Die schöne Müllerin* hat einen novellenartigen Aufbau. Überwiegen hier noch Strophenlieder und die anrührend schlichte Melodik des Volksliedes, besticht die *Winterreise* durch offene Liedformen und eine tief verzweifelte, geradezu modern anmutende Radikalität des Ausdrucks, die das musikalische Material weit über die Grenze des damals Vorstellbaren ausreizt.

Kein Wunder, dass Schuberts Freunde nach der Welturaufführung eher betreten dreinblicken.

»Schober sagte, es habe ihm nur ein Lied, *Der Lindenbaum*, gefallen. Schubert sprach hierauf nur: ›Mir gefallen diese Lieder mehr als alle, und sie werden euch auch noch gefallen‹« (Joseph von Spaun). Er sollte Recht behalten, die *Winterreise* gilt heute unbestritten als Opus magnum der Gattung Kunstlied. Darum lässt sich an diesem Werk besonders anschaulich demonstrieren, wie diffizil es sein kann, einen Liederzyklus angemessen aufzuführen. Jedes der Stücke gleicht einer meisterhaft gearbeiteten, in sich geschlossenen Miniatur. Es verbinden sie weder Leitmotive noch Zwischenspiele, auch ein harmonisches Schema wird man vergeblich suchen. Andererseits ergibt nur eines der Lieder, nämlich *Der Lindenbaum*, aus dem Zusammenhang gerissen wirklich einen Sinn. Die Klammer des Ganzen bildet allein die tragische Grundierung, die sich in unterschwelligen Tonartenbeziehungen, rhythmischen Äquivalenzen und subtilen Themenkorrespondenzen niederschlägt.

Aber welcher Nuancenreichtum findet sich auf Schuberts düsterer Palette, welche Achterbahnfahrt der Empfindungen muss der Sänger bewältigen:

Da ist die ironische Bissigkeit der *Wetterfahne* und die geballte Verzweiflung der *Gefrorenen Tränen*; auf rumorende, zur *Erstarrung* gerinnende Leidenschaft folgt das raffinierte Idyll des *Lindenbaumes*, hinter dessen Verheißung (»hier findest du deine Ruh«) Thomas Mann den Modergeruch des Grabes witterte; da ist der sehnsüchtige *Rückblick*, der in die feierliche Introspektion des Irrlichts mündet; das Lied vom *Greisen Kopf* steht spröde vor dem naturalistisch ausgeleuchteten Emotionskarussell der *Krähe*; die impressionistische Tonmalerei in der *Letzten Hoffnung* leitet das somnabule *Im Dorfe* ein; das Wüten des *Stürmischen Morgens* verebbt in der tänzerisch-spöttischen *Täuschung*. *Der Wegweiser* ist ein Musterexemplar wechselnder Dynamik mit einem Schluss, welcher nach schwellendem Terzenanstieg in sieben einzelnen Noten verhallt und so das Todesmotiv endgültig etabliert: »Einen Weiser seh ich stehn / unverrückt vor meinem Blick; / eine Straße muss ich gehen / die noch keiner ging zurück.« Der unmittelbar folgende Abstecher zum Friedhof, zum kühlen *Wirtshaus*, gleicht melodisch und formal einem gregorianischen Requiem. »Sind denn in diesem Hause / die Kammern all besetzt?«, hört man den Jüngling seufzen. Und weil das so ist, kratzt er (»weiter, nur weiter, mein treuer Wanderstab«) einen Rest *Mut* zusammen, leistet sich ein letztes blasphemisches Aufbäumen (»Will kein Gott auf Erden sein / sind wir selber Götter«), ehe er bestrahlt von mysteriösen *Nebensonnen* in den Fängen des *Leiermannes* landet.

Über diesen derangierten Musikus (»Barfuß auf dem Eise / wankt er hin und her«), den Schubert mit manisch drehorgelnden Zweitaktphrasen einführt, ist viel spekuliert worden. Wird uns ein romantischer Topos wie der einsame Wanderer präsentiert? Handelt es sich um eine Geistererscheinung? Tritt das Alter Ego des Komponisten auf, der hier seine desolate finanzielle und berufliche Situation ironisiert (»und sein kleiner Teller / bleibt für immer leer«)? Andere imaginieren in der einzig greifbaren Figur des Zyklus Gevatter Tod (»Keiner mag ihn hören, / keiner sieht ihn an«), wieder anderen ist der *Leiermann* Beleg für Schuberts illusionslose Analyse der postnapoleonischen Restaurationszeit, Nachhall »jenes fatalen Erkennens einer miserablen Wirklichkeit«, das er seinem Bruder Ferdinand 1824 per Post offenbart. Sei es, wie es wolle. Der Quintenbass schleppt eine trostlos redundante, auf den Wechsel von Tonika und Dominante reduzierte Harmonik über die Ziellinie, darüber verhallt die Gesangslinie im Nichts (»Wunderlicher Alter / soll ich mit dir gehen? / Willst du zu meinen Liedern / deine Leier drehn?«).

Die *Winterreise* war das erste Großwerk, das ich mir mit Frau Lehmann erarbeitet habe. Ich singe sie auch, als ich 1999, begleitet von Charles Spencer, mein Lied-Debüt im New Yorker Lincoln Center gebe, und sie wird mich bis an das Ende meiner Sängerkarriere begleiten. Wie oft ich das Stück schon gesungen habe? Ich kann es nicht sagen. Aber eins weiß ich genau: Man ist nie fertig damit. Man entdeckt immer wieder neue Schattierungen, ahnt Zusammenhänge und -klänge, harmonische Varianten, die erprobt sein wollen, für gut befunden oder beim nächsten Mal verworfen werden können. Es lassen sich – auch wenn das die Kritik oft nicht wahrhaben will – verschiedene durchaus schlüssige Interpretationen denken, einen gültigen Kanon gibt es nicht.

Der Nachwelt lässt Schubert ausrichten, man möge die *Winterreise* bitte »streng im Zeitmaß, ohne heftigen Ausdruck im Vortrag, lyrisch und nicht dramatisch« vortragen. Daran habe ich mich damals im Münchner Herkulessaal eisern gehalten und, wie berichtet, herbe Kritik einstecken müssen. Vielleicht hätte ich, statt tagaus, tagein Partituren zu studieren, mehr Fachlektüre wälzen sollen. Schließlich mangelt es nicht an Musikwissenschaftlern, die akribisch ausführen, wie man es besser macht. Ihre Schriften haben so schöne Titel wie: *Schuberts Lieder als Gesangproblem, Prinzipien des Schubertliedes, Franz Schubert oder die Melodie, Les Lieder de Franz Schubert, Auf den Spuren der Schubert-Lieder, Franz Schubert et le Lied, Das Schubertlied und seine Sänger, Schuberts's Song Technique* oder *Musikalischer Bau und Sprachvertonung in Schuberts Liedern.*

Sein berühmtester und auch von mir hoch geschätzter Interpret Dietrich Fischer-Dieskau hat selbst mindestens einen Meter Deutungsliteratur verfasst. Er spricht im Bezug auf die *Winterreise* von »Selbstentäußerung des Komponisten«, diagnostiziert »Züge der Empfindsamkeit, die das Pathologische streifen«, auch von »Wahnsinn« ist die Rede und von Schuberts »offensichtlicher Tendenz zur Selbstvernichtung« *(Franz Schubert und seine Lieder).*

Angesichts dieser mentalen Bankrotterklärung habe ich mich in meinen Anfangsjahren oft bänglich gefragt: Muss man, darf man das alles mitsingen? Heute frage ich mich: Stimmt das überhaupt? Verbürgt ist so viel: Schubert war ein überspannter Kauz und Schwarmgeist, und er trank oft viel zu viel. So kann man allerdings auch Hugo Wolf, E. T. A. Hoffmann oder Beethoven, eigentlich das Gros der dichtenden und notenschreibenden Zunft charakterisieren. Darüber hinaus kränkelte er oft und litt unter Depressionen. Aber ist das nicht normal, wenn einer zeitlebens in feuchten, zugigen Kammern hausen muss, für drei arbeitet und trotzdem nie Geld in der Tasche hat? Für den Pianisten und Kritiker Charles Rosen spielen derlei Psychologismen keine Rolle. Hauptsache, die *Winterreise* wird von einem Tenor gesungen. Denn nur »mit einem Tenor«, dekretiert Rosen in seiner *Musik der Romantik*, »kann der Zyklus seine volle Wirkung entfalten«. Selbst ein so wunderbarer lyrischer Bariton wie Hermann Prey setzte das Werk nicht ohne Gewissensbisse auf den Programmzettel, weil Schubert ursprünglich eine »hohe bis zum Gis und A reichende« Männerstimme vorschwebte. Erst der ebenso schuftige wie geizige Verleger Tobias Haslinger ließ die *Winterreise*-Lieder, von denen er im Übrigen nicht eines leiden mochte, der besseren Vermarktung halber heruntertransponieren. Prey tröstete sich schließlich damit, dass die Instrumente zu Schuberts Zeiten tiefer gestimmt waren als heute, und kam zu dem Schluss, »dass der Sänger diejenige Tonart wählen darf und soll, die seiner Stimme am meisten entgegenkommt«.

Da mag man nicht widersprechen. Ob man sich seiner Exegese des *Lindenbaumes* anschließt – nachzulesen in Preys Memoiren *Premierenfieber* –, ist eine andere Sache. Prey hat herausgefunden, das Lied sei »barförmig innerhalb der Barförmigkeit«, also »ein Beispiel für den so genannten potenzierten Reprisenbar«. Bei dieser Kompositionstechnik – sie basiert auf dem Großlai, einer aus dem Mittelalter überlieferten Form der liedhaften Verserzählung – werden verschiedene Formen, meist zwei melodiengleiche Abschnitte plus ein Abgesang wie Bergwerksstollen ineinander geschachtelt. Statt also einfach zu singen: »Am Brunnen vor dem Tore / da steht ein Lindenbaum; / ich träumt' in seinem Schatten / so manchen süßen Traum …«, hat sich der Sänger dieses Musterbeispiel liedhafter Innigkeit so vorzustellen:

»Innerhalb des übergeordneten Reprisenbars B1 + B2 + C + B1 (= Großstollen + Großstollen + großer Abgesang + Reprisenstollen) bildet
- das erste (barförmige) Gesätz b1 + b1 + c1 (= Kleinstollen + Kleinstollen + kleiner Abgesang) den ersten Großstollen B1
- das zweite (gleichfalls barförmige) Gesätz b2 + b2 + c1 den zweiten Großstollen B2
- die Imitationsgruppe d1 + d2 den großen Abgesang C, und schließlich
- das letzte (wiederum barförmige) Gesätz b1 + b1 + c1 den Reprisenstollen B1.«

Albert Einstein hätte daran sicherlich seine Freude gehabt, und ich habe das durchaus mit Interesse gelesen. In der Theorie kann man die so genannten Groß- und Reprisenstollen tatsächlich anhand der sechs Strophen verorten. Das triolische das Rauschen der Zweige und Blätter imitierende Vorspiel und die folgende Gesangsmelodie tauchen jeweils dreimal auf. Beim zweiten Mal wird die Regelmäßigkeit der Singstimme aber schon durch die wirbelnden Sechzehntel der Begleitung zerpflückt (»die kalten Winde bliesen«), ehe sich anlässlich der letzten Wiederholung Singstimme und Klaviereinleitung vereinen und die schöne Symmetrie endgültig durcheinander bringen. Es ist eben alles relativ. Auch im Reich der Musik.

Und was habe ich daraus gelernt? Ein Sänger muss seine Hausaufgaben machen, Sekundärliteratur heranziehen, Interpretationen vergleichen, Geschichte und Kontext eines Werkes studieren, aber sobald er eine Bühne betritt, sollte er sich seinen ganz persönlichen Reim auf die musikalische Vorlage gemacht haben.

Denn auch die bedeutendsten Köpfe sind nicht davor gefeit, groben Unfug in die Welt zu setzen, gerade wenn sie als Kunstrichter auftreten. Vladimir Horowitz beispielsweise ließ keine Gelegenheit aus, um an Schuberts B-Dur-Klaviersonate herumzukritteln. Sie war ihm schlicht zu einfach. Der ebenso begnadete wie exzentrische Glenn Gould beschimpfte Schubert, Schumann und Chopin als »Exhibitionisten«, nur weil sie sich nicht der strengen Zucht des Kontrapunktes unterwarfen. Robert Schumann wiederum, der Schuberts Sinfonien über alles liebte, ätzte über den Liedkomponisten: »Er hätte nach und nach wohl die ganze deutsche Literatur in Musik gesetzt, ... wo er hinfühlte, quoll Musik hervor.« Ähnlich rüde hat der Amateurpianist Friedrich Nietzsche die halbe Musikwelt angerempelt. Schumann war in seinen Augen allerdings gar nicht satisfaktionsfähig. Der Schöpfer des herrlichen Klavierkonzertes a-Moll op. 54 und der *Dichterliebe* sei nämlich im Gegensatz zu Mozart oder Wagner »kein europäisches Ereignis« gewesen.

Fehleinschätzungen dieser Art veranlassten Eckhard Henscheid, dann doch einmal grundsätzlich zu werden: »Ja, er war schon ein fast rundum inkompetenter Schmarrer, der Nietzsche, und wenn einer, der so wenig von beidem verstand, zum bekümmerungsvollen Großmeister von Literatur- und Musikkritik sich aufplusterte, dann heischt das retrospektiv schon fast wieder Bewunderung.« So weit der Autor der *Trilogie des laufenden Schwachsinns*. Henscheids ebenso komische wie geistreiche Invektiven zur klassischen Musik sind unter dem Titel *Musikplaudertasche* beziehungsweise ... *über Oper. Verdi ist der Mozart Wagners* erschienen und gehören in jede Hausbibliothek.

Ich habe die *Winterreise* 1998 begleitet von Charles Spencer für BMG eingesungen. Wenn ich die Aufnahme heute analysiere und überlege, ob sich meine Interpretation im

Lauf der Zeit grundlegend verändert hat, muss ich sagen: nein. Trotzdem klingt der Zyklus immer wieder anders und mit den Jahren, wie ich hoffe, immer gehaltvoller. Weil man ein bisschen reifer und weiser geworden ist, weil man sein Portefeuille um schöne und weniger schöne Erfahrungen bereichert hat, weil ein paar alte Kratzer vernarbt sind, andere immer noch schmerzen. Zum wechselnden Charakter eines Liederabends trägt auch die Persönlichkeit und Tagesform des Pianisten bei, nicht zu vergessen die eigene Gemütsverfassung – wie ich geschlafen und was ich geträumt habe, ob ich frisch verliebt oder gerade verlassen worden bin, mein Abendbrot mit zwei oder vier Bieren hinuntergespült habe. Dann ist da noch der Saal. Ist er groß? Ist er klein? Stimmt die Akustik? Produziert er viel Hall oder wenig? Hat er einen Orchestergraben? Oder singe ich mit Tuchfühlung zum Publikum? Und was sind das für Menschen, die eine Menge Geld ausgegeben haben, um Herrn Quasthoff singen zu hören? Distinguierte Großstadtflaneure, die Kulturveranstaltungen so selbstverständlich konsumieren wie ein teures Abendessen, der treue Pro-Musica-Abonnent, dem die Musik Erbauung und gesellschaftliches Highlight ist zwischen Büroalltag, Kinderaufzucht und Sonntags-*Tatort*, oder sind es Frauen und Männer in der Diaspora, wo ein klassisches Konzert immer noch bestaunt wird wie die Autogrammstunde des Fernsehpfarrers Fliege beim örtlichen Großdiscounter? Vielleicht spielen sogar das Wetter und die Jahreszeit eine Rolle. All das erzeugt atmosphärische Schwingungen, die unbewusst einfließen in den Gesang.

Man muss sich nur bewusst machen, dass es so ist, dann lässt sich mit diesen Einflüssen wunderbar arbeiten. Einigen sehr guten und sehr berühmten Kollegen ist diese Auffassung eher suspekt. Sie sind bestrebt, jedes Mal eine zeitlos gültige, sozusagen keimfreie Version zu präsentieren. Und dagegen ist auch nichts einzuwenden, sofern der Drang zum Idealischen künstlerisch überzeugende Resultate zeitigt und nicht zur musealen Weihestunde oder – schlimmer noch – zum Kunsthandwerk gerinnt. Ich dagegen bin eher ein intuitiver Sänger. Gerade wenn ich auf Tournee bin und täglich mit demselben Programm auftrete, möchte ich nicht nur mein Publikum überraschen, sondern auch mich selbst, möchte Routine ausschließen, spontanen Einfällen Raum geben und variable Akzente setzen, weil ich eben nicht jeden Abend dasselbe fühle.

Für mich gleicht die Aufführung einer *Winterreise* dem Besuch einer vertrauten Galerie, die mit den Seelenlandschaften Caspar David Friedrichs bestückt ist. Wie Schuberts Wanderer verlieren sich Friedrichs Figuren in der unberechenbaren Natur. Den Blick in die Ewigkeit gerichtet, stehen sie vor schrundigen Eiswänden und gewaltigen Felspanoramen, oder sie verschwinden im Dickicht verschatteter Eichenwälder, während über allem ein undurchdringliches, in gespenstische Farben gehülltes Himmelsgewölbe schwebt. Man hat die Szenerien dutzende Male betrachtet, fühlt sich heute von diesem, morgen von jenem Detail besonders angerührt, aber in der Gesamtschau verschmelzen die einzelnen Bilder zu einer Chiffre für die tragisch-romantische Haltung des Künstlers zur Welt.

Dieser Haltung glaubwürdig nachzuspüren, sie ins Heutige zu übertragen, ist meiner Auffassung nach die eigentliche Aufgabe des Sängers. Sie kann gelingen, wenn er die Elemente Technik, Reflexion, Inspiration und Erfahrung im richtigen Verhältnis ausbalanciert. Wobei die Technik nicht überbewertet werden sollte. Ich halte es da mit Karl Valentin: »Wenn man es kann, ist es keine Kunst. Wenn man es nicht kann, ist es erst recht keine Kunst.« Technische Fertigkeiten dienen der Inspiration als

Sprungbrett, dürfen das Fehlen derselben aber keinesfalls überspielen oder gar die Kunst an sich ersetzen. Auf der Bühne merke ich dann immer ziemlich schnell, ob das kreative Moment der Erdenschwere zu entkommen vermag. Das Publikum auch. »Wir machen Musik, da geht euch der Hut hoch, wir machen Musik, da geht euch der Bart ab«, heißt es in einem alten Chanson. Das muss man nicht wörtlich nehmen. Aber der Sänger spürt, wenn dieser besondere Moment eintritt. Dann hat der Vortrag den richtigen Drive entwickelt, und man kann die Stimme fliegen lassen.

Es gibt natürlich auch den entgegengesetzten Fall. Der Sänger hört die präludierenden Klaviertöne, macht den Mund auf und spürt: Oha, heute wird es schwer mit der ganz großen Kunst, heute hängen drei nasse Bademäntel an meinen Stimmbändern. Dann ist guter Rat teuer. Er kann ja schlecht an die Rampe treten, ein charmantes Lächeln aufsetzen und sagen: »Sorry, liebe Leute, hat keinen Sinn, bin nicht Form. Also tschö, arrivederci, goodbye, vielleicht klappt es ein andermal.« Schließlich ist der Saal rappelvoll, das Konzert muss weitergehen. Wären wir beim Fußball, würde er einfach die Ärmel hochkrempeln, die Schienbeinschoner festzurren und sich in die Partie hineinbeißen. »Quasthoff hat die erste Halbzeit komplett verschlafen, aber nach der Pause über den Kampf ins Spiel gefunden.« Leider wird so etwas nie in der Zeitung stehen. Ein Liederabend erlaubt – im Gegensatz zum Mannschaftssport Oper – weder resolutes Vorchecking noch die gemeine Blutgrätsche. Aber ich kann eine andere verlässliche Kategorie ins Feld führen: den Sound.

Mancher Klassikfreund wird erstaunt die Augenbrauen heben. Er kennt das Wort nur aus den Testberichten der HiFi-Magazine, wo es meist in Begleitung der Adjektive »brillant«, »gewöhnungsbedürftig« oder »grausam« auftritt. Der Begriff »Sound« stammt ursprünglich aus dem Jazz und hat später in der Popmusik Karriere gemacht. Man bezeichnet damit die individuelle Klangbildung und den Stil eines Künstlers beziehungsweise einer Band. Die Protagonisten der U-Musik sind immer schon der Ansicht gewesen, dass die Art und Weise, wie man etwas tut, mindestens genauso wichtig ist wie das, was man tut. Ein Standpunkt, der mir immer eingeleuchtet hat. Ich will auch erklären, warum.

Meine Stimme besitzt neben genetisch bedingten Eigenschaften wie Umfang und Kraft eine samtige Grundierung, an der ich hart gearbeitet habe. Weil sie mir eine dezente, im Jazz würde man sagen »coole«, und zugleich höchst geschmeidige Phrasierung ermöglicht. Darum denke ich, wann immer ich ein neues Lied einstudiere, zuerst darüber nach, welche Klangfarben ich benutzen kann, um die Komposition am besten zur Geltung zu bringen, ohne meinen Gesangsstil, meinen ganz persönlichen Sound, zu verbiegen.

Jetzt wirft er auch noch mit Binsenweisheiten um sich, wird der geneigte Leser denken. Nein, tut er nicht.

Nehmen wir uns zur Anschauung Goethens *Erlkönig* vor, die Schauerballade vom bösen Geist, der dem Vater und seinem Kinde im Nacken sitzt, während die beiden »durch Nacht und Wind« dem heimatlichen Anwesen entgegengaloppieren. Erst grauset's dem Junior, dann auch dem Senior, und so reitet er »geschwind, / er hält in den Armen das ächzende Kind, / erreicht den Hof mit Mühe und Not, / in seinen Armen das Kind war tot«. Hier gilt es vier Rollen zu gestalten: den Erzähler, den Vater, das Kind und den finsteren Dämon. Viele Sänger, gerade aus dem dramatisch aufgeladenen Opernfach, werfen sich – selbstverständlich nur bildlich gesprochen – auf das Gruselstückchen wie auf ein B-Movie. Die Versuchung ist ja auch groß, etwa die von Schubert mit einer abrupten harmonischen Rückung unterlegten Einflüsterungen der Spukgestalt (»Ich liebe dich«) in Vincent-Price-Manier herauszupressen, oder die horriblen Nonen, welche die Schreie des Kindes (»mein Vater, mein Vater«) begleiten, anzugehen, als handele es sich um Amando de Ossorios Horrorschocker *Die Nacht der reitenden Leichen*.

Ein guter Liedsänger wird unabhängig von der Tagesform Manierismen dieser Art vermeiden. Er wird »cool« bleiben und es darauf anlegen, die gestalterische Vielfalt mit seinem persönlichen Sound zusammenzubinden. Er wird sich sagen: Die vier Rollen liegen sowohl bei Schubert als auch in der Carl-Loewe-Fassung von den Tonarten her dicht beisammen. Schubert lässt anfangs g-Moll und c-Moll alternieren. Die Panik des Kindes kumuliert in h-Moll und cis-Moll. Des Erlkönigs Lockungen kommen erst in schmeichelndem B-Dur daher (»du liebes Kind, komm, geh mit mir«) dann – schon nachdrücklicher – in C-Dur (»mich reizt deine schöne Gestalt«). Loewe beginnt mit g-Moll und wechselt, sobald sich Vater und Sohn die Nackenhaare sträuben, zu d- und h-Moll. Sein Erlkönig säuselt in G-Dur, das kurz vor der tödlichen Berührung (»und bist du nicht willig, so brauch ich Gewalt«) nach g-Moll kippt. Ein Bariton transponiert die Originaltonarten natürlich herunter. Ich muss also jede Einzelstimme deutlich herausarbeiten, sie aber so arrangieren, dass keine aus dem Rahmen fällt und die Ballade am Ende ein formal geschlossenes Gesamtkunstwerk ergibt. Egal, ob Loewes *Erlkönig* eher ein süffiges, quasi kolportagehaftes Gespenster-Kolorit braucht oder Schubert die alle Sinne betörende Macht der Naturgewalten betont: Falsches Pathos sollte vermieden werden, die objektivierende Distanz, der Modus Operandi stets sichtbar bleiben.

Mit dieser »Coolness« lässt sich auch ein nicht ganz so strahlender Abend zur Befriedigung aller über die Runden bringen. Sie versetzt den Sänger darüber hinaus in die Lage, Edelkitsch wie Richard Straussens *Allerseelen* (»Und lass uns wieder von der Liebe reden, wie einst im Mai«), ein Lied, das ich im Frühjahr 2004 für meine CD *Romantische Lieder* aufgenommen habe, mit Genuss und Gewinn zu interpretieren. Denn jede Art von Musik, selbst ein Stück Kitsch, kann wahre Emotionen und Erkenntnis transportieren, wenn die Stimme im richtigen Soundkleid steckt. Der Sound ist die Basis der Interpretation.

Darauf hat auch Miles Davis gesetzt, als er 1957 den Arrangeur Gil Evans bat, seinen weichen, vibratolosen Trompetenton für eine Big-Band-Aufnahme zu inszenieren. Bevor Evans eine Note schrieb, ersetzte er den traditionellen Saxophonsatz durch eine Sektion aus Flöten, Klarinetten, Waldhörnern, einem Altsaxophon und einer Tuba. So entstand ein neoromantischer, lyrisch vergeistigter Orchesterklang, der laut Evans »wie eine Wolke« über dem Beat hing. Das war ziemlich gewagt, aber der Bläsersatz umschloss Davis' Trompetensound wie ein maßgeschneiderter Handschuh. Da die Arrangements tadellos swingten und sich obendrein wie warme Semmeln verkauften, sind die *Miles Ahead*-Aufnahmen schnell zu Klassikern geworden. Davis und Evans haben ihre Zusammenarbeit dann auf zwei weiteren Alben perfektioniert. Das bekannteste ist *Sketches of Spain*, dessen Material zum Gutteil auf dem klassischen *Concerto de Aranjuez* von Joan Rodrigo basiert. Vor den Ohren des Komponisten fand die LP allerdings keine Gnade, ein Umstand, den Davis in seiner Autobiografie folgendermaßen kommentiert:

»Ich sagte zu dem Typen, der mir das erzählte, lass uns mal abwarten. Vielleicht gefällt sie ihm, wenn die dicken Schecks aus den Tantiemen bei ihm ankommen.« Von Rodrigo sind keine weiteren Beschwerden bekannt geworden.

Solche Probleme kriegt ein klassischer Sänger ja eher selten, die meisten Komponisten liegen auf dem Friedhof. Trotzdem hat mir Davis' Chuzpe imponiert, weil sie nicht nur Weltklugheit verrät, sondern auch große Souveränität im Umgang mit dem musikalischen Material. Es gibt zwar auch im Jazz Traditionen, aber keinen verbindlichen Kanon, der vorschreibt, wie man ihnen zu dienen hat. Das Einzige, was zählt, sind Kreativität, künstlerische Freiheit und persönlicher Ausdruck.

Der geniale Tenorsaxophonist Lester Young wurde buchstäblich trübsinnig, als in den späten dreißiger Jahren etliche Tenoristen versuchten, seinen Stil zu imitieren. Im Birdland, wo Young eines Abends mit Paul »Lady Q« Quinichette, einem seiner geschicktesten Kopisten, spielte, hörte er sich ein paar Chorusse an, dann ging er entnervt von der Bühne und meinte: »Ich weiß nicht mehr, ob ich spielen soll wie ich oder wie ›Lady Q‹, weil er so sehr spielt wie ich.«

Quinichette haben die Raubkopien keinen Ruhm gebracht. Lester Young, Louis Armstrong, Count Basie, Duke Ellington, Coleman Hawkins, Charlie Parker, Bud Powell oder John Coltrane gelten als Meister ihres Faches, eben weil sie das Standardrepertoire auf unverwechselbare Weise interpretierten.

Die Jazzer (neben den Beatles und Soulsängern wie Stevie Wonder, Ray Charles, Aretha Franklin oder Al Green) haben meine Art zu musizieren nicht weniger beeinflusst als die bedeutenden Interpreten der klassischen Musik: Herman Prey, Fritz Wunderlich, Fischer-Dieskau,

Hans Hotter und Peter Schreier. Sie alle sind ebenfalls große Individualisten und sofort am eigenen Sound zu identifizieren.

Die erste Jazzplatte schenkt mir Patenonkel Bertold zur Konfirmation. *Louis Armstrong Memorial* ist ein Doppelalbum und enthält Aufnahmen der legendären Hot Five und Hot Seven, mit dem Klarinettisten Johnny Dodds, dem Posaunisten Kid Ory, Drummer Peanuts Hacko und Earl »Father« Hines am Klavier. Mein Bruder war da schon weiter. Er sammelte die Hardbopper Art Blakey, Horace Silver und Sunny Rollins. Irgendwann schleppt er dann die ersten Free-Jazz-Platten an, was Vaters Weltbild über Jahre erschüttert. Während Michas Klassenkameraden wenigstens auf berechenbare Weise aus der Art schlagen, ihre Eltern mit Haschischkonsum, Hardrock oder der Mitgliedschaft im Kommunistischen Bund Westdeutschlands erschrecken, trinkt sein Ältester Bier, schreibt merkwürdige Gedichte, sägt atonal auf dem Saxophon herum und gewinnt mit diesem …

»Krawall!«, hört man Vater waidwund stöhnen.

»Hänschen, mäßige dich!«, sagt Mama.

»Ich mäßige mich, ich mäßige mich seit Jahren. Trotzdem bleibt es Krawall.«

… gewinnt also mit diesem Krawall, begleitet von seinem Freund und Pianisten Achim, einen ersten Preis beim alljährlichen Musikwettbewerb des Andreanums.

»Puttchen, jetzt sind auch die Studienräte komplett verrückt geworden«, ruft Vater fassungslos, als mein Bruder ihm grinsend die Sieger-Urkunde unter die Nase hält. Immerhin kann ihn Mama überreden, einen Auftritt von Michas Combo Strange Tune Pictures in der Bischofmühle zu bemustern. Das Quintett spielt sich drei Sets lang die Finger wund. Mein alter Herr lehnt an einer Säule, saugt an seiner Pfeife und verzieht keine Miene. Als das Publikum nach Zugaben schreit, raunt er Mama ins Ohr: »Der Einzige, der bei denen arbeitet, ist der Schlagzeuger.«

Ein bisschen beeindruckt ist Vater aber doch. Jedenfalls hat er nichts dagegen, dass ich beim nächsten Konzert mit von der Partie bin. In zwei Wochen wird die Band nach Hamburg fahren, um im legendären Club Onkel Pö einen Live-Mitschnitt zu machen. Das Unternehmen steht allerdings unter keinem guten Stern. In Hamburg tobt ein Orkan, so dass niemand einen Fuß vor die Tür setzt, geschweige denn ins Onkel Pö. Der Laden ist bis auf ein Dutzend mitgereister Freunde leer, die Laune vor Konzertbeginn auf dem Gefrierpunkt. Sie bessert sich erst wieder, nachdem alle Freibiere vertilgt und die Jungs dazu übergegangen sind, ihre karge Abendgage gegen härtere Spirituosen zu tauschen. Da ist gerade mal das erste Set herum. Notgedrungen werden kompliziertere Arrangements über den Haufen geworfen, und es beginnt eine wilde Jam-Session. Ich erinnere noch, dass ich mir bei einer fünfundvierzigminütigen Version der Pharoah-Sanders-Nummer *Karma* die Lunge aus dem Hals gesungen habe. Wessen Karma dafür sorgte, dass im weiteren Verlaufe des Abends erst die Bandmaschine aus-, dann der riesige Onkel-Pö-Schriftzug über dem Eingang herunterfällt und in tausend Stücke zerspringt, ist nie geklärt worden. Die Antwort kennt wohl nur der Wind. Er wird auch wissen, wer eigentlich die Getränkerechnung bezahlt hat, die die Einnahmen der Band am Ende beträchtlich übersteigt. Wahrscheinlich niemand. Denn gegen drei Uhr morgens wirft uns der Wirt hinaus und macht dabei ein Gesicht, als wollte er sagen: »Kommt bloß nie wieder.«

Nicht weniger denkwürdig sind meine Gastspiele bei Stacy Mews und Tom Oz & The Wet, zwei Bands aus Hannover, in deren Diensten Micha ebenfalls das Saxophon bedient. Stacy Mews spielen mit zwei Schlagzeugern und einem klasse Pianisten namens Mike, der gerne trinkt, aber rein gar nichts verträgt. Es kommt schon mal vor, dass man mitten im Stück plötzlich das E-Piano vermisst, weil Mike sanft entschlummert ist. Aber der Mann ist ein Phänomen. Wenn man ihn mit einer leichten Kopfnuss weckt, weiß er sofort, wo wir sind, schüttelt einen eleganten Übergang aus dem Ärmel oder intoniert akkurat die zweite Stimme vom Refrain. Bei Tom Oz, der eigentlich Thomas Schmidt heißt, schläft niemand, obwohl die Konzerte regelmäßig an der Vier-Stunden-Marke kratzen. The Wet spielen Psychedelic-Funk, eine besonders suggestive Form schwarzer Tanzmusik. Die Auftritte gleichen tranceartigen Gottesdiensten, wie man sie aus dem tiefstem Süden der USA kennt, nur dass eben nicht einem höheren Wesen, sondern Lord Groove gehuldigt wird. Und sie sind im Gegensatz zu vielem, was heute leichthin so bezeichnet wird, tatsächlich Kult. Wenn der Funk-Preacher Schmidt ruft, setzen sich in München und Köln, Berlin und London viel beschäftigte Studiomusiker in Bewegung, um für wenig Geld und in irren Kostümen einen der raren Oz-Gigs zu absolvieren.

Höhepunkt seines Schaffens war zweifellos das Personalaufgebot für eine Show im Hamburger Westwerk. Kurz vor Beginn erscheint er mit zwölf Fotomodellen und drei Visagisten im Schlepptau. Die Damen sind außerirdisch schön, und so benehmen sie sich auch. Das heißt, sie blicken durch die Musiker hindurch, als wären es leere Kleiderständer. Herrn Schmidt kratzt das nicht. Er bugsiert den Haute-Couture-Tross mit triumphierendem Lächeln in die Garderobe.

Drinnen hört man den Kapellmeister flöten: »Nein, Kinderchen, ihr müsst euch nichts merken, seid einfach nur schön.« Der Band richtet er bündig aus: »Bitte nicht anfassen, Jungs. Die Püppchen werden tanzen.«

Spricht's und verschwindet, um sich mithilfe von einem Pfund Schminke, Patronengurt und Piratenkopftuch in Tom Oz zu verwandeln. Was er den Grazien über ihren Auftritt vorgegaukelt hat, ist allen ein Rätsel. Denn als Oz wie ein Tasmanischer Teufel aus wabernden Trockeneisschwaden zwischen die Damenriege springt und The Wet loswummern lässt, werden die eben noch so unnahbaren Models plötzlich sehr blass um die Nase. Statt sich anmutig zu bewegen, entwickeln sie Fluchtreflexe. Aber der Saal ist so voll, dass niemand die Bühne verlassen kann, ohne üble Quetschungen zu riskieren. Das hübsche Dutzend steckt in der Klemme. Unten johlt das Publikum, hinter ihnen brettert die Band Riffs im Akkord von der Bühne. Die Beautys stehen eine halbe Stunde schmollend im Soundgewitter, bis sie einsehen, dass das ziemlich bescheuert aussieht. Und bescheuert aussehen ist ja das Letzte, was Models wollen. Also fügen sie sich in ihr Schicksal und haben den Rest des Abends brav die Hüften geschwungen und dabei eine sehr gute Figur gemacht. Nach fünf frenetisch beklatschten Zugaben sind sie rechtschaffend »wet« geschwitzt. Sie sehen sogar glücklich aus und verteilen Küsschen. Mit Chanel-Geschmack. Die meisten kriegt natürlich Herr Schmidt ab. Da man so einen Abend kaum mehr toppen kann, wird Tom Oz kurz darauf begraben. Herr Schmidt wechselt in die Softwarebranche, heiratet (nein, kein Model), zeugt ein süßes Kind und ist für das Nachtleben verloren.

Ich dagegen habe Blut geleckt und ein eigenes Jazztrio zusammengestellt. Oliver Gross spielt Klavier, den Bass bedient Jürgen Attig, den alle nur Jaco nennen, nach Jaco Pastorius, dem Wunderbassisten der Jazzrock-Formation Weather Report. Da Jürgen seinem Vorbild wenig nachsteht und Oliver ebenfalls ein großartiger Musiker ist, gewinnen wir beim NDR-»Hörfest« auf Anhieb den ersten Preis. Außer einem kleinen Geldbetrag verschafft uns der Sieg eine Konzerttournee durch die norddeutschen Jazzclubs und ein paar Gigs bei größeren Festivals. Unter anderem dürfen wir im Rahmen der Hildesheimer »Jazztime« neben Miles-Davis-Schlagzeuger Tony Williams auftreten. Es interessiert sich sogar ein Schallplattenproduzent für uns. Dass er schmierig ist und fett, streng riecht, ästhetisch bedenkliche Anzüge trägt und insgesamt wirkt wie das Gestalt gewordene Unseriöse, stört uns nicht. Schließlich sind wir jung, dumm und schwerstbenebelt vom greifbar nahen Ruhm. Er braucht bloß mit dem Vertrag zu wedeln, schon haben wir unterschrieben. Leider ohne das Kleingedruckte auf der Rückseite zu lesen. Die Strafe folgt auf dem Fuße. Der Schuft schließt uns drei Tage und Nächte im Studio ein, wir müssen furchtbare Stücke einspielen und mit ansehen, wie unsere Namen auf das hässlichste Cover der Welt gedruckt werden. Als wir am Schluss das Thema Geld anschneiden, lässt satanisches Gelächter seine Speckbacken hüpfen.

»Wat für Geld. Ich kriech von euch noch 'nen Hunni für Bier, Kaffee und die Brötchen.«

Zu allem Unglück fällt das Produkt auch noch Frau Lehmann in die Hände. Wie ich schon erwähnte, hält meine Gesangslehrerin diese Art Musik für hochtoxisch und setzt das meinen Eltern nochmals detailliert auseinander. Sie sagen:

»Lieber Freund, wir leben in einem freien Land. Mach, was du willst. Nur eins muss klar sein: Wenn wir deine Stunden weiter zahlen sollen, ist erst einmal Feierabend mit dem Gejazze.« Das ist fair, führt aber, da mich das Jurastudium nicht auslastet und Konzerte im klassischen Fach noch rar gesät sind, zu schmerzlichen Entzugserscheinungen. Lange muss ich nicht leiden. Denn nun ruft die Kunst – schrill und laut wie mein Telefon. Micha ist dran. Er erzählt mir etwas von »Crossover-Art«, »audiovisuellen Medien«, »Schiedsrichtern«, »dem Wunder von Bern«, »Francis Ford Coppola« und irgendeinem Museum. Ich verstehe nur Bahnhof und sage ihm das auch.

»Macht nichts. Ist alles ein großer Spaß. Bist du dabei?« Wer könnte da nein sagen? Ich nicht.

Als wir später in Brüderchens Wohnung zusammensitzen, drückt mir Andi »Arbeit« Hahn, seines Zeichens prämierter Experimentalfilmer, Träger eines halben Hamburger Literaturpreises und Michas WG-Genosse, ein Exposé in die Hand. Es trägt den Titel *Kafka oder Tibor (Apoelyps Now) – ein M(H)ysterienspiel in zwei Halbzeiten.* Dem Text entnehme ich, dass es sich um eine Performance handelt, »die, wenn sie in ihrer barocken Fülle erst einmal in der Welt steht, das Verwischen und Ineinanderfließen literarischer, visueller und musikalischer Themen im reizüberfluteten Medienwald vorführt und geschmackvoll karikiert«.

»Ist das euer Ernst?«, frage ich.

»Nö«, sagen die beiden und kriegen einen Lachanfall. Wie sich herausstellt, haben sie das »traumatische Spektakel« anlässlich einer feuchtfröhlichen Balkonfeier entworfen und nach weiterer zügiger Getränkezufuhr in den Briefkasten geworfen. Adressat ist das »Literanover«. Der von renommierten Autoren meist weit umkurvte Lesereigen ist einer der vielen missglückten Versuche des Kulturamtsleiters, der niedersächsischen Landeshauptstadt so etwas wie Metropolenschnittigkeit zu verleihen. Heute ist der Mensch Dezernent.

»Und? Wird der Irrsinn etwa genommen?« Andi nickt, Micha seufzt. Damit haben die beiden nicht gerechnet. Aber wozu hat man Freunde? Das Ensemble ist schnell zusammentelefoniert, und schon am nächsten Morgen geht es zur ersten Probe ins Sprengel Museum Hannover, wo die Welturaufführung stattfinden soll.

Das Setting sieht folgendermaßen aus: Auf einer zweigeteilten Bühne liegt rechts der Urwald. Hier haust Tibor, die deutsche Version des Dschungelhelden Tarzan. Tibor liest seine Comicabenteuer vor, während seine Gefährtin dekorativ Schlangen beschwört. Auf einem Videomonitor ist Coppolas Vietnamdrama *Apocalypse Now* zu sehen. Links, »in einer anderen Welt (?)«, arbeiten Experimentalfilmer und Musiker am »totalen audiovisuellen Kunstwerk, der einzig wahren Filmmusik«. Das interessiert auch Franz Kafka, der sich – unermüdlich aus seinen Werken zitierend – an dem Jahrhundertwerk beteiligt. »Gemeinsam treiben sich Poet, Filmemacher und Musiker zu Höchstleistungen an.« Dann pfeift der Schiedsrichter die erste Halbzeit ab. Als es wieder losgeht, näht die Künstlerin Hiltrud im Dschungel eine Schweizer Fahne zusammen und Albert Einstein erklärt dem Publikum anhand seiner Relativitätstheorie, warum das »Wunder von Bern« kein Zufall war. »Die Musiker versuchen mit einem Tango auf dem Laufenden zu bleiben«, empfiehlt jetzt das Manuskript. Die süße Melodie lockt alle Beteiligten zum großen Finale auf die Bühne, nur seitenverkehrt. Kafka geht in den Urwald, Tibor und Gespielin zieht es zu visuellem Experiment und Free-Jazz-Orgien.

Das ist jedenfalls die Theorie. Sie erweist sich am Premierentag als erstaunlich haltbar. Abgesehen von unbedeutenden Korrekturen. Zum Leidwesen der Zoologiestudentin Hedi verbietet die Feuerwehr das Beschwören von echten Giftschlangen. Ich gebe den Einstein, kann mir aber die Relativitätstheorie nicht merken. Stattdessen sitze ich mit Künstlerin Hiltrud in einem Kanu und wir trällern die *Caprifischer*. Wirklich aus der Rolle fällt nur

Günther, unser Schiedsrichter. Er braucht eigentlich nichts weiter zu tun, als die Perfomance an- respektive abzupfeifen und in der Pause »eine Gedenkminute für die Väter des Grundgesetzes« zu verkünden. Aber er ist entschieden übermotiviert. In Durchgang eins hat er mosernden Zuschauern wiederholt die gelbe Karte gezeigt, in der zweiten Halbzeit sehen zwei von ihnen rot. Das heißt Feldverweis. Sie werden von dem vierschrötigen Kraftkerl kurzerhand aus dem Museum geworfen. Was Günther, der aus Hildesheim kommt, nicht wissen kann: Einer der beiden Banausen sitzt im hannoverschen Stadtrat. Der Christdemokrat tobt und droht mit einem juristischen Nachspiel. Hat er dann aber doch lieber gelassen, hat Manschetten gekriegt, das Weichei. Die Performance wird nämlich von der Lokalpresse als avantgardistische Spitzenleistung gepriesen.

Dieses Erlebnis ist tatsächlich der beste Literanover-Witz und führt stringent auf eine neue Spielwiese, die ich Anfang der achtziger Jahre für mich entdecke: das Kabarett. Die Themen liegen auf der Straße. Es ist die hohe Zeit der Anti-AKW-Proteste und Nachrüstungsdebatten. Während man in den Trutzburgen der Staatsmacht Schlagstock- und Wasserwerfereinsätze koordiniert, schwillt draußen im Land – ideologisch flankiert von Rudolf Bahros *Die Alternative* und Robert Jungks *Atomstaat* – eine Bewegung, der man in der Rückschau gewisse Züge des Grenzdebilen nicht absprechen kann. Das Spektrum reicht vom Neomystizismus eines Joseph Beuys, der urplötzlich aus der rheinischen Tiefebene auftaucht und mit ausgestopften Hasen Kreuze schlägt, bis zu den Hausbesetzern und Kampftrinkern der No-Future-Front, von trotzkistischen Land-WGs, Bioläden und India-Shops über Yoga-, Tantra- und Urschrei-Kurse bis hin zu feministischen Klitorisseminaren, männlichen Selbsterfahrungsgruppen und der Grün-Alternativen Liste: die BRD sieht aus wie ein veritables Therapiezentrum. Die Krankheit heißt je nach politischer Couleur *Mittelmaß und Wahn* (Hans Magnus Enzensberger) oder »Anspruchsdenken« (Franz J. Strauß). Und Ansprüche hat nur anzumelden, wer sie auch bezahlen kann, da ist sich die FDP mit den Christlichen einig. Feilt der sinistre und später im Zuge der Parteispendenaffäre rechtskräftig verurteilte Graf Lambsdorff nicht längst am Wendepapier? Genau so ist es.

Es steht ja schon 1981 schwarz auf weiß an der Wand vor dem Regierungssitz: »Modell Deutschland leicht beschädigt, gegenüber abzuholen bei Herrn Schmidt.« Hingemalt von einem der 300 000 Demonstranten, die geführt von Erhard Eppler, Heinrich Albertz und Carl Amery mitten in Bonn aufmarschieren: Künstler, Kirchentagsflagellanten, Friedensbewegte und anderweitig Hochbetroffene, die neuerdings quer durch die Republik Menschenketten bilden, vor Kasernen liegen und die Schlechtigkeit der Welt mit Tränen netzen. Ihr politischer Impetus manifestiert sich vorrangig im Absingen grässlicher Lieder. Das allergrässlichste ist die neue SPD-Parteihymne und heißt *Wir wollen wie das Wasser sein, weiches Wasser bricht den Stein.* Es stammt aus der Feder des einschlägig vorbelasteten Dieter Dehm, ebenfalls Genosse und unverdient reich geworden mit Smashhits für Deutschrocker Klaus Lage *(Und es hat Zoom gemacht).*

Und als ob das alles noch nicht reicht, um Kanzler Helmut Schmidt die Laune zu verderben, spielt auch der Rest der Welt verrückt. Die UdSSR überzieht Afghanistan mit Krieg, und Ronald Reagan bastelt an wahnwitzigen Weltraumwaffen. Selbst auf den Fußballfeldern sind die Symptome der Verrohung nicht mehr zu leugnen. Bei der WM '82 in Spanien werden Brasiliens Ballzauberer um

167

den genialen Zico von der Squadra Azzura kompromiss-
los aus dem Wettbewerb getreten. Der kongeniale End-
spielgegner Italiens heißt Deutschland, das die zweite
Runde überhaupt nur durch einen niederträchtigen
Nichtangriffspakt mit Österreich erreicht. Als Torwart
Schumacher im Halbfinale auch noch den Franzosen
Battiston vorsätzlich krankenhausreif schlägt, unkt Re-
porter Harry Valerien: »Wohl nie zuvor ist eine derart ver-
hasste Mannschaft in ein Finale eingezogen.« Man kann
dem Essayisten Norbert Seitz nur beipflichten, Jupp
Derwalls Mannen hätten »das Ende der sozialliberalen
Ära stilistisch antizipiert«. Das weiß auch der Kanzler, der
in Madrid Italiens WM-Sieg fast erleichtert mit ansieht.
Angesichts solcher Dekadenzerscheinungen rafft sich
Schmidt nur halbherzig auf, um seine Koalition durch die
so genannte »Operation 82« zu retten. Dahinter verbirgt
sich ein Sparpaket, das sich wie das Erste-Klasse-Begräb-
nis von hundert Jahren Sozialdemokratie ausnimmt und
uns heute wieder recht bekannt vorkommt: Kürzungen
beim Kindergeld, bei der Arbeitnehmersparzulage und
den Gesundheitskosten. Erhöht werden dagegen der Beitrag zur Arbeitslosenversicherung und die Steuern auf
Tabak, Branntwein und Sekt. Ein rechter Haken auf die
Leber des Proletariats. Dann ist alles sehr schnell vorbei.
Schmidt tritt zurück und am 1. Oktober beginnt das
Saumagenregiment des Helmut Kohl, der sofort eine
»Politik der Erneuerung« samt »Vaterlandsliebe« sowie
»Sauberkeit und Leistung« verordnet wider die »geistig-
moralische Verwahrlosung«, damit »das blanke Ich wie-
der aufgeht im Wir des Volkes«. Kurz: Kohl macht, laut
Kohl, »prima Politik«.

Da ich schon immer gut parodieren konnte, bildet der
Oggersheimer Sprachmüll die Basis meines Kabarett-Pro-
gramms. Man braucht nicht mal groß daran herumzufei-

len. Oder wie es Wolfgang Neuss formuliert: »Ich mache keine Witze mehr über Kohl. Ich lache gleich über ihn.« Allerdings möchte ich hier nicht den Eindruck erwecken, dass ich mich mit brillanten Satirikern vom Schlage Neuss oder Dieter Hildebrandt auf eine Stufe stellen will. Ich sehe nicht nur so aus, ich bin damals tatsächlich ein Klein-künstler, der das Gedankengut anderer zu Markte trägt. Mein Rest-Repertoire besteht nämlich größtenteils aus Karl-Valentin-Sketchen und Werken von Hanns Dieter Hüsch. Ich mag besonders seine *Hagenbuch*-Geschichten, weil sie das (nicht zuletzt dank der von Kohl sogleich in-stallierten Privatfunksender) immer vehementer und un-seliger um sich greifende öffentliche Klugschwätzen und Besserwissen so schön ad absurdum führen.

Damit auch die Neo-Karrieristen der Alt-68er ihr Fett abkriegen, habe ich den *Sommer der Liebe* im Programm. Der Song stammt aus der Feder meines Bruders. Der Text läuft anfangs über die Titelmelodie aus Fred Zinnemanns Edel-Western *12 Uhr mittags*:

»Wisst ihr noch, wie es damals war,
als erst ein Kaufhaus Feuer fing,
dann Baader kam und Schleyer starb
und Deutschland aus den Fugen ging.
›Deutscher Herbst‹ hieß das dann später,
doch es war damals ziemlich heiß,
die Amis schmissen Napalmbomben
auf dem Vietcong seinen Reis.«

Weiter geht es mit einer Akkordfolge der guten alten Troggs:

»Und Jimi Hendrix spielte *Wild Thing*,
wir stürmten los und haben die *Bild* verbrannt.

169

Dann wurde Dutschke angeschossen,
wir sind verstört davongerannt.
Meist war das Hirn ja schwer vernebelt,
von zu viel Marx und Habermas,
doch Genossen, Genossen gebt es zu,
wir hatten auch 'ne Menge Spaß.«

Refrain:

>>Das war der Sommer der Liebe,
und wir war'n dabei.«

>>Erinnert ihr euch noch an Teufel,
an Uschis Brüste, Ho Chi Minh,
heute beschimpft mich jeder Trottel,
dass ich dabei gewesen bin.
Wir wollten doch nur frei und high sein,
die Welt ein wenig besser machen,
die meisten mittels freier Liebe,
nur die RAF griff zu den Waffen.«

Den Abspann bildet wieder die traurige Western-Melodie:

>>Ensslin ging wohl ein bisschen weit.
Ich wusste, das wird sich nicht lohnen,
machte mich lieber auf den Marsch
durch die I-n-s-t-i-t-u-t-i-o-n-e-n.
Ich hab mich dabei nie verbogen,
ich kann nicht klagen, mir geht's fein,
heute wie damals heißt mein Motto:
Nicht Amboss, sondern Hammer sein.«

Die ersten Brettl-Auftritte habe ich mit dem Pianisten Hu-
bertus Conradi, später mit Freund Peter Müller im tav ab-

solviert. Die Hildesheimer Szenekneipe liegt nicht weit entfernt vom Stadttheater. Eines Abends schneit der Intendant Pierre Leon herein. Er amüsiert sich köstlich, spendiert ein Bier und fragt, ob wir unser Programm nicht mal auf der Studiobühne seines Hauses vorführen wollen. Natürlich wollen wir. Das Gastspiel ist ständig ausverkauft. Um dem Andrang Herr zu werden, müssen wir für die letzten beiden Vorstellungen sogar auf die Hauptbühne ausweichen. Danach sind wir reif für den Rest der Welt. Er liegt in unserem Fall ziemlich exakt zwischen Lüneburg und Holzminden. Zwei Jahre sind Peter und ich durch die Weiten Niedersachsens gezogen und haben mit Scherz, Satire, Ironie unser Bafög aufgebessert. Doch nach der hundertsten Vorstellung ist uns das Material ausgegangen. Wir konnten die alten Witze nicht mehr hören. Ich habe dann versucht, selbst Texte oder Songs zu schreiben, aber schnell eingesehen: dafür fehlt mir das Talent. Einvernehmlich beschließen wir, von der Kleinkunst die Finger zu lassen und uns auf die Klassik zu konzentrieren. Das Kabarett hat den Verlust ganz gut verkraftet.

Aber aus Tommi Quasthoff wäre ohne die Brettl-Erfahrung, ohne die Tingelei durch Kneipen und rauchige Jazzkeller ganz bestimmt ein anderer, ich vermute mal, ein weit schlechterer Sänger geworden. Was man dabei vor allem lernt, ist eine gewisse Lockerheit im Umgang mit dem Publikum sowie Durchsetzungsvermögen. Wer sich schon mal auf einem Kleinstadtfest Gehör verschaffen musste, bei strömendem Regen und Auge in Auge mit fünfhundert Freizeit-Rockern, die seit Stunden darauf warten, dass Peter Maffay erscheint, den kann nichts mehr erschüttern. Der weiß auch, dass man Leuten, die ausgerechnet in der Semperoper ihre Erbschaftsangelegenheiten regeln müssen, ruhig sagen darf: »Es ist sehr unhöflich, in die Musik zu quatschen, wir sind hier nicht bei der Hitparade.« Gleiches gilt für krankenschein-pflichtige Störmanöver. Als in der Hamburger Musikhalle Schumanns *Dichterliebe* unter katarrhalischem Bellen zu ersticken droht, bittet ich »alle Lungenkranken« nach-drücklich, »ihr Husten in die Pausen zu verlegen. Ich hus-te dann mit« – und schon ist Ruhe. Das klappt leider nicht immer. Anlässlich einer stark vergrippten *Winterreise* im Berliner Kammermusiksaal resümiert die *Berliner Morgen-post*: »Die röchelnden Ruhestörer lärmten sogar in die nachklingende grausige Stille des *Leiermannes* hinein, als wäre man beim Sechstagerennen.« Gegen Epidemien ist man machtlos. Gegen Übermüdung auch. Manchmal so-gar gegen Verspätungen.

Pianist Justus »Jussi« Zeyen, mein lieber Freund und Leib- und Magenpianist, mit dem ich heute die meisten Liederabende bestreite, ist eigentlich – wie ich – die Pünktlichkeit in Person. Aber wir sind beide wirklich sehr müde, als wir am Ende einer dreiwöchigen Lied-Tournee einmal viel zu spät in Luxemburg eintreffen. In Mainz ist uns ein Zug vor der Nase weggefahren. Im Hotel erfahren wir, dass unsere Koffer nicht angekommen sind. Oben lie-gen die Noten, unten frische Wäsche. Wir können uns nicht umziehen, wir können uns nicht frisch machen, wir haben nicht mal Zeit für einen Imbiss, wir müssen noch das Programm umstellen und im Übrigen sofort los. Vor der Tür wartet schon ein Taxi mit laufendem Motor, das uns zum Konzerthaus bringen soll. Es ist zum Haaraus-reißen, aber nicht zu ändern. Endlich angelangt, sehe ich im Garderobenspiegel mein verschwitztes Gesicht und denke: So kann man nicht arbeiten. Ich bin dann auf die Bühne gegangen, habe mich entschuldigt, den Sachver-halt erklärt und um ein wenig Geduld gebeten. Wir müss-ten noch zwanzig Minuten verschnaufen, dann würde es aber losgehen. Die Leute nehmen uns das nicht übel. Als wir wieder auftauchen, rauscht herzlicher Beifall auf, und auch der Rest des Abends gestaltet sich erfreulich. Nach vier Zugaben wollen uns die Luxemburger immer noch nicht von der Bühne lassen. Wir würden gerne noch etwas singen, aber es geht nicht mehr, die Akkus stehen auf null. Ich sage:

»Sie sind einfach großartig, aber wir sind stehend k.o. Wir haben Hunger und Durst, und wenn Sie einverstanden sind, heben wir uns den Rest für das nächste Mal auf.«

»Versprochen?«, ruft ein Mann in der ersten Reihe.

»Ehrenwort«, sage ich. Und das haben wir auch eingelöst.

Im *Luxemburger Wort* steht hernach zu lesen: »Überhaupt scheint der Sänger darauf bedacht, das steife Zeremoniell des konventionellen Liederabends zu durchbrechen«, und das sei ganz in Ordnung, »warum muss ein Liederabend immer so götterdämmrig ernst sein?« Ja, das ist eine gute Frage. Noch vor ein paar Jahren machten mir Kollegen Vorwürfe, weil ich gewagt hatte, Schuberts *Forelle* in Flensburg mit den Worten anzukündigen: »Jetzt kommt etwas Fischiges, das passt zur Gegend.« Zugegeben, in der Nordsee schwimmen gar keine Forellen. Aber das Zoologische haben die lieben Kollegen gar nicht gemeint. Es ging um die (innere) Haltung. Wer nicht wie sein eigenes Denkmal neben dem Flügel stand, galt als heikler Vogel und Schande der Zunft. Heutzutage weiß selbst so ein unbestechlicher Hüter bürgerlicher Etikette wie die *FAZ*, dass es nichts schadet, Brahms' *Vier ernste Gesänge* ein wenig zu entkrampfen. Es kann, schreibt das Blatt, Hörer und Interpret »zwischendurch vom Leidens- und Gestaltungsdruck entlasten«.

Der wächst naturgemäß ins Unermessliche, sollte Jussi oder mir – was selten, aber ab und an eben doch vorkommt – ein gröberer Schnitzer unterlaufen. Darum pflege ich solche Peinlichkeiten ebenfalls mit einem Scherz zu dekorieren.

»Wir sind seriöse Musiker, ehrlich«, sage ich dann immer, und die Leute lachen. Sie lachen, weil sie uns glauben, und sie lachen, weil wir uns nicht wichtiger als unbedingt nötig nehmen.

Wichtig ist die Kunst. Gleich danach kommt jedoch die Einsicht: Egal, ob es um Pop oder Klassik geht, ob Fritz Wunderlich oder Stevie Wonder auf der Bühne steht, letztlich sind wir immer auch Diener im Reich der Unterhaltung, wir sind immer auch Entertainer.

Aber der Weg zur Erkenntnis ist so beschwerlich wie der »Edle Achtfache Pfad« des Buddhisten. Bitte folgen Sie mir jetzt in den Lied-Meisterkurs einer beliebigen Musikhochschule. Im überfüllten »Studio« setzt ein Student aus Südkorea zum Vortrag an, nennen wir ihn Herrn Lee. Herr Lee hat die *Vier ernsten Gesänge* präpariert. Sie heißen nicht umsonst so, Johannes Brahms schrieb das Requiem für die sterbenskranke Clara Schumann, ewige Muse und einzige große Liebe des Komponisten. Er konnte das Werk seinen Freunden nicht vorsingen, ohne dass ihm die Tränen kamen. Herr Lee gibt dem Mann am Klavier ein Zeichen, holt Luft und donnert die ersten Zeilen schmissig an die Saaldecke: »Denn es geht dem Menschen wie dem Veeh. Wie dies stilbt, so stilbt er auch.«

Ich unterbreche und frage Herrn Lee, was er fühlt, wenn er das singt.

»Ich seh Bild, da sind Menschen und Tiele dlauf.«

»Schön«, sage ich. »Aber versuchen Sie sich daran zu erinnern, dass das Verse aus der Bibel sind. Brahms wollte keinen Ländler komponieren, er vertont hier einen Prediger-Text.«

174

Aber auch beim zweiten Versuch wird aus Herrn Lee kein Salomon. Er wird nur lauter. Bei seinen Lieblingsstellen sogar sehr laut. Dabei klumpen Noten und Buchstaben wie Nudeln in verkochter Suppe.

»Nicht Veeeh«, sage ich, »es heißt Vieh, eine Fee ist was anderes.«

So geht das noch eine halbe Stunde, dann versucht sich eine junge Dame an Schumanns *Nussbaum*. »Duuuftig« und »luuuftig« stelzt sie durch den romantischen Blütenzauber. Dabei muss es ganz natürlich klingen. »Dufftig« und »lufftig« mit vom Vokal gelöstem f. Eine andere Elevin garniert ihre wirklich aparte Stimme durch das Einschieben überflüssiger Zier- und Prunkvokale, die Hugo Wolf eigentlich nicht vorgesehen hat. »Heiß(ö) mich(ö) nicht(ä) reden, heiß(ö) mich(ö) schweigen.« Genau das möchte man manchmal tun.

Ich glaube schon, dass jeder halbwegs talentierte Mensch die klassische Singerei erlernen kann. Aber die deutschen Hochschulen machen es Studenten, die wirklich den Beruf des Konzert- oder Opernsängers anstreben, nicht leicht. Im Eifer des Gefechtes habe ich die Bildungsinstitute mal als »Brutstätten vokaler Manieriertheit« bezeichnet. Weil sie ihre Auszubildenden unnötig verwirren durch ein überdimensioniertes gesangspädagogisches Regelwerk, das den Weg zu echtem Kunstempfinden und individuellem Ausdruck eher verbaut.

Seit 1996 unterrichte ich an der Musikhochschule in Detmold. Ich muss sagen, viel geändert hat sich nicht. Große Probleme machen die zu kurzen Studienzeiten. Fünf Jahre sind definitiv zu wenig, um eine Stimme reifen zu lassen. Aber die Lehrpläne werden meist von Bürokraten entworfen, die von der Materie wenig bis gar nichts verstehen. Die Hochschulen wiederum sind bemüht, möglichst viele Studenten in relativ kurzer Zeit zum Abschluss zu bringen, weil die Diplomstückzahl den Aufsichtsbehörden als Nachweis effizienter Arbeit gilt. Und ebendiese kunstferne Effizienz ist heute das entscheidende Argument, wenn es um die Verteilung der immer knapper werdenden staatlichen Gelder geht. Es soll eben alles schnell gehen. Leider sehen das viele Studenten genauso. Sie wollen den schnellen Erfolg und singen zu früh zu schwere Partien und wundern sich dann, wenn die Stimmbänder ruiniert sind, ehe die Karriere richtig angefangen hat.

Von Sartre stammt der Satz: »Man ist nicht Tormann oder Läufer, wie man Lohnarbeiter ist.« Der Philosoph und Fußballconnaisseur will sagen, Ballkünstler zu sein ist kein normaler Beruf, sondern eine Berufung. Das gilt erst recht für den Sänger. Darum bin ich ein sehr strenger Lehrer. Wer sich für meine Klasse bewirbt, wird auf Herz und Nieren geprüft. Oft genug müssen die Kandidaten wieder gehen. Mir tut das jedes Mal furchtbar Leid. Aber wenn ich Studenten aufnehme, will ich sicher sein, dass sie durchhalten, dass ihre Stimmen sie dreißig, vierzig Jahre durch den Beruf tragen, dass sie von der Musik anständig leben können. Es bringt nichts, jungen Menschen etwas vorzumachen, ihnen Gefälligkeits- oder Nettigkeitszensuren zu geben, nur um sie hernach auf dem freien Markt scheitern zu sehen. Die Stellenangebote sind rar, entsprechend brutal ist die Konkurrenz. Wer den Anforderungen nicht genügt, ist ruck, zuck weg vom Fenster. Also fälle ich lieber ein ehrliches Urteil, getreu der Devise: Besser ein Ende mit Schrecken als ein Schrecken ohne Ende. Dann ist immer noch Zeit, sich etwas anderes zu suchen, anstatt weiter wertvolle Lebenszeit zu verschwenden.

Aber ich bin der Letzte, der behaupten würde, meine Auffassung sei der allein selig machende Schlüssel zum Erfolg. Meinen Schülern rate ich, haltet Augen und Ohren offen, schaut, was die Kollegen zu bieten haben, und wenn ihr glaubt, es bringt euch weiter, probiert es aus. Wir Professoren können euch zeigen, wie man schwimmen lernt. Aber wohin und wie schnell ihr schwimmen wollt, müsst ihr selbst entscheiden.

Ich habe das Glück gehabt, nach meiner Ausbildung bei Frau Lehmann in Helmuth Rilling einen Mentor zu finden, dessen Persönlichkeit unbedingtes Kunstwollen, Klugheit, Herzensbildung und gelassene Heiterkeit so selbstverständlich vereint wie der Friese heißen Tee, Kandis und kalte Milch. Rilling ist Gründer und Leiter der Internationalen Bachakademie Stuttgart, Dirigent von Weltrang, Lehrer von Format, Musikforscher und Wiederentdecker romantischer Chormusik und durch die regelmäßige Vergabe von Kompositionsaufträgen ein nimmermüder Förderer zeitgenössischer Musik.

Davon weiß ich aber so gut wie nichts, als er mich 1987 zum Vorsingen einlädt. Klar, ich habe von ihm gehört, schließlich gilt Rilling als *die* Autorität in Sachen Johann Sebastian Bach. Für mich ist er ein ehrfurchtgebietender Meister, der Sätze sagt wie: »Musik darf nie bequem sein, nicht museal, nicht beschwichtigend. Sie muss aufrütteln, die Menschen persönlich erreichen, sie zum Nachdenken bringen.«

Während der Bahnfahrt habe ich versucht, ihn mir zu imaginieren: Vor meinen Augen steht ein großer Mensch, asketisch, ernst und streng wie eine Fuge. Es gibt auch noch eine bauchige Version, die dem Thomaskantor ähnelt, nur ohne Perücke. In Stuttgart begrüßt mich dann ein kleiner freundlicher Herr mit schlohweißem Haar. Er blinzelt mit wachen Augen über den Rand seiner Lesebrille, trägt ein verschmitztes Lächeln im Gesicht und schwäbelt gemütlich:

»Ah, Sie müsse der Herr Quaschtoff sein. Hallöle, ich bin Helmuth Rilling.«

Das Vorsingen am nächsten Tag gerät zur mittleren Katastrophe. Die Aufregung ist mir wohl auf den Magen geschlagen. In der Nacht zuvor bekomme ich Durchfall, Schüttelfrost und kaum Schlaf. Morgens habe ich 39 Grad Fieber. Ich fühle mich wie ein nasser fauliger Sack, will aber nicht kneifen. Freund Peter Müller, der mitgereist ist, um mich am Klavier zu begleiten, schüttelt den Kopf:

»Wir spielen nicht. Du kannst so nicht singen. Du bist krank und gehörst ins Bett.« Er redet mit Engelszungen auf mich ein. Als er merkt, dass seine Ermahnungen nichts fruchten, hievt er das Elendsbündel schicksalsergeben in ein Taxi Richtung Bachakademie, um die Bass-Arie aus Händels *Joshua*-Oratorium doch noch an den Mann zu bringen. Anfangs geht auch alles gut, bis ich merke, dass Peter immer schneller wird. Oder werde ich langsamer? In meinem Fieberwahn vermag ich das nicht mehr zu beurteilen. Ich weiß nur noch, dass unter meiner Schädeldecke Großalarm herrscht:

»Oh Gott, was machen wir denn? Rilling denkt bestimmt, wir sind verrückt, Amateure, Nichtskönner. Das Thema Bachakademie ist ein für alle Mal erledigt.« Was danach vor sich geht, habe ich nicht mehr richtig wahrgenommen. Ich erinnere nur noch, dass ich völlig fertig in Hannover ankomme und für drei Wochen flachliege.

Von der Bachakademie höre ich ein Jahr nichts. Dann liegt eines Tages die Einladung für ein Kantatenwochenende in der Post. Was gesungen wird, ist mir entfallen. Ich weiß nur noch, dass es dieses Mal besser läuft. In einem der Stücke kommt ein tiefes C vor, und Helmuth strahlt jedes Mal, als hätte er im Lotto gewonnen, wenn dieses C sauber aus meinem Kehlkopf rollt. Kurz darauf bin ich mit der Bachakademie auf Tournee gegangen. Wir geben

Händels *Jephta* und gastieren in der damaligen CSSR und in Polen. Am Ende dieser Reise hat Helmuth mich gefragt:

»Sag, hascht Lust, mit mir die Matthäusch-Paschjon aufzuznääme?«

Dieses Bachsche Schlüsselwerk mit dem großen Rilling einzuspielen ist eine Art Ritterschlag und hat meiner Karriere nach dem ARD-Wettbewerb noch einmal einen gehörigen Schub versetzt. Unter seiner Stabführung singe ich auch erstmals das Brahms-Requiem, nicht zu vergessen Mendelssohns *Elias*, der im Gegensatz zu einem Bach-Oratorium nicht so üppig orchestriert ist, aber vom Sänger einen viel dramatischeren Einsatz erfordert. Ich kann mit Fug und Recht sagen, dass ich Helmuth und der Akademie einen Großteil meiner praktischen Ausbildung verdanke.

Im Lauf der Jahre ist daraus eine tiefe Beziehung gewachsen, die nicht nur auf der Liebe zur Musik basiert. Wir wissen beide einen guten Rotwein und ein gutes Fußballspiel zu schätzen. Helmuth ist glühender Anhänger des Stuttgarter VfB und versäumt, sofern es seine knappe Zeit erlaubt, kein Heimspiel. Außerdem hat er ein Faible für Cardinal-Mendoza-Cognac und Zigarren der Marke Davidoff, Genussmittel, die ich ihm gerne mitbringe, weil ich weiß, da fällt auch für mich immer etwas ab. Folglich führt mein erster Weg in den zollfreien Flughafenshop, als ich in Santiago de Compostela eintreffe, wo Helmuth mit der Real Filharmonia de Galicia den *Elias* aufführen wird. Sei es der schieren Genusssucht oder dem spirituellen Fluidum des berühmten Wahlfahrtsortes geschuldet, der ganze – eigentlich für drei Tage projektierte – Vorrat wird unter tätiger Mithilfe des Ehepaars Rilling und des geschätzten Bariton-Kollegen Matthias Goerne gleich am ersten Abend vernichtet.

Am nächsten Morgen treffe ich Helmuth nach dem Frühstück in der Lobby unseres Hotels. Er sagt nicht guten Morgen, sondern: »Tommi, isch dir au nach Flughafe zumute?« Wir sind dann gleich noch mal hingefahren.

Mit anderen Worten, Helmuth ist ein prima Reisekamerad. Inzwischen haben wir zusammen ein schönes Stück Weg zurückgelegt. Wir sind mehrmals durch die Iberische Halbinsel getourt, wir waren in Japan und haben die *Matthäus-Passion* in Buenos Aires, im Teatro Colón, einem der schönsten Opernhäuser der Welt, aufgeführt. Anschließend gebe ich dort noch einen Meisterkurs. Da die Bach-Tradition in Argentinien noch in den Kinderschuhen steckt, ist das sängerische Niveau, na, sagen wir, hochinteressant, und es gibt eine Menge zu tun. Unvergesslich wird mir ein zwei Meter großer schmalbrüstiger Jüngling bleiben. Er möchte Hugo Wolfs *Zur Ruh, zur Ruh* vortragen. Ich mache einige Atemübungen mit ihm und sehe, wie er blass und blasser wird. Nach der dritten Übung schaut er mich entrückt an, verdreht die Augen und fällt in Ohnmacht. Als er kurze Zeit später zu sich kommt, besteht er darauf, doch noch zu singen. Kaum hat er die ersten Töne herausgebracht, wird er wieder kreidebleich. Besorgt breche ich ab und empfehle ihm, sich lieber daheim »zur Ruh« zu legen, ehe er sich vor meinen Augen »gänzlich fort« macht »aus dem Raum der Erdenschmerzen«.

Helmuth hat mir auch auf dem nordamerikanischen Kontinent die Türen geöffnet. 1995 nimmt er mich mit nach Eugene, Oregon. In dem idyllischen Universitätsstädtchen hat er 1970 das Oregon Bach Festival, eines der profiliertesten Festivals in den USA, gegründet und leitet es bis heute. Ich bin seitdem oft dort gewesen. Unter anderem auch 1998, als Helmuth die Welturaufführung von Krzysztof Pendereckis *Credo* dirigiert, einer gewaltigen Messe für einhundertzehn Chorsänger, Orchester und fünf Solisten, die Julia Borchert, Milagro Vargas, Marietta Simpson, Rolf Romei und Tommi Quasthoff heißen. Die Atmosphäre ist etwas gespannt. Selbst Helmuth, den ansonsten nichts aus der Ruhe bringen kann, rauft sich mehr als einmal die Haare. Denn zwei Tage vor der Premiere hat Penderecki noch immer keine vollständige Partitur geliefert. Endlich am nächsten Morgen erscheint der Avantgardekomponist mit den Noten, drückt sie Helmuth in die Hand und setzt sich in die erste Reihe, um die Generalprobe zu verfolgen. Doch wir kommen nicht weit. Immer wieder unterbricht Penderecki, möchte hier den Chor etwas lauter, da eine Solostimme prägnanter und überhaupt die Streicher dynamischer haben. Der Dirigent nimmt es hin. Irgendwann haben wir tatsächlich fast einen kompletten Durchlauf geschafft, als Penderecki nochmals aufspringt und schreit:

»Trumpets! Too late! Too late! Too late!« Da reißt Helmuth der Geduldsfaden. Er brüllt zurück:

»Komponiert! Komponiert! Komponiert!«

Doch die nervenaufreibende Arbeit bleibt nicht unbelohnt. Das *Credo* ist der frenetisch bejubelte Höhepunkt des Festivals. Ein Live-Mitschnitt aus Krakau wird später auf CD gepresst, und Helmuth gewinnt mit dieser Aufnahme den Grammy Award für die beste Chor-Darbietung des Jahres 2000.

Zwei weitere Dirigenten, die großen Einfluss auf meine Art zu musizieren haben, sind Claudio Abbado und Simon Rattle. Abbado kann man im Vergleich zum überschäumenden Temperamentsbündel Rattle sicherlich einen introvertierten Orchesterleiter nennen. Aber er ist auf seine zurückhaltende Art genauso liebenswürdig, freundlich und warmherzig wie der Brite. Dass sein Horizont weit über den Rand des Orchestersaals hinausreicht, hat Abbado 1972 bewiesen, als er gegen größte Widerstände der betuchten Eliten und zum ersten Mal in der Geschichte Mailands die Scala für Studenten und Arbeiter öffnet und versucht diese Klientel mittels spezieller Programme für das Theater zu begeistern. Abbado besitzt eine natürliche Autorität, die sich aus seiner Musikalität und intellektuellen Redlichkeit speist. Er kennt keine Tricks oder Machtspielchen, ihm geht es immer um die Sache, um die Musik und um das Anliegen des Komponisten. Wenn er ans Pult tritt, kann man sicher sein, dass er eine Partitur mithilfe von Literaturstudium und wissenschaftlicher Recherche bis auf den Grund ausgeleuchtet und eine neue umfassende Lesart anzubieten hat. Das gilt für das klassische Repertoire des 19. Jahrhunderts ebenso wie für die Meister des frühen 20. Jahrhunderts oder die Neutöner Stockhausen, Berio oder Nono. Es gibt wohl kaum einen lebenden Dirigenten, der ein so breites Spektrum beherrscht. Egal, woran er gerade arbeitet, Abbado strebt stets mit höchster Intensität nach Klarheit von musikalischer Struktur und Stimmführung. Am faszinierendsten ist dabei seine unglaubliche Mimik und Körpersprache. Um zu vermitteln, was er mit einem Blick oder einer kleinen Geste ausdrücken kann, müssen andere den Taktstock schwingen wie die drei Musketiere ihre Degen. Ich habe den Chefdirigenten und künstlerischen Leiter des Berliner Philharmonischen Orchesters 1997 kennen gelernt, als er mich einlud, mit dem Chamber Orchestra of Europe bei den Berliner Festwochen zu musizieren. Dass ich unter seiner Leitung schon ein Jahr später Mahlers *Des Knaben Wunderhorn* für die Deutsche Grammophon aufnehmen darf, ist ein echter Glücksfall. Denn ich musiziere nicht nur mit den Berliner Philharmonikern und der grandiosen Sopranistin Anne Sofie von Otter, der CD wird auch noch der Grammy in der Kategorie »Beste klassische Gesangsdarbietung 1999« verliehen.

An Abbados Seite habe ich auch zwei meiner bewegendsten Konzerte gegeben. Mit den Berliner Philharmonikern sind wir 2001, zehn Tage nach den Anschlägen auf das World Trade Center, zu Gast in der Carnegie Hall, um die Konzertsaison zu eröffnen. Die Reise ist im Vorfeld sehr kontrovers diskutiert worden. An der Hudson Bay meinen nicht wenige, es sei pietätlos, so kurz nach dem grausamen Massaker an Konzerte zu denken; in Berlin gibt es Bedenken wegen der Sicherheitslage. Aber als die New Yorker beschließen, sich vom Terror nicht unterkriegen zu lassen und das Alltagsleben so normal wie möglich fortzusetzen, ist der Auftritt für Abbado und seine Musiker eine Frage von Solidarität und Ehre. Ich gebe zu, auch mir pocht beim Landeanflug auf den Kennedy-Airport das Herz ungewöhnlich heftig. Über Ground Zero steigt immer noch Rauch in den Himmel. Ich habe so viele Freunde in der Stadt, und die Vorstellung, es hätte einen von ihnen treffen können, macht mich traurig und wütend zugleich.

»Wir sind alle New Yorker«, steht im Programmheft, Kennedys berühmtes Berlin-Bekenntnis paraphrasierend, aber das Orchester widmet sein Konzert im Besonderen dem kürzlich verstorbenen Isaac Stern. Der eminente Violinvirtuose hat die Carnegie Hall vor dem Abriss gerettet und war danach lange Jahre ihr Präsident. An diesem Abend ist in dem ehrwürdigen Konzertsaal die metaphysische Kraft der Musik mit Händen zu greifen. Die Philharmoniker spielen Gustav Mahlers fünf Orchesterlieder, drei Beethoven-Sinfonien und das Klavierkonzert Nr. 1 d-Moll op. 15 von Johannes Brahms. Und sie spielen wie entrückt. Das Melos der *Eroica* entfaltet sich in einer irisierenden Atmosphäre, einer Melange aus Verletzlichkeit und Trost, Verzweiflung und Läuterung. Vielen Zuhörern rinnen Tränen über das Gesicht, aber am Ende stehen sie auf wie ein Mann und applaudieren begeistert: dem großartigen Orchester, vor allem aber wohl sich selbst. Ihrem Überlebenswillen und der Hoffnung, dass der Mensch fähig ist, letztlich auch den schlimmsten Schmerz zu überwinden.

Am 26. März 2002 habe ich dann die Ehre, dabei zu sein, als Claudio Abbado bei den Salzburger Osterfestspielen Abschied nimmt von seinen Berliner Philharmonikern. Er dirigiert Schumanns selten gespielte *Faust-Szenen*. Abbado ist in Hochform. Er hält das über zwölf Schaffensjahre mehr gewucherte als gewachsene Mammutwerk fest am Zügel und führt die Streicher mit Verve durch schrundige Passagen und Zuckerbäcker-Pianissimi, ohne dass die Trinität aus Chören, Rezitativ und Arioso jemals in Gefahr geriete, die Balance zu verlieren. Noch einmal entfaltet sich sein Sinn für Proportionen, brillante Klangfülle und für süffig zauberische Melodien. Am Schluss bemerkt jemand im Publikum: »Wunderbare Musik, nur der Text is a Schmarrn.« Ich hoffe, dass Abbado, den die *Süddeutsche Zeitung* mal liebevoll-schelmisch »Dr. Faustus des Südens« nannte, den Schmäh nicht gehört hat. Ansonsten ist sich der Maestro auch bei diesem Auftritt treu geblieben. Obwohl ihn die Salzburger zwanzig Minuten lang hochleben lassen, steht Abbado bescheiden am Bühnenrand, um den Ruhm den Solisten zu überlassen.

Simon Rattle, Abbados Nachfolger auf dem Berliner Dirigententhron, steht gern im Rampenlicht. Er ist ein Mensch mit einer ungeheuren Ausstrahlung. Wenn man ihn beim Dirigieren beobachtet, sieht man immer seine geöffnete linke Hand, die dem Orchester zugewandt ist. Die Geste sagt: »Ich bin offen für alles, seid ihr es auch.« Mit diesem »Spirit« kitzelt er Energien aus dem Orchester, die sich in den besten Momenten zu purem Expressionismus ballen und ein Publikum glatt aus den Sitzen fegen können. Gleichzeitig ist Simon liebenswert, einfühlsam, hochintelligent und bei aller musikalischen Genialität einer der witzigsten Zeitgenossen unter der Sonne. Davon bekomme ich gleich bei unserer ersten Zusammenarbeit eine Kostprobe.

Auf dem Programm steht Haydns *Schöpfung*. Es gibt da eine Stelle, wo der Erzengel Raphael zu singen hat: »Kriecht am Boden das Gewürm.« Man kann es auf einem hohen B enden lassen oder auf einem tiefen, Papa Haydn war beides recht. Normalerweise wird das hohe B bevorzugt. Auch von mir. Nach der ersten Klavierprobe fragt Rattle:

»Can you sing it also low?«

»Sure«, gebe ich zurück.

Als wir bei der folgenden Orchesterprobe an besagte Stelle kommen, bin ich so sehr damit beschäftigt, meine Partie fehlerlos zu bewältigen, dass ich seinen Wunsch total vergessen habe. Ich singe wieder ein hohes B. Simon stoppt die Musik-Maschinerie:

»Excuse me, can you sing it low?«

Ich bekomme einen roten Kopf und entschuldige mich. Doch ob meiner Nervosität wiederhole ich den Fehler auch auf der Generalprobe. Ich schwöre mir, im Konzert passiert dir das nicht. Und tatsächlich serviere ich ihm am entscheidenden Tag ein wunderbares tiefes B – extra large. Simon sagt kein Wort. Das Publikum amüsiert sich. Mitten im nächsten Stück dreht sich Simon, ohne das Dirigieren zu unterbrechen, zu mir um, verzieht das Gesicht zu einem breiten Grinsen und raunt:

»Asshole.«

Doch alle Frotzelei hat ein Ende, sobald es während der Proben an die eigentliche Kärrnerarbeit geht. Dann ist Simon Rattle ein manischer Feuerkopf, der Achtelnoten so lange wendet, zurechtfeilt und neu zusammensetzt, bis sie seiner Vision eines Werkes entsprechen. Niemals zuvor habe ich so eine perfekte Abstimmung der Instrumentengruppen gehört, wie sie die Berliner Philharmoniker unter seiner Leitung praktizieren, niemals zuvor ein so lebendiges Wogen des Orchesterapparates. Und ist ein Opus erst einmal bis zur Vorführungsreife runderneuert, sieht es einfach nicht mehr nach Arbeit aus, selbst Schwergewichtiges wie Mahler- oder Bruckner-Sinfonien wirkt spielerisch leicht. Wenn Simon dirigiert, ist das pure Magie. Wie frisch und anders er zu Werke geht, merkt man erst, wenn er einen hüftsteifen Oldie wie Haydns *Jahreszeiten* aufpoliert, die ich in Berlin mit Christiane Oelze und dem Tenor Ian Bostridge gesungen habe. Da schmettert sich der Chor bei aller Präzision wie aufgedreht durch die bukolische Szenerie, während das Orchester die wechselnden Landschaftsbilder in fast hyperrealistischer Brillanz nachzeichnet und doch zu einer barocken Fülle des Ausdrucks findet. Keine Spur mehr vom Bombast und Pathos der Karajan-Zeit, auch die panoramahaften Klangtableaus der Abbado-Ära sind perdu. Simon hat den Ballast einfach weggehobelt, hat den Klangkörper entschlackt, sodass der Blick jetzt auf all die funkelnden Details der Partitur fallen kann, die Simon ausstellt wie ein glücklicher Schatzsucher seine kostbare Beute. Das ist Tonmalerei in Vollendung. Und Karl Raab hat völlig Recht, wenn er schreibt, »es ist einfach wunderbar (und beinah köstlich kurzweilig), wie seine Musiker mit spürbar offensiver Neugier, Genauigkeit und allen erdenklichen instrumentatorischen Finessen diesem Zyklus des Jahreslaufes folgen. Simon Rattle kann wie ein Kind sein, das das Staunen noch nicht verlernt hat: das Staunen über die Natur und das Staunen über die Musik, die diese Natur imaginiert.«

Simon ist mir ein guter Freund und besonders enger musikalischer Bruder, weil er im Herzen bei aller Professionalität auch ein Romantiker ist. Und weil er in meiner Stimme immer wieder Möglichkeiten sieht, an die ich nicht im Traum zu denken wage. Zum Beispiel lässt er mich in der *Johannes-Passion* alle Bassrollen singen. Es sind fünf. Und jede muss mit einer anderen Tongebung vorgetragen werden. Ein Jesus darf nicht klingen wie ein Pilatus, ein Pilatus wiederum anders als ein Judas. Das ist schon die hohe Schule des Charakterfachs. Simon hat mich hineingeworfen, und ich habe es geschafft.

Im Sommer 2000 sind wir mit Beethovens Neunter Sinfonie in England unterwegs. Für den Chorpart ist der ehemalige Philharmonia Choir engagiert worden, den Otto Klemperer kurz nach dem Zweiten Weltkrieg gegründet hat. Als die würdigen Herren sich zur ersten Probe formieren, zwinkert Simon mir zu und sagt: »Wundere dich nicht, dass der Chor so tief klingt, es sind noch viele Gründungsmitglieder dabei.« Das letzte Konzert findet in der Ely-Cathedral statt, einer riesigen Kirche im Osten Englands. Auf dem Weg zum anschließenden Bankett hält Simon mich zurück und legt mir den Arm um die Schultern:

»Tommi, my friend, I believe now is the time we have to work in opera.«

Ich habe schon viele Angebote von großen Häusern bekommen, aber bisher alle abgelehnt, weil ich mich noch nicht reif genug fühlte und meine Behinderung nicht mehr als nötig ausstellen wollte.

Aber Simon vertraue ich, und ich weiß, dass er mich

nie zu etwas drängen würde, was er oder ich ästhetisch und musikalisch nicht verantworten können. Daher
habe ich dieses Mal gesagt: »Okay, Simon, what shall we
do?«

»Beethoven, *Fidelio*, 2003 in the Salzburg Festival-
house.«

Mitleid bekommt man umsonst,
Neid muss man sich erarbeiten

Der große Konzertsaal am Mönchsberg beherbergte zu glorreichen K.-u.-k.-Zeiten eine Reitschule. Jetzt regiert hier der diskrete Charme der Bourgeoisie. Von Juli bis August schwebt er über den Salzburger Festspielen, im April senkt er sich über die Osterfestspiele, die Herbert von Karajan 1967 aus der Taufe gehoben hat. Der unbedarfte Besucher spürt sein Wirken am Preisgefüge und an den dunklen S-Klasse-Limousinen, die vor den Premieren um den Block kreisen. Ich spüre ihn an den formvollendeten Buh-Rufen für Regisseur Nikolaus Lehnhoff, der den Oster-*Fidelio* 2003 partout nicht als historisierendes Singspiel auf die Bühne stellen mag, sondern ein abstraktes, sparsam dekoriertes Ideen-Drama inszeniert. Ihm zum Trost gereicht, dass es der Uraufführung nicht besser ging.

Beethovens einzige Oper »wird sehr kalt aufgenommen«, wie die Leipziger *Allgemeine Musikalische Zeitung* überliefert. Man schreibt das Jahr 1805. Europas Monarchien zittern vor dem Parvenü Napoleon, der sich die Kaiserkrone aufs Haupt gestülpt und dann in Marsch gesetzt hat, den Kontinent mittels Artilleriesalven und bürgerlichem Gesetzbuch umzukrempeln. Neun Jahre später sitzt der Korse auf Elba, in Wien lässt Restaurationskanzler Metternich den Kongress tanzen, und die Menschen geraten schier aus dem Häuschen, als Beethoven im Theater am Kärntnertor sein freiheitsbewegtes Schreckens- und Rettungsstück dirigiert. Damals war die Freiheit kostbar, heute ist sie grenzenlos. Außer auf der Opernbühne, wo

Polit-Häftling Florestan – zwecks zeitgeistiger Toppräsenz – wahrscheinlich aussehen müsste wie Knastbruder Edmond Dantès alias Graf von Monte Christo, den Alexandre Dumas bekanntlich als Hochstapler reüssieren und seine Feinde mit schierer Finanzkraft erledigen lässt.

Nun, darüber mache ich mir vorerst keine Gedanken. In meinem Kopf rumoren genug andere Probleme. Dass ich die Rolle stimmlich bewältige, weiß ich, weil ich den *Fidelio* 1996 schon auf CD gebannt habe, mit dem Symphonieorchester des Bayerischen Rundfunks unter Leitung von Sir Colin Davis. Aber als in Salzburg die ersten Proben anstehen, frage ich mich doch, ob mein Schauspieltalent und die körperliche Präsenz für die Opernbühne reichen. Denn trotz Simons Zuspruch nagt in schwachen Momenten immer noch die Furcht, mich mit meiner zwergenhaften Statur lächerlich zu machen. Schließlich soll ich den respektablen Minister Don Fernando geben.

»What happens?«, schlägt Freund Tony alle Bedenken in den Wind. Er sitzt in meinem Hotelzimmer und zieht genüsslich an einer Tüte schwarzem Afghanen.

»Remember all the fat old tenors, die hinterhersteigen young girls like Aida or Desdemona. That is the real ugly stuff. Not you, little big man.«

Er hat gut reden und mich noch nicht im Frack gesehen, den mir die Garderobiere heute Morgen verpasst hat. Das Ding ist schneeweiß und mindestens zwei Nummern zu groß. Statt würdevoller Schöße schleife ich zwei Stoffbahnen hinter mir her, die riesigen Insektenflügeln gleichen. Vormittags fühle ich mich wie Kafkas Käfer-Mann Gregor Samsa, abends wie der TV-Putzteufel Clementine, weil ich die Bühne nach jeder Probe besenrein hinterlasse. Diese modische Extravaganz kann man immerhin korrigieren – Kostümbildnerin Anna Eiermann lässt mir sofort ein passgenaues Exemplar in Schwarz auf den Leib schneidern –, aber gegen mein Lampenfieber hilft das erst einmal nicht. Vor allem wenn ich täglich erlebe, mit welch professioneller Hingabe Angela Denoke (Leonore/Fidelio) Jon Villar (Florestan) umgarnt und mit welch erotischer Verve sich Kollegin Juliane Banse (Marzelline) auf einem Container rekelt und das Liebesglück hinter dem Regenbogen besingt. Aber mit der Zeit wird es besser.

Regisseur Lehnhoff ist mit meiner Partie sehr zufrieden. Und auch Simon Rattle hat nichts auszusetzen. Im Gegenteil. Nach der Generalprobe haut er mir auf die Schulter und meint: »Tommi, the rehearsal was wunderbar. Don't be afraid. If something goes wrong, kick it off. Dann du gibst einfach weiter your concerts.«

Ich sage mir, wo er Recht hat, hat er Recht, und bin am Premierentag tatsächlich ganz ruhig. Da mein großer Auftritt erst im zweiten Akt erfolgt, begebe ich mich hinter die Bühne, um die Aufführung aus nächster Nähe zu verfolgen. Die Regie hat alle erklärenden Dialoge gestrichen, und schon das einleitende Tutti-Motiv zeigt, dass auch Simon gewillt ist, sein Orchester zum eigentlichen Deuter der Handlung zu machen. Er führt die Berliner Philharmoniker konzentriert unheroisch durch die Ouvertüre und umkurvt auch im Folgenden jedes hohle Pathos. Seine Tempi sind langsam, die Metri fließend, was besonders den Arien Ausdruck und Geschmeidigkeit verleiht, bis sich das Geschehen am Ende zum großen Freiheitshymnus verdichtet.

Um den Handlungsort, ein spanisches Staatsgefängnis in der Nähe von Sevilla, ins Bild zu setzen, reichen Lehnhoff drei glänzende Stahlwände. Den Bühnenboden bedecken ein paar alte Schuhe und Erdhaufen. Im Hintergrund ragt eine steile Falltreppe empor. Vor die tritt nun der junge Schließer Jaquino (Rainer Trost) und erklärt Marzelline seine Liebe (»Jetzt, Schätzelein, jetzt sind wir allein«). Sie singt auch prompt: »Oh, wär ich doch schon mit dir vereint«, meint aber nicht den armen Jaquino, sondern Fidelio, also die als Mann verkleidete Leonore. Marzellines Vater, der alte Kerkermeister Rocco (Laszlo Polgar), gibt der Verbindung seinen Segen. Als Fidelio/Leonore aufs Stichwort die Treppe hinabschreitet, erglühen die Stufen im morgendlichen Sonnenlicht und der Blick öffnet sich aus dem klaustrophobischen Bunker ins wüste, gefährlich Weite, wo der schurkische Gouverneur Don Pizarro (Alan Held) seine Fäden spinnt. Als Leonore die Stimme erhebt, ist das romantisierende Beziehungsgeplänkel mit einem Schlag vorbei, die Musik bekommt Beethovensche Wucht. »Wie groß ist die Gefahr«, lauten die ersten Worte der jungen Frau, die sich todesmutig in das Gefängnis geschlichen hat, weil ihr Herz nur einem gehört. Dem Gatten Florestan, Kämpfer für Freiheit und Gerechtigkeit und einziger Zeuge der Untaten Don Pizarros, der ihn genau darum in das tiefste Loch des Verlieses werfen ließ.

Und schon steht der Fiesling auf der Treppe, um Florestan endgültig mundtot zu machen. Denn aus der Hauptstadt kommt die Kunde, Minister Don Fernando, ein alter Freund des Florestan, beabsichtige, demnächst das Gefängnis zu inspizieren. Aber ich bin längst noch nicht dran. Erst muss das schlichte Gemüt Rocco überredet werden, dem Mörder Beihilfe zu leisten (»Dem Staate liegt daran«), nur um hernach von Leonore, die alles mit angehört hat, eingeflüstert zu bekommen, er habe nichts Dringlicheres zu tun, als die Zellen zu öffnen. Rocco tut ihr den Gefallen und verschafft dem Gefangenenchor die Gelegenheit, ein ergreifendes Lied zu intonieren (»Oh, welche Lust«). Doch die Freude wärt nicht lange. Als Pizarro von der unautorisierten Amnestie erfährt, schäumt er vor Wut und befiehlt, die Delinquenten schleunigst wieder wegzuschließen. Vor der Pause sehen wir noch, wie Leonore und Rocco in die Tiefen des Kerkers steigen. Er, um Florestan das Grab zu schaufeln, sie, um den Gatten zu befreien.

Der zweite Akt bringt das dramatisch besungene Wiedersehen der Liebenden, ein politisches Statement Florestans (»Wahrheit wagt' ich kühn zu sagen / Und die Ketten sind mein Lohn«), Pizarros Mordanschlag und – ehe es zum Schlimmsten kommt – die Wendung der Oper ins Utopisch-Wunderbare. Ein Trompetensignal lässt die Hand mit der meuchelnden Klinge in der Luft erstarren. Don Pizarro hat verspielt, der Minister naht, das heißt: Quasthoff muss arbeiten. Für meinen Auftritt hat sich Nikolaus Lehnhoff etwas wirklich Spektakuläres ausgedacht. Während sich die Gefangenen in Gestalt des Wiener Arnold-Schönberg-Chores zu einem Wall geschundener Seelen formieren, schleiche ich mich durch den Seiteneingang hinter die Menschenkette. Dann weicht sie zurück, ich trete – Blochs Prinzip Hoffnung auf zwei kurzen Beinen – aus dem Kreis der Entrechteten nach vorn und intoniere Don Fernandos jakobinisches Credo:

»Nicht länger kniet sklavisch nieder! / Tyrannenstrenge sei mir fern. / Es sucht der Bruder seine Brüder / und kann er helfen, hilft er gern.«

Die Liebenden sinken sich in die Arme, und alles ist gut. Na ja, fast alles. Die *Süddeutsche* bemäkelt einen »glatten Designer-Beethoven«, der Wiener Kritiker Volker Boser konstatiert, »das Publikum reagierte höflich, war aber nicht aus dem Häuschen«. Dafür berichtet der *Kölnische Stadtanzeiger*, man habe Simon Rattle mit »Bravo-Rufen« gefeiert und bescheinigt ihm »einen grandiosen Einstand als neuer Leiter der Salzburger Osterfestspiele«. Auch die *Welt* lobt einen »entschlackten *Fidelio*«, der »glänzend funktionierte«. Zu mir sind Publikum und Kritik ausgesprochen freundlich. Sogar die *SZ*, die in ihrem Generalverriss einräumt, Quasthoff habe »mit der Intelligenz des Liedsängers die Botschaft der Brüderlichkeit zumindest textverständlich und mit großem Ernst an sein Publikum gebracht«. Sybill Mahlke, der Rezensentin des Berliner *Tagesspiegels*, hat es besser gefallen. Sie schreibt, ich dürfe mir »in Zukunft getrost noch mehr Theater gönnen«.

Das hab ich dann auch getan. Fast auf den Tag genau ein Jahr später sendet *dpa* diese Meldung in die Redaktionsstuben:

»Wien (dpa) – Der gefeierte Bariton Thomas Quasthoff gibt am Donnerstag (8. April) sein Debüt an der Wiener Staatsoper. Der Grammy-Preisträger singt in der Neuinszenierung von Richard Wagners *Parsifal* (Regie: Christine Mielitz) den leidenden König Amfortas. Die Titelrolle singt Johan Botha, als Kundry ist Angela Denoke zu hören. Staatsoperndirektor Ioan Holender kündigte vor der Premiere an: ›Es wird kein glatter Abend werden. Aber wir müssen das tun, was wir für richtig halten.‹

Regisseurin Mielitz will Wagners letzte Oper nach eigenen Worten als ›gnadenlos-wissenden Abgesang auf Utopien‹ auf die Bühne bringen. Der als Liedsänger bekannt gewordene Quasthoff stand im April 2003 bei den Salzburger Osterfestspielen unter Simon Rattle erstmals auf der Opernbühne. Er hatte Auftritte in Opern bis dahin abgelehnt, um zu vermeiden, dass seine Contergan-Schädigung als Bühneneffekt genutzt würde. Sein Debüt am renommierten Haus an der Ringstraße kommentierte der vierundvierzigjährige

Sänger am Dienstag in der Wiener Zeitung *Kurier*: ›Es gibt Gott sei Dank viel wichtigere Dinge, als dass ich den Amfortas singe. Es geht nicht um mich. Es geht um die schönste Musik, die es auf diesem Planeten gibt.‹«

Ich muss bekennen, mir ist der Wagner-Kosmos lange Zeit so fern gewesen wie der NASA der Jupiter. Mein Theorie-Lehrer Ernst Huber-Contwig hat mich zwar ins Grundsätzliche eingeweiht, aber das Treiben auf dem Bayreuther Hügel ist mir eher suspekt: der sektenhafte Kult um die Aufführungen, das alljährliche Schaulaufen der bundesrepublikanischen Gernegroße, Wagners Judenhass, die Speichelleckerei des Bakunin-Freundes bei Ludwig II., sein politisches Spintisieren, das sich erst im Anarchismus, dann im deutschnationalen Urschlamm wälzt, um am Ende die Rettung des Sozialismus mithilfe von »Vegetariern«, »Tierschützern« und »Mäßigkeitspflegern« zu propagieren *(Über Religion und Kunst)*, vor allem hat mich die indiskutable Sympathie des Clans für die Naziideologie abgestoßen. Als Simon mir den Amfortas im *Parsifal* anbietet, komme ich aber nicht darum herum, mich mit Wagner intensiver auseinander zu setzen. Es dauert keine vier Wochen, da ist – was die rein musikalische Seite betrifft – aus dem Saulus ein Paulus geworden. In allen anderen Punkten will ich Thomas Manns Einschätzung gelten lassen: Wagners Œuvre sei eines der »fragwürdigsten, vieldeutigsten und faszinierendsten Phänomene der schöpferischen Welt«. Zumindest lässt sich schwerlich ein anderes Werk finden, in dem Wohl und Wehe, Würde und Wahn des 19. Jahrhunderts so dicht beieinander liegen. Wie wunderbar seine Musik klingen kann, erlebe ich noch im selben Jahr im Bayreuther Festspielhaus.

Tony, glühender Wagnerianer und seit Jahrzehnten

Dauergast der Wagner-Festspiele, hat mir eines der raren Tickets für die *Meistersinger* besorgt. Christian Thielemann dirigiert, und ich bin begeistert vom transparenten Orchesterklang und von der fast schon shakespearschen Heiterkeit der Lieder und Chöre. Am nächsten Tag verschafft uns Tonys Veteranenstatus eine Einladung zum Tee bei Wolfgang Wagner, dem greisen Vorstand der Erbengemeinschaft. Gerne würde ich jetzt mit ein paar Anekdoten aufwarten. Aber die Verständigung ist schwierig. Der würdige alte Herr spricht wenig. Wenn er doch mal etwas sagt, nuschelt er Sätze im konsonantenreichen Alt-Fränkisch und schiebt dabei auch noch Feingebäck von einer Backe in die andere. Außerdem hört er nicht mehr besonders gut. Was ich spätestens merke, als Tony seinen Standardvortrag in Sachen Musikgeschichte herunterrattert. Wolfgang Wagner blickt dabei aus dem Fenster, stippt unirdisch lächelnd Kekse in den Tee und lässt alle zwei Minuten den Kopf mechanisch nach unten sinken. Tonys obligatorischen Schlusssatz »I don't know what dieser Schönberg wollte!« kommentiert er so:

»Ja, ja, schö isser scho, aber bei uns soagt man net Beag, sondern Hüügl.«

Nach dem Bayreuth-Besuch habe ich Simon mit Freuden zugesagt. Das ist mir umso leichter gefallen, weil der *Parsifal* als das »unopernhafteste« Wagner-Großwerk gilt, man darf ruhig »Oratorium mit Kostümen« dazu sagen. Die Amfortas-Rolle habe ich auch gleich gemocht, weil sie einen sehr kantablen Charakter besitzt. Im Gegensatz beispielsweise zu Verdis verkrüppeltem *Rigoletto*, den ich oft angeboten bekomme, aber lieber nicht machen möchte.

Allerdings hätte ich nie gedacht, dass auch eine lyrische Wagner-Partie so anstrengend sein kann. Nach einem Monat Probenarbeit und sechs Aufführungen bin ich fast geneigt, Schopenhauer zuzustimmen, der die Oper

»eine Versammlung zum Zweck der Selbstpeinigung« ge-nannt hat. Die fünfstündige Inszenierung fordert nicht nur meiner Wenigkeit das Letzte ab. Auch der Drei-Zent-ner-Hüne Johan Botha, der den Parsifal singt, schaut am Ende abgekämpft aus seiner Rüstung. Es ist ja nicht allein die Länge, die an den Kräften zehrt. Viel schlimmer sind die Lichtbatterien. Jeder einzelne Scheinwerfer brennt mit 1000er-Wattzahlen von der Decke, sodass man allein beim Herumstehen schwitzt wie nach einem ausgiebigen Saunagang. In diesem Zustand soll man sich auch noch auf Wagners hochdramatische Gesangsstimmen konzen-trieren und schauspielern, als ginge es um den Gloria-Swanson-Gedächtnis-Preis.

Mir macht das alles besonders zu schaffen, weil sich meine Mutter unerwartet einer schweren Herzoperation unterziehen muss. Sie ist während des Umzugs meiner Eltern nach Hannover zusammengebrochen und schwebt eine Woche lang zwischen Leben und Tod. Auch Vater ist in einem desolaten Zustand. Obwohl ich weiß, dass Micha alles stehen und liegen gelassen hat, um sich um die beiden zu kümmern, kann ich vor Sorge kaum arbei-ten. Am liebsten würde ich sofort nach Hause fahren. Als ich Regisseurin Christine Mielitz mein Herz ausschütte, zögert sie keinen Moment:

»Ick versteh det jut. Wenn du gloobst, et jet nich mehr, fahr heem. Auf *Parsifal* brauchste keene Rücksicht nehm'. Auf mich schon jar nich.« Die ansonsten so burschikose Ostberlinerin hat ein großes Herz und ist rührend um mich besorgt. Das Gleiche gilt für die großartigen Kolle-gen, die mich während der Proben dick in Watte packen. Micha, der täglich das medizinische Bulletin durchtelefo-niert, rät mir, in Wien zu bleiben, solange Mamas Zustand kritisch, aber stabil ist. Auch Tony meint, ich solle nichts überstürzen. Hin- und hergerissen, beschließe ich, erst einmal weiterzuproben, aber eine große Stütze bin ich weder für die Regie noch für Dirigent Donald Runnicles. Drei Tage nach der Operation gibt Micha endlich Entwarnung, Mama ist aufgewacht, sie hat das Gröbste überstanden. Mir fällt ein ganzes Mittelgebirge vom Herzen, und ich stürze mich mit neuem Elan auf den Amfortas. Christine Mielitz hat schon angedeutet, dass er in ihrem Regiekonzept eine zentrale Rolle spielt, mir aber noch keine Details verraten.

»Ick muss erst mal wissen, wat de kannst!«

»Singen, denk ich doch!«

»Det weeß ick, Mensch. Ick meene, ob de mit deiner Behinderung loofen kannst, ob de auf der Bühne agieren kannst, oder ob wa den Amfortas von de Matratzengruft gleich in 'nen Sarg rollen müssen.«

»Keine Sorge, ich bin eine echte Sportskanone.«

Das hätte ich nicht sagen sollen. Denn jetzt wird der Gralskönig Kilometer fressen, anstatt seine ewig schwärende, von Klingsor geschlagene Wunde auf weichen Daunen zu pflegen und sich ansonsten von der Gralsknappschaft per Sänfte herumschleppen zu lassen. So steht es wenigstens im Libretto. Aber Frau Mielitz hat Amfortas Bewegung verordnet.

Ausgerechnet im dritten Akt wird mir, dem inzwischen Fast-Toten, die Sänfte gänzlich gestrichen. Stattdessen lässt sie einen Fahrstuhl bauen, der den Gralskönig vom Schnürboden effektvoll auf die Bühne bringen soll. Man erreicht das Gefährt nur über eine steile hohe Treppe hinter der Bühnenrückwand. Es ist eng dort und dunkel, und ich falle beim ersten Aufstieg fast in die Kulissen.

»Schraubt hier mal 'ne Lampe an«, brülle ich. »Es heißt doch immer, Amfortas darf nicht sterben.«

»Wenn de weiter so rumbrüllst, überleg ick mir det noch«, ruft meine Regisseurin. Als der Fahrstuhl mehrmals unter bedenklichem Ruckeln und Rucken drei Meter über dem Boden stecken bleibt, fürchte ich schon, sie meint es ernst.

»Reg dich nich uff«, beruhigt mich die Mielitz. »Runter kommste immer.«

»Fragt sich nur, in welchem Zustand. Wahrscheinlich braucht Amfortas dann nie mehr in die Maske.«

Man sieht, der Ton ist rau, aber herzlich. Was auch die Kollegen zu schätzen wissen. Jedenfalls folgen sie Christine Mielitz bedingungslos, die das Ensemble herumschiebt wie ein General seine Truppen, um den von ihr projektierten »Abgesang auf alle Utopien« angemessen zu bebildern. Nach der Generalprobe mustert sie zufrieden die Szenerie.

»So, det sah doch allet jut aus.« Auch Direktor Ioan Holender nickt und wappnet sich für die Premiere. Er ahnt, was auf ihn zukommen wird.

Am Abend des 8. April sind große Teile der Wiener Staatsoper fest in der Hand einer eingeschworenen Wagner-Gemeinde. Ihre Mitglieder sind den Gralsrittern gar nicht so unähnlich. Sie sitzen mit dem festen Willen im Gestühl, ein ästhetisches Ritual zu vollziehen und jede Schändung der heiligen Aufführungstradition abzustrafen, die in der Josefstadt seit fünfundzwanzig Jahren von August Everdings *Parsifal*-Inszenierung repräsentiert wird. Anfangs gibt es wenig Grund zur Klage.

Donald Runnicles lässt das von himmlischer Liebe und Kraft kündende As-Dur-Gralsmotiv aus den tiefen Registern der Streicher aufsteigen und an die Mauern der Gralsburg Montsalvat branden. Sie ist möbliert wie eine Kreuzung aus Schwimmbad und heruntergekommenem Fin-de-Siècle-Salon. Zwei Knappen schleppen Amfortas herein. Über des Königs Schulter liegt ein mit Bühnenblut getränktes Linnen. Ich nehme von Gurnemanz den Heilbalsam Kundrys entgegen und werde auch schon wieder hinausgetragen.

So muss der König wenigstens nicht mit ansehen, wie in der Burg langsam die Wände bröckeln. Als ich wieder auftrete, dämmert dem Publikum, dass auch das Verfallsdatum der Bewohner längst abgelaufen ist. Die Ritter sind mitnichten die göttlich gesegnete Elite des Abendlandes, sondern nur mehr ein dekadentes Machtkartell, eine Versammlung buchstäblich trüber Tassen, die so manche Leiche im Keller vergraben haben, Kinder entführen, kleinliche Händel austragen und den Frauen nachsteigen. Als Gralshüter haben sie abgewirtschaftet. Und mit ihnen der ideologische Überbau, den Wagner aus christlicher Heilslehre, Germanentum, persischer Mystik und Schopenhauer zum »Bühnenweihfestspiel« verlötet hat, um den Deutschen das Gesamtkunstwerk als Religions- und Politikersatz zu präsentieren. Folgerichtig mutieren die einst stolzen Recken zu kleinbürgerlichen Hosenträgern und tun sich dabei vorrangig selber Leid. Parsifal ist eher ein tumber als ein reiner Tor, Klingsor ein Bordellbesitzer, der Kundry und die Blumenmädchen zwingt, den Gralsrittern zu Willen zu sein, Zeremonienmeister Gurnemanz exekutiert das sinnentleerte Regelwerk der Gemeinschaft mit beamtenhafter Sturheit, und mein Amfortas entpuppt sich als reuiger Sünder, der nicht weiß, ob er mehr am unheiligen Weltgetriebe oder an der eigenen Unvollkommenheit leiden soll. Er zaudert sogar, die fällige Gralsenthüllung vorzunehmen, eine Prozedur, die ihm und seinen Spießgesellen das Überleben sichert. Und so muss erst der dank Gottes Gnade im eigenen Grabe höchst lebendig vor sich hin herumhomunkelnde Vater Titurel (Walter Fink) ein Machtwort sprechen, ehe der Sohnemann die heilige Handlung vollzieht. Mit zittrigen Händen fuhrwerkt Amfortas an der Reliquie herum, die dabei prompt irreparablen Schaden nimmt. Parsifal sieht es mit Staunen, vergisst aber die entscheidende Mitleidsfrage zu stellen und läutet so die erste Pause ein.

Die weitere Handlung spielt im Rotlichtviertel des Paten Klingsor. Der Großgangster und Medienzar hat alle Mitspieler im Griff, nur nicht den Naivling Parsifal, den er nun mithilfe der schönen Kundry zu verführen sucht. Anders als bei Wagner vorgesehen kriegt sie ihn tatsächlich zwischen die Schenkel, doch statt zum Höhepunkt kommt der Jüngling mit Dr. Freud zur Einsicht, dass höchste Lust nicht Triebabfuhr bedeutet, sondern Sublimierung. Und die gebietet ihm nun dringlich, den »Gral aus schuldbefleckten Händen« zu befreien. Da es im zweiten, ziemlich langen Aufzug für Amfortas nichts zu tun gibt, sitze ich hinter den Kulissen und habe ein gutes Buch dabei. Es bleibt aber auch in der sechsten Aufführung zugeklappt, weil ich immer wieder den Philharmonikern lausche, die unter Runnicles subtiler Stabführung den erotischen Showdown zwischen Kundry und Parsifal meisterhaft in Szene setzen.

Im dritten Akt, nach dem Intermezzo in der Karfreitagsaue, schickt mich Frau Mielitz ganz allein auf die Bühne. Begleitet nur von einem Trauermarsch und niedergedrückt von einer riesigen Gralskrone, schleppt sich Amfortas wie der irre gewordene Lear über die Heide. Es naht der Zug mit der Leiche Titurels. Der Sohn ist schuld am Tod des Titanen, weil er zum zweiten Mal die Enthüllung des Grals verweigert hat. Winselnd kriecht Amfortas in den Sarg des Vaters und schreit seinen Klagegesang heraus (»Mein Vater, mein Vater, Hochgesegneter der Helden«). Mir bleibt nur noch, die Ritter aufzufordern, meiner verpfuschten Existenz mit blankem Stahl ein Ende zu machen. Doch Parsifal, den man inzwischen zum Gralskönig gekürt hat, heilt meine Wunde durch die Berührung mit der heiligen Lanze. Noch einmal peitscht das Orchester mit dramatischer Grandezza durch die Schlussszene, dann lässt Runnicles das verklärende Gralsmotiv von As-Dur nach Des-Dur und zurück schwellen. Parsifals Lanze glüht auf wie das Schwert eines Jedi-Ritters. Das ist wahrlich »Höchsten Heiles Wunder« – die Erlösung winkt. Doch die Scheinwerfer kreisen suchend über den Besucherreihen, als wollten sie fragen: »Erlösung für wen? Erlösung von was? Erlösung? Wieso, weshalb, warum?«

Darüber lohnt es durchaus nachzudenken, findet zumindest ein Drittel des Publikums und applaudiert begeistert. Der Wagner-Gemeinde geht das entschieden über die Hutschnur. »Buh«, »Frechheit«, »Zumutung«, »Skandal«, heult es böse von den teuren Plätzen. Christine Mielitz nimmt es gelassen. Sie steht lächelnd an der Rampe und freut sich über den einmütigen Jubelsturm für die Sänger. »Phänomenal gesungen; interessant interpretiert«, urteilt tags darauf der *Wiener Kurier.* Auch in anderen Blättern ist von einem »überragenden Sänger-Ensemble« die Rede, respektive von »Weltklasse-Besetzung«. Und das haben die Kollegen, allen voran Angela Denoke und Johan Botha, auch verdient. Ich selbst bin nach einer Produktion wohl noch nie so matt und gleichzeitig so glücklich gewesen. Vor allem freut mich, dass Joachim Kaiser meinen Amfortas durchaus glaubwürdig findet. Er schreibt:

»Rasch nahmen wir Zuschauenden hin, dass der schwer verletzte, leidende Gralskönig ebenso sei, wie Quasthoff ihn verkörperte. Der Künstler bot die Partie souverän, hochmusikalisch phrasierend, bestechend deutlich in Diktion und Tongebung. Er verband Schubert-Melos mit wohlgesetzter musikdramatischer Emphase.«

Dass ihm letztlich aber doch »das Wagnerisch-Zehrende, das Erz, die selbstmörderische Wahnsinnsekstase« gefehlt hat, kann ich verstehen. Das ist reine Geschmackssache. Direktor Holender hätte die Rolle problemlos mit einem echten Wagner-Bariton besetzen können. Aber er wollte ausdrücklich einen lyrischen Sänger.

So sah das auch Eleonore Büning in der *Frankfurter Allgemeinen Zeitung*. »Weder die Regie noch Quasthoff selbst gaben den geringsten Raum für sensationslüsterne Effekte. Er sang seine Erzählung von Schuld, Strafe und Erlösung wie ein Liedsänger, der in wenige Töne das ganze Leid der Welt packen kann ... Parsifal hört den Ruf des Herzens und musste weinen. Allen, die zuhörten, ging es genauso.« Es gab natürlich auch Ausnahmen wie den Mann von *Associated Press*. Er befand kurz und bündig: »his voice, while pleasant, was occasionally not up to Wagnerian demands of sonority«.

Aber das hat mich nicht weiter gejuckt. Denn wenn man in fünfundzwanzig Berufsjahren eines lernt, dann dies: Es lohnt nicht, sich über Rezensenten aufzuregen. Auch wenn das Bewahren der Gemütsruhe oft schwer fällt. »Wer diese Zeilen liest, ist mir zu nahe getreten« – diesen Satz würde er am liebsten ans Ende seiner Bücher schreiben, hat das bayrische Originalgenie Herbert Achternbusch einem Interviewer gestanden. Hat er dann doch lieber gelassen, der Herbert, obwohl ihm die CSU-Kader im freistaatlichen Medienwald mehr als einmal unverdient und existenzbedrohend übel mitgespielt haben. Aperçus wie »die Kritik ist das Psychogramm eines Kritikers«, das der feinsinnige Will Quadflieg seinen Quälgeistern am liebsten auf die Stirn tätowiert hätte, mögen wahr sein, bringen aber niemanden weiter. Denn ohne Kritiker geht es nun einmal nicht. Das wissen alle, die ihre Kunst auf dem freien Markt feilbieten. Wo die Rezensenten-Zunft ausstirbt, das heißt wegrationalisiert wird, übernehmen die Pressebüros der Unterhaltungskonzerne oder Promo-Agenturen das Regiment. Was dabei herauskommt, ist in Stadtpostillen und Regionalzeitungen, in Privatradiosendern und TV-Anstalten längst zu besichtigen: kulturelle Wüsteneien, garniert mit der unredigierten Dreistigkeit des Event-Jargons.

Weit hilfreicher wäre es, dem Publikum klar zu machen, dass die Rezensentenkaste auch nur mit Wasser kocht. Manchmal auch nur mit heißer Luft. Wie diese Geschichte beweist: Als Theodor Fontane, damals schlecht bezahlter Redakteur einer Berliner Lokalgazette, am 18. April 1870 seine erste Theaterkritik (man gab *Wilhelm Tell*) an die große *Vossische Zeitung* schickte, lobte er die Aufführung, pries die Schauspieler und fabulierte etwas vom »animierten Publikum«. Im Tagebuch notierte der schlaue Fuchs dagegen, der Sums sei »ziemlich langweilig« gewesen. Er wusste genau: Verrisse schreiben ist nicht schwer. Das wahre Talent zeigt sich erst in der geschliffenen Belobigung. So sah das auch die *Vossische*. Fontane stieg schnell zum führenden Theatermann des Blattes auf und sorgte fortan dafür, dass sich Gerhart Hauptmann und mit ihm der Naturalismus auf deutschen Bühnen durchsetzte.

Was wiederum Beleg dafür ist, dass sich die Kritiker meistens redlich mühen. In der ARD konnte man einem von ihnen beim Rezensieren sogar einmal live über die Schulter gucken. Sehr beeindruckend, wie Joachim Kaiser von der *Süddeutschen* das machte. Das eisgrau befilzte Haupt an die Brust gedrückt, die Arme um die Schultern geschlungen, als müsste das Hemd am Rutschen gehindert werden, pantherte Kaiser durch sein Büro und zerkaute anscheinend selbstvergessen den Bügel seiner Lesebrille. Erst ging's drei Schritte nach rechts, dann vier

Schritte nach links, dann wieder zurück und so fort. Während der Rechtskehre hielt er jedes Mal vor einem sinnreich angebrachten Spiegel inne, linste, sein Charakterprofil ausgiebig prüfend, hinein, um hernach sichtlich gestärkt, aber schweigend den Gedankengang wieder aufzunehmen. Nach fünf weiteren Kilometern gebar Herr Kaiser tatsächlich – wenn auch nur unter erheblichem Knurren und Grummeln – ein Adjektiv. Es hieß, glaube ich, »mürbe«. Prompt hob ein munteres Klappern an, die Kamera schwenkte vorbei an einem Gummibaum drei Grad nach Westen auf einen Schreibtisch, wo die eilfertige Sekretärin ebenjene fünf kaiserlichen Buchstaben in die Schreibmaschine tippte. Ja, sagt uns diese Szene, hier ringt ein Gerechter mit den Göttern der Musik.

Wo die Eitelkeit anfängt, hört der Verstand auf, sagt der Volksmund. Und lügt wie gedruckt. Denn das Spreizen, Gaukeln und Selbstinszenieren gehört einfach zum Kulturbetrieb: vor, hinter oder auf der Bühne. Das kann jedermann höchstselbst im Theaterfoyer beobachten. Wenn die Besucher, das Sitzfleisch durch dezente Muskelkontraktionen lockernd, zur Pause heraustreten, geht es doch gleich los wie bei Herrn Kaiser. Die Herren versenken eine Pranke in der Hosentasche, die andere hält zwanghaft ein Pils, dann wird auf der Stelle getreten. Das Doppelkinn sinkt an den Schlipsknoten, die Stirn legt sich in Furchen, und nach langem Grübeln entringt sich der Kehle eine erste Einschätzung der ästhetischen Gemengelage: Meist ein heiseres »Nun ja«. Das kann alles bedeuten. Soll es auch. Denn es heißt erst einmal abwarten. Bis A) die Gattin, Mätresse oder die beste Freundin derselben, welche den gemeinsamen Kulturabend anberaumt hat, am Piccolo nippt und resolut verfügt: »Ist doch wunderbar«, B) vom Stehtisch der stadtbekannten Kritikergilde ein erstes

Urteil herüberweht oder C) man den »verehrten Herrn Direktor« respektive Ministerialdirigent oder Messe-Vorstand begrüßt und mit dem jovialen »Na, Krause, wie läuft's denn so?« auch ein »Wat sagen Se nu wieder zu diesem Regietheater-Unsinn« mit auf den Weg bekommt. Da wird man schnell ziemlich mürbe.

Dem mühsam ersessenen Urteil des Amateurbesuchers gebricht es keineswegs an Entschiedenheit. Aber sein Verdikt erreicht selten die Stilblütenpracht der professionellen Kritik. Da kommen »Verdis Cantabile-Passagen« daher »wie dunkelrot sprudelnder Chianti«, romantische Lieder schmecken »wie leckere Schnellgerichte und Thomas Quasthoff ist ein Meisterkoch«; da spielen Pianisten »pauschal«, Orchester »finden treffsicher den Weg in die Eingeweide ihrer Hörerschaft«, in Schuberts zartem *Frühlingstraum* »detonierte der dritte Teil beider Verse«, während Quasthoffs Stimme »mit dem allzu breit ausgesungenen Negro-Hit *Swing Low* nicht nur die Puristen entsetzte«, sondern »mitunter wie ein fahles Laubblatt auf herbstlichen Grund fällt. Eine irrwitzige Wirkung!« Noch irrer ist ein Sänger, der »die Zuschauer als eine emotionale Flutwelle überrollt und fast betäubt in den Polstern zurücklässt«. Anders gesagt: »wer unvorbereitet erscheint, sieht sich mit dem Unerwarteten konfrontiert«. Dabei hört mancher sogar »betörende Stimmen aus einer ganz anderen Welt«. Dann ist der Interpret entweder »eine Insel im Konzertbetrieb, von der man nicht gerettet werden möchte«, oder er laboriert an »Eintrübungen im Register-Bruchbereich«. Wenn er Pech hat, sitzt auch noch jener Wiener Rezensent im Saal, der eine Altistin durch dieses Urteil öffentlich hinrichtete: »Ihre Stimme klang wie ein Arschhaar. Rau und unsauber!«

Das ist natürlich weit unter der Gürtellinie, macht aber wenigstens semantisch Sinn. Was man von der Formulierung dieses fußballbegeisterten Kollegen nicht behaupten kann:

»Am Dienstagabend wäre an Simon Rattle auch nicht Stan Libuda vorbeigekommen. Auf dem Programm stand allerdings nicht Borussia Dortmund, sondern die *Gurrelieder* von Arnold Schönberg.« Ähnliche Treffsicherheit bewies eine Dame, die anlässlich der Fürther Kirchenmusiktage meine am Schlusstag vorgetragene *Winterreise* so zusammenfasste: »Damit füllte er die Lücken, die die Abende zum Thema Tod gelassen hatten.«

Zu ganz großer Form laufen die Schreiber auf, wenn es gilt, meinen Gesang mit meiner unorthodoxen Erscheinung zu verknüpfen. »Er ließ sich nicht behindern« heißen die subtilen Titelzeilen, »Behinderung ist kein Hindernis« oder »Behinderter nimmt alle Hürden«, gern auch »Behinderter mit Superstimme«. Die unübertroffenen Klassiker bleiben jedoch: »Der behinderte Zwerg Quasthoff hinkte auf die Bühne und erleuchtete *Paulus*« und das schon im ersten Kapitel erwähnte »Er sang, als ob Gott einen Betriebsunfall wieder gutmachen wollte«.

Um den Themenkreis endgültig abzurunden, möchte ich dem verehrten Leser zwei meiner liebsten Kritiken präsentieren. Die erste erschien unter der Überschrift »Große Totenmesse zum Weltspartag« in der *Wiener Zeitung*. Sie rührt durch den herkulischen Versuch des Autors, die Themen Bankenkrise, Totensonntag, Balkankrieg und das *Deutsche Requiem* von Brahms auf achtzig Zeilen zusammenzuzwingen.

»Wien. Betrübliche Kunde vom Weltspartag. Die Österreicher haben keinen Spaß mehr an ihren Sparbücheln. Wenn Banker Trauer tragen, ist ein Requiem fällig. Und über solche Unbill hinwegzutrösten, ist das *Deutsche Requiem* von Johannes Brahms durchaus in der Lage.

Die Sächsische Staatskapelle, verstärkt durch den Sing-verein der Gesellschaft der Musikfreunde Wien, ist im Goldenen Saal freilich zu Höherem angetreten und sollte den Totengedenktagen das passende Klang-ambiente verleihen. Doch die Klänge der Gegenwart dröhnen allerdings anders. Das aktuelle Instrumenta-rium besteht aus Flugzeugen und Raketen. Spreng-köpfe sind ihre Noten. Ihr Schlagzeug schlägt tot.

Da komponiert kein Brahms, da spielt kein Sachse und da singt kein Wiener drüber. Doch einer: Ein Ein-ziger bringt es zustande, in die Schluchten heutiger Erschütterung abzusteigen und aus diesen, wenn schon nicht tröstliche, so doch nicht minder erschüt-ternde Schönheit zu fördern. Es ist Thomas Quasthoff. Das Psalmwort ›Ach, wie gar nichts sind alle Men-schen, die doch so sicher leben‹, von ihm gesungen, wurde zur geistigen und emotionalen Coda dieses Abends …«

Besonders schön ist, dass ich so mir nichts, dir nichts zum Wiener geworden bin. Da wird sich mein Steuerberater freuen.

Den zweiten Artikel mag ich, weil ihn Micha geschrie-ben hat. Während seines Studiums bespricht er für die *Hannoversche Neue Presse* Platten, Bücher und Popkonzer-te. Als im Opernhaus Haydns *Schöpfung* auf dem Pro-gramm steht, liegt der E-Musik-Experte des Blattes mit Grippe im Bett. Sein Stellvertreter besucht ein Konzert in London. Also fragt der Ressortchef, ob Brüderchen sich eine Klassik-Rezension zutraut. Micha, der immer zu wenig Geld, aber mit Oratorien rein gar nichts am Hut hat, sagt:

»Klar, ich fürchte mich vor gar nichts«, fügt aber hinzu: »Sie wissen schon, dass mein Bruder den Raphael singt?«

»Ist das ein Problem?«

»Wenn es für Sie und die Oper keins ist, übernehme ich den Job.« Nachmittags fragt er vorsichtig an: »Sag mal, Tommi, wie lange wird das denn heute Abend dauern?«

»Knapp drei Stunden.« Micha seufzt und packt neben Stift und Block Chandlers *The Long Goodbye* in seine Tasche.

»Du sollst zuhören und nicht lesen«, mahne ich.

»Ist ja nur für den Notfall, falls es allzu transzendent wird. Aber keine Sorge, selbst wenn ich einschlafen sollte, wird es kein Verriss.« Er hält Wort und der *Neue Presse*-Leser am nächsten Morgen diesen Text in der Hand:

»›Vollendet ist das große Werk / der Schöpfer sieht's und freuet sich.‹ Nicht nur er. Auch von den voll besetzten Rängen des Opernhauses tönte frenetischer Beifall, als Oratorienchor, Staatsorchester und Solisten Haydns *Schöpfung* volltönend auf die Bühne stellten. Mit Recht. Nachdem die Symphoniker noch etwas orientierungslos durch das schwebende ›Urchaos‹ gestrichen waren, repräsentierte Dirigent Jöris spätestens vom hämmernden C-Dur-Einsatz an (»Und es ward Licht«) die ordnende Hand des Herrn. Souverän führte er den glänzend aufgelegten Chor durch die Partitur und bündelte Orchesterpart, Arien und Rezitative zu einem bewegenden Stück christlich-abendländischer Hochkunst. Höchstes Lob verdienen sich dabei vor allem zwei Erzengel. Sabine Paßows superb klingender Sopran federte schwerelos durch die Koloraturen der Gabriel-Rolle, und Bariton Thomas Quasthoff demonstrierte eindrucksvoll, dass große Sänger neben der Stimme eben doch noch ein Gran Soul mitbringen müssen, um den Raphael-Arien solch samtenen Glanz zu verleihen, wie er es tat. Seine geschmeidige, dabei stets kraftvoll-präsente Stimmführung machte selbst die Rezitative zu einem Genuss. So angeregt, sang sich ›Uriel‹ Aldo Baldin schnell das Klößchen aus dem Hals und hielt wacker mit.

Nur, was normalerweise als Höhepunkt der Schöpfung gehandelt wird, glich eher ungelenken Proben des Herrn. Manuela Benz knödelte ihre Eva auf Operettenniveau, während sich Rolf ›Adam‹ Zieglers Bass durch seine Zwei-Meter-Statur quälte wie durch ein hohles Fass. Heraus kam nur heiße Luft, die manchmal sogar einen Viertelton unter Normalnull lag. Aber, keine Schöpfung ist vollkommen.«

Als er mir das Werk zur Begutachtung vorlegt, sage ich: »Alle Achtung, gut getroffen. Liest sich, als hättest du nie etwas anderes gemacht.« Micha winkt ab.

»So 'ne Kurzkritik kann doch jeder zusammenklöppeln, wenn er ein bisschen Musikverstand und Reclams Konzertführer im Regal stehen hat.«

»Nur mein Part ist vielleicht ein bisschen dick aufgetragen, schließlich weiß morgen jeder, dass das mein Bruder geschrieben hat.«

»Erstens warst du wirklich klasse, zweitens habe ich mich ja nicht danach gedrängt, den Artikel zu übernehmen. Offensichtlich stört es keinen.«

Aber das ist ein Irrtum. Die beiden etwas formschwachen Kollegen sind stocksauer und intervenieren beim Intendanten, sie seien zu schlecht und Quasthoff zu gut weggekommen, was ja kein Wunder sei, wenn die Verwandtschaft die Kritiken schreibt. Der Intendant entblödet sich nicht, eine Gegendarstellung einzufordern. Bei der *Neuen Presse* beißt er allerdings auf Granit. Einige Redakteure haben ebenfalls im Konzert gesessen und finden den Text äußerst gelungen. Der Intendant schäumt und verhängt gegen Micha ein Jahr Hausverbot. Er hat darüber sehr gelacht. Er kennt das von den lokalen Veranstaltern aus der Popbranche, die auch sofort in der Chefredaktion anrufen, wenn der Rezensent ein Stadion voller PhilUdoGrönehagen-Fans nicht mit Superlativen beschmeißt.

»Der einzige Ton, den die gerne hören, ist das Klingeln der Registrierkasse. Ich hätte nur nicht gedacht, dass die Hochkultur genauso kleingeistig daherkommt.«

Hätte er alles bei Lessing in der *Emilia Galotti* nachlesen können.

»Was macht die Kunst«, fragt Prinz Gonzaga da.

»Die Kunst, Prinz, geht nach dem Brot«, antwortet Hofmaler Conti.

»Das muss sie nicht, das soll sie nicht«, trompetet Gonzaga stellvertretend für die Impresarios dieser Welt. Doch wie man weiß, ist der Mann ein skrupelloser Blender und notorischer Lügenbold.

Klassische Musik war und ist immer auch Big Business wie die bildende Kunst, das Fernsehen oder das Pop- und Rockgeschäft. Und dagegen ist auch nichts einzuwenden. Schließlich wollen alle Beteiligten Geld verdienen. Dass der Künstler seinen gerechten Anteil vom Kuchen erhält, stellen die Agenten sicher. Sie halten einem das Geschäft vom Leibe und werden dafür mit einem Teil der Einnahmen entlohnt.

Dass das ein faires Geschäft ist, erschließt sich mir erst nach einigen Umwegen. In meiner Anfangszeit habe ich nur mit kleinen, regionalen Konzertbüros zu tun. Und da geht schon eine Menge schief. Mal gibt es Terminchaos, mal warte ich monatelang auf die kargen Gagen. Daher bin ich nach dem ARD-Wettbewerb ganz froh, nicht an eine Agentur gebunden zu sein. Vorher hatte ich rund fünfzig Auftritte im Jahr, jetzt könnte ich auf einen Schlag zweihundert Konzerte geben. Ein windiger Agent hätte mich bestimmt zweimal quer durch die Republik gescheucht, um die Konjunktur zu nutzen. So aber sichte ich mit Frau Lehmann und ihrem Gatten Huber-Contwig in Ruhe die Angebote, und wir suchen uns die besten heraus.

Das geht so lange gut, bis Huber-Contwig sich in den Kopf setzt, an der Musikhochschule Hannover Professor zu werden. Das Problem ist, dass in jeder Stadt, wo ich auftrete, die Zeitungen Artikel über meinen musikalischen Werdegang schreiben. Selbstredend vergessen sie nie zu erwähnen, auf welch schnöde Weise Hochschulchef Jakobi das behinderte Talent seinerzeit abblitzen ließ. Jetzt steht Jakobi republikweit da wie der größte Depp, was ihm nur recht geschieht, Huber-Contwigs Chancen auf eine gut dotierte Verbeamtung aber nicht gerade erhöht. Er macht mir wegen der Presseberichte heftige Vorwürfe, dabei kann ich gar nichts dafür. Die Fakten sind nun einmal in der Welt, und die Journalisten ziehen sie jedes Mal genüsslich aus dem Archiv. Die Geschichte ist aus ihrer Sicht ja auch zu schön. Ich dränge sie niemandem auf, habe aber, wenn man mich danach fragt, keine Veranlassung, sie zu dementieren.

Huber-Contwig mag das nicht einsehen. Er wirkt zunehmend verbittert. Dass er sich neuerdings bei jeder Gelegenheit als mein großer Entdecker und Förderer anpreist, nehme ich hin, weil es Frau Lehmann, der diese Bezeichnung eigentlich zusteht, anscheinend nicht stört. Dass er obendrein anfängt, systematisch dumme Geschichten über mich in Umlauf zu bringen – Tenor: ich sei faul, arrogant und undankbar –, finde ich nicht mehr lustig. Ich sage ihm das, und ich sage es Frau Lehmann, die betroffen, aber etwas hilflos wirkt. Ändern tut sich jedenfalls nichts. Nach siebzehn Jahren enger Zusammenarbeit ist die Situation verfahren wie in einer überstrapazierten Ehe. Mir macht das sehr zu schaffen. Einerseits kann man so ein Verhalten nicht tolerieren, andererseits möchte ich meine Gesangslehrerin nicht verlieren. Aber das Fass läuft über, als es während eines Urlaubs in Locarno zu einem bizarren Auftritt kommt. Ich habe vorher mit Huber-Contwig *Entsorgt* einstudiert, ein Solostück für Bariton, das mir der Avantgarde-Komponist Aribert Reimann auf den Leib geschrieben hat. Der Text stammt von Nicolas Born. Unter dem Eindruck der Tschernobyl-Katastrophe zerlegt er den blinden Fortschrittsglauben der westlichen Welt in apokalyptische Bilder. Die Komposition ist so schwierig wie großartig, und ich freue mich auf die Uraufführung. Aber jetzt brauche ich eine Woche zum Abschalten. Am vierten Urlaubstag, ich sitze gerade mit Mama und Vater auf der Hotelterrasse, rauscht Huber-Contwig an – im Gepäck zwei frische Unterhosen und die Partitur. Er sagt nicht guten Tag, sondern rattert mit hochrotem Kopf Übungspläne herunter, die er für mich ausgearbeitet hat. *Entsorgt* sei so bedeutend für die Musikwelt, da könne man sich nicht einfach aus dem Staub machen und in die Sommerfrische fahren. Diese Suada lässt er obendrein in solcher Lautstärke vom Stapel, dass halb Locarno zuhören kann. Mein erster Reflex ist, schick ihn zum Teufel. Dann sehe ich meine Eltern an. Ihr Gesichtsausdruck sagt mir, sie glauben, er könnte Recht haben. Um des lieben Friedens willen verbringe ich den Resturlaub also mit dem Zerberus im Hotelzimmer und schmettere Born-Verse an die Zimmerdecke: »So wird der Schrecken ohne Ende langsam / normales Leben / Zuschauer blinzeln in den Hof / Im Mittagslicht …«

Nach der Premiere habe ich endgültig genug. Ich beschließe, dem Ehepaar Lehmann-Huber-Contwig zu kündigen und meinen Weg erst einmal allein zu gehen.

Die Luft riecht Ende der achtziger Jahre sowieso nach Veränderung. Und was kriegen wir nicht alles geboten: Lichterketten. Montagsdemos. Mauerfall. Kommunismus kaputt. Kalter Krieg vorbei. Weltgeschichte. Trabi-Trauma. Begrüßungsgeld. Die ersten Zonis in Hannovers Innenstadt: Rechts 'ne Plastiktüte, links 'ne Plastiktüte, Plaste- und Elaste-Jacke, Kolchosstulpen und Komsomolzenmütze – der wilde Osten, wie gemalt. Den wunderbaren *Titanic*-Gurken-Titel »Zonengabis erste Banane«. Das Triptychon Brandt, Kohl und Momper auf dem Balkon des Schöneberger Rathauses lauthals Haydns Deutschlandlied, ach was, die abendländische Musikkultur massakrierend. Kohl und Gorbi an der Wolga. Des Einheitskanzlers Strickzelt im »Haus der Geschichte«. Runde Tische in Jena. Goldene Wasserhähne in Wandlitz. Elend in Sorge und Sorge in Elend. Die Treuhand. Matthias Sammer in Stuttgart. Ulf Kirsten in Leverkusen – Ausverkauf bei Dynamo Dresden. Hansa Rostock in der ersten Bundesliga. Die Puhdys bei *Wetten, dass?* Honecker im chilenischen Exil. Mielke (»Ick liebe euch alle«) im Knast. Thierse im Bundestag. Menschen, Thesen, Sensationen: SED und PDS, Krenz und Gauck, Schorlemmer und Schabowski. Modrow. Merkel. De Maizière. Krause. Gysi. Bärbel Bohley. Täve Schur. Drei plus vier. Und dann 1990: Währungsunion, Wiedervereinigung, Fußball-Weltmeister in Rom. Großdeutschland wird »auf Jahre unschlagbar sein« (Franz Beckenbauer). Waaaaahnsinn!

Leider geht es mir wie unseren Brüdern und Schwestern in den Beitrittsgebieten. Nach dem Freiheitsrausch kommt der schwarze Kater. Ich arbeite zwar regelmäßig mit der Bachakademie, gebe Liederabende und werde von Leopold Hager und Peter Schreier zu Plattenaufnahmen (Haydns *Orpheus und Eurydike*, Mozarts *Krönungsmesse*) eingeladen. Aber ich merke bald, tagsüber mit Veranstaltern zu verhandeln und abends aufzutreten geht an die Substanz. Irgendwann muss ich die Stücke ja auch mal üben. Ein bisschen mehr Schlaf wäre ebenfalls nicht schlecht. Es muss schnellstens jemand her, der sich um die Geschäfte kümmert. Da kommt das Angebot einer Münchner Agentur gerade recht. Der Chef, nennen wir ihn Hinterseher, gibt sich wirklich große Mühe, mir den Vertragsabschluss schmackhaft zu machen. Bayern ist schön, schwurbeln die Reste eines Werbespots durch meinen Kopf, seine Landschaften typisch und seine Solidität weltberühmt, oder waren es die Bauten? Das Weißbier? Auf jeden Fall verspricht mir Hinterseher, dass ich in Kürze weltberühmt sein werde. Ich will einfach nur singen und unterschreibe. Danach knöpft mir Hinterseher erst einmal fünfhundert Mark ab. Die Aufnahmegebühr in die Weltklasse, denke ich und bin bass erstaunt, als er mir erklärt, dass der Betrag jeden Monat fällig wird.

»Das sind die üblichen Usancen«, lügt Hinterseher dem Greenhorn ins Gesicht. Danach habe ich ihn lange nicht mehr gesehen. Stattdessen tritt eine junge Dame in mein Leben, die mit Vornamen Christel und mit Nachnamen Personal Managerin heißt. Sie ist reizend, ganz neu bei der Agentur und nicht auf den Kopf gefallen. Wir führen lange Telefongespräche, gehen essen und schlendern heiter plaudernd durch den Englischen Garten. Öffentlich singen tue ich weniger. Denn wie sich herausstellt, versteht die Bürokauffrau vom Konzertgeschäft noch weniger als ich. Irgendwie habe ich mir mein Dasein als Hinterseher-Exklusiv-Künstler anders vorgestellt. Ein Blick auf mein Konto sagt mir: Ich kann mir den Mann nicht mehr leisten.

Ich wechsle auf Anraten von Kollegen zu einem Konzertbüro in Wien. Hier werde ich nicht mehr übers Ohr gehauen, hier habe ich einfach nur elendes Pech. Man lässt eine Agentin für mich arbeiten, die auch privat für Sänger schwärmt. Der aktuelle Favorit ist auch ein Bariton, sein Name steckt neben meinem in ihrer Kartei. Bis ich das durchschaue, vergeht eine Weile. In der Zwischenzeit wundere ich mich, warum ich keine guten Jobs bekomme. Ständig sprechen mich Kollegen an, sie hätten dieses oder jenes Konzert gesehen, alles sei sehr schön, nur der Bariton leider nicht ideal besetzt gewesen. Ich könnte platzen vor Wut. Ich habe mich auch noch nicht beruhigt, als ich im Büro des Agenturchefs vorstellig werde.

»So nicht«, tobe ich. Der Chef nickt und singsangt milde.

»Mein liaba junger Freund, regen S' sich net oaf. Nehmen S' erst amoal Platz und trinken S' aa Tasserl Kaffee.«

»Ich habe keinen Durst. Ich habe die Nase voll von dieser Vetternwirtschaft. Ich will, dass Ihr Büro vernünftige Auftritte besorgt!«

»Da ham S' joa rrächt, des is net die foaine Oart, des werma repariern.« Er ist ein alter Fahrensmann und kennt seine Pappenheimer. Zwei Tage später kümmert sich ein anderer Agent um mich, mit dem es zwar auch nicht optimal, aber besser läuft.

Heute arbeite ich mit der Agentur Schmid in meiner Heimatstadt Hannover und habe mein Glück gefunden. Natürlich gab es in den letzten zehn Jahren auch hier das eine oder andere Problem, aber mit Chefin Cornelia Schmid ist das spätestens nach einem gemeinsamen Mittagessen ausgeräumt. Sie ist eine integre und kompetente Geschäftsfrau und eine ebenso intelligente wie liebenswerte Weltbürgerin. Nicht ihr geringstes Verdienst ist es, dass sie in New York Linda Marder entdeckt hat, die mich in Amerika vertritt.

Aber mit dem Wechsel zur Agentur Schmid sind die

Abgründe des Gewerbes längst noch nicht durchschritten. Wie schartig sie wirklich sein können, wird mir 1997 eindrücklich vorgeführt. Im Sommer bekomme ich vom Büro der Berliner Philharmoniker die Zusage für ein Konzert mit Claudio Abbado und Sopranistin Anne Sofie von Otter. Es handelt sich um Mahlers *Des Knaben Wunderhorn.* Das ist ein begehrter Job, und ich freue mich ein ganzes Jahr darauf. Eine Woche vor Probenbeginn erfährt Cornelia Schmid, dass ein Agent aus Wiesbaden versucht, mich aus dem Vertrag zu kegeln und durch einen seiner Künstler zu ersetzen. Frage keiner, wie er das angestellt hat, aber es klappt. Die Konkurrenz steht auf der Bühne, ich gucke in die Röhre. Allerdings nicht lange. Mein Ersatzmann muss sich nicht gerade als Idealbesetzung empfohlen haben. Als Claudio Abbado das Stück drei Wochen später für die EMI einspielt, lässt er mich singen und verhilft mir zu meinem ersten Grammy.

So viel zum Thema Mitleidsbonus, der mir seit dem ARD-Wettbewerb anhängt wie ein Rucksack voller Mühlsteine. Schon damals giftet ein Kollege, den die Jury in der dritten Runde nicht mehr hören will: »Du verdankst den Sieg einzig und allein deiner Behinderung.«

Diese Person singt heute auf esoterischen Kongressen, ich in der Carnegie Hall. Und ich kann nicht sagen, dass mir das besonders Leid tut. Aber ich kann seine Verbitterung halbwegs verstehen. Das Musikgeschäft ist hart und selektiv. Gerade Sänger investieren eine Menge Zeit und Energie, um ein Niveau zu erreichen, das es einem ermöglicht, von der Kunst zu leben. Bleiben Erfolg und Anerkennung aus, kann das sehr demütigend sein. Ich selbst habe an dem Gerede vom Krüppelbonus lange zu knabbern gehabt. Bis ich merkte, es stimmt einfach nicht. Zweifellos gehört die Behinderung zu meiner Persönlichkeit, und sie beeinflusst auch die Art und Weise, wie mich die Menschen auf der Bühne wahrnehmen.

Meine Kollegin und gute Freundin Juliane Banse hat es so formuliert: »Thomas' Gestalt lenkt die Aufmerksamkeit automatisch auf die Musik.« Ich glaube, da ist etwas dran. Ich kann auf der Bühne keinen schicken Frack tragen, ich mache nichts her, mein Körper ist klein und unscheinbar, und für die beeindruckenden Gesten fehlen mir die Extremitäten. Meistens leuchtet im Scheinwerferkegel nichts weiter als mein verschwitzter Schädel und die große Klappe, aus der die Töne rollen. Aber entscheidend ist immer, *wie* sie herausrollen. Jemand, der aussieht wie der Glöckner von Notre-Dame, mag eine Saison lang als Kuriosität durchgehen, auf die Dauer akzeptiert das Publikum einen Künstler nur, wenn die Qualität stimmt, wenn er etwas zu sagen hat.

Mittlerweile sage ich mir, Mitleid bekommt man umsonst, Neid muss man sich erarbeiten, und ich versuche das Musikgeschäft wie ein großes Spiel zu sehen. Konkurrenz, Missgunst und Intrigen gehören genauso dazu wie die Trias *Glück, Glanz, Ruhm* (Robert Gernhardt). Die Kunst besteht darin, sich weder von den ernüchternden Seiten des Gewerbes noch von den Höhenräuschen aus dem Konzept bringen zu lassen. Ich beherrsche das inzwischen ganz gut. Ein Journalist hat mich mal gefragt:

»Was bedeuten Auszeichnungen für Sie?« Ich habe geantwortet:

»Vor allem Platzmangel im Regal.«

Zwischen meinen Büchern stehen unter anderem eine Goldene Kamera, zwei Echo-Preise und zwei Grammys. Ich freue mich natürlich riesig darüber und weiß, Ehrungen sind wichtig für das Renommee. Aber wenn ich drei Bier und einen Schnaps darauf getrunken habe, ist es gut, beziehungsweise bin ich dann blau und der dicke Kopf holt mich am nächsten Morgen zurück auf den Teppich. Allerdings wäre ich wenigstens bei einer der Grammy-Verleihungen gerne persönlich dabei gewesen, allein wegen der Chance, Ikonen wie Prince einmal die Hand zu schütteln. Leider ist nie etwas daraus geworden, weil an den entsprechenden Terminen immer Konzerte zu absolvieren waren. Vielleicht habe ich aber auch gar nichts versäumt, vielleicht sieht das Spektakel im Fernsehen viel eindrucksvoller aus, als es ist.

Bei den diversen Preis- und Promi-Versammlungen, an denen ich bisher teilgenommen habe, war das meistens so. In rundherum angenehmer Erinnerung sind mir tatsächlich nur zwei geblieben. Eine ist die Aids-Gala 2001 in Berlin, die von Loriot moderiert wird. Ich verbringe fast die ganze Show mit dem feinsinnigen Humor-Granden, weil er zwischen den Ansagen hinter der Bühne sitzt. Neben ihm hat es sich Otto Sander, sein Ersatzmann, gemütlich gemacht. Man hat Sander – das Fernsehen denkt ja an alles – engagiert, falls Vicco von Bülow, der gerade von einer schweren Krankheit genesen ist, schwächeln sollte. Aber das hätte nicht passieren dürfen. Otto Sander ist nämlich nicht nur ein bewundernswerter Schauspieler und schwer sympathischer Zeitgenosse, er ist auch ein großer Freund des Weines. Während das Programm abschnurrt, werden etliche Gläschen vernichtet. Nach meinem Auftritt bekomme ich auch etwas ab, und wir amüsieren uns prächtig. Jedes Mal, wenn Loriot wieder auf die Bühne muss, ruft Sander seinem Freund hinterher:

»Mensch, Vicco, halt dich gerade« oder »Gell, Vicco, du hältst durch«, und entkorkt feierlich eine neue Flasche.

So leger geht es 1999 beim G8-Gipfel nicht zu. Trotzdem ist es sehr unterhaltsam, man tummelt sich schließlich nicht jeden Tag im Dunstkreis der Weltenlenker. Kanzler Gerhard Schröder hat mich eingeladen, beim

Konzert für die Staatsoberhäupter in der Kölner Philharmonie mit dem Gürzenich-Orchester Brahms *Vier ernste Gesänge* vorzutragen. Die Veranstaltung läuft natürlich unter dem Rubrum »Hochsicherheitsstufe 1«. Rund um die Philharmonie patrouilliert ein Heer von Ordnungspolizisten und Kriminalern. Vor allem das Aufgebot der Amerikaner ist filmreif. Die FBI-Männer sehen aus wie ein Terminator-Regiment: Bürstenschnitt, Gesichtszüge wie der Mount Rushmore und Muskeln, vor denen sich die Klitschkos fürchten müssten. Dazu tragen sie dunkle Ray-Ban-Brillen und ihre großkalibrigen Colts dermaßen auffällig unter dem Jackett, dass die handverlesenen Gäste an den Herren vorbeistelzen, als hätten sie einen Stock verschluckt. Jeder denkt dasselbe: Jetzt bloß keine abrupte Bewegung, es könnte die letzte sein. Auf dem Empfang nach dem Konzert rutscht allen das Herz in die Hose, als die Bodyguards plötzlich anfangen, wie wild auf ihre Sprechfunkgeräte einzuschreien. Ich verstehe immer nur »Potus and Wotus. Potus and Wotus coming«, was sich anhört, als stürmten zwei wild gewordene Elefanten den Saal.

»Das bedeutet nur, die Clintons sind im Anmarsch«, beruhigt mich mein Freund Uwe Carsten Heye, Schröders Regierungssprecher.

»POTUS heißt President of the United States, WOTUS ist das Kürzel für Hillary, Wife of the United States.« Uwes Gattin Sabine erzählt mir schmunzelnd, wie das FBI am Abend vorher in der Nähe von Bonn einen halben Landkreis okkupiert hat, weil die Schröders und Clintons dort in einem berühmten Weinlokal dinieren. Draußen sichern Männer in Kampfanzügen das Terrain, drinnen sorgen sie in Zivil dafür, dass nichts Unvorhergesehenes passiert. Der Wirt bekommt fast einen Herzanfall, als er mit ansehen muss, wie seine antiken Deckenbalken angebohrt und mit Wanzen voll gestopft werden. Als sich die Agenten auch noch über seine Eichenfässer hermachen wollen, um nachzusehen, ob im Riesling ein Attentäter schwimmt, habe er sich aber todesmutig dazwischengeworfen und gerufen:

»Only over my dead body.«

Bill Clinton scheint der Sicherheitsaufwand nicht zu stören. Bei der Nachfeier bedankt er sich aufgeräumt für das Konzert und verspricht zu kommen, wenn ich im nächsten Jahr in Washington singe. Das hat dann doch nicht geklappt. Aber im Hotel werde ich ein Telegramm von Clinton finden, der mit sehr netten Worten bedauert, dass ihm unaufschiebbare Regierungsgeschäfte dazwischengekommen sind. Der Mann hat ohne Zweifel Stil und Charisma. In Köln ist Clinton unbestritten der Hahn im Korb. Während Chirac, Blair und die anderen Wichtigkeiten routiniert an ihren Gläsern nippen, beflirtet der Präsident die Damenwelt, knufft die Herren kumpelhaft in die Hüften und streut Witzchen unters Volk. Ähnlich ausgelassen ist nur noch Gerhard Schröder. Ich bin ihm in Hannover öfter begegnet, und auch Mama hat ihn schon einmal getroffen. Als er an unseren Tisch kommt, meine Mutter wie eine alte Bekannte begrüßt und mir das Du anbietet, macht er sogar bei Vater dicke Punkte, der ansonsten die Sozis für den Untergang des Abendlands hält.

Meine Eltern begleiten mich auch nach Berlin, wo ich 2001 von der Zeitschrift *Hörzu* die Goldene Kamera verliehen bekomme. Die anderen Preisträger sind Susanne von Borsody, die *Titanic*-Tränendrüse Kate Winslet, Sir Peter Ustinov, Ricky Martin, Sasha, Günther Jauch und die beiden Rundlinge Dieter Pfaff und Dirk Bach. Ich würde ja gern mit Sir Peter ein paar Worte wechseln. Aber ich fürchte, daraus wird nichts. Der Springer Verlag hat mir schon vor Monaten einen Aufmarschplan zugestellt, der dem Protokoll des Polit-Gipfels an Stringenz in nichts nachsteht.

10–12 Uhr:	Individuelle Anreise, Abholung durch persönlichen *Hörzu*-Betreuer mit Mercedes-Limousine. Hotel Vier Jahreszeiten
12.15 Uhr:	Probe der Regieanweisungen mit Kamera
15.30 Uhr:	Get-together mit Preisträgern, Promis, Jury und *Hörzu*-Chefredakteur im Axel-Springer-Haus
18.45 Uhr:	Cocktailempfang für Preisträger im Hotel Four Seasons, Salon »Langhans« mit Friede Springer und Konzernvorstand August A. Fischer
19.10 Uhr:	Fahrt im Konvoi zum Konzerthaus. Einzug auf dem roten Teppich
19.30 Uhr:	Warm-up mit Moderatorin Désirée Nosbusch
19.45 Uhr:	Make-up-Check, Beginn ZDF-Aufzeichnung (Regie: Utz Weber)
20 Uhr:	Preisverleihung

Wer schon einen Tag früher anreist, kann obendrein diese Toptermine mitnehmen:

21.30 Uhr:	Dinnerparty im Foyer Konzerthaus, Adlon Bar und Paris Bar geöffnet
0.00 Uhr:	Eröffnung Golden Dance Club im Foyer, danach alle in Harry's New York Bar

Später bekomme ich noch einen zweiten Brief aus dem Hause Springer. Die *Hörzu*-Redaktion fragt an, ob ich mir vor der Preisübergabe eine kleine Gesangseinlage mit Klavierbegleitung vorstellen könne. »Bitte berücksichtigen Sie, dass das Stück nicht länger als 1:30 Minuten sein soll.«

Ich greife zum Telefon und sage, ich könne mir fast alles vorstellen. »… aber bei 1:30 fällt mir nur *Good Golly Miss Molly* ein oder irgendetwas von Fats Domino. Und das ist doch wohl nicht …«

»Sorry, es geht gar nicht um 1:30«, unterbricht mich meine Gesprächspartnerin. »Regisseur Utz Weber hat den Sendeplan noch einmal überarbeitet. Sie hätten jetzt genau genommen 45 Sekunden.«

»Ach was«, sage ich, »in der Zeit könnte ich Ihnen die ersten vier Takte von *La Paloma* pfeifen. Soll ich?«

»Das ist jetzt ein Witz?«

»Das wollte ich auch gerade fragen. Ich glaube, wir vergessen das.«

Ich habe dann auch den Rest des Programms radikal zusammengestrichen und mich erst beim Cocktailempfang für die Preisträger eingeklinkt. Peter Ustinov ist auch da. Wir werden einander vorgestellt und plaudern eine ganze Weile über Filme, Musik und die Bedeutung des Wortes »Smalltalk«.

»Es muss verwandt sein mit das ›Kleingedruckte‹«, meint Sir Peter. »Man geht sehr leicht darüber weg, aber es kann böse Folgen haben«, spricht's, kneift ein Auge zu und späht mit dem anderen wie ein Hühnerhabicht in die Runde.

Es ist schön, dass ich ihn noch getroffen habe. Abends wäre ein Gespräch gar nicht mehr möglich gewesen, weil im Konzerthaus derartige Menschenmassen um- und durcheinander drängeln, dass man zehn Minuten braucht, um sich einen Meter vorwärts zu bewegen. Es ist einfach jeder da, der sein Gesicht schon mal für Geld vor eine Fernsehkamera gehalten hat. Als der offizielle Teil beginnt, sorgen die Tischkarten dafür, dass die gesellschaftliche Rangordnung wieder in die Reihe kommt. Die Gäste werden gut sortiert nach A-, B-, C- und D-Prominenz auf die sieben Stockwerke verteilt.

Ich begebe mich in den Backstage-Bereich, wo die Preisträger auf ihren Auftritt warten. Das Zeremoniell schreibt vor, dass jeder Geehrte von einem Laudator eingeführt wird. In meinem Fall schweben der *Hörzu* ursprünglich Claudio Abbado oder Daniel Barenboim vor. Was mich sehr freut. Ich habe mit beiden schon gearbeitet und schätze sie sehr. Aber die Maestros sind leider verhindert. Die Redaktion schickt mir daraufhin eine Liste mit Alternativ-Kandidaten. Warum Herbert Grönemeyer und Nina Hagen draufstehen, verstehe ich nicht so recht. Die Schauspielerin Meret Becker und die Herren José Carreras und Placido Domingo habe ich auch noch nie getroffen. Warum dann letztlich keiner von ihnen, sondern Kulturstaatsminister Julian Nida-Rümelin antritt, ist mir allerdings ein völliges Rätsel. Vielleicht hat ihn sein Imageberater getriezt, er müsse mal wieder ins Fernsehen. Denn Nida-Rümelin verspürt offensichtlich wenig Lust, sich mit meiner Person zu befassen. Den Text der Laudatio bestellt sein Büro – bei meinem Bruder. Er hätte ihn auch gleich vortragen sollen. Fünf Minuten vor unserem Auftritt sehe ich Nida-Rümelin hinter der Bühne herumwandern und auf ein Stück Papier starren. Wie es sich gehört, stelle ich mich vor und danke ihm, dass er meine Laudatio hält. Der gelernte Moralphilosoph mustert mich kurz, nickt knapp, dreht sich um und geht. Hoppla, denke ich, was war denn das? Unhöflich? Merkwürdig? Aber ehe ich mich zu einer Conclusio durchringen kann, steht Nida-Rümelin schon neben Désirée Nosbusch und scheitert bei dem Versuch, Michas Sätze fehlerfrei vom Blatt zu lesen. Dann hat Nida-Rümelin fertig. Er stopft den Spickzettel in die Hosentasche und wartet, dass die Moderatorin ruft: »… eine Goldene Kamera für Thomas Quasthoff.«

Ich schaue schnell noch mal auf den Springerschen Einsatzplan. Ah ja! »Nun tritt der Preisträger durch ein Pyramiden-Tor nach rechts auf, nimmt den Applaus in der Bühnenmitte entgegen und geht dann zum Moderatorenpult, wo der Laudator ihm die Goldene Kamera überreicht. Der Preisträger bedankt sich – für Ihre Dankesrede können Sie auch gern die beiden Teleprompter (Autocues) nutzen. Preisträger und Laudator gehen von der Bühne ab und zurück auf ihre Plätze im Parkett.«

Dort sitzen Mama und Vater, *Hörzu*-Leser der ersten Stunde, und strahlen. Kurz darauf beginnt die Schlacht am Luxusbüffet. Ich will gar nicht wissen, wie sie ausgeht. Als meine Eltern müde werden, fliehe ich aus dem Trubel in die hauseigene Paris Bar. Darauf sind auch schon andere gekommen. Zum Beispiel Hella von Sinnen. Die ulkige Person ist mir auf Anhieb sympathisch, und wir quatschen uns fest bis morgens um vier.

Was die Goldenen Kameras für das Fernsehen, sind die Echo-Preise für die Schallplattenindustrie. Leistungsschau, Promotion und Klassentreffen. In der Hamburger Musikhalle, wo die Klassik-Echos verliehen werden, ist alles ein bisschen kleiner: das Büffet, die Anzahl der Gäste und das Prominentenaufgebot. Weil das Fernsehen die Veranstaltung überträgt, darf das natürlich nicht auffallen. Also bemüht man sich jedes Jahr aufs Neue, wenigstens die ersten zehn Stuhlreihen mit allseits bekannten Gesichtern zu bestücken. Als ich 1998 in der Kategorie »Bester Sänger« nominiert bin, werden meine Eltern neben Inge Meysel platziert. Weil die Exmutter der Nation sofort einnickt, ist das Trio in der ZDF-Aufzeichnung leider nie zu sehen. Die Moderatoren Senta Berger und

Roger Willemsen können nichts dafür. Die Meysel schnarcht schon, bevor die Veranstaltung richtig losgegangen ist.

Berger und Willemsen geben ihr Bestes, um die »Kunststücke« der ausgezeichneten Musiker in günstiges Licht zu rücken. Das ist keine leichte Aufgabe. Das Angebot reicht von Klassik bis Jazz, von Chanson bis Tango, doch auffällig sind die vielen Mischformen, denen die Produzenten jede Kante weggeschliffen und alles Widerborstige ausgetrieben haben, sound-designte Ohrschmeichler, die in der Lage sind, gleich mehrere Konsumentenschichten anzusprechen. In den Marketingabteilungen firmiert dieser musikalische Kramladen unter dem Begriff »Crossover-Kultur«. Das hört sich trendy an, ist aber nur der neueste Rettungsanker, den die Unterhaltungskonzerne ausgeworfen haben, um die verheerenden Umsatzeinbrüche der letzten Jahre endlich zu stoppen.

Herausgekommen sind dabei Massenartikel wie André Rieu, Andrea Bocelli oder die »Wet T-Shirt«-Elfe Vanessa Mae, die ihre eher bescheidenen Fähigkeiten auf der Violine mit Modelposing kompensiert. Was an sich vollkommen in Ordnung geht, auf dem freien Markt ist ja Platz für jeden Schmarren. Man soll sie nur nicht mit Künstlern verwechseln. Sie sind Kunsthandwerker. Wenn diese Weichspüler im Klassikregal verkauft werden, ist das Etikettenschwindel, und es nimmt seriösen Interpreten die Chance, entsprechend ihren Fähigkeiten wahrgenommen zu werden.

Das Unheil begann mit dem heldischen Wagnertenor Peter Hofmann, der, das Karriereende vor Augen, wie Weiland Hagen von Tronje Tabula rasa machte und die Songs des großen Rockers Joe Cocker schändete, indem er sie auf Kurkonzertniveau herunterknödelte. Ein anderer, weit tragischerer Fall ist der David Helfgotts. Ein psychisch schwer kranker Mensch und mittelprächtiger Pianist, den skrupellose Manager erst zum Originalgenie hochjazzen, um ihn dann auf einer profitablen Welttournee an Rachmaninows drittem Klavierkonzert zerbrechen zu lassen. Helfgott hat sich davon nie wieder erholt.

Eine andere Variante dieser nur mehr von kühlen Finanzoptimierern dominierten Firmenpolitik sind auch die »Drei Tenöre« Placido Domingo, José Carreras und Luciano Pavarotti. Über die künstlerische Qualität ihrer Darbietungen möchte ich gar nichts sagen. Schließlich bin ich ein großer Fan von allen dreien gewesen. Mich stört nur, dass solche Spektakel Schule machen und mittlerweile einen Großteil der Sponsorengelder und Werbeetats vereinnahmen, die dann den leisen und ambitionierten Projekten fehlen. Und wenn sich mit wahllos zusammengeträllerten Canzonen, Prunk-Arien, Schlagern und Softrock-Schnulzen mühelos Millionen scheffeln lassen, warum sollten die Firmen überhaupt noch junge ernsthafte Interpreten fördern und geduldig warten, bis/ob eine Rendite fällig wird?

Diese Entwicklung ist schon abzusehen, als ich meine ersten holprigen Schritte in den Sängerberuf mache. Ich habe zwar das große Glück gehabt, von Helmuth Rilling an den Hänssler Verlag vermittelt zu werden, der auf geistliche Musik spezialisiert ist. Dort konnte ich in aller Ruhe CDs aufnehmen und künstlerisch reifen. Aber dem Liedinterpreten Quasthoff hat das erst einmal überhaupt nichts genützt. Ich singe für die EMI einige Loewe-Balladen (mit Norman Shetler) ein, die BMG produziert Schuberts *Winterreise*, seine Goethe-Lieder und die Schumann-CD *Dichterliebe – Liederkreis* (mit Roberto Szidon). Dann lande ich auf dem Abstellgleis. Vor allem BMG hat immer wieder vereinbarte Produktionen abgesagt oder fertiges Material gar nicht erst veröffentlicht, weil sich meine CDs angeblich nicht verkaufen. Darunter ist eine Auswahl von Brahms-Liedern, die ich später noch einmal für die Deutsche Grammophon eingesungen habe. Plötzlich geht die CD weg wie geschnitten Brot. Die Wahrheit ist, bei BMG hapert es schlicht am Vertrieb oder an der Motivation, die CDs unters Volk zu bringen. Jetzt verstehe ich auch, warum überall, wo ich auftrat, die Veranstalter klagten, sie könnten meine Aufnahmen im Handel nicht finden. Sie wurden gar nicht ausgeliefert. Fixiert auf wenige global vermarktbare Topacts, ist das Management an Kleinkram nicht mehr interessiert. Das rächt sich jetzt, da MP3-Technik und Raubkopierer das Absatzmonopol der Industrie bedrohen und den Leuten der Cent nicht mehr so locker in der Tasche sitzt, dass sie sich auch noch die 576. Neuaufnahme von Beethovens *Eroica* unterjubeln lassen. Dass es auch anders geht, demonstriert die Deutsche Grammophon. Als man dort die ersten Abmischungen von Abbados *Wunderhorn*-Einspielung hört, bietet man mir sofort einen langfristigen Vertrag an. Niemand hat geahnt, dass die Aufnahme so erfolgreich werden würde, was zählt, ist: ihnen gefällt der Sänger. Dass kurz nachdem die ersten Verkaufszahlen bekannt werden plötzlich auch BMG großes Interesse an einem Exklusivvertrag signalisiert, passt ins Bild. Aber wer zu spät kommt, den bestraft das Leben.

Unter diesem Gesichtspunkt ist die Absatzkrise der Musikindustrie auch eine Chance zum Umdenken. Ein anderes Mantra der Marketingstrategen lautet nämlich, der klassische Liedgesang ist nicht populär genug. Das sollen sie mal meinen Kollegen Matthias Goerne und Andreas Schmidt erzählen, die tippen sich an die Stirn. Ihre Konzerte sind nämlich ständig ausverkauft. Und auch ich muss eher selten in kariöse Stuhlreihen blicken. Ich vermute, es liegt daran, dass wir echte Liedsänger sind. Wenn das Genre zeitweilig ein bisschen in Verruf geraten ist, dann durch das so genannte Star-System. Durch Opernberühmtheiten, die glauben, man könne zwischen zwei *Zauberflöten* mal eben locker vom Hocker die *Dichterliebe* wegröhren, bloß weil ihnen das Fernsehen und der Boulevard dafür den roten Teppich ausrollen.

Der große Bariton Hans Hotter, der beide Fächer meisterlich beherrschte, wusste es besser:

»Ein Opernsänger kann erfolgreich sein, wenn er eine nur durchschnittliche Technik hat, ein nur durchschnittlicher Darsteller ist, aber eine wirklich schöne Stimme besitzt. Die Stimme ist entscheidend, und solange der Sänger es versteht, sich ihrer richtig zu bedienen, kann er ein so genannter Spitzensänger werden, ohne ansonsten bedeutend zu sein. Der Liedersänger muss ein Musiker sein. Die Technik ist die gleiche, muss aber im Liedgesang differenzierter eingesetzt werden. Der Sinn für Fantasie, für Geschmack, das Verständnis für Bedeutung und Stellenwert des Wortes – das alles ist ungemein wichtig. Nicht minder auch das Gefühl für die Qualität der Texte. Bei Opernsängern ist er oft unverständlich. Als Opernsänger kann man sich nicht um die Qualität des Librettos kümmern – das erwartet auch niemand. Doch beim Lied muss der Sänger auch solche Fragen bedenken und beurteilen, ob nicht etwa ein mittelmäßiges Gedicht durch das Genie des Komponisten höheren Wert bekommt.«

In diesem Sinne prophezeie ich hier und jetzt die Renaissance des Liedgesangs. Irgendwann werden auch die Marketingabteilungen merken, dass nicht nur die Qualität, sondern auch der Unterhaltungswert des Genres durchaus konkurrenzfähig ist. Ein Lied kann eine ganze Geschichte erzählen, während eine Arie immer nur einen Teil des Geschehens offeriert. Das heißt: In jedem Lied steckt eine kleine Oper. Und das Beste ist: Ein Liedsänger liefert pro Abend durchschnittlich zehn Miniopern zum Preis von einem *Rosenkavalier*. Last but not least beachte man das Themenspektrum. Besser kriegt es Hollywood auch nicht hin. Ein typisches Liedprogramm, das ich mit Jussi spiele, beginnt mit fünf Balladen von Carl Loewe. *Odins Meeresritt*, *Herr Oluf*, der *Nöck*, *Edward* und *Prinz Eugen*. Da wird vom Horrorschocker über Krieg, Vatermord, Liebe und Wahn bis zum berückenden Märchenzauber gleich alles geboten, was die Herzen der Kinofans höher schlagen lässt. Es folgen drei ähnlich balladesk-erzählende Stücke von Schubert: *Der Sänger, Szene aus Faust* und *Liedesend*. Sie kreisen um die klassischen Film-noir-Sujets Alkohol, Psychoterror und Künstlerelend. Brahms' *Vier ernste Gesänge* führen schließlich tief ins Existenzialistisch-Bodenlose. Fußend auf alttestamentarischen Texten, handeln die Lieder vom eitlen Treiben der Humanoiden (»Denn es geht dem Menschen wie dem Vieh«), von der Schlechtigkeit der Welt (»Ich wandte mich um und sah alle an, die Unrecht leiden unter der Sonne«), von der Vergänglichkeit (»Oh Tod, wie bitter bist du«) und von den letzten Dingen (»Wenn ich mit Menschen- und mit Engelszungen redete«). Falls Zugaben gewünscht werden, spielen wir Schuberts *Heideröslein*, seine *Forelle* und die *Sapphische Ode* von Brahms. Damit haben wir dann auch die Topthemen »Schändung der Natur«, »Die verführte Unschuld« und »Das Wunder weiblicher Schönheit« abgedeckt.

Da ich mich hier in Sachen Liedgesang schon so weit aus dem Fenster lehne, möchte ich auch noch ein Plädoyer für das Live-Singen anhängen. Musik ist im Gegensatz zu Literatur und Malerei ein sehr soziales Phänomen. Wenn ich die Wahl habe, mir dasselbe Programm auf CD oder im Konzertsaal anzuhören, würde ich immer den Konzertsaal vorziehen – egal, wie teuer meine HiFi-Anlage ist. Denn eine Studioaufnahme mag noch so gelungen sein, ich wüsste kein Stück, das ich live nicht noch besser hingekriegt hätte. Über die vielfältigen Faktoren, die den Vortrag beeinflussen, die jeden Abend eine neue, ganz eigene Atmosphäre schaffen, habe ich ja schon referiert. Dieses inspirierende Fluidum ist im Studio nur sehr schwer herzustellen.

Studioarbeit ist eine sehr genaue, fast mathematisch präzise Angelegenheit, weil man die Möglichkeit hat, an jedem Takt, an jeder Note herumzufeilen. Und wenn man zum ersten Mal das nüchterne, bis unter die Decke mit Technik voll gestopfte Reich betritt, ist man schnell bereit, jeden Trick zu nutzen, der hilft, die Aufnahme zu perfektionieren. Wie weit das heute gehen kann, ist für den Laien kaum vorstellbar. Mit dem Computer ist es kein Problem, jede eingesungene Note zu verändern: in der Tonhöhe, im Notenwert und ohne dass man die Charakteristik der Stimme verfälscht. Theoretisch wäre es möglich, Wagners *Ring* in seine Einzelteile zu zerlegen und digital neu zusammenzusetzen. Das will natürlich keiner, macht zu viel Arbeit. Bei Klassik-Produktionen wird dieses Verfahren auch nur sehr selten angewandt. Dafür sorgt schon der Toningenieur. Er weiß, dass es, um ein Werk zum Leben zu erwecken, mehr braucht als das saubere Umsetzen der Noten. Eine Aufnahme braucht einen gewissen Zug, und der geht verloren, wenn man zu viel herumdoktert. Ich habe mit meinem Pianisten Justus immer Wert darauf gelegt, die Einspielungen möglichst puristisch zu gestalten. Einen Zyklus wie Schuberts

Schwanengesang nehmen wir zwei, drei Mal durchgehend auf. Dann machen wir, wenn nötig, kleinere Korrekturen. Nicht digital, sondern wir wiederholen die betreffenden Stellen. Per Computer werden die neuen Takes lediglich eingefügt. So kommen wir mittlerweile mit einem Minimum an Schnitten aus.

Das sollte auch die Maxime bei Opernproduktionen sein. Eine *Aida*, wo König Amonasro seine Tonspur in einem Londoner Studio aufnimmt und an Amneris in Chicago schickt, die das Ganze nach getaner Arbeit Richtung Berlin weiterleitet, wo Radames wohnt, würde ich nicht mitmachen. Als ich die *Meistersinger* mit Christian Thielemann und dem Bariton Bryn Terfel einspielte, wollte eine amerikanische Kollegin ihre Rolle auf diese Art fixieren. Das lehnten sowohl Thielemann als auch die Deutsche Grammophon kategorisch ab. Bei einem Popsong mag das angehen. Aber wenn die Rollen miteinander agieren sollen, muss man im Studio Augenkontakt haben.

Ich möchte meinen Pianisten auch bei Liedaufnahmen ansehen können, daher hasse ich im Studio Trennwände oder geschlossene Schallkabinen. Ich brauche einfach ein Live-Gefühl. Ein guter Liedpianist muss ja nicht nur eine erstklassige Technik besitzen und zuhören können, er muss schon, bevor ich den Ton singe, wissen, was passiert. Antizipation heißt das Zauberwort. Geistesgegenwart ein anderes, betont Michael Raucheisen, einer der großen Begleiter des letzten Jahrhunderts, und erläutert das mit einer kleinen Geschichte:

»Einmal gab Erika Morini einen Geigenabend in Berlin und erlag einem Gedächtnisfehler. Ich flüsterte meinem Umwender, dem guten Burghard, der mir vierzig Jahre lang die Seiten umgeblättert hat, zu: ›Wenden Sie fünf Seiten!‹ Wie im Trancezustand habe ich die Stelle gefunden, und wir waren wieder beisammen.«

Dies quasi somnabule Verständnis setzt ein hohes Maß an Grundvertrauen voraus. Ich kann ohnehin nur mit Menschen gemeinsam musizieren, deren Spiel ich liebe und die ich auch persönlich mag. Das gilt für berühmte Pianisten wie Daniel Barenboim, Wolfram Rieger, András Schiff, Charles Spencer, Julius Drake oder Graham Johnson genauso wie für jene, die bald berühmt sein werden.

Ich habe viele Pianisten ausprobiert, aber immer das Glück gehabt, dass mir zum richtigen Zeitpunkt Könner über den Weg liefen, mit denen man Pferde stehlen kann. Der erste ist Norman Shetler, mit dem ich durch die Kirchen und Gemeindesäle Niedersachsens getingelt bin und meine erste Lieder-CD aufgenommen habe. Peter Müller habe ich durch Frau Lehmann kennen gelernt. Näher gekommen sind wir uns auf diversen Mensafeten und Kneipenbänken, wo die Themen Gott, die Welt und das Rätsel Frau mindestens genauso wichtig sind wie die Musik. Mit Peter habe ich viele Jahre musiziert und noch viel mehr Spaß gehabt. Ich habe ihm auch sehr viel zu verdanken, weil er so vielseitig ist. Er kann perfekt vom Blatt spielen und locker improvisieren, sodass wir uns von Pop bis Bop ein breites Repertoire »draufschaffen«, wie das unter Jazzern heißt. Im Lauf der Jahre hat dann jeder musikalisch andere Prioritäten gesetzt. Peter zieht es ins Theater. Auf diese Weise hat er es schnell ziemlich weit gebracht. Letzten Winter bis Kairo, wo er als Musical Director Brechts *Dreigroschenoper* auf die Bühne stellte. Als Peter aufhört, muss ich lange nach adäquatem Ersatz suchen. Bis ich Charles Spencer kennen und schätzen lerne. Er ist Professor für Liedinterpretation an der Wiener Musikhochschule, ein feiner Mensch und ein phänomenaler Pianist.

Entsprechend viele Sänger möchten mit ihm auftreten. Er hat Gundula Janowitz begleitet, mit Größen wie Jessye Norman, Marjana Wald und Thomas Hampson gearbeitet und war zwölf Jahre lang der ständige Liedbegleiter von Christa Ludwig. Wir nehmen CDs auf und spielen zusammen, wann immer es passt. Aber ich brauche noch jemanden, mit dem ich kontinuierlich arbeiten kann. Ich finde ihn, als ich im Herbst 1998 in Hannover einen Liederabend der Richard-Wagner-Stiftung besuche. Die Sängerin ist Mittelmaß, aber am Klavier sitzt ein echter Künstler. Er heißt Justus Zeyen. Ich frage ihn sofort, ob er mit mir beim Lockenhaus-Festival mit dem russischen Teufelsgeiger Gidon Kremer auftreten will. Er sagt Gott sei Dank ja. Seitdem sind wir unzertrennlich. Das heißt, er sieht Frau und Kinder seltener als mich, denn wir haben zusammen mindestens zweimal die Welt umrundet. Aber davon mehr im nächsten Kapitel.

Das Leben ist auch eine Reise

Aus Michael Stipe, Sänger der Rockband REM, brach am Ende einer anstrengenden Tournee der Fluch »Ich hasse mein Publikum«. Er hatte Pech. Reporter hörten mit. Später versicherte Stipe, er habe das nicht so gemeint und ihm tue alles entsetzlich Leid. Theatermenschen sind da aus ganz anderem Holz geschnitzt. Der Schauspieler Klaus Kinski etwa meinte stets, was er sagte, und ihm tat nie etwas Leid. Schon gar nicht das zahlende Publikum, das er ebenso wie Stipe für unheilbar ignorant hielt. In blanken Hass schlug seine Abneigung allerdings erst Ende der fünfziger Jahre um, als er beschloss, einen letzten Versuch zu wagen und auf deutschen Stadttheaterbühnen das Neue Testament zu rezitieren.

Wer sich an Kinskis Hang zum expressiven Überschwang erinnert, ahnt, was kommen musste. Man dankte es ihm nicht, sondern überschüttete den Mimen mit gellendem Gelächter. Am fünften Tourneetag – soweit ich weiß, war es in meiner Heimatstadt Hildesheim – ging Kinski dazu über, die Lästerer mit pfundschweren Bibeln zu bewerfen. Eine Performance, die seinen Ruf als solitärer Unhold und Quartalswahnsinniger festigte und ihn letztlich zum internationalen Filmstar machte (*Aguirre, der Zorn Gottes*). Trotzdem ist so etwas eigentlich intolerabel. Auch Günstlinge der Musen sollten die Geduld der Menschen nicht über Gebühr strapazieren. Schon gar nicht, wenn sie in fremde Länder reisen.

Diese Erkenntnis blieb auch dem berühmten Tenor Leo Slezak nicht erspart. Im Dienst der Metropolitan Opera tourte er Mitte der zwanziger Jahre mit Verdis *Othello* durch die USA. Alles lief wunderbar, bis die Produktion nach Georgia abbog, wo der Ku-Klux-Klan den farbigen Teil der Bevölkerung mit Hunden und Schrotflinten über die Baumwollfelder hetzte. In der Hauptstadt Atlanta, berichtete Slezak, habe der Bürgermeister den Manager angefleht, die Oper abzusagen oder wenigstens »den Mohren weiß« auftreten zu lassen, weil man sonst nicht für die Sicherheit des Künstlers garantieren könne. Man wisse aus Zeitungsberichten, dass Mr. Slezak die Rolle des Othello besonders brutal auffasse, und das hiesige Volk nehme es mehr als übel, wenn ein Schwarzer, und sei es ein falscher, eine weiße Frau küsst und ihr dann auch noch den Hals umdreht. Der Manager sagte Slezak davon lieber nichts. Als der Vorhang aufging, enterte er vorschriftsmäßig geschwärzt die Bühne, tat, was er tun musste, und brachte die Vorstellung ohne Zwischenfälle zu Ende. Die Rechnung präsentierte man ihm eine Stunde nach dem Abschminken. Als er in den Speisesaal seines Hotels schritt, zischte es Slezak hasserfüllt entgegen: »Here is no place for colored people.«

In dieser Hinsicht hat die Welt inzwischen eine Menge dazugelernt und der Künstler wenig zu befürchten. Es sei denn, man wollte die *Entführung aus dem Serail* ausgerechnet in Khartoum aufführen. Aber das will ja niemand, ist viel zu heiß da, in jeder Beziehung. Wir wollen H. Royce Saltzman, dem Executive Director des Oregon Bach Festival in Eugene, nur ein Jazzkonzert schmackhaft machen. Wir, das meint Jeffrey Kahane und meine Wenigkeit. Jeffrey ist Chef des Los Angeles Chamber Orchestra. Wir sind befreundet, seit ich 1995 zum ersten Mal in Eugene aufgetreten bin. Festival-Besucher kennen den kleinen Mann vor allem als Klaviervirtuosen, dessen Interpretation der Bachschen *Goldberg-Variationen* Vergleiche mit

Glenn Gould keineswegs zu scheuen braucht. Jeffrey teilt außerdem meine Liebe zum Jazz. Nach den Vorstellungen haben wir uns oft die halbe Nacht durch das Repertoire der Tin Pan Alley gejammt. Die Idee zu einem regulären Jazzabend entsteht 1999 auf dem Abschlussfest. Als fast alles ausgetrunken und das Gros der Kollegen längst zu Bett gegangen ist, sitzt Jeffrey am Flügel und perlt *One for my Baby and One for the Road* in die Tasten, Frank Sinatras melancholiesatte Hommage an den allerletzten Drink. Ich habe meinen müden Leib auf zwei Stühlen ausgebreitet, sauge an einer Weißweinschorle und bade in den lässig hingeworfenen Harmonien.

»It's a perfect song.«

»That's American classic«, sagt Jeffrey und lässt das Stück mit einem geschmackvollen Septakkord ausklingen.

»Wenn das so ist, spielen wir den Song nächstes Jahr im Festival-Programm.«

Jeffrey lacht nicht. Er sagt: »Okay. Ich werde es Mr. Saltzman und Helmuth Rilling vorschlagen. Cheers.«

Wir genehmigen uns noch »one for whatever«, dann trotten wir ebenfalls in die Betten. Ich muss in drei Stunden wieder aufstehen, um meinen Flieger zu erwischen. Als ich in Hannover lande, habe ich Kopfschmerzen und die Episode längst vergessen. Jeffrey nicht. Zwei Monate später ruft er mich an.

»Hi, Tommi, ich bereite unser Jazzkonzert im Hult Center vor. Der Titel ist *American Songbook.* Ich brauche eine Liste mit allen Nummern, die du singen willst.«

Ich bin von den Socken. Amerika ist zwar das Land der unbegrenzten Möglichkeiten, aber dass Jeffrey das Veranstalterkomitee dazu bewegen kann, mag ich kaum glauben. Genauso gut könnte man die Chefetage der Salzburger Festspiele fragen, ob sie für das Abschlusskonzert nicht mal B. B. King verpflichten wollen. Doch Jeffrey duldet keinen Widerspruch.

»Keep cool, my friend. Send me your list.«

Daran soll es nicht scheitern.

Die nächsten Monate wechseln immer neue Programm-Varianten über den Atlantik. Auch Micha, den ich gebeten habe, mir bei der der Auswahl des Materials zu helfen, ist Feuer und Flamme. Und bald nicht mehr zu bremsen. Fast täglich finde ich in meiner Mailbox endlose Song-Listen. Meine eigenen Entwürfe werden mit dem Furor des Fanatikers durch den Wolf gedreht.

»Kein Ray-Charles-Titel? Zehn Mal Sinatra, und nicht eine Nummer von Dr. John? Das ist nicht dein Ernst. Das ist Quatsch mit Soße. Das geht auf keinen Fall.«

»Doch das geht«, maile ich etwas verschnupft zurück.

Beeindrucken lässt sich Brüderchen davon nicht. Kurz darauf klingelt das Telefon: »Call the police, hurry, hurry!«, heult es aus der Muschel. »Call the police, quick, quick, quick! / Call the police, hurry, hurry, / Cause the guy has stolen my girl from me.«

»Was ist?«

»Das ist Nat King Cole!«

»Ja, Micha, deshalb brauchst du nicht so zu schreien. Ich kenne den Song, er läuft bei dir auf jeder zweiten Autokassette.«

»Und warum? Weil er großartig ist. Ein *American Songbook* ohne Nat King Cole, das geht nun überhaupt gar nicht!« Nachdem er mir im Lauf der nächsten Wochen das Gesamtwerk von Aaron Neville vorgesungen, zehn CDs mit »genialem« Underground-Soul kompiliert und die Country-Legende Willie Nelson als verkappten Jazzer enttarnt hat, erkläre ich ihm besser doch einmal, dass der erste Jazzabend in Rahmen des Bach-Festivals ein gewisses Maß an stilistischem Feingefühl erfordert. Schließlich muss Jeffrey das Programm dem guten Mr. Saltzman, der im Hauptberuf Professor für klassischen Chorgesang ist, verkaufen. Saltzman mag zwar ein toleranter gesetzter Gentleman sein, aber eben kein Soul-Bruder. Zusammen mit Jeffrey einigen wir uns schließlich auf eine eher konservative Auswahl, die man dem Festival-Publikum guten Gewissens anbieten kann. Darunter sind fünf Lieder aus Leonard Bernsteins *West Side Story*, die Sinatra-Hits *New York, New York* und *My Way*, Jerome Kerns *Ol' Man River*, Filmtitel wie *They Can't Take That Away From Me*, das George und Ira Gershwin für *Shall We Dance* geschrieben haben, Henry Mancinis *Moon River* aus *Frühstück bei Tiffany*, ein paar Stücke des Komponistengespanns Rogers/Hart und Traditionals wie *Swing Low, Sweet Chariot.*

Die Mischung stimmt, denn Ende des Jahres meldet Jeffrey, die Festival-Leitung hat das *American Songbook* akzeptiert. Doch damit fangen die Schwierigkeiten erst richtig an. Für die *West Side Story* braucht man ein großes Orchester, für das weitere Repertoire hat Jeffrey eine Big Band eingeplant. Das Orchester ist da, aber die Big-Band-Musiker werden ihm gestrichen. Geld, um Orchester-Arrangements der Jazzstücke einzukaufen, gibt es auch nicht. Da erinnert sich Jeffrey an James Taylor, Komponist und Interpret so großartiger Hits wie *Fire and Rain* oder *Country Road.* Jeffrey hat mit ihm öfter zusammengearbeitet, genauer gesagt, hat er das Orchester dirigiert, wenn Taylor im Studio oder bei Live-Auftritten Streicher verwendet. Jetzt revanchiert sich der Songwriter, indem er uns kostenlos einige Arrangements zur Verfügung stellt, darunter *Our Love is Here to Stay, Just the Way You Look Tonight* und *Fascinating Rhythm*, die wir dankbar ins Programm aufnehmen. Den Rest beschließen wir in Quintett-Besetzung zu spielen.

Als der große Tag naht, ist das Hult Center in Eugenes Innenstadt mit dreitausend Besuchern restlos ausgebucht. Jeffrey ist genauso nervös wie ich, was man daran merkt, dass er sich mit der Hand ständig über den Scheitel fährt, obwohl auf seinem Kopf nur ein tonsurartiges, von wirren Locken umtanztes Nichts glänzt. Während Mr. Saltzman das Auditorium begrüßt und den Sponsoren dankt, nuckeln wir in meiner Garderobe an einem dünnen Joint. Vor einem klassischen Konzert ist das selbstredend streng verpönt. Aber heute Abend sind Blue Notes gefragt, heute Abend ist »Jazztime«. Mit allem, was dazugehört.

»Ahhh«, der Qualm legt sich auch schon befruchtend auf das zentrale Nervensystem. Ich spucke Jeffrey über die rechte Schulter.

»Good luck.« Jeffrey spuckt zurück, atmet tief durch und trabt hinaus ins Ungewisse. Wir haben lange überlegt, ob wir uns von der kleinen Besetzung allegro con brio bis zum großen Orchesterfinale vorarbeiten oder besser die Überrumplungstaktik wählen, also Bernsteins Klangfeuerwerk gleich zu Beginn zünden sollen. Letzteres erweist sich als richtiger Schachzug. Die effektstarken Nummern der *West Side Story*, die alle Register zwischen Jazz, Oper und Sinfonik ziehen, bringen das Publikum auf die richtige Betriebstemperatur. Als wir die Gassenhauer *New York, New York* und *My Way* und gleich darauf die erstklassigen Taylor-Arrangements folgen lassen, schickt man uns mit brausendem Applaus in die Pause. Der erste Teil wäre also geschafft, das Orchesterpodium kann abgebaut werden. Backstage wartet schon mein Freund Rick Todd und bläst sich warm. Er wird unser Quintett mit seinem Waldhorn verstärken. Dass Rick dieses schwer zu intonierende Instrument leichtfüßig wie ein Kornett swingen lassen kann, habe ich ja schon erwähnt. Aber an diesem Abend übertrifft er sich selbst. Mal peitscht er die

Noten in Dizzy-Gillespie-Manier aus dem Horn, mal turnt er richtig funky durch die Skalen, dann nimmt er sich *Moon River* vor und haucht sein Solo zartbitter wie der junge Chet Baker ins Mikrofon. Wer es nicht glaubt, dem leihe ich gern den Mitschnitt des Konzertes. Nach zwei Stunden und fünf Zugaben stehen dreitausend Leute buchstäblich auf den Stühlen. Sie haben noch immer nicht genug.

Ich sehe Rick und Jeffrey an: »The last waltz?« Sie grinsen.

»*One for my Baby and One for the Road*«, sagt Rick. Eine gute Wahl. Danach weiß jeder, jetzt wird nichts mehr ausgeschenkt. Auch Mr. Saltzman, der hinter die Bühne geeilt ist, um uns allen gerührt die Hände zu schütteln.

»Wonderful«, murmelt er, »fantastic«, und will gar nicht aufhören, Jeffrey auf die Schultern zu klopfen. Aber wir haben es jetzt sehr eilig. Ich wechsle mein verschwitztes T-Shirt und sprinte zum Künstlereingang, wo Tonys Auto mit laufendem Motor wartet: »Anschnallen, Sweetheart!«

Und schon brausen wir durch die sternenklare Nacht, immer am Ufer des Willamette entlang bis an den hügeligen Stadtrand, wo John und Kazi Steinmetz ihr Domizil aufgeschlagen haben – mit Kind, Kegel und Promenadenmischung. In dem gemütlichen Holzhaus warten meine Musikerkollegen und ein zünftiges Barbecue. Die privaten After-Show-Partys sind ein gern gepflegtes Festival-Ritual. Gestern nach dem *Elias* hat Stevie Tunfisch gebraten, vorgestern, als ich mit Sibylle Rubens und Jussi Hugo Wolfs *Italienisches Liederbuch* gesungen habe, lagen bei den Todds saftige Hamburger auf dem Rost. Nur Jussi und ich sind echte Nassauer. Für uns zwei lohnt es sich nicht, ein ganzes Haus anzumieten, wir residieren während des Festivals im River Valley Inn. Der Name passt. Wer im

Westflügel wohnt, kann von seinem Zimmer aus mühelos in den Fluss spucken. Selbst Grillen ist hier allerdings streng verboten. Wir revanchieren uns bei den Kollegen mit Badespaß, Donuts und Softdrinks, die zwei weiß befrackte Kellner am Swimmingpool servieren.

Der Leser merkt schon, das 100 000-Seelen-Städtchen Eugene ist eine Oase der Geselligkeit. Aber das tut dem hohen musikalischen Standard keinen Abbruch. Der Grundstein des Bach-Gipfels wird vor dreißig Jahren im Schwäbischen gelegt. Royce Saltzman betreut dort im Auftrag der Universität Eugene eine Gruppe amerikanischer Musikstudenten, die für ein Studienjahr in Ludwigsburg weilen. Einer der Dozenten ist Helmuth Rilling. Saltzman fragt, ob Helmuth nicht Lust hätte, an seiner Uni Kurse zu geben. Das war 1970. Aus dem ersten Workshop für Chordirigenten ist gleich im nächsten Jahr ein kleines Festival geworden. Mittlerweile hat sich die Veranstaltung – wie die *Los Angeles Times* bemerkt – zu einem »musikalischen Unternehmen« gemausert, »das in Amerika seinesgleichen sucht«. Ich möchte behaupten, es gibt auf der ganzen Welt nichts Vergleichbares.

Keiner der Kollegen kommt hierher wegen des Geldes. Sie arbeiten zwar nicht umsonst, aber wenn man das Pensum der Orchestermusiker – in 17 Tagen sind 25 Konzerte zu absolvieren – nach Tarif bezahlen müsste, wäre das Festival erledigt. Die meisten sind gefragte Instrumentalisten und können es verschmerzen. Rick zum Beispiel gehört zu den hoch dotierten Spitzenkönnern, die in den Hollywood-Studios die Filmmusiken einspielen. Dennoch werden wir alle reichlich entschädigt. Durch die wunderbaren Konzerte, durch die familiäre Atmosphäre und durch eine großartige Umgebung. Ich bin in der privilegierten Lage, mich gründlich umzusehen, weil Solisten nicht ganz so viel zu tun haben. Eugene liegt mitten im

Willamette Valley, einer Schwemmlandebene, die im Süden durch die Klamath Mountains, im Nordwesten von den Cascades begrenzt wird. Über den bewaldeten Hängen des Gebirgszuges ragen der Mount Hood, die Three Sisters und der Mount McLoughlin dolomitenhoch in den Himmel. Von hier aus ist es nicht weit bis zu einem meiner Lieblingsplätze: Auf der Hochebene hinter dem Willamette Pass ruht umgeben von ewigem Schnee der Crater Lake, ein erloschener Vulkan, der in seinem kreisrunden Kegel Millionen Jahre altes Urwasser speichert. Wenn die Wolkenbänke über die Oberfläche ziehen und den Wasserspiegel von Ultramarin in glitzerndes Smaragdgrün changieren lassen, kann man verstehen, warum Crater Lake für die indianischen Ureinwohner heiliges Territorium ist. Eugene-Veteranen versäumen auch nie, den Highway 126 hinaufzufahren, um an einem der Wasserfälle des Mackenzie die Angel auszuwerfen. Wem die Zeit dabei zu lang wird, empfehle ich Richard Brautigans *Forellenfischen in Amerika* einzustecken. Der Dichter hat in der Beatnik-Ära das Mackenzie-Tal durchstreift und seine Erlebnisse in einem wunderbar lakonischen Erzählungsband festgehalten. Wer gut zu Fuß ist, kann ganze Tage lang in der »Wilderness« herumlaufen, ohne einer Menschenseele zu begegnen, sollte dabei aber keinesfalls einen Kompass und das Mückenspray vergessen. Leute, die es weniger abenteuerlich mögen, schleppen ihren Picknickkorb einfach an einen der zahlreichen Bergseen, die nicht nur alle Clear Lake heißen, sondern auch so aussehen. Wahlweise lenkt man das Auto zwei Stunden Richtung Westen bis Heceta Head und schaut zu, wie der Pazifik Brecher um Brecher an die Steilküste rollt.

Renate und Micha, die mich im Jahr 2000 in Oregon besuchen, sind nach Landessitte hoch zu Ross durch die Wälder getrabt. Ich persönlich habe ja eine Pferdeallergie und bin auch sonst eher ein fauler Knochen. Ich schwitze schon, wenn ich auf der Hotelterrasse liege und dem Trupp kenianischer Läufer zuwinke, der allmorgendlich ausrückt, um am Willamette entlangzuflitzen. Die sehnigen Männer wohnen auf derselben Etage wie ich und trainieren für die Prefontaine Classics. Das ist das letzte große Leichtathletik-Meeting vor den amerikanischen Meisterschaften. Alles, was Rang und Namen hat, tritt hier an. Ich habe schon Asse wie Carl Lewis, Marion Jones, den aktuellen Hundert-Meter-Weltrekordler Tim Montgomery und die Langstrecken-Olympiasiegerin Gabriela Szabo rennen sehen. Genauso gerne besuche ich mit Freund Stevie, der im Festival-Orchester Geige spielt, den Playground der Fighting Ducks. Obwohl er seit Jahren daran scheitert, mir die Baseball-Regeln zu erklären. Aber das ist egal. Bei diesem Spiel passiert die ersten drei Stunden eh so gut wie nichts. Entsprechend gleicht die Szenerie eher einem Volksfest. Die Menschen rekeln sich in der Sonne, schwatzen, trinken Bier, während das Aroma von Grillwurst und frischem Popcorn durch die Innings zieht. Dann halten alle wie vom Donner gerührt die Luft an und starren auf das Spielfeld. Im Stadion kann man jetzt das Gras wachsen hören. Dabei ist für den unbedarften Beobachter alles wie zuvor. Der Pitcher wirft, der Hitter trifft oder er trifft nicht, doch auf den Rängen bricht die Hölle los und ein Team hat gewonnen. Alles sehr verwirrend, aber insgesamt sehr entspannend. Noch entspannender finde ich das Golfen. In den Staaten ist dieser Sport kein Privileg der Großverdiener, sondern grunddemokratisch organisiert. Es gibt überall öffentliche Plätze und jedermann kann für wenig Geld ein paar Runden drehen. Als wir es versuchen, haben die Quasthoff-Brüder das Duo Renate und Jussi gleich um Längen geschlagen. Dank einer überlegenen Teamstrategie. Micha drischt die Bälle auf die Grüns, ich loch sie ein. Das muss natürlich gefeiert werden, zumal es für Renate und Micha der letzte Urlaubstag ist. Ich bleibe noch und gönne mir wie fast jedes Jahr zusammen mit Familie Steinmetz, Jussi, Rick, seiner Frau Marder und ihrem Töchterlein Haley – meinem süßen Patenkind – eine Woche Camping in den Pazifikdünen.

Am Abend vor der Abreise haben Jussi, Juliane Banse und ich noch einen Liederabend gegeben. Wir singen Debussy-Lieder und Mozart-Arien. Es muss ein denkwürdiges Ereignis gewesen sein, befindet jedenfalls der Rezensent des lokalen Tageblattes. Unter der Überschrift »The Banse-Quasthoff-Zeyen-Trio makes history« fasste er das Geschehen so zusammen:

»Am Donnerstag trat ein neues Ensemble auf der Bühne der Beall Hall in Erscheinung, bestehend aus der Sopranistin Juliane Banse, Bassbariton Thomas Quasthoff und Pianist Justus Zeyen. Sie lieferten ein Oregon-Bach-Festival-Konzert, das die Zuhörer für eine sehr, sehr lange Zeit im Gedächtnis behalten werden. Wie großartig es war? Nach zwei Zugaben und echten Standing Ovations (nicht eine von diesen ›Sich ducken, während der Nebenmann sowieso gerade aufsteht‹-Beifallskundgebungen), fiel das Publikum in eine Art rhythmisches Osteuropa-Klatschen, das an politische Kundgebungen in totalitären Staaten erinnert.«

Ich kolportiere das hier nicht aus Gründen der Selbstbeweihräucherung, sondern weil ich eine halbwegs elegante Überleitung brauche. Hier ist sie: In Osteuropa klatschen die Menschen tatsächlich anders Beifall als im Westen. Und daran hat sich auch nach dem Fall des Eisernen Vor-hangs nichts geändert. Ich habe das selbst zum ersten Mal in Petersburg erlebt, als ich mit dem Geiger Vladimir Spivakov aufgetreten bin. Am Ende der Vorstellung herrscht Totenstille. Ich gehe von der Bühne und frage Spivakov besorgt:

»Vladimir, was ist los? Die Leute klatschen nicht. Waren wir so schlecht, haben wir etwas falsch gemacht?«

Doch Spivakov steht seelenruhig da und brummt mit seinem im Dampf zehntausender Papyrossis geräucherten Bass: »Wait a moment. They will clap their hands!«

So ist es. Wie auf Kommando materialisiert sich Applaus, der wie ein russisches Garderegiment im Marschrhythmus durch den Saal paradiert – und den Lautstärkepegel zwanzig Minuten im Gleichmaß hält.

»Now«, brummt Spivakov, zieht mich an die Rampe und mustert mit stoischem Gesicht die jubelnden Massen.

Der kollektive Gleichklang kennzeichnet auch das Klatschen in Ungarn und Tschechien. Allerdings hebt und senkt sich das Volumen in diesen Gegenden eher wie eine Sinuskurve. Ein Phänomen, das wiederum in Polen völlig unbekannt ist. Hier unterscheiden sich die Beifallskundgebungen nicht wesentlich vom Applaus in anderen Ländern Mittel- und Nordwesteuropas. Egal, auf welchem Begeisterungsniveau man sich bewegt, das Über-Ich klatscht immer mit. Eine Ausnahme bildet allein der Wiener, der im Guten wie im Schlechten zu großem Enthusiasmus fähig ist und dem Vortragskünstler darüber hinaus nach dem Konzert gerne erklärt, was man gerade gesungen hat. So etwas würde den Menschen des romanischen Kulturkreises niemals einfallen. Sie halten es mit der Kultur wie mit dem Fußball und der Liebe. Es gibt nur hopp oder topp. Entweder du wirst ausgebuht oder man trägt dich auf Händen. Mir ist bis jetzt Gott sei Dank nur Letzteres widerfahren. Bei einem Gastspiel mit Helmuth Rilling im

Teatro Colón von Buenos Aires regnet es sogar Rosen. Erst auf der Bühne, später stehen die Argentinier am Künstlereingang Spalier und pfeffern uns die dornenreiche Ware en gros an die Köpfe.

»Sieschtde«, sagt Helmuth, »jetzt kannscht dich au mal fühle wie Maradona.«

Das ist aber alles nichts gegen den Affekthaushalt japanischer Konzertbesucher. Sie sind unberechenbar. Häufig applaudieren sie so manierlich wie eine Versammlung niedersächsischer Landfrauen, aber das Auditorium kann auch schier aus dem Häuschen geraten. Dann wird gelärmt und herumgetobt, als wären eben nicht das Personal der *Matthäus-Passion*, sondern die Jungs von Oasis aufgetreten. Noch erstaunlicher als im Konzertsaal wirkt dieses Verhalten im traditionellen Kabuki-Theater. Der Besuch ist ein gesellschaftliches Topereignis, sehr teuer und wird gemeinhin im Sonntagsstaat absolviert. Anfangs fühlt man sich auch an eine andächtige Kommunionsfeier erinnert. Die Zuschauer verfolgen regungslos, wie fantastisch kostümierte Protagonisten in höchst stilisierter Form sehr alte, mithin allseits bekannte Stücke aufführen. Sobald die Handlung jedoch ihrem dramatischen Höhepunkt entgegenstrebt, geht es schlagartig zu wie im Catcherzelt. Männer und Frauen springen auf, fuchteln mit den Fäusten und brüllen den Protagonisten zu: »Gib's ihm«, »Hau ihn um« oder »Mach sie fertig«.

Japan wird mir ein ewiges Rätsel bleiben, obwohl ich schon vier Mal dort gewesen bin. Einmal sogar drei Wochen am Stück, als Micha und ich mit Helmuth Rilling und der Prager Philharmonie von Tokio bis an den südlichen Zipfel der Insel Kyushu und wieder zurück gereist sind. Mich hat es dabei jedes Mal aufs Krankenlager geworfen, was ich aber keinesfalls den Japanern anlasten möchte, sondern meinem überaus empfindlichen Magen. Und der Unkenntnis der Landessprache. Einer der größten Irrtümer, dem Japanreisende immer wieder aufsitzen, ist nämlich der Glaube, man käme mit Englisch prima zurecht. Das ist falsch. Der Japaner spricht und versteht vorrangig Japanisch. Der Fremdling versteht vorrangig nichts. Mir geht es nicht anders, als nach dem Konzert in Osaka eine hagere Gestalt in die Garderobe stürmt. Der Mann trägt einen zerschlissenen schwarzen Anzug, verbeugt sich und beginnt, dringlich auf mich einzureden. Ich speichere nur, dass öfter von »kane«, »shinyo« und »bijinesu« die Rede ist.

»Das heißt Geld, Vertrauen und Geschäft«, erläutert Fräulein Noriko, die Pressefrau des örtlichen Veranstalters. Sie hat in Deutschland Musik studiert, und ich bin heilfroh, dass sie neben mir steht. Noriko weiß offensichtlich, was zu tun ist. Sie gibt der sinistren Figur eine knappe schneidende Antwort. Der dürre Mann starrt uns einen Moment lang grimmig an. Dann fletscht er die Zähne zu einem schiefen Lächeln, verbeugt sich wieder und geht. Ob ich gesehen habe, dass an seiner linken Hand zwei Fingerglieder fehlen, fragt Noriko.

»Er ist ein Yakuza, ein Gangster, und wollte wissen, ob Quasthoff-San einen Manager braucht.«

»Oh Gott, und was haben Sie ihm gesagt?«

»Kein Bedarf.«

»Und das hat er einfach so hingenommen?«

»Ja, natürlich.«

Ich bin sprachlos. Wie gesagt, der Fremdling versteht hier gar nichts. Die Japaner wissen das, und ich vermute, man tut ihnen ein bisschen Leid. Weshalb selbst Mafiosi die langnasigen Gaijin mit ausgesuchter Höflichkeit behandeln. Was sehr nett ist, aber nichts daran ändert, dass im Hotel schon das Bestellen eines gekochten Hühnereis zum Problemfall werden kann. Man sagt »tamago« (Ei) und »yuderu« (kochen). Aber es funktioniert nicht. Wahrscheinlich spreche ich die Wörter so komisch aus, wie das Englisch mancher Rezeptionsdamen nebulös ist. Die Quasthoff-Brüder haben sich mal erklären lassen, welche Bahnlinie nach Nikko führt. Im dortigen Tempel sind drei weltberühmte Affen zu besichtigen: Einer will nichts Böses sehen, einer nichts Böses sprechen, der dritte hält sich die Ohren zu. Genauso hätten wir es machen können. Die Irrfahrt wäre auch nicht schlimmer gewesen. Immerhin sind wir am Ende doch noch angekommen. Meinen gekochten Eiern gelang das nie. Ein Umstand, der mich sehr geschmerzt hat, weil andere Säulen der internationalen Gastronomie wie die zweisprachige Speisekarte auch in Großstädten wie Osaka kostbare Raritäten sind. Dafür bilden japanische Köche ihre Kreationen gern in Plastik nach und stellen sie im Schaufenster aus. Man weiß nur nicht, wie die Skulpturen heißen, geschweige denn wie sie schmecken.

»Man kann natürlich auch zum Italiener gehen«, schlägt Micha vor, als mich abends in Tokio der Hunger plagt.

»Ich bin dabei!« Jimmy Taylor reibt sich die Hände. Er hat zwar schon vor dem Konzert üppig gespeist, aber in den ebenso sympathischen wie pavarottirunden Tenor aus Houston, Texas, geht immer etwas hinein. Wir rufen ein Taxi. Der Fahrer hat wie alle japanischen Taxler weiße Handschuhe an und sein Fahrzeug mit Spitzendeckchen dekoriert. Sein Fahrstil ist weniger gemütlich. Um die obligatorischen Staus auf den Hauptstraßen zu vermeiden, rast er im Kamikazestil durch belebte Wohn- und Ladenviertel. Der Wagen passt gerade so eben zwischen die schmalen Bürgersteige. Wir sehen die Leute rechts und links in die Hauseingänge stürzen und sind heilfroh, dass er uns ohne Blutzoll vor einem Etablissement mit dem einladenden Schriftzug »Via Veneto« absetzt. Leider macht das Ristorante gerade zu. Jimmy fasst sich an den Kopf:

»What time is it?«

»Half past ten«, sagt mein Bruder und schaut den Kellner fragend an. Der Padrone zuckt mit den Schultern. Er sagt, dass die Gaststätten hier grundsätzlich um diese Zeit schließen. Oha! Micha und die ebenfalls von stetem Durst getriebenen Jungs von der Prager Philharmonie werden ihren Dämmerschoppen fürs Erste in einem der omnipräsenten Automatencenter einnehmen müssen, wo von der Literflasche Sapporo-Bier bis zum gebrauchten Damenschlüpfer alles im Angebot ist, was das Herz begehrt. Doch an diesem Abend haben wir Glück. Zwei Straßen weiter dringt aus einem japanischen Lokal noch Musik. Da ich wirklich großen Hunger habe, verdränge ich die letzte Magenverstimmung.

»Los, Jungs, hinein. Das ist für heute unsere letzte Chance.« Richtig. Denn auch hier beginnen die Kellner schon zusammenzuräumen. Wir streifen die Schuhe ab und werden in den Gastraum geleitet. Zwei Dutzend Geschäftsleute hocken im Schneidersitz vor kleinen Tischen. Sie haben Jacketts und Krawatten abgeworfen, ihre Köpfe, angeheizt von zügiger Bier- und Sakezufuhr, glühen und lasten sichtbar schwer auf den Schultern. Einige schlafen im Sitzen. Ein Kellner bringt uns die Speisekarte mit den landestypischen Schriftzeichen. Jimmy bestellt auf Englisch Huhn mit Reis. Der Kellner dienert und serviert ihm ein Schweinekotelett mit sauer eingelegten Rüben. Micha und ich haben Nudeln bestellt. Die kriegen wir auch. Sie sind kalt und grün wie die Beilagen: Seetang, Gurken und Meerrettich. Micha schmeckt es, ich gehe lieber hungrig ins Bett.

Nicht, dass man mich falsch versteht. Ich habe in Japan auch sehr gut gegessen. Vor allem in den Garküchen, die sich zahlreich um Bahnhöfe und U-Bahn-Stationen drängeln. Hier köchelt man bodenständige Suppen und deftige schnelle Fleisch- und Fischgerichte. Denn die Japaner haben es immer eilig. Weil sie entweder unterwegs zur Arbeit oder auf dem Weg nach Hause sind. Wer seine Heimstatt nicht mit der Bahn erreichen kann, hat es allerdings schwer. Der muss sich, von tumorartig wuchernden Baustellen behindert, im endlosen Stau über Betonpisten quälen, die drei- oder vierlagig übereinander geschichtet und verschlungen wie gordische Knoten das Stadtbild durchschneiden. Dass die Japaner dabei eine heroische Disziplin bewahren, ist bewundernswert. Viele erreichen ihr Ziel trotzdem nicht. Für diesen Fall hat man längs der Stadtautobahnen schmale Parkbuchten eingerichtet, wo der gestresste Autofahrer seinen Wagen abstellen und übernachten kann. Am nächsten Morgen wird gewendet und der Trott geht von vorne los. Das Verkehrschaos scheint auch der Grund zu sein, warum in Japan Konzert- und Theateraufführungen, Kino, Sport und Spiel sofort nach Arbeitsschluss beginnen. Und das Nachtleben spätestens um elf Uhr abends erloschen ist. Auch dabei darf man keine Zeit verlieren.

Eine der beliebtesten Feierabendvergnügungen ist Karaoke. Zu diesem Zweck geht man in einschlägige Bars. Oder besucht vorher einen der monumentalen Karaokepaläste. Ihre Fassaden zieren Drachen- und Samuraidarstellungen oder die Fabelwesen der Popwelt. Dahinter geht es nüchterner zu. Das Innenleben besteht aus winzigen schalldichten Waben, die alle mit CD-Spieler, TV-Gerät und je einem Japaner bestückt sind, der für den nächsten geselligen Abend Probe singt. Ebenso pompös, nur um Längen lärmiger sind die Pachinko-Hallen. Von außen verwechselt man die Prunkbauten leicht mit einer Großbank, sie enthalten aber nichts als hunderte unentwegt scheppernder Glücksspielautomaten. Überhaupt scheint Krach den Menschen richtig Spaß zu machen. So ist es durchaus normal, wenn im Schwitzraum einer Sauna das Radio plärrt oder sonntags im Stadtpark drei Rockbands nebeneinander stehen und gleichzeitig in die Saiten hauen. Womit wir wieder bei der unergründlichen Seele Nippons wären. Der Japaner schätzt den Lärm, aber er liebt die Stille. Bevor ich hierher kam, habe ich nicht gewusst, dass man Kontemplation so perfekt inszenieren kann. Man findet sie in den Teehäusern, wo man das Aufbrühen nach jahrhundertealten Regeln zelebriert, in kunstvollen Gärten und weitläufigen Parks und in den Tempelanlagen, die sich bewacht von mächtigen Zedern selbstbewusst neben den kapitalistischen Trutzburgen behaupten. Andererseits ist das kein so großes Kunststück. Sie sind schließlich selbst welche. Bevor die Mönche mit Glückssprüchen oder einem Orakel herausrücken, muss man bezahlen. Wer sich direkt an die Götter wendet, wird ebenfalls zur Kasse gebeten. In Tokio habe ich meine Münzen am liebsten in einen Shinto-Schrein auf dem Gelände des Asakusa-Tempels getragen. Die Hausherren sind drei übermannshohe, auf ihren hölzernen Hinterbeinen stehende Waschbären. Dem Trio hängt dasselbe unergründliche Grinsen im Gesicht wie der Edamer Katze, die Alice im Wunderland Folgendes mit auf den Weg gibt:

»Hier sind alle verrückt. Du bist verrückt. Ich bin verrückt.«

»Woher weißt du denn, dass ich verrückt bin?«, fragt Alice.

»Musst du ja sein«, sagt die Katze, »sonst wärst du doch gar nicht hier.«

Ich finde, ich habe mein Geld gut angelegt, weil mir

plötzlich klar wird, dass dem kauzigen Lewis Carroll nicht nur der Waschbärentempel gefallen hätte. Innerlich gestärkt ziehe ich von dannen und sehe das Treiben in Tokios Straßen mit ganz anderen Augen. Vor einem Volk, das die Zumutungen der Moderne auf so surreale und letztlich ja auch hochkomische Weise transzendiert, muss man einfach den Hut ziehen.

Der Philosoph Tetsuro Watsuji hat dazu bemerkt, die japanische Seelenlandschaft entspreche der geographischen, geologischen und klimatischen Beschaffenheit der Inseln. Und die sind ebenso vielseitig wie spektakulär. Ich sage nur: tropisch feuchtheiße Sommer, bitterkalte Winter, Monsun, Taifune, Erdbeben und Fudschijama! Deshalb, sagt Watsuji, sei der Japaner von Haus aus »zyklonähnlich« veranlagt, bewege sich »zwischen extremen Zuständen«, neige »zu abruptem Wechsel« und ruhe »niemals in stabilem Gleichgewicht«, setze aber »ungestümen, unkontrollierbaren Gewalten die Tugenden schweigenden Leidens« entgegen. Diese verblüffenden Thesen entnehme ich Kurt Singers famosem Buch *Spiegel, Schwert und Edelstein – Strukturen des japanischen Lebens*. Der Japankenner vermutet, dass sich diese Eigenschaften auch in der Lyrik wiederfinden. Vor allem im Haiku, jener klassischen, in drei Zeilen á fünf, sieben und wieder fünf Silben gegossenen Gedichtform. Der Asienkenner Singer bescheinigt dem Haiku »äußerste Empfindsamkeit, die plötzlich auflodert und ebenso plötzlich erstirbt; kurze Phasen einer extremen Spannung, die von einem Meer des Schweigens umhüllt sind«. Zur Anschauung ein Haiku des Dichters Buson (1715–1783):

»In seinem Glase
Der Goldfisch bass erstaunt blickt,
Dass heute Herbst ist.«

Dieses Exemplar stammt aus der Werkstatt von Meister Issa (1763–1827):

»Zum Abendmondschein
Ach, schreien dort im Schmortopf
Die Weinbergschnecken.«

Singer hat aus alldem gefolgert, die formale Strenge der Poetik wie das ausgefeilte gesellschaftliche Regelwerk Nippons seien entstanden, um die extreme Gefühlswelt seiner Bewohner einzuhegen. Im Umkehrschluss habe der Europäer seine fast durchweg aufgeräumte, lieblich bis platte geographische Disponiertheit mit grausamen Eroberungszügen, manischem Forscherdrang und zwischenmenschlicher Niedertracht kompensiert. Das sind interessante Überlegungen, die gerade zur Erhellung der deutschen Psyche einiges beitragen könnten. Zumal, wenn man in Betracht zieht, dass das Haiku-Schnitzen nach 1945 auch bei uns große Liebhaber gefunden hat. Einer der Geschicktesten ist der Berliner Dichter Uli Becker:

»Ein Pappteller, leer,
Von der Wurst nur der Schatten:
Wegwerfmemento.«

Auch bei den Quasthoff-Brüdern wird das Handwerk mit Eifer und, wie ich finde, auf ganz brauchbarem Niveau gepflegt. Hier ein Beitrag zum Thema Lebensabschnittspartner:

»Im Morgendämmer
Auf dem Nachttisch ihr Tampon:
Liebe macht nicht blind.«

Wenn wir beim Dichten im Wirtshaus sitzen, klingen die Haikus naturgemäß etwas flüssiger. Nämlich so:

>Seht meinen Schatten,
In schöner Koinzidenz
Trinkt er auf mein Wohl.«

Oder so:

>Stets zur rechten Zeit
Vor der Brust der Kellnerin:
Ein Herrengedeck.«

Darüber, was dieser japanisch-deutsche Kulturtransfer völkerpsychologisch zu bedeuten hat, will ich nicht weiter spekulieren. Schließlich bin ich weder Geschichtsphilosoph noch Sabine Christiansen. Sondern nur ein reisender Liedsänger.

Wenn das bisher Geschilderte suggeriert, die Globetrotterei beschere unsereinem ein Leben in Saus und Braus, muss ich den Eindruck korrigieren. Der Tourneealltag ist normalerweise gar nicht lustig. Er ist anstrengend und wie bei Leistungssportlern geprägt von enervierender Redundanz. Jussi und ich steigen morgens irgendwo in den Zug oder ins Flugzeug, kommen am Nachmittag gerädert irgendwo an und fahren ins Hotel, um ein wenig auszuruhen. Oft genug sind die Zimmer noch nicht frei, dann drücken wir uns im Foyer herum oder traben durch die ewig gleichen Shoppingmalls der Innenstädte. Wenn ich mein Haupt endlich auf ein frisches Laken betten könnte, steht die erste Probe an. Also mache ich einen kurzen Check, ob alles so ist, wie meine Agentur bestellt hat: Sind Handtücher da? Ist das Waschbecken tief genug für mich?

Wenn nicht, gibt es eine Fußbank? Komme ich ohne Hilfe in die Dusche? Wenn ich Pech habe, muss ich das Zimmer tauschen. Und weil die Verhandlungen dauern, hetze ich meistens wie von Furien gejagt zur Probe. Anschließend wird eine Kleinigkeit gegessen und wir gehen, nein, eben nicht um die Häuser, sondern schlafen. Denn am nächsten Tag heißt es auftreten. Da sind verräucherte Räume und Alkohol eher kontraproduktiv. Haben wir das Konzert zur Zufriedenheit aller Beteiligten hinter uns gebracht, gibt es zur Belohnung ein Glas Wein, dann ist Zapfen-streich. Weil sich die Stimme erholen muss, weil wir früh raus – und zum Bahnhof oder zum Flugplatz müssen, um wieder irgendwo anzukommen, die Koffer ins Hotel zu stellen, zur Probe zu fahren und so weiter und so fort.

Schlägt man ausnahmsweise über die Stränge, wird das gemeinhin sofort bestraft. Wie in Madrid, wo Pianist Peter Müller und ich nach einem Liederabend tatsächlich mal gründlich versackt sind. Zurück im Hotel, wankt Peter ins Zimmer, nuschelt »Utenacht« und drückt die Tür zu. Ich höre noch, wie er den Schlüssel herumdreht, das Ding wieder aus dem Schloss fingert und mit Karacho auf sein Bett fällt.

»Idiot«, rufe ich. »Ich wohndochauhier.« Denn um Geld zu sparen, haben wir diesmal ein Doppelzimmer ge-mietet. Aber Peter rührt sich nicht. Immerhin gibt es einen Zweitschlüssel. Nur wo? Ich durchforste meine Westen-taschen – einmal, zweimal und auch noch ein drittes Mal. Nichts.

»Das kann nicht sein, ein Schlüssel kann sich nicht in Luft auflösen«, ramentert es durch mein beduseltes Hirn. »Rioja verschwindet, Tapas verschwinden, Cognac ebenso. Aber Dinge? Dinge können verloren gehen, ver-schwinden im Sinne von nicht mehr da sein, das können sie nicht.«

Also tigere ich fünfmal über den Korridor, spähe in alle Ecken und inspiziere jede Teppichfliese. Ich stiere auf das Türschloss, vielleicht habe ich den Schlüssel doch schon hineingesteckt. Nein, so betrunken bin ich auch wieder nicht. Dann fällt es mir wie Schuppen von den Augen: Peter muss auch das zweite Exemplar eingesteckt haben. Ich klopfe an der Tür, ich bearbeite das Pressholz mit dem Schuh, ich schreie seinen Namen. Vergeblich. Das Einzige, was aus dem Zimmer dringt, ist Peters seliges Schnarchen. Mir bleibt nichts weiter übrig, als hinunter zur Rezeption zu fahren und den Nachtportier um einen Drittschlüssel zu bitten. Ich betrete den Aufzug und strecke mich nach der Bedienungstastatur. Gottlob kann ich den unteren Rand gerade so eben erreichen. Die Kabine setzt sich in Bewegung, passiert anstandslos acht Etagen, dann ruckt es ungut und der Fahrstuhl hält. Ich hänge irgendwo zwischen dem ersten und zweiten Stock. Zumindest glaube ich das. Denn die Tür geht nicht auf und im Display glimmt die Ziffer Zwei. Ich bin schlagartig wieder nüchtern. Stattdessen kriecht mir Panik in den Nacken. Mit Aufzügen hab ich es ja eh nicht so. Ich weiß auch genau, warum. Sie können stecken bleiben und der Notknopf der Sprechanlage klebt meistens dreißig Zentimeter über der E-Taste an der Wand. Unerreichbar für meine armlose Kleinheit. Hier ist es nicht anders. Ich sehe nur zwei Möglichkeiten: Warten, bis ein Frühaufsteher die Panne bemerkt, oder Krawall schlagen. Da ich klaustrophobisch veranlagt bin, bleibt nur Nummer zwei. Ich hole tief Luft und beginne, das Hotel nach allen Regeln der Kunst zusammenzubrüllen. Nach zehn Minuten machen sich die jahrelangen Stimmübungen bezahlt. Der Portier meldet sich aus dem Lautsprecher und verspricht schnelle Hilfe. Er übertreibt leider maßlos, ich bekomme Tobsuchtsanfälle. Als man den Aufzug nach zwei Stunden endlich repariert hat, bin ich mental und stimmlich ein Wrack. Den letzten Rest meines Organs ruiniere ich mir auf dem Zimmer. Peter, der zwischenzeitlich aus dem Koma erwacht ist, muss sich wütend anbellen lassen. Dabei kann der arme Kerl gar nichts dafür. Als er längst wieder schnarcht, fällt mir ein, dass ich ihn ausdrücklich gebeten habe, den Schlüssel für mich aufzubewahren. Gut, dass er sich am nächsten Morgen an meine Schimpfkanonade partout nicht mehr erinnern kann. Manchmal hat ein Brummschädel eben auch segensreiche Wirkungen. Unser zweites Madrid-Konzert bringen Peter und ich aber nur mit Ach und Krach über die Bühne. Trotzdem bekommen wir tolle Kritiken, weil die Journalisten alle schon am Vortag da gewesen sind. Wir haben ein ziemlich schlechtes Gewissen und schwören uns, Ausfälle dieser Art zukünftig Rockern wie den Scorpions zu überlassen.

Der hannoversche Exportschlager kriegt so etwas nämlich auch alkoholfrei hin. Dass ich das live erleben darf, verdanke ich meinem Bruder und seiner Exfreundin Sabine Haack. Sabine arbeitet in der Pressestelle der niedersächsischen Staatskanzlei, wo seit kurzem Gerhard Schröder residiert. Anfang 1992 muss sie sich mit der Weltausstellung befassen, die im Sommer in Sevilla stattfindet. Kanzler Kohl hat verfügt, die Kultur im deutschen Pavillon soll von den Landesregierungen bezahlt werden. Im Gegenzug darf jedes Bundesland eine Woche lang das Programm gestalten. Da Sabine eigentlich weit dringlichere Aufgaben zu erledigen hat, heuert sie Micha an. Der ist Feuilletonist, kennt die meisten Szenefiguren und arbeitet ab und an als Texter für die Staatskanzlei. Was den Vorteil hat, dass er obendrein weiß, wie der Auftraggeber tickt. Weltoffen soll der EXPO-Auftritt sein, kulturell werthaltig, aber nicht zu kopflastig und fern der schollenschweren Verstocktheit, die die alte, schwarzgelbe Regierung mit dem notorischen Absingen der inoffiziellen Landeshymne, dem Niedersachsenlied, kultivierte (»Wo fielen die römischen Schergen? / Wo versank die welsche Brut? / In Niedersachsen Bergen, / an Niedersachsen Wut. / Wir sind die Niedersachsen, / sturmfest und erdverwachsen«).

Micha macht sich auch gleich daran, mithilfe des EXPO-Budgets einen weltoffenen und grundsympathischen Nepotismus zu installieren. Ich bin der Erste, den er verpflichtet, der zweite ist Kumpel Thomas Hauck. Er steht Frecc-Frecc vor, einem Performance-Kollektiv mit sechs Musikern aus drei Bundesländern. Für die bildende Kunst tritt seine Thekenbekanntschaft Thomas Kuhlenbeck nebst den liebreizenden Damen Antonia Jacobsen und Katja Schmiedeskamp an. Internationale Kurzfilme repräsentieren die Sparte »Bewegte Bilder«. Sie werden in Hannover von Avantgarde-Regisseur Ecki Kähne vertrieben. Dank der Gage kann er endlich seine Deckelschulden bei Micha abtragen. Die Bluesband Captain Crayfish stammt aus der Rattenfängerstadt Hameln, wie ein Kollege von Sabine.

Halt, stopp! Hochverehrtes Publikum, das ist natürlich nur Spaß und alles gar nicht wahr. Brüderchen ist zwar mit einigen Künstlern per Du, aber für die EXPO qualifizieren sich nur Kulturschaffende, deren Format durch diverse Preise oder stete Feuilleton-Elogen untermauert wird. Die freie Theatergruppe Mahagonny gehört in die erste Liga der Republik, ein Prädikat, das auch für den hannoverschen Kinderzirkus gilt. Altsaxophonist Uli Orth belegt in den Rankings der Fachzeitschriften regelmäßig vordere Plätze und auch die oben erwähnten Kandidaten sind ausgewiesene Spitzenkräfte. Anders ginge es auch gar nicht, da Niedersachsens konservative Zeitungsverleger die Abwahl »des schwarzen Abtes« Ernst Albrecht ziemlich übel nehmen und dem rotgrünen Regiment mit Argusaugen auf die Finger sehen.

Lediglich die Scorpions reisen auf dem Goodwill-Ticket von Gerhard Schröder nach Sevilla. Sänger Klaus Meine gehört zur Stammtischbesetzung des Ministerpräsidenten. Niemand sonst will sie mitnehmen. Micha nicht, Sabine nicht und auch nicht Regierungssprecher Uwe Heye, der für das Programm letztlich den Kopf hinhalten muss. Es geht dabei weniger um Geschmacksfragen. Das Amphitheater im deutschen Pavillon fasst nur zweihundertfünfzig Zuschauer und ist auch akustisch nicht für eine Heavy-Metal-Show konzipiert. Im Gegenteil. Man setzt eher auf familienfreundliches Entertainment. Der Eintritt ist frei und die Menschen sollen hereinschlendern können, ohne sich erst langwierigen Sicherheitskontrollen unterziehen zu müssen. Die Scorpions haben aber gerade mit der Glasnost-Schmonzette *Wind of Change* einen globalen Monsterhit gelandet. Jeder kann sich ausrechnen, was passiert, wenn ihr Auftritt publik wird. Der Ansturm der Fans wäre nicht mehr zu kontrollieren und die Spanier würden mit Recht fragen, warum die Niedersachsen so dumm sind, diesen Topact in den viel zu kleinen Pavillon zu stecken. Aber Gerhard Schröder sagt nicht: »Ich habe verstanden«, sondern: »Basta! Die Scorpions fahren mit.« Die Band hätte ihm versprochen, mit leichtem Gepäck zu reisen und unplugged (akustisch) aufzutreten. Obendrein versuchen Sabine und Micha das Management mit Engelszungen zu überreden, den Auftritt nicht groß in der Welt, speziell nicht auf der Iberischen Halbinsel herumzuposaunen. Das Management stimmt zu, wird sich am Ende aber einen Deubel darum scheren.

Dass das nicht gut gehen würde, hätten abergläubische

Menschen gleich geahnt, als Hannovers bunte Kultur-truppe Ende August in Malaga landet. Nicht nur mein Eröffnungskonzert wäre fast ins Wasser gefallen, weil die Lufthansa zwei Drittel aller Instrumente, darunter einen Bechstein-Flügel, nach Istanbul geschickt hat. Zum Glück stellt uns der holländische Pavillon wenigstens ein Kla-vier zur Verfügung. Deutschland revanchiert sich im Gruppenspiel der gleichzeitig im Schwedischen ausgetra-genen Fußball-Europameisterschaft mit einer indiskutab-len Defensivleistung, die unseren Nachbarn ein 3 : 1 er-möglicht (genützt hat es nichts, die Holländer schaffen es nicht einmal ins Finale, das die Deutschen gegen Außen-seiter Dänemark 0 : 2 verlieren). Nach dem Spiel lassen es sich die Oranjes aber nicht nehmen, noch mal im deut-schen Pavillon vorbeizuschauen – den Magen randvoll mit Genever und auf den Lippen wüste Spottgesänge.

Für die Scorpions bleibt die Logistikpanne ohne Fol-gen. Sie werden kurz vor ihrem Auftritt mit einer eigenen Chartermaschine eingeflogen. Der Rest der Künstler macht lange Gesichter und muss auf die nächste Direkt-verbindung Istanbul – Malaga warten. Die Mienen hellen sich erst wieder auf, als wir unser Quartier zu sehen be-kommen. Die weitläufige Bungalowanlage mit Pool, Bar und Restaurant lässt keine Wünsche offen. Ich beziehe einen der weißen Kästen zusammen mit Freundin Eva. In das blonde Geschöpf bin ich seit einem halben Jahr ver-liebt bis über beide Ohren. Und umgekehrt. Für mich ist sie nicht nur die schönste Frau der Welt (obwohl die Se-ñoritas Andalusiens an Grazie kaum zu übertreffen sind), für mich ist sie einfach perfekt. Denn abgesehen davon, dass Eva an der Musikhochschule Hannover in der Kla-vier-Meisterklasse sitzt, liest sie auch noch regelmäßig den *Kicker*, Deutschlands auflagenstärkstes Fußballfach-blatt. Sie kickt auch selbst gern. Wenn wir nicht gerade im

Amphitheater italienische Arien feilbieten, organisieren wir mit den Jungs von Frec Frec ein Spielchen oder laufen Händchen haltend durch die Altstadt von Sevilla. Sie liegt am Ufer des mächtigen Guadalquivir direkt gegenüber dem EXPO-Gelände. Das ist sehr praktisch. In den schattigen Gassen findet man Schutz vor der brütenden Hitze und stößt an jeder Ecke auf traubenbehangene Bodegas, wo sich die Siesta bei einem Glas Portwein prima verdämmern lässt. Abends nach getaner Arbeit schlendern wir über die EXPO-Plaza. Wenn die Pavillons geschlossen haben, verwandeln die Spanier das Gelände in eine Partyzone für Jung und Alt. Die Veteranen nippen Rotwein aus bauchigen Korbflaschen und begutachten kennerisch die Flamenco-Gruppen, Sevillas Jugend tanzt bis in die Morgenstunden vor der Salsabühne, auf der zwei fulminante kubanische Big Bands um die Wette grooven. Oder das junge Glück sitzt turtelnd im Hotelgarten und sieht zu, wie seine Mitstreiter sich an den Osborne-Portionen abarbeiten, die das Restaurant ebenso billig wie großzügig ausschenkt.

Die Einzigen, die den Ausflug nicht richtig genießen können, heißen Sabine und Micha. Die beiden sind Herbergsvater und Herbergsmutter, Kummerkasten und Auskunftsbüro. Sie verteilen Aspirin, sie sorgen dafür, dass jeder rechtzeitig auf der Bühne steht, sie betreuen die Journalisten und sie vermitteln, wenn sich der Münchner Edelwirt Auer wieder mal lautstark beschwert, weil die Musiker seinen VIP-Gästen ins Essen spielen. Als ihm der zwei Meter große Performer Hauck beim nächsten Gemecker ein blaues Auge verspricht, geht Auer zum Pavillonchef und petzt. Der Chef de Mission heißt Herbert Hegelein. Mit seinen grauen Schläfen, zu denen er stets einen weißen Anzug trägt, sieht Hegelein nicht nur aus wie ein Diplomat der alten Schule. Er ist auch einer – im Botschafterrang. Das Gezeter des Haxenbräters erträgt er mit professioneller Contenance. Dann hebt er die rechte Augenbraue und spricht so:

»Gehen S', Herr Auer, lesen Sie Ihren Mietvertrag. Mit dem Programm müssen Sie leben. Wenn Sie das nicht können, beschweren Sie sich im Außenministerium. Ich schlage vor, Sie knöpfen Ihrer Nobelkundschaft einfach zehn Peso mehr fürs Essen ab und schreiben auf die Speisekarte ›Leberkäse mit Musik‹.«

Hegelein war jahrelang in Südamerika stationiert. Er hat zu viel Elend gesehen, um sich von Sponsoren, Medienpartnern oder sonstigen Windmachern auf der Nase herumtanzen zu lassen. Ein ganz besonderes Früchtchen ist Margarita Mathiopoulos. Republikweit bekannt geworden als erste Frau, die es schaffte, den alten Willy Brandt fast um den Verstand zu bringen, konnte sie den frühen Ruhm halbwegs konservieren, indem sie mit der Merkel-Sprechblase Friedbert Pflüger vor den Traualtar trat. Heute ist sie geschieden und auf dem absteigenden Ast beziehungsweise für die FDP unterwegs. Im Sommer '92 stöckelt sie im Dienst der Norddeutschen Landesbank über das EXPO-Gelände. Das Geldinstitut sponsert Niedersachsens Kulturwoche. Frau Mathiopoulos hat an allem etwas auszusetzen. An der Platzierung der Nord-LB-Logos, an der Größe der Nord-LB-Logos, am Protokoll der Eröffnungsfeier, am Kulturprogramm und an der Art, wie man sie behandelt. Eine Enormität ihres Kalibers kriegt nämlich Pickel, wenn sie mit Domestiken verhandeln muss. Unter Herrn Hegelein macht sie es nicht. Noch lieber wäre ihr allerdings Staatssekretär Uwe Heye, aber nur, wenn der Ministerpräsident keine Zeit hat.

Meist trifft es Hegelein. Freund Uwe pflegt die Nervensäge nämlich weiträumig zu umkurven. Er ist gerade mit Gerhard Schröder und Gattin Hiltrud eingetroffen, um nachzusehen, wie sich die Niedersachsen unter Spaniens Sonne schlagen. Er kann zufrieden sein. Die Länderwoche hat eine gute Presse. Die meisten Punkte bei den Sevillanern machen die Künstler. Sie »fälschen« Werke spanischer Meister auf witzige Art und versteigern die Bilder für einen guten Zweck. Einen Tag nach dem Ministerpräsidenten rücken auch die Scorpions an. Ab diesem Zeitpunkt geht im deutschen Pavillon gar nichts mehr. Die Roadies schichten tonnenschweres Equipment auf die Bühne und lassen sich dabei auch nicht von meinen Verdi-Arien stören. Nach dem dritten Stück habe ich keine Lust mehr und breche ab. Auch Uli Orth weigert sich aufzutreten. Derweil hockt das Schwermetall-Quintett in Auers Grillstube und lässt sich feiern. Zu diesem Zweck haben sie zwei Dutzend Claqueure mitgebracht. Die Bräute stecken in Lederhosen und Leoparden-Tops, aus denen üppig das Brustfleisch quillt, die Herren tragen den Schmerbauch nabelfrei oder sehen aus wie der späte Udo Lindenberg. Ohne Hut. Nachdem man sich mit ein paar Weizenbieren aufgewärmt hat, ruft ihr Manager zur internationalen Pressekonferenz. Da so eine EXPO – einmal eröffnet – erschreckend ereignisarm vor sich hin dämmert, sind die Scorpions für die akkreditierten Journalisten (und für Wirt Auer) ein gefundenes Fressen. Der Konferenzsaal im Pavillon ist voll gepackt mit TV-Kameras und Laptops, als Gitarrist Schenker und Sänger Meine aufs Podium schlurfen. Sie haben drei Dinge zu verkünden. Erstens: Lower Saxony ist ein »echt dufter place«. Zweitens: genauso dufte sei der *Wind of Change*, der dank tätiger Mithilfe der Scorpions jetzt »echt heavy und freedom-mäßig« an der Moskwa weht. Drittens: die Scorpions finden es superdufte, dass »… der Gerd uns nach Sevilla eingeladen hat, um den deutschen Pavillon zu rocken. Und ihr dürft alle wiederkommen«, näselt Meine, »wenn wir heute Abend um zwanzig Uhr für Niedersachsen, für Spanien, für den Weltfrieden und für den Gerd eine tolle Gratisshow geben.«

Raten Sie mal, was davon in der Weltpresse erschienen ist. Genau! Gar nichts. Aber in den Mittagsmagazinen der andalusischen TV- und Radio-Stationen ist die Sache mit dem Gratiskonzert der Aufmacher.

Zwei Stunden später stehen die ersten Fans vor der Tür. Nachmittags sind es Hundertschaften, am frühen Abend belagern tausende den Pavillon. In Hegeleins Büro tagt der Krisenstab. Um dem Chaos Herr zu werden, bleibt ihm nichts weiter übrig, als bei der EXPO-Leitung Polizei anzufordern. Doch die kommt nicht. Stattdessen rückt die Guardia Civil an. Die paramilitärische Truppe gilt nicht gerade als zimperlich, und sie macht ihrem Ruf alle Ehre. Mit gezücktem Schlagstock räumen die Barettträger das Pavillongelände, umstellen das Gebäude und zählen vierhundert Personen ab, die wieder hineindürfen. Die Hardrocker stört das alles nicht. Sie verbarrikadieren sich in der Garderobe und feilen an ihrer Show. Die Combo hat sich Unerhörtes ausgedacht: »The Scorpions meet Elvis Presley«, einen Streifzug durch das Werk des King of Rock 'n' Roll. Unerhört ist auch der Aufwand, den sie betreiben, um die Drei-Akkord-Hits »unplugged« nachzustellen. Vor den Verstärkertürmen hat die Crew einen ganzen Percussionpark und fünfundzwanzig Gitarren aufgebaut, damit sich die Virtuosen nicht auf dem Griffbrett verirren, wenn beim nächsten Stück die Tonart wechselt. Genützt hat es nichts. Denn was sich da auf der Bühne abspielt, nachdem Meine ein kerniges »Hallo, Sevilla. We are the Scorpions from Lower Saxony. Hope you feel good« in den Abendhimmel gekräht hat, lässt sich mit Worten kaum beschreiben. Ich versuche es trotzdem.

Der verehrte Leser imaginiere bitte vor seinem geistigen Ohr *Hound Dog*, in der Originalfassung, die Elvis 1956 für das Sun-Label aufgenommen hat: das zornig vibrierende, aber stets geschmeidige Organ des Kings, Joe Fontanas treibendes Drumset, die mitreißend shuffelnde Rhythmusgitarre Scotty Moores, die er mit eleganten Single-Notes synkopiert. Haben Sie es? »You are nothing but a hound dog« – dúb dábdudu dúb, you are crying all the time – dúb dábdudu dúb …« Nun stelle man sich vor, wie das Stück klingt, wenn der Scorpions-Frontmann sein Kastratenfalsett anwirft, Schenkers Akustikgitarre klingt, als ginge es nicht um *den* Rhythm-and-Blues-Klassiker, sondern um *Neanderthal Man* von den Hotlegs und Schlagwerker Rarebell dem eigentlich staubtrockenen Groove auf zwei Bongos hinterherklöppelt. Höhepunkt der Darbietung ist das Gitarrensolo von Herrn Jabs, der vergessen hat, dass ein Bluesschema nur zwölf Takte hat. In diesem Stil vergehen sich die Scorpions an *Jailhouse Rock, Love Me Tender, Don't be Cruel* und fünfzehn weiteren Perlen des Kings. Man kann Elvis the Pelvis förmlich im Grabe rotieren hören.

Immerhin, Gerhard Schröder ist begeistert. Weil ihn *In the Ghetto* immer an seine harte Jugend erinnert, damals zu Mossenberg im Lippischen, als »wir den Kitt aus Fenstern fressen« mussten, wie der zukünftige Kanzler in sentimentalen Momenten gern einmal erzählt. Aber man muss ihm das nachsehen. Er hat es nicht so mit der Musik, er sammelt Kunst. Niedersachsens EXPO-Delegation atmet jedenfalls auf, als der Spuk vorbei ist und die Scorpions am nächsten Tag zusammenpacken. Die nächsten fünf Tage haben wir das kleine Amphitheater wieder für uns. Dann kommen die Thüringer.

Der Abschied fällt schwer. Weil die Spanier tolle Gastgeber waren, weil sich die neu gewonnenen Freunde in alle Richtungen zerstreuen, und weil En-suite-Engagements immer viel schöner sind als das tägliche Herumzigeunern auf normalen Tourneen. Aber das Leben ist eine Reise, und da geht es halt mal bergauf und mal bergab. Ich will auch gar nicht jammern. Die nächste EXPO wird erst wieder im Jahr 2000 in Hannover stattfinden, dafür steht im nächsten Frühjahr meine erste Kreuzfahrt mit der *Mermoz* auf dem Programm. Das Schiff ist mir im Laufe der Zeit wirklich ans Herz gewachsen.

Wenn man mich fragt, was denn die *Mermoz* von ihren Brüdern und Schwestern unterscheidet, die mittlerweile in D-Day-Stärke vor den Stränden cruisen und dem Pauschalurlauber den sauer ersparten Seeblick trüben, sage ich: Das kann man nicht sehen, das muss man fühlen. Für mich ist die *Mermoz* wie Eugene, nur mit Wasser drunter. Ich freue mich jedes Mal, wenn ich dort arbeiten kann. Ich schaffe es nicht jedes Jahr, aber wenn ich an Bord gehe, treffe ich gute alte Freunde, lerne neue großartige Kollegen kennen wie den Cellisten Boris Pergamenschikow, die Sopranistin Andrea Rost, den Pianisten Byron Janis oder die famose Jazzvokalistin Maria Joao und empfange dafür auch noch fürstlichen Lohn. Inklusive Sonne, exquisiter Speisung und Freigetränken, so viele mein Magen verträgt. Der Mann, der das möglich macht, ist ein ungarischer Konzertveranstalter namens André Borosc. Ich habe ihn erstmals in Paris getroffen, im Haus des Kunstmäzens Marc Smeja. Smeja veranstaltet regelmäßig Hauskonzerte, und Borosc gehört zu den Gästen, als ich dort 1993 auftrete. Er erzählt mir, dass er ein kleines, aber kommodes Schiffchen besitzt. Es böte Platz für eine Hand voll betuchter Kunden, die eine Menge Geld bezahlen, damit er sie mit klassischer Musikbegleitung durchs Mittelmeer schippert. Ob das etwas für mich und die *Winterreise* wäre? Ich bin skeptisch. Den Pausenclown machen auf einem

Kreuzfahrtschiff? Ist das nicht das Endlager des Unterhaltungsgewerbes? Noch schlimmer als Bädertourneen oder die Gesangseinlage beim sechzigsten Geburtstag eines Sparkassengiroverbandsvorsitzenden? Borosc, ein Mensch mit feinen Manieren und dem ironischen Charme des weltläufigen Impresarios, ahnt, was mir durch den Kopf geht:

»Bittasärr, Härr Quuuaasthoff, Sie kännän mich noch nicht. Abärrr ich bin särriösär Mensch, fragen Sie mänä Frrreund Vladi.«

Er streckt den Arm aus und zeigt auf den berühmten Geiger Vladimir Spivakov, der einsam neben der Bowle steht und melancholisch in die Runde guckt. Spivakov winkt müde lächelnd herüber. Ich bin beeindruckt. Restlos überzeugt hat mich Borosc, als er die Vertragsbedingungen spezifiert und ganz nebenbei fallen lässt, dass ich, sofern mir sein Angebot gefällt, buchstäblich im selben Boot sitzen würde wie der Cello-Gott Rostropowitsch und seine Gattin, die Ausnahmesopranistin Galina Wischnewskaja. Sie ist eine der drei Künstlerpersönlichkeiten, für die Benjamin Britten sein pazifistisches Großwerk *War Requiem* geschrieben hat. Die anderen beiden sind Dietrich Fischer-Dieskau und der britische Tenor Peter Pears. Die Premiere am 30. Mai 1962 in der Westminster Abtei musste allerdings ohne die Russin stattfinden. Chruschtschow verweigerte ihr die Teilnahme. Da ich ein großer Fan der Wischnewskaja bin, verspreche ich Borosc, dabei zu sein, wenn sein Schiff im Mai in See sticht. Aufgeregt rufe ich noch am selben Abend Charles Spencer an. Er muss mitfahren, damit wenigstens am Klavier das Weltniveau gesichert ist.

Die *Mermoz* liegt in Marseille. Als ich mich in Begleitung von Charles an einem strahlenden Frühlingsmorgen einschiffe, hätte ich mir nicht träumen lassen, dass ich zwei Tage später zu Rostropowitsch Slawa sagen darf. Nach meinem ersten Konzert umarmt mich das Ehepaar zu Tränen gerührt, und Rostropowitsch meint:

»Chuunger Mann, we have to do some work together.«

Zuerst einmal heißt das freilich zusammen trinken. Und zwar Wodka aus Wassergläsern. Die Portion zu hundertfünfzig Gramm. Mir schnürt sich der Magen zusammen, ich bekomme feuchte Hände. Doch der fast siebzigjährige Rostropowitsch klopft mir aufmunternd auf die Schulter.

»Chou have to drink this. This is Russian mentality. And now call me Slawa.« Dann lässt er sein Glas gegen meines scheppern und stürzt den Inhalt in einem Zug hinunter.

»I am Tommi«, murmele ich ergriffen. Todesverachtend packe ich mein Glas und tue es ihm gleich. Man will sich ja vor einem Genie nicht blamieren. Mein neuer Freund schenkt gleich noch mal nach. Was nach dem dritten Glas passiert ist, habe ich komplett vergessen. Am nächsten Morgen wecken mich stürmischer Seegang, Übelkeit und rasende Kopfschmerzen. Als ich mein fahles Gesicht im Spiegel betrachte, bin ich sicher, ich habe das alles nur geträumt. Doch kaum bin ich an Deck geschlittert, sehe ich Rostropowitsch schon wieder putzmunter an der Reling stehen. Er hält den Charakterkopf in den Wind und brüllt:

»Aaaaah, gutt morning, Tommi. You sleep too long. I see you need other lessons in Russian style.« Ich lächele gequält und verspüre akuten Brechreiz. Aber die Reling ist zu hoch für mich. Ich mache grußlos kehrt und schaffe es gerade noch zurück in meine Kabine.

Später sitze ich mit Slawa und seiner Frau im Salon. Die beiden trinken Campari, ich bestelle Pfefferminztee.

Galina Wischnewskaja erzählt eine Geschichte, die zeigt, aus welchem Holz der Schiffseigner geschnitzt ist. André Borosc habe mit der christlichen Seefahrt eigentlich nie etwas zu schaffen gehabt. Ins Kreuzfahrtgeschäft ist er eingestiegen, als sein Freund Rostropowitsch aus Russland emigrieren und sich eine neue Existenz aufbauen musste. Borosc hat gewusst, dass die musikalischen Rundreisen für beide ein einträgliches Geschäft sein werden. Slawa ist eine ebenso treue Seele. Wir haben eine Woche lang zusammen viel Spaß gehabt, aber ich hätte nie gedacht, dass er sein Angebot, demnächst gemeinsam zu musizieren, ernst meint. Doch ich bin kaum eine Woche zu Hause, da klingelt das Telefon.

»Here is Rostropowitsch«, sagt die Stimme. Ich vermute einen Scherz von meinen Freunden, denen ich die Kreuzfahrergeschichten zu oft in schillernden Farben ausgemalt habe. Also antworte ich.

»Yes, here is the Queen of Saba.«

»Really, here is Slawa«, gurgelt die Stimme wieder.

»I know, and here is the Queen of Saba speaking.«

»Thomas, don't be redicoulus«, tönt es etwas ungehalten zurück und ich merke, er ist es tatsächlich. Ich kann es nicht fassen. Slawa lädt mich ein, den Baritonpart im *War Requiem* zu singen, das er in Tokio dirigieren wird.

Mittlerweile habe ich ihn oft getroffen. Er ist nämlich Stammgast auf der *Mermoz*. Und ich muss sagen, mit Slawa ist es nie langweilig. Ein steter Quell der Heiterkeit sind die Anfälle von Konsumwahn, die seine bessere Hälfte unvermittelt heimsuchen und selbst den von Haus aus sehr freigiebigen Slawa zur Verzweiflung treiben können. Als die *Mermoz* vor Casablanca ankert, wird ihm da wieder einiges zugemutet. Auf dem Programm steht ein Landgang. Slawa und ich halten auf dem Oberdeck lieber zwei Liegestühle besetzt und essen Eis. Für alles andere ist es viel zu heiß. Nicht für Galina. Sie hat schon vor dem Frühstück ein Taxi geordert. Jetzt lässt sie sich von ihrem Gatten ein Dollarbündel aushändigen und fährt shoppen. Nach zwanzig Minuten steht sie wieder auf dem Oberdeck und verlangt einen Nachschlag. Grummelnd zieht er eine Hand voll Hundert-Dollar-Noten aus der Tasche. Als die Wischnewskaja nach einer Stunde wiederkommt, hängt hinter dem Taxi ein Anhänger. Slawa schüttelt den Kopf:

»I don't believe it.«

»Oh, darling, it's not for me, it's for the walls in your office.« Sie hat ihren Slawa mit sage und schreibe dreihundert Meter kostbarem Damaststoff für sein Arbeitszimmer in Sankt Petersburg beglückt. Danach ist ihm die Lust auf Eis vergangen. Er steht auf und verschwindet Richtung Bordbar. Abends sitzt er immer noch dort. Inzwischen haben sich fünf bis sechs Irish Coffee in seinem Inneren verteilt, nicht ohne eine gewisse Wirkung zu hinterlassen. Auf die Frage, wie es ihm geht, antwortet er:

»Oh, very gutt. My wife is sleeping and can't buy anything.«

Sollte ich mich doch einmal an Land bequemen, lande ich, zerrüttet von Hitze, Staub und dem Basargewimmel, meist im nächsten Kaffeehaus. Jedes Mal, wenn Jussi auf der *Mermoz* Klavier spielt, brauche ich dort nicht allein zu sitzen. Er ist ebenso schlecht zu Fuß wie ich. Darum fahren wir so gern nach Marrakesch. Dort steht das Mamudiah, eines der fünf besten Hotels der Welt. Wir klettern aus dem Bus, stiefeln durch die Lobby in den herrlichen Garten und lassen uns unter Palmen nieder. Nach einem Erfrischungsgetränk werden wir schwimmen gehen. Denn was es heißt, in Luxus zu baden, haben Jussi und ich erstmals gemerkt, als wir uns im Mamudiah in den riesigen

Pool geworfen haben. Immer wenn man an den Rand des Beckens paddelt, steht ein Kellner bei Fuß, der fragt, was er für einen tun kann. Wir haben das weidlich ausgenutzt und die alkoholfreie Cocktailkarte vor- und rückwärts durchprobiert. Nur als der Ruf des Muezzins über die Anlage gellt, da ordern wir Bier. Das ist Christenpflicht.

1996 bereichert auch das junge Piano-Genie Jewgenij Kissin den Konzertkalender der *Mermoz*. Er ist ein feiner Kerl, leider kann er das nicht so oft zeigen. Denn stets pirschen Mutter und eine herbe Klavierlehrerin in seiner Spur. Der zweiköpfige Zerberus passt auf, dass sein Schützling mit den Versuchungen des Lebens, die da heißen Wein, Weib und unkeuscher Gesang, gar nicht erst in Berührung kommt. Der Geiger Shlomo Mintz, Bratschist Juri Baschmet und ich sehen uns das vier Tage an. Er tut uns furchtbar Leid. Eines Abends, als Jewgenij wieder einmal traurig und die beiden Erinnyen im Schlepptau um die Borddisco schleicht, wird er einfach gekidnappt. Juri postiert sich hinter der Tür, und als der Pianist vorbeigeht, zieht er ihn entschlossen hinein. Wir nehmen unseren Fang in die Mitte und flüchten durch einen Seiteneingang ins Restaurant. Die Wachhunde verlieren auch prompt die Spur. Auf den gelungenen Coup bestellen wir Bier. Jewgenij mundet es ausgezeichnet. Wir bestellen noch eins, und er trinkt auch das mit Genuss. Schließlich haben wir bis morgens um fünf geredet, in der Disco herumgetanzt und weitere Biere geköpft. Am nächsten Morgen stiefelt der Zerberus mit zwei finsteren Mienen über das Deck und wirft uns tödliche Blicke zu. Jewgenij erscheint Stunden später. Er geht wie in Zeitlupe, über seine Augen hat er eine dicke Sonnenbrille gezogen.

»Na, wie fühlst du dich?«, fragt Shlomo lachend. Jewgenij strahlt über beide Wangen:

»Terrible, but it was a great night.«

Im nächsten Jahr registrieren Juri und ich befriedigt, dass er seine Wachhunde endgültig abgeschüttelt hat.

Über meinen alten Freund Juri Baschmet könnte man ein eigenes Buch schreiben. Der Mann ist ein musikalisches Urviech, ein Original und Lebenskünstler und dabei einer der großherzigsten und liebenswertesten Zeitgenossen, den ich kenne. Fachleute zählen Juri zu den besten Bratschisten der Welt, und es sind nicht die Dümmsten, die behaupten, die Schönheit seines Spiels habe etwas Unirdisches. Weshalb man Neider zuweilen munkeln hört, er habe seine Seele dem Teufel verkauft. Das mag daran liegen, dass Juris Gesamterscheinung – kohlrabenschwarzes Haar, dunkel funkelnde Augen, Adlerprofil und ein herausfordernd majestätisches Auftreten – etwas Dämonisches, sprich Paganinihaftes anhaftet. Nahrung erhält dieser Eindruck, wenn man weiß, dass Juri das Klavier und die Violine ebenso gut beherrscht wie die Bratsche. Ich habe selbst erlebt, wie der Dirigent Baschmet einem bekannten Geigen-Virtuosen heimleuchtete. Der Mann bekam ein paar äußerst schwierige Takte, ich glaube, es ging um Bartóks Violinkonzert in C, einfach nicht so hin, wie Juri sich das vorstellte. Man probierte es wieder und wieder, bis Juri der Kragen platzte. Er entriss dem Virtuosen das Instrument und fidelte die tückische Stelle prima vista und mit unschlagbarer Grandezza herunter. Der so Gedemütigte kriegte den Mund vor Staunen nicht mehr zu. Juri durchbohrte ihn mit seinen schwarzen Augen, drückte ihm Geige und Bogen an die Brust und raunzte verächtlich:

»You have to do it in this way.«

Juri könnte als Solist Millionen scheffeln. Stattdessen ernährt er in Sankt Petersburg einen ganzen Tross von Musikern, mit denen er als Orchesterleiter durch die Welt zieht. Ich habe Juri und seine Familie ein paar Mal besucht und gesehen, was sein Engagement für die Kollegen bedeutet. Die Stadt ist voller wunderbarer Musiker, aber die meisten leben seit dem Zusammenbruch der Sowjetunion in Verhältnissen, die im Westen niemand aushalten würde. Viele der einst ruhmreichen Rundfunk- und Staatsorchester sind aufgelöst worden, abgewickelt von der neuen Zeit, die für die Segnungen der Kultur kein Geld und keinen Bedarf mehr hat. Damit sind auch ihre Protagonisten obsolet geworden. Es gibt keine Arbeit, weil es kein Publikum mehr gibt. Und so bietet ihnen Juri eine der wenigen Möglichkeiten, in Würde weiterzuspielen und zu leben.

Wenn man ihn fragt, warum er sich den Stress antut, anstatt eine der lukrativen Agentenofferten anzunehmen und als gefeierter Star über die Bühnen der Musiktheater zu ziehen, zuckt er nur mit den Schultern.

»Tell me, what is a star. A star is so far from all human being, a cold glittering light in universe. I want to stay on the bottom.«

Das ist schön gesagt. Doch manchmal gerät auch Juris anrührende Bodenständigkeit arg ins Wanken und kollidiert mit seiner promethischen Künstlernatur. Dann kann er, gepeinigt von der Trostlosigkeit des Seins im Allgemeinen und des Musikgewerbes im Besonderen, in weiße Wut, wahlweise tagelang in schwarze Melancholie fallen. Zum Beispiel wenn es darum geht, Proben zu organisieren, Terminabsprachen ernst zu nehmen oder seinen formschwankenden Orchesterapparat im Gleichgewicht zu halten. Im Konzertsaal und außerhalb.

Als ich Juri und sein Orchester auf Schloss Elmau wieder treffe, herrscht gerade die melancholische Phase. Sie wird ausgiebig mit Alkohol gewässert, sodass das Petersburger Ensemble einen schönen Kontrast bildet zur auf-

geräumten Gästeschar, die das Hotel über Neujahr be-
völkert. Wie Eugene ist die Elmau ein Ort mit Persönlichkeit. Elmau heißt nicht nur das Schloß, sondern ein
ganzes Hochtal. Es liegt, versteckt zwischen den Kalk-
steinwänden von Karwendel- und Wettersteingebirge,
in der Nähe von Mittenwald. Gründervater der freundlichen Herberge ist der Wanderprediger und Sinnsucher
Johannes Müller. Um 1900 durchstreift er das Süddeutsche und fischt Menschenseelen. Das ist damals in den
Kreisen des von der Industrialisierung tief verunsicherten
Bürgertums ein Volkssport. Aber Müller hat – im Gegensatz zu den meisten Konkurrenten – mit seiner kauzigen,
aber gut gemeinten Mixtur aus »Zurück zur Natur«-Ap-
pellen und eigenwilligen Bibelauslegungen nachhaltigen
Erfolg. Vor allem bei Damen. Als er das stille Elmautal
entdeckt, scheint ihm das der richtige Ort, um eine
lebensreformerische Kommune zu errichten. Eine seiner
solventen Verehrerinnen, die Gräfin Waldersee, baut ihm
das schlossähnliche Haupthaus neben den Ferchenbach,
und mit der Zeit wächst die Elmau zu einer Begegnungs-
stätte mit sozialtherapeutischen Ambitionen, welche sich
aber zum Glück für die erholungsbedürftige Klientel auf
die Müllersche Generalmaxime reduzieren: »Leben ist
mehr als Werk, und das Sein ist wichtiger als das Tun.«
Solch ein sinnesfrohes Credo kann sich aber schon zu
Müllers Zeiten nicht jedermann leisten. Und so sorgt ein
illustres Völkchen aus Künstlern, Ministerialen und
Großverdienern aller Couleur dafür, dass sich im Lauf der
Zeit jenes Fluidum herausschält, das noch heute die Räume durchweht. Es ist eine leicht museale Abart großbür-
gerlicher Feinsinnigkeit (kein Fernsehen!), gewürzt mit
Wellness, Esoterik light, Lesungen, Podiumsdiskussionen
zur Weltlage und last but not least einem erstklassigen
Musikprogramm zwischen Klassik und modernem Jazz.

Ich habe auf Schloss Elmau das erste Mal kurz nach dem Gewinn des ARD-Wettbewerbs gesungen. Seitdem verbringe ich hier fast jeden zweiten Jahreswechsel. Es ist jedes Mal wie ein großer Familienausflug. Jussi reist mit Frau und drei Kindern an, ich bringe Mama und Vater mit. Manchmal sind auch Micha und Renate mit von der Partie. Die beiden stapfen durch den Schnee hinunter zur Partnachklamm oder hinauf zur Schachenhütte, die Ludwig Zwo erbauen ließ, um ungestört von seinen Bayern in den Tag zu träumen. Ich bleibe lieber im Kaminzimmer und gucke lebende Prominente. Ein paar sind immer da. Loriot, der grundsympathische Achim Rohde oder Peter Glotz. Glotz ist im Jahr 2002 einfach nicht zu übersehen. Der Quer- und Schwerdenker wandert seit Tagen rastlos über das Parkett, die Stirn zerknittert, den Blick zu Boden gerichtet, als suche er einen abgefallenen Hosenknopf. Unter dem Arm trägt er einen gewaltigen Aktenordner. Er enthält ein Manuskript. Das weiß ich, weil Glotz den Ordner des Öfteren wie absichtslos und immer dekorativ aufgeschlagen liegen lässt, um dann drei Pfund leichter weiterzuwandern und Knöpfe zu suchen. Einmal sehe ich hinein und lese Sachen wie »ein europäisches Problem neu erzählen«, »Volkstumskämpfe«, »sudetendeutsches Problem« und »gegen den Strom schwimmen«.

»Ach, du grüne Neune«, seufzt Micha, als ich ihm davon erzähle, »da können wir uns im nächsten Bücherherbst ja wieder auf einiges gefasst machen.« Und tatsächlich, ein paar Wochen später setzt sich der Genosse an die Spitze einer Bewegung, die es mit ihrer Idee, in Berlin ein Vertriebenen-Mahnmal neben die Holocaust-Gedenkstätte zu setzen, fertig bringt, das deutsch-polnische Verhältnis auf den Stand von 1945 zurückzuwerfen.

Nicht halb so vergreist hält am Tag darauf die Dichterin Hilde Domin Hof. Dabei ist die zierliche Dame fast doppelt so alt wie Glotzens Peter. Der Unterschied ist, ihre Werke, die in jeder guten Lyrik-Anthologie stehen, werden überdauern. Sie hat Stil und muss niemandem mehr etwas beweisen. Und so hat sie auch die Lesung serviert. Was heißt Lesung? Eigentlich war es eine Performance, und zwar eine der besten, die ich je gesehen habe. Als die Domin auf die Bühne tippelt, habe ich gleich gemerkt, Tommi pass auf, hier kannst du noch etwas lernen. Ihre Haltung – Rückgrat und eisgrauer Dutt bilden eine gerade Line – ist ebenso vorbildlich wie der Tonfall, mit dem sie den Auftritt eröffnet und das Publikum in die Defensive zwingt, ohne dass es die Leute krumm nehmen: verbindlich, aber sehr bestimmt, rasant, aber jedes Wort präzise artikulierend. Frau Domin ist jederzeit Herrin der Lage.

»Ich lese jetzt mein erstes veröffentlichtes Gedicht«, hebt sie an.

»Ich lese es zweimal. Ich lese immer alles zweimal. Wer mich schon einmal lesen gehört hat, weiß das.«

Sie liest aber gar nicht, sondern erzählt jetzt erst einmal etwas Persönliches.

»Ich bin ja Zeitzeugin«, sagt die Domin. »Ich darf das.«

Dann erzählt sie, dass Kollegin Marie Luise Kaschnitz gelegentlich einen ziemlichen Summs zusammengereimt habe. Wenn die Kaschnitz schrieb, »es liefen zwei Löwen durchs Zimmer«, habe sie gefragt:

»Luise, stimmt das?«

»Ne.«

»Siehste.«

Ja, so sei das gewesen bei der Gruppe 47. Ihr selbst kämen ja die Gedichte einfach so zugeflogen, wer sich mit Lyrik beschäftigt, weiß, wie das ist. Für alle anderen werde sie jetzt zu Demonstrationszwecken tatsächlich eines ihrer Gedichte vorlesen.

»Oder zwei. Na gut, zwei. Eins aus dem Jahre 1947, mein erstes veröffentlichtes Gedicht, das andere aus dem Jahr 1958. Beziehungsweise lese ich erst das eine zweimal, dann das andere zweimal.«

Denn das müsse man wissen, sie, die Domin, lese alles zweimal vor.

»Und nie länger als 59 Minuten. Ob mir mal jemand sagen kann, wie spät es ist?«

»Viertel vor fünf«, ruft jemand.

»Ah, dann müssen wir uns sputen. Also lese ich jetzt zwei ganz kurze Gedichte. Sie sind Virginia Woolf gewidmet, einer Selbstmörderin.«

Aber auch dazu fällt Hilde Domin wieder eine Schnurre ein. Und so geht es fort und fort. Es war großartig. Leider holt mich Jussi zur Probe ab, bevor ich feststellen kann, ob sie ihre Lesung tatsächlich zu Ende bringt, ohne ein einziges Gedicht vorzutragen.

Ich habe mich jedenfalls sehr gefreut, sie in einer der vorderen Reihen sitzen zu sehen, als ich abends mit Sibylle Rubens und Jussi Hugo Wolfs *Italienisches Liederbuch* vortrage. Sibylle ist nicht nur eine meiner ältesten musikalischen Weggefährtinnen, sie hat auch eine der schönsten Sopranstimmen, die ich kenne. Für das Liederbuch ist sie die ideale Partnerin, weil sie wie ich Spaß daran hat, dieser süß-sauren »Beziehungskiste« auch mimisch Zucker zu geben. Wir ernten jedenfalls mehrmals große Lacher. Auch Juri Baschmets Stimmungsbarometer steht inzwischen wieder auf heiter. Unser Arienabend wird ein schönes Erlebnis, weil die Petersburger wieder einmal zu großer Form auflaufen. Nach dem Konzert sitzen Juri, meine Eltern und ich noch lange beisammen. Ich kann mir das leisten, meine Arbeit ist getan. Jetzt beginnt das Vergnügen. Und das heißt auf der Elmau immer, den Jazzcracks zuzuhören. In diesem Jahr ist der schwedische

Pianist Esbjörn Svensson zu Gast. Ich habe ihn schon letzte Saison mit dem Posaunisten Nils Landgren gesehen, der auch auf eine bezwingend lakonische Weise Jazzstandards singt. Manchmal sitzen die Jazzer auch in den klassischen Konzerten, oder man jammt und trifft sich anschließend in der Bar. Es herrscht echte Festival-Atmosphäre. Der Höhepunkt ist zweifellos die Silvesterfeier. Wenn er nicht gerade auf Tournee ist oder an einem südlichen Strand liegt, schneit Klaus Doldinger herein. Deutschlands bekanntester Jazzmusiker und Filmkomponist wohnt in der Nähe und hat immer sein Saxophon dabei. Dann wird das neue Jahr mit einer wilden Session eingeläutet.

Das entspannte Zusammenwirken von Klassik-Interpreten und Jazzern bestätigt wieder einmal, wie überflüssig das deutsche Schubladendenken ist. Es gibt tatsächlich nur gute oder schlechte Musik. Und was man vorrangig als singender Reisekader lernt, ist, dass gute Musik, egal welcher Spielart, die Menschen im Innersten anrührt und verbindet, ob in Berlin, Moskau, Tokio, Houston, Johannesburg oder Timbuktu.

So ist es auch bei dem umstrittensten Konzert, das ich je mitgemacht habe. Am 7. Mai 2000, dem Befreiungstag des Konzentrationslagers Mauthausen, spielen Simon Rattle und die Wiener Philharmoniker im Steinbruch unterhalb der »Todesstiege« Beethovens Neunte Sinfonie und die *Ode an die Freude*.

Im Vorfeld gibt es wütende Proteste. Ausgerechnet Beethoven und Schiller, argumentieren die Opferverbände. Zwei unverfrorener von den Nazis vereinnahmte Künstler hätte man nicht finden können. Diese Musik an einem Ort zu hören, wo 105 000 Menschen ermordet wurden, sei unerträglich. Auch der renommierte Jazzmusiker

Joe Zawinul, der 1998 an gleicher Stelle seine Komposition *Vom Großen Sterben hören* aufführte, meldet Bedenken an.

»Ich fände es besser, wenn die Philharmoniker etwas Neues spielen würden und nicht Beethoven. Das haben auch die Nazis spielen lassen.« Unterstützung bekommt er von dem Historiker Niklas Perzi:

»Zawinul hat sich musikalisch intensiv mit Mauthausen auseinander gesetzt, die Philharmoniker hingegen wollen einfach Beethoven über das KZ legen.«

Beethoven und Schiller waren keine Nazis, hält Simon dagegen. Ich persönlich finde, es ist eine schwierige Entscheidung. Aber letztlich überzeugt mich Simons Haltung, der mit seinem Credo »Die Musik bedeutet Erinnerung, Reue und Respekt. Musik ist da, um zu heilen« alle Bedenken vom Tisch wischt. Niemand weiß das besser als ich, weil die Musik mir über so vieles Unerfreuliche in meinem Leben hinweggeholfen hat.

Dietrich Fischer-Dieskau, der die Aufführung am TV-Gerät verfolgt, hat der *FAZ* seine Eindrücke später so beschrieben:

»Die Wiener Philharmoniker waren fabelhaft. Da brachte übrigens das Fernsehen eine unglaubliche Atmosphäre mit herüber. Man sah diesen Steinbruch, in dem die Menschen gefoltert wurden. Und man sah am Schluss die Leute ohne Beifall dasitzen nach all diesem Freudenjubel. Sie saßen da still, jeder sein Kerzchen im Schoß, in vollkommener, absoluter Ruhe. Viele tausende. Und Millionen sahen zu. Das ist schon erschütternd. Die Neunte ist schließlich immer noch ein haariges Stück für den Chor. Für die Solisten auch. Aber so ein Ereignis in alle Häuser zu tragen, das ist schon etwas Besonderes. Es funktioniert besser als jedes Mahnmal, worum sich die Fachleute streiten. Es erschüttert alle, die es erreicht.«

Fischer-Dieskau hat es sehr gut getroffen. Welche magischen und kathartischen, ja gleichsam seelsorgerischen Kräfte der Musik innewohnen, habe ich schon öfter erfahren. Am intensivsten in Erinnerung geblieben ist mir eine Begebenheit, die sich vor zehn Jahren in Israel zugetragen hat. Ich bin mit Karl-Friedrich Beringer und dem Windsbacher Knabenchor unterwegs gewesen. Nach drei Konzerten in Tel Aviv wollen wir die *Matthäus-Passion* auf einem großen Festival am See Genezareth aufführen. Bachs Meisterwerk ist hierzulande sehr umstritten. Einige Textzeilen, besonders im Choral *O Haupt voll Blut und Wunden*, bezeichnen die Juden eindeutig und in recht unschöner Weise als Gottesmörder. Ultrareligiöse Fanatiker nehmen die alten Bibelstellen persönlich. Sie drohen uns Demonstrationen und Schlimmeres an. Beringer lässt sich aber nicht beirren, wir spielen das Stück. Nach dem Konzert tritt ein älterer Mann in meine Garderobe. Er hat ein kurzes Hemd an, und ich kann sehen, dass auf seinem rechten Arm eine ausgeblichene blaue Ziffernfolge eintätowiert ist – die Kennungsnummer der KZ-Insassen. Der Mann erzählt in gebrochenem Deutsch, dass er auch Musiker ist und in Bergen-Belsen interniert war. Über sein Gesicht laufen Tränen. Dann nimmt er meine Hand, drückt sie minutenlang und sagt:

»Nach fünfzig Jahren habe ich heute zum ersten Mal wieder geweint. Dafür danke ich Bach, und ich danke Ihnen!«

Ich habe den Mann dann fünf Wochen später bei einem meiner Liederabende in München wiedergesehen. Er ist extra aus Israel angereist, um mich noch einmal zu hören. Da kann *ich* die Tränen kaum zurückhalten. Aber der alte

Herr hat gar keine Sentimentalitäten aufkommen lassen und mir einen schönen Musiker-Witz erzählt:

Ein israelischer Dirigent geht am Strand spazieren und findet eine verschlossene Flasche. Er macht sie auf, heraus kommt ein Dschinn. Der Flaschengeist sagt:

»Du hast mich nach dreihundert Jahren aus der Flasche befreit. Nun darfst du dir etwas wünschen.« Der Dirigent überlegt lange, dann zieht er eine Landkarte aus der Jackentasche und breitet sie am Strand aus.

»Schau mal, hier ist Israel, hier ist Palästina, hier Syrien, da liegt Ägypten. Seit Jahrzehnten regiert hier Gewalt und Unfrieden. Wenn du es fertig bringst, dass endlich Friede herrscht, wäre ich zufrieden.«

Der Geist reibt sich nachdenklich das Kinn:

»Hm, eine sehr schwere Aufgabe. Ich bin erst seit einer Minute aus der Flasche heraus und etwas aus der Übung. Hast du vielleicht noch einen anderen Wunsch?«

Der Dirigent überlegt: »Ich leite ein Orchester und habe wie alle Dirigenten ein Problem mit den Bratschisten. Sie kommen immer zu spät, fordern die meisten Pausen und die höchsten Gagen, können aber ihr Instrument nicht richtig spielen. Wenn das aufhört, wäre ich dir sehr dankbar.«

Der Geist kratzt sich am Kopf und sagt: »Zeig mir lieber noch mal die Landkarte.«

Das Leben ist ein Gesamtkunstwerk

»Bei uns in Detmold is äne Jesangs-Professur frei, die Schtelle is wie für disch jemacht.« Hilde Kronstein-Uhrmacher lacht mir ins Gesicht. Dabei sollte die rheinische Frohnatur lieber nach vorn schauen, wo ihr Benz bedenklich Richtung Leitplanke driftet.

»Pass auf, der Wagen ...«, rufe ich mit geschlossenen Augen, während mir der Angstschweiß in den Nacken läuft. Hilde lässt sich nicht beirren:

»Räsch disch nisch auf, hör mir lieber zu. Bewürb disch und mer sin näschtet Jahr Kolleschen.«

Wieder gerät der Benz aus der Spur, diesmal rasiert er fast den rechten Grünstreifen. Hilde kann einfach nicht geradeaus fahren. Wieder klingelt ihr Singsang in meinen Ohren:

»Bewürb disch, verjiss et nisch.« Ich transpiriere schweigend vor mich hin und versuche, meinen Mageninhalt unter Kontrolle zu halten. So geht es hin und fort im Schlingerkurs von Hamburg bis Hannover. Als wir am Aegidientorplatz halten, steige ich wie gerädert aus der Karosse.

»Tschö, Tommi, bis später.« Sie kurbelt das Fenster herunter. »Und verjiss Detmold nisch!«

»Ja, Hildchen«, das werde ich bestimmt nie vergessen. Dann wanke ich in die Garderobe des Theaters am Aegi, wo Hildes Gatte, Herr Kronstein, Intendant ist und einen Liederabend für mich und Jussi organisiert hat. Die Dozentin Hilde Kronstein-Uhrmacher schätze ich, seit wir Ende der achtziger Jahre einen langweiligen Kongress der

Gesangspädagogen in der Cafeteria ausgesessen haben. Später, als wir tatsächlich Kollegen sind, wird sie mich häufiger durchs kurvenreiche Weserbergland in den Verwaltungssitz des Landkreises Lippe chauffieren. Ich habe gelernt, mich mit ihrem Fahrstil zu arrangieren. Denn mit der Bahn dauert die Reise fast zweieinhalb Stunden, weil man zwei Mal umsteigen und auf Anschlusszüge warten muss.

Das Unterrichten hat mir schon immer großen Spaß gemacht. Nach dem ARD-Wettbewerb fragen mich viele junge Sänger, ob ich ihnen weiterhelfen kann. Die Begabtesten nehme ich gerne an, obwohl mir zwischen den Reisen nicht viel Zeit bleibt. Anscheinend verfüge ich über ein bisschen pädagogisches Talent. Meine erste Klientin, Katharina Petz, hat es gleich zum festen Ensemblemitglied an der Züricher Oper gebracht. Trotzdem habe ich damals lange überlegt, ob ich wirklich eine Bewerbung an die Musikhochschule Detmold abschicken soll. Zum einen habe ich mich gerade an das Dasein als nomadisierender Liedsänger gewöhnt, zum anderen ist das Wenige, was ich über Detmold weiß, nicht gerade dazu angetan, mir den Umzug in den Teutoburger Wald besonders schmackhaft zu machen.

Das Städtchen wirbt mit dem größten Freilichtmuseum Deutschlands, das den Besuchern neben historischen Bauernkaten Attraktionen wie die Lippegans und das Bentheimer Landschwein zu bieten hat. Ein weiteres Juwel ist die Bundesanstalt für Getreide-, Kartoffel- und Fettforschung. Darüber hinaus listet der Stadtführer diverse Möbelfabriken und Brauereien auf, ein Dreispartentheater, eine spätgotische Stadtkirche, das Residenzschloss der Grafen zu Lippe aus dem 16. Jahrhundert und 72 600 zu einem Gutteil verbeamtete Einwohner. Mit ihren

Vorfahren hat es der Komponist und Hofschauspieler Albert Lortzing sieben Jahre lang ausgehalten, ist dabei aber ständig abwesend, will heißen mit dem Theater im Westfälischen unterwegs gewesen.

Johannes Brahms, der Pfingsten 1857 in die Residenzstadt kommt, um im Schloss eine Stelle als Chordirigent und Pianist anzutreten, bringt es auf drei Jahre. Zumindest nominell. In Wirklichkeit flieht der junge Mann, sooft es seine Pflichten erlauben, nach Göttingen, wo er nach dem etwas unentschlossenen und folglich ergebnislosen Werben um Clara Schumann Trost bei der Professorentochter Agathe von Siebold findet. Als der Herr Papa von Verlobung spricht, sucht Brahms allerdings schnell das Weite. Immerhin ist die Detmolder Episode keine gänzlich verlorene Zeit. Brahms geht viel spazieren, komponiert zwei Serenaden (op. 11 und 16), sein Erstes Klavierkonzert und einige romantische Lieder. Das romantischste, *Unter Blüten des Mais spielt ich mit ihrer Hand*, ist der schönen Agathe gewidmet. Als er sie sitzen lässt, klagt Clara Schumann: »Ach lieber Johannes, hättest du es nicht so weit kommen lassen.«

Doch Brahms liebt »nur die Musik«, wie er an die immer noch hochverehrte Freundin meldet: »Ich denke nichts als sie und nur an anderes, wenn es die Musik mir schöner macht.« Dass er die Fast-Verlobte in seinem Streichsextett in G-Dur verewigt, ist immerhin ein nobler Zug. Im Seitenthema des ersten Satzes erscheint das Motiv a-g-a-h-e.

Am abschreckendsten wirkt das Beispiel Christian Dietrich Grabbes. Als schiere Geldnot Detmolds größten Sohn und Deutschlands bedeutendsten Vormärz-Dichter neben Heinrich Heine aus Berlin zurück an die Ufer von Werre und Berlebecke zwingt, klagt Grabbe einem Freund, er fühlte sich verbannt in ein »tristes Neste«, »wo man einen gebildeten Menschen für einen verschlechterten Mastochsen hält« und »dessen Namen ich vor Ingrimm kaum ausschreiben kann«. In »diesem Detmold, wo ich abgeschnitten von aller Literatur, Phantasie, Freunden und Vernunft bin, stehe ich (dir ins Ohr gesagt) am Rande des Verderbens«. Zwar schreibt er demselben Freund einige Monate später: »Wer weiß, ob ich im Lippischen nicht aller Vorurteile ungeachtet in eine erträgliche Karriere gerate …?«, aber daraus wird nichts werden. Der Brotberuf des Militärrichters ist ihm mindestens so zuwider wie Ehefrau Louise, sodass er seine Tage und Nächte lieber gleich in der Schankwirtschaft Posthaus, wahlweise in der Punschhöhle Zur Stadt Frankfurt verbringt. 1836, kurz nach Vollendung seines Dramas *Hermannschlacht*, stirbt Grabbe noch nicht einmal fünfunddreißigjährig an gebrochenem Herzen und ruinierten Leberwerten.

Ein anderer berühmter Detmolder, der Poet und 48er Revolutionär Ferdinand Freiligrath, macht es besser und sich sofort nach der Schulzeit auf Nimmerwiedersehen ins Niederrheinische davon. Dass er seiner Heimatstadt ein Kaff wie Unkel vorgezogen hat, spricht ja wohl Bände.

Jedenfalls sitze ich mit gemischten Gefühlen in Hildes Wagen, als wir an der Abfahrt Bielefeld Zentrum von der A2 abbiegen und über die Bundesstraßen 66 und 239 in die City von Detmold einrollen. Hilde hat sich bereit erklärt, mir die Schokoladenseiten der Stadt persönlich nahe zu bringen. Mit Erfolg. Erleichtert stelle ich fest, dass sich in den letzten hundertsechzig Jahren doch einiges zum Besseren gewendet hat. Das polierte Fachwerk grüßt heimelig, die Menschen sind freundlich und aufgeschlossen, und in und um Detmold herum sprießt üppiges Grün. Auch die Musikhochschule, an der seit mehr als fünfzig Jahren Koryphäen wie der moderne Komponist Günter Bialas unterrichten, bietet ein überaus freundliches Bild. Die Lehrgebäude ruhen oberhalb eines Wiesenhangs unter den Baumkronen des Englischen Hofgartens. Das gräfliche Palais beherbergt die Pianisten und Organisten, die Musikwissenschaftler bewohnen eine Jugendstilvilla am Gartenrand, alle anderen Fraktionen residieren in maßgeschneiderten Flachbauten, die wie hingewürfelt auf dem weitläufigen Campus liegen. Gesangsschülern steht für Podiumstraining und szenische Aufführungen das ebenfalls am Rande des Campus gelegene historische Sommertheater zur freien Verfügung. Es gibt auch einen großen Konzertsaal mit professionell eingerichteten Tonmeister-Studios.

Am Ende der Besichtigungstour regelt Hilde auch gleich die Wohnungsfrage: »Falls de hier anfängst, brauchst de nit mal wat anzumieten. Mach et wie ich. Hock disch einfach ins Hotel und lass dir allet von den feschen Mädsche vor de Nase tragen.«

Kurz darauf sitzen wir in Schusters Bistro im rustikalen Detmolder Hof, über dessen Tür in güldenen Lettern das Baujahr 1560 eingraviert ist. Bei einem Pils und vorzüglichem Hirschrahm besprechen wir ein eventuelles Arrangement. Herr Schuster bietet mir ein Zimmer zum Vorzugspreis, das man auch, wenn ich auf Reisen bin, freihalten will. In dem Familienbetrieb werde ich mich die nächsten acht Jahre pudelwohl fühlen. Denn da mir Hilde, meine Eltern und Micha vehement zuraten, habe ich meine Bewerbung tatsächlich losgeschickt und bin prompt angenommen worden. Auslösendes Moment für meinen Sinneswandel ist nicht zuletzt die Trennung von meiner Freundin Eva. Wir haben fast sechs Jahre zusammengelebt. Nun geht der Bruch mit höchst unschönen Szenen vonstatten und mir sehr nahe. Man kann auch sagen, ich leide wie ein Hund (das ist anscheinend mein Karma bei Beziehungsstress). Ich habe dann versucht, mein Elend mit Arbeit zu kompensieren. Nach drei Wochen bin ich zusammengebrochen und muss für einen Monat alle Auftritte absagen.

Als ich wieder auf dem Damm bin, scheint mir eine neue berufliche Herausforderung nebst Ortswechsel nicht das Schlechteste zu sein. Im Sommersemester 1996 begrüßt mich Dekan Professor Martin Redel im Kreis der Kollegen. Die meisten beäugen den Neuen erst einmal mit skeptischen Gesichtern. Einen Behinderten als Dozenten haben sie noch nie gesehen. Außerdem bin ich der Einzige im Kollegium, der professionell musiziert, was dazu führt, dass meine Lehrmethoden und Beurteilungen eher unorthodox, also praxisnah ausfallen.

Zum Beispiel habe ich meine Klasse gleich zu Beginn in die Seminare der Kollegen geführt. Nicht die einzige Maßnahme, die bei manchem Unverständnis und ärgerliches Kopfschütteln hervorruft, weil mir unterstellt wird, ich wolle lediglich demonstrieren, dass ich es besser könne. Aber das ist grober Unfug, ich tue das, damit sich die Studenten ein Bild machen können über die Bandbreite des pädagogischen Angebots und selbstständig entscheiden lernen, was gut für sie ist. Schließlich habe ich die Weisheit nicht gepachtet und bin keinem böse, der meine Klasse verlässt. Auch sind mir die meisten akademischen Riten, gegen die ich angeblich verstoße, ein Buch mit sieben Siegeln.

Aber der Mensch gewöhnt sich an alles, selbst an so ein Unikum wie meine Wenigkeit. Nach ein paar Wochen legen sich die Irritationen, und es beginnt die schönste Zeit meines Lebens. Die Hälfte des Jahres toure ich um die Welt, den Rest der Zeit verbringe ich mit meinen Studenten, die sehr gute Fortschritte machen. Überhaupt sind die

Absolventen der Detmolder Hochschule überproportional häufig unter den Preisträgern herausragender Wettbewerbe zu finden und auf allen bedeutenden Bühnen und Podien der Welt vertreten. Einer der Gründe dafür ist, dass hier seit jeher besonderer Wert auf die praktische öffentliche Musikausübung gelegt wird. Die Hochschule organisiert mehr als zweihundertfünfzig Konzerte pro Jahr, bespielt zahlreiche Konzertsäle, Studiobühnen und das Detmolder Theater.

Auch privat geht es rapide aufwärts. In einem meiner öffentlichen Kurse lerne ich Nadja aus Limburg kennen. Sie ist Sängerin, trägt einen kessen Kurzhaarschnitt und bereichert mein Dasein mit ihren zwei kleinen Kindern. Wir verstehen uns prächtig. Bald sind wir ein Paar, und da das Trio genauso gerne essen geht wie ich, verhelfen wir der Gastronomie von Detmold zu einer kleinen Hausse. Nach zwei rauschhaften Sommern des Verliebtseins beginnen jedoch die Probleme. Nadja möchte eine festere Bindung. Und sie möchte, dass ich nach Limburg ziehe, weil sie dort ein Haus besitzt, in dem allerdings auch ihr geschiedener Mann eine Wohnung unterhält. Ich mag ihre Kinder Maja und Jaro sehr gern und kann mir einen Familienbetrieb in Zukunft durchaus vorstellen, aber in dieser Konstellation erst einmal nicht. Außerdem ist mein Terminkalender durch die Tourneen und den Lehrauftrag so prall gefüllt, dass sich solche Planspiele auch von dieser Seite erübrigen. Ich liebe meinen Beruf und bin noch nicht bereit, für was auch immer zurückzustecken, weil ich fühle, ich habe mein musikalisches Potential noch längst nicht ausgeschöpft. Ich sage ihr das in aller Offenheit. Nadja, die zum Radikal-Vegetarismus konvertiert ist, sagt immer öfter »Du riechst nach Fleisch« und drängt mich ebenfalls zu rein pflanzlicher Nahrungsaufnahme.

Das Resultat ist vorhersehbar. Nach drei Jahren trauter Zweisamkeit gehen wir wieder getrennte Wege. Dafür habe ich in Detmold Freunde gefunden, die ich bis an mein Lebensende nicht mehr missen möchte.

Einer heißt Joachim Thalmann und fungiert als Pressesprecher der Universität. Das gemütliche Häuschen der Thalmanns am Detmolder Stadtrand ist mir ein zweites Zuhause geworden. Ich werde mindestens einmal pro Woche von Achims ebenso patenter wie reizender Gattin Eva bewirtet. Von mir wird nichts weiter verlangt als gesunder Appetit und nach dem Dessert ein Fußballmatch gegen Thalmanns Junior Jannick, was ich mit Freuden erledige. Der andere Herzensfreund ist Clemens Luhmann. Seines Zeichens Doktor der Medizin, Kneipenwirt und Sprössling des Soziologen Niklas Luhmann. Ich habe den bedeutenden Systemtheoretiker kurz vor seinem Tod noch kennen lernen dürfen. Er war ein profunder Kenner der Musik und der bildenden Kunst und wie Sohn Clemens ein durch und durch feiner Mensch, der sich auf seinen Ruhm nicht das Geringste einbildete.

Ich hoffe, dass auch mir die paar Preise und lobenden Kritiken nicht über Gebühr zu Kopf gestiegen sind. Obwohl es bestimmt einige Kritikusse gibt, die das Ende meiner Detmolder Zeit genauso deuten wollen. Ich werde zum Wintersemester 2004 meine Zelte im Teutoburger Wald abbrechen, um einer Berufung an die Hanns-Eisler-Hochschule in Berlin zu folgen. Das hat nichts mit Überdruss an der Provinz zu tun, sondern vor allem mit praktischen Erwägungen. Ich bin seit einem Jahr stolzer Besitzer eines wunderschönen Hauses im hannoverschen Ortsteil Kirchrode. Ich habe es erworben, weil ich in der Leinestadt alt werden möchte. Hier leben mittlerweile meine Eltern, hier wohnen Bruder Micha mit seiner Freundin Renate und eine Menge guter Freunde. Aber mindestens ebenso viele mir wichtige Menschen sind mittlerweile nach Berlin gezogen, wie Uwe Heye und seine Frau Sabine, der Künstler Andi »Arbeit« Hahn und die Schriftstellerin Felicitas Hoppe. Sie alle habe ich in den letzten Jahren viel zu wenig gesehen, weil ich immer auf Reisen oder in Detmold war. Das soll jetzt anders werden. Ich muss nicht einmal fürchten, dass mir eine Überdosis Hauptstadttrubel die Laune verhagelt. Seit die ICE-Strecke Berlin-Hannover fertig ist, kann ich in zwei Stunden wieder daheim in meinem Garten sitzen. Das ist die Hälfte der Zeit, die mich die Reise Detmold-Hannover gekostet hat. Ein weiteres gewichtiges Argument für den Wechsel ist der exzellente Ruf der Hanns-Eisler-Hochschule. Sie gilt als eine der besten Ausbildungsstätten Europas. Eine Professur an diesem Institut kann man eigentlich nicht ablehnen. Ich schon gar nicht. Denn an der »Eisler« lehren viele Musiker der Berliner Philharmoniker, mit denen ich in Zukunft – wie mir Simon Rattle versichert hat – viel zu tun bekommen werde. Ich glaube, das darf man sagen, ohne dass einem gleich Starallüren unterstellt werden. Womit wir auch schon beim letzten Themenkomplex meiner Ausführungen angekommen wären. Zum Einstieg des Ausstieges gibt es ein kleines Rätsel:

»Ich werde nie vergessen, wie diese Dame richtig ausflippte. Sie sprang auf die Bühne und legte mich flach. Sie war größer als ich. Da lag ich nun auf dem Rücken, und sie saß rittlings auf mir. Ich konnte nicht aufstehen, und sie wurde richtig wild. Schließlich konnten John und Scott sie losreißen und von der Bühne zerren.« Verehrter Leser, wer hat diese Geschichte wohl erzählt? Arturo Toscanini? Herbert von Karajan? Luciano Pavarotti? Oder Elvis Presley? Die Antwort dürfte auf der Hand liegen: das sind die Erinnerungen des Kings. Rock-'n'-Roller haben Fans, Fußballer und Filmstars auch, vielleicht hat sogar ein Guido Westerwelle Fans. Aber klassische Bühnenkünstler? Haben Dirigenten, Solisten, Opern- oder Konzertsänger heutzutage wirklich echte Fans? Ich glaube nicht. Bekanntlich leitet sich das Wort vom lateinischen »fanaticus« (schwärmend, besessen) ab, mit dem man von der Antike bis in die Neuzeit Ketzer, Häretiker, Utopisten, kurz: Störer des allgemeinen Betriebsfriedens disqualifizierte. Damals fiel dieser Menschenschlag in das Ressort der Inquisition. Neuerdings beschäftigen Fans und Fanatiker die Psychologie. Sie attestiert ihnen »neurotische Selbstunsicherheit« und »psychotische Züge«, die unbedingt der Behandlung bedürfen.

Das scheint nicht ganz fair, weil zumindest den psychoanalytischen Zweigen dieser Wissenschaft ein Hang zum Fanatismus nicht ganz fremd ist. Aber Freudianer, auch wenn sie herdenweise in Kongresszentren auftreten, verfügen berufsbedingt über ein gewisses Maß an Selbstkontrolle. Das lehnt der Fan rundheraus ab. Richtige Fans enthemmen sich mit allerlei Drogen, fallen scharenweise in Ohnmacht, reißen sich die Haare aus, brüllen wie am Spieß und schwenken semantisch fragwürdige Transparente. Sie werfen mit nasser Unterwäsche oder zerhauen gern mal einen bestuhlten Saal, um hernach auch die anrückende Ordnungsmacht nach Strich und Faden zu vermöbeln. Der gemeine Fan hat somit im Theater oder Konzertsaal nichts, aber auch rein gar nichts zu suchen. Gott sei Dank geht er selten hin. Ein Grund könnte sein, dass der Fan schlicht nicht denkbar ist ohne die Objekte seiner Verehrung, die so genannten Hausgötter oder Idole. Man erkennt ein Idol an zwei untrüglichen Merkmalen: zum einen an seiner unbegreiflichen, unirdischen Wesenheit, auf die bekanntlich schon Martin Luther hingewiesen hat, zum anderen an einer nahezu kompromisslosen Verherr-

lichung seines Wirkens. Jeder kennt ein paar solcher Ge-
stalten. Margret Thatcher, Heidi Klum, die Helden von
Bern, Zinedine Zidane, der Dalai-Lama, John Lennon,
Madonna, Kim Il Sung und Dean Martin, an dem die
Frauen einen Narren gefressen hatten, obwohl er Sachen
sang wie *When the Moon Hits Your Eye like a Big Pizza Pie,
that's Amore*, oder jenen Schalker Flügelstürmer, dessen
Fans den Slogan eines protestantischen Werbeplakates
»An Jesus kommt niemand vorbei« mit dem Zusatz
»außer Libuda« ergänzten.

Sagen wir, wie es ist: Idole dieser Dimension sind seit
Maria Callas' Zeiten im klassischen Musikbetrieb selten
geworden. Und das scheint mir – angesichts der oben ge-
schilderten Fan-Exzesse – auch ganz gut so. Heutzutage
sind klassische Interpreten höchstens prominent. Das
heißt, sie erregen über ein Special-Interest-Publikum hinaus ein gewisses Maß an Aufmerksamkeit. Dafür reicht
es, seinen Kopf zwei bis drei Mal ins Fernsehen zu halten,
und schon grüßt einen der Bäcker am nächsten Morgen
wie einen lieben Verwandten. Aber die Brötchen gibt es
trotzdem nicht billiger. Warum auch? Prominenz an sich
ist ja kein Verdienst. Denn für erhöhte Aufmerksamkeit in
unserer Mediengesellschaft sorgt meistens nicht mehr
»die denkbar höchste Kompetenz«, sondern allein »der
Bekanntheitsgrad«, egal, ob jemand durch segensreiches
öffentliches Wirken oder nur durch chronische Gimpelei
auffällig geworden ist. Sagt jedenfalls der Kulturphilo-
soph Thomas H. Macho in seiner Schrift *Container der
Aufmerksamkeit – Reflexionen über die Aufrichtigkeit in der
Politik*. Und beschreibt ein Phänomen, welches so genannten »Partyludern« oder den fast schon wieder vergesse-
nen Popliteraten ein auskömmliches Dasein beschert und
dazu geführt hat, dass ein Dieter Bohlen im TV ungestraft
über politische Themen räsonieren darf.

Spätestens mit der medialen Unentbehrlichkeit dieses eitlen Pflaumenaugusts hat die schiere Prominenz den akademischen Titel von der Geltungsskala getilgt. Obwohl er als Bedeutungsindikator im erzkatholischen Passau bis ins Jahr 1996 nachzuweisen ist. Ich bin seinerzeit dorthin gefahren, um einen Meisterkurs zu geben, und habe von meiner Agentur ein Hotelzimmer reservieren lassen. Als ich das Etablissement betrete, mustert die Rezeptionsdame meine unorthodoxe Gestalt wie einen laufenden Müllbeutel. Es ist nicht zu übersehen, sie mag keine Zwerge. Dabei sieht sie auch nicht gerade aus wie Miss Donau, sondern gleicht einem quellenden Hefestück mit Haarbesatz.

»Sis alles belägt«, raunzt die unförmige Matrone, ehe ich überhaupt den Mund aufmachen kann.

Mit der Reservierung konfrontiert, findet sie meinen Namen in ihrer Liste und grunzt missmutig. Sie muss den Homunkulus tatsächlich beherbergen. Sie weist den Pagen an, mein Gepäck sieben Stockwerke hoch in eine Kammer zu tragen, die Gästezimmer zu nennen jede Almhütte auf das Tödlichste beleidigen würde. Die Butze ist klein, muffig und finster, das Bad starrt vor Dreck. So riecht es auch. Ich habe die Koffer gar nicht erst ausgepackt und bin gleich wieder runter an die Rezeption, um – argwöhnisch beäugt von dem Hefekloß – meinen Pianisten Charles Spencer abzupassen, der jeden Augenblick eintreffen muss. Lange brauche ich nicht zu warten. Charles federt herein und begrüßt mich mit gewohntem Überschwang:

»Na, Herr Professor, hocherfreut, dich zu sehen«.

»Ganz meinerseits. Aber deine Koffer kannst du gleich wieder rausbringen. Hier sind wir nicht erwünscht.«

Die Matrone steht wie vom Schlag gerührt. Ihr Teint

wechselt von Hefegrau ins Mehlschwitzige. »Jesus Maria«, höre ich sie stammeln.

»Nein«, sage ich, »nur Professor Quasthoff von der Musikhochschule Detmold. Und der möchte, dass sein Gepäck umgehend aus der Rumpelkammer ins Foyer expediert wird.« Sie zwängt ihre Pfunde hinter dem Tresen hervor:

»Tschuldigen S', Härr Professor, tschuldigen S' vielmals. Dös is mir jetza sähr unangenehm.« Dann grummelt sie etwas von »sofort dös Zimmer austauschen« und »peinlichem Irrtum«. Diesmal mustere ich sie wie eine lästige Stubenfliege:

»Gute Frau, peinlich ist das schon, aber bestimmt kein Irrtum. Bitte rufen Sie ein Taxi. Ich ziehe aus.«

So etwas ist mir später nie wieder passiert. Denn auch ich habe meinen Kopf ins Fernsehen gehalten und ein Stückchen Prominenz abgeerntet. Ich bilde mir darauf nichts ein. Aber es hilft manchmal, der Quasthoffschen Kleinheit den nötigen Respekt zu verschaffen. Seitdem ich ein paar Mal in dem Kasten aufgetaucht bin, hat es beispielsweise kein Bahn-AG-Schaffner mehr gewagt, im Kasernenton Strafzahlungen einzufordern, nur weil ich meinen Behindertenausweis vergessen habe. Im Gegenteil. Man behandelt mich wie ein rohes Ei. Und das ist, um meine Lieblingsstelle aus Helmut Dietls *Rossini* zu zitieren, »ein wirklich gutes Gefühl«.

Dass es so weit kommen konnte, erstaunt mich immer wieder. Als ich nach dem Gewinn des ARD-Wettbewerbs meinen ersten Tonträger eingesungen habe, unternimmt die Plattenfirma ein paar zaghafte Versuche, das Produkt über Musik- und Talkshows zu promoten. Aber man winkt allseits ab. Ende der achtziger Jahre gilt ein singender Gnom nicht als sendefähig. Weder öffentlich-rechtlich noch privat. Jedenfalls nicht als ernsthafter Künstler.

Der einzige Fernsehmann, der sich für mich interessiert, ist Alfred Biolek. 1992 fragt seine Redaktion an, ob Freundin Eva und ich in seiner Talkshow *Boulevard Bio* auftreten möchten. Es geht natürlich nicht um Musik, sondern um Contergan, recht eigentlich aber um Menschen, denen auch schwerste Behinderungen nicht die gute Laune verderben können. Meine Begeisterung hält sich in Grenzen. Schließlich kenne ich die Geschichten vom fröhlich trällernden Pillenopfer aus der Presse. Ich bin ja tatsächlich keine Trauerweide, mich stört lediglich, wenn ich als Vorzeigebehinderter präsentiert werden soll.

Das ist nämlich pure Augenwischerei. Ich tauge weder zum Vorbild noch zum Lebensberater. Schon gar nicht will ich als Alibi für eine Gesellschaft herhalten, die Finanz- und Ordnungsämter mit behindertengerechten Eingängen ausstattet, ihre Versehrten aber ansonsten mit Nichtachtung straft. Was nützen meine Erfahrungen einem Contergangeschädigten ohne Arme und Beine, wenn er nicht singen oder mit dem Mund malen kann wie Picasso? Gar nichts. Unspektakulär Behinderte bekommen in diesem Land immer noch sehr schwer einen Arbeitsplatz, weil sich die Arbeitgeber, die eigentlich einen bestimmten Anteil Behinderter beschäftigen müssen, mittels lächerlicher Strafzahlungen aus der Verantwortung stehlen können. Die meisten Versehrten vegetieren immer noch auf Sozialhilfeniveau, sie werden in Heimen oder betreuten Werkstätten verwahrt und mit Billigarbeit ausgebeutet. Seit meinem neunten Geburtstag bin ich diesem Ghetto entflohen. Dank der liebevollen Förderung meiner Eltern, dank meiner musikalischen Begabung, dank der Toleranz einiger weniger Personen und mit viel, viel Glück. Darum erscheint es mir verlogen, einer Behindertenorganisation beizutreten und das Contergan als Motto über mein Leben zu nageln. Denn anders als die meisten meiner Schicksalsgenossen habe ich die Gelegenheit bekommen, die körperlichen Defizite nicht als Handicap, sondern einfach als Faktum hinzunehmen wie andere Leute ihre Hühneraugen. Auch wenn das ein langer, schmerzlicher Prozess gewesen ist.

Der Leser, der mir geduldig bis hierher gefolgt ist, weiß, dass ich kein typisches Versehrtenleben geführt habe. Ich bekam dieselben Kopfnüsse wie mein Bruder, hatte die gleichen normalen Freunde, dieselben Probleme und prägenden Erlebnisse: den ersten Bierrausch, die erste Zigarette, das entscheidende Tor, das ich mal bei einem Match gegen die Gang aus dem Nachbarviertel geschossen habe, den ersten verliebten Kuss und die Musik. Wenn Presse, Funk und Fernsehen immer wieder mit den alten Handicap-Geschichten kommen, finde ich das mittlerweile einfach nur noch anstrengend und knurre meinen Standardsatz:

»Ich bin einer von achtzig Millionen behinderten Deutschen. Mir sieht man es nur gleich an.«

Zu Biolek sind wir dann aber doch gegangen, weil meine Agentur mich darum gebeten hat und weil ich, begleitet von Peter Müller, den *Erlkönig* singen darf. Bereuen muss ich den Auftritt nicht. Bio ist ein charmanter Gastgeber, und die Infos, die ihm die Redakteure über Eva und meine Person auf seine Kartons geschrieben haben, stimmen. Etwas mulmig wird mir nur, als der Star-Talker sein Gesicht zusammenfaltet und auf seine vernuschelt harmlose Tour beginnt, den Intimbereich unseres Verhältnisses anzusteuern.

»Sagen Sie, liebe Eva«, hebt Bio an und lässt den markanten Unterkiefer mahlen, »dass Sie beide sich wunderbar verstehen, können unsere Zuschauer ja sehen. Doch wie war das denn so, als Sie, mmh, nun, wie soll ich sagen, zum ersten Mal, als Sie mmh, mmmh zusammen übernachtet …?«

Ich werfe mich sofort peinlich berührt dazwischen und lüge, dass ich Sex in einer Beziehung nur für dritt- oder viertrangig halte. Doch Eva lässt sich nicht ins Bockshorn jagen: »Das finde ich gar nicht. Mir gefällt Thomas auch körperlich. Er sieht gut aus und hat einen wunderbaren Kussmund.«

Das ist sehr süß. Mein Kopf färbt sich trotzdem ketchuprot.

»War doch wunderbar«, sagt Bio, als wir nach der Sendung in einer Kölner Altstadtkneipe zusammensitzen, die der viel beschäftigte Medienprofessor, TV-Mann und Kochbuchautor praktischerweise sein Eigen nennt. Na ja, wunderbar ist übertrieben, aber ich hatte es mir schlimmer vorgestellt. Bio entpuppt sich auch privat als äußerst angenehmer Zeitgenosse, der hinter den Kulissen weit mehr schrägen Witz entwickelt als vor der Kamera. Wenn man mit ihm bis in die frühen Morgenstunden schwatzt, ist einem klar, warum ausgerechnet er die britische Komikertruppe Monty Python für Deutschland entdeckt hat. Inzwischen sind wir ganz gute Freunde. Er hat mich schon bekocht, und so habe ich sofort zugesagt, als er mich einlädt, bei seiner letzten Talkshow dabei zu sein. Neben mir sitzen Babs Becker, drei junge Südafrikaner, die ein Aids-Projekt betreuen, und – offensiv schwanger – Verona Feldbusch. Seitdem kann ich die viel diskutierte Theorie widerlegen, dass sich hinter der Maske der komplett meschuggenen Blubb-Mamsell eine Intelligenzbestie verbirgt. Definitiv nein.

Nach meinem ersten Grammy-Gewinn flattern mir auch Einladungen von Johannes B. Kerner und Reinhold Beckmann ins Haus, und ich begreife, warum ihre Sendungen »Premium-Talkshows« heißen. In Hamburg bei

Kerner beispielsweise verfrachten sie einen ins noble Atlantic Hotel Kempinski, und man muss sich verpflichten, vier Wochen vorher in keiner anderen Plauderrunde aus dem Unterhaltungsbereich aufzutreten. Diese Klausel wird allerdings eher lax gehandhabt, wie man beim Durchzappen der Programme unschwer feststellen kann. Ich gebe zu, ich bin mit Vorbehalten an die Elbe gefahren, weil Kerner auch Sportreporter ist und mir die hurra-patriotische Brille, die der flotte Herr Poschmann den ZDF-Fußballkommentatoren verordnet hat, regelmäßig die Länderspiele verhagelt. Aber das ist Geschmackssache. Der Talkmaster Kerner ist wie sein Kollege Beckmann hinter den Kulissen ein netter Mensch, und beide sind bestens vorbereitet. Manchmal ist das aber vergebliche Liebesmüh. Als die Kerner-Show aufgezeichnet wird, kommt zwischen mir und dem grünen Vollwerthedonisten Rezzo Schlauch ein blondes TV-Starlet zu sitzen, dessen Stärken allzu offensichtlich nicht im Rhetorischen liegen. Ihr grammatikalischer Waffelbruch muss dreimal wiederholt und trotzdem auf ein Minimum zusammengeschnitten werden.

In einer echten Live-Sendung geht das nicht. Ein Umstand, der oft zu schönen, weil irreparablen Hanswurstiaden führt, die ja – geben wir es ruhig zu – den eigentlichen Reiz dieser Unterhaltungsform ausmachen. Bei *Riverboat*, einem in Dresden auf der Elbe schaukelnden Talktreff des MDR, bin ich mal mit Schlager-Oldie Bernhard Brink aneinander geraten. Und das kommt so: Kurz bevor es losgeht, kreuzt der Mann an der Reling des Ausflugsdampfers meinen Weg. Ich habe ihn nie zuvor gesehen. Er mich anscheinend schon. Brink bleibt stehen, starrt mich trübe an, dann bläht er mir unvermittelt ins Gesicht:

»Ich versteh nicht, wie sich ein Behinderter auch noch auf die Opernbühne stellen kann.« Dass in seiner Blut-

bahn ein paar Bierchen zu viel zirkulieren, kann man riechen. Was sie unter seiner Schädeldecke noch so alles
anrichten, will man sich lieber gar nicht erst ausmalen.
Also bleibe ich ganz ruhig und sage:

»Ich wusste gar nicht, dass wir uns duzen.«

Brink indes vernimmt es nicht. Er hat längst kehrt-
gemacht und wankt davon, wahrscheinlich in Richtung
Riverboat-Kantine.

Während der Sendung hockt er mit leerem Blick in seiner Sofaecke. Ab und an nimmt er Flüssigkeit auf und
wirft schale Witze in die Runde, über die niemand lacht.
Das Moderatorentrio versucht ihn so gut es geht zu ignorieren. Aber als sich die Sendezeit neigt, muss irgend-
jemand mit ihm reden. Brink darf sein neuestes Produkt
vorstellen. Es handelt sich um eine Schmähschrift über
Dieter Bohlen, der Herrn Brink vor Dekaden als Chauf-
feur zu Diensten war. Dem Werk liegt eine CD mit frühen
Demoaufnahmen des Modern-Talking-Chefs bei, die ent-
hüllt, was die Welt seit langem weiß: der Mensch kann
nicht singen. Brink verkauft diesen Versuch, seiner Karriere im Sog der gerade erschienenen Bohlen-Memoiren ein
wenig auf die Sprünge zu helfen, als uneigennützige Hel-
dentat, weil der Erlös angeblich sozialen Einrichtungen
zugute kommen soll. Ich beschließe, ihm das nicht durchgehen zu lassen. Als die CD abgespielt wird, krakeele ich:

»Haben wir in diesem Land keine anderen Sorgen, als
uns monatelang mit Herrn Bohlen zu beschäftigen? Ich
kann den Mist nicht mehr hören.«

Das Publikum johlt. Als Jörg Kachelmann, ARD-Wet-
terfrosch und *Riverboat*-Kapitän in Personalunion, von
Brink eine Antwort einfordert, entbrennt eine wilde Debatte über das Unterhaltungsbedürfnis des Volkes im Allgemeinen und Brinks Sozialverträglichkeit im Besonderen.
Am Ende giftet er mich an:

»Wir sitzen doch alle hier, um etwas zu verkaufen. Sie auch.« Um Brink wird es plötzlich sehr einsam. In der Talkrunde sinkt die Stimmung auf den Gefrierpunkt.

»Mich hat man eingeladen, um über meinen Grammy zu reden«, gebe ich lächelnd zurück und registriere befriedigt, dass Brink mich wieder siezt. Im Prinzip hat er ja Recht. Aber Strafe muss sein.

In der Radio-Bremen-Talkshow *III nach Neun* bin ich höchstpersönlich der Gelackmeierte und obendrein selbst schuld. Denn mein erster Impuls war, gar nicht hinzugehen, weil das Herumhocken in Fernsehstudios so spannend nun auch wieder nicht ist. Außerdem stecke ich gerade in den Proben für Schönbergs *Gurrelieder*, die Simon Rattle mit den Berliner Philharmonikern einspielen wird. Es ist ein ebenso diffiziles wie monströses Werk, das sogar Straussens *Elektra* und Mahlers Achte Sinfonie an spätromantischem Breitwandformat übertrifft. Ich singe den Sprecher und den Bauern und habe entsprechend viel zu tun. Ich hätte auf die innere Eingebung hören sollen. Stattdessen lasse ich mich von der Deutschen Grammophon zur Teilnahme überreden, die gerade meine neue CD mit Schubert- und Brahms-Liedern herausgebracht hat. Das Desaster beginnt damit, dass tagelang ein Redakteur der Sendung mein Handy blockiert, um den Termin für ein persönliches Vorgespräch abzustimmen. Das ist an sich nicht üblich und widerstrebt mir zutiefst, aber weil es der Fernsehmensch so dringlich macht, schwänze ich eine Probe. Im Gegenzug bitte ich darum, das Thema Behinderung auszuklammern, die Ablehnung der Uni Hannover nicht nochmals durchzukauen und auch über die Arbeit von Kollegen kein Wort zu verlieren. All das hätte ich schon bei Bio, bei Kerner und neulich auch dem Magazin *Stern* erzählt.

»Geht klar«, versichert der Redakteur. »Moderator Giovanni di Lorenzo wird mit Ihnen über das Musikgeschäft und die neue Platte reden.«

Da bin ich in guten Händen. Di Lorenzo stammt aus Hannover und schrieb, ehe er erst zum *Tagesspiegel*-, dann zum *Zeit*-Chefredakteur aufstieg, erstklassige Reportagen für die *Süddeutsche Zeitung*. Aber was passiert? Nicht di Lorenzo führt das Gespräch, sondern seine Co-Moderatorin Amelie Fried. Sie verfasst hauptberuflich Frauenromane, ist in der Show fürs Menscheln zuständig und hat nur drei Themen auf dem Spickzettel: meine Behinderungen, die Ablehnung der Uni Hannover und was ich über die Arbeit der Kollegen denke. Ich fühle mich übers Ohr gehauen. Aber das kann man der Moderatorin ja nicht vor laufender Kamera an den Kopf werfen. Am liebsten würde ich gar nichts mehr sagen und gehen. Aber das traue ich mich auch wieder nicht. Also verlege ich mich darauf, verdruckste Hauptsätze zu bilden, die mit Subjekt, Prädikat und Objekt auskommen. Nach fünf Minuten merkt Frau Fried, dass es so nicht weitergehen kann. Ich merke das auch und hoffe, sie gibt auf. Tut sie aber nicht, sie versucht, wenigstens noch ein bisschen Kollegenschelte aus mir herauszuquetschen. Ich erkläre, dass ich dazu wirklich nichts sagen möchte. Fried ignoriert meinen Einwand souverän und bohrt so lange weiter, bis sich meine wirklich sehr schlechte Laune in einer Tirade wider die Schmalztöpfe Bocelli, Rieu und Konsorten entlädt. Davon muss ich nichts zurücknehmen, aber blöd war es doch, weil ich mich habe provozieren lassen. Der Redakteur, den ich hinterher wegen der gebrochenen Absprache zur Rede stelle, gibt mir dann einen wertvollen Lehrsatz mit auf den Weg:

»Tja, so ist Fernsehen.«

Das habe ich mir gemerkt und mich bei weiteren Talkeinsätzen über nichts mehr gewundert, geschweige denn aufgeregt, und die Plaudereien als das genommen, was sie sind: ein Geschäft auf Gegenseitigkeit. Ich kann für meine Arbeit werben, die Sender bekommen Futter zum Versenden, und wenn sich beide Mühe geben, bescheren sie dem Gebührenzahler eine Stunde entspannte Unterhaltung.

Welche Macht das Fernsehen hat, wird mir erstmals klar, als Jussi und ich 1998 unsere erste Liedtournee durch die USA absolvieren. Die CBS dreht über uns einen Beitrag für ihre Newsshow *Sixty Minutes*. Sie läuft täglich um 19 Uhr und wird regelmäßig von dreißig bis vierzig Millionen Zuschauern gesehen. Für den Rest der Tournee fühlen wir uns nicht nur prominent, sondern wie echte Stars. Wir werden auf der Straße gegrüßt und müssen, wo wir auftauchen, Autogramme schreiben. Als die ARD *Die Stimme* ausstrahlt, ein Porträt, das mein Freund Michael Harder gedreht hat, nimmt es in Deutschland zwei Tage lang ähnliche Dimensionen an. Dann sinkt der Aufmerksamkeitspegel Gott sei Dank wieder auf Normalmaß. Der Nachteil ist, dass in TV-Redaktionen ob dieser Wirkungsmacht manchmal der Größenwahn epidemisch wird. Dann kosten sie einen den letzten Nerv.

So geht es Jussi und mir mit den Strategen von *Unser Land*, einem Vorabendmagazin des Kieler Funkhauses. Sie schicken ein Team, das unseren Auftritt beim Schleswig-Holstein-Musikfestival dokumentieren soll. Die Crew rückt mittags an, kippt ihr Equipment in das Konzerthaus und belegt sofort die gesamte Haustechnik, den Hausmeister und die Kantine mit Beschlag. Als wir auf die Bühne wollen, um den Flügel einzuspielen und noch ein wenig zu proben, mustert uns die Redakteurin wie zwei Außerirdische.

»Sie sehen doch, das geht jetzt auf gar keinen Fall, wir müssen erst alles fertig einrichten«, spricht's und haut uns die Tür vor der Nase zu. Das Einrichten dauert Stunden. Die Probe können wir vergessen. Umso erstaunter sind wir am Abend. Wir haben kaum angefangen zu spielen, da packt das Team schon wieder ein und rumpelt mitten in der Piano-Stelle eines Schumann-Lieds aus dem Saal. Gesendet hat *Unser Land* anderntags genau zwei Minuten.

Noch unverfrorener treibt es einmal der WDR. Der Sender möchte ein Porträt von mir für das ARD-Frühstücksfernsehen drehen.

»Wie lang soll es denn werden?«, frage ich argwöhnisch.

»Drei Minuten. Höchstens!«

Die ausgesandte Redakteurin filmt mich zu Hause, sie filmt mich bei einem Klassik-Konzert, sie filmt mich in der Kneipe beim Frühstück. Ihr Team rückt mir zwei Tage nicht von der Pelle. Dann hört sie, dass ich nächste Woche im Künstlerhaus Hannover im Rahmen der Fitz-Oblong-Weihnachtsgala etwas vorlesen und ein, zwei Popsongs singen werde. Ein paar Shots von der Veranstaltung, findet sie, könnten den Film runden. Gut, sage ich, das mache ich auch noch mit, erkläre ihr aber, eingedenk des Affentheaters mit *Unser Land*, dass dort außer mir noch zehn andere Künstler auftreten, die pünktlich zum Soundcheck auf die Bühne wollen. Sie müsse den Aufwand so gering wie möglich halten.

»Logisch, null problemo. Wir haben eh schon viel Material.«

Da ich das genauso sehe, begebe ich mich am Premierentag bester Dinge ins Künstlerhaus. Vor der Tür sehe ich Micha und seinen Freund Dietrich wütend durch den Schneematsch stapfen.

»Schön, dass du so prominent bist«, wettert mein Bruder. »Aber eins sage ich dir: halt mir in Zukunft die Fernsehfritzen vom Hals, sonst nenn ich dich Abel, und du darfst Kain zu mir sagen.«

Micha und Dietrich zur Nedden sind nämlich Gastgeber der Fitz-Oblong-Show. Ich habe die beiden natürlich gefragt, ob der WDR drehen darf. Sie waren einverstanden – unter der Bedingung, dass der etwas komplizierte Ablauf nicht gestört wird. Aber nun müssen sie mit ansehen, wie der WDR seit Mittag das Künstlerhaus blockiert. Erst als Micha mehrmals mit Handgreiflichkeiten droht, rückt das Team vorübergehend ab. Abends stehen sie wieder auf der Matte und mögen – anders als in Kiel – leider nicht nach zwei Minuten das Feld räumen. Im Gegenteil. Man kriecht den Vortragenden mit geschulterter Kamera zwischen den Beinen herum, hält das Gerät angstbleichen Zuschauern ins Gesicht und bringt mehrmals die Gesangsanlage zum Kollabieren, weil der Ton nicht fernsehtauglich ist. Mir tut das alles furchtbar Leid. Am meisten schmerzt mich jedoch, dass ich Micha davon abgehalten habe, dem Kameramann tatsächlich eine Watschen zu verpassen. Stellvertretend für die Redakteurin. Denn das Frühstücksfernsehen hat das Porträt niemals ausgestrahlt.

Ansonsten ist die Fitz-Oblong-Show für mich ein steter Quell der Freude. Der Name stammt aus Robert Bolts Kinderbuchklassiker *Der kleine dicke Ritter Oblong Fitz Oblong*, in der schwarzweißen Fernsehfassung der Augsburger Puppenkiste ein prägendes Ereignis unserer vorpubertären Tage. Dietrich und Micha betreiben die Oblong-Show seit mehr als zehn Jahren. Erst im Künstlerhaus, jetzt in der Cumberlandschen Galerie des Schauspielhauses. Die »Literarische Nummernrevue« sieht ungefähr so aus wie jene Veranstaltungen, die das

Großfeuilleton neuerdings in Berlin als »kultig« emp-fiehlt. Sie sitzen hinter einem schlichten Tisch und bieten Shortstorys, Feuilletons, Gedichte und Songs feil. Bob-Dylan-Exeget Dietrich gibt dabei den messerscharfen Analytiker unserer Multioptionsgesellschaft. Seine Songs heißen ... *und irgendwo bellt immer ein Hund, Denkwerkstatt Deutschland* oder *Wenn das Umfeld umfällt*:

> »Ob Profikicker oder Tennisqueen,
> Showmaster, Maurer, Referent,
> ob Klofrau, Zahnarzt oder Ergotherapeutin,
> ohne intaktes Umfeld loost selbst der Präsident.
> Erfolg ist heute schlicht ein Gruppending,
> die Parole heißt: nur gemeinsam sind wir stark,
> wenn das Umfeld stimmt, ja dann ist alles klar,
> geht's andersrum, gibt's nur Magerquark.«

Refrain:

> »Wenn das Umfeld umfällt, bist du plötzlich sehr allein.
> Wenn das Umfeld umfällt, fühlst du dich ganz klein.
> Wenn das Umfeld umfällt, nimmt von dir keiner mehr 'nen Scheck.
> Wenn das Umfeld umfällt, bist du nur der letzte Dreck.«

Micha dagegen pflegt eher den melancholischen Hedonis-mus des heißen amerikanischen Südens, selbst wenn er den mitteleuropäischen Winter besingt:

> »Rundrum Grabesstille, wo gestern Vögel sangen,
> Gestern da war Sommer, jetzt ist er gegangen.
> Du drehst an der Heizung, trinkst deinen Rum mit Tee,
> Hockst tagelang am Fenster, wartest auf den ersten Schnee, oh je.

And're warten auf Reformen, den Mann von Bofrost,
   auf Godot,
Auf das Glück im Lotto, freie Fahrt nach Stopp and Go,
Sie warten auf die Liebe, auf den Bus, auf ich weiß
   nicht was,
mancher wartet ewig und beißt drüber hin ins Gras.

Und du sitzt noch am Fenster, den Rum trinkst du jetzt
   pur,
Du tust dir entsetzlich Leid, und fragst dich, warum
   nur?
Da fällst es dir ein mit einem Ruck:«

Refrain:

»Willkommen im Club der Melancholie!
Legen Se doch ab, wir warten schon auf Sie.
Links ist der Trübsaal, das Klo, das ist gleich da.
Willkommen im Club, wir seh'n uns an der Bar.

Wir trinken Scotch auf all die Damen, die uns ein
   Lächeln schenkten,
Und noch zwei Tequila, auf alle, die uns kränkten.
Drei Pils auf jeden Elfer, den wir in den Himmel schos-
   sen,
Und bitte bring'n Se einen Lappen, jetzt ham wir was
   vergossen.
Das Allgemeine seh'n wir doppelt, dem Besond'ren
   fehlt Kontur,
wir tun uns entsetzlich Leid und fragen: Warum nur?
Vielleicht fällt es uns ein beim nächsten Schluck!«

Sooft es mein Terminkalender zulässt, bin ich mit von der
Partie, trage Geschichten vor und übernehme den Ge-

sangspart. Die Texte lese ich prima vista, für die Songs reicht ein kurzes Ansingen eine halbe Stunde vor dem Auftritt. Die Oblongs und ich verstehen uns blind, und Micha vertritt sowieso die Ansicht, wer mit über dreißig noch proben muss, der soll es sein lassen. So ähnlich klang das aber schon, als er fünfundzwanzig war. Auf den Oblong-CDs, die am Ende eines jeden Jahres die Songernte dokumentieren, geben wir uns natürlich ein bisschen mehr Mühe. Damit es den beiden Protagonisten nicht langweilig wird, bitten sie jedes Mal einen Gastautor an ihren Tisch: was obendrein den Vorteil hat, dass auch ich fast jeden Monat interessante neue Bekanntschaften mache, die sich mit Gegeneinladungen revanchieren (müssen). In der letzten Dekade ist da ein kleiner Kosmos deutscher Gegenwartsliteratur zusammengekommen, wobei die Statuten sagen, dass Schwerblüter wie Durs Grünbein wegen mangelnder Selbstironie außen vor bleiben müssen. Unter anderem waren zum Teil mehrfach dabei: die unvergleichlichen Damen Felicitas Hoppe, Susanne Fischer, Fanny Müller und Jan Kusminski, die Satiriker Gerhard Henschel, Wiglaf Droste, Fritz Eckenga und Jürgen Roth, die Dichter Andi »Arbeit« Hahn, Franz Dobler, Horst Tomayer und Thomas Gsella, Frank Schulz, Schöpfer der Kultromane *Kolks blonde Bräute* und *Morbus Fontikuli*, *Rolling Stone*-Autor Frank Schäfer, die Schauspieler Marek Jera und Hanspeter Bader, Essayist Norbert Seeßlen, die Pianisten Hans Gierschik und Peter Müller und last but not least Bernd Rauschenbach und Jörg Gronius. Das berühmt-berüchtigte Dramatiker-Duo gehört sozusagen zum Inventar der Fitz-Oblong-Show. Die Herren fehlen bei keiner der legendären und Monate im Voraus ausverkauften Weihnachtsrevuen, die stets am Tag vor Heiligabend die Highlights des vergangenen Jahres nochmals auf die Bühne stellen. Rauschenbach ist haupt-

beruflich Chef der Arno-Schmidt-Stiftung in Bargfeld/El-
dingen und besitzt eine viel gefragte Stimme für Hör-
bücher. Gronius verdient Geld und Meriten als Opern-
librettist, Dramaturg und freier Schriftsteller. Seit ihrer
gemeinsamen Schulzeit schreiben Gronius und Rauschenbach absurde Theaterstücke und zwar die kürzesten
der Welt. Das allerkürzeste heißt *Sine Loco et Anno* und
geht so:

> *Wenn der Vorhang aufgeht,*
> *sieht man weder Zeit noch Raum.*
> *Dunkel.*
> *Vorhang.*

Die beiden können aber auch länger. Für die EXPO 2000
haben sie das Mammutwerk *Stellen aus der Welt* geschaf-
fen. Es enthält exakt 2000 (kurze) Akte. *Sein Wunder, sein
Maß: Ehrhard* kommt mit einunddreißig Bildern aus.
Dafür haben sie mir die *Heinz-Ludwig-Ehrhardt-Revue* auf
den kleinen Leib geschrieben. Das ist eine große Ehre und
ein Heidenspaß. Außerdem ist *Sein Wunder, sein Maß* ein
großartiges Stück mit pfiffigen Couplets, für das der Gat-
tungsbegriff surrealer Realismus erfunden werden müsste. Allein die Besetzungsliste liest sich wie ein verspätetes
Dadatreffen der wilden Fünfziger. Es treten auf:

Ludwig der Stammler, Ludwig der Fromme, Ludwig
XIV., Ludwig XV., Louis Günther Guillaume, Helmut
Ludwig Schnauze, genannt »Schmidt«, Helmut Ludwig
Lafontaine, genannt »Hosenkohl«, Sepp Luigi Moser,
Luigi Waldleitner, Gerhard Ludwig Schröder, Ludwig
Brenningkmeyer, Ludwig Butter Gott Lindner, Ludovico
Amerigo Vespucci, Robert Louis Stevenson, Jean Paul
Ludwig Richter, Peter Ludwig Rühmkorf, Ernst Ludwig
Jünger, Heiner Ludwig Goebbels, Harry Ludwig Bela-
fonte, Fred Ludwig Bertelsmann, Heinz Ludwig Arnold

Schwarzenegger, Frieder Ludwig Hentsch und die Zypris, Heinz Ludwig Ehrhardt, Louise Ehrhard-Miller, Kurtisane am Bonner Hof.

Unser Ehrgeiz ist, das gesamte Personalaufgebot mit der Sitzgruppe Gronius/Rauschenbach/Quasthoff zu spielen, Pianist Hans Gierschik hat genug mit der Begleitung zu tun. Es klappt auch alles wie am Schnürchen, als die Revue am 25. September 2001 im Pavillon zu Hannover Weltpremiere hat. Der Abend wird aufgezeichnet und eine Woche später vom Audience-Label als Hörbuch herausgebracht. Wir haben mit der Revue anschließend noch in Wien, Berlin und in Detmold gastiert. Mit großem Erfolg, weshalb wir *Sein Wunder, sein Maß* so lange durch die Lande tragen wollen, bis der nächste Aufschwung kommt oder bis das Soziale der Marktwirtschaft endgültig an der Biegung des Rheins begraben wird.

An dieser Stelle lassen wir Ludwig Erhard aber in Frieden ruhen. Kommen wir nun zu den lebenden Vertretern der Politik, denen ein Semi-Prominenter wie ich eigentlich gar nicht ausweichen kann. Kommt es zur Kollision, halten sich Freud und Leid dabei so ziemlich die Waage.

Gerhard Schröder beispielsweise habe ich als schlagfertigen, kunstsinnigen und entgegen seinem Image durchaus ernsthaften Menschen kennen gelernt, als ich einige Benefizkonzerte für die Stiftung »Kinder von Tschernobyl« gesungen habe. Das tue ich heute noch und habe mittlerweile auch von seiner Exgattin Hiltrud die Schirmherrschaft übernommen.

Die Stiftung ist 1992 von der niedersächsischen Landesregierung ins Leben gerufen worden, als die schrecklichen Folgeschäden der Reaktorkatastrophe offenbar wurden. In der Gegend um Tschernobyl und in den angrenzenden Provinzen Russlands und der Ukraine sind

2,5 Millionen Menschen unmittelbar betroffen. 115 000 Menschen wurden umgesiedelt. Viel zu wenige und meistens viel zu spät. Pro Quadratmeter gingen damals eine Million Becquerel Cäsium, Strontium und Plutonium nieder, eine Dosis, die dreihundertmal höher als in Hiroshima ist. Aber der Vergleich hinkt. In Tschernobyl ist ja keine Atombombe explodiert, sondern – Folge eines fahrlässigen Experiments – Knallgas. Dabei riss das Reaktorgehäuse. Die Brennstäbe begannen zu schmelzen und setzten nicht nur Radioaktivität frei, sondern auch Unmengen von Schwermetallen und chemischen Verbindungen. Niemand weiß genau, was wo und in welcher Menge im Boden steckt. Die Folgen für Mensch und Natur sind unberechenbar. Im Minsker Institut für Radiologie existiert eine Karte, die den Verseuchungsgrad der einzelnen Landesteile so gut es geht erfasst. Sie ist, soweit ich weiß, bis heute nicht veröffentlicht. Diese Art der Öffentlichkeitsarbeit hatte von Anfang an Methode. Als das schwedische Kraftwerk Forsmark am 28. April 1986, zwei Tage nach dem Bersten des Reaktors, einen erhöhten Jod-131-Fallout registrierte und die Welt alarmierte, wurde eine beispiellose Vertuschungsaktion inszeniert. Die Regierungen in Moskau und Minsk kappten die Telefonleitungen in die ukrainische Hauptstadt Kiew und verhängten eine Informationssperre. Um den Arbeitern die Maifeiern nicht zu verderben, weigerte man sich in Weißrussland, 30 000 Tonnen kontaminiertes Fleisch aus dem Verkehr zu ziehen. Den lokalen Behörden wurde die Anweisung erteilt, es im Verhältnis eins zu zehn unter die Wurstwaren zu mischen. Flankierend setzte das Gesundheitsministerium per Eilerlass die für den Bürger maximal zulässige Strahlendosis herauf, um die Notstandsgebiete möglichst klein zu halten. Hauptleidtragende sind nach wie vor die Kinder. Anfang der neunziger Jahre waren von 800 000 Jugendlichen 700 000 krank. Und die Lage ist nicht viel besser geworden. Besonders bedrohlich ist der Anstieg von Schilddrüsenkrebs bei Kleinkindern. Oft kann er gar nicht diagnostiziert werden, weil Ultraschallgeräte fehlen. Die Stiftung hat sich zum Ziel gesetzt, diese Geräte heranzuschaffen, Arznei- und Hilfsmittel für die Nachbehandlung von Schilddrüsenoperationen zur Verfügung zu stellen und die Ärzte in der Diagnostik zu schulen. Weil die Therapiemöglichkeiten in den GUS-Staaten immer noch sehr begrenzt sind, sammelt die Stiftung auch Geld, um schwer erkrankte Kinder in Deutschland zu behandeln. Jeder noch so kleine Beitrag ist willkommen und kann auf das Konto 101 473 999 bei der Norddeutschen Landesbank, Bankleitzahl 250 500 00, eingezahlt werden.

Schröders Nachfolger auf dem Stuhl des niedersächsischen Ministerpräsidenten, Sigmar Gabriel, ist trotz seiner fassrunden Gewichtigkeit eher ein Kleinformat. Ein halbes Jahr vor der Landtagswahl beruft er mich in einen Beraterkreis für Kulturfragen. Meine Mitberater sind Kulturpromis wie die Schriftstellerin Thea Dorn, *Zeit*-Herausgeber Michael Naumann, Ulrich Krempel, der Direktor des Sprengel Museum Hannover, Viva-Chef Dieter Gorny und noch ein paar andere Figuren, deren Namen ich vergessen habe, weil sie gar nicht erst aufgetaucht sind. Ich bin auch nur zweimal da gewesen. Das Catering in der Landesvertretung bewegt sich immerhin auf dem angepeilten Topniveau. Was man von dem Einleitungsreferat des Herrn Gorny nicht behaupten kann. Das ehemalige Mitglied der Bochumer Symphoniker zerkaut neoliberales Vokabular wie »Bench-Marking«, »Employability« und »Webucation«, »triggert« dauernd irgendwelche Projekte und propagiert halbseidene Thesen über Image-Optionismus und Crossover-Marketing. Das erste Mal habe ich noch gedacht: Okay, der Medienguru hat einfach noch nicht gemerkt, dass der New-Economy-Sprech so out ist wie eine Take-That-CD, aber wenigstens gibt es einen Ministerpräsidenten, der über Kultur nachdenken lässt. Als ich bei meinem zweiten Besuch das MP-Trumm mit offenen Augen schnarchen höre, kann ich mich nicht des Eindrucks erwehren, dass der Akkordredner Gorny gar nicht so falsch liegt und wir hier nur Kasperltheater zur Imageoptimierung des wahlkämpfenden Sozen aufführen. Zumal der Beraterkreis inoffiziellen Status haben soll, Gabriels Presseabteilung aber unermüdlich mit der Teilnehmerliste durch die Medienhäuser zieht.

Er hat die Wahl mit Pauken und Trompeten verloren. Jetzt dirigiert der Christdemokrat Christian Wulff die Staatskanzlei. Ein Mann, dessen kultureller Horizont sich am »Tag der Niedersachsen«, zwischen eingelegten Gurken, Oldie-Rock und Bauerntanz, exakt vermessen lässt. Seitdem er mit den Freidemokraten regiert, gilt für die Kulturschaffenden Alarmstufe rot. Letztlich deckt sich das auch mit meinen Erfahrungen, die ich an der Hochschule Detmold sammeln konnte.

Es ist immer das Gleiche im Land der Dichter und Denker: Wenn die Finanzen knapp sind, geht es zuerst der Kultur an den Beutel, obwohl sie in den Haushalten nur mit verschwindend geringen Summen zu Buche schlägt. Da ist eine sofort zu vollziehende Zwei-Millionen-Euro-Kürzung, die das Land dem Staatstheater Hannover aufdrückt, ein genauso schlechter Witz wie Wulffens Kulturverweser Lutz Stratmann, der nicht weiß, dass es auch in der Branche der schönen Künste langfristige Verträge und Verpflichtungen gibt, die man nicht eben mal in den Orkus treten kann. Aber genau das hat Stratmann verlangt. Trotzdem macht er große Augen, als wütende Demonstrationszüge wochenlang seinen Dienstsitz belagern. An der

Abschlusskundgebung vor dem Opernhaus habe auch ich teilgenommen. Aber da ist längst klar, dass Stratmann an der kurzen Leine des Ministerpräsidenten hängt und die Kürzungen nicht zurücknehmen darf.

»Jedes gesungene Wort in diesem Hause berührt mich mehr als jedes gesprochene Wort eines Politikers«, ruft Bürger Quasthoff etwas pathetisch in die Menge. Präziser umreißt der Dramatiker Marius von Meyenburg die Strategie des Christdemokraten:

»Man setzt eine Kulturinstitution auf die Abschussliste, zuerst regen sich die Menschen auf, aber schon wenn die Institution zum zweiten Mal ins Gerede kommt, werden die Stimmen leiser, und schließlich hört man nur noch ein Murren.«

Dazu passt, dass ausgerechnet der in die Jahre gekommene Krautrocker Heinz Rudolf »Warum bin ich nicht Grönemeyer« Kunze (Werke unter anderen *Abrissbirne, Armutszeugnis, Brotlose Kunst*) im Auftrag des städtischen Kulturamtes Shakespeares *Was ihr wollt* zum Musical dekonstruieren darf, während gleichzeitig das Land dem Sprengel Museum Hannover 220 000 Euro aus dem Etat streicht. Das Museum ist eine der wenigen überregional bedeutenden Kulturinstitutionen Niedersachsens. Mein Bruder betreut dort die Öffentlichkeitsarbeit. Er mag gar nicht mehr hinsehen, wenn die politischen Kleinsparer zur Eröffnung der großen Ausstellungen ans Rednerpult drängeln, um erst das Publikum mit öden Phrasen zu langweilen und dann mit dem Künstler und Herrn Direktor für die Presse zu posieren.

Wie es um den Kulturbegriff im Niedersächsischen bestellt ist, zeigt eine Posse, die sich im Jahr 2001 abgespielt hat. Im Mittelpunkt steht eine Kunstinvestition von 800 000 DM. Für diese Summe erwirbt der Verkehrsverein (!) acht Bronzestatuen des Straßendekorateurs Se-ward Johnson. Es handelt sich dabei um grobschlächtige und völlig ironiefreie Darstellungen menschlichen Mittelmaßes, die schon während der EXPO 2000 auf Leihbasis vor Karstadt Kameras, Hüte und Einkaufstüten schwenken durften. Man kann auch sagen, um »ästhetischen Sperrmüll«, wie Sprengel-Direktor Krempel öffentlich anmerkt und damit eine wütende Leserbrief-Debatte entfacht. Unverbildete Zeitgenossen halten die Homunkuli nämlich für »Kunst«, die »tausenden Menschen Freude macht«. Unter anderem auch die CDU-Fraktion im Stadtrat. Die Christdemokraten versteigen sich sogar dazu, Johnsons Figuren via Leitantrag als »Mitmenschen« einzugemeinden.

Der Grund liegt auf der Hand. Der Leinestädter fühlt sich gut getroffen. Und – Kunst oder nicht – eins muss man Johnson lassen: Die Skulpturen wirken erschreckend lebensecht. Hannovers Oberbürgermeister Schmalstieg wird wiederholt beobachtet, wie er versucht, einem der Bronzekameraden die sozialdemokratische Kommunalwahlbroschüre *Hannover überrascht* in die Hand zu drücken. Im Gegenzug fallen Menschen, sobald sie des OBs ansichtig werden, in reglose Starre, wie um dem aufdringlichen Amtsträger durch morphologische und mentale Versteinerung zu entrinnen.

Das sind die ersten Symptome der großen Politikverdrossenheit, die sich bald wie Mehltau über das Land legen wird, während über den globalen Marktplatz ein schneidender Wind fegt und keinen Stein auf dem anderen lässt. Nur am Standort Deutschland herrscht Flaute. Dabei sollen wir doch längst in einer besseren, weil rotgrünen Republik leben. Zumindest sieht sie besser aus. Gerhard Schröder hat im Garten des Bonner Kanzleramtes die ausgedienten Stützstrümpfe des Kohl-Kabinetts verbrennen lassen. Das Kabinett trägt jetzt Brioni und Chanel und Regierungsstiefel aus dem Unterschenkelleder ungarischer Jungstuten. Dazu raucht man kubanische Cohibas und hat die gesammelten Tony-Blair-Papiere plus vier Jahre Aufschwung bestellt. Hoch motiviert fabriziert die neue Regierung auch sofort lustige Steuergesetze und verwickelt eine Bundeswehr, die neunundvierzig Jahre lang nichts außer Bierkästen vernichtet hat, in den Balkankrieg. Gerhard Schröder spricht das historische Machtwort: »Wir kriegen das hin.«

Auch der deutsche Finanzminister ist gut drauf. Während die Weltwirtschaft von einer Krise in die nächste taumelt, versteigert Hans Eichel die UMTS-Mobilfunklizenzen für irre 98,8 Milliarden Mark an ein paar superirre Firmenvorstände. Gleichzeitig fällt der deutsche Kleinanleger in einen megairren Aktienrausch und investiert das letzte Hemd in Anteile der Kommunikationsbranche. Da kann ja nichts schief gehen, weil er selbst so gern telefoniert und Team-Telekom-Pedaleur Jan Ullrich als erster Deutscher die Tour de France gewinnt. Als sich diese extravagante Conclusio als Trugschluss erweist, stürzt das Land in eine tiefe Depression. Doch es kommt noch dicker. Es kommt der Rinderwahn. Die Deutschen leben von Broccoli, Zwieback und Schweinekotelett. Da macht selbst der zehnte Jahrestag der Einheit keine Freude mehr. In Hannover herrscht Schneetreiben und Eiseskälte. Der Polizeipräsident hat alle freien Parkplätze mit bewaffneten Truppen besetzen lassen. Es gibt erschreckende Engpässe auf dem Wurst- und Glühweinsektor. Das Militär pöbelt, das Volk hungert. Elf Jahre nach dem Fall der Mauer Zustände wie in der Zone. Quo vadis, Deutschland?

Am 11. September 2001 fliegen zwei Boeings in die Türme des World Trade Center, und nun ist tatsächlich nichts mehr, wie es war. Sagt der *Spiegel*. Sagt Peter Hahne und sagt Frau Christiansen. »Jetzt führen wir Krieg gegen den Terror«, sagt der Präsident der Amerikaner. »Wir sind alle Amerikaner«, sagt die *Bild*. Die Deutschen grillen wieder Rindfleisch und boykottieren Kebab. Die Amerikaner machen in Afghanistan alles kaputt. Schröder schickt die Bundeswehr nach Kabul zum Trümmerräumen. Der DFB schickt Rudi Völler nach Japan. Die Deutschen werden Vizeweltmeister und beschließen, sich von nichts und niemand mehr Bange machen zu lassen. Weder von der großen Oderflut noch von Edmund Stoiber. Nur ein bisschen vom drohenden Krieg im Irak. Schröder und Fischer sagen: »Krieg, nein danke«, und gewinnen auch die nächste Bundestagswahl. Bald herrschen Krieg und Chaos im Irak. Die Börsenkurse fallen ins Bodenlose und eine Million deutsche Arbeitslose fallen dank Hartz IV aus dem sozialen Netz. Noch tiefer fällt der deutsche Fußball. Rudis Elf gewinnt im Sommer 2004 bei der EM in Portugal kein Spiel, schießt in drei Spielen nur zwei Tore und scheidet in der Vorrunde aus.

»Die Welt ist arm, der Mensch ist schlecht / Da hab ich eben leider Recht.« Sagt Brecht. Und stöhnt Micha, der gekleidet in Portugals Farben fassungslos vor dem Fernseher kniet und mit ansehen muss, wie Außenseiter Griechenland mit altdeutschen Tugenden und dem noch älteren Otto Rehhagel auf der Trainerbank dem Ballkünstler Luis Figo den Sieg im Endspiel stiehlt.

Für mich dagegen könnte die Welt nicht schöner sein. Ich verehre Figo, aber ich liebe nur die blonde Claudia. Sie sitzt neben mir auf dem Sofa und knabbert Chips. Ich knabbere an ihrem Ohrläppchen, während Töchterlein Lotte durch den Garten tobt. Ich bin also doch noch zu einer Kleinfamilie gekommen und fühle mich pudelwohl dabei. Claudia ist Redakteurin beim MDR, wohnt in Leipzig und war abkommandiert, Sänger Quasthoff auf dem schwankenden *Riverboat* zu betreuen. Ich stand sofort in hellen Flammen, was zum Glück auf Gegenseitigkeit beruhte. Es hat allerdings eine Weile gedauert, bis das beide Teile mitbekommen haben. Inzwischen steht fest, dass wir gerne ins Kino gehen, fanatische Bücherwürmer sind, eine Schwäche fürs Kochen haben, am liebsten an der See urlauben und überhaupt alles passt wie der sprichwörtliche Deckel auf den Topf. Nur meine Spielkonsole mustert die kleine Lotti mit weit mehr Begeisterung als ihre Mutter. Ich bin mir sicher, diesmal habe ich die Frau fürs Leben gefunden. Die beiden haben auch schon den Elterntest mit Bravour bestanden. Dass Lotti Mama und Vater im Sturm erobern würde, war klar. Bei Claudia bin ich mir da gar nicht so sicher gewesen, weil vor allem Vater der Ansicht ist, mein Urteilsvermögen gegenüber der Damenwelt leide zeitweilig unter schwerer Eintrübung. Doch als wir zum Antrittsbesuch erscheinen, ruht sein Auge mit Wohlgefallen auf meiner Auserwählten. Vater gibt den Charmeur alter Schule und offeriert Claudia und Lotti auf dem goldenen Hochzeitsfest, das meine Eltern im Juli gefeiert haben, gleich zwei Ehrenplätze neben den Jubilaren.

Könnte ich die Zeit anhalten und würde mich vor den Spiegel stellen, ich sähe tatsächlich einen glücklichen Menschen. Und das Schönste ist: Das private Hoch schwebt auch über dem beruflichen Wellental. Meine Stimme funktioniert wie geschmiert, und die Auftragsbücher sind voll bis 2010.

Wenn Christian Thielemann demnächst die *Die Meistersinger* produziert, darf ich den Beckmesser geben, mein großartiger Bariton-Kollege Bryn Terfel den Hans Sachs. Des Weiteren ist geplant, dass Claudio Abbado den *Tristan* mit Ben Heppner und Deborah Polaski aufnehmen wird und mich als Kurwenal vorgesehen hat. Ich werde weiter fleißig Liederabende geben und eines schönen Tages auch meine Traumpartie, den Wozzeck, singen – ein Projekt, das ich unbedingt mit Simon Rattle realisieren möchte. Auch für Rollen wie Macbeth, Sarastro oder Germont, den Sprecher in der *Zauberflöte*, fühle ich mich reif genug.

Ich bete nur, dass meine Eltern sich noch lange daran freuen können, dass ich mein Leben gemeistert habe. Ich möchte natürlich auch selbst gesund bleiben, um all die musikalischen Projekte zu verwirklichen, die mich reizen. Allerdings merke ich, dass sich aufgrund meiner Behinderung die ersten Verschleißerscheinungen in den Körper gefressen haben. Da heißt es, schnell auf Holz geklopft und dreimal über die Schulter gespuckt. Jedenfalls möchte ich nie wieder erleben, dass ich mitten in einem Konzert mit den Berliner Philharmonikern meine Stimme verliere. Ich musste damals von der Bühne gehen und habe zwei Tage in schierer Panik verbracht, bis mir ein Arzt sagte, dass meine Stimmbänder nur ein wenig Schonung brauchten. Als ich mich bei Simon, der am Pult gestanden hat, entschuldigen will, zuckt er nur mit den Schultern:

»There's no reason why, Tommi. Take it easy.«

Simon meint, er selbst habe aufgehört, sich über Widrigkeiten, die man nicht ändern kann und die man nicht verschuldet hat, aufzuregen. Seitdem gehe es ihm entschieden besser. Wie gut, wenn in solchen Situation ein Freund mit Trost und Rat zur Stelle ist.

Freund Dietrich behauptet ja immer, »jeder ist eine Insel«. Das ist ein schönes Bild. Trotzdem finde ich, die menschliche Existenz hat eher etwas Planetarisches. Trudeln wir nicht alle von Geburt an als unbehauste Körper im stummen schwarzen Nichts? Mit heißen oder erkalteten Oberflächen, mit Ringen um den Hüften und ein paar narbigen Monden in der Krone. Ab und an schlägt ein anderer Himmelskörper ein, dann ist die Hölle los. Hat sich der Rauch verzogen, ellipst man bald wieder am Nasenring der Schwerkraft einsam und eselig um die Sonne auf der Suche nach ein bisschen Wärme. Und fragt sich oft, wozu das alles gut sein soll. Da ist es beruhigend, wenn einer wenigstens weiß, wo er hingehört. Das ist in unserer unsteten Welt nichts Geringes. Ich habe ja ein schönes Haus mit einer hohen Mauer drum herum, ich habe einen Pool und eine Sauna, um jeglichen Wetterunbilden des Universums zu trotzen. Aber wenn es um die innere Temperierung geht, muss man doch ab und an sein Heim verlassen und jene Orte aufsuchen, die im Englischen Pub, im Italienischen Bar und im Deutschen Gastwirtschaft heißen.

Verehrter, duldsamer Leser, der Sie meine Geschichte noch immer nicht aus der Hand gelegt haben. Zu guter Letzt, sozusagen als Bonus und um die gemeinsam verbrachten Stunden abzurunden, möchte ich Sie in meine absolute Lieblingswirtschaft führen. Sie finden sie im Quadranten M8 des Stadtplans von Hannover. Die Gegend ist berüchtigt für ihre schwarzen Löcher. Sie tarnen sich als Friseursalons, Nagel- und Sonnenstudios, Lottoannahmestellen und Fahrschulen. Das tiefste Loch ist ein indisches Restaurant. Dort verschwinden regelmäßig Köche. Bis heute vermisst man acht Inder, drei Vietnamesen und zwei Ghanaer. Zuletzt brühte ein Tscheche den Basmatireis. Seit einer Woche ist auch er nicht mehr aufzufinden.

Mit anderen Worten, es wäre im Quadranten M8 gar nicht auszuhalten, funkelte nicht an der Ecke Laves-/ Warmbüchenstraße der gastronomische Fixstern Vater und Sohn. Allerdings ist auch Wirtsvater Guido längst in ein schwarzes Loch gefallen. Dem Sohn Aribert vererbte der Alte neben der Schanklizenz ein Grünkohlfeld, eine Bratkartoffelplantage, zentnerweise Sauerfleisch, eine Schiffsladung Bratheringe und seine schneeweiße Schürze. Aribert trägt sie mit Würde, genau wie den gepflegten Schnauzbart. Sein Motto heißt: »Bitte nicht hetzen, wir sind bei der Arbeit und nicht auf der Flucht.« Hält man sich daran, fließen Köpi, Herrenhäuser und Weihenstephan wie ein stiller breiter Strom. Wenn nicht … Nun, sagen wir es so: Aribert wird ungemütlich. Dann hagelt es Lokalverbote. Wer je einen der seltenen Ausbrüche des Menschenfreundes erlebt hat, erzählt davon nur im Flüsterton. Es heißt, er könne wie eine explodierende Supernova aus der Durchreiche zur Küche fahren und Renitenzler zu Sternenstaub zermahlen.

»Das wird ein furrrrchtbares Ende nehmen«, orakelt Hansen, der einmal dabei gewesen sein will. Das »r« schmirgelt dabei durch seine Kehle, als sei sie ein rostiges Abflussrohr. So ist es auch. Hansen, ein schrundiger Geselle, dessen Leberwerte »prrraktisch garrr nich mehr errrfassbarrr« sind, gibt sozusagen den Uranus im Vater-und-Sohn-System. Deshalb wettet die Stammkundschaft auch seit Jahren darauf, dass es vor allem mit Hansen furchtbar enden wird. Aber am nächsten Abend ahasvert er doch wieder Heine oder die Stones zitierend durch das Lokal. Dezent behütet, das heißt unter- und noch öfter ausgehalten von Richie Krauskopf, seinem freundlichen Konterpart. Richie ist einer meiner besten Freunde, kugelrund, der Gatte von Chefkellnerin Anne und das Humane in persona. Leider ist er auch ein rechter Unglücksvogel, dem der Sinnspruch des Mittelstürmers Jürgen »Kobra« Wegmann das Schicksal verdunkelt. »Erst hatten wir kein Glück, dann kam auch noch Pech dazu.« Weshalb er öfter bandagiert auftritt.

Die Stammkundschaft nimmt das Lokalkolorit gelassen. Dafür sorgt Anne, das Herzstück der Wirtschaft. Der treuen Seele unterliegt das operative Geschäft. Sie bändigt Stammtische, Landespolitiker, sensible Schauspieler und andere Wichtigkeiten, die Ariberts exzellente Speisekarte abarbeiten, mit gleich bleibend milder Bestimmtheit. Und komplimentiert sie rechtzeitig hinaus, wenn Mitternacht naht, die blaue Stunde, zu der das Vater und Sohn seine wahre Pracht entfaltet und sich mein soziales Umfeld um den Tresen drängt. Schlag zwölf kann man vor dem Tresen Gestalten wie Herrn zur Nedden erkennen, der funkelnde Biere ins Licht hält. Und wie von Zauberhand gelenkt erscheint das Dramatiker-Duo Gronius und Rauschenbach mit barockem Durst und Appetit, um mit noch barockeren Geschichten aus fernen Galaxien zu prunken. Nach der Oblong-Show schaut der Dichter Gerhard Henschel herein und zeigt Interessierten gern gegen ein Gratispils Fotos seiner Kleinfamilie, während Herr Foxx – vergeblich wie immer – versucht, mittels hektografierter Kunstwerke seine Deckelschulden auszulösen. In ganz besonderen Nächten kann man Andi Hahn mit Aribert zarte Kochrezepte singen hören und die Dichterin Felicitas Hoppe spielt dazu am Klavier in Moll. Dann weinen durchreisende Berliner Theaterkritiker und runde bayrische Künstlerinnen, weil es eine solche Schönheit bei ihnen zu Hause gar nicht mehr gibt. Zum Trost spendiert Aribert Wodka satt, und alle Frauen sehen plötzlich aus wie Sharon Stone. In solchen Momenten begreife selbst ich, was es mit Heisenbergs Unschärferelation auf sich hat. Getreu dem Lessingschen Wahlspruch: »Zu viel kann man wohl trinken, doch trinkt man nie genug.«

Vielleicht treffen wir uns dort einmal. Oder in einem Konzertsaal Ihrer Wahl. Ich würde mich freuen.

Also bis demnächst!

Anhang

Diskografie

A Portrait (Bach, Beethoven, Mozart, Schubert), Charles Spencer, BMG, Oktober 2001

Johann Sebastian **Bach**: Edition Bachakademie Vol. 66 (Weltliche Kantaten), Bach-Collegium Stuttgart, Helmuth Rilling, Hänssler, Juni 1999

Johann Sebastian Bach: Edition Bachakademie Vol. 67 (Weltliche Kantaten), Bach-Collegium Stuttgart, Helmuth Rilling, Hänssler, Februar 2000

Johann Sebastian Bach: Edition Bachakademie (Weltliche Kantaten), Bach-Collegium Stuttgart, Helmuth Rilling, Hänssler, November 1997

Johann Sebastian Bach: Edition Bachakademie (Weltliche Kantaten), Gächinger Kantorei Stuttgart, Helmuth Rilling, Hänssler, Juli 2001

Johann Sebastian Bach: Edition Bachakademie Vol. 73 Magnificat, Lukas-Passion, Gächinger Kantorei Stuttgart, Helmuth Rilling, Hänssler, Januar 2000

Johann Sebastian Bach: Edition Bachakademie Vol. 74 (Matthäus-Passion), Gächinger Kantorei Stuttgart, Helmuth Rilling, Hänssler, Juni 1999

Johann Sebastian Bach: Jagd-/Kaffee-Kantate, Gächinger Kantorei Stuttgart, Bach-Collegium Stuttgart, Helmuth Rilling, Hänssler, Mai 1997

Johann Sebastian Bach: Johannes-Passion, Chorgemeinschaft Neubeuern, Bach-Collegium München, Enoch zu Guttenberg, BMG, Januar 1992

Johann Sebastian Bach: Kantaten, Windsbacher Knabenchor, Münchener Bach-Solisten, Karl-Friedrich Beringer, BR, Januar 1991

Johann Sebastian Bach: Lateinische Kirchenmusik 2, Messe in g-Moll, Messe in G-Dur, Sanctus C-Dur, mit Gächinger Kantorei Stuttgart, Helmuth Rilling, Hänssler, September 1999

Johann Sebastian Bach: Magnificat D-Dur, Gächinger Kantorei Stuttgart, Bach-Collegium Stuttgart, Helmuth Rilling, Hänssler, Januar 1997

Johann Sebastian Bach: Matthäus-Passion, Bach-Collegium Stuttgart, Helmuth Rilling, Hänssler, Januar 1997

Johann Sebastian Bach: Matthäus-Passion, Tokyo Opera Singers, Saito Kinen Orchestra, Seiji Ozawa, Philips, Februar 1999

Johann Sebastian Bach: Messe, Gächinger Kantorei Stuttgart, Helmut Rilling, Hänssler, Oktober 1999

Johann Sebastian Bach: Messe in F-Dur und A-Dur, Gächinger Kantorei Stuttgart, Bach-Collegium Stuttgart, Helmuth Rilling, Hänssler, Januar 1997

Johann Sebastian Bach: Messe in F-Dur und A-Dur, Gächinger Kantorei Stuttgart, Helmuth Rilling, Hänssler, August 1999

Johann Sebastian Bach: Messe in g-Moll und G-Dur, Bach-Collegium Stuttgart, Stuttgarter Kammerorchester, Helmuth Rilling, Hänssler, Januar 1997

Johann Sebastian Bach: Messe in h-Moll, Windsbacher Knabenchor, Deutsche Kammerakademie Neuss, Karl-Friedrich Beringer, Hänssler, Januar 1997

Johann Sebastian Bach: Messe in h-Moll, Windsbacher Knabenchor, Deutsche Kammerakademie Neuss, Karl-Friedrich Beringer, Hänssler, Oktober 1999

Johann Sebastian Bach: Messe in h-Moll, Windsbacher Knabenchor, Deutsche Kammerakademie Neuss, Karl-Friedrich Beringer, Rop, November 2003

Johann Sebastian Bach: Weihnachtsoratorium, mit Windsbacher Knabenchor, Karl-Friedrich Beringer, Teldec, Oktober 1994

Ludwig van **Beethoven**: Neunte Sinfonie, Eric Ericson Chamber Choir, Schwedischer Rundfunkchor, Berliner Philharmoniker, Claudio Abbado, Deutsche Grammophon, April 2002

Johannes **Brahms**, Franz Liszt: Lieder, mit Justus Zeyen, Deutsche Grammophon, Februar 2000

Antonio Casimir **Cartellieri**: Gioas, Bachchor Gütersloh, Detmolder Kammerorchester, Gernot Schmalfuss, Mdg, September 1997

Antonin **Dvorak**: Stabat Mater, Bach Festival Oregon Chor, Helmuth Rilling, Hänssler, Januar 1997

Georg Friedrich **Händel**: Der Messias, Oregon Bach Festival Chor und Orchester, Helmuth Rilling, Hänssler, Dezember 1997

Georg Friedrich Händel: Der Messias, Oregon Bach Festival Chor und Orchester, Helmuth Rilling, Hänssler, April 2002

Joseph **Haydn**: Orfeo und Euridice, Leopold Hager, Orfeo, Mai 1994

Carl **Loewe**: Balladen, Norman Shetler, EMI, November 1989

Gustav **Mahler**: Des Knaben Wunderhorn, Anne Sofie von Otter, Berliner Philharmoniker, Claudio Abbado, Deutsche Grammophon, April 1999

Wolfgang Amadeus **Mozart**: Arien, Württembergisches Kammerorchester, Jorg Faerber, BMG, September 1997
Wolfgang Amadeus Mozart: Credo-Messe, Profil 2004
Wolfgang Amadeus Mozart: Krönungsmesse, Rundfunkchor Leipzig, Staatskapelle Dresden, Peter Schreier, Philips, Oktober 1993

Krzysztof **Penderecki**: Credo, Oregon Bach Festival Chor und Orchester, Helmuth Rilling, Hänssler, September 1998

Thomas **Quasthoff** sings Händel & Bach, Helmuth Rilling, Hänssler, Juli 2002

Aribert **Reimann**: Lieder, Christine Schäfer, Ursula Hesse, Claudia Barainsky, Axel Bauni, Orfeo, März 1996

Romantische Lieder (Schubert, Wolf, Schumann, Strauß), Justus Zeyen, Deutsche Grammophon, März 2004

Arnold **Schönberg**: Gurrelieder, Berliner Philharmoniker, Simon Rattle, EMI, April 2002

Franz **Schubert**: Goethe-Lieder, Charles Spencer, BMG, März 1995
Franz Schubert: Schubert-Lieder, Anne Sofie von Otter, Chamber Orchestra of Europe, Claudio Abbado, Deutsche Grammophon, April 2003
Franz Schubert: Schwanengesang; Johannes Brahms: Vier ernste Gesänge, mit Justus Zeyen, Deutsche Grammophon, April 2001

Franz Schubert: Die Winterreise, Charles Spencer, BMG, Oktober 1998

Robert **Schumann**: Genoveva, Arnold-Schönberg-Chor, Cleveland Orchestra, Nikolaus Harnoncourt, Teldec, September 1997

Robert Schumann: Schumann Liederkreis, Robert Szidon, BMG, August 1993

Die **Stimme** (Deutsche romantische Arien), Orchester der Deutschen Oper Berlin, Christian Thielemann, Deutsche Grammophon, März 2002

Personenregister

Ronnith Neuman
Tod auf Korfu

Kriminalroman. www.list-taschenbuch.de
ISBN 978-3-548-60811-2

In Agros auf Korfu stirbt ein krankes Kind. Wenige Tage später wird an einem einsamen Strandstück eine nackte männliche Leiche angeschwemmt. Hauptkommissar Alexandros Kasantzakis, der Grieche vom Festland, dem die Gewohnheiten der Inselbewohner noch immer fremd sind, beginnt zu ermitteln. Die blutigen Spuren deuten auf eine lange zurückliegende Tragödie in der deutsch-griechischen Vergangenheit hin.

»Mitten in der Urlaubsidylle wartet der Mörder. Sie entdecken die Insel durch die Augen von Hauptkommissar Alexandros Kasantzakis. Gänsehaut garantiert.«
tz, München

List Taschenbuch

L336